On Playing the Flute

JOHANN JOACHIM QUANTZ

On Playing The Flute

SECOND EDITION

Translated with notes and an introduction

BY

EDWARD R. REILLY

SCHIRMER BOOKS

A Division of Macmillan, Inc.

NEW YORK

Schirmer Books
A Division of Macmillan, Inc.
866 Third Avenue, New York, N.Y. 10022

First American publication of this second edition 1985
First published in the United States of America 1966
by The Free Press, A Division of Macmillan, Inc.
Library of Congress Catalog Card No.: 85–8840
Printed and bound in Great Britain
printing number (hc)
1   2   3   4   5   6   7   8   9   10
printing number (pbk)
1   2   3   4   5   6   7   8   9   10

Library of Congress Cataloging in Publication Data

Quantz, Johann Joachim 1697–1773.
On playing the flute.

Translation of: Versuch einer Anweisung die Flöte
traversiere zu spielen.
Bibliography: p.
Includes index.
1. Flute—methods—Early works to 1800. 2. Flute
music—Interpretation (Phrasing, dynamics, etc.)—
Early works to 1800. 3. Musical accompaniment—
Early works to 1800. I. Reilly, Edward R. II. Title.
MT342.Q313 1985   788'.51'071   85–8840
ISBN 0–02–872920–X
ISBN 0–02–870160–7 (pbk.)

CONTENTS

ILLUSTRATIONS

INTRODUCTION

THE value of Quantz's *Essay of a Method for Playing the Transverse Flute* as a major source of information about eighteenth-century musical practice and thought has been long recognized. The work has been repeatedly cited on a wide range of topics from the time that musicians and scholars first began to comprehend fully that an understanding of earlier approaches to performance might have a vital bearing on the convincing re-creation of music of the past.

The reasons that the *Essay* has been so frequently singled out, rather than one of the other flute tutors of the period, lie in the unusual scope of the treatise, and in the detailed treatment that Quantz accords his subject. If the work were no more than a reproduction of the standard material found in most eighteenth-century flute methods, it would probably be considered only as a particularly good example of a commonly encountered type. But Quantz was an exceptional teacher, and his treatise was conceived as far more than an introduction to flute playing. In the *Essay* he offers his readers a comprehensive programme of studies for the performing musician.

Quantz's aim was that of good music teachers everywhere, 'to train a skilled and intelligent musician, and not just a mechanical . . . player . . .'.[1] To provide a basis for the realization of this goal he organized the *Essay* as three more or less separate but closely interrelated treatises. Each deals with an important phase of the performer's training, but each is also designed so that it can be read independently of the others. The first is devoted to the education of the solo musician, the second to accompanying, and the third to forms and styles.

The first of these three divisions (Chapters I–XVI) is carefully arranged in two sequences of chapters. The first ten begin by introducing the student to the history, the structure, and the mechanics of his instrument, that is, embouchure, tone production, fingering, and articulation. The basic forms of ornamentation, appoggiaturas and shakes, are then dealt with; and a general review, with some remarks on individual practice, concludes the exposition of the rudiments of flute playing.

The next six chapters of the opening treatise form more advanced stages of the performer's training. In them Quantz is primarily concerned with developing the ability of the student to recognize and convey the character of each work that he performs. The various types of fast and slow pieces and their appropriate execution are explored, as well as dynamics, free ornamentation, and cadenzas. Discussion of these areas leads naturally to the final chapter of this portion of the *Essay*, in which

[1] See the Preface to the *Essay*.

the student is advised on problems associated with his performance in public.

Having provided the flautist with a solid musical and technical foundation on his own instrument in the first part of his work, Quantz then directs the attention of his pupil to those instruments that would accompany him in concerts. Chapter XVII, which forms roughly one-third of the book, consists of a number of separate sections devoted to the 'duties' of the leader of an ensemble, each member of the string family, the keyboard player, and accompanists in general. In turn many important subjects are taken up in addition to matters connected with the technique of each individual instrument. Tempo markings, intonation, problems of balance, the size and arrangement of an ensemble, and many other matters are considered in detail.

In the concluding portion of the *Essay* (Chapter XVIII), Quantz rounds out his student's training with a lengthy discussion of contemporary forms and styles. The first half of this discussion is devoted to clearly worded descriptions of most of the principal types of composition then cultivated, especially those favoured in the courts of central and northern Germany. The remainder consists of a comparison and evaluation of Italian, French, and German styles of performance and composition.

The *Essay* as a whole is preceded by an excellent introduction on 'The Qualities Required of Those Who Would Dedicate Themselves to Music'. This section, like many others in the *Essay*, vividly brings home the constancy of certain aspects of musical life, and still offers much sound advice to those interested in becoming professional musicians.

That Quantz intended his work for musicians of all kinds is clear both from the manner in which the *Essay* is organized and his own Preface. Only about 50 pages of the original 334 are devoted exclusively to the flute. Although the first of the three main divisions of the work was conceived specifically for the flute, most of the material after Chapter VII is equally applicable to other instruments and to singing. The preceding discussions of notation, breathing, and articulation, however, also contain much valuable information for performers other than flautists.

Quantz's actual treatment of the various subjects with which he deals matches the breadth of his basic plan. As an experienced teacher he had obviously recognized the need to be clear and specific. He also strove diligently to avoid the superficiality of those methods that offered quick mastery of an instrument with little effort. In many areas he provides much more concrete information about important points of performance than either his immediate predecessors or his followers; and his attention to detail—even if at times it becomes pedantic—considerably enhances the value of the *Essay* as a guide for modern performers. Subjects such as extempore embellishments, dynamics, cadenzas, and tempo are explored more fully than in any other treatise of the time. The valuable works of

C. P. E. Bach[1] and Leopold Mozart,[2] which appeared shortly after that of Quantz, show a considerable extension of the treatment of the keyboard and violin as well as of some other matters, but frequently seem to assume some knowledge of Quantz's treatise.

The unique combination of breadth and detail found in the *Essay* could scarcely have been better designed to provide a more stimulating introduction to musical thought, performance, and style in the eighteenth century, and more than justifies a long overdue complete translation into English. Yet, important as the treatise is, modern performers must remember that the work is the synthesis of the experience of one man active at a particular period in time and in a certain milieu. Solutions to the various problems of performance were as diverse during that time as they are today.

Quantz's general approach in his *Essay*, and his specific treatment of the many subjects that he examines, grew out of years of personal experience in all the phases of music that he discusses. During his long career he was active and successful as a solo and orchestral performer on a variety of instruments, as a composer, as a teacher and writer on music, as a director of a chamber ensemble, and as a maker of flutes. To see the *Essay* in its historical context, a picture of his life and musical training, and a knowledge of some of his compositions are both valuable. In Quantz's case the catch-all label 'teacher of Frederick the Great' has done much to obscure recognition and study of the crucial quarter-century that he spent at Dresden, as well as to link subjective feelings about Frederick with estimates of Quantz. The old maxim that 'theory is always fifty years behind practice' has also tended to cloud the fact that Quantz was very much a part of his time, and that his work was conceived in relation to the music cultivated during his prime. Happily, Quantz himself has provided many of the essentials of his background in a short autobiography, written in 1754 and published the following year.[3] This work forms the basis for much of the brief sketch that follows.

Born (30 January 1697) the son of a blacksmith in the village of Oberscheden in Hanover, Quantz's early love of music grew out of his en-

---

[1] *Essay on the True Art of Playing Keyboard Instruments*, translated and edited by William J. Mitchell (New York: W. W. Norton, 1949).

[2] *A Treatise on the Fundamental Principles of Violin Playing*, translated by Editha Knocker (London: Oxford University Press, 1948).

[3] 'Herrn Johann Joachim Quantzens Lebenslauf, von ihm selbst entworfen', in F. W. Marpurg, *Historisch-kritische Beyträge zur Aufnahme der Musik*, i (1755), pp. 197–250. This work forms the primary basis for all later accounts of Quantz's life, from that of Hiller to those found in current reference works. A facsimile reprint is included in W. Kahl, *Selbstbiographien deutscher Musiker des XVIII. Jahrhunderts* (Cologne: Staufen-Verlag, 1948), pp. 104–57, with an introduction and many useful notes by the editor. An English translation appears in P. Nettl, *Forgotten Musicians* (New York: Philosophical Library, 1951), pp. 280–319. A partial translation and paraphrase is also included in C. Burney, *The Present State of Music in Germany, the Netherlands, and United Provinces* (1773). See *Dr. Burney's Musical Tours in Europe*, edited by Percy A. Scholes (2 vols.; London: Oxford University Press, 1959), ii, pp. 183–95. The passages quoted in this introduction, however, have been freshly translated by the present writer.

counters with it at village festivals. These he attended with a brother, Jost
Matthies,[1] who occasionally took the place of one of the village musicians.
But Quantz's father opposed the boy's interest, and when the child was
9 insisted that he should begin work in the family trade. The death of the
father in the following year, 1707, suddenly gave the reluctant apprentice
the opportunity to escape from the career laid out for him. An uncle,
Justus Quantz, who was a town musician at Merseburg, offered to take
him in and train him.

   Although the uncle also died only a few months after his nephew's
arrival in Merseburg, Quantz continued his apprenticeship for the next
five years under Johann Adolf Fleischhack (dates unknown), son-in-law
and successor to Justus. Fleischhack was apparently an indifferent master,
but Quantz during his Merseburg years gained a useful practical foundation in his chosen profession. Orphaned at so early an age, he seems to
have turned all of his energies to music. The main requirement of a town
musician was passable proficiency on a variety of instruments. During
his apprenticeship Quantz studied the violin, oboe, trumpet, cornett,
trombone, horn, recorder, bassoon, 'cello, viola da gamba, and double
bass. On the violin, his principal instrument, he gained sufficient technical mastery to play works by Heinrich Biber (1644–1704), Johann Jakob
Walther (c. 1650–1717), Henrico Albicastro (c. 1670–c. 1738), Arcangelo
Corelli (1653–1713), and Georg Philipp Telemann (1681–1767). Among
the other instruments the oboe and trumpet were those on which he
became most competent. On his own initiative he made his first attempts
at composition, and studied the harpsichord under Johann Friedrich
Kiesewetter (d. 1712), a relative who was organist at the church of St.
Maximi. Kiesewetter introduced him to the latest works of Telemann,
Melchior Hofmann (d. 1715), and Johann David Heinichen (1683–1729).

   Quantz completed his apprenticeship at the age of 16, and then remained with Fleischhack as a journeyman for two years and four months.
During this time he already aspired to a higher level of musicianship than
he found in Merseburg, and hoped to go to Berlin or Dresden to continue his studies. In 1714, when the death of the brother of the Duke of
Saxony-Merseburg caused a temporary suspension of musical activities,
Quantz travelled to Dresden.[2] He attempted without success to discover
an opening in the beautiful *Residenzstadt* of Augustus II, the Elector of
Saxony (under the title Frederick Augustus I) and King of Poland. Eventually he found work in Pirna, under the town musician Georg Schalle
(1670–1720), and while there he came to know the director of the Dresden
town band, Gottfried Heyne or Heine (d. 1738), who employed him when
additional players were needed for weddings.

   [1] For further information on Quantz's family and his early teachers, see W. Nagel, 'Miscellanea', *Monatshefte für Musikgeschichte*, xxix (1897), pp. 69–78.
   [2] Quantz's choice of Dresden was probably influenced by the fact that the Royal Chapel in
Berlin was disbanded by Frederick William I in 1713.

Quantz's brief stay in the vicinity of Dresden in 1714 marked a turning-point in his career as both performer and composer. His acquaintance-ship with Heyne became the first step towards a position in Dresden. And while at Pirna he first encountered the concertos of Antonio Vivaldi (1678–1741), works which were to have a decisive influence on his development as a composer. His reaction to them, noted in his autobiography, reflects that of a whole generation of German composers: 'As a then completely new species of musical pieces, they made more than a slight impression on me. I did not fail to collect a considerable assortment of them. In the future the splendid ritornellos of Vivaldi provided me with good models.'[1]

Returning to Merseburg in September 1714 Quantz completed the remaining year and a half of his service as a journeyman. In the year following the conclusion of his formal training, he received several different offers for positions as a violinist, oboist, or trumpet player. The realization that he would be 'the best among bad'[2] performers made him wait for a more attractive opening to appear. In March 1716 his hopes were rewarded by an offer from Heyne to become a member of the Dresden town band.

The twenty-five years from 1716 to 1741, during which Dresden remained the centre of Quantz's activities, constitute the most interesting and critical era in his life. The rich cultural environment of the city during the reigns of Augustus II (1670–1733) and Augustus III (Frederick Augustus II; 1696–1763) provided him with both the stimulus and the opportunity to develop into a mature performer and composer. The strong impression made by the high standards that the young man encountered in the Dresden orchestra (not the town band to which he at first belonged) is most vividly conveyed in his own words:

Thus in March 1716 I went to Dresden. Here I soon perceived that merely hitting the notes as the composer wrote them was still far from the greatest excellence of a musical artist.

The Royal Orchestra at that time was already in a particularly flourishing state. Through the French equal style of execution introduced by Volumier,[3] the concertmaster at that time, it already distinguished itself from many other orchestras; and later, under the direction of the following concertmaster, Mr. Pisendel,[4] it achieved, through the introduction of a mixed style, such refinement of performance that, in all my later travels, I heard none better. At that time it boasted various celebrated instrumentalists, such as Pisendel and Veracini[5]

---

[1] Quantz, 'Lebenslauf', p. 205. On the influence of Vivaldi's concertos in Germany, see M. Pincherle, *Vivaldi, Genius of the Baroque* (New York: W. W. Norton, 1957), pp. 219–66, and A. Hutchings, *The Baroque Concerto* (New York: W. W. Norton, 1961), pp. 201–25.

[2] Quantz, 'Lebenslauf', p. 205.

[3] Jean Baptiste Volumier (c. 1670–1728). Volumier had come to Dresden in 1709 from Berlin.

[4] Johann Georg Pisendel (1687–1755).

[5] Francesco Veracini (1690–1768) was in Dresden from 1717 to 1722. His Op. 1, *Sonate a violino solo e basso*, appeared there in 1721. ←

on violin, Pantaleon Hebenstreit[1] on the pantalon, Sylvius Leopold Weiss[2] on the lute and theorbo, Richter[3] on the oboe, and Buffardin[4] on the transverse flute, to say nothing of the good violoncellists, bassoonists, horn players, and double bass players.

Hearing these celebrated people I was profoundly impressed, and my zeal to inquire further into music was redoubled. I sought in time to put myself in a position to become a passable member of so excellent a society. For although I otherwise enjoyed the way of life of the town musician, the tiresome playing of dances, which is so harmful to more refined performance, made me yearn for a release from it.[5]

In the year after his removal to Dresden, Quantz took advantage of the freedom offered by another period of mourning to continue his training in composition. He went to Vienna, and there studied counterpoint briefly with Fux's pupil Jan Dismas Zelenka (1679–1745),[6] who was later to become one of the court composers at Dresden.

In March 1718, at the age of 21, the young and ambitious town musician was able to move into the fringe of the illustrious circle of the court orchestra. After an audition he was accepted as an oboist in the newly formed *Kleine Kammermusik* known as the 'Polish Chapel'. This small ensemble of twelve musicians accompanied the King on his visits to Warsaw, but also remained in Dresden for substantial periods. Besides improving Quantz's salary and standing, the new position was decisive in other ways. Seeing no prospect for advancement as an oboist because of the seniority of other members of the ensemble, he turned seriously to the study of the transverse flute, since the flautist in the group willingly allowed him the first chair. Quantz's only formal instruction on the instrument came from the renowned French player, Buffardin, with whom he studied for four months. Buffardin's speciality, he notes, lay in the execution of fast pieces.

Quantz's activities in the Polish Chapel also strengthened his interest in composition, especially of works for the transverse flute. At that time the instrument had a rather small repertoire of pieces specifically written for it. Unable to secure promised instruction from one of the two masters of the Dresden chapel, Johann Christoph Schmidt (1664–1728), and hesitant to approach his rival Heinichen,[7] Quantz taught himself by studying the scores of established masters, 'attempting, without plagiary, to imitate their manner of writing in trios and concertos'.[8]

The strongest personal influence that he acknowledges in his musical

---

[1] Pantaleon Hebenstreit (1667–1750). The pantalon, or pantaleon, was a large dulcimer with 185 strings, played with two small hammers.

[2] Sylvius Leopold Weiss (1686–1750).   [3] Johann Christian Richter (1689–1744).

[4] Pierre Gabriel Buffardin (*c.* 1690–1768).   [5] Quantz, 'Lebenslauf', pp. 206–7.

[6] Quantz was not a pupil of Fux, as is incorrectly stated in some reference works. He did, however, use Fux's *Gradus ad Parnassum* in the training of his students in composition.

[7] The fullest account of musical life at the Dresden court, with its two *Kapellmeister*, is still found in M. Fürstenau, *Zur Geschichte der Musik und des Theaters am Hofe zu Dresden* (2 vols.; Dresden: R. Kuntze, 1861–2).   [8] Quantz, 'Lebenslauf', p. 210.

development is that of the violinist noted above, Johann Georg Pisendel, a pupil of Torelli, Vivaldi, and Montanari, whose friendship he gained in his early years at the Dresden court. He praises Pisendel, at that time Volumier's second in command in the direction of the Royal Orchestra, warmly as both man and artist:

From this equally great violinist, worthy concertmaster,[1] excellent musical artist, and truly honest man, I not only learned how to execute the Adagio,[2] but from him profited most fully in connection with the selection of compositions[3] and the performance of music in general. By him I was encouraged to venture further in composition. His style then was already a mixture of the Italian and the French, for he had already travelled through both countries as a man of ripe powers of discernment. In his tender years he sang as a chapel boy in Ansbach under the excellent singer and singing master Franc. Antonio Pistocchi,[4] and thus had the opportunity to lay the best foundation for good style. At the same place, however, he learned the violin from Torelli.[5] His example took such deep root in me that I have since always preferred the mixed style in music to the national styles. In matters of style I am also not a little indebted to the attention that I have always paid to good singers.[6]

This acknowledgement gives the clearest possible evidence of Quantz's obligation to Pisendel for certain basic features of his approach to performance and for his notions about the mixture of national styles. It also confirms the fact that Quantz's style was strongly affected by his experiences at Dresden and thus, to a considerable extent, reflects the practices of one of the most important musical centres in Germany from about 1720 to 1740.

Quantz's perception of the significant differences between Italian and French modes of performance and composition developed from his contact with each at Dresden. The orchestra under Volumier was grounded in the French discipline of orchestral playing used, from the time of Lully, in the performance of French overtures and dances.[7] Quantz's only instruction on the flute also came from a Frenchman, Buffardin. But French influences, which were strong at the Saxon court in the first decades of the century, were gradually submerged by the increasing importation of Italian opera and opera singers, and by the wide dissemination of the sonatas and concertos of Corelli, Torelli, Vivaldi, and Albinoni, to cite only a few of the most significant composers.

Quantz had become familiar with the concertos of Vivaldi in 1714, and there can be little question that they formed an important part of the repertoire of the Dresden orchestra. At least one concerto was written

---

[1] Pisendel became concertmaster of the Dresden orchestra officially in 1729.

[2] i.e. slow movements. See the *Essay*, Chapter XIV.

[3] *Das Ausnehmen der Sätze*. This phrase is not clear. Burney translates it as 'to compose in many parts'; Nettl gives 'the interpretation of movements'.

[4] Francesco Antonio Mamiliano Pistocchi (1659–1726). See the *Essay*, Chapter XVIII, § 56.

[5] Giuseppe Torelli (1658–1709). See the *Essay*, Chapter XVIII, §§ 30 and 58.

[6] Quantz, 'Lebenslauf', pp. 210–11.

[7] See the *Essay*, Chapter XVII, Section II, § 1, and the accompanying footnote.

specifically for the Dresden company, and a number of concertos and
sonatas were written expressly for his friend Pisendel (who has left an
interesting ornamented version of at least one Vivaldi adagio).[1] Quantz's
genuine appreciation of the richness of the Italian style of singing and
vocal composition dates from 1719, when two operas, *Ascanio*[2] and
Teofane, by the Venetian composer Antonio Lotti (*c*. 1667–1740), were performed as part of the marriage festivities of Crown Prince Frederick
Augustus and Maria Josepha, eldest daughter of Emperor Joseph I of
Austria. For the occasion a brilliant group of Italian singers, including
Francesco Bernardi (Senesino, *c*. 1680–*c*. 1759), Matteo Berselli (dates
unknown), Vittoria Tesi (1700–75), and Margherita Durastanti (dates unknown), was engaged, a group that also attracted Handel to Dresden in
his quest for singers for the Royal Academy of Music in London.[3]
Although a dispute between Senesino and Heinichen, perhaps precipitated
by the agreement which Handel reached with Senesino and Berselli,
brought about a suspension of further Italian opera productions for
several years, the impressions that Quantz had already gained were among
the most important in forming his ideals of performance. In the years that
followed he constantly studied the styles of the best vocalists of his day.

After his entry into the Polish Chapel, Quantz gradually established
himself as a player of more than average abilities, and gained the support
of several patrons. A planned visit to Italy, supported by some Polish
nobles, fell through in 1722. But the following year Quantz, together with
the lutenist Weiss and Carl Heinrich Graun (1704–59), the future *Kapellmeister* of Frederick the Great, was able to journey to Prague for the
coronation of Charles VI. All took part as orchestral players in the
performance of the opera *Costanza e fortezza* by Johann Joseph Fux (1660–
1741), the noted composer and theorist who headed the musical establishment of the Viennese court. The work was produced in a magnificent
style, with spectacular staging, a large chorus (with the youthful Franz
Benda, a later friend of Quantz and concertmaster of Frederick the Great,
among its members) and orchestra, and an excellent cast of singers.[4]
Quantz was thus given further opportunities to hear many of the best
singers and instrumentalists of his day. Also while at Prague he heard the
already celebrated violinist Tartini (1692–1770), who had recently entered
the service of Count Kinsky.

In 1724 Quantz finally saw his hopes for a period of study in Italy
fulfilled. Prince Lubomirsky, one of his supporters at court, obtained

---

[1] See Pincherle, *Vivaldi*, pp. 43, 51, 84, 95–96, 247.

[2] *Ascanio* was first performed in 1718, but was repeated on 7 Sept. 1719.

[3] See O. E. Deutsch, *Handel, a Documentary Biography* (London: A. & C. Black, 1955),
pp. 89–99.

[4] The opera has been reprinted in *Denkmäler der Tonkunst in Österreich*, Jahrgang XVII, with
reproductions of the striking original sets. For Quantz's interesting comments on the work and
the singers who participated in the performance, see 'Lebenslauf', pp. 216–20, and Nettl,
Forgotten Musicians, pp. 294–7.

permission for him to make the southward journey in the suite of Count von Lagnasco, the new Polish minister to Rome. But what began as a visit to Italy was gradually extended into a three-year grand tour, with stays in France and England as well. During these travels Quantz took advantage of every occasion on which he could familiarize himself with the works of the most well-known composers and the styles of the most famous singers and instrumentalists.

The greater part of his sojourn in Italy was spent in Rome, where he studied counterpoint under Francesco Gasparini (1668–1727), *maestro di cappella* at St. John Lateran, and author of a useful manual on thorough-bass, *L'armonico pratico al cimbalo* (1708). But he also visited almost every town where he could hear interesting music. Naples, Florence, Leghorn, Bologna, Ferrara, Padua, Venice, Modena, Reggio, Parma, Milan, and Turin all formed part of his itinerary.

A list of composers whose works he heard includes most of the important figures of the day: Alessandro Scarlatti (1660–1725), his son Domenico (1685–1757), and his student Joharu Adolph Hasse (1699–1783), Giuseppe Ottavio Pittoni (1657–1743), Pietro Paolo Bencini (d. 1755), Giovanni Battista San Martino (Sammartini, 1701–75), Giovanni Andrea Fiorini (dates unknown), Francesco Mancini (1672–1737), Leonardo Leo (1694–1744), Francesco Feo (1691–1761), Nicola Antonio Porpora (1686–1768), Leonardo Vinci (*c.* 1690–1730), Antonio Vivaldi, Giovanni Maria Capelli (d. 1726), Domenico Sarro (1679–1744), Benedetto Marcello (1686–1739), Tomaso Albinoni (1671–1751), and Antonio Lotti.

In Naples he became friendly with Hasse,[1] who within a few years was to become the most popular operatic composer in Italy and Germany, and *Kapellmeister* at Dresden. Through Hasse he was introduced to Alessandro Scarlatti and won his favour in spite of an initial unwillingness to listen to wind players because of the frequency of bad intonation.

Among performers Quantz gave the greatest attention to singers. The most impressive was the castrato Carlo Broschi (1705–82), known as Farinelli, then at the beginning of his career. Quantz heard him on a number of occasions, and they became personally acquainted.[2] Perhaps an indication of Quantz's own skill at the time is found in the fact that at Naples he was invited to perform in a concert which featured Hasse, Farinelli, the contralto Tesi, and the 'incomparable' 'cellist Franciscello (1691–1739). Other notable singers whom he heard were Carestini, already familiar from Dresden, Anna Maria Strada (*c.* 1700–1773), Giovanni Battista Pinacci (dates unknown), Annibale Pio Fabri (1697–1760), Nicolò Grimaldi (Nicolini, 1673–1732), Marianna Gaberini (Romanina; d. 1734), and Giovanni Paita (dates unknown).

[1] Stylistically Quantz's works are probably closest to those of Hasse, although Hasse carries the process of simplification a step further.

[2] For some examples of Farinelli's repertoire and his style of embellishing vocal parts, see F. Haböck, *Die Gesangskunst der Kastraten* (Vienna: Universal-Edition, 1923). The stylistic similarities between some of Quantz's works and the arias presented here is worth noting.

With the exception of the oboist Giuseppe Sammartini (1695–1750), Quantz found Italy lacking in good performers on woodwind instruments, but was able to hear excellent string players such as the 'cellists Giovannini (dates unknown) and Franciscello, and the violinists Vivaldi, Francesco Montanari (d. 1730), Luigi Madonis (*c.* 1693–*c.* 1770), Giovanni Battista Somis (1686–1763) and his young pupil, Jean-Marie Leclair (1697–1764). As may be seen in the *Essay*[1] he disapproved of some of the tendencies that he noticed in Italian instrumental performance, and in general preferred the best Italian singers as models for his own style, but there can be no question that he was influenced to some extent by the works and execution of these artists.

After a stay of almost two years in Italy Quantz moved on to France, arriving at Paris in August 1726. There he remained for seven months. His reactions to French musical life were typical of many Germans of his day. French opera he found in a poor state, suffering from too great an adherence to Lully's works, a poor orchestra, and bad singing methods. On the other hand he was impressed by French acting, staging, and dancing, and especially by the excellence of many individual instrumentalists. In Paris he encountered many good performers on the transverse flute, including among others Jean Christophe Naudot (d. 1762), and Michel Blavet (1700–68). A warm friendship developed with Blavet, the finest French flute player of his day and an excellent composer for the instrument. Among other performers Quantz singles out the gambists Antoine Fortcroix (Forcqueray, 1672–1745) and Roland Marais (*c.* 1680–*c.* 1750), and the violinists Giovanni Pietro Guignon (1702–74), an Italian player active mainly in France, and Jean-Jacques-Baptiste Anet (1676–1755), also noting that 'there was no dearth of good organists, clavier players, and violoncellists'.[2]

During the period of his visit to Paris, Quantz also made his first attempt to improve the structure and intonation of his flutes by adding another key to the one-keyed instrument then in use, a modification that he explains at some length in the *Essay*.[3]

In spite of orders to return to Dresden early in 1727, the now well-travelled performer and composer found himself unable to resist the impulse to extend his journey to England. His brief visit there lasted from 20 March to 1 June, and more than justified his expectations. He found Italian opera, as presented by the Royal Academy of Music under Handel's direction, in its 'fullest bloom'.[4] He heard G. B. Bononcini's *Astyanax* and the 'splendid music'[5] of Handel's *Admetus*, and was strongly impressed both by Handel's direction of the opera orchestra and by his music. He witnessed and gives a good account of the famous rivalry between the prima donnas Faustina and Cuzzoni, although in later years he was perhaps a little biased in favour of Faustina, whom he had frequent opportunities

[1] See Chapter XVIII, §§ 59–61.   [2] 'Lebenslauf', p. 239.
[3] See the *Essay*, Chapter III, §§ 8–11.   [4] 'Lebenslauf', p. 239.   [5] Loc. cit.

to hear in Dresden after she had become the wife of his friend Hasse. Solo instrumentalists heard in England included Handel on the harpsichord and organ, the violinists Francesco Geminiani (1687–1762), his pupil Matthew Dubourg (1703–67), the brothers Pietro (1679–1752) and Prospero (d. 1760) Castrucci, and Mauro d'Alais (dates unknown), and the flautists Karl Friedrich Weidemann (d. 1782) and John Festing (d. 1772).

Quantz seems to have been sorely tempted to remain in England, and was urged to do so by Handel. But his sense of obligation to Augustus II won out, and on 1 June 1727 he began the return trip to Dresden, travelling through Holland (with visits to Amsterdam, the Hague, Leiden, and Rotterdam), Hanover, and Brunswick. His three-year European tour ended with his arrival at Dresden on 23 July 1727.

Quantz's travels form the final stage of his training, and mark the beginning of his international reputation as a performer and composer. During his journeys he had been able to hear an astonishing number of the best composers and performers of his day. At the same time he seems to have made a considerable impression on those who heard him. Within a year or two of his visits, printed collections of his music began to appear in France, England, and Holland. At least seventeen collections have been preserved from the years 1728 to about 1750, and several others are known to have been issued. Nearly all seem to contain relatively youthful works of the composer. Although Quantz specifically disavowed some of the compositions published in England and Holland, the authenticity of about half can be established; and the fact that some spurious works were issued under his name simply confirms the general esteem in which he was held.[1]

While travelling Quantz had continued his study of composition by imitating the styles that he encountered at the places he visited. At Dresden he began to review his experiences, 'to put [his] ideas in order', and to set about 'forming an individual style'.[2] At present we know that forty trio sonatas, some of which are duplicated in the prints mentioned above, and ten concertos, all preserved in manuscripts in the *Sächsische Landesbibliothek*, definitely belong to the years from 1716 to 1741. A considerable group of the solo sonatas and concertos later incorporated into the collection of Frederick the Great may also belong to this period. Unfortunately the chronology of these manuscripts cannot be definitely fixed as yet, although the printed works seem to form a key to a solution of this problem in some cases. Thus it is difficult to trace a full picture of the various phases of Quantz's development as a composer during these formative years.[3]

---

[1] For a list and discussion of eighteenth-century editions of Quantz's compositions, see Appendix II of my *Quantz and His Versuch: Three Studies* (New York: American Musicological Society, 1971), pp. 144–54, and the supplement to this list provided below, pp. 388–92.

[2] 'Lebenslauf', p. 244.

[3] An interesting study of a group of Quantz's trio sonatas, together with a thematic catalogue of Quantz's forty-seven works in this form, is contained in Karl-Heinz Köhler, 'Die Triosonate

After his return to Dresden his position again improved considerably. In March 1728 he was made a member of the main Saxon *Kapelle* at Dresden, with a salary of 250 thalers in addition to his former stipend of 216 thalers, and was no longer required to double as an oboist. Thenceforth he seems to have been singled out as one of the outstanding performers in the Dresden orchestra.

The young virtuoso's thirty-first year also saw the beginning of an important new relationship. The King of Prussia, Frederick William I, paid a state visit to Dresden together with his 16-year-old son, Frederick. In May 1728 Augustus II paid a return visit to Berlin, and brought with him a group of his best musicians, including Pisendel, Weiss, Buffardin, and Quantz. Quantz made a particularly strong impression on Crown Prince Frederick (and his sister Wilhelmine), and their mother offered him a good position. Quantz claims that he could not secure his freedom from the Dresden establishment. From that time, however, he was allowed to visit Berlin, and later Ruppin and Rheinsberg, each year in order to teach Frederick the flute.

Although Quantz's tutelage of Frederick began in 1728, it must be emphasized that his home and the centre of his activities remained in Dresden for another thirteen years, and that Dresden in these years entered its most flourishing period of musical activity. In 1725 Italian opera was cultivated again, with the active support of the Crown Prince and future King, Augustus III. In 1731 his friend Hasse, who had meanwhile achieved an enormous success in Italy, was appointed *Kapellmeister*; and Hasse's wife, the notable singer Faustina, became one of the principal singers in the company. Also during these years Quantz had several opportunities to hear Johann Sebastian Bach perform on the organ; and as the *Essay* shows, he was not to forget the strong impression made by the great musician as a performer, although his estimate of Bach as a composer is uncertain. A few lines from the autobiography suggest how much he enjoyed and benefited from the musical life in which he participated: 'The beautiful church music, the excellent operas, and the extraordinary virtuoso singers that I was able to hear in Dresden brought me ever new pleasures, and constantly excited new enthusiasm.'[1]

It seems unlikely that Quantz would have seriously considered ex-

bei den Dresdener Zeitgenossen Johann Sebastian Bachs', unpublished dissertation, Friedrich-Schiller-Universität Jena, 1956, pp. 20–26, 39–41, 81–102 and, in the volume of examples, pp. 41–47. The most extended study of Quantz's music attempted thus far is found in Adolf Raskin, 'Johann Joachim Quantz. Sein Leben und seine Kompositionen', unpublished dissertation, Universität Köln, 1923. Although very useful as a preliminary study, the portion of this work devoted to Quantz's compositions leaves many basic questions unanswered, and the author's attempt at a general chronology fails to take a number of factors into account. An extensive but incomplete list of compositions is included, but the thematic incipits are lacking in the copy available to me. For a review of the current state of our knowledge of Quantz's work as a composer, together with detailed lists of manuscripts, eighteenth-century editions, and modern editions, see *Quantz and His Versuch*, pp. 1–39, 134–63, and the additions provided below, pp. 387–94.

[1] 'Lebenslauf', p. 245.

changing this position for a much less stimulating and much more tenu-
ous one under Crown Prince Frederick without considerable rewards.
Frederick's artistic activities as a young man were brutally opposed by his
father. And only after his imprisonment in the fortress of Küstrin in 1730,
and his apparent submission to his father's wishes, was he able to gradually begin the secret organization of his own private musical ensemble.
On Quantz's recommendation his friend, the violinist Franz Benda, was
employed by Frederick in 1733.[1] But in that same year when Augustus II
of Saxony was succeeded by his son, Quantz retained his Dresden post.
He reports that his salary was raised to 800 thalers, and permission was
granted to continue his visits to Frederick, as well as to the Margrave of
Bayreuth, who was now counted among his pupils; but he was not
allowed to leave the service of the new Elector and King, Augustus III.
A passage in a letter of 6 November 1733 by Frederick to his sister Wilhelmine suggests, however, that Quantz may have been playing a familiar
game, and also indicates that the relationship between teacher and student
was not without moments of strain. 'Quantz is probably pleased that his
new lord has ascended the throne,' Frederick writes. 'Since he does not
wish to change from horse to donkey, he has considered it advisable to
break his word to me; for he had promised to enter my service.'[2]

Quantz conveyed his appreciation of the benevolence of his 'new lord'
and sought his continued favour the following year by dedicating a
printed collection of sonatas to him, entitled *Sei sonate a flauto traversiere
solo, e cembalo, dedicate alla Maestà d'Augusto III. Re di Pollonia, Elettore di
Sassonia ... Opera prima* (Dresden, 1734).[3] These sonatas form the first collection for which the composer himself was directly responsible, and reflect
his care in preparing works for publication. In his preface he reports that
some of the solo sonatas already published under his name in England and
Holland are spurious, and that the others contain numerous printer's errors.

The remaining years of the now successful performer, composer, and
teacher at Dresden are marked by only two other recorded events. In
1737, at the age of 40, he was married, or, if a story published after
his death is true,[4] was tricked into marriage to Anna Rosina Carolina

---

[1] See Benda's autobiography in Nettl, *Forgotten Musicians*, pp. 222–4.

[2] Quoted in Kahl, *Selbstbiographien*, pp. 275–6. Quantz's original petition for a raise in
salary, dated 27 March 1733, is preserved in the *Sächsisches Landeshauptarchiv* in Dresden, and
has been reprinted in La Mara, *Musikerbriefe aus fünf Jahrhunderten* (2 vols.; Leipzig: Breitkopf
& Härtel, 1886), i, pp. 185–6. A second petition, along the same lines as the first, dated 9 July
1733, and the order for the salary increase, dated 21 September 1733, are also preserved in
the same archives.

[3] The first five of these sonatas have been issued in a modern edition 'revised' by Oscar
Fischer (Leipzig: Forberg, 1921). The edition, however, reflects an almost total indifference to
Quantz's teaching, as well as poor editorial practices in general. Better versions of the first and
fourth sonatas are presented as the first two of *Drei Sonaten* by Quantz, ed. by F. Schroeder
(Leipzig: VEB Breitkopf & Härtel, 1963).

[4] See F. W. Marpurg, *Legende einiger Musikheiligen* (Breslau: Korn, 1786), p. 67, and E. L.
Gerber, *Historisch-biographisches Lexicon der Tonkünstler* (2 vols.; Leipzig: Breitkopf, 1790–2),
ii, pp. 212–13.

Schindler (*née* Hölzel), probably the widow of a horn player in the Dresden orchestra. The meagre evidence preserved suggests that the union was not a happy one.*

Two years later, in 1739, he expanded his already rich field of activities to include the boring and tuning of flutes, a business that he also managed with considerable success for the remainder of his life.[1]

The concluding period of Quantz's life coincides with the rise of Prussia to the position of a major European power under the ambitious leadership of Frederick the Great. After he became King in 1740 the active young ruler was able to offer Quantz terms which his Saxon patron could not match, and which the musician could not refuse. In Berlin he was to have a position rarely equalled by an instrumental performer and composer in the eighteenth century. It was stipulated that he should receive

a stipend of two thousand thalers a year for life, in addition to a special payment for my compositions, a hundred ducats for each flute that I would supply, and the privilege of playing only in the Royal Chamber Ensemble, not in the [opera] orchestra, and of taking orders from none but the King. . . .[2]

Few musicians could have asked for more, and probably few could have failed to be somewhat envious of both the salary and prerogatives. Quantz obtained a release from the King of Poland, and officially entered the service of Frederick in December 1741.

From this time Quantz's life settled down into a pattern which seems to have remained more or less constant for his remaining thirty-two years. The outer routine was dictated by Frederick's own inflexible schedule in musical as well as other matters. According to one reliable witness

the months of December and January, together with the 27th of March, the birthday of Her Majesty the Queen Mother, were set aside for regular theatrical entertainments . . . and performances [of opera] occur every Monday and Friday of these two months. On the other days of the week during Carnival time masquerades, concerts, comedies and other entertainments alternate at court. At other times every day in the evening from 7 until 9 a regular concert is performed in the chamber of the King, in which His Majesty himself is accustomed to demonstrate his penetrating and exquisite taste, and his exceptional facility on the flute.[3]

This basic pattern seems to have been modified only by affairs of state. Opera productions were suspended during the Seven Years' War (1756–

[1] On Quantz's flutes, see *Quantz and His Versuch*, pp. 93–104, and Appendix n. 31, fn. 1, p. 358.

[2] 'Lebenslauf', p. 248. Quantz's salary is confirmed by contemporary records now preserved in the Merseburg division of the *Deutsches Zentralarchiv*. See the former Br. Pr. Hausarchiv, Rep. 12 B Nr. 3 and Nr. 10. Other records show that Frederick inquired after, or helped to obtain, stipends for Quantz from various towns in 1742, 1744, and 1748. See the former Geh. Pr. Staatsarchiv, Rep. 33 n 70B, Rep. 34 n 144a, and Rep. 52 n 27c.

[3] Marpurg, *Historisch-kritische Beyträge*, i, p. 75.

63), but Frederick seems to have continued to enjoy the recreation provided by the concerts, whenever he was able, at Berlin or Potsdam, and occasionally the Royal musicians attended him elsewhere. In 1746 Quantz accompanied him to Bad Pyrmont, and in 1760–1 joined him at his winter quarters at Leipzig.

As he was not required to play in the opera orchestra, the centre of Quantz's activities throughout the Berlin years remained the evening chamber concerts. While the operas presented by Frederick were public, and served as a public manifestation of his patronage, the concerts were private and intended entirely for his own enjoyment and relaxation. Only a few specially invited guests seem to have been allowed to attend. Although little reliable evidence has been discovered about the works performed in the earlier years of Frederick's ensemble, the main repertoire in the later decades consisted of works by Quantz and Frederick himself. Quantz personally set the tempos for the works performed and perhaps took part in the performance on occasion.[1] He was granted the exclusive privilege of approving or disapproving of the King's playing by conferring or withholding a 'bravo'. At other times he undoubtedly had to make himself available whenever the King wished to play sonatas or duets, or when he desired musical instruction or advice.

His principal duties, in addition to those that required his personal attendance, involved the continued creation of new compositions for the King, and the manufacture of new flutes. At the time of Quantz's death the joint catalogue that Frederick used as a guide to his own and his teacher's works included 361 flute sonatas, 153 by Quantz, and 300 concertos, all but 4 by Quantz.[2] Several volumes of studies, written jointly with Frederick,[3] and contributions to one or two collaborative compositions by several members of Frederick's musical establishment[4] also belong to his output for the King. At one time most of these compositions were believed destroyed in the Second World War. Some were lost, but the main body of Quantz's works formerly owned by Frederick were preserved, and are now located in the Deutsche Staatsbibliothek in East Berlin and the Staatsbibliothek Preußischer Kulturbesitz in West Berlin.

The majority of the compositions that Quantz wrote after his entry into Frederick's service were intended solely for the use of the King. Nevertheless, some reached a wider public in manuscript copies and printed editions. Fifty-two manuscript solos, trio sonatas, and concertos, including a considerable number written for Frederick,[5] were advertised in the

[1] Several concertos for two flutes and strings form a part of Frederick's collection.
[2] See the list of mss. in *Quantz and His Versuch*, pp. 134–43 and the additions on pp. 387–8.
[3] A selection of these exercises has been published as *Das Flötenbuch Friedrichs des Großen*, edited by E. Schwarz-Reiflingen (Leipzig: Breitkopf & Härtel, 1934).
[4] See F. Bose, 'Quantz', in *Die Musik in Geschichte und Gegenwart*, 10, col. 1801, and E. E. Helm, *Music at the Court of Frederick the Great* (Norman: University of Oklahoma Press, 1960), pp. 40–41, 61, 104–5, 123.
[5] A note in the German edition of Burney's *The Present State of Music in Germany* indicates that none of Quantz's concertos 'became generally known until sixteen or twenty years after it

catalogues of Breitkopf from 1762 to 1784, and a smaller group was published in Berlin in the seventeen-fifties and -sixties. Among the published works the most important are the *Sei duetti a due flauti traversi . . . opera seconda*,[1] published in 1759 by Winter with a lengthy preface dealing with the value of duets in the training of good students. The implication that the duets were intended as a musical adjunct to the *Essay* seems unmistakable. Other printed works from this period include a handful of songs, a series of *Neue Kirchen-Melodien zu denen geistlichen Liedern des Herrn Professor Gellerts . . .* (Berlin, Winter, 1760),[2] and a flute sonata published in the *Musikalisches Allerley* of 1761 (Berlin, Birnstiel).[3]

Although Quantz's considerable output of flute compositions is frequently cited with the imputation that such numbers automatically preclude any thought of quality, it must be remembered that these works were created over a period of about fifty years, and that, today, they are relatively little known. Quantz is hardly likely to enjoy again the reputation as a composer that he earned in his own day, but he has not yet been given the benefit of a study that clarifies the development of his style or separates his best work from the merely routine. Such a study could be illuminating in many ways, especially since Quantz's activity as a composer spanned a long and particularly interesting phase in the evolution of musical styles.

While the works available in modern editions seem to have been selected all too haphazardly, and provide only a limited idea of Quantz's efforts as a composer, study of several of his solos, duets, trio sonatas, and concertos in conjunction with the *Essay* will do much to deepen the modern student's insight into Quantz's meanings. They will serve more effectively than any number of words to place him in his proper musical and historical milieu, that charming if somewhat superficial *galant* world that emerged in the German courts in the early decades of the eighteenth century. Without advocating an undesirable wholesale revival of Quantz's compositions, it should be clear that his combined efforts as a teacher and composer offer an unrivalled opportunity to explore the interrelationships between musical thought and musical practice. Experimentation with Quantz's precepts on tempo, dynamics, ornamentation, articulation,

---

was written'. Thus the works advertised by Breitkopf may be relatively early compositions. See *Dr. Burney's Musical Tours*, ii, p. 163, n. 1.

[1] Several modern editions of these duets have been published, but none is entirely satisfactory. The facsimile of the original edition published in 1967 by Gregg Press is preferable to all other versions. A translation of the full preface to the collection is presented in my article 'Further Musical Examples for Quantz's *Versuch*', *Journal of the American Musicological Society*, xvii (1964), pp. 157–69. These duets were also published *c.* 1770 in England, as 'collected by Mr. Tacet', but with no acknowledgement of Quantz as the composer.

[2] The Preface to this collection contains a letter of Quantz in which he explains his aims in composing these congregational songs.

[3] The third movement of this sonata is reproduced in E. Bücken, *Die Musik des Rokokos und der Klassik* (Potsdam: Akademische Verlagsgesellschaft Athenaion, 1929), pp. 80–84. The complete sonata appears as the third of the *Drei Sonaten* by Quantz, ed. by F. Schroeder (Leipzig: VEB Breitkopf & Härtel, 1963).

and other matters quickly shows how effective they are in animating his
own works, even when the composition appears unpromising on paper.
And because many aspects of Quantz's style are not especially original,
but common to many other major and lesser figures of the late Baroque
and pre-Classic eras, his compositions provide an excellent basis from
which the student may see where his teachings are best applied, and where
one must be cautious about their appropriateness in other works. They
also form the soundest guide in suggesting just how literally certain rules
should be interpreted, provide concrete examples of the various forms that
he describes, and do much to clarify the musical realizations of that
language of the passions which underlies his aesthetic theory.[1]

Quantz's influential position at Frederick's court apparently changed
very little during the last thirty years of his life, but the relationship between Frederick's musical tastes and those found in other parts of Europe
altered significantly after his return from the Seven Years' War.[2] In the
earlier years of his reign Frederick almost single-handedly made Berlin an
important musical centre. A first-rate orchestra was formed, on the basis of
his Rheinsberg ensemble, with many outstanding performers and composers such as C. P. E. Bach (1714–88), Franz Benda (1709–86), and J. G.
Graun (1702/3–71). A beautiful opera house was built, and good singers and
dancers were imported to perform works by the two most popular German composers of Italian opera, J. A. Hasse and his own *Kapellmeister* Carl
Heinrich Graun. Frederick himself played an active role in musical and
dramatic productions,[3] and did his utmost to make Berlin rival the musical
splendour achieved at Dresden by Augustus III, whose musical establishment formed the model for his own. The musical life of the Saxon
court, which ironically Frederick destroyed in the course of the Seven
Years' War, directly and indirectly influenced his tastes and standards, as it
had those of Quantz. Many of Frederick's musicians had been active there
at one time, and many of his composers perpetuated the styles cultivated
in Dresden. Far from seeming conservative, however, the preferences of
Dresden and Berlin, and of Frederick, coincided with those of much of
Europe in the seventeen-forties and -fifties.

After the Seven Years' War, during which C. H. Graun died, Frederick's
interest in music gradually waned, and he did little more than perpetuate
the pattern that he had already created. While important musical developments were taking place around him, he held tenaciously to the opinions
and preferences of his youth. The operas of Hasse and Graun continued
to be performed, and his own and Quantz's works remained the staples

[1] On Quantz's aesthetics, see R. Schäfke, 'Quantz als Ästhetiker', *Archiv für Musikwissenschaft*, vi (1924), pp. 213–42.
[2] For general surveys of Frederick's musical activities and attitudes, see E. E. Helm, *Music at
the Court of Frederick the Great*, and G. Thouret, *Friedrich der Große als Musikfreund und Musiker*
(Leipzig: Breitkopf & Härtel, 1898).
[3] On Frederick's activities as composer and librettist, see Helm, *Music at the Court of Frederick
the Great*, pp. 39–80.

of his private concerts. Thus Frederick and many of the musicians whom he had gathered together in their prime grew old together, and Berlin became increasingly conservative in relation to the newer styles emerging in *opera buffa*, the reform operas of Gluck and the Mannheim symphonists, to say nothing of the works of Haydn and the youthful Mozart. By the late seventeen-sixties the styles preserved in Berlin, with the exception of that of C. P. E. Bach, who escaped to Hamburg in 1767, seemed quite old-fashioned to those aware of musical currents elsewhere.

As would seem natural if not admirable in a man of his age, Quantz's attitudes in his last years seem to have coincided to a certain extent with those of his master. Burney, writing in 1772, provides a generally excellent if one-sided picture of musical life in Berlin in its declining years, and he remarks that Quantz's opinions 'when he wrote his book, more than twenty years ago . . . were enlarged and liberal, which is not the case at present . . .'.[1] As is so often true with the advance of age, it seems that Quantz, having worked diligently to develop and codify his own ideas about performance and composition, was unable to accept other views then emerging, and could see in them only a decline in the standards and ideals of his own generation. To what extent he continued to develop as a composer, however, is a question that must remain unanswered until the chronology of his compositions is settled. The few works that can be dated suggest that there are some changes in style, but that fundamentally he continued to adhere to the *galant* idiom of the second quarter of the century.

Details about Quantz's relations with other members of Frederick's musical establishment are scarce, and not always as clear as some writers imply. He was on friendly terms with Franz Benda and C. H. Graun before he or they entered Frederick's service, and there is no reason to believe that the friendship diminished. Johann Friedrich Agricola (1720–74) and Christoph Nichelmann (1717–61/2), both pupils of J. S. Bach, were among Quantz's students in composition, and also seem to have been good friends. That a more creative composer such as C. P. E. Bach may well have been irritated by Frederick's exclusive devotion to Quantz's works is certainly probable, but the personal relationship between C. P. E. Bach and Quantz is in many respects uncertain; and one must be careful about accepting the frequently contradictory testimony of the opportunist Johann Friedrich Reichardt (1752–1814) or the amusing (and damning) *Gedenkrede auf Friedrich den Großen* (1809) of Carl Friedrich Zelter (1758–1832) at their face value. Both belong to a generation that rebelled against everything that Frederick represented in the arts, even though Reichardt served for a time as his *Kapellmeister* and apologist; and both were infants during the best years of Frederick's musical patronage. C. P. E. Bach does not hesitate to call upon Quantz as a witness to his father's skill, while Quantz's open admiration of J. S. Bach as a performer hardly suggests a vindictive attitude towards the son.[2]

[1] *Dr. Burney's Musical Tours*, ii, p. 207. [2] See the *Essay*, Chapter XVIII, § 83.

Outside court Quantz seems to have taken an active part in the musical life of Berlin up to the last decade of his life. His musical publications during this period have already been noted, and there is no question that they were highly regarded. After the appearance of the *Essay* in 1752 he contributed a number of articles to the periodicals of the critic and theorist Friedrich Wilhelm Marpurg (1718–95), and became involved in several of the controversies that formed a staple of Berlin musical life. The autobiography appeared in 1755, a reply to an attack on the *Essay* in 1758,[1] and a series of letters dealing with the harmonic theories of Georg Andreas Sorge, Marpurg, and Rameau in 1759 and 1760.[2] On the occasion of the publication of the *Sei duetti* of 1759, Johann Philipp Kirnberger (1721–83), another pupil of J. S. Bach and court musician to Princess Amalia of Prussia, precipitated a public dispute on the nature of 'true' duets. Judging from the reports published by Marpurg, public sympathy seems to have been entirely on Quantz's side.

Of his personal life during his years at Berlin and Potsdam very little is known. A letter from the noted author Lessing (1729–81) to the poet Ramler (1725–98) closes with greetings to Quantz and Agricola, and refers to a club that met regularly on Friday evenings.[3] The two musicians, Ramler, Lessing, the aesthetician Christian Gottfried Krause (1719–70), and perhaps the author and publisher Christoph Friedrich Nicolai (1733–1811) were among its members, but unfortunately no further details of Quantz's position in this interesting group have as yet been uncovered.

One personal letter of Quantz, dated 5 August 1755, was preserved and reproduced by a nineteenth-century descendant of the family.[4] Written to the wife of a recently deceased cousin, it combines pious reflection with practical advice on the disposal of her husband's property, and gives notice that 20 thalers are being sent to cover burial and other expenses. A letter to the publisher Nicolai, dated 7 February 1767, conveys thanks for the publication of an engraved portrait of the composer by Johann David Schleuen (fl. 1740–74) as frontispiece to the fourth volume (1767) of the *Allgemeine Deutsche Bibliothek*.[5] And four recently uncovered letters

[1] 'Hrn. Johann Joachim Quanzens Antwort auf des Herrn von Moldenit gedrucktes so genanntes Schreiben an Hrn. Quanz . . .' in Marpurg, *Historisch-kritische Beyträge*, iv (1759), pp. 153–91.

[2] *Kritische Briefe über die Tonkunst* (3 vols.; Berlin: Birnstiel, 1760–4), i, pp. 25–28, 57–60, 75–80, 135–7. Some doubts as to whether Quantz was actually the author of these letters are raised by the fact that Sorge states that he believes that they were the work of Marpurg, and that the 'Neologos' under whose name they appeared was only one of several different pseudonyms used by Marpurg. See G. A. Sorge, *Compendium harmonicum* (Lobenstein: published by the author, 1760), p. 121.

[3] See Richard Benz, *Die Zeit der deutschen Klassik* (Stuttgart: Reclam, 1953), pp. 157–8.

[4] Quoted in A. Quantz, *Leben und Werke des Flötisten Johann Joachim Quantz* (Berlin: R. Oppenheim, 1877), pp. 41–42.

[5] This portrait is reproduced in Bücken, *Die Musik des Rokokos und der Klassik*, p. 78. At least two other portraits of Quantz have been preserved, one an attractive oil painting of him as a relatively young man, by an unidentified artist, now in Schloß Kronberg in the Taunus, the other a less flattering sketch by Heinrich Franke (1738–92) now in the Deutsche Staatsbibliothek. The

from Quantz to the celebrated music historian Padre Martini (1706–84) now in the Civico Museo Bibliografico, Bologna, show that in the years from 1761 to 1765 the two musicians exchanged literary and musical works, and that Martini requested information about Quantz for inclusion in his history.

On the basis of this limited evidence, it is impossible to draw a full picture of Quantz's personality and character. It is perhaps appropriate that most of what we know about him has to do with the musician rather than the details of his private life. The most attractive side of his personality is his complete devotion to his art. The whole record of his life shows a man who was interested in all aspects of music and spared no pains to learn all that he could about every phase of it. His musical limitations seem to have been the result of the natural tendency to become more conservative with the passing of years, and of the belief that his generation of musicians had discovered more permanent artistic values and standards than their predecessors or followers. The success that was the reward of his industry and musical sensitivity gave him an obvious pride in accomplishment that stands out on nearly every page of his autobiography. His habit of quoting salaries and dropping names in that work forms an unpleasant aspect of this quality, but is an understandable trait in a man who, largely through his own efforts, advanced from very poor beginnings to a position beyond the dreams of most instrumentalists of his day. His career is indeed a classic illustration of the virtues and rewards of hard work, and might well form the subject of a series of engravings along the lines of Hogarth's 'Industry and Idleness'.

In contrast to his pupil, Frederick, a strong element of piety, with an accompanying belief in an ultimately benevolent Providence, is noticeable in some of his writings; and his active interest in church music is reflected in his *Neue Kirchen-Melodien* and his sharp comments in the *Essay* on the position of cantors in the German churches of his day.[1] That he was shrewdly aware of the need to please one's patrons is also evident in several passages in the *Essay*;[2] but Frederick's letters and one or two apparently reliable stories of Quantz's relationship with Frederick indicate that he was anything but a fawning courtier. The breadth of his knowledge, his musical sensitivity, and his practical wisdom are fully apparent in the *Essay* itself.

References in the *Essay* and in his other literary works also indicate a considerable familiarity with contemporary writing on music. And although first-hand experience in all of the fields he discusses forms the essential basis of Quantz's teaching, a few of the works that form a background for certain portions of the *Essay* may be mentioned here for those

former, to my knowledge, was first reproduced in the Bärenreiter Music Calendar of 1960; the latter is found in Bose, 'Quantz', *MGG*, 10, cols. 1797–9, where Quantz's letter to Nicolai also appears.

[1] See his note to § 80 in Chapter XVIII.
[2] See Chapter XIV, § 1, and Chapter XVI, §§ 20–23.

interested in exploring further the connexions between the treatise and other works that preceded it.

The only significant tutors for the transverse flute before Quantz's work were the two complementary guides of Jacques Hotteterre, 'le Romain' (*c.* 1674–1762), the *Principes de la flute traversiere, ou flute d'Allemagne* (1707), and *L'Art de preluder sur la flûte traversiere* (1719), and M. Corrette's *Methode pour apprendre aisément à joüer de la flute traversiere* (*c.* 1740). ◄ The general areas discussed in Quantz's first ten chapters may have been suggested in part by these brief works, but his treatment goes far beyond them in every respect, and differs from them in many particulars.

Some of the material in the chapters on execution (XI to XVI) parallel portions of Pier Francesco Tosi's *Opinioni de' cantori antichi, e moderni* (1723),[1] which Quantz knew and which his pupil Agricola translated into German with many valuable notes, and also a series of articles on execution in Marpurg's *Des critischen Musicus an der Spree erster Band* (1749–50).[2] The treatment of extempore variations may have been prompted by a number of sources, the embellished versions of Corelli's Op. V which he himself cites, or perhaps Telemann's *Sonates methodiques* (1728–32)[3] and *Trietti metodichi* (1731).[4] Quantz speaks highly of Telemann's works in a number of genres, and is also listed among the subscribers to his *Tafelmusik.*

No real precedent has been discovered for the sections on accompanying instruments, unless they were perhaps conceived as extensions of rudimentary methods for a variety of instruments such as J. F. B. C. Majer's *Museum musicum* (1732).

Antecedents of Quantz's discussions of musical forms are found in portions of Johann Mattheson's *Der vollkommene Capellmeister* (1739),[5] and especially in articles scattered throughout the *Critischer Musicus* (1737–40) of the much maligned, but extremely interesting critic J. A. Scheibe.[6]

Stylistic comparisons of French and Italian music go back to the beginning of the century, with the *Paralèle des italiens et des françois* (1702) of François Raguenet, and the *Comparaison de la musique italienne et de la musique française* (1704–6) of Le Cerf de la Viéville,[7] both of which were

---

[1] See Chapters i, iv, vi, viii, and ix of J. E. Galliard's translation of Tosi, under the title *Observations on the Florid Song* (2nd ed.; London: J. Wilcox, 1743). A number of specific relevant passages are indicated in the footnotes to the translation.

[2] See pp. 208–10, 215–18, 223–6.

[3] See G. P. Telemann, *Musikalische Werke* (Kassel: Bärenreiter, 1950-), vol. 1. A reference to 'den mir überaus lieben Herrn Quantz' in a letter from Telemann to C. H. Graun, dated 15 November 1751, suggests that Quantz and Telemann may have been personally acquainted. ◄ See *Denkmäler deutscher Tonkunst*, xxviii, p. lxx.

[4] *III trietti metodichi e III scherzi*, ed. by Max Schneider (3 vols.; Leipzig: Breitkopf & Härtel, 1948). For references to further examples of this type of ornamentation, see the note accompanying § 44 in Chapter XIII of the *Essay*.

[5] See especially pp. 210–34.

[6] The individual sections are indicated in the notes to the translation.

[7] For English translations of a portion of the latter and the entire former work, see O. Strunk, *Source Readings in Music History* (New York: W. W. Norton, 1950), pp. 473–507.

well known in Germany. Extensions of these comparisons to include references to German style are found in articles by both Scheibe[1] and Marpurg.[2]

While the works noted and others cited in the various articles of Quantz confirm his familiarity with contemporary musical thought and writing, comparison with them shows that he never merely copied what others had to say. Quantz's treatment is generally both richer and more concrete, and although not essentially an original thinker, through experience and reflection he made the material with which he dealt his own. Unfortunately no record of the contents of his library has been located. It might throw still more light on his interests, reading, and musical taste.[3]

Less than a year after the eminent English music historian Charles Burney visited Berlin and Potsdam and reported Quantz as enjoying 'an uncommon portion of health and vigour' for a man of his age, and as still able to execute 'rapid movements with great precision',[4] the long career of the celebrated musician reached its end. He died on 12 July 1773, when a musical era far different in many respects from that of his own prime had already come into being. Haydn was 41 and had already completed the 'Sun' quartets, Mozart a precocious 17.

Obituaries praising both the man and the musician appeared in the newspapers, a funeral cantata was written,[5] and Frederick later had a statue by the Ränz brothers erected in his memory.[6] The passing of the famed composer and teacher, and Frederick's homage, were noted even in London, where they were duly reported in the daily press.[7] As a more personal tribute Frederick also completed the attractive concerto which had occupied Quantz's last days. When playing the slow movement he is reported to have turned to Franz Benda and remarked 'You see, Quantz departed this world with very good ideas'.[8]

Although the particular style of composition and performance represented by Quantz and his generation was outmoded even at the time of his death, and his musical works disappeared gradually from the repertoire, he left the generations that followed a more enduring legacy. His *Essay*,

[1] *Critischer Musikus, neue, vermehrte und verbesserte Auflage* (Leipzig: B. C. Breitkopf, 1745), pp. 141–50.

[2] *Des critischen Musicus an der Spree erster Band* (Berlin: Haude & Spener, 1750), pp. 1 ff.

[3] C. F. D. Schubart, *Ideen zu einer Ästhetik der Tonkunst*, ed. by P. A. Merbach (Leipzig: Wolkenwanderer Verlag, 1924), p. 55, indicates that Quantz's library was purchased by Frederick for 20,000 thalers. Although Schubart was none too reliable, he may have been at least partly correct in this instance. A document (the former Geh. Pr. Staatsarchiv, Rep. 21 n 124) now in the Merseburg division of the *Deutsches Zentralarchiv* indicates that Frederick did have *Abschoßgelder* sent to the magistrate at Potsdam for Quantz's *Nachlaß*.

[4] *Dr. Burney's Musical Tours*, ii, pp. 180, 182.

[5] See A. Quantz, *J. J. Quantz*, pp. 40–41, 43–45.

[6] A picture is reproduced in Bücken, *Die Musik des Rokokos und der Klassik*, p. 79.

[7] See *The Daily Advertiser*, Wednesday, 25 Aug. 1773.

[8] An as yet unpublished edition of this concerto has been prepared by the present writer. An account of Frederick's completion of the work as well as a description of Quantz's working habits is found in C. F. Nicolai, *Anekdoten von König Friedrich II. von Preußen, und von einigen Personen, die um ihn waren* (6 vols.; Berlin and Stettin: F. Nicolai, 1788–92), iii, pp. 250, 258–9.

like the treatises of Leopold Mozart and C. P. E. Bach, continued to be highly esteemed until the end of the century, and was never really equalled by the works of later teachers.

Just as Quantz's biography and music provide a glimpse of the rich fund of experience that went into the *Essay*, the various editions of the work offer a picture of the authority which it obtained. An extended list of the editions of the treatise or of portions of it, and of works that draw material directly from it, is presented in a separate section in the bibliography of the present volume, both to indicate the continuing fame of the work and to establish a more complete record than that currently available in standard reference works.

The considerable reputation enjoyed by the *Essay* that this list suggests is confirmed in numerous references to the work in the writings of other authors. The longest review thus far discovered is contained in an article in the *Bibliothek der schönen Wissenschaften* devoted to the three works of Quantz, C. P. E. Bach, and L. Mozart. The unnamed reviewer gives high praise to the work as a whole, and raises a question or two about several points in the latter part of the work:

Truth, genius, and good taste, qualities which do not characterize all performers and music masters, distinguish the authors [Mozart, Quantz, and C. P. E. Bach] and their writings. Yet one notes a particular distinctive feature in Mr. Quantz's *Essay*: it is almost a general work, for it does not merely expound and illustrate most accurately and forthrightly the principles of playing the flute, but explains thoroughly and clearly all the basic rules and interests of performers of every type, and everything related to the performance of a musical piece. All kinds of instrumentalists, as well as singers, and the leader and director of an ensemble, find their qualities, their virtues, and their faults cited in it. All can learn from it, composers not excepted. Even the characteristics of various musical pieces and various styles are found characterized with particular accuracy. Mr. Quantz concludes with an historical–critical report on the present style of music. Here there is neither time nor opportunity to go into his views properly, but we must mention that the epoch when the Germans began to educate themselves in vocal composition must actually be much earlier than Mr. Quantz supposes. . . . In this regard we know, from the period of Opitz, the father of German poetry, that even before the year 1627 German operas were performed in Germany; and was not Schütz, the master of the chapel at Dresden, who brought Opitz's *Daphne* to the lyric stage, a German? On the other hand, we laud with pleasure the judgment of Mr. Quantz when he calls the present good style of music, which is a kind of mixed style, the style of the Germans; for they were the first who fell upon arranging and adorning [this style] which, for some years now, has found favour not only in Germany, but even in Italy and France. Before we leave this fine work, we must further note, however, that some important remarks might be made about Mr. Quantz's views in Chapter XVII, where the placement and complement of a good musical ensemble are discussed. In the performance of a large vocal piece with a strong instrumental accompaniment in a large hall, it might well be very disadvantageous to the good effect that is one's goal if the plan given were followed. Very well-founded physical reasons also might be cited as to why care must be taken to give the flutes and oboes a position quite distant from the high vocal parts in small and large vocal pieces. No musical instruments swallow up the tone and the words of high voices as much as flutes and oboes, if they are too near to the singers, although no instruments are more useful for strengthening and supporting them than the oboes, and none provide greater amenity than the flutes. Hence a skilful leader must be all the more careful to insist that the instruments are judiciously placed, for otherwise the benefits which a musical piece derives from the instruments fall away entirely. The notes and the words of the singers of both sexes are the principal matter to which everything must be directed, and where these are suppressed or even weakened everything else is to no purpose and without point.[1]

The work as a whole and various portions of it are also recommended by Marpurg, Agricola, Mattheson, G. M. Telemann, Adlung, Reichardt, Forkel, Sulzer and, in a particularly charming way, by C. G. Schröter.[2]

But criticisms of certain parts of the *Essay* must also be noted, as they emphasize the variety of opinion and practice of the time, a variety that must be constantly stressed for the benefit of those who seek to dogmatize about the performance of music in the past, or expect to find 'definitive' solutions to artistic problems. Unfortunately, however, the lengthiest dispute about the *Essay* was precipitated by a charlatan bent on irritating his former teacher. In 1753 Joachim von Moldenit published in Hamburg a work entitled *Sei sonate da flauto traverso e basso continuo, con un discorso sopra la maniera di sonar il flauto traverso*. In the sonatas he demanded a range exceeding that customary on the flutes of the day, and in his *discorso* attacked Quantz's method of articulating with the tongue, explaining that he had a new approach based on the use of the lower lip (*sic*). Caustic reports of Moldenit's work appeared in Marpurg's *Historisch-kritische Beyträge* which precipitated another work by Moldenit directly attacking Quantz, whom he felt responsible for Marpurg's review. Moldenit's article finally aroused Quantz's ire, and he replied with a sharp rebuttal in which he skilfully examined Moldenit's contentions point by point.[3] In the course of his reply Quantz challenged Moldenit to a public contest with one of his pupils in which Telemann's unaccompanied flute *Fantasias*[4] were to be performed before a group of connoisseurs. Moldenit, of course, failed to appear, and his failure to support his claims in person was publicly reported by Marpurg, thus putting an end to this amusing tempest in a teapot. The most valuable result of the argument is found in Quantz's article, which provides a few more particulars about his teaching.

More pertinent criticism is found in the article *Anmerkungen über Herrn Quanzens, Königl. Preußischen Kammermusici dis und es Klappe auf der Querflöte* (Remarks on the Royal Chamber Musician Mr. Quantz's D sharp and

---

[1] *Bibliothek der schönen Wissenschaften*, x (1763), pp. 50–53.
[2] For further details, see Reilly, *Quantz and His Versuch*, pp. 54–5.
[3] See p. xxvii, n. 1 above.
[4] See G. P. Telemann, *Musikalische Werke* (Kassel: Bärenreiter, 1950–), vol. 6.

E flat Keys on the Transverse Flute) of the organist Georg Andreas Sorge.[1] Sorge attempts to correct Quantz's reckoning of the difference between conjunct sharp and flat notes, and advocates the use of the tempered system of tuning which would have made Quantz's second key unnecessary. The article emphasizes the differences of opinion about tempered tuning which persisted long after its acceptance by keyboard players.

In addition to these direct criticisms, disagreements in some later works indicate changes which affected the validity of Quantz's teaching on certain points. One interesting reference is found in a review of Schlegel's 1788 adaptation of the *Essay*[2] in which Schlegel is severely criticized for not bringing some portions of the work up to date, especially the treatment of appoggiaturas. The reviewer exclaims: 'How incomplete about them are [Quantz's] instructions with regard to our present style! In this respect the editor might justly have made use of other more recent instruction books, and could have enlarged and corrected the treatment of appoggiaturas preserved in Quantz's *Essay*.'[3] And as early as 1772 Burney suggests that Quantz's approach to appoggiaturas and several other matters was old-fashioned to those familiar with current fashions:

Without giving in to tricks and caprice, and even allowing composition to have been arrived at its *acme* of perfection, forty years ago, yet a simple melody may surely be embellished by the modern manner of taking *appogiaturas* [*sic*], or preparing and returning shakes, of gradually enforcing and diminishing whole passages, as well as single notes, and, above all, by the variety of expression arising from that superiority in the use of the bow, which violin players of this age possess over those of any other period since its invention.[4]

After recommending Quantz's work generally, Reichardt in his *Ueber die Pflichten des Ripien-Violinisten* (On the Duties of the Ripieno Violinist, 1776) also suggests a different approach to bowing: 'I must, however, warn everyone against the frequent detaching of the bow, which in my opinion is just as erroneous as for a violinist to consider it his first duty to be able to give equal significance to the up-stroke and the down-stroke.'[5] Criticisms of this sort are most useful in suggesting those areas of musical performance in which basic changes were occurring.

In considering the relationship between Quantz and the authors of two other important tutors of his own time, C. P. E. Bach and L. Mozart, it is obvious that the works of the three authors complement one another in striking fashion. Although differences of opinion exist on certain points, they are usually minor.[6] Quantz's work was the first to appear, and seems

[1] See Marpurg, *Historisch-kritische Beyträge*, iv, pp. 1–7.
[2] See the list of editions in part I of the bibliography.
[3] *Allgemeine Deutsche Bibliothek*, cx (1792), pp. 118–19.
[4] *Dr. Burney's Musical Tours*, ii, p. 182.
[5] J. F. Reichardt, *Ueber die Pflichten des Ripien-Violinisten* (Berlin and Leipzig: G. J. Decker, 1776), pp. 28–29.
[6] A number of differences are pointed out in the notes to the translation.

to have suggested the approach of the other two. C. P. E. Bach and
L. Mozart seem to have been intent on applying Quantz's detailed treatment to their own instruments without attempting to equal the range of
his coverage. In general Quantz's work, because it takes up so many
phases of music-making, provides the best foundation for a perceptive
understanding of many points in the other two works, or, for that matter,
of many other treatises on music which appeared in the eighteenth century.

The matter of Quantz's influence outside Germany is too complex to
be considered in detail here. Editions and borrowings make it clear that
the *Essay* was known and respected in Holland, England, France, and
Italy; but it is unlikely that it ever achieved the popularity of the simpler
native methods.[1] Of all the notices of the *Essay* examined, however, the
best is that of Burney, who in a few words manages to touch upon many
of the essential points concerning both the background of the author and
the values of the treatise. Burney's lines may still serve as an apt summary
and conclusion to the present introduction:

In 1752, Quantz, who had the honour of being the late King of Prussia's
master on the German-flute, published in German and French on the art of
playing that instrument; a work not only useful to flute-players, but to every
kind of musician. His counsels to young students in Music are built upon good
sense and experience; and though his genius for composition was not original,
he was a keen observer of the beauties and defects of others, both in composition
and performance. His advantages in hearing at Dresden, in the most flourishing
time of that court, the greatest performers then living, and afterwards travelling
through Europe for improvement, with an acute understanding and an insatiable thirst for knowledge, enable him to embellish his instructions with
anecdotes and observations, which, notwithstanding the vicissitudes of taste and
style, are still extremely valuable.[2]

[1] See Reilly, *Quantz and His Versuch*, pp. 54–5.
[2] C. Burney, *A General History of Music from the Earliest Ages to the Present*, 2nd ed., edited by
F. Mercer (2 vols.; New York: Harcourt, Brace and Co., 1935), ii, pp. 949–50.

INTRODUCTION TO THE NEW EDITION

WHEN I first became interested in Quantz's treatise—now many years ago—it was not simply with a view to producing a translation of the volume. Rather, I wished to attempt a study of the work which involved what was then a new method of approach. I hoped to shed light on Quantz's views by exploring them from a variety of different perspectives: Quantz's specific training as a performer and composer; the stylistic features of his compositions and their implications with respect to performance; professional reactions to the work as a whole and to specific points in it in the eighteenth century; and finally, the similarities and differences in Quantz's views on a wide range of topics in relation to predecessors, contemporaries and followers.

Because of the size and expense of producing the entire work when it was initially completed in 1958, it could not be published as a single unit. Ultimately, certain of the materials were condensed in the introduction and notes of the present volume, and after a delay of several years, a companion volume, *Quantz and His Versuch: Three Studies*, was published in 1972 by the American Musicological Society. In these studies much more detailed and comprehensive information was presented about Quantz's work as a composer, the dissemination of the *Versuch* and the critical reaction to it in different countries, and the specific background for several major areas of musical discussion in the work (Quantz's flutes and his treatment of ornamentation, dynamics and tempo).

In this new edition of the translation I have tried to make known the material now available in the companion volume cited above and in the more recent studies of other scholars, and to correct any slips of fact or translation that have been discovered. The works of Robert Donington, Frederick Neumann and, for woodwind players, especially those of Betty Bang Mather and David Lasocki, have added substantially to the evidence available to modern players, and at the appropriate places in the translation I have done my best to draw attention to at least some of the most important pertinent research by these and other scholars. Readers may easily supplement the references included here by making use of the excellent Select Bibliography in the new version (1974) of Donington's *The Interpretation of Early Music* and the valuable work edited by Mary Vinquist and Neal Zaslaw, *Performance Practice: A Bibliography* (New York: W. W. Norton, 1970), with its supplements in *Current Musicology*, No. 12 (1971) and No. 15 (1973). Since 1973 the journal *Early Music* has become a stimulating forum for discussions of a wide range of matters connected with the performance of music of earlier periods.

The past few years have also been more specifically important with regard to the location of new material connected with Quantz and his work. In this period, manuscripts of a group of *Solfeggi* with instructions by Quantz, and of sets of unaccompanied *Capricci, Fantasias*, and other pieces for flute, have at last been located in the Danish Royal Library in Copenhagen. Modern editions of all of these works have already been published. Although *Solfeggi* are a well-known genre in the eighteenth century, this collection is unique in the range of its examples, the majority of which are drawn from actual compositions by Quantz and at least eighteen other composers, and in its wealth of comments by Quantz on concrete matters of rhythm, articulation, phrasing, dynamics and tone quality. The collection thus provides an extraordinarily important musical supplement to the instructions found in the *Versuch*; and the specific comments on individual musical passages vividly demonstrate the flexibility with which Quantz interpreted his own principles. The *Fantasias* and *Capricci* restore to us a substantial group of compositions previously believed lost. These add an attractive and interesting further dimension to Quantz's work as a composer. If, now, examples of his quartets can be traced, the most important remaining gap in our knowledge of his output will be filled.

The appearance of volume 7 of *Einzeldrucke vor 1800* (Printed Editions of the Works of Individual Composers Before 1800) of the *International Inventory of Musical Sources* (RISM) has made possible the location of six further editions of Quantz's solo sonatas, extending the total number of surviving collections (excluding works in anthologies) from fifteen to twenty-one. This number even more clearly suggests Quantz's popularity as a composer in Paris, London, and Amsterdam, although it adds few compositions to those already known. Two of the newly located volumes are in fact French editions of Quantz's own *Sei Sonate ... Opera prima,* published in Dresden in 1734. Others further complicate the already complicated question of which sonatas are genuine in several English, Dutch and French editions. Details about these volumes, and also about recent modern editions of Quantz's music, are provided in the supplements to my previous lists of manuscripts and printed editions in *Quantz and His Versuch*. These supplements appear at the end of the new material appended to this edition of the translation.

In the area of Quantz's activity as a designer of flutes, additional information is also available. Although I have not yet been able to establish a comprehensive list of all of the known surviving instruments made under his supervision, it is now possible to indicate the location of four of his type of two-keyed flutes. The notes of Dayton C. Miller on the instruments he examined in Germany before World War II provide further valuable information on twice that number. Most recently the distinguished modern instrument maker, Friedrich von Huene, has produced replicas of Quantz's two-keyed flutes, which now permit players to familiarize themselves directly with the distinctive qualities of his instruments. Reports received thus far confirm those of Quantz's contemporaries. The fact that replicas of Quantz's flutes are available, and even more important, that there are growing numbers of performers who can play eighteenth-century flutes well, suggests most concretely what a startling growth of interest has developed in the sonorities of earlier music and in modern skills in recreating the music of earlier times with the appropriate instruments.

Wherever space permitted, corrections and alterations in this edition were made in the appropriate places on the page. Additions or modifications which required further space are indicated by a small arrow (→) at the proper place in the margin of the text, and are located in the Appendix at the back of the volume. For my original Bibliography, I have also drawn attention to a few pertinent bits of new information and to many of the numerous reprints of works to which I referred. In the supplementary Bibliography I have confined myself largely to the new books and articles that I have cited in this edition; many further items are noted in the works of Donington and Vinquist mentioned earlier. And since I am still convinced that the study of Quantz's treatise is initially best undertaken in conjunction with his own music, I have continued to encourage a greater familiarity with his works by bringing up to date the lists of manuscripts, eighteenth-century editions, and modern editions included in my *Three Studies*. Finally, for this edition Quantz's own index, included in the first edition, has been expanded to include additional material by the editor in the introduction and notes as well as any omissions noted in the references to the text of the treatise itself. References to chapters, sections, and paragraphs in the original index have also been replaced by page references in this edition.

I must again happily acknowledge my debt to all those who provided so much assistance in the preparation of this work when it first appeared. I cannot single out all of these kind people again here. I would, however, like to acknowledge a special debt to two men, Gustave Reese and Frederick Freedman, who played important roles in finding a publisher for this volume. Although both are now dead, the memory of their generous assistance should not be forgotten. And for the period since publication, I am especially indebted to Betty Bang Mather and David Lasocki, whose excellent works have added much to our knowledge of eighteenth-century performance. May they and others like them continue their efforts! It is my greatest hope that this translation of Quantz's work may continue to inspire in others his own high standards for the vivid re-creation of the music of his time.

Edward R. Reilly
Vassar College
Poughkeepsie, New York
1 June 1980/15 July 1984

PREFACE TO THE TRANSLATION

THE first draft of the present translation was made from a microfilm of the first German edition (1752) of the *Essay*. Revisions were made with the aid of the subsequently published facsimile of the third German edition of 1789, which is identical textually with the first edition. Finally, the entire work was carefully compared with the French translation issued in Berlin simultaneously with the original German edition of 1752. This French translation, published at the instigation of Quantz himself, and an unusually careful piece of work for the period, has been most helpful in clarifying the meanings of a number of words and sentences, and in cases where the wording or sentence structure of the French edition makes the meaning of the author clearer I have not hesitated to follow the French text. Slight variations between the French and German texts have not been ← singled out in the footnotes except on a few occasions when they seem pertinent. Wherever the text remains somewhat ambiguous, however, both German and French versions are presented in italics in the footnotes. The German and French equivalents of the most important technical terms have also been indicated in italics in the footnotes at the points where they seem most relevant, in order to facilitate comparative study with other treatises of the period. If, at a later point in the text, the reader wishes to check on a German or French equivalent, he may refer to the index, where they are inserted in brackets immediately after their English translation. Except for the initial capitals in the footnotes and a few other special cases, the capitalization, spelling, and accents of the original German and French texts have been preserved in both the text itself and the notes. In these matters numerous deviations from modern practice are encountered as well as a few slips that go back to Quantz and his French translator.

In format and typography the original German and French texts have been followed as closely as possible. Each chapter of the *Essay* was originally divided into a series of numbered paragraphs, the numbering starting over again with each new chapter, or with each new section in cases where the chapter is subdivided. The same procedure has been followed in the translation. Thus the reader may locate a passage in any of the various German editions or in the French translation with no difficulty. Cross-references are likewise made in terms of chapter and paragraph numbers. As in the original German and French texts, Quantz's own footnotes appear after each paragraph rather than at the bottom of the page, and are set off by smaller print and special indentation. In some instances they refer to a particular sentence marked with an asterisk. In other cases they form additions to the paragraph as a whole and no special marking is found. For purposes of emphasis Quantz had some words set in bolder type. In the translation these words are italicized. Although modern practice also requires italics for certain foreign terms, Quantz's special cases are clearly distinguishable.

The only point in which the translation substantially differs from the first German and French editions is in the matter of musical examples. These originally appeared in a set of numbered tables at the back of the volume. To spare the reader the cumbersome task of constantly referring from text to examples, the latter have been inserted in the text at the appropriate places. Where several references to the same example are made at different places, footnotes indicate where it is placed.

The style and language of the original German text are fairly typical of didactic works of nearly every type appearing in Germany at the time when the *Essay* was first published. By modern standards, this style is often redundant and wordy, and frequently relies on over-long sentence structure. Nevertheless, the *Essay* is generally quite clear in both German and French, and seems simple and terse when compared with works of the earlier part of the century, such as those of Johann Mattheson or Johann David Heinichen. In the translation no attempt has been made to prettify the original style: at the same time, however, it has not been made more difficult by a false literality that ignores the differences between German and English. Where necessary, sentences have been broken up, or their structure modified. In general, if a long sentence seems clear, it has been left long; if it is not clear, it has been broken up. In a large number of cases modifications of this type have been suggested by the French translation. Genuine paraphrase has been kept to a minimum.

As a matter of convenience a few special terms and practices in the translation that may require some comment are listed and discussed briefly here, to avoid repetitious notes in the main body of the work.

The Allegro, the Adagio. Quantz uses these terms as generic designations for all types of quick pieces or movements on the one hand, and all types of slow pieces on the other. To set them off with this meaning, they have been capitalized throughout the translation.

Concertante. This term is regularly used to designate an undoubled part, that is, a solo part in a composition, or the performer of such a part. Thus *concertante* normally indicates the solo part or parts of a concerto, or undoubled parts in chamber works such as sonatas, trios, and quartets, or the performers of these parts. The antitheses of concertante part and concertante performer are ripieno part and ripienist. On Quantz's use of the term *solo*, see below.

The Forte and Piano. For Quantz this expression is synonymous with the term 'dynamics'. Since the alternation and contrast of these two levels form the basis of Quantz's conception of dynamics, his usage is quite understandable. At the same time one must remember that the many other degrees of dynamic shading that Quantz explains are implicit in this phrase.

Musical establishment. The German word *Musik* was used in a number of different senses in Quantz's day, indicating a composition, a concert, a small ensemble, an orchestra, or the entire body of musicians that formed the *Kapelle* of a lord or prince. Which meaning is intended is usually clear from the context, but one or several of these meanings may serve at times as equally appropriate alternatives.

Passions, sentiments. One of the most difficult problems for the modern reader of the *Essay* is to grasp the emotional climate of the author and the period. This difficulty stems from several sources. The descriptive terms for the emotions differed somewhat from those used today, and, in a number of cases, the musical associations of these terms are not what some readers might expect. Instead of speaking of the mood, the emotional content, or the character of a piece of music, Quantz and his contemporaries spoke of its passion(s) or sentiment(s) (German, *Leidenschaften, Affecten;* French, *passions, sentiments*). The two terms were used interchangeably, and a good definition for both is 'one of the feelings natural to all men, such as fear, love, hate, or joy' (Webster). The principal passions or sentiments mentioned by Quantz are gaiety, melancholy, boldness, flattery, and majesty. Some of these sentiments no longer seem 'natural' to the modern student, and he must therefore try to discover their musical equivalents from Quantz himself. The dominance of Italian opera throughout much of Europe in Quantz's day should be kept in mind. Much purely instrumental music had its emotional background in opera, where these sentiments were more directly characterized. Although I have consciously tried to avoid imposing my own interpretations of these emotional states, I would like to note that in Quantz's view majesty and liveliness were not inimical, and flattery had no ethical or moral overtones in reference to music. In its general sense 'flattery' refers to that which caresses or gratifies the senses, or to a sensation that is charming or beguiling. Since Quantz has specific notions about what constitutes a flattering style in music (see, for example, Chapter XII, § 24), and since the whole network of his references to this sentiment cannot be preserved through other possible translations of the German and French terms, I have preferred to use this equivalent.

Proportions. The phrase 'the proportions of the notes' refers to the mathematical ratios underlying musical intervals, and is used by Quantz much as we would use the expression 'the exact pitches of the notes'.

Science. In the eighteenth century the German word *Wissenschaft*, like the English *science*, had a wide variety of meanings. Few of these meanings are closely related to *science* as it is popularly used today, although they are still included in some dictionaries. *Wissenschaft*, as used by Quantz, may have any of the following meanings : (1) knowledge in general; (2) a particular branch of knowledge; (3) an art or a particular skill; (4) one of the arts; (5) a discipline related to the arts. Where one of the specific meanings seems clearly indicated by the context, or is suggested by the French translation, it has been employed. In other cases the word has been left as it stands.

Solo. Quantz normally uses this word only as a noun, referring in nearly all cases to a solo sonata. It is rarely used to indicate a solo part, a solo section, or a solo performer.

Style, taste. In Quantz's day the word *Geschmack* embraced the meanings of both style and taste as used today; and the same was also true of the French *goût* and the English *taste*. In the translation both modern equivalents have been used, depending upon the context. In some cases *taste* refers more specifically to the performer's ability to improvise appropriate embellishments in a composition.

To tip, tipping. This verb indicates the process of articulating one or several notes with the tongue in playing the flute. Although known and used in the eighteenth century, it is now, unfortunately, uncommon. *Tipping* has been used in preference to *tonguing* because it is a more agreeable word that suggests the physical process more graphically, and because it helps to avoid a number of clumsy phrases in the translation.

Tongue-stroke. Curiously, no word seems to have evolved in English to indicate the individual tongue movements required for articulation on wind instruments. Thus, to translate the German *Zungenstoß* and the French *coup de langue*, this rather clumsy composite had to be created.

Upbeat, downbeat. These terms evolved from the practice of beating time with the hand or foot, and originally indicated the actual up and down movements of either, rather than the beat in the modern sense. With this point in mind, the few cases in which Quantz's usage does not correspond exactly with that of today are readily understandable.

Unison. With this term Quantz refers both to actual unisons and to octave doublings. As a noun it is frequently used to refer to musical phrases doubled at the unison or octave.

In conclusion, I would like to express my gratitude for all the help that I have received from so many people in the course of this work. My thanks must go to all the members of my doctoral committee, which supervised the original work in which the translation, in a slightly different version, formed a part. A very special debt is owed to Dr. Louise E. Cuyler, who worked unstintingly to help make the entire work better than it would have been, and to Dr. Otto Graf, who, with German text in hand, patiently listened for many hours to my droning reading of the translation, in order to ensure its greater accuracy. Responsibility for any errors that have crept in, however, must remain my own. I would also like to express my sincere appreciation to Mr. Robert Donington, whose straightforward assessment of my original translation and commentary provided an excellent basis for many important revisions, and also a needed stimulus to persist in my work; to Mrs. Helen Snyder, who read the entire translation and made many valuable suggestions for improving style and language; to Mr. Bernard Wilson, who read a portion of the translation and was helpful in many ways when I was trying to locate many small bits of information; and to Dr. Edith Borroff, who offered much encouragement and stimulated thought in many directions with her fresh point of view on many subjects.

In the continuing search for material on Quantz, his music, and his *Essay*, I would especially like to thank the following scholars and librarians who have helped to locate further information: Dr. Fritz Bose of the Staatliches Institut für Musikforschung, Berlin; Dr. Karl-Heinz Köhler of the Deutsche Staatsbibliothek, Berlin; Dr. Wolfgang Reich of the Sächsische Landesbibliothek, Dresden; Professor Napoleone Fanti of the Civico Museo Bibliografico Musicale, Bologna; and the librarians of the British Library, the Library of Congress, the University of California, the Staats- und Universitäts-Bibliothek, Hamburg, the Universitätsbibliothek, Cologne, the Niedersächsische Staats- und Universitäts-Bibliothek, Göttingen, and the Staatsbibliothek Preußischer Kulturbesitz, West Berlin.

To my wife, who has patiently endured an all too extended preoccupation with Quantz and his *Essay*, and who has contributed so much towards the completion of the present work, I owe much more than I can express in words. Finally, my sincere thanks must go to Professor Gustave Reese and the Publication Committee of the American Musicological Society for their interest in this work, and for all their help in finding a publisher for it.

E. R. REILLY

Johann Joachim Quantzens,

Königl. Preußischen Kammermusikus,

Versuch einer Anweisung

die

Flöte traversiere

zu spielen;

mit verschiedenen,

zur Beförderung des guten Geschmackes

in der praktischen Musik

dienlichen Anmerkungen

begleitet,

und mit Exempeln erläutert.

Nebst XXIV. Kupfertafeln.

✦✧✦✧✦✧✦✧✦✧✦✧✦✧✦✧✦✧✦✧✦✧✦✧✦✧✦✧✦✧✦

BERLIN,

bey Johann Friedrich Voß. 1752.

THE TITLE-PAGE OF THE FIRST GERMAN EDITION

ESSAY OF A METHOD

FOR

PLAYING
The Transverse Flute,

ACCOMPANIED

by several Remarks of service
for the Improvement of Good Taste
in Practical Music,
and illustrated with examples.

With XXIV copperplate tables.

By

JOHANN JOACHIM QUANTZ

Royal Prussian Chamber Musician

BERLIN,

JOHANN FRIEDRICH VOSS

1752

*T*O the most Serene, Great and Mighty Prince and Lord, Lord FREDERICK, King in Prussia; Margrave at Brandenburg; Chamberlain and Elector of the Holy Roman Empire; Sovereign and High Duke of Silesia; Sovereign Prince of Orange, Neufchatel and Valengin, and also of the Earldom of Glaz; Duke in Geldern, at Magdeburg, Cleve, Jülich, Berg, Stettin, Pomerania, of Cassuben and Wenden, at Mecklenburg, and at Crossen; Burgrave at Nürnberg; Prince at Halberstadt, Mindin, Camin, Wenden, Schwerin, Ratzeburg, Ostfriesland and Moeurs; Count at Hohenzollern, Ruppin, the Mark, Ravensberg, Hohenstein, Tecklenburg, Lingen, Schwerin, Bühren and Lehrdam; Lord at Ravenstein, of the region of Rostock, Stargard, Lauenburg, Bütow, Arlay and Breda.

My most gracious King and Master.

Most Serene,
Great and Mighty King,
Most Gracious King and Master,

IN deepest humility, may I venture to dedicate the present pages to Your Royal Highness, although they contain in part only the first rudiments of an instrument that Your Highness has brought to such particular perfection.

The protection, and the high favour, which Your Royal Highness has vouchsafed the sciences in general, and music in particular, allow me to hope that Your Royal Highness will not refuse the same protection to my efforts also, and that a favourable eye may be found for that which I have projected here, according to my slight powers, in the service of music.

This most humble request is united with the most faithful desire for the preservation of Your Sacred Person,

Most Serene,
Great and Mighty King,
Most Gracious King and Master,
Your Royal Majesty,

your most humble and
obedient servant,

JOHANN JOACHIM QUANTZ.

PREFACE

I PRESENT here to the lovers of music a method for playing the transverse flute. I have tried to teach clearly and from the first rudiments everything required for the practice of this instrument.

I have therefore also ventured rather extensively into the precepts of good taste in practical music. And although I have applied them specifically only to the transverse flute, they can be useful to all those who make a profession of singing or of the practice of other instruments, and wish to apply themselves to good musical execution. Each person so inclined need only choose and apply that which is suited to his voice or instrument.

Because the effectiveness of a musical composition does not depend entirely upon those who play the principal or concertante parts, and because the accompanying instrumentalists must also attend to their parts, I have added a special chapter in which I show how the principal parts must be properly accompanied.

In doing this I do not believe I have ventured too far afield. Since I am endeavouring to train a skilled and intelligent musician, and not just a mechanical flute player, I must try not only to educate his lips, tongue, and fingers, but must also try to form his taste, and sharpen his discernment. A knowledge of how to accompany well is particularly necessary, not only because the player may be frequently obliged to perform this function, but also because he is entitled to know his claims upon those who accompany and support him when he performs a solo part.

The last chapter proceeded from similar motives. In it I show how a musician and a musical composition must be judged. The first part can serve a beginner in music as a mirror from which he can inquire into himself, and see the judgement that just and reasonable connoisseurs might pass upon him. The second part may serve as a guide in the choice of the pieces he wishes to play, and protect him from the danger of taking dross for gold.

But these were not the only reasons that induced me to add the two final chapters. I have already said that all musicians who perform principal parts can profit from this method in some way. I hope that my book will gain still wider general utility if those instrumentalists who apply themselves primarily to accompaniment by preference also find in it instruction as to that which they must observe if they wish to accompany well. Beginners in composition will find in the last chapter outlines from which they can trace out the pieces they wish to write.

I do not pretend, however, to prescribe rules for those musicians who have acquired general approbation either in composition or in performance. On the contrary, I publish their merits, and those of their compositions, through the particulars that I give about what distinguishes them from so many others, thus showing the young people who devote themselves to music how they must proceed if they wish to imitate these celebrated men, and follow in their footsteps.

If at times I seem to stray from the material that I treat, and if I make slight digressions, I hope I will be pardoned because of my determination to correct defects still in vogue in music, and because of my desire to make use of this opportunity to communicate various remarks which will be of service in the improvement of good taste in practical music.

Occasionally I seem to speak rather dictatorially, supporting my tenets only with a simple *'one must'*, without advancing other proofs. Here one should remember that at times it would take too long, at times it would be impossible, to give demonstrative proofs of matters that nearly always depend upon taste. Anyone who does not wish to trust my taste, which I have diligently endeavoured to purify through long experience and reflection, is free to try the opposite of that which I teach, and then choose what seems best to him.

I do not, however, wish to set myself up as infallible. If someone convinces me with reason and moderation of something better than what I have said, I will be the first to approve and accept it. I will continue to investigate the materials that I have treated here, and whatever I may find to add may, perhaps, be communicated in supplements printed separately. Then I will either make use of the remarks which I here invite good friends to give me, if I think they are well founded, or I will reply to them. I will not, however, trouble myself to reply to anyone who dwells only on insignificant trifles, or criticizes me simply for the sake of criticizing. I am particularly unwilling to enter into disputes about words.

Although in this essay I believe I have stated everything, as regards the transverse flute, that is necessary to learn this instrument, I am far from maintaining that somebody can learn the flute well from it by himself without further instructions and without having a teacher at hand. And since I have always presumed that one will be assisted by a teacher, I have omitted some of the rudiments of music, and have gone into detail only where I have found some advantages to disclose, or something particular to call to mind. Frequently a treatment of some point that may seem too ample or even superfluous to one person another will find hardly sufficient. For this reason I have preferred to say certain things twice, if they pertain to two different chapters, when it could be done without prolixity, than to tax the patience of some of my readers with the necessity of making frequent references for the sake of a trifle.

If in this work I make use of some foreign words at times, I do so to be more easily understood. German translations of the technical terms of music still have not been introduced everywhere, and thus are not familiar to all musicians. Until they become more customary and general, the usual technical terms borrowed from foreign languages must be retained.

Since much in this treatise may not be so intelligible if the examples are not at hand, my readers would do well to have the copperplate tables bound separately, so that they are always close by, and may be compared more conveniently with what I say in the book.[1]

So that my book, which I have written in German, may be useful to other nations, I have had it translated into French; and for the same reason it was necessary to employ two styles of denominating the notes.

For the rest, I doubt not a favourable reception for these my labours, and the account that I render of the use I have made until now[2] of my previous leisure hours.

> Berlin,
> written in September
> 1752

QUANTZ

[1] The following paragraph appears only in the French text. Sol-fa syllables were added after the pitch letters in the French translation.

[2] French text: 'for several years'.

PYTHAGORAS AT THE FORGE, DISCOVERING THE LAWS OF PITCH

From an engraving by G. F. Schmidt in the first German and French editions of the *Essay of a Method for Playing the Transverse Flute*

INTRODUCTION

Of the Qualities Required of Those Who Would Dedicate Themselves to Music

§ 1

Before I begin my instructions for playing the flute, and for becoming a good musician at the same time, I feel that it is necessary to give those who wish to apply themselves to music, and by that means make themselves useful members of society, some rules by which they may determine whether they are gifted with all the qualities necessary to a good musician. In this way they will not err in the choice of this profession, and need fear none of the unhappy consequences that would result from an unwise choice.

§ 2

I speak here only of those who truly wish to make music their profession and with time to become excellent in it. Less, of course, is required of those who wish to devote themselves to it only as an avocation and for their own enjoyment, but they will acquire so much the more honour and pleasure if they are willing and able to profit from what is said here and in the following pages.

§ 3

The choice of a profession, and the decision to enter into that of music or any other, must be made with great circumspection. Very few persons have the good fortune to be dedicated to that science[1] or profession for which they are best suited by nature. Frequently this misfortune is due to lack of knowledge on the part of parents or superiors. They often force young people into something in which only they, the superiors, have pleasure; or they imagine that this or that science or profession brings more honour, or greater advantages, than another; or they demand that the children learn just the same trade as their parents, thus forcing them to enter into a way of life for which they, the children, have neither love nor aptitude. Hence it is not surprising that exceptional scholars and particularly distinguished artists are so rare. If we paid diligent attention to the inclinations of young people, sought to find out how they spontaneously preferred to occupy themselves, and gave them the freedom to choose for

[1] *Wissenschaft* (*science*). On the various meanings of this term, see the Preface to the Translation.

themselves that occupation for which they showed the greatest inclination, we would find more happy and truly useful people in the world. It is quite evident that, if the proper decision had been made, many so-called scholars or artists would have been at best ordinary artisans, while many artisans could have become scholars or able artists. I myself know of two musicians who studied at the same time with the same master, about forty years ago. The fathers of both were blacksmiths. The first was dedicated to music by a father who was wealthy and did not wish his son to become a common artisan. He spared no expense, retaining several masters to instruct his son in the science of thorough-bass, in composition, and on various instruments. Although the apprentice himself showed a great inclination for music, and applied himself to it assiduously, he remained a very ordinary musician, and would have been much better at his father's trade than at music. The second musician,[1] on the other hand, was destined by his father, who was less wealthy, for the blacksmith's trade. And this would certainly have been his fate, if the premature death of his father had not left him free to choose his profession in accordance with his own wishes. To that end his relatives sought to learn whether he wished to become a smith, a tailor, or a musician, or if he desired an academic career, for there were some among his relatives in each of these professions. Because he felt the greatest inclination for music, he happily embraced that art, and was apprenticed to the master mentioned above. What he lacked in instruction, and in the means to retain other masters, was supplied by his talent, inclination, eagerness, and industry, as well as by the happy circumstance that he soon found himself in places where he could hear much that was good, and share the society of many worthy connoisseurs. Had his father lived only a few years longer, this blacksmith's son would have had to become a smith also, and as a result his talent for music would have been buried, and the musical works he was later to fashion would never have seen the light. I will not mention here the many other instances of people who have devoted half of their lives to music, and made it their profession, only to turn in their mature years to another art in which, without special instruction, they were more successful than in music. Had these people been led in youth to the profession that they afterwards adopted, they would surely have become very great artists.

§ 4

The first quality[2] required of someone who wishes to become a good musician is a particularly good talent, or natural gift. He who wishes to

---

[1] The second musician is Quantz himself. Here he gives an anonymous account of his own youthful experiences. See 'The Life of Herr Johann Joachim Quantz as Sketched by Himself', in P. Nettl, *Forgotten Musicians* (New York: Philosophical Library, 1951), pp. 280–1. A facsimile of the German text of this autobiography is found in W. Kahl, *Selbstbiographien deutscher Musiker des XVIII. Jahrhunderts* (Cologne: Staufen Verlag, 1948), pp. 104–57.

[2] For related discussions of the various qualities demanded of different types of musicians, see chapter iv of Wolfgang Kaspar Printz's *Phrynis Mytilenæus, oder ander Theil des satyrischen*

devote himself to composition must have a lively and fiery spirit, united with a soul capable of tender feeling; a good mixture, without too much melancholy, of what scholars call the temperaments; much imagination, inventiveness, judgement, and discernment; a good memory; a good and delicate ear; a sharp and quick eye; and a receptive mind that grasps everything quickly and easily. Someone who wishes to devote himself to an instrument must be equipped with various physical endowments, according to the nature of the instrument, in addition to many of the qualities of spirit mentioned above. For example, a wind instrument, and the flute in particular, requires a completely healthy body; strong and open lungs; prolonged breath; even teeth that are neither too long nor too short; lips that are thin, smooth, and delicate rather than puffed out and thick, which have neither too much nor too little flesh, and with which one may cover the mouth easily; a fluent and skilful tongue; well-formed fingers that are neither too long nor too short, too corpulent or too pointed, but are provided with good tendons; and an unobstructed nasal passage for inhaling and exhaling with ease. A singer must have the strong chest, the long breath, and the ready tongue in common with the wind player, while the players of stringed and bowed instruments must have the able fingers and the strong tendons; in addition the first must be gifted with a beautiful voice, and the second with supple joints in his hands and arms.

§ 5

If, then, these qualities are found in a person, he is indeed generally qualified for music; but since natural gifts are so varied, and are seldom all present in so full a measure in the same person, it will always be found that one person is more disposed to one thing, another to something else. For example, one person may have a natural bent for composition, but may not be qualified for the handling of instruments, while a second may possess more ability for instruments, but have no capacity at all for composition; a third may have more talent for one instrument than for another, a fourth have ability for all instruments, and a fifth have it for none. If somebody has the necessary talent for composition, for singing, and for instruments, it may be said, in the most exact sense, that he is born to music.

§ 6

Hence it is necessary for each person, before he settles upon something in music, to explore carefully the area to which his talent most inclines him. If this matter were always properly considered, there would be less imperfection in music than there is at the present time, and will perhaps

Componisten (Sagan: C. Okels, 1677), which deals with the *Requisiten eines guten Componistens*. See also chapter ii of the same author's *Musica modulatoria vocales* (Schweidnitz: C. Okels, 1678), which deals with the *Requisiten eines Sängers und sonderlich von der Lust zur Musik und natürlicher Geschicklichkeit*.

continue to be. He who devotes himself to a branch of music for which he lacks the gifts will always remain a mediocre musician in spite of the best instruction and application.

§ 7

It is clear from what has been said above that a special talent is required if one is to become an able and learned musician. By the words 'able musician'[1] I mean a good singer or instrumentalist: 'learned musician'[2] on the other hand, I apply to someone who has learned composition thoroughly. Since, however, we do not always need musicians of the highest excellence, and a musician of moderate ability can serve as a good ripienist or performer of middle parts, it should be noted that less talent is required of someone who aspires to be no more than a good ripienist.* Whoever has a healthy body, with well-disposed and healthy limbs, and yet is not stupid or of unsound mind can, with much industry, learn what is called the mechanics of music, and these are the proper qualifications of a ripienist. Everything he needs to know—for example, tempo,[3] the value and division of the notes, and the matters connected with them, the bow-stroke upon stringed instruments, and the tongue-stroke, embouchure, and fingering upon wind instruments—may be understood through rules that can be clearly and fully explained. The many who have no proper understanding of one or another of these things usually have only themselves to blame: it is astonishing that many musicians of mature years should, with no lack of opportunity for improvement, still be deficient in matters that they might have learned in two or three years' time. What I have just said must not be interpreted as a disparagement of good ripienists. There are many who have talent, are industrious, distinguish themselves above others, and are often worthy and capable of leading an orchestra, yet must suffer the misfortune of being so harassed and thwarted, as a result of jealousy, avarice, and countless other reasons, that their talent can never achieve maturity. Those who, despite their inclination for music, possess no exceptional gifts for it, may note by way of consolation that if nature has not permitted them to become bright stars in the world of music, they may still be very useful people if they become good ripienists. But whoever has been given a completely wooden and unfeeling spirit, hopelessly clumsy fingers, and no ear for music, would do better to learn some other art.

---

⁴ * We apologize to the reader for the word *ripienist*; it will be new to him, but will be intelligible from the description given here.

¹ *Geschickter Musikus (habile Musicien).*
² *Gelehrter Musikus (savant Musicien).*
³ In the French text the word 'metre' is substituted for 'tempo'. Both terms may have been used in a broader sense to indicate 'time'.
⁴ The following note appears only in the French text.

§ 8

Furthermore, he who wishes to excel in music must feel in himself a perpetual and untiring love for it, a willingness and eagerness to spare neither industry nor pains, and to bear steadfastly all the difficulties that present themselves in this mode of life. Music seldom procures the same advantages as the other arts, and even if some prosper in it, this prosperity is most often subject to inconstancy. Changes of taste, the weakening of bodily powers, vanishing youth, the loss of a patron—upon whom the entire fortune of many a musician depends—are all capable of hindering the progress of music. Experience sufficiently confirms this, if we think back only about half a century. How many are the changes in the musical life of Germany! At many courts, and in many towns where music previously flourished, so that a good number of able people were trained in it, now nothing but ignorance prevails. At the majority of courts formerly provided with some moderately able people, and even with some very celebrated ones, the unfortunate custom has been introduced of giving the first places in the musical establishment to persons who do not merit even the last positions in a good orchestra, to persons whose office does indeed bring them some consideration among the ignorant who allow themselves to be blinded by titles, but who do no honour to their office, bring no advantage to music, and do not advance the pleasure of those upon whom their fortune depends. Although music is a science that can never be studied and investigated too thoroughly, it does not have the good fortune of other sciences, in part higher, in part on the same level, of being taught publicly. Some cloudy-minded modern philosophers do not, like the ancients,[1] consider knowledge of it a necessity. People of means do not cultivate it, and the poor do not have the means to retain good masters at the outset, or to travel to places where music of good taste is in vogue. Nevertheless, at some places music has again begun to receive greater esteem. There once more it has its noble connoisseurs, protectors, and patrons. Its honour is beginning to be restored by those enlightened philosophers who again count it among the fine arts. The taste for these fine arts, particularly in Germany, is becoming increasingly enlightened[2] and widespread. Those who have decent training can always earn a living.

§ 9

Someone who has the talent and the inclination for music must make every effort to secure a good master.[3] It would take too long if I were to

---

[1] Here Quantz probably refers to the Greek philosophers. Elsewhere he uses the term simply to indicate any earlier generation of musicians, in the sense of 'elders'.

[2] *Aufgeheitert (éclairé)*.

[3] For a related discussion of teachers, see P. F. Tosi, *Observations on the Florid Song*, trans. by Galliard (2nd ed.; London: J. Wilcox, 1743), pp. 10–30. The original Italian treatise of Tosi was published in Bologna in 1723, and Quantz visited Bologna in 1724. Quantz also met Tosi when they were both in England in 1727. See Nettl, *Forgotten Musicians*, pp. 299, 314.

treat of masters in every branch of music. As an example, I will only take
the time to discuss the type of master required for the study of the flute. It
is true that this instrument has become very common in the last thirty to
forty years, especially in Germany. As was not the case when it first came
into vogue, we no longer suffer any lack of pieces[1] through which a
student may learn with but slight difficulty the skill necessary on the
instrument to control his tongue, fingers, and embouchure. In spite of this,
there are still very few who know how to play it in accordance with its
nature, and in its proper style. It seems as if the majority of flute players
today have fingers and tongues, to be sure, but are deficient in brains, does
it not? It is absolutely necessary for anyone who wishes to learn the
instrument adequately to have a good master, and I expressly demand it
of anyone who wishes to make use of my method. But how many are
there upon whom the title of master may be justly conferred? Are not the
majority, when closely observed, still students in their science? How,
then, can they teach music, if they themselves remain in a state of ignorance? To be sure, there are some who play the instrument well, or at least
passably; many, however, lack the ability to impart to others that which
they know themselves. It is possible that somebody who plays quite well
knows little of how to teach. Someone else may teach better than he plays.
And since a student is not able to judge whether a master instructs well
or poorly, he is fortunate indeed if by chance he selects the best. The
attributes of a teacher who will train good students are difficult to define
in detail, but an approximate idea may be gained from the following list
of defects that he must avoid. A beginner will also do well to ask the
advice of persons who are impartial, yet have insight into music. The
student must beware of a master who understands nothing of harmony
and who is no more than an instrumentalist; who has not learned his
science thoroughly, and according to correct principles; who has no clear
notion of embouchure, fingering, breathing, and tonguing; who does not
know how to play the passage-work[2] in the Allegro or the little embellishments and niceties in the Adagio[3] distinctly and roundly; who does not
have an agreeable and distinct execution, or a refined taste in general;
who possesses no knowledge of the proportions of the notes needed for
playing the flute with correct intonation; who does not know how to
observe tempo with the greatest strictness; who does not know how to
play a plain air coherently, and to introduce the appoggiaturas, *pincemens*,

[1] In the first half of the century violin music was frequently adapted for the flute. M. Corrette in his *Methode pour apprendre aisément à joüer de la flute traversiere* (Paris: Boivin, *c.* 1740),
p. 50, provides a brief discussion of how this was done, and gives an illustration from Corelli's
Op. 5. Quantz also mentions the lack of good music specifically intended for the transverse
flute in his autobiography. See Nettl, *Forgotten Musicians*, p. 289.

[2] *Passagien (passages)*. Passage-work was at this time considered a normal and important part
of composition which gave the performer an opportunity to demonstrate his skill. As used
here, the term has no derogatory connotations.

[3] On Quantz's use of 'the Allegro', 'the Adagio', and the phrase 'the proportions of the
notes' that appears below, see the Preface to the Translation.

battemens, flattemens, doublés, and shakes at the proper places; who in an Adagio does not know how to add extempore graces to the plain air (that is, one written without embellishments)[1] as the air and the harmony require and who is unable to sustain light and shadow through the alternation of Forte and Piano as well as through the graces. The student must avoid a master who is not in a position to explain clearly and thoroughly everything that the student finds difficult to understand, and seeks to impart everything by ear, and through imitation, as we train birds; a master who flatters the apprentice, and overlooks all defects; who does not have the patience to show the student the same thing frequently, and have him repeat it; who does not know how to choose the pieces that are suited at one time or another to the capacity of the student, and how to play each piece in its style; who seeks to delay the student; who does not prefer honour to self-interest, hardship to comfort, and unselfish service to jealousy and envy; or who in general does not have the progress of music as his goal. Masters with these defects cannot train good students. If, however, one is found whose students not only play truly and distinctly, but are also quite sure in tempo, you have substantial reasons to expect much of him.

§ 10

Whoever wishes to apply himself to music profitably will enjoy a considerable advantage if he falls into the hands of a good master *at the very beginning.* There are some who have the harmful delusion that at the outset it is unnecessary to have a good master in order to learn the fundamental principles. For the sake of economy they often take whoever is cheapest, and often someone who himself knows nothing at all, so that one blind man leads another. I advise the opposite course. The best master should be secured at the very beginning, even if he must be paid two or three times as much as others. It will cost no more in the end, and both time and effort will be saved. More can be accomplished in a year with a good master than in ten years with a poor one.

§ 11

Although, as has been shown here, much depends upon a good master who can instruct his apprentices thoroughly, still more depends upon the students themselves. There are frequent examples of good masters who have trained poor students, and, on the contrary, of poor masters who have trained good students. It is well known that many excellent musicians have distinguished themselves who have had no other master than their great natural ability, and the opportunity to hear much that is good; these musicians have advanced further through their own effort, industry, diligence, and constant inquiry than many who have been instructed by

---

[1] Translator's parentheses.

several masters. Thus a special industry and attentiveness are also required of a student. Anyone who lacks them should be advised not to occupy himself with music, at least if he proposes to make his fortune through it. No success can be promised to anyone who loves idleness, slothfulness, or other such futile things more than music. Many who dedicate themselves to music deceive themselves in this regard. They shrink from the inevitable hardships. They would like to become skilful, but they do not wish to exert the necessary effort. They imagine that music is all pleasure, that to learn it is child's play, that neither physical nor mental powers are needed, that neither knowledge nor experience appertains to it, and that everything depends entirely upon inclination and good natural ability. It is true that innate ability and inclination are the primary foundations upon which solid understanding must be built. But thorough instruction, and, on the part of the student, much industry and reflection, are absolutely necessary to erect the entire structure. If a novice has had the good fortune to find a good master at the outset, he must place all his confidence in him. He must be tractable rather than obstinate; he must seek zealously and eagerly not only to carry out and copy what his master prescribes during the lesson, but also to repeat it frequently by himself with much diligence; and if he has not properly understood something, or has forgotten it, he must ask the master about it at the following lesson. A novice must not allow himself to be vexed if he is frequently admonished about the same matter, but must rather take such admonitions as a sign of his own carelessness and of the zeal of his teacher, and hold that master the best who corrects him most frequently. Hence the student must pay close attention to his defects; for when he begins to recognize them, half the battle is won. If it is necessary for the master to correct him too often about the same matter, he may be safely assured that he will have little success in music; for there are countless things which no master will teach him, or can teach him, and which he must, as it were, 'lift' from others. Indeed it is this licensed thievery that produces the greatest artists.[1] The student must not drop anything that has been the subject of much criticism before he can play it as the master demands. He must not prescribe to the master what kind of pieces should be given him; it is for the master to know best what can be of advantage to the student. If, as I presuppose, he has had the good fortune to find a good master, he must seek to retain him as long as he has need of instruction. There is nothing more injurious than for a student to betake himself for instruction to one master after another. Different kinds of execution and different ways of playing confuse the beginner, since he must, so to speak, constantly start over again. There are many who like to boast of having studied with many great masters, but they will seldom be found to have profited much from it. Whoever runs from one master to another is satisfied with none,

[1] For a clearer idea of the importance that Quantz attaches to the study of others through listening, see Chapter X, § 20.

and has confidence in none; and no one wishes to accept the precepts of a person in whom he has no confidence. Having placed the proper confidence in a good master, and allowed him sufficient time to manifest his knowledge, the student with a genuine desire to perfect himself will discover from time to time new benefits that he had been previously unable to perceive, which will stimulate him to further inquiry.

§ 12

Inquiry of this sort must also be warmly recommended to the beginning musician. Industry alone is not enough. He may have good natural ability, good instruction, great industry, and good opportunities to hear much that is beautiful, yet never rise above mediocrity. He may compose a great deal, and sing and play frequently, without increasing his knowledge and skill. For everything in music that is done without reflection and deliberation, and simply, as it were, as a pastime, is without profit. Industry founded upon ardent love and insatiable enthusiasm for music must be united with constant and diligent inquiry, and mature reflection and examination. In this respect a noble pride must prevent the beginner from being easily satisfied, and must inspire him to gradually perfect himself. Anyone who only cares to devote himself to music haphazardly, as to a trade rather than an art, will remain a lifelong bungler.

§ 13

Impatience must not intrude upon the endeavour to progress, making the student want to begin only where others leave off. Some commit this error. They either choose for their practice very difficult pieces for which they are not yet prepared, and which lead them into the habit of rushing over the notes and executing them indistinctly, or, in the wish to be *galant*, they lapse into pieces which are so easy that their only advantage is that of flattering the ear. Those pieces, on the other hand, which sharpen their musical discernment, deepen their insight into harmony, make their bow-stroke, tongue-stroke, embouchure, and fingers adept, which are good for learning how to read and correctly divide notes and how to judge tempo without immediately tickling the senses, pieces of this sort, I say, they neglect and even consider a waste of time, although neither good execution nor good taste may be achieved without them.

§ 14

Too great a dependence upon talent is a great obstacle to industry and subsequent reflection. Experience teaches that we encounter more ignorant persons among those who possess especially good natural gifts than among those who enhance mediocre talents through industry and reflection. Indeed, good natural ability is for many a detriment rather than an advantage. For convincing proof, consider the majority of fashionable modern composers. How many does one find who have learned the art of composition in accordance with principles? Do not the majority rely almost entirely upon instinct? With at most a slight understanding of thorough-bass, they believe that so profound a science as composition involves no more than the insight and ability to avoid forbidden fifths and octaves, and perhaps to make a drum bass[1] and set to it one or two feeble middle parts; all the rest they consider harmful pedantry that only hinders good taste and good melody. If no technical skill is necessary, and pure natural ability is sufficient, why then do the pieces of experienced composers make a stronger impression, gain a wider dissemination, and remain in vogue longer than those of untutored instinctive writers; and why do the finished products of every good composer show a great improvement over his first sketches? Is this to be attributed to pure natural ability, or to ability and skill combined? Natural ability is innate, while technical skill is learned through good instruction and diligent inquiry, and both are necessary to a good composer. Although the operatic style has brought about an improvement in taste, it has produced a decline in technical skill. Since it is believed that genius and invention are more essential in this kind of music than knowledge of composition, and since operatic music generally finds greater favour among the amateurs than instrumental music or music composed for the church, the young and untutored composers in Italy have for the most part occupied themselves with it, both to acquire a reputation quickly, and in the briefest possible time to pass for masters, or, as they say, *maestri*. But the premature endeavour to obtain this title makes *maestri* of the majority before they have been students, for they have learned no correct principles to begin with, and after having received the applause of the ignorant are ashamed to receive instruction. Hence they imitate each other, copy each other's works, or even present another's work as their own, as experience will show, especially if such instinctive composers find it necessary to seek their fortune in foreign lands. They bring along their inventions not in their heads but in their luggage. And if by any chance they have the capacity to invent something out of their own heads, without decking themselves out in another's plumes, they seldom spend the time demanded by such an extended work as an opera: on the contrary, it is often considered a special mark of cleverness to be able to scribble out an entire opera in ten or twelve days, without caring whether it is either beautiful or reasonable, if it is only somewhat novel. It is easy to imagine the quality of things produced in such haste. Indeed ideas must be, so to speak, snapped out of the air, as a beast of prey pounces upon a bird.[2] What happens to the order,

[1] *Trummelbaß*. Quantz refers to a bass in which single notes are repeated at length, suggesting drum beats in their monotony. The French translator substitutes the phrase 'make a bass as in a tambourin', referring to the French dance form in which the bass frequently remained for long periods on the same note.

[2] French text: 'like birds of prey that subsist on whatever they find to their liking'.

coherence, and nicety of the ideas? As a result, there are no longer as many excellent composers to be found in Italy as formerly. And if experienced composers are lacking, how can good taste be preserved or perpetuated? Anyone who knows the requirements of a perfect opera must admit that a work such as this requires an experienced composer rather than a beginner, and more time than a few days. On the other hand, if composers begin to write reasonably, and put aside that which is wild and bold, the majority are unfortunately accused of having lost their fire, of having exhausted themselves, showing less ingenuity, or of being poor in invention. These things may be true of many, but if you were to inquire closely into the matter, you would find that such misfortunes happen only to the composers described above who have never learned composition thoroughly. An edifice built upon poor foundations will not last very long. But if talent, technical skill, and experience are combined, they will form an almost inexhaustible source of tasteful invention.[1] Since experience is so highly regarded in all trades, all sciences, and professions, why not also in music, and in composition in particular? Anybody who imagines that everything in composition depends upon luck and blind fancy errs greatly, and has not the slightest comprehension of the matter. It is true that inventions and fancies are fortuitous, and cannot be acquired through instruction; but the nicety and propriety, and the choice and mixture of ideas are not fortuitous, and are learned through knowledge and experience. These are the principal accomplishments that distinguish a master from a student, and that a great number of composers still lack. Everyone can learn the rules of composition and the principles of harmony, even without applying much time to them. Counterpoint may retain its invariable rules as long as music exists: the nicety, propriety, coherence, order, and mixture of ideas, on the other hand, require new rules in almost every piece. Thus those who have recourse to plagiarism often miss their mark; for it is easy to perceive whether their ideas are all the original inventions of the same mind, or whether they are simply put together in a mechanical way.

§ 15

In former times composition was not so little esteemed as at present, but there were then fewer bunglers encountered than nowadays. Our elders did not believe that composition could be learned without instruction. They considered it necessary to know thorough-bass, but did not think it sufficient by itself for learning composition. There were only a few who occupied themselves with composition, and those who undertook it endeavoured to learn it thoroughly. Today almost anyone who knows how to play an instrument passably pretends at the same time to have learned composition. In consequence so many monstrosities come into the world that it would be no surprise if music were to decline rather than

[1] The last three words of this sentence are found only in the French text.

progress. For if learned and experienced composers gradually disappear; if modern composers rely entirely upon natural ability, as many do at present, and consider learning the rules of composition superfluous or even harmful to good taste and good melody; and if the operatic style, although good in itself, is abused, and interspersed in pieces where it does not belong, so that church and instrumental compositions are adapted to it and everything must smack of operatic arias, as already happens in Italy, we may justifiably fear that music may gradually lose its former splendour, and that the art may finally suffer the same fate among the Germans, and among other peoples, as that suffered by other lost arts. In former times the Italians always said, in favour of the Germans, that even if they did not possess much taste, they at least understood the rules of composition more thoroughly than their neighbours. Should not the German nation, in which good taste in the arts spreads from day to day, strive to avoid a reproach which eventually might be made against it if its young composers neglect instruction and diligent inquiry, and place an absolute trust in pure natural ability? Should it not endeavour to preserve the laudable qualities of its ancestors? Only if exceptional natural ability is supported by thorough instruction, by industry, pains, and inquiry; only in this fashion, I repeat, can a special degree of excellence be achieved.

§ 16

None must imagine, however, that I demand that every piece must be composed in accordance with the rigid rules of double counterpoint, that is, in accordance with the rules that prescribe how to adjust the parts so that they are inverted, exchanged, and transposed in an harmonious manner. This would be a reprehensible kind of pedantry. I maintain only that it is the duty of every composer to know such rules; that he should seek to use these artifices only at places where good melody permits, so that no rupture is felt either in the beauty of the melody or in its good effect;[1] and that the listeners should perceive no laborious industry, but nature alone shining forth everywhere. The word counterpoint usually makes a disagreeable impression upon the majority of those who propose to follow only their innate ability; they consider it bookish pedantry. The reason is that they know only the name, and not the nature of the subject and its benefits. Had they acquired only a little understanding of it, the word would sound less frightful. I do not wish to play the part of panegyrist for all kinds of double counterpoint, although each, employed in a certain manner and at a suitable time, may have its uses. I cannot, however, refrain from rendering justice to counterpoint *all'ottava*, and strongly recommending exact knowledge of it as an indispensable matter for every young composer, since this form of counterpoint is not only

---

[1] *Ausnahme (effet)*. Here and at several other points in the text *Ausnahme* seems to be a misprint of *Aufnahme*.

most necessary in fugues and other artful pieces,[1] but is also of excellent service in many *galant* imitations and exchanges of parts. It is true that earlier composers occupied themselves too much with musical artifices, and pushed their use so far that they almost neglected the most essential part of music, that which is intended to move and please. But should counterpoint be blamed if the contrapuntists do not know how to make proper use if it, or if they abuse it? Should counterpoint be blamed if amateurs do not have a taste for it because of their lack of understanding? Is it not a point common to all sciences, including counterpoint, that without knowledge of them we may also find no pleasure in them? Who can say, for example, whether he would ever have acquired a taste for trigonometry or algebra, if he had learned nothing about them? It is with knowledge and insight that esteem and love for a subject grow. Distinguished persons do not always have their children instructed in many of the sciences with the object that they make a profession of them, but rather that they may have enough insight into them to be able to discuss them when the occasion requires. If, then, all teachers of music were at the same time connoisseurs of it; if they knew how to impart proper notions of artful music to their pupils; if they had their pupils play pieces that are skilfully worked out soon enough, and explained their contents to them; then amateurs not only would gradually accustom themselves to music of this kind, but would also acquire greater insight into music in general, and find more pleasure in it. In consequence, music would be more highly esteemed than at present, and true musicians would earn more thanks for their labours. Since, however, the majority of amateurs only learn music mechanically, these benefits are suppressed; and since we lack both good masters and willing students, the state of music remains very imperfect.[2]

§ 17

If you were to ask what the true object of inquiry and reflection should be, my answer would be as follows. If a young composer has thoroughly learned the rules of harmony (as already stated, the slightest and easiest part of composition, though many lack knowledge of them),[3] he must strive to hit upon a good choice and mixture of ideas from beginning to end in accordance with the purpose of each piece. He must express the different passions of the soul properly. He must preserve a flowing melody, and be fresh and yet natural in progression,[4] and correct in metrics;[5] he

---

[1] *Künstliche Stücke (pièces faites avec art)*, i.e. pieces in which contrapuntal artifices are an essential part of the structure.

[2] Many of the complaints expressed in §§ 14 to 16 are also voiced by Tosi, *Observations*, pp. 117–25.

[3] Translator's parentheses.

[4] *Modulation (modulation)*. In eighteenth-century usage this term frequently indicates progression or movement in general. It does not necessarily imply movement to different keys.

[5] *Metrum (mesure)*. Elsewhere the French translator uses *metrum*. Quantz's term embraces metre in general, and metrical phrase-structure in particular.

must maintain light and shadow constantly, limit his inventions to a moderate length, commit no abuses with regard to caesuras and the repetition of ideas, and write comfortably for both voices and instruments. He must write in conformity with the length of the syllables and the sense of the words in vocal music, and acquire a satisfactory knowledge both of singing methods and of the qualities of each instrument. A singer or an instrumentalist must endeavour to make himself complete master of his voice or instrument, must learn to know the proportions of the notes, become truly secure in holding the tempo and in reading the notes, learn harmony thoroughly and, especially, put into practice all the particulars required to achieve good execution.

§ 18

He who wishes to distinguish himself in music must not begin the study of it too late. If he sets about it at an age when his energies are no longer vigorous, or when his throat or fingers are no longer flexible, and thus cannot acquire sufficient facility to perform the shakes, the little refined embellishments or *propretés*,[1] and the passage-work roundly and distinctly, he will not go very far.

§ 19

Furthermore, a musician must not occupy himself with too many other things. Almost every science requires the whole man. My meaning here, however, is by no means that it is impossible to excel in more than one science at the same time, but that this requires a quite extraordinary talent, of a kind that nature seldom produces. Many people make this mistake. Some want to learn everything, and, because of the changeability of their temperaments, turn from one matter to another, now to this or that instrument, now to composition, then to something other than music; and because of their inconstancy, they learn nothing thoroughly. Some who devote themselves to one of the higher sciences begin by treating music as an avocation for many years. They cannot devote to music the time that it requires, and have neither the opportunity nor the means to retain a good master, or to hear good things. Frequently they have learned no more than to read notes, and to humbug their listeners with some difficult things poorly executed and in poor taste; and if by chance they have the good fortune to become one-eyed kings in the land of the blind and to receive some applause, their lack of knowledge deludes them into thinking that, because of their other skills, they merit preference over other musicians who, though not trained at universities, really know

---

[1] *Propretäten.* The German term is a direct borrowing from French, and is one of several synonyms used for the essential graces described in Chapter VIII. The French translator substitutes the word *roulemens* in this sentence, but uses *propretés* in all other cases. *Roulemens* was used for graces or passage-work which moved by step rather than by leap.

more about music. Some practise music simply because they need a livelihood, without having the slightest pleasure in it. Others have learned
music in their youth more through their own practice than through correct principles, and in later years are ashamed to receive instruction, or
believe they have no further need of it. Disliking correction, they prefer
to win praise disguised as 'amateurs'. They[1] are forced to turn to music
because fate has denied them success through their other skills; but just
as they were formerly only half scholars, they now remain only half
musicians, because of the time lost in applying themselves to other
sciences. Their talent, which was insufficient for other fields of endeavour,
is still less adequate for music, and their prejudice and conceit make
them unwilling to endure any correction from others. He who does not
possess sufficient natural gifts for academic study probably has even fewer
gifts for music. Yet if someone who gives himself to academic studies has
sufficient talent for music, and devotes just as much industry to it as to the
former, he not only has an advantage over other musicians, but also can
be of greater service to music in general than others, as can be demonstrated with many examples. Whoever is aware of how much influence
mathematics and the other related sciences, such as philosophy, poetry,
and oratory, have upon music, will have to own not only that music has a
greater compass than many imagine, but also that the evident lack of
knowledge about the above-mentioned sciences among the majority of
professional musicians is a great obstacle to their further advancement,
and the reason why music has not yet been brought to a more perfect
state. This seems inevitable, since those who have a command of theory
are seldom strong in practice, and those who excel in practice can seldom
pretend to be masters of theory. In these circumstances is it possible to
bring music to some degree of perfection? To do so, serious counsel must
be given to young people who dedicate themselves to music that they endeavour not to remain strangers at least to those sciences mentioned
above, and some foreign languages besides, even if time does not permit
them to engage in all academic studies. And for those who propose to
make composition their goal, a thorough knowledge of acting will not be
unserviceable.

§ 20

My last counsel for someone who wishes to excel in music is to control
his vanity, and to hold it in check. Immoderate and uncontrolled vanity is
very harmful in general, since it can easily cloud the mind and obstruct
true understanding. It is equally harmful in music, and becomes increasingly so the more it steals in. It finds greater nourishment in music than in
other professions, in which one does not, as in music, allow oneself to
be taken in and inflated by a mere bravo. How many disorders has it not
already caused in music? In the beginning we usually please ourselves

---

[1] French text: 'Still others'.

more than others. We are satisfied if perhaps we can merely double a part on occasion. Then we allow ourselves to be deluded by untimely and excessive praise, and come to take it for a merited recompense. We do not wish to tolerate any contradiction, any admonition or correction. Should somebody undertake something of this sort from necessity, or with good intent, the rash fellow is immediately considered an enemy. Some persons with very little knowledge frequently flatter themselves that they know a great deal, and seek to elevate themselves above those from whom they could still learn. Indeed, from jealousy, envy, and malice, they even go so far as to scorn the latter. But if this pretended knowledge is carefully investigated, in many cases it will be found to be nothing but quackery: these persons have memorized a few technical terms from theoretical writings, or they are able to talk about musical artifices a little, but do not know how to produce them. In this fashion, it is true, they may gain some authority among the ignorant, but they also run the risk of making themselves ridiculous among connoisseurs, since they resemble those artisans who know how to name their tools, but use them poorly. Some persons who are in a position to discourse at length about an art or science are in point of fact more embarrassed in practice than others who do not brag half as much. And if one has finally succeeded through good instruction in meriting some applause, he immediately counts himself among the multitude of virtuosi, and believes that he has already reached the first step of Parnassus. In consequence he is ashamed to receive further instruction, or holds it unnecessary. He quits his master at the most favourable time, in the flower of growth. He does not seek to profit from the judgement of experienced persons, but prefers to remain in ignorance rather than to condescend a little and take lessons again. And even if he deigns to consult somebody else about any of his doubts, it is more often done with a view to hearing praise than to hearing the truth. This perverted vanity causes untold harm. Suffice it to say that vanity produces a false satisfaction, and that it is one of the greatest obstacles to growth in music.

§ 21

Before concluding I must set right those who have the mistaken notion that playing the flute is harmful to the chest or lungs. Far from being harmful, it is, on the contrary, salutary and beneficial. It expands and strengthens the chest. Were it necessary, I could show by means of examples that some young people who were very short of wind, and scarcely capable of playing two measures in a single breath, succeeded in a few years in achieving the capacity to play more than twenty measures in the same breath. It can only be concluded that blowing upon the flute is as little harmful to the lungs as riding, fencing, dancing, and running. The player must merely not overdo it, and must neither play too soon after mealtime, nor take a cold drink immediately after playing, when his lungs are still highly stimulated. None will deny that the trumpet requires stronger lungs and far more physical power than the flute. Nevertheless, experience shows that people who occupy themselves with the trumpet for the most part attain a very great age. From my youth I remember a young fellow[1] of very weak physical constitution who became a trumpeter, and who not only practised his instrument very diligently, but also became quite good on it. He is not only still alive, but vigorous and in good health. Although it is undeniable that the practice of the flute or the trumpet requires as healthy a body as the athletic pursuits previously mentioned, it will not, of course, cure anyone who already has consumption, nor should it be recommended for that purpose. I have already stated above that in general, regardless of the instrument a musician wishes to play, he must have a perfectly healthy body and not a weak or sickly one, and that he must also have a lively and vigorous spirit, since both must work together.

[1] Quantz again may be referring to himself. In his earlier years the trumpet was one of his principal instruments. See Nettl, *Forgotten Musicians*, p. 218.

Fig. 15.

Fig. 16.

CHAPTER I

Short History and Description of the Transverse Flute

§ 1

I will not waste time here with fabulous and uncertain tales of the origin of flutes that are held crossways before the mouth. Since we have no absolutely certain information about the matter, it is immaterial whether the Phrygian King *Midas*[1] or someone else is supposed to have invented them. Likewise, I cannot determine whether the invention was first suggested by a draught of wind striking a hollow branch of an elder-bush, broken off at the top, in which rot had made a little opening in the side, or whether it was due to some other circumstance.

§ 2

It is beyond all doubt, however, that in Occidental lands the Germans were the first to revive, if not to establish, the basic principles of the transverse flute as well as of many other wind instruments. Thus the English call the instrument the *German flute*, and the French designate it *la flute allemande* (see *Principes de la flute traversiere, ou de la flute allemande, par Mr. Hotteterre le Romain*).[2]

§ 3

Michael Praetorius, in his *Theatrum instrumentorum*, published in Wolfenbüttel in 1620,[3] when none of the present keys were used, calls this flute the

---

[1] J. G. Walther, *Musikalisches Lexikon* (Leipzig: Wolffgang Deer, 1732), p. 248, states that the invention of the transverse flute is attributed to King Midas in Polydorus Vergilius, *lib. I de inventoribus rerum*, c. 15.

[2] Hotteterre's *Principes* was the first, and the most popular, tutor designed specifically for the transverse flute. It first appeared in France in 1707, and was translated into English in 1729. It appeared in numerous editions for over half a century in both countries. Quantz's version of the title is not quite accurate. The title of the first edition is as follows: *Principes de la flute traversiere, ou flute d'Allemagne, de la flute a bec, ou flute douce, et du hautbois, divisez par traitez. Par le sieur Hotteterre-le-Romain, ordinaire de la musique du roy. A Paris, chez Christophe Ballard. . . . M. DCCVII.* The association of the transverse flute with the Germans can be traced back at least to the fifteenth century. In 1441 the Duke of Este mentions a special *flauto alemano* used in Germany. See C. Sachs, *Handbuch der Musikinstrumentenkunde* (Leipzig: Breitkopf & Härtel. 1920), p. 303. For further information on the history of the transverse flute, see A. Baines, *Woodwind Instruments and their History*, 3rd ed. (London: Faber and Faber, 1967), pp. 52–75, 171–88, 239–40, 290–5.

[3] The *Theatrum instrumentorum* of Praetorius is a volume of illustrations for the second

cross-flute.[1] In contradistinction to it, the instrument still used today among soldiers to accompany the drum is termed the *Swiss pipe*.[2]

§ 4

Thus the structure of the transverse flute was formerly not the same as it is now. Since the key indispensable for the semitone D sharp was lacking,[3] one could not play in all tonalities upon it. I myself possess one of this kind, fashioned in Germany about sixty years ago, which is a fourth lower than ordinary flutes. The French, by the addition of a key, were the first to make the instrument more serviceable than it had been previously among the Germans.

§ 5

The exact time when this improvement was made, and who its originator was, cannot be fixed with certainty, although I have spared no pains to discover reliable answers. In all probability the improvement was made less than a century ago; it was, no doubt, undertaken in France at the same time that the shawm[4] was developed into the oboe, and the bombard[5] into the bassoon.

§ 6

In France the first to distinguish himself and to make himself celebrated and popular upon the improved transverse flute was *Philibert*,[6] well known as a result of his singular experiences. After him came *la Barre*[7] and *Hotteterre le Romain*.[8] They were followed by *Buffardin*[9] and *Blavet*,[10] who greatly excelled their predecessors in the practice of the instrument.

volume of the *Syntagma Musicum*, entitled *De Organographia* (Wolfenbüttel: Helwein, 1619). The instruments Quantz mentions are found depicted in figs. 3 and 4 in plate IX of the *Theatrum*.

[1] *Die Querflöte* (*Flute en travers*).

[2] *Die Schweitzerpfeife* (*la Flute des Suisses*).

[3] D sharp and E flat were distinguished in both theory and practice at this time. The majority of eighteenth-century flutes had only one key, and this was called the D sharp key. The addition of this key gave the flute a full chromatic scale, although some pitches had to be corrected through adjustment of the embouchure.

[4] *Schallmey* (*Chalemie*).

[5] *Bombard* (*Bombardo*).

[6] Philibert Rebillé (*fl.* 1667–1717). Philibert was involved in a murder, was imprisoned, and later pardoned. For details about his life, see J.-G. Prod'homme, *Écrits de musiciens* (Paris: Mercure de France, 1912), p. 244.

[7] Michel de la Barre (*c.* 1675–1743/4). An interesting letter of de la Barre, which confirms Quantz's statements in this and the preceding paragraph, is found in Prod'homme, *Écrits*, pp. 242–5.

[8] Jacques Hotteterre (*dit* le Romain) (*c.* 1674–*c.* 1763).

[9] Pierre Gabriel Buffardin (*c.* 1690–1768). Buffardin was the principal flute player in Dresden during Quantz's younger days, and is the only teacher whom Quantz acknowledges in his study of the transverse flute. See Nettl, *Forgotten Musicians*, p. 289.

[10] Michel Blavet (1700–68). Blavet was the most esteemed flute player of his day in France. Quantz became acquainted with him during his visit to Paris in 1726–7, and praises him highly in his autobiography. See Nettl, *Forgotten Musicians*, p. 311.

§ 7

Although the French musicians just enumerated were the first to play the instrument well and with some understanding of its peculiarities, the Germans reacquired it about fifty or sixty years ago in its improved form, that is, with a single key. The particular approbation and the great inclination which the Germans have always cherished for wind instruments have now made the transverse flute as common in Germany as it is in France.

§ 8

As yet the flute had only one key. When I gradually learned to understand the peculiarities of the instrument, however, I found that there remained a slight impurity in certain tones, which could be remedied only by the addition of a second key. I added this second key in the year 1726.* And in this fashion the transverse flute illustrated in Tab. I, Fig. 1, came into being.[1]

*I explain the reasons for this second key more fully in § 8 of Chapter III.

§ 9

In earlier times the transverse flute consisted of only a single piece, like the Swiss pipe still used today, or the so-called soldiers' cross-pipe,[2] although it was an octave lower than the latter. But when in France the single key was added, to make the flute as well as other instruments more serviceable for music, it not only received a better exterior form, but was also, for the sake of greater convenience, divided into three parts, namely a head piece in which the mouth hole was found, a middle piece with six holes, and a foot piece on which the key was found. If the same pitch had prevailed everywhere, these three pieces would have sufficed.[3] About thirty years ago, however, the flute was supplied with several interchangeable middle pieces, necessitated by the fact that the pitch to which we tune is so varied that a different tuning or prevailing pitch has been introduced not only in every country, but in almost every province and city, while even at the very same place the harpsichord is tuned high at one time, low at another, by careless tuners. Accordingly, the long middle piece with six holes was divided into two parts, to make the flute more convenient to

[1] For Quantz's illustration, see Chapter III, § 4. A more detailed and clearer illustration of Quantz's instrument is presented here in Plate III, reproduced from the *Recueil de planches*, vol. xii, of Diderot's *Encyclopédie*, where it was used to illustrate an article on Quantz's flutes in vol. iii (1777) of the *Supplément*. A translation of this interesting article is found in E. Halfpenny, 'A French Commentary on Quantz', *Music & Letters*, xxxvii (1956), pp. 61–66. Quantz entered seriously into the business of making flutes in 1739. See Nettl, *Forgotten Musicians*, pp. 317–18. ←

[2] *Die Querpfeiffe* (*le Fifre*).

[3] For further information on the various pitches used in Quantz's day, see Chapter XVII, Section VII, §§ 6–7.

carry about in one's pocket;[1] and to take the place of one of these two parts, namely the upper section, two or three others were fashioned, one shorter than another, so that they differed from one another by about a semitone; for the length or shortness of the flute makes its pitch respectively lower or higher. When the instrument still could not be tuned correctly, one piece often being too low, the other too high, the upper middle piece had to be pulled out a little from the head piece. Since the difference between these middle pieces was still too great, however, and the middle pieces had to be drawn out further than the structure of the flute permitted, making it false, means were finally found to add still more middle pieces, each differing from one another by no more than a comma, or the ninth part of a whole tone. Six middle pieces now form an interval a little larger than a major semitone, which the construction of the flute permits with no detriment to true intonation; and if it is necessary, two more middle pieces can be added.

§ 10

In the head piece of the flute, between the cap and the mouth hole, a cork plug is found which may be pushed in or pulled out at will.[2] This plug is indispensable in the flute, and produces the very same effect as that made in the violin by the sound-post, that is, the little piece of wood standing upright beneath the bridge. The latter makes the tone either good or bad, depending upon whether it is correctly or incorrectly placed; and the former, if pressed in too deeply or drawn out too far, is obstructive not only to good tone, but to true intonation in general.

§ 11

When the flute is shortened or lengthened with the middle pieces, the true intonation of its octaves will be lost if the plug always remains in the same position. It must be drawn further back from the mouth hole for each shorter middle piece, and must be pressed in closer to the mouth hole for each longer piece. To manage this more conveniently, a screw must be attached to the plug and the cap; with it the plug can be more easily pushed in or pulled out.[3]

§ 12

To determine whether the plug stands at the correct place, test the low D[4] against the middle and highest D. If these two octaves are true, it is

[1] The division of the middle piece must have occurred by about 1735, since it is illustrated in M. Corrette's *Methode*, p. 9. 'In one's pocket' is found only in the French text.

[2] A. Mahaut, in his *Nieuwe manier om binnen korten tyd op de dwarsfluit te leeren speelen — Nouvelle Méthode pour apprendre en peu de tems a jouer de la flute traversiere* (Amsterdam: J. J. Hummel, *c.* 1759); p. 2, attributes the invention of the movable plug to Quantz's teacher Buffardin. The text of Mahaut's work appears in parallel Dutch and French columns.

[3] For a clear illustration of the plug and the screw, see Fig. 16 in Plate II.

[4] For an explanation of Quantz's system of pitch designations, see Chapter III, § 2.

correctly placed. But if the highest D is too high, and therefore the low one too deep, draw the plug back until they are true. If on the other hand the highest D is too low, and the low one too high, press the plug further in until the intonation of both octaves is true.

§ 13

When pulling out the middle pieces,[1] you must be careful not to go too far, or C'[2] and the shake upon it, as well as that upon C sharp, will become too harsh. Thus, as already stated above, the middle pieces must differ from one another by no more than a comma, or the intervening empty space must be filled out with a ring as thick as the tenon. Only the broad end of the middle piece which goes into the head piece may be pulled out. If the narrow end, or the one next to the foot, were pulled out, the intonation of the entire flute would be upset, since the increased distance between the holes makes the resulting tones higher.

§ 14

Not very long ago an invention appeared by virtue of which the foot can be made longer or shorter by dividing it into two parts which, like a pin case, can be pulled apart about a half-inch and pushed together again.[3] The joint is placed below the holes upon which the keys lie.[4] The purpose is supposed to be to make the foot a little shorter for each shorter middle piece, so that with the help of six middle pieces the flute might be raised or lowered by a whole tone. If it stood the test, the invention would have its value. But since only the D becomes higher as a result of shortening the foot, while the intonation of the following notes, such as D sharp, E, F, G, &c., remains unchanged for the most part and does not rise with the D in the proper proportion, it follows that the flute does indeed become a whole note higher, but also that it becomes completely false, with the exception of the notes produced with the holes[5] of the first piece. For these reasons, and for those cited in the previous paragraph, this invention must be rejected as most harmful and detrimental. It serves no other purpose than to make it possible for somebody with thriftiness in mind to manage upon

[1] In the French text the word 'plug' is substituted for 'middle pieces'.
[2] C' here should probably read C'', unless Quantz intended a note produced artificially with the embouchure. The normal lowest note on the transverse flute at this time is D'. See Chapter III, § 4.
[3] A. Mahaut, *Nieuwe manier*, p. 2, also ascribes the invention of the divided foot-piece to Buffardin, and defends its use. J. G. Tromlitz, in his *Ausführlicher und gründlicher Unterricht die Flöte zu spielen* (Leipzig: A. F. Böhme, 1791), pp. 23–24, also defends the use of a divided foot-piece, which he calls a *Register*. For those interested in the history and structure of the flute, the entire first chapter of Tromlitz's work provides a valuable and detailed supplement to the present chapter of Quantz.
[4] *Das Ausziehen geschieht unter den Löchern worauf die Klappen liegen.* (On les tire dehors au dessous des troux que les clefs couvrent.)
[5] The preceding four words occur in the French text.

a single badly tuned flute what would otherwise require two flutes, that is, a low one and a high one. But anyone who wanted to make use of this invention would run the risk of greatly offending the ear; and its originator reveals that he neither understands the proportions of the notes, nor possesses a good musical ear.

§ 15

Shortening and lengthening of this kind could be better introduced in the head piece than in the foot, that is, by dividing the head piece into two parts, and making the tenon of the lower part a little longer than that of the middle part. By inserting this tenon into the upper part of the head, the head can be made shorter or longer without detriment to the intonation, and the advantage sought for in vain through the aforementioned invention can be obtained with ease. I have tested this myself, and have found it trustworthy.[1]

§ 16

About thirty years ago some persons tried to add yet another note, namely C,[2] to the low register of the flute. To this end they lengthened the foot as much as was required for a whole tone, and, in order to have the C sharp, added another key. Since this seems to have been detrimental to the true intonation of the flute as well as its tone, the pretended improvement was not widely accepted and disappeared.[3]

§ 17

Besides the usual transverse flutes, there are various other less usual kinds, both larger and smaller in size. There are low *Quartflöten, flutes d'amour*, little *Quartflöten*, &c. The first type is a fourth, the second a minor third lower than the ordinary flute, while the third type is a fourth higher. Of these, the *flutes d'amour* are still the best. At present, however, none approaches the regular transverse flute in trueness and beauty of tone. But if anyone wishes to practise upon one of these uncommon flutes, he has only to imagine a different clef for the notes; he then can manage everything else as upon the regular transverse flute.

§ 18

Flutes are fashioned out of different kinds of hard wood, such as boxwood, ebony, kingwood, lignum sanctum, granadilla, &c. Boxwood is the most common and durable wood for flutes. Ebony, however, produces the

---

[1] For an illustration of this tuning slide, see Plate III, Fig. 16. Quantz claims it as his invention in his autobiography. See Nettl, *Forgotten Musicians*, p. 318. Tromlitz, *Unterricht*, pp. 19–20, strongly opposes its use.

[2] C' is meant.

[3] A flute of this type is illustrated with a picture and fingering chart in J. F. B. C. Majer's *Museum musicum theoretico practicum* (Schwäbisch Hall: G. M. Majer, 1732), p. 33.

clearest and most beautiful tone.[1] Anyone who wishes to make the tone of the flute shrill, rude, and disagreeable can have it cased with brass, as some have tried.

§ 19

Since harmful moisture forms in the flute when it is blown, it must be frequently and carefully cleaned with a rag attached to a little stick. And so that the moisture is not absorbed by the wood, it must be smeared occasionally with oil of almonds.

[1] See Corrette, *Methode*, p. 7, for further information on the materials used for making flutes.

CHAPTER II

Of Holding the Flute, and Placing
the Fingers

§ 1

To explain myself clearly here, it will be necessary to give each finger a number, enabling you to see without difficulty to which fingers I refer in the engraving of the flute found in Table I.[1] I therefore designate the forefinger of the left hand 1, and the following two fingers 2 and 3; the little finger of this hand is not used. The forefinger of the right hand I mark 4, the following two fingers 5 and 6. The numbers 7 and 8 are reserved for the little finger of the right hand. When marked 7 it touches the little key, and when designated 8 it touches the bent key. Henceforth, when dealing with fingering (*application*)[2] and in *all other cases*, the fingers will be designated in this manner. It should be noted, however, that the fingers marked 1 to 6 cover the holes of the flute, while the one marked 7 and 8 depresses the keys, and thus opens the holes.[3]

§ 2

If the flute is to be held and played naturally, when it is screwed together the holes of the two middle pieces must stand in a straight line with the hole covered by the bent key, so that the little finger of the right hand can reach both of the keys comfortably. The head piece must be turned in towards the mouth so that it deviates from the straight line approximately the distance of the section of the mouth hole.

§ 3

Place the left thumb almost directly below the finger marked 2, with the tip of the thumb curved inwards. Lay the flute between the ball[4] at the base of the first finger and its second member in such a way that when you place the first finger on the flute it can cover the upper hole comfortably. In this fashion, when you place the flute to your mouth you will not only be able to press it against your mouth comfortably and hold it firmly with

---

[1] The illustration of the flute, with the numbers for each hole, is found in Chapter III, § 4.

[2] On the meaning of this term, see Chapter III, note 1.

[3] In the fingering charts of some other writers the little finger is marked when it leaves the hole covered by the little key closed rather than open.

[4] i.e. the fleshy portion of the first joint of the finger.

finger 1 and the left thumb (which forms the point of equilibrium)[1] without the aid of the other fingers or of the right hand, but will also be able to strike shakes with each finger of the left hand without the assistance of the right.

§ 4

As to the right hand, place the thumb, bent and curved outwards, with the tip beneath finger 4. Place the other fingers of this hand, as well as those of the left hand, over the holes in a curved arch; do not use the tips of the fingers, however, or you will not be able to cover the holes so that no air can escape. The arching of the fingers serves to give you more strength to strike the shakes quickly and evenly.

§ 5

The head must be held constantly erect, yet naturally, so that respiration is not impaired.[2] You must hold your arms a little outwards and up, the left more than the right, and must not press them against your body, lest you be compelled to hold your head obliquely toward the right side; for this not only produces bad posture, but also impedes your blowing, since the throat is constricted, and respiration is not as easy as it should be.

§ 6

You must always hold the flute firmly against your mouth, and must not turn it alternately in and out, which makes the tone either lower or higher.

§ 7

If you are to avoid all unnecessary and diffuse movements, you must hold the fingers directly above the holes, and must never contract them inwards or extend them outwards. Hence you must always set your right thumb at the same place, not to sustain the flute, for which the left thumb alone is appointed, but so that the other fingers also can hold their places surely, and can find the holes more easily. In general you must also tense the tendons of the fingers a little in order to strike the shakes evenly and brilliantly.

§ 8

It is also necessary to pay diligent attention to your fingers, so that you do not become accustomed to raising them too high, or to lifting one finger higher than the others; this would make it impossible to execute passage-work very quickly, roundly,[3] and distinctly, and these matters are

---

[1] Translator's parentheses.

[2] *Damit der Wind im Steigen nicht verhindert werde (afin que le vent ne soit pas empeché de monter).* Literally, 'so that the wind is not obstructed in rising'.

[3] For a clearer understanding of Quantz's use of the terms 'round' and 'roundly', see Chapter XI, § 11.

extremely important in playing. Yet the fingers must not be held too close to the holes; if the clarity and trueness of the tone are not to be impaired, they must be held at least the breadth of the little finger above the holes.

<h1 style="text-align:center">§ 9</h1>

In holding the flute, guard against coming to the aid of the left hand with the right, and even more against allowing the little finger to remain on one of the keys when it should be closed, in order to hold the flute firmly. The latter defect I have perceived among a great many players who make a profession of this instrument. It is a harmful custom; for if in quick passage-work, where one hand works in alternation with the other, you allow the little finger to remain on the key, and thus hold it open, for E′ and E″ and for F′ and F″ (see the fingering chart of the flute),[1] these notes become a comma, or a ninth of a tone, too high, which is not at all agreeable to the ear. In F sharp″, G″, A″, B flat″, and B natural″ opening the key causes no harm.

[1] See Chapter III, § 4.

CHAPTER III

Of the Fingering or *Application*,[1] and the Gamut or Scale of the Flute

§ 1

In several places in the following chapter, which treats of embouchure, I must presuppose a knowledge of fingering, without which the rules given there could not be carried out; hence I must explain fingering here first. The system of fingering is that which I employ myself and that which I consider the best.

§ 2

As is well known, the names of the principal notes*[2] are *C, D, E, F, G, A,* and *B.*** These are repeated in all the octaves. Two among them, that is, F to E and C to B, are semitones, the others whole tones. The lowest octave that occurs on the flute is the one customarily designated by placing a dash above the letters, and called the *one-line* octave. Two dashes are placed above the letters in the following octave, and it is called the *two-line* octave. In the next octave three dashes are placed above the letters, and it is given the name *three-line* octave.[3] This manner of designating notes had its beginnings in the German tablature formerly used for the keyboard. These seven notes are represented on a staff of five lines, which for the flute are appointed with a G clef on the second line, so that a note for one pitch always occupies one line, and the note for the neighbouring pitch occupies the adjoining space. Therefore D′, the lowest regular note of the flute, occupies the space below the lowest line. The other notes follow it upon alternative lines and spaces up to G″. When notes lying above this one occur, it is customary to add another line, and thus make another space, proceeding in the same fashion to the highest possible register (see Tab. I, Fig. 1).[4]

[1] The German term *Application* is a contraction of the French phrase *l'application des doigts*, which refers to the process of applying the fingers to the flute in order to stop the proper holes for each note.

[2] When discussing ornamentation, Quantz later uses the term 'principal notes' to indicate the unembellished notes of a melody.

[3] The German designations of the three octaves beginning with middle C are *eingestrichen*, *zweygestrichen*, and *dreygestrichen*. As explained in the text, these lines were normally placed above the notes. Throughout the treatise Quantz frequently uses the written-out designations. To avoid the frequent repetition of these clumsy phrases, however, the modern system of dashes to the side of the notes has been substituted. Thus A′ in the translation is equivalent to 'one-line A' in the original text.   [4] See § 4 of this chapter for this illustration.

*I call them principal notes since they were the first to be used, and appear as such on the staff of five lines on which the notes are placed, before it is altered through accidentals.[1] The Germans name each note by only a single letter, but the French name the notes in two different manners. In the first they add two sol-fa syllables to the letter of the note, thus saying C sol ut, D la re, E si mi, F ut fa, G re sol, A mi la, B fa si. Their second manner is to say only the last syllable, that is, ut, re, mi, fa, sol, la, si. When a sharp or flat is found before a note, they say *diese* or *b mol* after the syllable, that is, ut diese, re b mol, &c. But since the latter manner is more common at present, I will make use of it. The French designation will always be enclosed in parentheses. In the following pages you will find certain names which are not known to everyone, such as C flat, E sharp, &c.[2] But since differences between the keys demand that the notes be marked at some times with sharps, at others with flats, and, in fact, that there be a difference between these tones, it is also proper to give them different names. This will be discussed in the following paragraph.

**In designating the notes I will make use of large German capitals throughout the entire book, and, where necessary, will indicate with words the octave in which they stand. This is done partly for the sake of convenience of printing, partly in order not to cause any confusion at certain places.[3] It has long been the custom among the Germans to call the lowest octave of the keyboard *the great octave*; and in indicating it with letters, large letters, such as C, D, E, &c., are used. The following octave above is indicated by small letters, such as c, d, e, &c., and in German is called *the octave with no line*, since there is nothing above its letters, while above those which mark the third octave there is a little dash—c̄, d̄, ē, &c.; for this reason it is called *the one-line octave*. For each of the succeeding octaves an additional dash is added above the letters. This designation of the notes has become common for all instruments, but the notes of the flute begin only with the third octave, or one-line octave of the keyboard.

§ 3

Between the whole tones of these seven principal notes lie five other notes which divide the space between the principal notes into two halves, albeit unequal halves at some places, and thus form large or small semitones in relation to the neighbouring upper or lower principal notes.* Just because of this inequality they are given two names, are written in two ways, and are produced in two ways in accordance with true intonation. In German they are designated by two syllables, *-es* or *-is*, attached to the principal notes, and are indicated with either flats or sharps on the line or space of the principal note. If one of these notes is a semitone below the principal note, the syllable *-es* is attached to the letter of the principal note, and a *round b*,[4] called a *flat*, is placed before the note. This means that the semitone must always be stopped below the principal tone. A and E, to which only *-s* is attached, form exceptions to the regular designation with

---

[1] The remainder of this note occurs only in the French text.

[2] Throughout the treatise, and particularly in the present chapter, it must be remembered that Quantz favours mean-tone tuning, and carefully distinguishes raised semitones and lowered semitones.

[3] The remainder of this note appears only in the French text, where it takes the place of the German note.

[4] The flat sign and the natural sign were considered two forms of the letter *b*. The flat is called the 'round *b*', the natural the 'quadrant *b*'. See the latter part of the present paragraph.

the syllable -*es*, and the semitone below H is usually simply called B.[1] Thus the designations are as follows: *Des, Es, Ges, As*, and *B*. When these semitones are mingled with the principal notes, the distinction produced by them is necessarily extended to the two semitones found in the natural scale, and in consequence *Ces* and *Fes* arise (see Tab. 1, Fig. 2).[2] But if you must take the semitone above the principal note, a *double cross* or diesis, which is called a *sharp*, is placed before the note; and in the designation of these tones the syllable -*is* is attached to the letters of the principal notes, which are thus called *Cis, Dis, Fis, Gis*, and *Ais*. For the above reasons, these are also joined by *Eis* and *His* (see Tab. I, Fig. 3). Occasionally before Fis and Cis a *plain large cross* is found (see Tab. I, Fig. 3, the fourth and ninth notes). This raises the principal note by two small semitones, and when the principal note is already raised by a semitone, this single cross is used to avoid confusion, and in order not to have to place two double crosses before a note. The first note, *Fis*, is transformed into G, and the second into D, on both the keyboard and the flute. Therefore the first could be called G fis, and the second D cis, since to my knowledge there is no accepted designation for them. If, however, a principal note is to be lowered by two small semitones, as may occur at times with B [flat] and Es, no special sign has as yet been established to do so. Some composers make use of a somewhat larger round *b* instead of two round *b*'s in this situation. On the flute these notes are stopped like the principal note found below the semitone, B [double flat] like A, and E [double flat] like D.** If the tonality requires that one or another of the principal notes be constantly lowered or raised, the flat and sharp are placed, for ease of writing, at the very beginning of the piece on the first staff, on the lines and spaces [of the notes] to be raised or lowered. If one of these lowered or raised principal notes is to be returned to its natural form, a special sign, called *the quadrant b, the angular b, the revocation sign*, or also *the natural sign*, is used, since it returns an altered principal note to its natural place; it is formed as in the second measure of Fig. 3 in Tab. XXI.[3]

*It is true that the designation of the large and small semitones appears to be somewhat contradictory. For two parts of a whole which are not perfectly equal, and in which the division is not exact, cannot be called halves in the strictest sense. Nevertheless this designation has long been accepted, and I do not believe I would be as easily understood without it. Thus I hope that these little apparent inconsistencies will be allowed to slip through until a more exact and precise designation becomes common.

[4] **In solmization Ces, Des, Es, Fes, Ges, As, B, are called *ut b mol, re b mol, mi b mol, fa b mol, sol b mol, la b mol, si b mol*, and Cis, Dis, Eis, Fis, Gis, Ais, His, are called *ut diese, re diese, mi diese, fa diese, sol diese, la diese, si diese*. When *fa* is already raised a semi-

[1] In German terminology H is B natural and B is B flat. Except in this paragraph, normal English terminology is used in the present translation.
[2] Fig. 2 and the other examples mentioned in this paragraph are found in § 4.
[3] Fig. 3, Tab. XXI, is found in Chapter XV, § 27.
[4] The following note appears only in the French text.

tone, and has a single cross before it in addition, it is changed into *sol*, and in the
same circumstances, *ut* is changed into *re*. They may also be called *fa deux dieses*, and
ut deux dieses. *Si b mol* when lowered another semitone may only be called *la*, but
mi b mol in the same circumstances is called either *re* or *mi deux b mols*.

§ 4

How all these notes must be stopped upon the flute you may see from
→ Figs. 1, 2, and 3 of the first table. The principal or diatonic notes are
found in Fig. 1, the notes indicated by the round *b* in Fig. 2, and the notes
indicated by sharps, which are called chromatic and enharmonic,[1] in Fig. 3.
As already mentioned in the previous chapter, the figures beneath the
notes indicate which fingers must cover the holes required for each pitch.
Where horizontal dashes take the place of figures, the holes remain open.
The little finger, marked 7 and 8, opens its keys when these figures appear,
but when a dash is found, it leaves them closed. If C sharp''' follows
B sharp'' (see Tab. 1, Fig. 3), you need only raise finger 5 and the C sharp
will be perfectly true. On other occasions this B sharp may also be taken
with fingers 2, 3, 4, 5, and 7, half covering the first hole. The first way,
however, is better than the second. Thus you need only remark which
figures stand opposite each hole in the flute illustrated in this table to see
which fingers must be used for each note.

TABLE I

FIG. 1

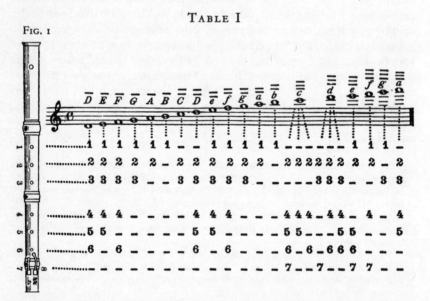

If the F''' in Fig. 1 does not speak readily, you may cover the fifth hole half-way.

---

[1] Quantz uses the terms 'chromatic' and 'enharmonic' here simply to indicate tones raised
with sharps. See Walther's discussion of these words in his *Musikalisches Lexikon*, pp. 163,
225. Both were commonly used to refer to any chromatic alterations.

FIG. 2

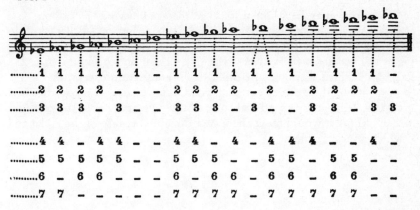

FIG. 3

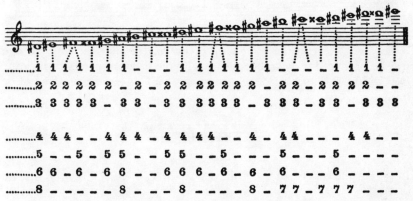

The ordinary C sharp''' in Fig. 3, with fingers 2, 3, 4, and 7, is a little too high. But if you half cover the first hole, or take the C sharp mentioned with fingers 2, 3, 4, 6, and 7, it is true, although the latter stopping is possible only where the movement is slow. The irregular C sharp''', in which all the holes remain open, is too low, on the other hand, and you must therefore turn the flute outwards.

§ 5

From these tables you will be able to perceive that the notes indicated with flats are a comma higher than those with sharps. In consequence the minor keys lying between D and E, and between G and A, and the major keys between C and D, which are sometimes written with flats, sometimes with sharps, must be stopped in different ways, so that D flat is a comma higher than C sharp, E flat is a comma higher than D sharp, and A flat is a comma higher than G sharp.

§ 6

Some notes may be stopped in more than one way. For example, C'''
and D''' may be taken in three ways (see Tab. I, Fig. 1),[1] B flat'' in two
ways (see Fig. 2), and F sharp', F sharp'', and C sharp''' in two ways (see
Fig. 3). The first way is always the most usual and common one; the
second and third ways, on the other hand, are used in exceptional cases,
to make it possible to play certain passages more easily and comfortably.
For example, if you were to make use of the regular B flat in the passages
in Table II (*a*), it would make them very difficult, because of the A flat and
C which appear in them.

TABLE II

FIG. 1

If, however, you take the B flat in the exceptional fashion, the same passage
may be produced truly and distinctly with the greatest speed. In the leaps
E–C and D–C in Fig. 1 (*b*) the second way for C is easier than the first or
third.

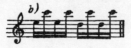

In (*c*), on the other hand, the third way for C is easier than the first or
second.

There are some flutes upon which this C can be produced in yet another
way, namely, with the third finger and the key. This is very comfortable
if you have a passage of several notes that ascend or descend stepwise in a
quick tempo in which B flat, C, and D occur in the high register. The
passage in (*d*) could not be produced rapidly with the ordinary C sharp.
But if you use the second way, it is very easy.

---

[1] See the fingering charts in § 4 above.

In (*e*) the D can be taken in the second way, and in (*f*) in the third way.

In (*g*) the B flat in the first three figures can be taken with fingers 1 and 3, and in the fourth figure with fingers 1, 3, 4, and 6, moderating the wind a little for the B flat, since otherwise it is too high.

If you test the alternative methods, you will find that passages of this kind are not to be produced with the conventional fingering.

§ 7

These few examples may give occasion for further inquiry. You must be constantly attentive to the sequence of the notes, and then choose the kind of fingering that requires the fewest fingers in relation to the movement of the hands. For example, if the B flat in the passage in (*a*) were to be taken in the regular way, six fingers would be brought into motion from C to B flat, and four from A flat to B flat. But if the B flat is taken in the second way, only one finger comes into motion in both the first and second cases, and greater speed is more easily obtainable as a result. If you investigate the remaining passages in (*b*), (*c*), (*d*), (*e*), (*f*), and (*g*), you will find this same ease. The second or irregular F sharp is used more in slow and cantabile passages than in quick ones. It is mainly encountered when either ascending or descending notes like those in Table II (*h*) or (*i*) follow one another.

The ordinary F sharp on the flute is too low in relation to both the G sharp and the E sharp. If the flute does not sound this F sharp without the little key, however, you must open the large key for it, and moderate the wind. Once you have allowed this irregular F sharp to be heard, you must continue to use it as long as the piece remains in E major, C sharp minor, F sharp minor, G sharp minor, B major, and F sharp major. At such places you must not take the regular F sharp at one time, the irregular one at another. If, however, the key changes, so that the G sharp becomes G, you must use the regular F sharp again, at first sounding it a little higher than usual, until the ear is again accustomed to it.

§ 8

The motive which induced me to add yet another key, not previously used, to the flute, stems from the difference between large and small semitones. When a note on the same line or space as another note is raised with a sharp (see Table II (*k*)), or lowered with a flat (see (*l*)), the difference between the altered note and the principal note consists of a small semitone.

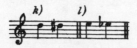

When, on the other hand, one note stands on the line while the other stands a step higher, and is lowered with a flat (see (*m*)); or if one note stands on the line, and is raised with a sharp, while the other stands on the space a step higher, and remains natural (see (*n*)), the difference amounts to a large semitone.

The large semitone has five commas, the small one only four. Therefore E flat must be a comma higher than D sharp. If there were only one key on the flute, both the E flat and the D sharp would have to be tempered,[1] as on the keyboard, where they are struck on a single key, so that neither the E flat to the B flat, the ascending fifth, nor the D sharp to the B, the descending major third, would sound truly. To mark this difference, and to stop the notes in their true proportions,[2] it was necessary to add another key to the flute. In consequence, the semitones produced by adding flats to the principal notes are stopped differently from those indicated by sharps. For example, B flat' is stopped differently from A sharp', C'' differently from B sharp', D flat'' (in which the flute is turned outward) differently from C sharp'', F flat differently from E, G flat'' differently from F sharp'', A flat'' (with the small key) differently from G sharp'' (with the large key), C flat''' differently from B'', &c. It is true that this distinction cannot be made on the keyboard, where each pair of notes differentiated here is struck with a single key, and recourse must be taken to tempering. Nevertheless, since the distinction is based on the nature of the notes, and since singers and string players can observe it without difficulty, it may be reasonably introduced on the flute; and this cannot be done without the second key. Knowledge of the key is needed by all who wish to develop a genuinely refined musical ear. Perhaps in time it will be of even greater utility.

---

[1] *Schwebend gestimmet werden* (*entonner l'un & l'autre . . . de la même façon*).
[2] See the Preface to the Translation on the meaning of this term.

§ 9

Although I introduced the use of this second key more than twenty years ago, it still has not been generally accepted. Perhaps not all its uses have been perceived; perhaps it has been thought to make playing much more difficult. But since the bent key is used only for the four notes found in Table II (*q*) when a sharp stands before them, while the little key serves for all the other natural, sharpened, or flattened notes, which need only one key, you can see that there is little to this imagined difficulty.[1]

§ 10

From the illustration of the flute in the first table[2] you will be able to see that the bent key must be placed above, in a straight line with the holes, and the little key must be placed immediately next to it, opposite the little finger. If someone plays left-handed,[3] the curved portion of the large key must be bent to the other side, and the little key also must be placed there; and they must be placed in such a way that both keys may be reached comfortably with the little finger whether they are on one side or the other. Therefore the crook[4] of the bent key must not be too long; the bent key must be only the breadth of a little finger longer than the small key, not projecting over it, so that the little key may be depressed without touching the bent one. If you make a bent key with two crooks, like the C key on the oboe, and place an additional little key on the other side of the flute, it can be used by anyone, whether he plays right-handed or left-handed.

§ 11

To tune the holes for the two keys truly, you must test the third, G, and the fifth, B flat (see Table II (*o*)) for the little key, and the B and F sharp, in which this D sharp forms the major third (see (*p*)), for the bent one.

---

[1] For further comment on Quantz's second key, see Halfpenny, 'A French Commentary on Quantz', pp. 61–65.

[2] See § 4 above, and also Plate III.

[3] Left-handed playing seems to have been fairly common in Quantz's day. Blavet was a left-handed performer.

[4] The 'crook' is the bent portion of the key. See Plate III.

§ 12

Since the fingering of the transverse flute strongly resembles that of the oboe, many believe that anyone who plays the oboe can learn the transverse flute by himself; and from this fallacy there arise many wrong fingerings and awkward sorts of embouchure. As anyone may easily perceive, the characteristics of these two instruments differ greatly; thus you must not allow yourself to be misled by the misconception just cited.

CHAPTER IV

Of the Embouchure[1]

§ 1

The structure of the flute resembles that of the windpipe, and the formation of the tone in the flute resembles the formation of the tone in the human windpipe.[2] The human voice is produced by the exhalation of air from the lungs, and by the motion of the larynx. The diverse attitudes of the various parts of the mouth, such as the palate, the uvula, the cheeks, the teeth, the lips, and of the nose as well, cause the tone to be produced in diverse ways, either well or poorly. A low note results when you expand the opening of the windpipe by means of the appropriate muscles, and thus depress the five cartilages of which the larynx consists so that the said larynx is shortened slightly while you simultaneously exhale the air rather slowly from the lungs; the depth of this note depends upon the degree of expansion of the opening of the windpipe. A higher note results when you contract the opening of the windpipe, with the aid of the other muscles appointed for this purpose, and in consequence the aforementioned five cartilages in the larynx rise, making the windpipe somewhat narrower and longer, while you simultaneously exhale the air from the lungs more rapidly; the height of this note depends upon the narrowness of the opening. If you press the tongue against the palate, or clamp the teeth together so that the mouth is not sufficiently open, an obstruction of the tone results which gives rise to the principal defects of singing, that is, the so-called throaty voice and the nasal voice.

§ 2

On the flute the tone is formed by the movement of the lips, in accordance with the degree to which they are contracted during the exhalation

---

[1] *Ansatz. Embouchure* appears in parentheses in the German text.

[2] In his 'Antwort auf des Herrn von Moldenit gedrucktes so genanntes Schreiben an Hrn. Quanz', in Marpurg's *Historisch-kritische Beyträge zur Aufnahme der Musik* (Berlin: G. A. Lange), iv (1759), pp. 153–91, Quantz cites the *Naturlehre* (3 vols., 1740–9) of Jean-Gottlob Krüger (1715–59) and unspecified works of Denis Dodart (1634–1707) and Antoine Ferrein (1693–1769) as the authoritative sources of information on the subject of voice production. The works of Dodart which he had in mind were probably 'Sur les causes de la voix de l'homme et de ses différents tons', *Mémoires de l'Académie royale des Sciences* (Paris: Martin, 1700), pp. 244–93; 'Suppléments au mémoire sur la voix et sur les tons', ibid. (1706), pp. 136–48; (1707), p. 66; and 'De la différence des tons de la parole et de la voix du chant, par rapport au recitatif, et, par occasion, des expressions de la musique et de la musique modern', ibid. (1706), pp. 388–410. Ferrein was the author of an article entitled 'De la formation de la voix de l'homme' which appeared in the *Mémoires* of the year 1741, pp. 409–32.

of the air into the mouth hole of the flute. The mouth and its parts, however, may also modify the tone in many ways. Hence, if you are not to imitate the above-mentioned defects found in some human voices, you must take care to avoid all the mistakes which are possible in this connexion. They will be more fully indicated below.

§ 3

In general the most pleasing tone quality (*sonus*) on the flute is that which more nearly resembles a contralto than a soprano, or which imitates the chest tones of the human voice.[1] You must strive as much as possible to acquire the tone quality of those flute players who know how to produce a clear, penetrating, thick, round, masculine, and withal pleasing sound from the instrument.

§ 4

Much depends upon the flute itself, and whether its tone has the necessary similarity to the human voice. If it lacks this, no one can improve the tone quality, even with very adroit lips, just as no singer can make a poor natural voice beautiful. Some flutes give out a strong and thick tone, others a weak and thin one. The strength and clarity of the tone depend upon the quality of the wood, that is, whether it is dense or compact, hard, and heavy. A thick and masculine tone depends upon the interior diameter of the flute, and upon the proportionate thickness of the wood. A thin, weak tone results from the opposite features: porous and light wood, a narrow interior bore, and thin wood. The trueness of the octaves depends entirely upon the interior bore, which also contributes much to the beauty and agreeability of the tone. If the bore of the flute is too narrow, the high notes become too high in relation to the low ones. But if the interior diameter is not narrow enough, the high notes become too low in relation to the low ones. Likewise the mouth hole must be well cut. Pure intonation from one note to another depends upon a firm and secure embouchure, a good musical ear, and upon a good understanding of the proportions of the notes. Whoever possesses this knowledge and also plays well is in a position to make a good, accurately tuned flute. But since the majority of flute makers are not able to do so, it is difficult not only to get hold of a good flute, but also to acquire a good ear, even with frequent playing. Hence it is most advantageous for the flute player if he knows how to make flutes himself, or at least how to tune them. A new flute contracts with blowing, and its interior bore frequently changes; in consequence it must be re-bored to preserve the trueness of its octaves. In former times it was mistakenly believed that only a bad player, and not a good one, could spoil the intonation of an instrument and make it false,

[1] Majer, *Museum musicum*, p. 33, states that the flute is 'that *instrument* which, according to informed opinion, will come closest to a *moderated* human voice . . .'.

in spite of the fact that the wood changes in the hands of one player as well as another, whether he plays loudly or softly, with true or false intonation. In general a good and accurately tuned flute that has been frequently played is always preferable to a new one. Anyone who has a flute with all the good qualities recounted here is more than fortunate, for a good instrument that is tuned truly reduces the task of playing by half.

§ 5

Frequently, however, more depends upon the player than upon the instrument. If many persons play in succession upon the same instrument, it will be found that each produces a distinctive and different tone quality. This quality does not depend upon the instrument, but upon him who plays it. Many possess a gift for imitating both the quality of voice and the language of other people. With close scrutiny, however, it is found that the voice quality is not their own, but an imitation. It follows that each person naturally possesses a particular voice quality, and upon instruments a particular tone quality which he cannot entirely alter. I do not wish to deny that with great industry and much exact observation you can change your tone quality, and can to a degree achieve some semblance of the tone quality of another player, especially if you apply yourself to it from the beginning; yet I know from my own experience that the tone quality of one person always remains a little different from that of another, even if both play together for many years. This is apparent not only on the flute and all the other instruments upon which the tone is produced by embouchure or bow-stroke, but even on the harpsichord and the lute.

§ 6

Everyone will discover that his embouchure on the flute is not always the same or equally good, and that his tone is regularly clearer and more pleasing at one time than at another. At times the tone even changes during playing, if the sharp edge of the rim of the mouth hole has made too deep an impression upon the lip; at other times it does not change. This depends upon the state of the lips. The weather, some foods and beverages, fever, and other circumstances may easily damage the lips for a considerable time, making them too hard, too soft, or too swollen. In these circumstances, only patience, and avoidance of those things which might be harmful, can be advised.

§ 7

Hence you can see that it is not an easy matter to give certain and specific rules for a good embouchure. Many acquire one very easily through natural aptitude, many have much difficulty, and many have almost no success. Much depends upon the natural constitution and disposition of

the lips and teeth. If the lips are very thick, and the teeth short and uneven, great difficulty is experienced. I shall, nevertheless, try to discuss the
subject as fully as possible.

§ 8

When you put the flute to your mouth, first contract your cheeks so
that your lips become smooth. Then place the upper lip above the mouth
hole, on its rim. Press the lower lip to the upper, and then draw it down to
the mouth hole until you feel the lower rim of the mouth hole is almost in
the middle of the red[1] of the lower lip, and the hole is half covered by the
lower lip (after the flute first has been turned a little away from the upper
lip).[2] When you blow, half the air must pass into the mouth hole, and half
must pass over it, so that the sharp edge of the mouth hole divides the
[column of] air; for this is what produces the sound. If the hole remains
too far open, the tone becomes strong but unpleasant and wooden; if, on
the contrary, you cover it too much with the lower lip, and do not hold
your head up, the tone is too weak, and is not clear enough. Pressing the
lips and teeth together too tightly makes a hissing tone, while dilating the
mouth and throat too much makes a dull one.

§ 9

When you play, your chin and lips must constantly move backwards or
forwards, in accordance with the proportions of the ascending and descending notes. To produce a full and penetrating tone in the low register,
from D'' down to D', the lips must be drawn back gradually, and the
opening of the lips must be made a little longer and wider. From D'' up to
D''' the chin and both lips must gradually be pushed forwards, in snch
fashion that the lower lip projects a little more than the upper, and the
opening of the lips becomes a little smaller and narrower. Do not press
the lips together too tightly, however, lest the hiss of the air be heard.

§ 10

Those who have very thick lips would do well to try their embouchure
a little to the left rather than in the middle of the lips; for the wind receives more edge[3] when it is directed against the angle to the left of the
mouth hole, a circumstance better demonstrated by experience than by
description.

§ 11

I wish now to give a general rule for how much you must withdraw or
advance your chin and lips in each octave. Examine the drawing of the

---

[1] *Das Roth (le rouge)*. The portion of the lip meant is probably the philtrum.
[2] The parentheses appear in the French text.
[3] *Der Wind bekömmt alsdenn mehr Schärfe (le vent en est rendu plus aigu)*.

mouth hole (*embouchure*)[1] in Tab. II, Fig. 2; it represents the proper size the hole must have on the flute.[2] In it you will discover four horizontal lines. The second line from the bottom indicates the middle, and how much of the mouth hole must be covered with the lips for D''. The lowest line shows how far both lips must be drawn back to produce D'. The third line indicates how far the lips must be pushed forwards for D'''. And the fourth line, only half as far away, shows how much further the lips must be pushed forwards for G''' than is necessary for D'''. The opening of the mouth hole then remains no larger than the space here between the fourth line and rim of the circle.

FIG. 2

Since the movement of the lips through an octave covers no greater distance than the space here between the lines, it is not possible to mark the six intervening tones with individual lines. To locate them you must use your judgement and your ear.

§ 12

If you wish now to begin to form your embouchure, and have placed the flute to your lips in the manner described above, so that the mouth hole is covered up to the second line, that is, half-way, you must blow in this position without placing the fingers upon the holes, using the same embouchure until the lower lip becomes weary, so to speak, and the lower rim of the mouth hole has made an impression upon it. So that you may get the feeling of finding the same place again, and can produce the note immediately without great difficulty, you must not change this impression of the sharp edge of the rim either to the side or up and down. D'' is sounded in this fashion. Next play the descending notes in the first octave down to D', drawing the lips back, together with the chin, to the lowest line, in the proportion indicated above. Then reverse the procedure and play the same notes in their ascending order up to the previous D'', pushing the lips and chin forwards just as they were earlier drawn back. Continue this exercise until you can produce all these notes surely one after the other.

§ 13

From D'' play the following high notes up to D''', pushing the chin forwards, and the lips away from the teeth, to the third line, in just the same

[1] The French term *embouchure*, which appears in parentheses in the German text, can mean the mouth hole itself as well as the manner of applying the lips to the hole, and tone production in general on wind instruments.

[2] The reproduction of Fig. 2 is slightly reduced in size.

proportion as is used in the low octave when moving to the second line. If you continue to advance the chin and lips from the third line to the fourth, the notes of the third octave, up to G''', can be made to speak very easily. These should not be attempted, however, until you are able to produce the first two octaves with ease.

§ 14

In producing the notes mentioned in the previous paragraph, on no account must the wind be increased or doubled, as Mr. *Vaucanson* erroneously teaches in his *Mechanical Flute Player*,[1] asserting that the octaves can be produced in no other way on the transverse flute. Actually they must be effected by the compression of the air in the mouth hole, which results from advancing the chin and lips : hence the former opinion is a completely false and harmful one. Its falseness is also evident from the fact that you can sustain your breath longer in the upper register than in the lower; hence it is impossible that more wind is used in it. I admit that Mr. *Vaucanson's* method is necessary for a flute played by a machine, since the movements of its lips are limited. From experience I also know, however, that the rule that the low notes must be played strongly and the upper ones weakly is disregarded on such mechanical flute players. If the octaves were to be produced by strengthening and doubling the wind, it would follow that the high notes would have to be blown more strongly than the low ones, which is contrary to the nature of the flute, and makes the high notes exceedingly coarse and unpleasant. Thus you must not allow yourself to be misled[2] by the reasoning of Mr. *Vaucanson*.

§ 15

It is true that there are many flute players who transgress against these rules. Bad embouchure is the cause. Instead of covering half of the mouth hole with their lips, these players leave it open too far, so that they are prevented from withdrawing the lips sufficiently in the low notes, and from advancing them sufficiently in the high notes. Thus, because the mouth hole is open too far, they must necessarily force out the high notes with stronger blowing. They know nothing of the necessary movement of the chin and lips, and allow them to remain constantly fixed, although playing in tune on the flute mainly depends upon movement of this kind. With a larger or smaller opening of the mouth hole, you can play the flute a quarter, half, or even a whole tone higher or lower; and in

[1] Quantz refers to a brief work of Jacques de Vaucanson entitled *Le Mécanisme du fluteur automate* (Paris : Jacques Guerin, 1738). In it the author explains the structure of a mechanical flute player that he actually built. It enjoyed a considerable fame, and was apparently exhibited in France, Germany, and England. Several German and English translations of the article were published. Vaucanson, however, was not the only person to advocate strengthening or doubling the wind. Among others, Corrette, *Methode*, p. 10, suggests the same procedure.
[2] The remainder of this sentence is found only in the French text.

the flute itself the inner bore must be constructed so that the octaves are a little sharp, so that if you wish to play them as truly as the ear demands you are forced to blow the low notes more strongly and the high ones more weakly to correct the intonation of these sharp octaves. To do this you must move your chin and lips. If the lower lip covers the mouth hole as much as is necessary for the high notes, the low ones cannot be played strongly or truly. If, however, the lip is drawn back as far as the low notes require, and you play in the upper register without moving your chin and lips, you lapse into the error indicated above, that is, you make your tone quality hissing and dull, and generally too strong and unpleasant for the instrument.

§ 16

Since only a minority of flute players properly observe these rules, many are of the opinion that these matters depend entirely upon the instrument, which is not the case. It is true that the flute has certain imperfections in several chromatic keys.[1] This defect can be easily remedied, however, if the player possesses a good embouchure, a good musical ear, a correct system of fingering, and an adequate knowledge of the proportions of the notes.

§ 17

It has been stated above that the octaves on the flute must not be produced by strengthening and doubling the wind, but by advancing the chin and lips. In this respect the flute again somewhat resembles the human voice. There are two kinds of voice, the chest voice and the falsetto or fistula voice.[2] With the latter, in which the larynx is even more compressed than is ordinarily the case, you can, without straining yourself, produce several more notes in the upper register than is possible with the chest voice. The Italians and several other nations unite this falsetto with the chest voice, and make use of it to great advantage in singing :[3] among the French, however, it is not customary, and for that reason their singing in the high register is often transformed into a disagreeable shrieking, the

---

[1] i.e. keys that have accidentals in their key signatures. See Chapter III, § 4.

[2] Galliard, in his translation of Tosi, *Observations*, p. 22, distinguishes three types of voices: '*Voce di Petto* is a full Voice, which comes from the Breast by Strength, and is the most sonorous and expressive. *Voce di Testa* comes more from the Throat, than from the Breast, and is capable of more Volubility. *Falsetto* is a feigned Voice, which is entirely formed in the Throat, has more Volubility than any, but of no Substance.'

[3] Tosi, *Observations*, pp. 23–24, provides the following information on the two types of voice mentioned by Quantz: 'A diligent Master, knowing that a *Soprano*, without the *Falsetto*, is constrained to sing within the narrow Compass of a few Notes, ought not only to endeavour to help him to it, but also to leave no Means untried so to unite the feigned and the natural voice, that they may not be distinguished; for if they do not perfectly unite, the Voice will be of divers Registers, and must consequently lose its Beauty. The extent of the full natural Voice terminates generally upon the fourth Space, which is C; or on the fifth Line, which is D; and there the feigned Voice becomes of Use, as well in going up to the high Notes, as returning to the natural Voice; the Difficulty consists in uniting them.'

effect of which is exactly the same as that created when you do not cover the mouth hole sufficiently on the flute, and when you try to force out the high notes by blowing more strongly. The chest voice is the natural one used in speaking.* The falsetto, however, is artificial, and is used only in singing. It begins where the chest voice ends. Although the larynx also becomes somewhat narrower and longer at each degree when you ascend into the upper register with the chest voice, with the falsetto it is considerably more contracted, and in the high register is kept contracted. The air is forced out of the lungs a little more quickly rather than more strongly. The tone quality, however, becomes only a little weaker than in the natural voice.

* For this reason experienced composers have established a rule that you should not, except in cases of necessity or in other special situations, give the singer words to pronounce in arias—much less recitatives—outside of the range of the chest voice, especially if the vowels *u* or *i* occur in them. When the falsetto voice is used, the position of the mouth in the pronunciation of both of these vowels can be adjusted to the position of the larynx only with positive discomfort among the majority of singers.

§ 18

Just as the larynx becomes narrower in the falsetto notes, advancing the chin and lips makes the mouth hole narrower on the flute; in this fashion, having previously sounded a low note, you can make its upper octave speak without tipping it with the tongue.[1] The low octave of the flute could be compared with the chest voice, and the high one with the falsetto. Hence in general the flute corresponds with the human voice in that in the latter the larynx must be contracted or expanded in accordance with the proportion of the interval when you sing ascending or descending notes, while in the former the opening of the mouth hole must be made narrower for the ascending notes by advancing and compressing the lips and chin, and wider for descending notes by withdrawing and separating the lips. For without this movement the high notes become too strong, the low ones too weak, and the octaves untrue.

§ 19

If you wish to form an exercise to learn how to produce the octaves on the flute truly, place the flute to your mouth so that the mouth hole is covered by the lips as far as the second line,[2] and then withdraw the lips and chin to the lowest line and tip D'. Continue to blow with the same strength, and when you wish to raise the first finger for D" at the same time advance the lips and chin to the second line; you will then find that the D" speaks of itself. Repeat this exercise until you learn to feel how far you must advance the lips and chin. The D octave is the easiest to practise,

[1] *Ohne mit der Zunge anzustoßen (sans qu'il soit necessaire d'un coup de langue).* On the use of the expression 'to tip', see the Preface to the Translation.
[2] Quantz refers to the lines in Fig. 2 in § 11.

since opening the hole of the first finger facilitates it somewhat. Then try the exercise a tone higher, that is, from E' to E''. Here the lips, together with the chin, must be withdrawn not quite to the first line, and must be advanced slightly above the second line for the octave. Proceed in accordance with the proportion explained in § 11 with all the notes that have octaves above them. The example in Tab. II, Fig. 3, may be used as a model, and can be transposed into all keys.

FIG. 3

§ 20

The highest usable note that you can invariably produce is E'''.[1] Those which are higher require a particularly good embouchure. The high register is much easier for players with thin and narrow lips. Thick lips, on the other hand, are advantageous in the low register. But if you know how surely to find the proper distance to advance the lips on the mouth hole, as indicated by the rules given with the lines, it will no longer be difficult to produce all the notes in both the high and the low registers.

§ 21

It is self-evident, therefore, that the lips must move gradually for notes which ascend or descend by step, while in leaps they must vary their movements in accordance with the size of the leaps if the appointed place on the mouth hole is always to be hit with certainty. Note especially that the notes in the low octave must always be played more strongly than those in the high octave. This is particularly important in passage-work in leaps.

§ 22

In producing octaves no strengthening of wind is necessary. If, however, you wish to produce a louder or softer tone, whether high or low, note that strengthening the wind, and withdrawing the lips from the appointed place for each note on the mouth hole, make the tone higher, while moderating the wind and advancing the lips make the tone lower. Thus if you wish to produce a long note softly and then increase its strength, you must first withdraw the lips, or turn the flute outwards, as much as is necessary for the note to remain in tune with the other instruments. And when you blow more strongly, advance the lips or turn the flute inwards; otherwise

[1] In his 'Antwort', Quantz gives fingerings for the notes up to E'''' to supplement his original fingering chart in Chapter III, § 4. He states again, however, that these tones are too difficult to produce to be of any practical value.

the note will be first too low, then too high. If, however, you wish to end the same note softly again, you must again withdraw the lips in the proper proportion, or turn the flute outwards.

§ 23

The flute has the innate defect that some of its notes when sharpened are not quite true, some being a little too low, some a little too high. For in tuning the flute you must first see to it that the natural[1] notes are tuned truly in accordance with their proportions. The faulty ones you must, as much as possible, seek to play in tune with the help of your embouchure and your ear. A little has been said of this matter in the previous chapter, but in order that you may know to which notes you must give the most attention, I will specify them here.

E sharp' and E sharp", F sharp' and F sharp" stopped in the exceptional way, and G sharp" and A sharp" are too high. Hence you must moderate your wind, and turn the flute inwards.

The regular F sharp' and F sharp" are too low, and hence must be raised by rotating the flute outwards, or by strengthening your wind.

D flat" and C flat" are too low. For them you must rotate the flute perceptibly outwards.

[2]For the low F, which is the weakest note on the flute, and which is too high on the majority of flutes because of an unavoidable flaw in their inner structure, you must rotate the flute inwards, and advance your upper lip a little.[3]

If in a piece you play softly and loudly by turns, in the first case you must rotate the flute as much outwards, in the second case as much inwards, as weak blowing lowers the notes, and strong blowing raises them.

§ 24

If you pay close attention to all of these admonitions, you will never play too high or too low, and the flute will always remain in tune; otherwise this will be impossible. And if you train your ear to perceive those major thirds that must be a little sharp, you can very easily acquire all the advantages [of correct intonation].[4]

[1] i.e. 'diatonic'. In other words, the player must make sure that the diatonic notes are accurate before he worries about sharps or flats. See the report on Quantz's flutes in Halfpenny, 'A French Commentary on Quantz', p. 66.

[2] The following paragraph is omitted in the French text.

[3] Literally, 'shove your upper lip inwards a little'.

[4] *Und so fern man sich die großen Terzen, so etwas über sich schweben müssen, im Gehöre recht bekannt machet; so kann man sehr leicht hinter diese Vortheile kommen.* (*Et pourvû que l'oreille fasse bien attention aux Tierces majeures, qui doivent être un peu hautes, on pourra se mettre au fait de tous ces avantages.*) Quantz probably refers to the pitches F sharp', F sharp", D flat", and C flat" mentioned in § 23.

§ 25

You can also considerably improve the tone quality of the flute through the action of your chest. You must not use a violent, that is, a trembling action, however, but a calm one. Otherwise the tone will become too loud. A proportional opening of the teeth and mouth, and expansion of the throat, produce a thick, round, and masculine tone quality. The forward and backward motion of the lips makes the tone true and pleasing. In the second octave avoid advancing the upper lip beyond the lower.

§ 26

In concluding it remains to be noted that if you wish to moderate the tone of the flute and play somewhat more softly, as is required in the Adagio, you must cover the mouth hole with your lips a little more than has been suggested above. Since, however, the flute becomes a little lower as a result, you must also have a screw attached to the plug found in the head piece with which you can press the plug the breadth of a good knife-back further into the flute, in order to raise the flute from its normal level as much as your softer playing and the increased covering of the mouth hole require (see §§ 10, 11, and 12 of Chapter I). This makes the flute shorter, and thus higher; and in this fashion you can always remain in tune with the other instruments.

CHAPTER V

Of Notes, their Values, Metre, Rests, and Other Musical Signs

§ 1

In § 2 of Chapter III I have already indicated how notes are written on five closely spaced horizontal lines, and have shown which clef is employed for the flute. I need only remark here that there are *nine musical clefs* in all. These are divided into three classes, the *G clefs*, the *C clefs*, and the *F clefs*. In the first of these classes the line upon which the clef stands is always G′; the C clef makes the line upon which it stands C′; and the F clef makes its line F. For the flute you need actually know only the group of G clefs. There are two kinds of G clefs, the French clef, and the Italian indicated earlier. The latter is also called the standard violin clef. The former, that is, the French clef, stands on the lowest line, and is generally used for the flute only in France.

§ 2

The four kinds of C clefs and the three kinds of F clefs are used at times for the notes of the voice parts, at times for other instruments. They are not wholly useless to the flautist for transpositions, and may be learned without difficulty either through oral instruction, or from books treating of the rudiments of music, by those who wish to become more closely acquainted with them.[1]

§ 3

In Chapter III, § 3, I have also indicated the form and use of key signatures, by means of which you may quickly distinguish the tonalities used when they are placed at the beginning of the staff of five lines.

§ 4

As is well known, *mode*[2] is of two kinds, hard and soft, commonly called *dur* and *moll*. These modes could be designated more precisely, as in Latin, by the words *major* and *minor*. The major mode has the major third in its accord, the minor mode has the minor third.[3]

[1] For one of many eighteenth-century explanations of transposition, see Corrette, *Methode*, p. 49.

[2] *Tonart* (mode). Quantz uses this term for both 'mode' and 'key'

[3] *Die Tonart Dur hat die große, und die Tonart Moll, die kleine Terze in ihrem Accord.* By *Accord*,

§ 5

With respect to the notes that occur within its gamut, and also in its key signature, each major key is like the minor key that lies a minor third below it. C major, for example, is like A minor, F major like D minor, &c. The signatures for these keys are found in Tab. II, Fig. 4. The fundamental notes[1] of the major and minor keys that are alike are found one above the other. The upper note is the fundamental note of the major key, and the lower one the fundamental note of the minor key.

FIG. 4

§ 6

Reckoning upward from the fundamental note, each major key has the major second, major third, perfect fourth, perfect fifth, major sixth, and major seventh in its gamut. Again reckoning upward from the fundamental note, each minor key has the major second, minor third, perfect fourth, perfect fifth, minor sixth, and minor seventh in its gamut. In C major and A minor, but not in the other keys, all these notes lie in the diatonic scale. Hence for each key either as many sharps or as many flats must be prefixed to the staff as are necessary to form the intended gamut. From C major and A minor to G flat major and E flat minor a flat is regularly added to the signature of each key that lies a fourth above the preceding one, each being major or minor like the key a fourth below; and from C major and A minor to F sharp major and D sharp minor one more sharp than is found in the preceding key is added to the key lying a fifth above it. See the illustration in Tab. II, Fig. 4.[2]

§ 7

In former times, the gamuts of the modes were composed entirely of diatonic notes, and in consequence the sixth had to be major in many minor modes, while in others the second had to be minor (as, for example, in the Dorian and Phrygian modes, D and E minor).[3] Thus when the

Quantz here seems to mean 'tonic chord'. In other words, the major mode has the major third in its tonic chord, the minor mode the minor third.

[1] *Die Grundtöne (les tons fondamentaux).* This term is used to refer to the tonic notes of each key. In some other cases, it means the root of a chord.

[2] The illustration is found in the preceding paragraph.

[3] Translator's parentheses. Here there is an apparent confusion of the terms 'mode' and

modes were transposed by one or several tones, and preserved their gamuts, at times one less sharp or one less flat was marked than is usual today, and none but the Ionian and Aeolian modes (C major and A minor)[1] accorded with our present modes *per se* and when transposed. If in progressions ordered in the modern style you imitated old signatures of this kind, as some composers did not very long ago, you would create much unnecessary labour for yourself in writing; for afterwards you would have to add the flats and sharps separately to each note that required them.

§ 8

If you wish to remember easily the *values of the notes* illustrated in Tab. II, Fig. 6, imagine the round white note without a stem, which has the value of a full bar in common time, as a semibreve [whole note] (see Fig. 6 (*a*)). A white note with a stem, two of which notes fill a bar, may be thought of as half of this whole (see (*b*)). A black note without a crook, which is called a crotchet [quarter], four of which fill a bar, may be thought of as a quarter of this whole (see (*c*)). In the rest, namely the quavers [eighths] (see (*d*)), semiquavers [sixteenths] (see (*e*)), and demisemiquavers [thirty-seconds] (see (*f*)), the names already indicate what part of the whole they form, and that, as they follow each other here, one always amounts to half of the preceding one, and hence is half as long in value. It is also the custom to call them one-, two-, and three-crook notes,[2] in accordance with the number of crooks each has. Each crook doubles the number of notes in a bar, and therefore halves the time of their duration. Hence notes with three, four, and five crooks are still shorter; but these never occur in great numbers. When several notes with crooks follow one another, two, four, or eight are joined together, and then called figures (see Tab. II, Fig. 6 (*d*), (*e*), and (*f*)).

F IG. 6

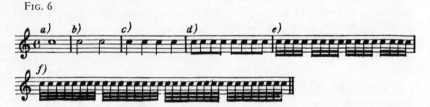

'key'. It may be explained, however, by the fact that the terms 'major' and 'minor' originally meant only modes with major and minor thirds above the tonic (see § 4). The Dorian and Phrygian modes have minor thirds above their tonics, and thus are minor or *moll* in this sense. The phrase might be clearer if it were to read 'as for example in the Dorian and Phrygian modes, the D and E modes with minor thirds above their tonics'. The practice referred to here is, of course, that of modal signatures, which were common in the seventeenth and early eighteenth centuries. On the various uses of the word 'mode', see Walther, *Lexicon*, pp. 409–17.

[1] Translator's parentheses.

[2] *Ein- zwey- und dreygeschwänzte Noten* (*Croches, Double croches, Triple croches*).

§ 9

A *dot* standing after a note has half the value of the preceding note, or the same value as the following one (see Tab. II, Fig. 7).[1]

§ 10

The *rests*, which take the place of notes, indicate that you must remain silent as long as the value of each requires in relation to the tempo. Their values are as follows. A thick stroke that touches the space between three lines has the value of four bars, as indicated by the notes beneath it (see Tab. II, Fig. 9 (*a*)).

FIG. 9

A thick stroke between two lines has the value of two bars (see (*b*)).

A thick stroke below a line has the value of a whole bar (see (*c*)).

One which stands above the line has the value of a half bar (see (*d*)).

The other rests (see (*e*)) have the values of the notes beneath them, that is, of a crotchet, quaver, semiquaver, and demisemiquaver.

It is the custom to place dots after these latter kinds of rests at times, and as with notes they have half the value of the preceding rest (see (*f*)). This is

---

[1] This illustration is found in §§ 20 and 21 of this chapter. As L. Mozart, *A Treatise on the Fundamental Principles of Violin Playing*, trans. by E. Knocker (London: Oxford University Press, 1948), pp. 40–41, points out, the latter half of this rule has a number of exceptions.

done mainly for the sake of convenience, however, in order to avoid placing two rests in a row.

When a semicircle with a dot beneath it stands above a rest, it is a general pause or *fermata*, or sign of repose. Here all parts remain still as long as they think proper, without adhering to the beat (see (*g*)). Consult § 43, Section VII, Chapter XVII, upon this point.

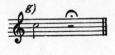

§ 11

The proper measurement and division of slow and quick notes is called *metre*[1] (*la mesure*); *tempo*[2] (*le mouvement*), on the other hand, is the law governing the slow and quick movement of the beat.

§ 12

Metre in general is of two kinds, *duple* and *triple*.[3] Duple metre permits regular divisions in even parts, while in triple the division is odd. Triple is generally called *triple time*. When a bar comes to an end, it is the custom in writing to place a *bar line* after the notes; hence all the notes found between two of these lines form a measure of some kind in accordance with the metre sign placed after the key signature at the beginning of a piece (see Tab. II, Fig. 6).[4]

§ 13

Duple metre is again of two kinds, four-four time and two-four time. Four-four time, which is also called *common* or imperfect time, is indicated with a large C at the beginning of a piece, and two-four with $\frac{2}{4}$. In four-four time it is important to note that if a stroke goes through the C, as illustrated in Tab. II, Fig. 10, the notes receive a different value, so to speak, and must be played twice as fast as when the C has no stroke through it.

---

[1] *Der Tact*. This is one of the most troublesome of all German musical terms, since it can also mean 'beat', 'measure', or 'bar', or simply 'time'. The last equivalent would also be appropriate here.

[2] *Das Zeitmaaß*.

[3] In German the terms for 'duple' and 'triple' are *gerade* and *ungerade*, that is, 'equal' and 'unequal'. Thus in the original text the following sentences are less redundant.

[4] This illustration is found in § 8 of the present chapter.

FIG. 10

This metre is called *alla breve*,[1] or *alla cappella*. Since many people through ignorance commit errors with respect to the metre just mentioned, it is advisable to make yourself thoroughly acquainted with this difference. It is a metre that is more common in the *galant* style of the present day than it was in former times.

§ 14

There are various kinds of triple time, as the following fractions indicate: $\frac{3}{1}$, three-one time; $\frac{3}{2}$, three-two time; $\frac{3}{4}$, three-four time; $\frac{6}{4}$, six-four time; $\frac{3}{8}$, three-eight time; $\frac{6}{8}$, six-eight time; $\frac{9}{8}$, nine-eight time; $\frac{12}{8}$, twelve-eight time, &c.[2]

§ 15

There is a kind of figure in which three equal notes are joined together, and hence resemble triple time, although they occur in both duple and triple time. These figures are called *triplets*. Here (see Tab. II, Fig. 7 (*l*)) three quavers make a crotchet, three semiquavers a quaver (see (*m*)), and three demisemiquavers a semiquaver (see (*n*)), as the upper notes indicate. Although unnecessary, it is also the custom to place the number 3 above them, as may be seen in (*l*).

§ 16

Although I have now pointed out the values of the notes and rests, and the various kinds of metres, it is still necessary to show how each note and rest must be properly divided in the bar, and how one may learn to do so easily. The majority look upon this as a simple matter, and believe that it is learned gradually through practice. But since many still err, even after they have studied the matter a long time, obviously it must not be one of the easiest things in music. The harmonious execution of a piece depends largely upon such knowledge, and whoever does not acquire it in good time through correct principles will remain in a constant state of uncertainty, and will often be embarrassed in small matters that he does not encounter daily. It is not to be denied that in this regard verbal instructions,

[1] Judging from Quantz's tempo indications in Chapter XVII, Section VII, § 51, alla breve time does not always imply a basic duple beat for Quantz.
[2] Quantz classifies compound metres with triple metres.

if thorough, are of better service than a written method. But since many who are supposed to instruct others may not be familiar with the proper mode of teaching this point, I will indicate a method here.

§ 17

First accustom yourself to making regular beats with the tip of your foot, for which you may use the pulse beat of your hand as your guide. Then divide common or four-four time into quavers with the foot, again with the guidance of the pulse beat. On the first beat, tip the white note without a stem (see Tab. II, Fig. 6 (a))[1] with your tongue, and sustain the tone until you have mentally counted 1, 2, 3, 4, 5, 6, 7, 8 in accordance with the beat of your foot; this bar will then receive its proper time. If you continue beating your foot in this manner, and count 1, 2, 3, 4 for the first white note with a stem (see (b)), and 1, 2, 3, 4 again for the second white note, these two minims will also be correct. For crotchets (see (c)) there are two beats to a note. For quavers (see (d)) each note receives a beat. For semiquavers (see (e)) there are two notes to a beat, and if you count both the rise and the fall of the foot, there will be a semiquaver on each. For demisemiquavers (see (f)) there are two notes on the downbeat and two on the upbeat.[2]

§ 18

In all slow pieces you may govern yourself, in accordance with the requirements of the tempo, by this division into eight beats. In quick pieces, however, you can divide common time into four parts, in which downbeats and upbeats of the foot form quavers, while triple time may be divided into three parts.

§ 19

In alla breve time the minims receive as much time as the crotchets in common time, and the crotchets take as much as the quavers in common time; hence only the minims are marked with the foot.

§ 20

The dotted minim (see Tab. II, Fig. 7 (a)) receives six beats with the foot, and the following crotchet receives two beats. The dotted crotchet (see (b)) receives three beats, and the following quaver only one beat.

[1] Fig. 6 is found in § 8 of this chapter.

[2] Quantz's explanation of beating time and the division of notes is important in gaining an understanding of his use of the terms 'upbeat' and 'downbeat'. As he uses them, these two terms refer to the up or down movement of the foot or hand in beating time. Since he begins his explanation with a divided beat, and presupposes a slow tempo, 'upbeat' may mean the weak part of any of the four beats, and 'downbeat' may mean the strong portion of these beats. In a quick tempo, on the other hand, the second and fourth beats are upbeats.

FIG. 7

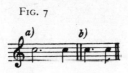

§ 21

In dotted quavers, semiquavers, and demisemiquavers (see (*c*), (*d*), and (*e*)) you depart from the general rule, because of the animation that these notes must express. It is particularly important to observe that the notes after the dots in (*c*) and (*d*) must be played just as short as those [after the dots] in (*e*), whether the tempo is slow or fast.

As a result, the dotted notes in (*c*) receive almost the time of a full crotchet, and those in (*d*) the time of a quaver, since the time of the short notes after the dots cannot actually be fixed with complete exactness. To grasp this more clearly, play the lower notes in (*f*) and (*g*) slowly, yet in accordance with their proper duration in each example, that is, those in (*g*) twice as fast as those in (*f*), those in (*h*) twice as fast as those in (*g*), and imagine that the upper notes are dotted. Then turn this round, play the upper notes, and hold each dotted note until the time of the lower dotted note has passed. Make the note after the dot just as short as the hemidemisemiquaver below it.[1] In this manner you will see that the upper dotted notes in (*f*) receive the time of three semiquavers and a dotted demisemiquaver, those in (*g*) the time of a semiquaver and a dotted demisemiquaver, and those in (*h*) only the time of a demisemiquaver with a dot and a half, since double dots are found in the lower notes, and the following notes have an additional crook.[2]

[1] Although the text reads literally 'the notes with the dots', it is clear from the examples that the notes after the dots are meant.

[2] The practice of lengthening the normal value of dots is also explained in L. Mozart, *A Treatise*, pp. 41–42, and in C. P. E. Bach, *Essay on the True Art of Playing Keyboard Instruments*, trans. by W. J. Mitchell (New York: W. W. Norton, 1949), pp. 157–8. It should be noted, however, that Quantz suggests lengthening dots only in the case of dotted quavers and shorter values. For a review of the subject, see R. Donington, *The Interpretation of Early Music*, new version (London: Faber and Faber, 1974, pp. 441–51, and the articles of F. Neumann and M. Collins cited on p. 451.

22

This rule likewise must be observed when there are triplets in one part and dotted notes against them in the other part (see (*i*)).

Hence you must not strike the short note after the dot with the third note of the triplet, but after it.[1] Otherwise it will sound like six-eight or twelve-eight time, as in (*k*).

The two passages must be treated quite differently, since a quaver triplet equals a crotchet, a semiquaver triplet equals a quaver, and a demisemiquaver triplet a semiquaver, as the single upper notes in (*l*), (*m*), and (*n*)[2] show, while in six-eight or twelve-eight time three quavers equal a crotchet and a quaver (see (*k*)). If you were to play all the dotted notes found beneath the triplets in accordance with their ordinary value, the expression would be very lame and insipid, rather than brilliant and majestic.

23

With regard to the length of the dot and the shortness of the first note, the notes in Fig. 8, where the dot stands after every second note, are similar to the dotted notes mentioned above. Their order is simply reversed. The notes D and C in (*a*) must be just as short as those in (*c*), whether the tempo is slow or quick.

FIG. 8

The two quick notes in (*b*) and (*d*) are treated in the same manner, two quick notes here receiving no more time than one in the examples above.[3]

---

[1] Quantz's position on this point was not universal. C. P. E. Bach, *Essay*, p. 160, suggests an interpretation like that in (*k*).   [2] These examples are found in § 15.

[3] As Quantz points out in his index, Figs. (*a*), (*b*), (*c*), and (*d*) are examples of what was known as the Lombardic style. See also Chapter XVIII, § 58.

In (*e*) and (*f*) the notes after the dots are played just as quickly and precipitately as those before the dotted notes in (*b*) and (*d*).

The shorter you make the first notes in (*a*), (*b*), (*c*), and (*d*), the livelier and bolder is the expression. The longer the dots in (*e*) and (*f*) are held, on the other hand, the more flattering and pleasing notes of this kind sound.

§ 24

With regard to rests, it has already been stated that where they appear you remain silent for the time required by their value. It will not be necessary to explain those of one or more bars, since you need only conform to the [normal] time beat (see Fig. 9 (*a*), (*b*), and (*c*)).[1] If you have a minim rest, however, count 1, 2, 3, 4 in accordance with the beat of the foot, as for a semibreve, and tip the following note on the fifth beat (see (*h*)). For a crotchet rest count 1, 2, and tip the following note on the third beat (see (*i*)). For a quaver say 1, and tip the note on the second beat (see (*k*)). For a semiquaver also say 1, and tip the note on the rise of the foot (see (*l*)). For a demisemiquaver rest again say 1. But since here two notes come in the fall and two in the rise of the foot, the note after the rest must be tipped during the fall (see (*m*)).

§ 25

After you have practised enough in this manner in a slow tempo, gradually play these examples a little more quickly, until you have acquired the ability to undertake something more. Eventually the division of the notes will become so easy that you will be able to completely dispense with the use of the foot in beating time.

§ 26

Precise and exact indications for the different kinds of tempos are found in Section VII of Chapter XVII, § 45 to § 59.

§ 27

There are various sorts of *repeat signs*. If two straight lines stand next to one another without dots (see Fig. 5 (*b*)), they signify that the piece

[1] See above, § 10.

consists of two parts, and that the first must be repeated, but not before the piece has first been played from beginning to end. Then the first part is repeated to the double bar, or to the note that precedes it (which amounts to the same thing),[1] above which there stands a semicircle with a dot (see (*a*)). In such pieces *da capo* is written at the end of the second part. If four dots follow one bar line (see (*c*)), they signify that the following notes, from there to another bar line which has four dots before it, are to be repeated. Often the word *bis* is also written above notes such as these which are to be repeated. If there are two dots on each side of a double bar (see (*d*)), they signify that the piece consists of two parts, and that each part must be played twice. Finally, if there are one or two *semicircles* with dots (see (*e*)), they signify that the piece ends at that point. The sign on the E (see (*f*)) is called the *custos*, and indicates the placement of the first note on the staff that follows.

FIG. 5

[1] Translator's parentheses.

CHAPTER VI

Of the Use of the Tongue in Blowing upon the Flute

§ 1

The tongue is the means by which we give animation to the execution of the notes upon the flute. It is indispensable for musical articulation, and serves the same purpose as the bow-stroke upon the violin. Its use so distinguishes one flute player from another that if a single piece is played in turn by several persons, the differences in their execution frequently make the work almost unrecognizable. The majority of these differences rest upon the correct or incorrect use of the tongue. It is true that much also depends upon the fingers. They are necessary not only to fix the height or depth of each note and to distinguish intervals, but also to give each note its proper duration. The liveliness of the execution, however, depends less upon the fingers than upon the tongue. It is the latter which must animate the expression of the passions in pieces of every sort, whatever they may be: sublime or melancholy, gay or pleasing.

§ 2

To make the tone of the flute speak properly with the aid of the tongue and the wind that it allows to escape, you must, as you blow, pronounce certain syllables, in accordance with the nature of the notes to be played. These syllables are of three kinds. The first is *ti* or *di*, the second *tiri*, and the third *did'll*.[1] The last is usually called the *double tongue*, while the first is called the *single tongue*. The manner in which each is to be learned and applied will be treated in separate sections. And since the use of the tongue on the oboe and bassoon has much in common with its use on the flute, I will add a supplement designed for those who play these instruments; there I will indicate how they should make use of the tongue and any other particulars that they should observe.

SECTION I

Of the Use of the Tongue with the Syllable ti *or* di

§ 1

Since some notes must be tipped firmly and others gently, it is important to remember that *ti* is used for short, equal, lively, and quick notes. *Di*,

---

[1] In German the *i* resembles the English vowel in *bit*.

on the contrary, must be used when the melody is slow, and even when it is gay, provided that it is still pleasing and sustained. In the Adagio *di* is always used, except in dotted notes, which require *ti*. Those accustomed to the Upper Saxon dialect must take particular care not to confuse the *t* with the *d*.[1]

§ 2

Ti is called a tongue-stroke.[2] To make it, both sides of the tongue must be pressed firmly against the palate, the tip curved up and placed in front near the teeth, so that the wind is stopped or held in check. When the note is to be produced, you draw only the tip of the tongue away from the palate, the rear part of the tongue remaining on the palate; the impact of the stopped wind is the result of this withdrawal, rather than of the stroke of the tongue itself, as many mistakenly believe.[3]

§ 3

Some have a way of placing the tongue between the lips and making the stroke by withdrawing it. This I consider wrong. It prevents a full, round, and masculine tone, particularly in the low register, and the tongue also must make an excessive forward or backward movement, which impedes quickness.

§ 4

To give each note its proper expression, from the low register to the high, you must use the tongue just as you use the lips and the chin, that is to say, in playing an ascending scale from the lowest note to the highest, you must place the tongue a good thumb's breadth back from the teeth, curved against the palate; for the lowest note you must greatly enlarge the mouth, and for each higher one must make the stroke with the tongue a little further forward on the palate, and gradually compress the mouth. Continue in this fashion until you reach the highest B, where the tongue comes very close to the teeth. From the highest C on, however, the stroke must no longer be made with a curved tongue, but with a straight one, between the teeth against the lips. If you attempt the opposite method, drawing the tongue far back for the highest note, or making the stroke with it between the teeth for the lowest note, you will find that the high notes sound hissing, and do not speak well, while the low ones become weak and thin.

---

[1] In this dialect *t* is pronounced *d*.   [2] *Zungenstoß (coup de langue)*.
[3] In this sentence the words 'impact' and 'stroke' are the same word in German, *Stoß*. The terms *Zungenstoß*, *coup de langue*, and 'tongue-stroke', are all misleading, and Quantz correctly points out that the note is produced by the air released by the tongue, rather than by the tongue itself. Quantz's syllable *ti* is probably a modification of Hotteterre's *tu*. For earlier examples of articulation on the flute, see Hotteterre, *Principes*, pp. 22–30. The fullest discussion of articulation found in a flute treatise after Quantz is that of Tromlitz, *Unterricht*, pp. 154–237. Tromlitz uses the syllables *ta*, *da*, *tara*, and *tad'll*.

§ 5

If you wish to make the notes very short, you must use the *ti*, since the tip of the tongue must spring back against the palate immediately, in order to check the wind again. You can note this process best if, without blowing, you quickly pronounce *ti-ti-ti-ti* several times in succession.

§ 6

For slow and sustained (*nourrissantes*) notes, the stroke must not be firm;[1] hence you must use *di* instead of *ti*. It should be noted that while in the *ti* the tongue immediately springs back against the palate, in the *di* it must remain free in the middle of the mouth, so that the wind is not kept from sustaining the tone.

§ 7

If leaps are formed by the quavers in the Allegro, *ti* is used for them. If, however, other notes follow which ascend or descend by step, whether they are quavers, crotchets, or minims, *di* is used (see Tab. III, Fig. 1).

TABLE III

FIG. 1

ti ti ti ti ti ti ti ti ti di di di   di   di   di

If strokes[2] are placed above the crotchets, *ti* is kept (see Tab. III, Fig. 2).

FIG. 2

ti ti   ti   ti   ti   ti

If an appoggiatura is found next to a note, it is tipped with the same kind of tongue-stroke as the preceding note, whether firm or gentle (see Tab. III, Figs. 3 and 4).

FIG. 3   FIG. 4

ti ti ti ti ti＿ ti ti＿   di di di＿ di di＿ di di＿

§ 8

It is a general rule that there must be a slight separation between the appoggiatura and the note that precedes it, particularly if both are on

[1] *Hart (rude).*

[2] 'Strokes' indicate a kind of staccato, but not necessarily a very short staccato. For further information on the use of staccato marks, see Chapter XVII, Section II, §§ 12 and 27.

the same pitch, so that the appoggiatura can be heard distinctly. Hence the tongue must spring back to the palate immediately after tipping the preceding note, thereby checking the wind, making the note shorter and the appoggiatura more distinct.

§ 9

In quick passage-work the single tongue does not have a good effect, since it makes all the notes alike, and to conform with good taste they must be a little unequal (see Chapter XI, § 12).[1] Thus the other two ways of using the tongue may be employed, that is, *tiri* for dotted notes and moderately quick passage-work, and *did'll* for very quick passage-work.

§ 10

All notes do not have to be tipped: if an arc stands above two or more, → they must be slurred. Thus you must remember that only the note on which the slur begins needs to be tipped; the others found beneath the arc are slurred to it, and the tongue meanwhile has nothing to do. Ordinarily *di* rather than *ti* is used for slurred notes (see Tab. III, Fig. 5).

FIG. 5

di — di — di — di — di

If, however, a stroke stands above the note preceding the slur, both the first and the following note receive *ti* (see Fig. 6).

FIG. 6

ti ti —— di —— ti ti

If the slur begins on the second note, and the unstressed note is slurred to the stressed one, play them as is to be seen in Fig. 7. But if this happens in a quick tempo, use *ti* instead of *di*.

FIG. 7

di di — di — di — di —

---

[1] The reference to § 11 in the original text is incorrect.

§ 11

If a slur is found above notes which are repeated (see Fig. 8), they must be expressed by exhalation, with chest action.[1]

Fig. 8

di ———

If, however, dots also stand above such notes (see Fig. 9), the notes must be expressed much more sharply, and, so to speak, articulated from the chest.[2]

Fig. 9

di ———

§ 12

It is impossible to define fully in words either the difference between *ti* or *di*, upon which a considerable part of the expression of the passions depends, or all of the different kinds of tongue-strokes. Meanwhile, individual reflection will suffice to convince everyone that, just as there are various shades between black and white, there is more than one intermediate degree between a firm and a gentle tongue-stroke. Hence you can also express *ti* and *di* in diverse ways with the tongue. You simply must try to make the tongue supple enough to be able to tip the notes more firmly at one time, more gently at another, in accordance with their nature. This is accomplished both by the quicker or slower withdrawal of the tongue from the palate, and by the stronger or weaker exhalation of the wind.

§ 13

In a large place which reverberates, and where the listeners are at a great distance, you must in general mark the notes with the tongue with greater force and sharpness than in a small place, especially if several notes appear on the same pitch, otherwise they will sound as if they are produced only by exhalation from the chest.

[1] *Durch das Hauchen, mit Bewegung der Brust* (*par des souflemens qui ne viennent que du mouvement de la poitrine*). The French text adds 'without employing the tongue'.
[2] *Mit der Brust gestoßen werden* (*par des coups de poitrine*). J. S. Petri, *Anleitung zur praktischen Musik* (2nd ed.; Leipzig: J. G. I. Breitkopf, 1782), p. 479, uses the syllable *he* to suggest articulation of this kind, the *h* being produced from the chest.

SECTION II

Of the Use of the Tongue with the Word tiri

§ 1

This kind of tongue-stroke is most useful in passage-work of moderate quickness, especially since the quickest notes in them must always be played a little unequally (see Chapter XI, § 12).[1]

§ 2

In the previous section I have already indicated how the syllable *ti* is to be formed with the tongue. In the tongue-stroke treated here *ri* is added to it. You must seek to pronounce the letter *r* very sharply. To the ear it produces the same effect as when the single tongue *di* is used, although it does not appear the same to the player.

§ 3

Tiri is indispensable for dotted notes; it expresses them in a much sharper and livelier fashion than is possible with any other kind of tonguing.

§ 4

In this word *tiri* the accent falls on the second syllable; the *ti* is short, and the *ri* long. Hence the *ri* must always be used for the note on the downbeat, and the *ti* for the note on the upbeat.[2] Thus in four semiquavers the *ri* always comes on the first and third notes, and the *ti* on the second and fourth.

§ 5

Since, however, you can never begin with *ri*, you must tip the first two notes with *ti*. In the remaining notes of this kind, you continue with *tiri* until a variation in the notes or a rest occurs. The following examples will show how notes of this kind must be articulated with the tongue (see Tab. III, Figs. 10, 11, and 12). If a rest takes the place of the first note, as is to be seen in the last example, you continue with *tiri*. But since here the dots cease in the second crotchet, and the two demisemiquavers E–F come on the upbeat, each has a *ti*. The following G on the downbeat has *ri*; and since it is not dotted, and thus is equal to the following F, the following dotted note receives *ti* instead of *ri*.

---

[1] The reference to § 11 in the original text is incorrect.

[2] This statement is somewhat misleading. Even with Quantz's system of beating time, the syllables do not necessarily fall on upbeats or downbeats.

FIG. 10

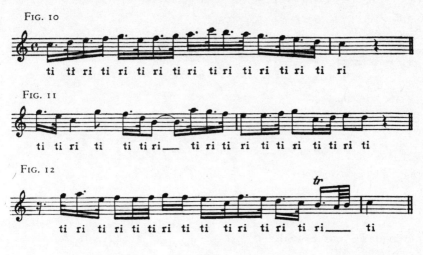

ti tt ri ti ri ti ri ti ri ti ri ti ri ti ri ti ri

FIG. 11

ti ti ri ti   ti ti ri___   ti ri ti ri ti ti ri ti ti ri ti

FIG. 12

ti ri ti ri ti ti ri ti ti ti ri ti ri ti ri___ ti

§ 6

The same rule applies in triple time (see Tab. III, Figs. 13 and 14).

FIG. 13　　　　　　　　　　　　　FIG. 14

ti ti ri ti ri ti ri ti　　　ti ri ti ri ti ri ti

If in three-four, three-eight, six-eight, nine-eight, or twelve-eight time the first note in a figure of three is dotted, as occurs in gigues, the first two notes have *ti*, and the last has *ri* (see Tab. III, Figs. 15, 16, 17, and 18).

FIG. 15　　　　　　　　　　　　　FIG. 16

ti ti ri ti ti ri ti　　　ti ri ti ti ri ti ti ri ti

FIG. 17　　　　　　　　　　　　　FIG. 18

ti ti ri ti ti ri ti　　　ti ti ri ti ti ti ri ti ti

§ 7

In notes without dots *di* can be used in place of *ti*. Quickness does not permit articulation with *ti* in passage-work; for there it would strike the ear disagreeably, and would eventually make the notes all too unequal. The first note, however, always keeps *ti*, and the others *diri*. If leaps in quavers follow semiquavers, *ti* is used, in stepwise quavers *di* (see Figs. 19 and 20).

FIG. 19

ti di ri di ri di ri di ri di ri di ri di ri di ri ti ti ti ti ti di di di di

FIG. 20

di ri di ri di ri di ri   di ri di ri di ri

§ 8

If the passage-work must be played more quickly than *diri* can be articulated, you must slur either the third and fourth notes, or the first and second (see Figs. 21 and 22).

FIG. 21   FIG. 22

ti ti ri— ti ti ri— ti ti   ti— ri ti ti— ri ti ti

The latter way, where the first and fourth notes have *ti*, and the third has *ri*, is most strongly recommended, since you can use it in various kinds of passage-work in both leaps and stepwise notes. In slurring the second note the tongue rests, and hence can continue for a longer period without tiring, while it soon becomes tired when *diri* is constantly used, and quickness is impeded. In this regard see the examples in Tab. III, Figs. 23, 24, 25, 26, 27, 28, and 29.

FIG. 23   FIG. 24

ti— ri ti ti— ri ti ti   ti— ri ti ti— ri ti ti

FIG. 25   FIG. 26

ti— ri ti ti— ri ti ti   ti— ri ti ti— ri ti ti

FIG. 27   FIG. 28   FIG. 29

ti di ri di ri di ri di ri di ri   ti ti ri— ti ti ti— ri ti ti ti

§ 9

The last kind [of tonguing], that in Fig. 29, is the most convenient for speed in triple time. In general, however, you must adjust to the leaps. If after a note two quicker ones follow, the first two may have *di*, and the third may have *ri*. The same applies to three equal quavers, or to triplets (see Tab. III, Figs. 30, 31, 32, 33, and 34).

SECTION III

Of the Use of the Tongue with the Word did'll, *or the so-called Double Tongue*

§ 1

The double tongue is used only for the very quickest passage-work. Although easy to explain orally, and simple for the ear to grasp, it is difficult to teach in writing. The word *did'll* which is articulated in it should consist of two syllables. In the second, however, no vowel is present; hence it must be pronounced *did'll* rather than *didel* or *dili*, suppressing the vowel which should appear in the second syllable. But the *d'll* must not be articulated with the tip of the tongue like the *di*.

§ 2

I have indicated in the first section of this chapter how the *di* must be formed. I refer you to that section here. To articulate *did'll*, first say *di*, and while the tip of the tongue springs forward to the palate, quickly draw the middle portion of the tongue downward a little on both sides, away from the palate, so that the wind is expelled on both sides obliquely between the teeth. This withdrawal of the tongue will then produce the stroke of the second syllable *d'll*; but it can never be articulated without the preceding *di*. If you pronounce *did'll* quickly several times in a row, you will hear how it should sound better than I can express it in writing.

§ 3

In its use *did'll* is the opposite of *tiri*. In *tiri* the accent lies on the second syllable, in *did'll* it falls on the first, and always comes on the note on the downbeat, the so-called *good note*.

§ 4

If you wish to learn how to execute *did'll*, you must first play several notes on the same pitch, without moving your fingers, and in the middle register; for this kind of tonguing will be a little prejudicial to tone or embouchure at the beginning. You can use the following notes at the beginning, articulating the *did'll* while you blow as indicated beneath the notes (see Tab. IV, Fig. 1).

TABLE IV

Fig. 1

did'll   di   did'll   di   did'll   di   did'll   di

Practise this example until you can produce all the notes distinctly. Then add a few more notes (see Tab. IV, Fig. 2).

Fig. 2

did'll   did'll   di   did'll   did'll   di

And when you have mastered this, take some notes by step (see Figs. 3, 4, 5, and 6).

Fig. 3   Fig. 4

did'll did'll di   did'll did'll di   did'll did'll   did'll did'll did'll did'll di

Fig. 5   Fig. 6

did'll did'll di did'll did'll di   did'll did'll did'll did'll did'll did'll   did'll did'll di

§ 5

You must be very careful that the tongue does not anticipate the fingers, as frequently happens in the beginning. You must rather seek always to hold on to the first note with *di* a little, and to make the second, with *d'll*, slightly shorter. For through the quick withdrawal of the tongue, the *d'll* receives a sharper stroke.

§ 6

I hope that the above examples will be sufficient for the mastery of this tongue-stroke. The following ones should show you how you can apply it in all sorts of passage-work.

§ 7

When the passage-work continues with notes of the same value, and without large leaps, the first note on the downbeat always receives *di*, and the second *d'll*, &c., as Fig. 7 shows.

Fig. 7

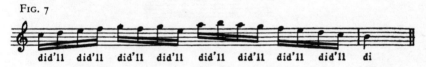

did'll   did'll   did'll   did'll   did'll   did'll   did'll   did'll   di

§ 8

If a rest takes the place of the first note, the two notes that follow must be tipped with *ti*. The others, however, again receive *di* (see Fig. 8).

Fig. 8

ti   tid'll   did'll did'll di   ti   tid'll   did'll did'll di

§ 9

If the first two notes are the same, the first three must be tipped with *ti*. If the last two are the same, the third is tipped with *di*, and the fourth with *ti* (see Figs. 9 and 10).

Fig. 9   Fig. 10

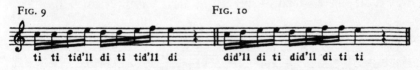

ti   ti   tid'll   di   ti   tid'll   di   did'll   di   ti   did'll   di   ti   ti

§ 10

If the last note [of four] makes an ascending leap, it also can be tipped with *ti* (see Fig. 11).

Fig. 11

did'll   di   ti   tid'll   di   ti   tid'll   di   ti   tid'll   di   ti

§ 11

If the first of the quick notes is tied to a long note preceding it, or if a dot is substituted for it, you must express it with a breath from the chest, saying *hi* instead of *di* (see Figs. 12 and 13).

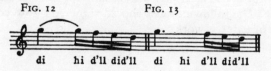

FIG. 12   FIG. 13

di   hi d'll did'll   di   hi d'll did'll

You can also tip the two notes after the dot with *ti* (see Fig. 14).[1]

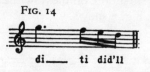

FIG. 14

di___   ti did'll

§ 12

In the following examples I will try to cite the most important types of passage-work that require a change of tonguing. But since it is impossible to set down all the passages that might occur, I must leave others to the individual reflection of the player.

§ 13

From the examples in Figs. 15 to 24 in Table IV, and Figs. 1 to 11 in Table V, you can see that occasions for changes in tonguing are produced by extended ascending or descending leaps, by rests, or by two notes on the same pitch, where *ti* must also be repeated.

FIG. 15

di ti tid'll   did'll   did'll   di ti tid'll   did'll   did'll   di

FIG. 16   FIG. 17

did'll did'll di ti tid'll di   did'll did'll di ti ti d'll did'll di

FIG. 18

ti   ti - d'll   di - d'll   di - d'll   di

[1] The *di* below the note E might be articulated with *ti*.

FIG. 19

di ti tid'll did'll did'll di ti tid'll di ti tid'll di

FIG. 20 FIG. 21

di ti tid'll di ti tid'll di did'll did'll di ti tid'll di

FIG. 22

di____ ti tid'll did'll did'll did'll did'll did'll di ti

FIG. 23 FIG. 24

di ti tid'll di ti tid'll di did'll did'll did'll did'll di

TABLE V

FIG. 1 FIG. 2

did'll di did'll di did'll did'll did'll di ti tid'll did'll di

FIG. 3 FIG. 4

did'll di ti tid'll di ti di did'll did'll did'll

FIG. 4 (*cont.*) FIG. 5

di did'll did'll di di did'll did'll di ti tid'll did'll di

FIG. 6 FIG. 7

did'll di ti tid'll did'll di did'll did'll di ti

FIG. 7 (*cont.*)   FIG. 8

ti ti tid'll did'll   di   did'll did'll di ti   tid'll did'll di ti

FIG. 9

did'll   did'll   did'll   did'll   did'll   did'll   did'll   did'll

FIG. 10   FIG. 11

di did'll di did'll di   di did'll di did'll di

§ 14

In three equal notes, whether they occur as triplets or appear in six-eight and other similar metres, it is to be observed that the first two notes always receive *did'll* and the third receives *di*, whatever the intervals may be (see Tab. V, Figs. 12 and 13).

FIG. 12   FIG. 13

did'll   di did'll   di   did'll   di did'll   di

If, however, the second note makes a very large descending leap, the first must be given *di*, and the last two *did'll* (see Fig. 14).

FIG. 14

di did'll   did'll   di did'll   di

If a rest takes the place of the first note, the two following notes are given *did'll* (see Fig. 15).

FIG. 15

did'll   did'll   di did'll   di

§ 15

The first note of each figure, whether it consists of three, four, or six notes, must always be held a little, to keep the movement of the tongue and fingers in accord, and so that each note receives its proper time.

§ 16

Four or more quick notes that are repeated may serve as a test of whether you are practising the double tongue correctly, that is, of whether the second note is being tipped just as sharply as the first. If this is not the case, you cannot execute roulades[1] brilliantly or vivaciously enough.

SUPPLEMENT

Several Remarks for the Use of the Oboe and Bassoon

§ 1

Except in matters of *fingering* and *embouchure*, the oboe and bassoon have much in common with the transverse flute. Hence those who apply themselves to one of these two instruments may profit not only from the instructions given for the use of the two kinds of tongue-strokes with *ti* and *tiri*, but, in general, from the entire method for the flute, in so far as it does not have to do with fingering and embouchure.

§ 2

They need only note in the tongue-stroke with *ti* that, since the reed is taken between the lips, they must extend the tongue directly forwards, instead of curving the tip of the tongue and pressing it upward against the palate, as on the flute. The opening of the reed must be closed with the tip of the tongue in order to stop or check the wind. As on the flute, the withdrawal of the tongue produces the stroke.

§ 3

The bassoonist has the advantage over the oboist in that he can also use the double tongue *did'll* like the flautist. He must simply note that on the bassoon wide ascending leaps, with the exception of those that do not go above the C below middle C, cannot be slurred as on the flute. All the upper notes of leaps made from the lowest octave must be tipped. In the second octave, that is, from D below middle C, a few notes forming leaps can indeed be slurred, but the leaps must not ascend above A below middle C unless you have a particularly good reed and a very firm embouchure.

§ 4

As to the tone on both of these instruments, much depends upon a good reed, that is, whether it is made of good and seasoned wood, whether it has the proper concavity, whether it is neither too wide nor too narrow,

---

[1] *Die rollenden Passagien (les passages roulants).*

neither too long nor too short, and whether, when shaved, it is made neither too thick nor too thin. If the front of the reed is too wide and too long, the high notes become too low in relation to the low ones; but if it is too narrow and too short, they become too high. Even if all these conditions have been observed, however, the lips, and manner of taking the reed between the lips, are of even greater importance. You must not bite the lips in between the teeth too much or too little. In the first case, the tone becomes dull, in the second it becomes too blaring and strident.

§ 5

Some players, particularly bassoonists, have a way of taking the reed between their lips rather obliquely, so that they can express the high notes more easily. This not only produces a poor and hissing tone, but also frequently makes the disagreeable hiss of the wind that escapes at the side of the reed audible at a distance. Hence it is much better to take the reed straight between the lips, so that a sustained and pleasing tone can be drawn from the instrument.

§ 6

In holding both of these instruments you must be mindful of a good natural posture. Hold the arms away from the body, and extend them forwards, so that the head need not hang down, constricting the throat and hampering breathing. In an orchestra the oboist must hold his instrument up as much as possible. If he pokes it below the stand, the tone loses its force.

CHAPTER VII

Of Taking Breath, in the Practice of the Flute

§ 1

Taking breath at the proper time is essential in playing wind instruments as well as in singing. Because of frequently encountered abuses in this regard, melodies that should be coherent are often broken up, the composition is spoiled, and the listener is robbed of part of his pleasure. To separate several notes that belong together is just as bad as to take a breath in reading [words] before the sense is clear, or in the middle of a word of two or three syllables. While separation of this kind is not met with in reading, it is unfortunately all too common among wind players.

§ 2

Since, however, it is not always possible to play in a single breath everything that belongs together, either because the composition has not been written with the prudence necessary in this regard, or because its performer does not possess sufficient capacity for conserving his breath, I will cite some examples here from which you will be able to perceive at which notes breath may be taken most conveniently. Subsequently you will be able to deduce general rules from these examples.

§ 3

As explained more fully in Chapter XI, § 12,[1] to which you may refer in this connexion, the quickest notes of the same value in a piece must be played a little unequally. This practice is the basis for the rule that breath must be taken between a long and a short note.[2] It should never be taken after a short note, much less after the last note in the bar; for no matter how briefly you may tip these notes, taking breath occupies too much time. Triplets are exceptions if they ascend or descend by step, and if they must be played very quickly. In this case necessity often requires that breath be taken after the last note in the bar. If, however, the leap of a third or the like is present, it may be taken between the notes of the leap.

[1] In the original German and French texts, the paragraph number is mistakenly given as 11 rather than 12.

[2] 'Long' should be taken here in a very relative sense, as may be seen from the examples in § 7.

§ 4

If a piece begins with a note on the upbeat (whether the opening note is the last note in the bar or a rest precedes it on the beat)[1] or if there is a cadence and a new idea begins, breath must be taken before the repetition of the principal subject or the beginning of the new idea, so that the end of the preceding idea and the beginning of the one that follows are separated from one another.

§ 5

If you have a note of one or more bars to sustain, you may take breath before the held note, even if a short note precedes it. If a quaver is tied to the long note, and two semiquavers and another tied note follow (see Tab. V, Fig. 16), you may make two semiquavers on the same pitch out of the quaver (see Tab. V, Fig. 17), and take breath between them.

FIG. 16   FIG. 17

You may do the same, as often as is necessary, with all tied notes (ligatures)[2] whether crotchets, quavers, or semiquavers. But if another tied note does not follow the one after the minim[3] (see Fig. 18), breath may be taken after the note tied to the long one without dividing it into two parts.

FIG. 18

§ 6

To play long passage-work you must slowly inhale a good supply of breath. To this end you must enlarge your throat and expand your chest fully, draw up your shoulders, and try to retain the breath in your chest as fully as possible, blowing it very economically into the flute. But if you still find it necessary to take breath between quick notes, you must make the preceding note very short, inhale the breath rapidly only as far as the throat, and rush the following two or three notes a little, so that the beat

---

[1] In other words if, in common time, the opening note appears on the fourth beat or *after* a short rest on the fourth beat. Translator's parentheses.

[2] The German terms for tied notes, *gebundene Noten* and *Bindungen*, like the English term 'binding' of the same period, may mean either tied notes or suspensions, or both. The examples given here are typical suspension figures. The term 'ligatures' occurs in parentheses in the original text. At this time it is merely another name for tied notes.

[3] Actually a semibreve appears in the original text. The engraver apparently forgot to add a stem to the note.

is not retarded and none of the notes is omitted. If you think beforehand that you will not be able to play the passage-work in a single breath, you will do well to take breath tranquilly and in due time, rather than wait until the last moment. The more often you take quick breaths, the more uncomfortable they become, and the less they help.

§ 7

From the following examples (Fig. 19 to the end of Table V) you will be able to see clearly the notes after which breath may be taken most conveniently. They are always those with a stroke above them. It is self-evident that you must take breath only when necessity requires, and not whenever notes like these occur.

FIG. 19

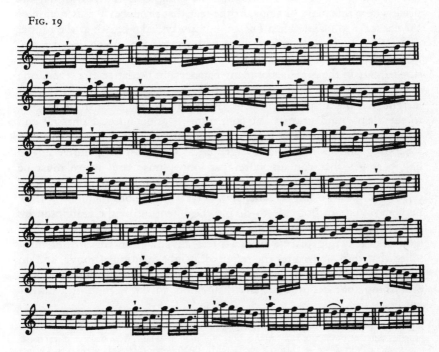

§ 8

Although you may take breath during the first, second, third, or last crotchet of each bar, it is always better to do so in the first crotchet, and indeed after the first note [in the time of the crotchet], unless the first four notes[1] move by step, while those that follow move by leaps. For wide intervals are best suited for taking breath.

---

[1] i.e. the four semiquavers in the time of the first crotchet. See the preceding examples.

§ 9

If you familiarize yourself well with the examples from Fig. 16 to the end of Table V, you will learn to take breath at the right places, and in → time will acquire the ability to negotiate any passages that may occur.

§ 10

If space permitted, the subject of taking breath would merit illustration with additional examples, since both singers and wind players commit such an abundance of errors in this regard. But who could determine all the situations where one cannot play everything in a single breath that should be played that way? The reasons why one cannot are so diverse that it is not always possible to say whether the composer, the performer, the place where one plays or sings, or the fear that produces a constriction of the chest, is to blame when one cannot always take breath at the proper time. What is certain is that you can produce twice as much, if not more, in a single breath when you sing or play for yourself than when you must sing or play in the presence of many listeners. In the latter case, therefore, you must know how to make use of all the imaginable skills that your insight into the art of performance offers. Hence you must strive to learn to see clearly and grasp what constitutes a good musical phrase,[1] and what must therefore hang together. You must be just as careful to avoid separating phrases that belong together, as you must be attentive not to link passages that contain more than one phrase, and hence must be divided; for a great part of true expression in performance depends upon this matter. Those singers and wind players (of whom there are a large number) who are not able to divine the intention of the composer are always in danger of committing errors in this respect, and betraying their weaknesses. String players have a great advantage in this matter, provided that they strive after the required insight mentioned above, and do not allow themselves to be misled by the bad example of those who join everything together without any distinction, in the fashion of a hurdy-gurdy.

---

[1] *Was einen musikalischen Sinn ausmache (ce qui fait un sens musical)*. 'Phrase' is not a literal or general rendering of the word *Sinn*, and is more limited in meaning. 'What makes musical sense' may come a little closer to Quantz's meaning. In the following sentence, however, Quantz seems to use the term in a narrower sense to mean 'phrase' or 'idea'.

CHAPTER VIII

Of the Appoggiaturas,[1] and the Little Essential Graces[2] Related to Them

§ 1

In performance appoggiaturas (Italian, *appoggiature*, French, *ports de voix*) are both ornamental and essential. Without appoggiaturas a melody would often sound very meagre and plain. If it is to have a *galant*[3] air, it must contain more consonances than dissonances; but if many of the former occur in succession, and several rapid notes are followed by a long one that is also a consonance, the ear may easily be wearied by them. Hence dissonances must be used from time to time to rouse the ear. And in this connexion appoggiaturas can be of considerable assistance, since they are transformed into dissonances, such as fourths and sevenths, if they stand before thirds or sixths reckoned from the bass, and are then properly resolved by the following notes.

§ 2

To avoid confusion with ordinary notes, they are marked with very small notes, and they receive their value from the notes before which they stand. It is of little importance whether they have one or two crooks.[4]

[1] The German term for appoggiatura, *Vorschlag*, means simply 'fore-beat', and thus does not have the connotation of 'leaning' found in the Italian word. Quantz and other German writers of the eighteenth century use it to refer to several different types of graces prefixed to a principal note, some of which do not fall within the modern usage of the word 'appoggiatura'.

[2] *Wesentliche Manieren.* The essential graces are those embellishments that have a limited compass and relatively fixed form, such as appoggiaturas, turns, mordents, and shakes. They are so designated to distinguish them from the *willkührliche Veränderungen* (extempore or arbitrary variations), discussed in Chapter XIII, which might have a wider compass and a variable form. Throughout the treatise four terms are used for ornamentation. These have been consistently translated in the following manner: *Manieren* (graces), *Veränderungen* (variations), *Verzierungen* (embellishments), *Zierrathen* (ornaments). *Manieren* is nearly always used in connexion with the small fixed graces, and *Veränderungen* in connexion with free variations. The two remaining terms apply to any type of ornamentation.

[3] On the use of the term 'galant', see Donington, *Interpretation*, pp. 108–9. *Grazioso*, the equivalent used in the manuscript Italian translation of the *Essay*, suggests Quantz's meaning most clearly.

[4] The practice of systematically indicating the actual value of appoggiaturas by using small minims, crotchets, quavers, semiquavers, and so forth, was first strongly advocated by C. P. E. Bach in the year following the appearance of Quantz's *Versuch*. See C. P. E. Bach, *Essay*, p. 87. Quantz here shows himself a member of an earlier generation in relying more on the performer. The *Sei duetti*, Op. 2 (1759), however, indicate that his attitude changed somewhat after the *Versuch* was published.

Usually they have only one. Semiquavers are generally used only before notes that must not be deprived of any[1] of their value. For example, with two or more long repeated notes, whether crotchets or minims (see Tab. VI, Fig. 25), these little semiquavers, taken either from above or below, are expressed very briefly, and tipped in place of the principal notes on the beat.

TABLE VI

FIG. 25

§ 3

Appoggiaturas are [normally] retardations of the prefixed notes.[2] Therefore they can be taken from either above or below, depending upon the position of the prefixed note (see Tab. VI, Figs. 1 and 2).

FIG. 1   FIG. 2

If the preceding [ordinary] note stands one or two steps higher than that which follows, before which the appoggiatura is found, the appoggiatura is taken from above (see Tab. VI, Fig. 3).

FIG. 3

But if the preceding note is lower than the following one, the appoggiatura must be taken from below (see Fig. 4); it generally becomes a ninth,[3] resolving to the third above, or a fourth, resolving to the fifth above.

FIG. 4

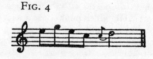

[1] Quantz is not careful in his wording here. The following sentence makes it clear that the notes were actually deprived of a small portion of their value.

[2] *Die Vorschläge sind eine Aufhaltung der vorigen Note.* (*Les Ports de voix sont un retardement de la note précédente.*) Quantz's wording is again confusing. *Vorigen*, I believe, refers to the prefixed note itself, and not to the note preceding the appoggiatura. A paraphrase of this sentence in Tromlitz, *Unterricht*, p. 240 is worth noting: *Der Vorhalt oder Vorschlag ist eine Aufhaltung einer Note durch eine vorhergehende.* 'The *Vorhalt* or appoggiatura is a retardation of a note through a preceding one.'

[3] That Quantz distinguished between seconds and ninths is indicated in Chapter XVII, Section VI, § 21.

§ 4

Appoggiaturas must be tipped gently with the tongue, allowing them to swell in volume if time permits; the following notes are slurred a little more softly. This type of embellishment is called the *Abzug*;[1] it originated with the Italians.

§ 5

There are two kinds of appoggiaturas. Some are tipped as accented notes, or notes on the downbeat, others as passing notes, or on the upbeat. The former may be called *accented*,[2] the latter, *passing appoggiaturas*.[3]

§ 6

Passing appoggiaturas[4] occur when several notes of the same value descend in leaps of thirds (see Tab. VI, Fig. 5).

FIG. 5

When performed they are expressed as illustrated in Fig. 6.

FIG. 6

The dots are lengthened, and the notes on which the slurs begin, that is, the second, fourth, and sixth, are tipped. Notes of this kind must not be

---

[1] The *Abzug* is not a new or separate type of ornament, but a normal, long appoggiatura performed in a special way, that is, with a swell and a diminuendo. See Tromlitz, *Unterricht*, p. 242: 'In practice the accent always falls on the long appoggiatura, and if you have time you sound the appoggiatura softly, allow it to grow in strength, and slur it to the following tone very softly, allowing it to decrescendo at the same time. This is called an *Abzug*.' In the French text the term *accent* is used. Quantz's detailed instructions on dynamics in Chapter XIV, §§ 26–43, provide some examples of where *Abzüge* appear and how they are treated.

[2] *Anschlagende Vorschläge* (*Ports de voix frappants*).

[3] *Durchgehende Vorschläge* (*Ports de voix passagers*).

[4] To some modern readers 'passing' appoggiaturas seem to be a contradiction in terms. As illustrated in Fig. 6 they seem to be no more than passing notes. It should be noted, however, that these appoggiaturas require a special kind of articulation. Also, as indicated above, the term *Vorschlag* does not have exactly the same connotations as the word 'appoggiatura'. In the English translation of Hotteterre's *Principes*, the passing appoggiatura is called a 'slide'. In France it was commonly designated a *coulé*. C. P. E. Bach, *Essay*, pp. 97–98, disagrees strongly with Quantz's realization of appoggiaturas of this type. He places most of them in his class of invariable appoggiaturas, in which the appoggiatura is performed as quickly as possible on the beat rather than before it. Many other German and French writers also advocate performance on the beat, although they differ as to duration. L. Mozart, *A Treatise*, pp. 177–8, gives some examples that agree with those of Quantz, as do J. J. Rousseau and a number of writers on music.

confused with those in which a dot appears after the second,[1] and which express almost the same melody (see Fig. 7).

FIG. 7

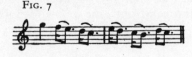

In this figure the second, fourth, and following short notes fall on the downbeat, as dissonances against the bass; when performed, they are executed boldly and briskly, while the appoggiaturas discussed here require, on the contrary, a flattering expression. Were the little notes in Fig. 5 lengthened, and tipped in the time of the following principal notes, the melody would be completely altered, and would sound as illustrated in Fig. 8.[2]

FIG. 8

But this[3] would be opposed to the French style of playing, to which these appoggiaturas owe their origin, hence to the intention of their inventors, who have met with almost universal approbation in this regard. Often two appoggiaturas are also found before a note, the first marked with a small note, but the second by a note reckoned as part of the beat; they occur at caesuras (see Fig. 9).

FIG. 9

Here the little note is again tipped briefly, and reckoned in the time of the previous note in the upbeat. Thus the notes in Fig. 9 are played as illustrated in Fig. 10.[4]

FIG. 10

[1] Fig. 7 is an example of the so-called 'Lombardian snap'. See Chapter V, § 23, and Chapter XVIII, § 58.

[2] This figure, in other words, should be written as it is to be performed.

[3] i.e. the lengthening of the appoggiaturas illustrated in Fig. 8. Judging from Quantz's insistence that the performance of passing appoggiaturas in the time of the preceding note is part of the French style of playing, he probably heard them performed in that manner, at least by flute players, during his visit to Paris in 1726 and 1727.

[4] In his review of the subject of passing appoggiaturas in Chapter XVII, Section II, § 20, Quantz introduces another important example of where they should be used. Before any attempt is made to apply Quantz's rules about appoggiaturas, the paragraph cited should be studied. Other important references to the subject are found in Chapter XIII, §§ 30, 42, and 43.

§ 7

Accented appoggiaturas, or appoggiaturas which fall on the downbeat, are found before a long note on the downbeat following a short one on the upbeat (see Tab. VI, Fig. 11).

FIG. 11

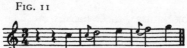

Here the appoggiatura is held for half the value of the following principal note, and is played as illustrated in Fig. 12.

FIG. 12

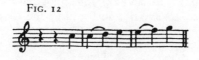

§ 8

If the note to be ornamented by the appoggiatura is dotted, it is divisible into three parts. The appoggiatura receives two of these parts, but the note itself only one part, that is, the value of the dot. Therefore the notes in Fig. 13 are played as illustrated in Fig. 14.

FIG. 13   FIG. 14

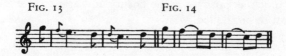

These rules, and those given in the preceding paragraph, are generally applicable,[1] regardless of the species of notes or of the position of the appoggiaturas above or below them.

§ 9

If in six-eight or six-four time two notes are tied together upon the same pitch, and the first is dotted, as occurs in gigues, the appoggiaturas are held for the value of the first dotted note (see Figs. 15 and 17).

FIG. 15   FIG. 17

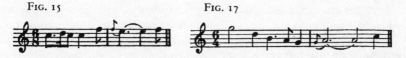

[1] None of Quantz's rules is without its exceptions, however, and the context of the harmony and the movement of the other parts must always be taken into consideration. For example, see § 10 below.

They are played as illustrated in Figs. 16 and 18, and thus depart from the preceding rule.

FIG. 16   FIG. 18

With regard to appoggiaturas, these metres must be considered as duple rather than triple.[1]

§ 10

If there are shakes upon notes which form dissonances against the bass, whether the augmented fourth, the diminished fifth, the seventh, or the second (see Figs. 19, 20, 21, and 22), the appoggiaturas before the shakes must be very short, to avoid transforming the dissonances into consonances.

FIG. 19   FIG. 20   FIG. 21   FIG. 22

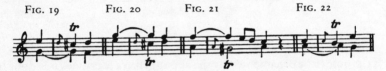

For example, if in Fig. 21 the appoggiatura A were held half as long as the following G sharp with the shake, the sixth, F to A, would be heard instead of the seventh, F to G sharp, which should be heard; this must be avoided as much as possible if the beauty and agreeableness of the harmony are not to be spoiled.

§ 11

If a rest follows a note, the appoggiatura receives the time of the note, and the note the time of the rest, unless the need to take breath makes this impossible.[2] The three kinds of notes in Fig. 23 are thus played as illustrated in Fig. 24.

FIG. 23   FIG. 24

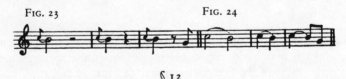

§ 12

It is not enough to be able to play the different types of appoggiaturas with their proper values when they are marked. You must also know how

[1] In Chapter V, § 14, Quantz classifies six-eight and six-four among the triple metres. If they were considered triple here (that is, four bars of triple time), the appoggiatura would have the value of a crotchet in Fig. 15 and that of a minim in Fig. 17.

[2] The qualifying phrase at the end of this sentence should be stressed. There are also many other cases where this rule cannot be applied, either because of the harmonic context or the metrical structure.

to add them at the appropriate places when they are not indicated. To learn this, make the following rule your guide: if a *long*[1] note follows one or more *short* notes on the downbeat or upbeat, and remains in a consonant harmony, an appoggiatura may be placed before the long note, in order to constantly maintain the agreeability of the melody. The preceding note will show whether it must be taken from above or below.

§ 13

I would now like to give a short example which includes most of the different kinds of appoggiaturas (see Fig. 26).[2]

FIG. 26

If you wish to be convinced of the necessity and effectiveness of appoggiaturas, play this example first with the designated appoggiaturas, then without them. You will perceive very distinctly the difference in style. The example will also make it clear that the appoggiaturas are placed for the most part before notes which have quicker notes either before or after them, and also that appoggiaturas are required in the majority of shakes.

§ 14

Several other little embellishments stemming from the appoggiaturas, such as the *half-shake*[3] (see Tab. VI, Figs. 27 and 28), the *pincé* (the mordent;[4]

---

[1] The word 'long' is used in a very relative sense.

[2] Quantz has cited all the necessary rules for the realization of this example except one. In the examples in Chapter XVII, Section II, § 20, he indicates that he considers appoggiaturas of the type found at the beginning of the third and fifth measures to be passing rather than accented appoggiaturas. Thus they do not receive half of the value of the quavers. They are performed very quickly in the time of the preceding notes.   [3] *Der halbe Triller (demi tremblement).*

[4] Quantz uses the French term *pincé* in the German text with the German *der Mordant* in parentheses.

see Figs. 29 and 30), and the *doublé* or *turn*[1] (see Fig. 31) are customary
in the French style for giving brilliance to a piece.

FIG. 27   FIG. 28   FIG. 29   FIG. 30   FIG. 31

The half-shakes are of two kinds (see Figs. 27 and 28), and may be added
to upper appoggiaturas in place of the simple *Abzug*. The *pincés* are also
of two sorts and, like the *doublés*, may be added to lower appoggiaturas.

§ 15

The *battemens* (see Figs. 32 and 33) may be introduced in leaps, where
appoggiaturas are not permitted, to enliven the notes and make them
brilliant.[2]

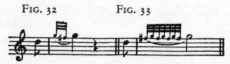

FIG. 32   FIG. 33

On the flute the first must be produced with a simultaneous blow of the
finger and stroke of the tongue, and may be introduced in quick notes as
well as slow ones. The second is more suitable for rather slow notes than
for rapid ones; but the demisemiquavers must still be produced with
the greatest speed, and thus the fingers must not be raised too high.

§ 16

The embellishments or graces which I have described in the fourteenth
and fifteenth paragraphs serve, in accordance with the temper of the piece,
to excite cheer and gaiety, while the simple appoggiaturas, on the contrary,
arouse tenderness and melancholy. Since music should now rouse the
passions, now still them again, the utility and necessity of these graces in
a plain and unadorned melody is self-evident.

§ 17

If you wish now to mix the graces described in the fourteenth and
fifteenth paragraphs with the pure appoggiaturas used in the example in
Tab. VI, Fig. 26,[3] and introduce them after the appoggiaturas, you may do

---

[1] *Der Doppelschlag.* For further discussions of these and some other graces, see Chapter
XIII,§§ 32, 40 and 41, and Chapter XVII, Section II,§§ 21–25. For comparative examples
→ of half-shakes, mordents, and turns, see Donington, *Interpretation*, pp. 250–3, 260–7, 272–6.

[2] As illustrated by Quantz the *battemens* differ from the *pincés* in that they lack an opening
long appoggiatura. In Fig. 33 the embellishment begins with a lower neighbour, which
makes it seem almost the ornamenting of a lower appoggiatura. For a description of
battemens and a list of fingerings for them, see Corrette, *Methode*, pp. 32–33 (pp. 44–45 in
Farrar's translation).

[3] See § 13 above.

so in the following manner at the notes that have letters above them. The grace in Fig. 27[1] may be introduced at the notes beneath (*c*), (*d*), (*f*), (*i*), and (*n*). That in Fig. 28 is proper with the note at (*k*). That in Fig. 29 is made at the notes beneath (*g*) and (*m*). That in Fig. 30 should be heard at (*e*), but that in Fig. 31 at (*b*). That in Fig. 32 may be joined to the notes beneath (*a*) and (*l*), and that in Fig. 33 to the note under (*h*). It is obvious that the graces must everywhere be transposed to the notes indicated by the appoggiaturas.

§ 18

In this mixture of the simple appoggiaturas with the little graces, or French *propretés*,[2] it will be found that the melody is much more lively and brilliant with the latter than without them. The mixture, however, must be undertaken with discernment; for a considerable part of good execution depends upon it.

§ 19

Some persons greatly abuse the use of the extempore embellishments as well as the appoggiaturas and the other essential graces described here. They allow hardly a single note to be heard without some addition, wherever the time or their fingers permit it. They make the melody either too weak through an excessive load of appoggiaturas and *Abzüge*, or too variegated through a superabundance of whole and half shakes, mordents, turns, *battemens*, &c. These they frequently introduce upon notes which even an insensitive[3] musical ear recognizes as inappropriate. If it happens that a celebrated singer has a particularly pleasing manner of introducing appoggiaturas, at once half the singers of his country begin to howl, and to dampen the fire of their liveliest pieces with their offensive wailings; and in this fashion they believe they are approaching, if not surpassing, the merits of that celebrated singer. It is true that the ornaments described above are absolutely necessary for good execution. But they must be used sparingly or they become too much of a good thing. The rarest and most tasteful delicacies produce nausea if over-indulged. The same is true of musical embellishments if we use them too profusely, and attempt to overwhelm the ear. A sublime, majestic, and vigorous air can be made common and insipid through poorly introduced appoggiaturas, and a melancholy and tender air, on the contrary, too gay and bold through an excessive load of shakes and other little graces, thus spoiling the balanced design of the composer. Hence it is apparent that embellishments may both improve a piece where it is necessary, and mar it if used inappropriately. Those who wish to display good taste but do not possess it are the first to fall into this error. Because of their lack of sensitivity they

---

[1] See § 14 above for this and the following figures.
[2] *Propretäten*. Both the French and German words refer to the embellishments described in §§ 14 and 15 of this chapter.
[3] *Halb gesund* (lit. 'half-healthy').

are unable to deal with a simple melody. They are, so to speak, bored with noble simplicity. Those who would avoid such blunders should early accustom themselves to singing and playing neither too simply nor too colourfully, always mixing simplicity and brilliance. The little embellishments should be used like seasoning at a meal; if the prevailing sentiment is taken as the guiding principle, propriety will be maintained, and one passion will never be transformed into another.[1]

[1] Tromlitz, in his *Unterricht*, pp. 237–65, offers a useful discussion of embellishments that parallels the present chapter in some respects, and indicates some of the changes in interpretation that appeared in the latter half of the eighteenth century.

CHAPTER IX

Of Shakes

§ 1

Shakes[1] add great lustre to one's playing, and, like appoggiaturas, are quite indispensable. If an instrumentalist or singer were to possess all the skill required by good taste in performance, and yet could not strike good shakes, his total art would be incomplete. While nature stands one person in good stead in this respect, another must learn the shake through much application. Some players succeed with all their fingers, some with only a few, and for still others the shake remains throughout life a stumbling-block presumably more dependent upon the constitution of the man's tendons than upon his will. With industry, however, many improvements can be made, if the player does not expect the shake to come by itself, and if, while his fingers are still growing, he takes the requisite pains to perfect it.

§ 2

All shakes do not have to be struck with the same speed; in this matter you must be governed by the place in which you are playing, as well as by the piece to be performed. If playing in a large place which reverberates strongly, a somewhat slower shake will be more effective than a quicker one; for too rapid an alternation of notes is confused through the reverberation, and this makes the shake indistinct. In a small or tapestried room, on the other hand, where the listeners are close by, a quicker shake will be better than a slower one. In addition, you must be able to distinguish the character of each piece you play, so that you do not confuse those of one sort with those of another, as many do. In melancholy pieces the shake must be struck more slowly, in gay ones, more quickly.[2]

§ 3

Slowness or quickness, however, must not be excessive. The very slow shake is customary only in French singing, and is of as little use as the very quick, trembling one, which the French call *chevroté* (bleating).[3] You must

---

[1] *Die Triller (les Tremblements)*.

[2] L. Mozart, *A Treatise*, p. 189, follows Quantz very closely in his discussion of shakes. C. P. E. Bach, *Essay*, p. 101, states that 'A rapid trill is always preferable to a slow one. In sad pieces the trill may be broadened slightly, but elsewhere its rapidity contributes much to the melody.'

[3] This type of shake was also known as the *Bockstriller* or 'goat's trill'. See L. Mozart, *A*

not be misled even if some of the greatest and most celebrated singers
execute the shake chiefly in the latter fashion. Although many, from ignorance, indeed consider this bleating shake a special merit, they do not know
that a moderately quick and even shake is much more difficult to learn
than the very fast trembling one, and that the latter must therefore be
considered a defect.

§ 4

The *shake in thirds*[1] in which the third, instead of the adjacent second, is
struck above the principal note, although customary of old, and still the
mode nowadays among some Italian violinists and oboists, must not be
used either in singing or playing (except, perhaps, upon the bagpipe). Each
shake must take up no more than the interval of a whole tone or a semitone, as is required by the key, and by the note upon which the shake
originates.

§ 5

If the shake is to be genuinely beautiful, it must be played evenly, or at
a uniform and moderate speed.[2] Upon instruments, therefore, the fingers
must never be raised higher at one stroke than at another.

§ 6

To fix precisely the proper speed of a good regular shake is rather difficult. Yet I believe that a *long* shake which prepares a cadence will be
neither too slow nor too quick if it is so struck that the finger makes not
many more than *four* movements in the time of a pulse beat,[3] and thus
makes *eight* notes, as illustrated in Tab. VII, Fig. 1.[4]

TABLE VII

FIG. 1

In fast and gay pieces, however, brief shakes can be struck a little more
quickly. Here the finger may be raised, in the time of a pulse-beat, once or

Treatise, p. 189. Tosi, *Observations*, p. 48, writes that the shake sung 'like the Quivering of a
Goat makes one laugh'.

[1] *Der Terzentriller (le tremblement de la Tierce)*. Tosi, loc. cit., also disapproves of this type of
shake.

[2] Some writers advocate a shake that gradually increases in speed. Corrette, *Methode*, p. 22,
gives an illustration of this type. On the other hand, Tosi, *Observations*, p. 42, says 'let the Master
. . . strive that the Scholar may attain one that is equal, distinctly mark'd, easy, and moderately
quick, which are its most beautiful Qualifications'. For further comments on this point, and
others connected with the performance of shakes, see Donington, *Interpretation*, pp. 239–50.

[3] In Chapter XVII, Section VII, § 55, Quantz establishes approximately eighty pulse beats a
minute as the norm.

[4] In this example Quantz omits the opening appoggiatura. That he expected the performer
➤ to add this appoggiatura is clearly stated in the following paragraph.

at most twice more.¹ But this latter type is permissible only upon short notes, and when there are several short notes in succession.

> With regard to the speed of shakes in general, it might also be mentioned, perhaps unnecessarily, that you must adjust to the height and depth of the notes. Taking the four octaves of the harpsichord as the gauge, I believe that if the shake is struck at the speed described above in the octave C′ to C″, it can be struck a little more quickly in the octave above; in the octave below it can be struck a little more slowly, and in the lowest octave still more slowly. In the case of the human voice, I might further conclude that the soprano could execute the shake more quickly than the alto and, in the proper proportion, the tenor and bass could execute it more slowly than the soprano and alto. Shakes on the violin, viola, violoncello, and double bass could correspond to the shakes of the four voice parts. On the flute and oboe the shake could be executed as quickly as the soprano executes it, and the shake on the bassoon could have the same quickness as the shake of the tenor. I grant everyone the choice of accepting or rejecting this notion. Although some may censure subtleties of this sort as useless, I will be satisfied if only a few persons of refined taste, ripe critical sense, and much experience are not completely opposed to me.

§ 7

Each shake begins with the appoggiatura that precedes its note, and as explained in the previous chapter, the appoggiatura may be taken from above or below. The ending of each shake consists of two little notes which follow the notes of the shake, and are added to it at the same speed (see Tab. VII, Fig. 2). They are called the *termination*.²

FIG. 2

This termination is sometimes written out with separate notes (see Fig. 3).

FIG. 3

If, however, only a plain note is found (as in Fig. 4), both the appoggiatura and termination are implied, since without them the shake would be neither complete nor sufficiently brilliant.³

FIG. 4

---

¹ i.e. once or twice more than the normal four times mentioned earlier.

² *Der Nachschlag* (*le coup d'après*). The term means literally 'afterbeat', and was used by other writers to describe several different types of graces. See, for example, L. Mozart, *A Treatise*, p. 185, and C. P. E. Bach, *Essay*, p. 98.

³ For some important additional remarks on terminations and shakes, see Chapter XIII, §§ 35 and 36, and Chapter XVII, Section II, § 24.

§ 8

Sometimes the appoggiatura of the shake is just as fast as the other notes which form the shake; for example, when, after a rest, a new idea begins with a shake.[1] Whether the appoggiatura is long or short, however, it must always be tipped with the tongue; the shake and its termination, on the other hand, must be slurred to the appoggiatura.

§ 9

The preparations,[2] or appoggiaturas, of shakes are of two kinds, consisting either of whole tones or semitones. A whole tone is usually heard on the flute when you raise your finger naturally. Hence in shakes consisting of semitones the breath must be moderated, and the finger must be struck quickly at a short distance from the hole, so that the ear perceives only a semitone. Thus the preparation must be kept firmly in mind, and must be produced with full wind. But as soon as the finger is to strike, the wind must be moderated, and the finger must scarcely leave the wood.

§ 10

By way of further illustration, and to facilitate understanding, I shall list here the most important notes with appoggiaturas of semitones. The appoggiatura F before E (see Fig. 5) will be transformed into F sharp if the fifth finger is raised too high. Similarly, the D sharp will be transformed into E (in Fig. 6), the C into C sharp (in Fig. 7), the B flat into B (in Fig. 8), the A flat into A (in Fig. 9), and the A into B flat (in Fig. 10), whether they appear in the high register or in the low one.

FIG. 5   FIG. 6   FIG. 7   FIG. 8   FIG. 9   FIG. 10

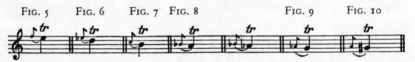

In this fashion all of these shakes that consist of semitones would be made false. If you follow the rule given above, however, they can all be struck truly. Although this observation seems to be unknown to many flute players, I consider it most necessary. Without purity of intonation in playing the ear can never be completely satisfied. Poor intonation is contrary to the proportions of the notes, and because of this weakness on the part of its performers the flute has fallen into disrepute among many connoisseurs who comprehend neither the characteristics nor the difficulties of the instrument, and suppose that it cannot be played more truly than has, until now, been the case among the majority. I have made these

[1] For another case in which the appoggiatura of the shake is performed quickly, see Chapter VIII, § 10, and the accompanying illustrations.

[2] *Vorhaltenden Noten (les notes qui précédent)*.

remarks for the benefit of those who are concerned with greater trueness of execution on the instrument. Individual practice can lead each player to further insights in this regard.

§ 11

Which fingers must be used for each shake on the flute through its entire scale may be seen in Tab. VII, Figs. 22, 23, and 24. The numbers below the notes indicate which finger must be used for each note. I presuppose here that, before attempting to learn shakes, the player has acquired a knowledge of the fingers required in stopping each note in accordance with the instructions for Table I.[1]

In the shake on D'' you must raise the first finger slightly;[2] the shake will then be clearer and more brilliant.

FIG. 22

FIG. 23

FIG. 24

---

[1] See Chapter III, § 4. To compare Quantz's fingering of shakes with that of his predecessors, see Hotteterre, *Principes*, pp. 10–12, 17–22, and Corrette, *Methode*, pp. 24–29. For detailed discussion of shakes dating from the late eighteenth century, see Tromlitz, *Unterricht*, pp. 266–93.
[2] *Muß man mit dem 1. Finger ein wenig Luft machen (il faut donner un peu d'air avec le doigt 1).*

Some shakes cannot be explained clearly enough with figures alone. Hence I shall indicate here the particular manner in which each must be struck. In the shake on C″ (see Fig. 11), you must first tip the appoggiatura D, then hold fingers 2, 3, 5, and 6, and strike the shake with 4. For the termination raise all the fingers simultaneously, and sound the two little notes B–C, at the same speed as the shake.

FIG. 11

If a flat is found before the little note (see Fig. 12), you must turn the flute outwards for the appoggiatura, and inwards during the shake, and must moderate your breath so that the semitone does not become a whole tone. For the termination, B♭–C, if you raise your right hand and the second finger, hold 3, close and open 1, and then close 2, the C is finally heard alone.

FIG. 12

In the shake on C‴ (see Fig. 13), close the first hole half-way, and the second and third completely; leave 7 open and strike 4 and 5 together, making the termination with 6. This shake may also be struck in another way, namely, after the appoggiatura D close 4, 5, and 6, and strike 4 and 5 together, making the termination with 1.

FIG. 13

For the shake without an appoggiatura on D‴ (see Fig. 14), close 1 half-way, and 2 and 3 completely; leave the little key open; strike the shake with 3 and then hold it, making the termination with 4 and 5 together. This shake, and the one on E‴, should be used only in cases of necessity, since on the flute both can consist only of semitones rather than whole tones.

FIG. 14

On D flat" (see Fig. 15), first take E flat and hold the right hand; close 1 half-way, and strike the shake with 2 and 3 together; then raise all the fingers simultaneously, and make the termination with 1.

FIG. 15

In the shake on C sharp" (see Fig. 16), you proceed in the same fashion, but use the large key instead of the little one. In general these two shakes occur infrequently, since they sound very harsh, especially the first one. But if the little finger is raised slightly during the shake, so that the key is a little closer to the hole, the shake speaks easily.

FIG. 16

On B sharp' (see Fig. 17), after the appoggiatura cover 2, 3, 4, 5, and 6, and make the shake with 4; then raise all these fingers again and make the termination with 1. During the shake you must moderate your breath, so that D is not heard instead of C sharp.

FIG. 17

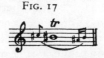

On F sharp' (see Fig. 18), and likewise at the octave above, the shake is struck with the third finger, because of the appoggiatura G sharp.

FIG. 18

In Fig. 19, however, because the following E is sharpened, the F sharp is stopped with 1, 2, 3, 5, 6, and 8, and the shake is made with 3. In the octave below you do the same, but do not depress the key. This fingering is only to be used in the Adagio, however, and then the flute must be turned inwards for the F sharp, and the breath moderated. In the Allegro the shake is struck as in Fig. 18.

FIG. 19

If the shake on either E' or E" starts on F sharp, it is struck not with 5 but with 4. Since this shake, like the F sharp shake in Fig. 18, tends to become a third, you must strike it very quickly, and must not raise the fingers high.

In the shake on C sharp" (see Fig. 20), tip the appoggiatura, hold 4, 5, and 6, and strike the shake with 2 and 3 together. Then raise all fingers, and make the termination with 1.

FIG. 20

In the shake on B sharp" (see Fig. 21), stop the C sharp with 2, 3, 4, and 7; for the shake cover 5 and 6 also, and then make the shake either with 5 or with 4 and 5 together, it makes no difference which. Finger 1 makes the termination while all the other fingers are held.

FIG. 21

§ 13

If a close[1] (cadence) follows the shake, whether it is in the middle of the piece or at the end, an appoggiatura is not permitted between the closing note and the termination of the shake, particularly if the note of the shake is a step higher than the closing note. For example, if a shake were struck on D", in order to close on C, and the appoggiatura D were made before this concluding note, it would sound quite ineffectual, and you would be immediately enlisted among the musical rabble, since this error is never committed by a person of refined taste.

[1] *Ein Schluß.* In the German text *Cadenz* appears in parentheses. In the French text *Cadence* alone is used. It is possible that Quantz refers only to full cadences which conclude the major sections of a piece. L. Mozart, *A Treatise*, p. 191, gives the same rule. C. P. E. Bach, *Essay*, p. 97, endorses the use of appoggiaturas before the closing note.

CHAPTER X

What a Beginner Must Observe in His Independent Practice

§ 1

I have already said, and I repeat, that a beginner who proposes to learn to play the flute thoroughly requires oral instruction from a good master in addition to my method. Rules given in writing do indeed show the surest way to learn a subject, but they do not correct the mistakes so often made in practice, especially at the beginning. The beginner is not always aware of these mistakes himself, and if the master is not careful to point them out constantly, they turn into a habit with the pupil, and eventually become second nature. Then more effort and industry are required to cast off that which is bad than to embrace that which is good. But if the student does not know how to help himself in his independent practice; if he does not understand what his teacher has taught him, or has forgotten it; or if the principles of his master are unfortunately incorrect, he may, through the present instructions, disabuse himself of his errors, and remain on the correct path. In each of the sciences, however—not only those which must be grasped by the mind, but those in which the senses and the body contribute their share—several so-called aptitudes are also essential.[1]

§ 2

I shall first summarize briefly the most important of the principles that I have explained more fully in the previous chapters, so that you may find them with greater ease in a single place, may read them over frequently, and hence may remember them more easily.

§ 3

A beginner must remember to hold the flute firmly with the left thumb. He must press the flute firmly to his mouth. He must take care not to allow the little finger to remain on the key in playing either the low or the middle E and F. He must not form the careless habit of allowing any of the fingers of the right hand to cover the holes in notes that require only the left hand.

[1] *Sogenannte Handgriffe.* A paraphrase appears in the French text: 'both skill and practice are essential.'

He must not raise the fingers unequally or too high. He can best note whether he is avoiding these faults by standing in front of a mirror when he practises passages in which both hands are employed by turns. The fingers must not be held too closely above the holes, however, since this will make the notes flat and untrue, and will give them a hissing sound.

The flute must not be turned in at one time and out at another,[1] or the notes will become either lower or higher than they should be.

A beginner must not allow his head to fall forwards and down when playing, so that the mouth hole is covered too far, and the upward passage of the wind is obstructed.

The arms must be held up, and a little away from the body.

A beginner must guard against making any unnecessary or constrained gestures with his head, body, or arms; although this is not a vital matter, they may produce a disagreeable effect upon the listeners.

He must produce the notes truly through proper fingering as well as proper blowing.

He must pay close attention to the movement of the chin and lips in ascending and descending notes.

He must blow the flute weakly in the high notes, in accordance with their proportions,[2] and strongly in the low ones, especially in passages that consist of leaps.

With regard to force of tone, he must take special care never to play a piece so loudly or so softly that he cannot, if it should be necessary, play a Fortissimo after a Forte, and a Pianissimo after a Piano. This can be done only by increasing or by moderating the wind. Playing always on the same level would soon become tedious.

The player must not allow the action of his chest or lungs to become sluggish, but must try to sustain the vitality of his wind by strengthening and moderating it by turns, especially in the Allegro.

He must never wait until the last moment to take breath, much less take it at the wrong time. If he does so, he will interrupt the course of every melody and make it incomprehensible.

He must always mark the beat—that is, the quaver in slow pieces and the crotchet in quick ones—with his foot.

The tongue must always accord with the fingers,[3] and must not become accustomed to laziness or indolence. The liveliness and distinctness of the execution depend upon this. Hence the tongue must be exercised most frequently with *ti*.

In passage-work the beginner must be mindful not only of the notes, but of the particular fingers required for them, so that he does not raise the

---

[1] i.e. it must not be turned inadvertently or without special intent. There are cases in which the flute must be turned in or out. See Chapter IX, §§ 12 ff.

[2] i.e. the mathematical ratios of the notes. See the Preface to the Translation.

[3] The meaning of this phrase is clearer if one reads 'The movement of the tongue must always accord with that of the fingers. . . .' For further information on this point, see Chapter XII, § 6.

fingers when he should cover the holes. This mistake is easy to make if he is not sufficiently practised in his reading or in his time.

He must never play a piece more quickly than he is able to perform it in a uniform tempo; the notes must be expressed distinctly, and whatever the fingers are at first unable to manage must be frequently repeated.

§ 4

The master also must pay diligent attention during lessons to all the matters discussed here, so that he does not allow the student to overlook anything, or to become accustomed to such errors. Therefore, in order to perceive everything more easily, the master must sit on the right hand of the student when he plays.

§ 5

A beginner must choose very short and easy pieces at first for exercising his embouchure, tongue, and fingers, so that he does not tax his memory more than he does his tongue and fingers. These pieces may be set in easy keys such as G major, C major, A minor, F major, B minor, D major, and E minor. But as soon as he has achieved some facility with his embouchure, tongue, and fingers, he may venture to play in more difficult keys, for example in A major, E major, B major, C sharp minor, B flat major, G minor, C minor, D sharp major, F minor, B flat minor, and A sharp major.[1] To be sure, these keys will seem rather difficult to the beginner, but since everything will appear difficult to him, he will not find them as hard as he would if he were to undertake to play in the keys mentioned after he had already acquired some facility in performance;[2] for then he would be subjected to unaccustomed difficulties which might hold him back for a considerable time.

§ 6

To form the habit of making the simple tongue-strokes *ti* equal, the best pieces are those which consist of a single class of notes moving in leaps; these notes may be quavers or semiquavers, either in common time or, as in gigues, in six-eight or twelve-eight time.

§ 7

For the tongue-stroke with *tiri*, on the other hand, dotted notes are more suitable than those of equal value, as the examples in the second section of Chapter VI show. Hence pieces [with dotted notes] in both

[1] In Quantz's view D sharp major and A sharp major existed independently of E flat major and B flat major.

[2] In other words, the beginner is not as conscious of the particular difficulties involved as the practised performer.

duple and triple time, and also gigues and canaries, should be used for practice.

§ 8

If the beginner has acquired some facility in the use of his fingers and in reading notes, he can then devote himself more fully to the double tongue with *did'll*; this he can perfect by playing some longer and more difficult passage-work in accordance with the rules given previously. At the beginning he must select, from solos and concertos, easy passages that move more by step than by leap, playing them slowly at first, and then more and more quickly, so that the action of the tongue and fingers coincide.

§ 9

In order to avoid the natural inclination of the tongue to anticipate the fingers, the notes on which the *di* of the double tongue falls must always be held slightly, and stressed (see Chapter VI, Section III, §§ 5 and 15). Thus in common time the following notes are stressed: the first of four semiquavers, the first note of three in triplets, and first of eight in demi-semiquavers; in alla breve, the first of four quavers; and in triple time, the first note on the downbeat, whether the notes are quavers or semiquavers. This not only helps to regulate the tongue, but also serves to accustom one not to rush, a great defect in playing which often keeps the principal notes of the melody from coinciding as they should with the bass notes set to them, and, as is easy to perceive, produces a very disagreeable effect.

§ 10

To develop the necessary facility with his tongue and fingers, the beginner must for a considerable time play only pieces that consist entirely of difficult passages in leaps and runs, in both minor and major keys. Shakes he must practice daily in all keys, in order to make each finger fluent. If he neglects these two matters, he will never be able to play an Adagio accurately and in tune. For even greater quickness is required for the little graces than for the passages.

§ 11

No beginner should be advised to meddle prematurely with *galant* pieces, or with the Adagio. Some few amateurs of music understand this, but the majority want to begin where others end, that is, with concertos and solos in which the Adagio is embellished with many graces that they have not yet grasped. Indeed they consider the best masters to be those who are most prodigal in this respect. In consequence, however, they go backwards rather than forwards, and after having martyred themselves for many years must begin anew, that is to say, must begin to learn fundamental principles. If initially they had had the necessary patience for this science,[1] they would have advanced further in two years than they actually have in many.

§ 12

It is also unfortunate if a beginner wishes to be heard in public before he has acquired the necessary sureness in time and in reading notes. For as a result of the fear born of his incertitude, he will form many bad habits from which he cannot easily free himself.

§ 13

After the beginner has exercised his tongue, fingers, and sense of time for a considerable period in the manner described above, let him take up pieces which are more melodious than those mentioned above, and in which both appoggiaturas and shakes may be introduced, so that he may learn to play an air in a cantabile and *nourrissant* manner,[2] that is, with the melody sustained. French pieces, or those composed in this style, are much more advantageous in this respect than Italian ones. For pieces in the French style are for the most part *pièces caractérisées*,[3] and are composed with appoggiaturas and shakes[4] in such a fashion that almost nothing may be added to what the composer has already written. In music after the Italian style, however, much is left to the caprice, and to the ability, of the performer. In this regard the performance of French music is also more slavish[5] and difficult than that of Italian music as it is written today, since, with the exception of the passage-work, the plain airs of the former are written out with the graces indicated. A beginner is not to be advised, however, to undertake solos in the Italian style prematurely, before he has achieved an understanding of harmony, if he does not wish to retard his own growth; for although neither the science of thorough-bass nor an insight into composition is required for the performance of French pieces, they are, on the contrary, most necessary for Italian works, particularly for certain passages that are intentionally set very plainly and dryly to give the performer the freedom to vary them several times in accordance with his insight and pleasure, and by this means constantly excite the listeners with new inventions.

§ 14

Thus, in accordance with the instructions given in the previous paragraph, the player should take for practice well-elaborated duets and trios

---

[1] Quantz may mean the science (or art) of music here, or simply skill in introducing embellishments.   [2] Literally, 'nourishingly'.

[3] *Die Stücke . . . sind . . . charakterisiret.* Quantz refers to the various types of French dances. The meaning and derivation of this term are clarified in Chapter XVII, Section VII, § 56.

[4] i.e. with indications of where the embellishments are to be introduced. The graces themselves were not generally written out.

[5] *Sklavischer (plus servile).* 'Permitting or manifesting no freedom of choice or judgement' (Webster).

which contain fugues and are composed by solid masters, and should continue with them for a considerable time. They will improve his ability to read notes and rests and to keep time. For this practice I wish to especially recommend *Telemann's* trios written in the French style, many of which he had already fashioned thirty or more years ago. Unfortunately, they may be difficult to obtain, since they were not engraved. It seems that so-called elaborate music,[1] and fugues in particular, are considered pedantic nowadays among the majority of musicians and amateurs, perhaps because only a few comprehend their value and utility. But anyone eager to learn must not allow himself to be frightened away from them because of this prejudice; he can be assured, on the contrary, that the pains they require will profit him greatly. For no reasonable musician will deny that so-called elaborate music that is good is one of the principal means of developing insight into harmony, and into the science of executing well, and making more beautiful, an air that is natural and good in itself. Through such pieces the player also learns to read at sight, or as we say to play *à livre ouvert*, more quickly than through melodious solos that can be easily memorized, but which make those who use them slaves to memory for a long period. A flautist has much less opportunity to learn to play at sight than other instrumentalists, since, as is well known, the flute is used more for solos and for concertante parts than for ripieno parts. Hence the beginner is to be advised to play along with the ripieno parts in public concerts whenever he has the opportunity to do so.

§ 15

In practising duets, trios, &c., the beginner will find it very helpful to play the first and second parts alternately. By playing the second part he not only learns how best to duplicate, because of the imitations of the first,[2] the execution of his master, but also to avoid accustoming himself to memorizing, which is obstructive to reading. He must constantly direct his ear to those who play with him, particularly to the bass; in this fashion he will be able to learn harmony, time, and purity of intonation so much the more easily. If he neglects this practice, his playing will always remain defective.

§ 16

A beginner will also derive great advantage from familiarizing himself with the different kinds of transpositions in passage-work, in which one bar resembles another.[3] In this fashion he can often anticipate the continuation of the passages for several bars without looking at each individual note, which is not always possible in a very fast tempo.

[1] *Gearbeitete Musik (Musique travaillée)*, i.e. music written in an imitative or contrapuntal style.

[2] i.e. the imitative entries in the music itself.   [3] i.e. sequential passages.

§ 17

After the beginner has practised passage-work and pieces in the elaborate style for a considerable time, has made his tongue and fingers fluent, and has made himself so familiar with that which I have explained thus far that it has become second nature, he can then undertake some solos and concertos in the Italian style; the Adagios in these works must not move too slowly, however, and the Allegros must be set with short and easy passage-work. He should seek to embellish the plain air in the Adagio with appoggiaturas, shakes, and little graces in the manner explained in the two preceding chapters, and should continue in this fashion until he becomes adept in their use, and is able to play an unembellished melody correctly and pleasingly without too many extempore additions. If ornamentation of this kind does not seem sufficient in certain Adagios that are perhaps set very flatly and dryly, I refer him to Chapters XIII and XIV, on extempore variations, and on the manner of playing the Adagio, where he will find fuller instructions.

§ 18

The beginner will acquire a greater perfection in this matter if, together with the flute, he studies at least the science of thorough-bass, if not composition. And if he has the opportunity to study the art of singing, either before or at the same time that he studies the flute, I strongly recommend that he do so. Through it he will acquire good execution in his playing so much the more easily; and the insight that the art of singing provides will give him a particularly great advantage in the reasonable embellishment of an Adagio. Then he will not remain just a simple player of the flute, but will be on the way to becoming, in time, a musician in the true sense.

§ 19

If the beginner is to acquire a general understanding of the differences in taste in music, however, it is not sufficient for him to practise only pieces composed for the flute; he must acquaint himself with the pieces characteristic of different nations and provinces, and learn to play each in the style appropriate to it. In time this will be of greater profit to him than he may at first realize. There is a greater diversity of *pièces caractérisées* in French and German music than in that of the Italians and some other peoples. Italian music is less circumscribed than any other, while the French is almost too much so, which is perhaps why in French music the new so often seems to resemble the old. Yet the manner of *playing*[1] of the French is not to be scorned; on the contrary, the beginner is to be

---

[1] 'Playing' is emphasized here because Quantz had different ideas about French singing. He liked French playing and Italian singing, but disliked French singing and Italian playing. For a fuller exposition of his views on this subject, see Chapter XVIII, §§ 56–77.

advised to use French propriety and clarity to temper the obscurity[1] of the *playing* of the Italians, chiefly caused by their bowing, and by the excessive addition of graces, a matter in which the Italian instrumentalists go too far, and the French in general do not go far enough. By this means his taste will become more universal. For universal good taste is not to be encountered in single nations, as each flatters itself; it must be formed and shaped through the mixture and through the reasonable choice of good ideas and good methods of playing from different nations. Each nation has in its musical idiom[2] something both of the agreeable and pleasing, and of the disagreeable. He who knows how to choose that which is best will not be led astray by that which is common, low, and bad. I will deal with this matter more fully in Chapter XVIII.

§ 20

The beginner must therefore seek also to listen to as many good and generally approved compositions as possible. By this means he will greatly facilitate his path toward good taste in music. He must seek to profit not only from good instrumentalists of every kind, but also from good singers. For that purpose he must first learn to distinguish the different keys; and when, for example, he hears someone play the flute, he must immediately note the principal key of the piece, so that he can determine those that follow more easily. To tell whether he has divined the key, he can occasionally look at the player's fingers. Divining each key in this fashion will become still easier if from time to time he has his master play short passages over for him, so that he may duplicate them without looking at the master's fingers; this exercise he must continue until he can immediately repeat everything he hears. In this way he will be able to imitate the good things he hears from different persons and profit from them. This will be still easier if he already has some understanding of the keyboard and the violin, since few compositions are performed without these instruments.

§ 21

The beginner should collect as many good musical pieces as he can afford, and use them for his daily practice; through them his taste will gradually be formed along good lines, and he will learn to distinguish the bad from the good. The most necessary information about the requisite qualities of each type of piece, if it is to be considered good, is found in Chapter XVIII of this method. For his practice the beginner will also do well to choose only pieces that are suited to his instrument, and which have been fashioned by composers whose merits are generally recognized. He must not pay any attention to whether a piece is quite new or already

---

[1] Quantz seems to use this term to refer to lack of clarity and distinctness.
[2] *Musikalische Denkart* (*pensées de Musique*).

somewhat out of date. Let it suffice him if it is simply good. For every-thing that is new is not necessarily also beautiful. He should especially guard against the pieces of self-taught composers who have not learned composition through either oral or written instruction; for neither con-tinuity of melody nor correct harmony will be found in them. The majority consist of a hodgepodge of borrowed and patched-up ideas. Many of these untutored composers write only the upper part themselves, and make others add the remaining ones. Hence it is easy to deduce that neither an orderly association of ideas nor orderly progression[1] will be observed, and in consequence violence must be done to the other parts at many places. In this respect the pieces of composers who are just beginning also are not to be relied upon. If, however, a composer has learned composition methodically, and from someone who has the ability to instruct others, and if he understands how to compose neatly in four parts, one may have greater confidence in his works.

§ 22

The beginner must particularly endeavour to learn to play everything he undertakes distinctly and roundly, whether rapid passage-work in the Allegro, graces in the Adagio, or notes of some other kind. This means that he must not stumble over the notes, or raise or lower two or three fingers instead of one, thus swallowing up several notes; he must play each note throughout the entire piece in accordance with its true value, and in the correct tempo. In short, he must strive to achieve good execu-tion,[2] a matter that will be dealt with more fully in the following chapters. This good execution is both the most essential and the most difficult element in playing. If it is lacking, a performance will always remain defective, regardless of how artful and astonishing it may appear, and the player will never obtain the approbation of connoisseurs. A beginner must therefore be constantly attentive when he plays, and must take care that he hears each note as he sees it with his eyes, and as its value and expression require. Inner feeling—the singing of the soul—yields a great advantage in this regard. The beginner must therefore seek gradually to arouse this feeling in himself. For if he is not himself moved by what he plays, he cannot hope for any profit from his efforts, and he will never move others through his playing, which should be his real aim. To be sure, this ability cannot be required in any degree of perfection from a beginner, since he must still think too much of his fingers, tongue, and embouchure, and more than a few years are needed to acquire it. Neverthe-less, the beginner must strive in good season to have this aim in view, so that he does not lapse into indifference. In his practice he must always imagine that he has listeners before him who can advance his fortune.

[1] *Modulation (modulation)*, i.e. harmonic progression in a general sense.
[2] *Vortrag (expression)*. On Quantz's use of this term, see Chapter XI, § 1.

§ 23

How much time beginners need to practise each day cannot be fixed exactly. Some grasp a matter more easily than others. Thus each person must settle this question in accordance with his ability and talent. It is possible, however, to go too far as well as not far enough in this regard. If, in order to reach his goal quickly, the beginner plays the entire day, it not only can be harmful to his health, but can exhaust both the tendons of his fingers and his senses prematurely. But if he contents himself with one hour a day, any profit may be slow in coming. I maintain that it is neither too much nor too little if the beginner fixes two hours in the morning for his practice, and an equal number in the afternoon, in addition always resting a little during practice. When one has reached the point where one can produce all the passage-work that may appear truly and distinctly with no trouble, an hour a day is sufficient for independent practice, to keep the tongue, fingers, and embouchure in proper condition. Excessive playing, especially when one has already reached a certain age, weakens the body, blunts the senses, and destroys the desire and appetite to perform a piece with true fervour. The too-constant execution of shakes makes the tendons of the fingers become stiff, just as a knife becomes jagged when one continually sharpens it without occasionally cutting with it. Those who know how to take a moderate course in all these things will enjoy the advantage of playing the flute several more years than would otherwise be possible.

CHAPTER XI

Of Good Execution in General in Singing and Playing

§ 1

Musical execution[1] may be compared with the delivery of an orator. The orator and the musician have, at bottom, the same aim in regard to both the preparation and the final execution of their productions, namely to make themselves masters of the hearts of their listeners, to arouse or still their passions, and to transport them now to this sentiment, now to that. Thus it is advantageous to both, if each has some knowledge of the duties of the other.

§ 2

We know the effect in a discourse of good delivery upon the minds of the listeners; we also know how poor delivery injures the most beautifully written discourse; and we know again that a discourse delivered with the very same words by two different persons will sound much better from one than from the other. The same is true of musical execution: a piece sung or played by two different people may produce two quite different effects.

§ 3

As to delivery, we demand that an orator have an audible, clear, and true voice; that he have distinct and perfectly true pronunciation, not confusing some letters with others, or swallowing them; that he aim at a pleasing variety in voice and language; that he avoid monotony in the discourse, rather allowing the tone of the syllables and words to be heard now loudly, now softly, now quickly, now slowly; and that he raise his voice in words requiring emphasis, subdue it in others. He must express each sentiment with an appropriate vocal inflexion, and in general adapt himself to the place where he speaks, to the listeners before him, and to the content of the discourse he delivers. Thus he must know, for example, how to make the proper distinction between a funeral oration, a panegyric, a jocular discourse, &c. Finally, he must assume a good outward bearing.

[1] *Vortrag* (*expression*). The Dutch translator of the *Versuch*, J. W. Lustig, makes the following remark about Quantz's use of the term: 'the expression musical *execution*, which is often used by the author, deserves to be admitted as a new and concise technical term signifying the *manner of performance*.' See Quantz, *Grondig onderwys van den aardt en de regte behandeling der dwarsfluit* (Amsterdam: A. Olofsen, 1754), unnumbered page in the preface.

§ 4

I shall try to show that all of these things are also required in good musical execution, after I have first said something of the necessity of good execution, and of the faults that disfigure it.

§ 5

The good effect of a piece of music depends almost as much upon the performer as upon the composer himself. The best composition may be marred by poor execution, just as a mediocre composition may be improved and enhanced by good execution. Often you hear a piece sung or played in which the composition is not to be scorned, in which the embellishments in the Adagio accord with the rules of harmony, and in which the passage-work in the Allegro is played rapidly enough; yet it pleases only a few persons. But if someone else plays the same piece, using exactly the same instrument, the very same graces, and showing no greater facility, it may sound much more agreeable. Only the different manners of execution can account for this.

§ 6

Some persons believe that they will appear learned[1] if they crowd an Adagio with many graces, and twist them around in such fashion that all too often hardly one note among ten harmonizes with the bass, and little of the principal air can be perceived. Yet in this they err greatly, and show their lack of true feeling for good taste. They pay as little attention to the rules of composition, which require not only that each dissonance must be well prepared, but also must receive its proper resolution, if it is to preserve its agreeable character; for otherwise it would become and remain a most disagreeable sound. Finally, they are ignorant that there is more art in saying much with little, than little with much. If Adagios of this sort[2] do not please, the execution is once more to blame.

§ 7

Reason teaches that if in speaking we demand something from someone, we must make use of such expressions as the other understands. Now music is nothing but an artificial language through which we seek to acquaint the listener with our *musical*[3] ideas. If we execute these ideas in an obscure and bizarre manner which is incomprehensible to the listener and arouses no feeling, of what use are our perpetual efforts to be thought learned? If we were to demand that all our listeners be connoisseurs and

---

[1] On Quantz's use of this word see the Introduction, § 7. Here it is used in the sense of someone who impresses others through his knowledge.

[2] i.e. with the defects cited at the beginning of this paragraph.

[3] Italicized in the French text.

musical scholars, their number would not be very great; we would have to seek them out, one at a time, among the professional musicians. And from the latter it would be most unwise to hope for many benefits. For they could do no more than acquaint the amateurs with the skill of the performer by their approval. Yet how rare and unlikely is this! The majority are so carried away by passion, and particularly by envy, that they are neither able to perceive the merits of their equals, nor willing to make them known to others. If, on the other hand, every amateur knew as much as the professional should know, there again would be no advantage, since there would be little or no further need of the professional artist. Thus it is most important that the professional musician seek to play each piece distinctly, and with such expression that it becomes intelligible to both the learned and the unlearned, and hence may please them both.

§ 8

Good execution is indispensable not only for those who perform principal parts, but also for those who only wish to be ripienists, and content themselves with accompanying the former. Each in his sphere must observe both general and particular rules. Many people believe that if they are able to play a studied solo, or to read at sight a ripieno part placed before them, without making serious errors, nothing more may be demanded of them. I believe, on the other hand, that it is easier to play a solo extempore[1] than to perform a ripieno part, where the player has less freedom and must join with many others to interpret the piece according to the intention of the composer. If then, you lack good principles in execution, you will never do justice to the piece. For this reason all able music masters, and especially those who are violinists, should see to it that they do not introduce their pupils to solo playing until they are already good ripienists. Good execution of simple ripieno parts prepares the way for playing solos; and many a dully played solo would reach the senses of the listeners more distinctly and agreeably if the performer followed the example set in the art of painting, where you must first learn how to make a good drawing of a picture before you consider the embellishments. Few beginners, however, can bide their time. Eager to be counted among the multitude of virtuosi, they too often begin the wrong way round, namely with solo playing, and martyr themselves with many elaborate ornaments and difficult feats for which they are not yet quite ready, obscuring their execution instead of learning to make it distinct. The masters themselves are often to blame for this, that is, if they plume themselves on their ability to teach their students several solos in a short period. If these students are afterwards used as ripienists, this ability does not always do such teachers much honour. Matters of good execution which ripienists in particular must observe are discussed in detail in Chapter XVII of this method.

[1] *Willkührlich (arbitrairement).* Quantz refers to the practice of performing a solo with the addition of free variations. The procedure is discussed in detail in Chapter XIII.

§ 9

Almost everyone has an individual style of execution. The reason for this is found not only in musical training, but in the particular temperament[1] that distinguishes one person from another. Suppose, for example, that several persons have learned music from a single master at the same time, and from the same basic principles, and that they have played in the same manner for the first three or four years. Later, after they have not heard their master for several years, it will be found that each will adopt a particular execution suitable to his own natural talent, in so far as they do not wish to remain simply copies of their master. And one of these players will always hit upon a better style of execution than the others.

§ 10

We shall now investigate the principal qualities of good execution in general. Good execution must be first of all *true and distinct*.[2] Not only must each note be heard, but each note must be sounded with its true intonation, so that all will be intelligible to the listener. Not one must be left out. You must try to make each sound as beautiful as possible. You must guard with particular care against faulty fingering. The importance of embouchure and tonguing in this respect has been explained earlier. You must avoid slurring notes that ought to be articulated, and articulating those that ought to be slurred. The notes must not seem stuck together. The tonguing on wind instruments, and the bowing on bowed instruments, must always be used in conformity with the aims of the composer, in accordance with his indications of slurs and strokes; this puts life into the notes. [Articulation of this sort] distinguishes these instruments from the bagpipe,[3] which is played without tonguing. The fingers, no matter how smoothly or animatedly they move, cannot convey musical articulation by themselves, if the tongue or the bow does not contribute its greater share, by proper movements suitable to the piece to be performed. Musical ideas that belong together must not be separated; on the other hand, you must separate those ideas in which one musical thought ends and a new idea begins, even if there is no rest or caesura. This is especially true when the final note of the preceding phrase and opening note of the following one are on the same pitch.

---

[1] Quantz's classification of temperaments follows the old division into sanguine, phlegmatic, choleric, and melancholic. Temperament was determined by the 'humours'. See § 17 of this chapter, and Chapter XVI, § 22.

[2] *Rein und deutlich (nette & distincte)*. In the German and French texts the terms *rein* and *nette* nearly always refer to intonation; the same is true of the use of the word 'true' in the present translation. In eighteenth-century English the term 'nice' and the phrase 'to play with nicety' were frequently used in similar situations to refer to intonation.

[3] *Sackpfeife (Cornemuse)*.

§ 11

Good execution must be *rounded* and *complete*.[1] Each note must be expressed with its true value, and in its correct tempo. If this is properly observed, the notes will sound as the composer intended them; for the latter is also bound by rules. Many players are not attentive in this regard. From ignorance, or a corrupt taste, they often give the following note something of the time that belongs to the preceding. Sustained and flattering notes must be slurred to one another, but gay and leaping notes must be detached and separated from one another. The shakes and the little graces must all be completed truly and in a lively manner.

§ 12

Here I must make a necessary observation concerning the length of time each note must be held. You must know how to make a distinction in execution between the *principal notes*, ordinarily called *accented* or in the Italian manner, *good* notes, and those that *pass*, which some foreigners call *bad* notes. Where it is possible, the principal notes always must be emphasized more than the passing. In consequence of this rule, the quickest notes in every piece of *moderate tempo*, or even in the *Adagio*, though they seem to have the same value, must be played a little unequally, so that the stressed notes of each figure, namely the first, third, fifth, and seventh, are held slightly longer than the passing, namely the second, fourth, sixth, and eighth, although this lengthening must not be as much as if the notes were dotted. Among these quickest notes I include the crotchet in three-two time, the quaver in three-four and the semiquaver in three-eight time, the quaver in alla breve, and the semiquaver or demisemiquaver in two-four or common duple time: but these are included only as long as no figures of still more rapid notes, or doubly quick ones, are intermingled in each metre, for then the latter must be executed in the manner described above. For example, if the eight semiquavers beneath the letters (*k*), (*m*), and (*n*) in Tab. IX, Fig. 1 are played slowly with the same value, they will not sound as pleasing as if the first and third of four are heard a little longer, and with a stronger tone, than the second and fourth.

TABLE IX

FIG. 1

Excepted from the rule, however, is first, quick passage-work in a very fast tempo in which the time does not permit unequal execution, and in which

---

[1] *Rund und vollständig (ronde & complete).*

length and strength must therefore be applied only to the first of every four notes. Also excepted is all quick passage-work which must be executed by the human voice, unless it is supposed to be slurred. Since every note of passage-work of this kind for the voice must be performed distinctly and stressed by a gentle breath of air from the chest, there can be no inequality in them. Further excepted are the notes above which strokes or dots are found. The same exception must be made when several notes follow one another upon the same pitch; or when there is a slur above more than two notes, that is, above four, six, or eight; and finally with regard to quavers in gigues. All of these notes must be executed equally, that is, one as long as the other.[1]

§ 13

Execution also must be *easy and flowing*.[2] No matter how difficult the notes performed may be, this difficulty must not be apparent in their performer. Everything of a coarse, forced disposition in singing and playing must be avoided with great care. You must guard against all grimaces and, as much as possible, try to preserve in yourself a constant composure.

§ 14

No less must good execution be *varied*.[3] Light and shadow must be constantly maintained. No listener will be particularly moved by someone who always produces the notes with the same force or weakness and, so to speak, plays always in the same colour, or by someone who does not know how to raise or moderate the tone at the proper time. Thus a continual alternation of the Forte and Piano must be observed. Since this is a matter of great importance, I will show, by examples at the end of Chapter XIV, how you must proceed note by note.

§ 15

Finally, good execution must be *expressive, and appropriate to each passion that one encounters*.[4] In the Allegro, and in all the gay pieces of this type, liveliness must rule, but in the Adagio, and pieces of this character, delicacy must prevail, and the notes must be drawn out or sustained in an agreeable manner.[5] The performer of a piece must seek to enter into

---

[1] The practice of slightly lengthening certain notes described in this paragraph is probably related to the French practice of *notes inégales*. For French discussions of the subject, see Hotteterre, *L'Art de preluder sur la flûte traversiere* (Paris: pub. by the author, 1719), pp. 57–61, and Corrette, *Methode*, pp. 4–6. The latter and a number of other useful passages are quoted in Donington, *Interpretation*, pp. 452–63 and 665–70. See also Sol Babitz, 'A Problem of Rhythm in Baroque Music', *The Musical Quarterly*, xxxviii (1952), pp. 533–65.

[2] *Leicht und fließend (aisée & coulante).*   [3] *Mannigfaltig (diversifiée).*

[4] *Ausdrückend, und jeder vorkommenden Leidenschaft gemäß seyn (expressive & convenable à chaque passion qui se rencontre).*

[5] *Muß . . . ein angenehmes Ziehen oder Tragen der Stimme herrschen (que les tons soient traités & portés d'une maniére agréable).*

the principal and related passions that he is to express. And since in the majority of pieces one passion constantly alternates with another, the performer must know how to judge the nature of the passion that each idea contains, and constantly make his execution conform to it.[1] Only in this manner will he do justice to the intentions of the composer, and to the ideas that he had in mind when he wrote the piece. There are even various degrees of liveliness and melancholy. For example, where a furious emotion prevails, the execution must have much more fire than in jocular pieces, although it must be lively in both; and the situation is the same in the opposite kind of music. The addition of the embellishments with which you seek to adorn, and to further enhance, the prescribed air or plain melody must also be adjusted accordingly. These embellishments, whether essential or extempore, must never contradict the prevailing sentiments in the principal melody; and thus the sustained and drawn-out melody must not be confused with the playful, pleasing, half-gay, and lively one, the bold with the flattering, &c. The appoggiaturas connect the melody and augment the harmony; the shakes and the other little embellishments such as half-shakes, mordents, turns, and *battemens* enliven it. The alternation of Piano and Forte heightens some notes at one time, at another arouses tenderness. Flattering[2] passages in the Adagio must not be attacked too rudely with the stroke of the tongue and bow, and on the other hand joyful and distinguished ideas in the Allegro must not be dragged, slurred, or attacked too gently.

§ 16

I will now indicate some particular features by which, taken together, you can usually, if not always, perceive the dominant sentiment of a piece, and in consequence how it should be performed, that is, whether it must be flattering, melancholy, tender, gay, bold, serious, &c. This may be determined by (1) whether the key is major or minor. Generally a major key is used for the expression of what is gay, bold, serious, and sublime, and a minor one for the expression of the flattering, melancholy, and tender (see § 6 of Chapter XIV). This rule has its exceptions, however; thus you must also consider the following characteristics. The passion may be discerned by (2) whether the intervals between the notes are great or small, and whether the notes themselves ought to be slurred or articulated. Flattery, melancholy, and tenderness are expressed by slurred and close intervals, gaiety and boldness by brief articulated notes, or those forming distant leaps, as well as by figures in which dots appear regularly after the second note.[3] Dotted and sustained notes express the serious and the pathetic;

[1] Those imbued with the notion that Baroque compositions are limited to the expression of one passion or sentiment in any given movement might well note this passage.
[2] Quantz explains the musical expression of 'flattery' and other sentiments in the following paragraph.
[3] i.e. figures with the rhythm of the Lombardian snap:

long notes, such as semibreves or minims, intermingled with quick ones express the majestic and sublime. (3) The passions may be perceived from the dissonances. These are not all the same; they always produce a variety of different effects. I have explained this matter at length, and have illustrated it with an example, in Section VI of Chapter XVII. Since this knowledge is indispensable not only to accompanists, but to all performers, I wish to draw special attention to § 13 and those that follow to § 17 of the section mentioned. (4) The fourth indication of the dominant sentiment is the word found at the beginning of each piece,[1] such as Allegro, Allegro non tanto, — assai, — di molto, — moderato, Presto, Allegretto, Andante, Andantino, Arioso, Cantabile, Spiritoso, Affettuoso, Grave, Adagio, Adagio assai, Lento, Mesto, and so forth. Each of these words, if carefully prescribed, requires a particular execution in performance. In addition, as I have said above, each piece which has the character of one of those mentioned previously may have in it diverse mixtures of pathetic, flattering, gay, majestic, or jocular ideas. Hence you must, so to speak, adopt a different sentiment at each bar, so that you can imagine yourself now melancholy, now gay, now serious, &c. Such dissembling is most necessary in music. He who can truly fathom this art is not likely to be wanting in approval from his listeners, and his execution will always be *moving*. One should not imagine, however, that this fine discrimination can be acquired in a short time. It can hardly be demanded at all from young people, who in this respect are usually too hasty and impatient. It comes only with the growth of feeling and judgement.

§ 17

In this respect each person must also regulate himself in accordance with his innate temperament, and know how to govern it properly. A rash and hot-tempered person, especially inclined to the majestic and serious, and to immoderate quickness,[2] must try to moderate his fire in the Adagio. On the other hand, a melancholy and dejected person, if he is to play an Allegro in a lively manner, would do well to try to assume some of the surplus fire of the former. And if a merry or sanguine person knows how to procure for himself a reasonable mixture of the temperaments of the former two, and does not allow himself to be deterred from the necessary exertion by his *amour propre* and complacency, he will make the greatest progress in good execution, and in music in general. But those who have from birth that happy mixture of the humours which includes something

[1] Many so-called tempo markings in Quantz's day had stronger connotations of emotional character than they have at the present time. See the passages quoted in Donington, *Interpretation*, pp. 386–90.

[2] In referring to 'the majestic and serious, and to immoderate quickness', Quantz here may be indicating two particular traits that are more or less independent. Elsewhere, however, 'majesty' and 'quickness' are frequently associated in the same phrase. Majesty in Quantz's thinking did not necessarily connote slowness. In most cases, the opposite would seem to be the case.

of the qualities of all the persons described above, have all of the advantages that could possibly be hoped for in music; for that which is inborn is always better and more permanent than that which is assumed.

§ 18

I have stated above that melodies must be enriched and heightened by the addition of graces. Care must be taken, however, that the air is not overburdened or crushed by them. The all too colourful performance, like the all too plain, may in the end become offensive to the ear. Hence both the extempore embellishments and the essential graces must be used sparingly, and not too extravagantly. Observance of this rule is particularly important in very quick passages, where the time does not permit many additions, if they are not to become indistinct and distasteful. Some singers for whom the shake is easy, even if it is not of the best quality, are badly addicted to this fault of over-abundant shakes.

§ 19

Each instrumentalist must strive to execute that which is cantabile as a good singer executes it. The singer, on the other hand, must try in lively pieces to achieve the fire of good instrumentalists, as much as the voice is capable of it.

§ 20

These, then, are the universal rules of good execution in singing and playing in general. I will next apply them separately to the principal kinds of pieces. From them proceed the following three chapters, on the Allegro, on extempore variations, and on the Adagio. Much of Chapter XVII, on the duties of accompanists, also relates to this one. I shall illustrate all with examples, and shall explain these examples as fully as possible.

§ 21

Poor execution is the opposite of that which is required for good execution. I will sum up its principal characteristics here, so that you may more easily survey them all together, and in consequence may avoid them with greater care. Execution is poor, if the intonation is untrue and the tone is forced; if the notes are executed indistinctly, obscurely, unintelligibly, without articulation, feebly, sluggishly, tediously, sleepily, coarsely, and dryly; if all the notes are slurred or attacked indiscriminately; if tempo is not observed, and the notes do not receive their true value. It is poor if the graces in the Adagio are too protracted, and do not accord with the harmony; if the graces are poorly concluded, or rushed, or if the dissonances are neither properly prepared nor so resolved; if the passage-work is not performed roundly and distinctly, rather than heavily, anxiously, tediously, or precipitately and blunderingly, and if it is accompanied by all sorts of grimaces. Execution is poor, if everything is sung without warmth or played on the same level, with no alternation of Piano and Forte; if you contradict the passions that should be expressed, or in general execute everything without feeling, without sentiment, and without being moved yourself, so that you have the aspect of having to sing or play in commission for someone else. The listener who hears a piece thus poorly rendered is more apt to be overcome with drowsiness than sustained and diverted, and will be glad when it is over.

CHAPTER XII

Of the Manner of Playing the Allegro

§ 1

The word *Allegro*, used in opposition to *Adagio*, has a very broad meaning in the designation of musical pieces, and in this sense applies to many kinds of quick pieces, such as the Allegro, Allegro assai, Allegro di molto, Allegro non presto, Allegro ma non tanto, Allegro moderato, Vivace, Allegretto, Presto, Prestissimo, &c. We take it in this broad sense here, and understand by it all kinds of lively and quick works. We do not concern ourselves here with its special sense when it characterizes an individual kind of rapid movement.

§ 2

Since, however, the above epithets are often used by many composers more out of habit than to accurately characterize the matter itself, and to make the tempo clear[1] to the performer, cases may occur in which they are not at all times binding, and the intention of the composer must be discovered instead from the content of the piece.

§ 3

The principal character of the Allegro is one of gaiety and liveliness, just as that of the Adagio, on the contrary, is one of tenderness and melancholy.

§ 4

In the Allegro the quick passage-work must be played above all roundly, correctly, and distinctly, and with liveliness and articulation. The liveliness of the tonguing, and the action of the chest and lips are of considerable help in this regard on wind instruments, and on bowed instruments, the bow-stroke. On the flute the tongue must tip firmly at one time, gently at another, as the species[2] of notes require; and the movements of the tongue and fingers must always be simultaneous, so that several notes are not omitted here and there in the passages. Thus all the fingers must be raised equally and not too high.

[1] French text: 'to characterize the true movement of pieces'.
[2] That is, quavers, semiquavers, and so forth. For a fuller discussion of articulation on the flute, see Chapter VI.

§ 5

Pains must be taken to play each note with its proper value, and to avoid carefully either hurrying or dragging. To this end, the player should keep the tempo in mind at each crotchet, and should not believe it sufficient to be in accord with the other parts only at the beginning and end of the bar. Hurrying of passage-work may occur, particularly in ascending notes, if the fingers are raised too quickly. To avoid this, the first note of quick figures must be stressed and held slightly (see Chapter X, § 9), especially since the principal notes should always be heard a little longer than the passing ones. To this end, the principal notes which form the fundamental melody may also be stressed from time to time through chest action. As to which notes must be played unequally, I refer you to § 12 of the previous chapter.

§ 6

The defect of hurrying also frequently results from inattentiveness to the tongue-stroke. Some imagine that the stroke occurs at the exact moment when the tongue is placed against the palate. Thus they raise their fingers with the movement of the tongue. But this is false; for in this fashion the fingers anticipate the tongue. The movement of the fingers must take place with the withdrawal of the tongue that produces the tone.

§ 7

Particular care must be taken not to hurry slow and singing notes[1] interspersed in the passage-work.

§ 8

No attempt ought to be made to play the Allegro more quickly than the passage-work can be played with uniform quickness, lest you be forced to play some passages, perhaps more difficult than others, more slowly, which causes a disagreeable alteration of the tempo. Thus the tempo must be set in accordance with the most difficult passage-work.[2]

§ 9

If in an Allegro passage-work in semiquavers or demisemiquavers is interspersed with quaver or semiquaver triplets, you must regulate your speed by the passage-work rather than by the triplets; for otherwise you will find yourself short of time, since sixteen equal notes in one measure require more time than four triplets. Hence the latter must be moderated.

---

[1] i.e. phrases with slower time-values performed in a cantabile style, and frequently slurred.

[2] This statement should be kept in mind when reading Quantz's discussion of tempo in Chapter XVII, Section VII, §§ 45–59. His recommendations for various tempos are not intended to be categorical rules.

§ 10

You must take care to make the triplets quite round and equal, and must not hurry the first two notes in them, lest they sound as though they have yet another crook; for in this fashion they would no longer remain triplets.[1] Thus the first note of a triplet, since it is a principal note in the chord, may be held slightly, so that the tempo is not forced, and the execution in consequence distorted.

§ 11

Notwithstanding all the liveliness required in the Allegro, you must never lose your composure. For everything that is hurriedly played causes your listeners anxiety rather than satisfaction. Your principal goal must always be the expression of the sentiment, not quick playing. With skill a musical machine[2] could be constructed that would play certain pieces with a quickness and exactitude so remarkable that no human being could equal it either with his fingers or with his tongue. Indeed it would excite astonishment,[3] but it would never move you; and having heard it several times, and understood its construction, you would even cease to be astonished. Accordingly, those who wish to maintain their superiority over the machine, and wish to touch people, must play each piece with its proper fire; but they must also avoid immoderate haste, if the piece is not to lose all its agreeableness.

§ 12

Care must be taken not to begin prematurely the notes following short rests that occur in the place of the principal notes on the downbeat. For example, if there is a rest in the place of the first of four semiquavers, you must wait half as long again as the rest appears to last, since the following note must be shorter than the first one. The proportion is the same in demisemiquavers.[4]

§ 13

You must take breath always at the proper time, and learn how to use it economically, so that you do not disjoin a connected air by untimely breathing.

---

[1] In other words ♩♩♩ should not be performed ♫♩

[2] See Quantz's reference to the *fluteur automate* in Chapter IV, § 14.

[3] *Verwunderung* may mean either 'astonishment' or 'admiration'. Here it probably has a bit of both meanings.

[4] The rule stated in this paragraph grows out of Quantz's earlier rules about the length of accented notes and passing notes. See Chapter XI, § 12.

§ 14

In gay musical ideas the shakes must be played happily and quickly. And if in the passage-work several notes descend by step, and time permits, half-shakes may be introduced from time to time on the first or third notes; if the notes ascend, *battemens* may be employed. Both impart greater liveliness and shimmer to the passage-work. Yet you must not abuse them if you would not cause distaste (see Chapter VIII, § 19).

§ 15

How appoggiaturas ought to be distinguished from the notes that precede them has already been explained in Chapter VI, Section I, § 8.

§ 16

In passage-work where the principal notes ascend and the passing descend,[1] the former must be slightly held and stressed, and must be sounded with more force than the latter, since the melody lies in the former. The latter, on the other hand, may be slurred gently to the former.

§ 17

The deeper the leaps made in passage-work, the more strongly the low notes must be executed, partly because they are principal notes in the harmony, partly because the low notes on the flute are not as cutting and penetrating as the high ones.

§ 18

Long notes must be sustained in an elevated manner by swelling and diminishing the strength of the tone, but the succeeding quick notes must be set off from them by a gay execution.

§ 19

If a long note unexpectedly follows several quick ones, interrupting the air, it must be stressed with particular emphasis. In the ensuing notes the strength of the tone may be somewhat moderated again.

§ 20

If, however, after quick notes several slow singing ones follow, the player's fire must be moderated immediately, and the slow notes executed with the requisite sentiment, so that they do not become boring.

[1] A mistake appears here in the German text, where the word 'ascend' is repeated. It is corrected in the French translation.

§ 21

Slurred notes must be played as they are indicated, since a particular expression is often sought through them. On the other hand, those that require tonguing also must not be slurred.

§ 22

If in an Allegro assai semiquavers are the quickest notes, the quavers must be tipped briefly[1] for the most part, while the crotchets must be played in a singing and sustained manner.* But in an Allegretto where semidemiquaver triplets occur, the semiquavers must be tipped briefly, and the quavers played in a singing fashion.

* When we speak of tipping short notes, such as quavers and semiquavers, the hard tongue-stroke with *ti* is always understood on the flute. But in slow singing notes the tongue-stroke with *di* is understood, which I would have you remember once and for all.

§ 23

If in an Allegro the principal subject (*thema*)[2] frequently recurs it must always be clearly differentiated in its execution from the auxiliary ideas. Whether majestic or flattering, gay or bold,[3] the subject can always be made sensible to the ear in a different manner by the liveliness or moderation of the movements of the tongue, chest, and lips, and also by the Piano and Forte. In repetitions generally, the alternation of Piano and Forte does good service.

§ 24

The passions change frequently in the Allegro just as in the Adagio. The performer must therefore seek to transport himself into each of these passions, and to express it suitably. Hence it is necessary to investigate whether the piece to be played consists entirely of gay ideas, or whether these are joined to others of a different kind. In the first case, constant liveliness must be maintained in the piece. In the second, however, the foregoing rule holds good. *Gaiety*[4] is represented with short notes—quavers, semiquavers, or, in alla breve time, crotchets, according to the requirements of the metre—which move both by leap and step; it is expressed by lively tonguing. *Majesty*[5] is represented both with long notes during which the other parts have quick motion, and with dotted notes. The dotted notes must be attacked sharply, and must be executed in a lively fashion. The dots are held long, and the following notes are made very short (see Chapter V, §§ 21 and 22). Shakes also may be introduced from time to time during the dots. *Boldness*[6] is represented with notes the second

[1] The notes must be articulated in a semi-staccato manner. [2] *Hauptsatz (sujet)*.
[3] On the musical implications of these words, see the following paragraph.
[4] *Das Lustige (le gai)*. [5] *Das Prächtige (le majestueux)*. [6] *Das Freche (le hardi)*. ◄

or third of which is dotted, and, in consequence, in which the first is pre-cipitated.[1] Here you must take care not to hurry too greatly, lest the effect be that of common dance music. In a concertante part the sentiment can be moderated somewhat, and made agreeable by discreet execution. *Flattery*[2] is expressed with slurred notes that ascend or descend by step, and also with syncopated notes, in which the first half of the note must be sounded softly, and the second reinforced by chest and lip action.

§ 25

Principal ideas must be clearly distinguished from those interspersed with them; they are, indeed, the best guide to the expression. If there are more gay than majestic or flattering ideas in an Allegro, it must be played happily and quickly for the most part. But if majesty is the character of the principal ideas, in general the piece must be played more seriously. If the principal sentiment is flattery, greater composure must prevail.

§ 26

In the Allegro, as in the Adagio, the plain air must be embellished and made more agreeable by appoggiaturas, and by the other little essential graces, as the passion of the moment demands.[3] The majestic admits few additions, but those that are appropriate must be executed in an elevated style. Flattery requires appoggiaturas, slurred notes, and a tender[4] expres-sion. Gaiety, on the other hand, demands neatly ended shakes, mordents, and a jocular execution.

§ 27

Few extempore variations[5] are allowed in the Allegro, since it is usually composed with melodies and passages of a kind that leave little room for im-provement. But if you still want to make some variations, you must not do so before the repetition; this is most conveniently practicable in a solo where the Allegro consists of two reprises.[6] Beautiful singing ideas, how-ever, which are not likely to become tiresome, and brilliant passages which contain sufficiently agreeable melodies must not be varied; only ideas of the

---

[1] Quantz again refers to the Lombardian snap rhythm: ♪. ♪. or ♫. ♫.

[2] *Das Schmeichelnde (le flatteur)*. 'Flattery' in this sense refers to that which is charming or beguiling.

[3] By 'passion' Quantz means the emotional character of any composition or portion of a composition. The most common passions in quick pieces are described in § 24.

[4] The German term *zärtlich* may also mean 'delicate'.

[5] Quantz refers to the free variations described in Chapter XIII as opposed to the essential graces discussed in Chapter VIII. The latter may be added quite freely in the Allegro. The former are more appropriate in slow pieces.

[6] 'Reprises' here means 'repeated sections'. A large proportion of quick movements in the first half of the eighteenth century consisted of two reprises, that is, were written in the well-known two-part form, both parts of which were repeated.

kind that leave but a slight impression require variations. For the listener is moved not so much by the skill of the performer as by the beauty which he knows how to express with his skill. If, however, through the oversight of the composer, too-frequent repetitions do occur, which could easily arouse displeasure, the performer is in this case justified in improving them through his skill. I say improve, not disfigure. Many believe that to remedy something they need do no more than vary it, although by doing this they often spoil more than they improve.

CHAPTER XIII

Of Extempore Variations[1] on Simple Intervals

§ 1

The difference between a melody set in the Italian style and one set in the French, in so far as this difference extends to the embellishment of the air, has been indicated in passing in Chapter X.[2] There it will be seen that the melodies of those who compose in the Italian style, as opposed to those of French composers, are not written out with all the graces; hence that further additions and improvements are possible. Thus there are other embellishments, depending upon the skill and inclination of the performer, beyond the essential graces explained in Chapters VIII and IX.

§ 2

Almost no one who devotes himself to the study of music, particularly outside France, is content to perform only the essential graces; the majority feel moved to invent variations or extempore embellishments. In itself this inclination is not to be condemned, but it cannot be realized without an understanding of composition, or, at least, of thorough-bass. Since, however, most musicians lack the necessary instruction, progress is slow; and so many incorrect and awkward ideas appear that it would be better in many cases to play the melody as the composer has set it rather than to spoil it repeatedly with such wretched variations.

§ 3

To remedy this abuse somewhat, I shall give some instructions, for those who still lack the requisite knowledge, as to how variations may be made in diverse ways on plain notes in the majority of the most common intervals, without contravening the harmony of the bass.

[1] *Willkührliche Veränderungen* (*changemens ou des variations arbitraires*). These terms are sometimes translated as 'arbitrary variations'. In using the word 'extempore' (four syllables) the present translator has followed the anonymous eighteenth-century translation of Chapters XIII and XV published under the title *Easy and Fundamental Instructions*. . . . Although the more usual adjectival form today is 'extemporary', Fowler still indicates that 'extempore' is to be preferred. The term is used with the meaning 'originated for or at the occasion' (Webster). The essential graces had more or less fixed melodic forms and could be used in nearly all types of compositions. The extempore variations had no fixed melodic form and were created for each composition that the performer felt required them. Different variations also might be introduced in different performances of the same composition. See Chapter VIII, § 1.
[2] See Chapter X, § 13.

§ 4

To this end I have gathered together in a table the most common kinds of intervals, together with the basses appropriate to them (see Table VIII) and above the basses have figured the harmony for them, so that the variations stemming naturally from these numbers or figures will be seen clearly in the following tables, and thus may be transposed easily into all the keys in which you may have to play.

TABLE VIII

§ 5

I do not pretend to have created in these few examples all the variations it is possible to discover on these intervals; I present them only as an introduction for the novice. Those who have advanced to the point where they know how to use these properly will not find it difficult to invent more.

§ 6

Although, to avoid prolixity, these examples have been set for the most part only in major keys, they are also to be used in minor keys; thus it is necessary that you familiarize yourself thoroughly with the key in which you wish to play them, so that you are immediately able to imagine the flats or sharps that must be prefixed in each key, without confusing whole tones with halves or halves with wholes in the transpositions, and hence do not act out of conformity with the proportions[1] of the keys. Close attention also must be paid to the bass, to whether a major or minor third should be present above the fundamental note, and, when the latter has a sixth against the upper part, to whether the sixth is major or minor, which may be seen more fully in Tab. XIII, Fig. 13, and in Tab. XIV, Fig. 14.[2]

The examples in which several figures are enclosed under a single slur require the same variations, since each has the same bass for its foundation. But if the bass is raised with a sharp, the upper part then must be treated in the same way.[3]

You must pay attention to whether the movement of the notes remains at the unison,[4] or whether the intervals make either an ascending or descending second, third, fourth, fifth, sixth, or seventh, as is to be seen from the first bar of each example; for these intervals form the basis of the variations.

§ 7

In general you must always see to it in the variations that the principal notes, on which the variations are made, are not obscured. If variations are introduced on crotchets, usually the first note of the variation must be the same as the plain note; and you proceed in the same fashion with all the other values, whether they are greater or less than a crotchet. To be sure, another note may be chosen from the harmony of the bass, but the principal note must then be heard immediately after it.

§ 8

Gay and bold variations must never be interspersed in a melancholy and modest melody, unless you seek to render them agreeable through your execution, in which case they are not to be condemned.

---

[1] On the term 'proportions', see the Preface to the Translation.

[2] For these illustrations see §§ 26 and 27 of this chapter.

[3] In other words, if the bass part has a sharpened note, the same note must be sharpened in the upper part.

[4] i.e. whether the notes remain on the same pitch.

§ 9

Variations must be undertaken only after the plain air has already been heard; otherwise the listener cannot know if variations are actually present. A well-written melody, which is already sufficiently pleasing in itself, must never be varied, unless you believe it can be improved. If you wish to vary something, you must always do it in such fashion that the addition is still more agreeable in the singing phrases, and still more brilliant in the passage-work, than they stand as written. Not a little insight and experience are required for this. Without an understanding of composition, success is impossible. Those who lack this skill will always do better to prefer the invention of the composer to their own fancies. A long series of quick notes does not always suffice. They may, indeed, excite admiration, but they do not touch the heart as easily as the plain notes, and this, after all, is the true object of music, and the most difficult one. Here also a great abuse has crept in. Therefore my advice is not to give yourself over too much to variations, but rather to apply yourself to playing a plain air nobly, truly, and clearly. If you indulge a passion for variation prematurely, before having acquired some taste in music, your spirit becomes so accustomed to this excess of motley notes, that eventually it can no longer endure a plain air. The same is true of your tongue in this regard. Once having accustomed it to strongly spiced foods, it can no longer taste healthy, simple ones. If a noble, plain air does not touch him who executes it, it can make but a slight impression on his listeners.

§ 10

Although I believe the majority of the examples given that are pertinent here are sufficiently clear to demonstrate the diversity with which the intervals may be varied, I shall give, in addition, a brief explanation of each example after its kind, to make it more useful and understandable for those desirous of instruction.

§ 11

To determine both how they are to be understood, and how they are to be used, study the examples of the variations and the basses belonging to them from the Tables in sequence. In each section the numbers indicate the examples of the plain phrases from the beginning of the Table; these phrases consist of crotchets, and are the notes upon which the variations are to be made. The multiple notes without stems placed above each other indicate the harmony of each note to be varied, and the intervals both above and below each that form the basis of the variations. The notes with upward stems found in the middle of the harmonies are the principal notes of the plain air. The remaining notes, with letters above them, are the

variations proper on the crotchets at the beginning of each example, as
may be seen from what follows.

Notice here that if I cite intervals in the description of the principal notes of the
harmony, I do not reckon them, as in thorough-bass, from the fundamental note,
but count either up or down from the note to be varied in the upper part.

Those who understand nothing at all of harmony and thorough-bass, and must
vary entirely by ear, for whose sake chiefly I am rather prolix here, may familiarize
themselves with the intervals in Figs. 27 and 28 of Tab. XVI,[1] so that they can at
least recognize them at sight. They can recognize them from the distance between
the notes, which stand either on lines or spaces, and from the size of the leaps. From
one space to the next is a third; from the space to the second line, a fourth; to the
third space, a fifth; from the space to the third line, a sixth; to the fourth space, a
seventh; from the space to the fourth line, an octave. To be sure that you remember
this example, it would be well to transpose it a tone higher or lower, since the notes
on the spaces will then be on the lines, and vice versa. In this fashion you can familiarize yourself with each kind of interval. Yet it is always better to learn them through
the study of thorough-bass.[2]

§ 12

TABLE IX

Fig. 1

The unison,[3] as is to be seen here, suffers no other variations than those
that lie in its harmony, if, that is, the bass remains stationary on the funda-

---

[1] See §§ 42 and 43 of this chapter.

[2] For detailed instructions about the dynamic interpretation of the following examples, see
→ Chapter XIV, §§ 26–39.

[3] 'The unison' here seems to mean repeated notes on the same pitch. The duplication of the
same notes in the bass, however, is also implied.

mental note,[1] or descends by step. But if the bass has melodic notes that ascend or descend either by leap or step in quavers or semiquavers, only (*a*), (*h*), (*s*), (*t*), and (*u*) of these variations may be used, if you do not wish to produce discordant sounds.

§ 13

FIG. 2

Of these three notes, which ascend from the fundamental note, C, through the second, D, into the third, E, the first has in its harmony the third and fifth above it, and the fourth and sixth (which are simply a reiteration of the third and fifth) below it. And since the chord consists of three notes, that is, the fundamental note and the third and fifth above it, the notes in it may be reiterated in either the upper or the lower octave, a rule which I would have you remember once and for all. The second note, D, has the third and fifth (which fifth is the fundamental note in the bass) below it, but the fourth and sixth above it. The third note, E (as the third above the bass), has the third and sixth both above and below it; and in this fashion the variations are made, (*n*) showing the upper, and (*z*) the lower intervals of the harmony.[2]

---

[1] 'Fundamental note' usually refers to the root of a triad or seventh chord. To see the harmonic movement of this figure, and of those that follow, the reader should refer back to § 4, where each figure is given with its bass part.

[2] In (*f*) demisemiquavers appear mistakenly instead of hemidemisemiquavers in the original musical examples.

§ 14

FIG. 3

TABLE X

The situation is different in these three descending notes, since they begin on the fifth above the bass, and descend by step to the third; the first note, D, then has the third and fifth (which fifth is the fundamental note in the bass) below it, but the fourth and sixth above it. The second note, C, has the third, diminished fifth, and seventh (which last is the fundamental note of the bass) below it, but the augmented fourth and sixth above it. The third note, B (as third above the bass), has the third and sixth both above and below it; (*v*) in Table X shows the upper, and (*w*) the lower intervals of the harmony.

§ 15

FIG. 4

Although these four notes appear to be similar to the three in Fig. 2, their bass parts distinguish them, since these begin on the third and those in Fig. 2 begin on the fundamental note, so that the first note has the interval of a fourth below it (see (*e*) in Fig. 2); each note of the figure here has a third both above and below it (see (*a*) and (*b*)), which is why the same variations are not acceptable in both. The first note, E, thus has the third and sixth both above and below it in its chord. The second note, F, has the third and diminished fifth below, and the augmented fourth and sixth above it. The third note, G, has the third and fifth below, and the fourth and sixth above it. The fourth note, A, has the third above, and the third, fifth, and sixth below it, since the descending interval from A to B forms a seventh, of which something more will be reported in Fig. 13.

§ 16

FIG. 5

These five descending notes have as little similarity with the three in Fig. 3 as the previous notes in Fig. 4 have with those in Fig. 2. Although the first, A, is the third above the bass note, F, it must be regarded as a sixth from the fundamental note, C, since this phrase is in the key of C, and not in F; otherwise B flat would have to be taken between A and C instead of the passing-note B natural. The first note, A, has the third and sixth both above and below it in its harmony. The second note, G, has the third and fifth below, and the fourth and sixth above it. The third note, F, has the third and diminished fifth below, and the augmented fourth and sixth above it. The fourth note, E, has the third and sixth both above and below it. The fifth note, D, has the third and fifth below, and the fourth and sixth above it; and at (*l*) the proper harmony for each note is to be found expressed in semiquavers.

§ 17

TABLE XI

FIG. 6

These three notes likewise must not be confused with those in Fig. 4. Although both figures begin on the third, and ascend by step, Fig. 4 remains in its natural key, while Fig. 6 modulates to the key of G through the augmented fourth, F sharp.[1] And since the bass remains on the same pitch while the upper part proceeds from the third to the fourth, both the sixth and the second above the bass may be taken, in either the upper or lower octave, in place of the fourth, since they belong to the harmony of the bass, (see (*h*) and (*ll*)). The first note in the bass may have both the pure

---

[1] F sharp is an augmented fourth against the bass note C. See the bass for this example in Tab. VIII, Fig. 6 in § 4 of this chapter.

chord[1] and the fifth and sixth in the harmony above it without disadvantage to the variations; the first note, E, then has the third, fifth, and sixth below it, and the third, fourth, and sixth above it. The second note, F sharp, has the third and sixth above and below it. The third note, G, has the fourth and sixth below, and the third and fifth above it. The two notes, G and A, found in the chord of the first note, E, form a fifth and sixth in thorough-bass, and hence a dissonance which can only be expressed with broken notes on wind instruments (see (*m*) and (*q*)); in (*m*) the second note, G, is the fifth, and the fourth note, A, the sixth above the bass, while in (*q*), on the other hand, the third note is the sixth, and the fourth note the fifth above the bass.

§ 18

Since the augmented fourth (reckoned from the bass) is usually accompanied by the second and sixth, variations like those found on this F sharp may be introduced on all similar occasions, provided that you first look to see whether the bass is longer or shorter than a crotchet. This point governs whether the variations are to be played faster or slower[2] or, where it is possible, whether they are to be repeated. (*c*), (*f*), (*g*), (*l*), (*t*), (*u*), and (*v*) of this figure are suitable for this purpose.

§ 19

For the easy recognition of these three notes, the second, fourth, and sixth of the harmony, it facilitates matters for the beginner to observe that, since they are leaps of thirds, they all stand either on lines or between lines. That which is on a line in the upper register is ordinarily between the lines in the octave below, as may be seen clearly in the notes placed beneath one another. These notes by themselves, without the bass, make a pure chord, but with the bass they form a dissonance, since the bass stands a tone lower than the chord. Therefore the bass must be resolved downwards, and the upper part upwards.

§ 20

Fig. 7

---

[1] That is, a plain triad.
[2] That is, whether the values of the notes are shorter or longer.

Of these two notes, the first, E, has the third and sixth both above and below it. The second note, D, has the third and fifth below, and the fourth and sixth above it; and the variation of the first note can be expressed with broken notes as is illustrated in (*c*) and (*e*). If the harmony remains on the E longer than the value of a crotchet, the variations may be made more slowly, or also repeated, as you prefer. If the former is necessary, you need only imagine that the notes have one less crook.[1] (*a*), (*b*), (*c*), (*e*), (*f*), (*g*), (*h*), (*i*), (*k*), (*l*), (*ll*), (*m*), (*n*), (*o*), and (*u*) may be repeated.[2]

§ 21

TABLE XII

FIG. 8

---

[1] That is, the player must imagine the semiquavers to be quavers, the demisemiquavers to be semiquavers, and so forth.

[2] The opening crotchet rest at the beginning of (*g*) was inadvertently omitted in the original musical examples.

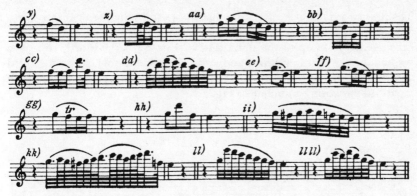

Although the leaps which in this example are enclosed beneath a single slur consist of three different intervals, the fifth, seventh, and octave, they all have the same bass notes underlying them, and thus, as the multiple notes above one another indicate, also have the same harmony, with the exception of the leap of the seventh which, in concluding a grace, must be heard distinctly before the resolution to the third, in order to distinguish it from the octave leap. With this exception, the variations found here may be used interchangeably for the different intervals. For the sake of order I have appended six variations for each example, those in (*a*), (*b*), (*c*), (*d*), (*e*), and (*f*) belonging to the leap of the fifth, those in (*g*), (*h*), (*i*), (*k*), (*l*), and (*ll*) to the seventh, and those in (*m*), (*n*), (*o*), (*p*), (*q*), and (*r*) to the octave. Should there be a rest in place of the first note, G, in these three examples, the second note of each, D, F, or G, still retains the same chord; the variations on the note replaced by the rest can then be omitted, and those belonging to the second crotchet used, in accordance with the nature of the interval, in the following manner: those in (*s*), (*t*), (*u*), (*v*), (*w*), and (*x*) on D to E, those in (*y*), (*z*), (*aa*), (*bb*), (*cc*), and (*dd*) on F to E, and those in (*ee*), (*ff*), (*gg*), (*hh*), (*ii*), and (*kk*) on G to E.

§ 22

FIG. 9

The first two notes have the same harmony, since the bass beneath them remains on the same pitch, and the movement of the upper part is from the fundamental note up to the third. The first note has the fourth and sixth below, and the third and fifth above it. The second note, E, as the third above the bass, has the third and sixth both above and below it, and with regard to variations is similar to Fig. 7.

§ 23

TABLE XIII

FIG. 10

The first two of these notes, lying in the key of F, also have the same bass, and since the first is the fifth above the bass, it has the third and fifth below, and the fourth and sixth above it. The second note has the fourth and sixth below, and the third and fifth above it. The third note, as the third above C, has the third and sixth both below and above it.

§ 24

FIG. 11

In these three notes the situation is different, since the first interval ascends a fifth, and the second descends a third. And since the first proceeds from the fundamental note, both notes cannot have the same bass;

ordinarily the second note, G, which makes a leap of a third back to E, must be the sixth above the bass, and the following note, E, the third above the bass. It can be seen from the chords that the C has the fourth and sixth below, and the third and fifth above it; the G, the fourth and sixth below, and the third and fifth above it; and the E, the third and sixth both above and below it. If there is a rest in place of the first note, the last two notes, G and E, are of the same nature as those in the third example in Fig. 8, and admit the same variations.

§ 25

FIG. 12

The first of these two notes, which form a descending leap of a sixth, is the fifth above the bass, and thus has in its chord the third and fifth below it, and the fourth and sixth above it. The second note, as the third above the bass, has the third and sixth both above and below it. Wherever the first note in these intervals is on a space, the principal notes belonging to it also occur on spaces, and vice versa (see (*b*)). If you wish to fill out this interval with several notes, those on the lines, that is, F and D, are used as passing notes (see (*c*)). If you wish to fill it out with two triplets, the two types in (*i*) and (*n*) may serve as examples.

§ 26

FIG. 13

For these notes, A–B, which leap a seventh downwards, the bass ordinarily has the third, usually figured with the fifth and sixth, as is to be seen in Table VIII.[1] The two notes form thirds against the fundamental notes, the first having in its chord the third above, and the third, fifth, sixth, and octave below it, the second having the third and sixth both above and below it. You must remember, however, that the bass note is frequently raised by a sharp, to which the upper part must be regulated, so as not to mix F with F sharp, which would occasion an offensive sound. Use the two variations in (*m*) and (*n*) as models, since the one has an F and the other an F sharp in it. If the notes in this interval stand either on lines or on spaces, those belonging to the chord (as in Fig. 12) likewise fall on lines or spaces, depending on the position of the first note (see (*a*) and (*c*)). Six notes proceeding by step may be used to fill out this interval (see (*k*)); two triplets also may be used (see (*ll*)), or demisemiquavers proceeding either by step (see (*f*) and (*g*)), or in leaps of thirds (see (*i*)).

§ 27

TABLE XIV

FIG. 14

With respect to the interval, this example is the same as Fig. 13, except that the latter is in the major mode, and this one is in the minor. And since the bass is the same for the first two intervals, they may also have the same variations. In the third of these three intervals, where the bass is raised by a sharp (see (*t*)), and the upper part consequently becomes a minor instead of a major sixth, the G must be changed into G sharp, and the B flat into B natural (see (*u*)). To acquaint yourself thoroughly with this interval, which occurs very frequently before caesuras, take the present and preceding

---

[1] See § 4 above.

examples as models. If, that is, two such notes forming a downward leap of a third stand on lines, the principal notes of the graces likewise occur on lines, and if they stand on spaces, the principal notes occur on the same also. The bass of the first note ordinarily has a sixth in its harmony. If it is a major sixth, and the bass ascends a whole tone, a minor third is used above the upper part, and you may go still another third higher to make a grace, thus forming a fifth from the first note. This fifth is a third above the bass, and, if the third is minor, the fifth must be diminished (see (*m*)). But if the minor sixth is present in the harmony, and the bass is raised by a sharp, as in this example, and ascends only a semitone, the diminished fifth mentioned likewise must be raised and changed into a perfect fifth (see (*u*)).[1] These differences occur only in minor keys. In major keys the major third and perfect fifth are always used for the embellishment of the note in the upper part.

§ 28

FIG. 15

In ligatures,[2] or suspensions, where the seventh is suspended against the bass and resolved either to the sixth or third—to which is immaterial with regard to the upper part—the first progression after the tied note generally may be made by the leap of a fourth upward, which is the third above the bass; and you may do this twice, but the third time the sixth must be taken instead of the fourth (see (*a*)). The lower seventh or fifth

---

[1] In the German and French texts (*n*) is mistakenly indicated instead of (*u*).
[2] i.e. 'tied notes' or 'suspensions'.

also may be taken instead of the fourth (see (*e*) and (*k*)); and the more frequently these intervals are used in alternation, from above or below, the more pleasing it is to the ear. If you wish, the intermediate space between the simple intervals of the graces also may be filled out with notes. The other variations may be introduced arbitrarily.

§ 29

FIG. 16

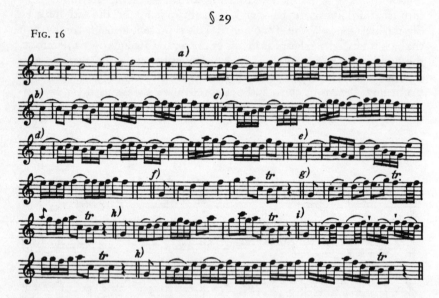

Without some addition, this phrase, in which the fifth and sixth[1] alternate would eventually become distasteful to the ear. The examples from (*a*) to (*e*) may serve as models for variations. You will see at the same time that subsequent variations must not be always of the same sort. This is particularly important in the repetition of the same ideas, in which you must add or omit something the second time the ideas appear. If, for example, the two measures in (*f*) were to be repeated, and were played a second time just as they are written, the listener would be less satisfied than if you were to choose one of the following variations under (*g*), (*h*), (*i*), or (*k*) instead of the plain air. For if the *thema* or principal subject is lengthened by transposition,[2] you must not continue the variations with a single species of notes; you must soon change and in the continuation try to create variations that are different from the preceding ones. The ear is not satisfied by what it has anticipated, but wishes to be continually deceived.

[1] Quantz refers to the fifth and sixth above the bass. See § 4.
[2] i.e. by sequential extensions.

§ 30

TABLE XV

FIG. 17

If in a slow tempo several short notes ascend or descend by step but do not appear to be cantabile enough on certain occasions, a little note may be added after the first and third notes, to make the melody more agreeable (see (*a*) and (*c*)). With the additions they must be expressed as is to be seen in (*b*) and (*d*). Fig. 17 (*e*) and (*f*) are variations on this phrase. The situation is the same with descending notes, and those in (*g*) and (*i*) must be played as in (*h*) and (*k*). Fig. 17 (*l*), (*ll*), and (*m*) are variations on these falling notes.

§ 31

FIG. 18

If notes like these consist of falling (see (*a*)) or rising leaps of thirds (see (*i*)), a little note, in French called *port de voix*, may be added after each note (see (*b*)) and (*k*)). From (*c*) to (*h*) there are other graces on falling leaps of thirds, from (*l*) to (*p*) on rising leaps of thirds. Whether notes of this kind have greater or lesser value, you can still make use of variations on them such as these, if they are in cantabile style. My concern is only with those intervals that occur most frequently in cantabile pieces. If many of these follow one another and you do not add something to them, the listener will soon be wearied. The two notes in (*q*) are the same as the last two semiquavers in (*a*); thus the variations which belong in the time of the second quaver from (*a*) to (*h*) may be made on them. The two notes in (*r*) have the same relationship with those from (*i*) to (*p*).

§ 32

FIG. 19

If in a slow tempo several triplets ascend or descend by step, so that the third note of one triplet and the first note of the following are either on the same pitch, or the first note of the following triplet is a step higher than the preceding, you may always make an appoggiatura before the first note (see (*a*)). But if many triplets descend in succession, you can always make a half-shake[1] without a termination (in which the finger falls only twice) on the first note of each, and slur the following two notes to it (see (*b*)). If you wish to transform the triplets into quicker notes, imagine those in (*c*) as in six-eight time instead of two-four, and add another note to each quaver, as the semiquavers in (*d*) indicate.[2] Various kinds of triplets can be treated in this manner, as the intervals permit.

§ 33

In notes which do not continually ascend or descend by step, but in which two notes are found on the same pitch, the first in the upbeat, either an appoggiatura (see (*e*)) or (*g*)), or a shake (see (*f*) and (*h*)), may be used on the second note, on the downbeat, with the following note slurred to it. But if some notes descend by step, an appoggiatura may be used before each (see (*i*)), or a shake may be used before those on the downbeat (see (*k*)).

[1] See Chapter VIII, § 14.
[2] Three-eight appears in the original examples, but six-eight was apparently intended.

§ 34

FIG. 20

If the interval of an ascending fourth begins on the upbeat, and occurs in a slow tempo when the bass rests, the variations in (*a*), (*b*), (*c*), (*d*), and (*e*) may be made on it. If the key is minor, semitones may be employed (see (*f*) and (*g*)). If two notes ascend or descend in succession by step in a slow tempo, whether they have a rest or a note of greater value preceding them, or whether the third note, with or without a dot, ascends or descends, you may always place a little note between the two, which, if the notes descend (see (*h*)), comes a step higher,[1] and if they ascend (see (*i*)), comes two steps higher.

§ 35

FIG. 21

In caesuras in a slow tempo, where the air is interrupted by a rest preceded by one (see (*a*)) or two notes (see (*b*)), the latter making a descending leap of a third (it may be a major or minor third, on the upbeat or downbeat), it is to be noted that the single note (see (*a*)), demands both an appoggiatura and a shake. Leaps of thirds are treated in the same fashion (see (*b*)), but you must make the shake without a termination, in its place slurring the note lacking in the third to the shake. This leap of a third must nearly always be viewed as though the little note were present in the middle, as the composers of the present day are for the most part in the habit of writing it, since the third in itself is not sufficiently singing in a slow tempo.

§ 36

If in either the Allegro or the Adagio a slur with a dot occurs above a rest, which is called a *fermata, pausa generalis*, or *ad libitum*, you may strike

---

[1] The note comes a step higher than the preceding note.

a rather long shake if you wish, but it must be without a termination; the notes that follow do not allow it, since they must conclude in a quiet and flattering manner (see (*c*)). Since, however, this is more difficult in practice than it appears to the eye, and since everyone does not have the necessary insight into how it should actually be played in accordance with the rule established a long time ago, I consider it necessary first to indicate it with notes (see (*d*)), and then to explain it with a few remarks. The latter are as follows: take the two little semiquavers before the minim shake with the same quickness as the shake, allow the tone to swell and diminish during the shake, and imagine the time of the shake as four slow quavers. After these have passed, let the finger that has made the shake remain on the hole while diminishing the tone, but for no longer than the time required for the first of the four demisemiquavers, and then make the second of the four demisemiquavers. In the appoggiatura before the third note, give a little emphasis or breath with the chest, and complete the remaining two notes with a diminishing Piano. For the remaining caesuras in (*e*), (*f*), (*g*), and (*h*), which demand only appoggiaturas or shakes for the most part, you may employ the examples that follow in Figs. 22, 23, and 24, on the intervals of the descending third, fourth, and fifth, as variations in a slow tempo.

§ 37

FIG. 22

Although these two plain notes, E–C, are crotchets, the variations that follow can also be used on the caesura in (*e*) from Fig. 21, which is in quavers. You need only imagine that the notes of the variations have additional crooks.[1] These variations, with the exception of those in (*a*), (*b*), (*f*), and (*o*), are also acceptable in the caesura in (*f*) from the same example, where the interval descends only a tone; and then the plain note C need only be changed into D. If you also wish to employ the two variations in (*f*) and (*o*), you must take the upper F instead of the last note, D.

---

[1] In other words, imagine the quavers as semiquavers, the semiquavers as demisemiquavers, and so forth. Fig. 21 is found in § 35 of this chapter.

§ 38

TABLE XVI

FIG. 23

These variations may be introduced in the same manner on the caesura in
(*g*), Fig. 21,[1] since the bass note usually remains in the harmony of the
first note, F.

§ 39

FIG. 24

These variations on the leap of a fifth may be used on the caesura at (*h*) in
Fig. 21.[2] If the first two notes of each of these examples, that is, E–C,
F–C, and G–C, are found in succession in a melody, you can seek out the
variations that are of the same sort in each example, and use one after the
other. Since the second note, C, has no variations in these three examples,
the notes of the variations made on the previous note (with the exception
of the first note) may be repeated if necessary. For example, if you wish to
introduce the variation in (*e*) from Fig. 22,[3] where the first notes read
E–G–E, you make a quaver of the crotchet C, and repeat the two semiquavers, G and E.[4] If the same is done in (*e*) from Fig. 23,[5] and if in (*d*)
from Fig. 24 the last three semiquavers before the note C (which likewise

---

[1] See § 35.   [2] See § 35.   [3] See § 37.
[4] Quantz has his time-values wrong here. 'Quaver' should read 'dotted quaver' and 'semiquavers' should read 'demisemiquavers'.
[5] See the preceding paragraph.

becomes a semiquaver) are repeated, the varied air will retain its coherence. All of these variations may be put to use in this manner, provided that you observe the types of notes that go together, and choose from each example the variation you believe most suitable in the place you wish to embellish, and thus, like the bees, gather the honey from different flowers.

§ 40

FIG. 25

Very slow dotted semiquavers may easily become distasteful to the ear, especially if they consist entirely of consonances, such as thirds, fifths, sixths, and octaves. To be sure, consonances set the passions at rest, but at length they become unpleasant if they are not interspersed from time to time with some dissonances, such as seconds, fourths, sevenths, and ninths; these dissonances give rise to appoggiaturas and are sometimes terminated with half-shakes or mordents. From this example you may see the manner in which dotted notes, usually more suitable for majesty and seriousness than for that which is cantabile, may be played agreeably. You must allow the notes that are dotted, and thus which are heard the longest, to grow in volume, but moderate your breath during the dot. The note after the dot must always be very short. If an appoggiatura appears before the dotted note, it must be treated as has just been stated with regard to the long note, since it is held instead of the note before which it stands. The note itself then receives the time of the dot, and thus must be weaker than the appoggiatura (see (*a*)). Of the three little notes in (*b*), which form a mordent,[1] the first, with the dot, must be held as long as the time required for the following large note. The other two little notes, together with the large note, then come in the time of the dot, and are quickly made with a double rise and fall of the finger. The breath also must be moderated during this movement. The four little notes in (*c*) form a turn; since the last

---

[1] The mordent, and the turn and half-shake mentioned below, are also discussed in Chapter VIII, § 14.

of them comes in the time of the dot, it also must be held in its stead. Moderation of the breath likewise must take place during the little notes. The case is the same with the remaining examples from (*d*) to (*ll*),[1] except that the little notes in (*e*) and (*f*) form half-shakes. The notes in (*m*) and (*n*) occur frequently in cadences, where the turns are very appropriate.

§ 41

FIG. 26

These two little notes (see (*a*), (*b*), (*c*), (*d*), (*e*), (*f*), and (*g*)), which form leaps of thirds, are called the *Anschlag*,[2] and are used by singers in extended leaps to hit the high note surely. It may be introduced in rising intervals, such as the second, third, fourth, fifth, sixth, seventh, or octave, before long notes on either the upbeat or downbeat, wherever you do not wish to make some other grace. It must be very quickly, yet weakly, tied to the note. The note itself must be a little stronger than the two little ones. Used in the intervals of the second, fourth, or seventh (see (*a*), (*c*), and (*f*)), the *Anschlag* is more agreeable than in the others; thus it has a better effect if the first little note is a semitone rather than a whole tone below the principal note (see (*c*) and (*f*)). Although the *Anschlag* expresses a tender, sighing, and pleasing sentiment in singing and playing, I do not advise that it be used too lavishly; it is better to introduce it infrequently, since one quickly remembers that which is very pleasing to the ear, while something in excess, no matter how beautiful it may be, may eventually engender distaste.

§ 42

FIG. 27

If long notes form leaps, and you do not wish to make any other variations, the leaps can be filled out with the intervening principal and passing notes.

---

[1] In (*ll*) an extra cross bar was apparently added by mistake to the first four principal notes in the original examples.

[2] *Une espèce d'accent.* In the *Easy and Fundamental Instructions* . . ., p. 18, they are called 'double Apogiaturas'.

The little quavers and semiquavers in (*a*) indicate the passing notes, and the crotchets the principal notes belonging to the chord; the former belong in the time of the preceding notes, and must be slurred briefly to them. In (*b*) to (*g*) both the principal and passing notes are expressed with the values into which they must be divided in the bar. The two intervals of the third and fourth have no principal notes from the chord within them; they have only passing notes.

§ 43

FIG. 28

In falling intervals the passing and principal notes are treated in this manner: the little or passing notes belong in the time of the following notes, and also must be slurred to them.[1] Those within either ascending or descending leaps of fourths, however, belong in the time of the preceding notes. In the intervals of this kind, where neither suspension nor shake is acceptable, the little preparatory notes[2] depart from the rules in Chapter VIII; there they last half the value of the following notes, here they must be made very short.

§ 44

All the rules just given for variations are designed chiefly for the Adagio, since it is there that you have the greatest time and opportunity to introduce variations. You will, however, be able to use many of them in the Allegro too. Those suitable for the Allegro I leave to the consideration of each individual. But how some of the variations described above are to be applied in an Adagio I show in the chapter on the Adagio, in an example especially prepared for it.[3] The kind of execution to be used in all of these

---

[1] In the cases where the harmonic notes form leaps of thirds, Quantz seems to depart from the rules given for passing appoggiaturas in Chapter VIII, § 6. The appoggiaturas between the thirds are apparently played very short, but on the beat. Quantz confuses the issue in the last sentence of this paragraph by referring to the rule for long appoggiaturas.

[2] *Die vorhaltenden kleinen Noten (ces petites notes).* In the French text the first phrase of this sentence is omitted. The French text reads: 'In these little notes where neither shake nor suspension is permitted. . .'.

[3] See Chapter XIV, §§ 23–24.

variations, with particular regard to the strengthening or weakening of the tone, is indicated for each figure in §§ 25 to 43 at the end of the chapter on the Adagio.[1]

[1] Hans-Peter Schmitz, *Die Kunst der Verzierung im 18. Jahrhundert* (Kassel: Bärenreiter, 1955), Ernest T. Ferand, *Improvisation in Nine Centuries of Western Music*, 'Anthology of Music' (Cologne: Arno Volk Verlag, 1961), and B. B. Mather and D. Lasocki, *Free Ornamentation in Woodwind Music 1700–1775*, cited above, contain a considerable number of written-out examples of the variation techniques described in this chapter. And since Quantz so often stresses vocal models, examples such as those included in Hellmuth Christian Wolff, *Original Vocal Improvisations from the 16th–18th Centuries*, trans. A. C. Howie, 'Anthology of Music' (Cologne: Arno Volk Verlag, 1972), especially those for works by Handel, Graupner, Hasse (by Faustina Bordoni and by Frederick the Great) and Telemann, pp. 101–70, should receive special attention. How problematic the interpretation of some of these documents can be may be seen by comparing Wolff's interpretation of the background and transcription of the embellishments found in the Handel arias, pp. 109–32, with the edition of the same works by Winton Dean in G. F. Handel, *Three Ornamental Arias* (London: Oxford University Press, 1976); see also Dean's 'Vocal Embellishment in a Handel Aria', in *Studies in Eighteenth-Century Music: A Tribute to Karl Geiringer on his Seventeenth Birthday*, ed. H. C. Robbins Landon and Roger E. Chapman (New York: Oxford University Press, 1970), pp. 151–9. Other valuable additions to the repertoire of examples of extempore variations located in recent years are found in David D. Boyden, 'Corelli's Solo Violin Sonatas "Grac'd" by Dubourg', in *Festskrift Jens Peter Larsen* (Copenhagen: W. Hansen, 1972), pp. 113–25, and George J. Buelow, 'A Lesson in Operatic Performance Practice by Madame Faustina Bordoni', in *A Musical Offering: Essays in Honor of Martin Bernstein*, ed. by E. H. Clinkscale and C. Brook (New York: Pendragon Press, 1977), pp. 79–96. A complete set of *Six Embellished Sonatas for Violin and Continuo*, by Quantz's good friend and colleague Franz Benda, has been edited by Douglas A. Lee and published in the series *Recent Researches in the Music of the Classical Era* (Madison, Wisconsin: A-R Editions, 1981). For a good, brief practical introduction to the subject of embellishing Baroque music, see B. B. Mather, 'Making Up Your Own Baroque Ornamentation', *The American Recorder*, xxii (1981), pp. 55–9. The example of the procedure found in the 1791 treatise on flute playing by J. G. Tromlitz is reproduced in Thomas E. Warner, 'Tromlitz's Flute Treatise: A Neglected Source of Eighteenth-Century Performance Practice', also in *A Musical Offering*, pp. 261–73. Howard Mayer Brown, *Embellishing 16th-Century Music*, 'Early Music Series', 1 (London: Oxford University Press, 1976), now provides a valuable introduction to earlier practice, and Donington, *Interpretation*, pp. 161–84, and Neumann, *Ornamentation*, pp. 525–73, offer reviews of some of the surviving Baroque material and its interpretation.

CHAPTER XIV

Of the Manner of Playing the Adagio

§ 1

The Adagio[1] ordinarily affords persons who are simple amateurs[2] of music the least pleasure. There are even some professional musicians who, lacking the necessary feeling and insight, are gratified to see the end of the Adagio arrive. Yet a true musician may distinguish himself by the manner in which he plays the Adagio, may greatly please true connoisseurs and sensitive and feeling amateurs, and may demonstrate his skill to those who know composition. Since it does remain a stumbling-block, however, intelligent musicians will, without my advice, accommodate themselves to their listeners and to the amateurs, not only to earn more easily the respect befitting their skill, but also to ingratiate themselves.

§ 2

The Adagio may be viewed in two ways with respect to the manner in which it should be played and embellished; that is, it may be viewed in accordance with the French or the Italian style. The first requires a clean and sustained execution of the air, and embellishment with the essential graces, such as appoggiaturas, whole and half-shakes, mordents, turns, *battemens, flattemens*, &c., but no extensive passage-work or significant addition of extempore embellishments. The example in Tab. VI, Fig. 26,[3] played slowly, may serve as a model for playing in this manner. In the second manner, that is, the Italian, extensive artificial graces that accord with the harmony are introduced in the Adagio in addition to the little French embellishments. Here the example in Tables XVII, XVIII, XIX,[4] in which all of these extempore embellishments are directly indicated with notes, may serve as a model; it will be treated more fully below. If the plain air of this example is played with the addition of only the essential graces already frequently named, we have another illustration of the French manner of playing. You will also notice, however, that this manner is inadequate for an Adagio composed in this fashion.

---

[1] Just as 'the Allegro' refers to any type of quick movement or piece, 'the Adagio' refers to any kind of slow movement or piece.

[2] The German word *Liebhabern* and the French *amateurs* used here do not have the derogatory connotations of the English word.

[3] This example is presented in Chapter VIII, § 13.

[4] These tables follow § 24 of this chapter.

§ 3

With good instruction the French manner of embellishing the Adagio may be learned without understanding harmony. For the Italian manner, on the other hand, knowledge of harmony is indispensable, or, as is the mode with most singers, you must keep a master constantly at hand from whom you can learn variations for each Adagio; and if you do this, you will remain a student all your life, and will never become a master yourself. But you must know the French manner before you venture upon the Italian. Anyone who does not know either how to introduce the little graces at the correct places, or how to execute them well, will have little success with the large embellishments. And it is from a mixture of small and large embellishments that a universally pleasing, reasonable and good style in singing and playing arises.

§ 4

It has already been stated that French composers usually write the embellishments with the air, and the performer thus needs only to concern himself with executing them well. In the Italian style in former times no embellishments at all were set down, and everything was left to the caprice of the performer; an Adagio then looked approximately like the plain air in the example in Tables XVII, XVIII, and XIX.[1] For some time, however, those who follow the Italian manner have also begun to indicate the most necessary embellishments, probably because it was found that the Adagio was much disfigured by many inexperienced performers, and this reduced and tarnished the honour and reputation of the composers. Thus it is undeniable that in Italian music just about as much depends upon the performer as upon the composer, while in French music far more depends upon the composer than upon the performer, if the piece is to be completely effective.

§ 5

To play an Adagio well, you must enter as much as possible into a calm and almost melancholy mood, so that you execute what you have to play in the same state of mind as that in which the composer wrote it. A true Adagio must resemble a flattering petition. For just as anyone who wishes to request something from a person to whom he owes particular respect will scarcely achieve his object with bold and impudent threats, so here you will scarcely engage, soften, and touch your listeners with a bold and bizarre manner of playing. For that which does not come from the heart does not easily reach the heart.

---

[1] See § 24 of this chapter.

§ 6

The kinds of slow pieces are diverse. Some are very slow and melancholy, while others are a little more lively, and hence more pleasing and agreeable. In both kinds the style of execution[1] depends greatly upon the keys in which they are written. A minor, C minor, D sharp major,[2] and F minor express a melancholy sentiment much better than other minor keys; and this is why composers usually employ the keys cited for that purpose. The other major and minor keys, on the other hand, are used for pleasing, singing, and arioso pieces.

There is no agreement as to whether certain keys, either major or minor, have particular individual effects. The ancients were of the opinion that each key had its particular quality, and its particular emotional expression. Because the scales of their keys were not all alike—since, for example, the Dorian and the Phrygian, two keys with the minor third, differ to such an extent that the former has a major second and major sixth in its compass while the latter has a minor second and sixth—and because almost every key as a result had its special way of cadencing, this opinion was adequately justified. In recent times, however, when the scales of all the major keys and likewise those of all the minor keys are similar,[3] the question is whether the same situation exists with regard to the qualities of the keys. Some still accede to the opinion of the ancients; others repudiate it, and assert that each passion can be expressed as well in one key as in the others, provided that the composer possesses sufficient capacity. It is true that they have examples to exhibit, and proofs that many a passion has been expressed very well in a key that does not seem to be exactly the most suitable one for it. But who knows whether the same piece would not have an even better effect if it were written in another key more suitable to the subject? Exceptional instances do not establish a universal rule in this matter. It would take me too long to go into this question thoroughly here. But I would like to propose a test that is based both on experience and on individual perception. For example, transpose a quite successful piece written in F minor into G, A, E, and D minor, or transpose another piece written in E major into F, G, D sharp, D, and C major. If, then, these two pieces have the same effect in each key, the followers of the ancients are incorrect. But if it is found that these pieces produce a different effect in each key, seek to profit from this experience rather than to contest it. As for myself, until I can be convinced of the contrary, I will trust to my experience, which assures me of the different effects of different keys [4]

§ 7

Hence in playing you must regulate yourself in accordance with the prevailing sentiment, so that you do not play a very melancholy Adagio too quickly or a cantabile Adagio too slowly. Thus the following kinds of

[1] 'The style of execution' is found only in the French text.

[2] On Quantz's distinction between D sharp and E flat, see Chapter III, § 8.

[3] 'Major' and 'minor' are used to indicate keys or modes with the major or minor third above the tonic. For an explanation of the apparent confusion between 'mode' and 'key' see Chapter V, § 7.

[4] This footnote of Quantz is a direct refutation of a passage in Johann David Heinichen's *Der General-Bass in der Composition* (Dresden: published by the author, 1728), footnote on pp. 83-87, in which Heinichen tries to prove that different keys do not have different emotional effects.

slow pieces, that is, the *Cantabile, Arioso, Affettuoso, Andante, Andantino, Largo, Larghetto,* &c., must be very clearly distinguished from a pathetic Adagio. As to tempo or *mouvement,* you must judge the requirements of each piece by the individual context. The key and the metre (that is, whether it is duple or triple)[1] throw some light on the matter. In accordance with what was said above, slow movements in G minor, A minor, C minor, D sharp major, and F minor must be played more mournfully, and therefore more slowly, than those in other major and minor keys. A slow piece in two-four or six-eight time is played a little more quickly, and one in alla breve or three-two time is played more slowly, than one in common time or in three-four time.

§ 8

If the setting of the Adagio is very melancholy, as is usually indicated by the words *Adagio di molto* or *Lento assai,* it must be embellished more with slurred notes than with extensive leaps or shakes, since the latter incite gaiety in us more than they move us to melancholy. Yet shakes must not be wholly avoided, lest the listener be lulled to sleep; you must vary the air in such a way that you provoke melancholy a little more at one time, and subdue it again at another.

§ 9

In this matter the alternation of Piano and Forte may contribute greatly; together with the skilfully varied addition of a mixture of small and large graces, it here[2] forms the musical light and shadow to be expressed by the performer, and is of the greatest necessity. It must be used with great discernment, however, lest you go from one to the other with too much vehemence rather than swell and diminish the tone imperceptibly.

§ 10

If you must hold a long note for either a whole or a half bar, which the Italians call *messa di voce,*[3] you must first tip it gently with the tongue, scarcely exhaling; then you begin pianissimo, allow the strength of the tone to swell to the middle of the note, and from there diminish it to the end of the note in the same fashion, making a vibrato[4] with the finger on

---

[1] Translator's parentheses.   [2] i.e. in the Adagio.

[3] Tosi, *Observations,* pp. 27-28, makes the following remarks about the *messa di voce:* 'A beautiful *Messa di Voce,* from a Singer that uses it sparingly, and only on the open Vowels, can never fail of having an exquisite Effect. Very few of the present Singers find it to their Taste, either from the Instability of their Voice, or in order to avoid all Manner of Resemblance of the *odious Ancients.* It is, however, a manifest Injury they do to the Nightingale, who was the Origin of it, and the only thing which the Voice can well imitate. But perhaps they have found some other of the feathered Kind worthy their Imitation, that sing quite after the New Mode.' ←

[4] *Bebung (flattement).* The original text reads: *auch neben dem nächsten offenen Loche mit dem Finger eine Bebung machen (& on fait en même tems au trou ouvert le plus proche, un flattement avec le doigt).* This passage is one of Quantz's rare references to the *Bebung,* which is discussed more

the nearest open hole. To keep the tone from becoming higher or lower during the crescendo and diminuendo, however (a defect which could originate in the nature of the flute), the rule given in § 22 of Chapter IV must be applied here; the tone will then always remain in tune with the accompanying instruments, whether you blow strongly or weakly.

§ 11

The singing notes that follow a long note may be played a little more prominently. Yet each note, whether it is a crotchet, quaver, or semi-quaver, must have its own Piano and Forte, to the extent that the time permits. If, however, several long notes are found in succession where, in strengthening the tone, the time does not permit you to swell each note individually, you can still swell and diminish the tone during notes like this so that some sound louder and others softer. And this change in the strength of the tone must be made from the chest, that is, through exhalation.

§ 12

You must also be careful to sustain the melody constantly, and to take breath at the proper time. Especially when you encounter rests you must not leave the note immediately; it is better to hold the last note a little longer than its value requires, unless the bass meanwhile has several cantabile notes that compensate the ear for what it loses through the silence of the upper part. The effect produced is good, however, if the upper part draws out and concludes the last note with a diminuendo, and then begins the following notes with renewed force, continuing in the manner described above until another caesura or conclusion of an idea occurs.

§ 13

All the notes in the Adagio must be caressed and flattered, so to speak; they must never be tipped harshly with the tongue, unless perhaps the composer wishes several notes briefly articulated to revive the listener who may have dozed off.

§ 14

If the setting of the Adagio is very flat, and more harmonic than melodic, and you want to add several notes here and there in the melody, you must never do so in excess, lest the principal notes be obscured, and the plain air be made unrecognizable. You must play the principal subject at the very beginning just as it is written.[1] If it returns frequently, a few

fully by Hotteterre and Corrette. The *Bebung* is not a vibrato in the modern sense. In the eighteenth century it was considered a special kind of embellishment similar to the shake. Fingerings for it on the flute are given in Hotteterre, *Principes*, pp. 30–33, and Corrette, *Methode*, pp. 30–31 (pp. 43–44 in trans.). See also, Tromlitz, *Unterricht*, pp. 239–40, and Mather, *Interpretation*, pp. 65–66.

[1] Tosi, *Observations*, pp. 93–94, gives the same rule.

notes may be added the first time, and still more the second, forming either running passage-work, or passage-work broken through the harmony. The third time you must again desist and add almost nothing, in order to maintain the constant attention of the listeners.

§ 15

The rest of the air also may be treated in this manner, so that indolent[1] notes lying close together alternate with prominent notes that outline the harmony and lie at a greater distance from one another. And if an idea is repeated in the same key, and no variations immediately occur to you, you may remedy the resulting deficiency with the Piano and with slurred notes.

§ 16

When playing these graces you must not hurry the tempo; they must be completed with great care and composure, since hurrying makes even the most beautiful ideas imperfect. Hence it is most necessary to pay close attention to the movement of the accompanying parts : it is better to allow yourself to be carried forward by them than to anticipate them.

§ 17

A *Grave*, in which the air consists of dotted notes, must be played in a rather elevated and lively manner, and embellished from time to time with passage-work outlining the harmony. The dotted notes must be swelled up to the dot, and, if the interval is not too great, must be slurred softly and briefly to the following notes; in very large leaps, however, each note must be articulated separately. If such notes ascend or descend by step, appoggiaturas may be used before the long notes; these are usually consonances, and might easily displease the ear if unduly protracted.[2]

§ 18

An *Adagio spiritoso* is usually written in triple time with dotted notes, and frequently has many caesuras; its performance requires still more liveliness than that demanded in the preceding paragraph. Hence more of the notes must be articulated than slurred, and fewer graces must be used. Appoggiaturas concluded with half-shakes are particularly appropriate. But should several cantabile ideas be interspersed besides those of this sort,[3] as a finely developed taste in composition requires, you must regulate yourself accordingly, and vary the serious with the flattering.

[1] *Schläfrige* (*assoupissants*). Literally 'sleepy' or 'drowsy'.
[2] A few pertinent remarks on the bowing of this type of slow movement, and the other types discussed in the following paragraphs, are found in Chapter XVII, Section II, § 26.
[3] i.e. with dotted notes.

§ 19

Since it has already been stated above, it is unnecessary to repeat here that these and other kinds of slow pieces, such as the Cantabile, Arioso, Andante, Andantino, Affettuoso, Largo, Larghetto, &c., must be clearly distinguished in playing from a melancholy and pathetic Adagio.

§ 20

If in a *Cantabile* or *Arioso* in three-eight time many semiquavers ascend or descend by step, and the bass continually shifts from one note to another, you cannot make extensive additions of the kind used in a plain air; you must try to execute such notes in a simple and flattering manner with the alternation of Piano and Forte. If leaps in quavers are found, which make the air dry and do not sustain it, the leaps of thirds may be filled out with appoggiaturas or triplets. When the bass sometimes remains with several notes on the same pitch and harmony for an entire bar, the upper part then receives the freedom to make more graces; but these graces must never depart from the general style in which you are playing.

§ 21

An *Andante* or *Larghetto* in three-four time in which the air consists of crotchet leaps, accompanied by a bass in quavers, six of which usually remain on the same pitch or harmony, may be played a little more seriously, and with more graces, than an *Arioso*. But if the bass ascends and descends by step, you must pay closer attention to the graces, so that you do not make forbidden fifths and octaves with the bass.

§ 22

An *alla Siciliana* in twelve-eight time, with dotted notes interspersed, must be played very simply, not too slowly, and with almost no shakes. Since it is an imitation of a Sicilian shepherd's dance, few graces may be introduced other than some slurred semiquavers and appoggiaturas. This rule also applies to French musettes and bergeries.

§ 23

If this description does not suffice to make the manner in which an Adagio may be embellished with graces intelligible to everyone, the description may be further enlarged with the example found in Tables XVII, XVIII, and XIX. From Tables IX to XVI[1] I have taken the variations most appropriate to the plain air found here, and from them have fashioned a coherent melody with embellishments. It may be taken as an illustration of how these individual variations may be combined. The plain air is on the

---

[1] See Chapter XIII, §§ 12–43.

first staff, and the air with variations is on the second. The numbers beneath the latter indicate the numerals or figures of the examples in the
preceding tables, the letters above, the placement of the variations [in each
figure]. Among these examples of variations, there are some that are not
in the same keys as in the tables; they are written either higher or
lower in order to show, as has been mentioned above, that the variations
may be transposed into both major and minor keys.

§ 24

I certainly do not expect this style of variation from a raw beginner
who does not yet know how to play a plain air correctly; this example is
presented only for the investigation of those who have already had some
practice, but who lack good instruction, so that they may gradually perfect themselves. Neither do I demand that all Adagios be ordered like
this one, and thus overloaded with graces; the graces should be introduced
only where the simple air renders them necessary, as is the case here. In
other respects I remain of the opinion previously mentioned: the more
simply and correctly an Adagio is played with feeling, the more it charms
the listeners, and the less it obscures or destroys the good ideas that the
composer has created with care and reflection. For when you are playing
it is unlikely that you will, on the spur of the moment, improve upon the
inventions of a composer who may have considered his work at length.

TABLE XVII

TABLE XVIII

TABLE XIX

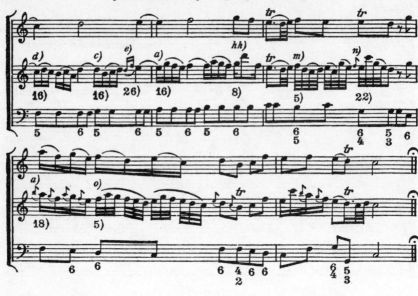

§ 25

Now I must also show the proper execution for each note in this example, with particular regard to the alternation of Forte and Piano. Here I give the illustration of the *variety* of good execution promised in § 14 of Chapter XI; and since I do not believe it will be offensive to lovers of good execution, I will go through all the variations that have been given on the simple intervals in this manner, noting what it is possible to express in words, and leaving the remainder to the judgement and individual perception of the attentive performer. The numerals refer to the tables and the principal examples or figures for each interval; the letters refer to the passages found in them which will be discussed. I remind the reader in advance that as long as nothing is said of the Allegro, the slow tempo must always be understood. The abbreviated words are to be understood as follows: *cr.*—*crescendo*, or with an increasing volume of tone; *decr.*—*decrescendo*, or with a decreasing volume of tone; *str.*—*strong*; *strgr.*—*stronger*; *wk.*—*weak*.[1] In practice when the words strong or weak occur, you must adjust your tonguing or bowing in such fashion that you give each note greater or less stress. But you must not always take these words in their extreme degree; you must proceed as in painting, where so-called *mezze tinte* or half-tints, by which the dark is imperceptibly joined to the

---

[1] 'Strong' and 'weak' have not been equated here with 'Forte' and 'Piano' since Quantz himself knew the latter and chose not to use them. Later he does use them. See Chapter XVII, Section VI, § 14, where the subject of dynamics is taken up again, with specific reference to keyboard accompanying, and Chapter XVII, Section VII, § 19, where all of the various dynamic levels are enumerated. Here Quantz may have wished to avoid the suggestion of too much contrast.

light, are employed to express light and shadow. In singing and playing you must use the diminuendo and crescendo like half-tints, since this variety is indispensable for good execution in music. Now, to business.[1]

§ 26

Tab. IX, Fig. 1. The three demisemiquavers in (*a*) wk., the crotchets C-C-C cr. In (*b*) the dotted C cr., the following short notes and the first C wk., the following C str., the crotchet cr. (*c*) in the same manner. In (*e*) the principal notes cr., the little notes wk. In (*h*) the shake str., the termination[2] wk. In (*l*) C cr., F and E decr., E str., G wk., B str., C wk. In (*ll*) C and E cr., F wk., G-E-C cr., the little notes wk. In (*o*) C cr., decr. during the run, C-C-C str. In (*p*) the first note str., the following three wk., G str., F-E-D wk., C cr. In (*r*) the first note str., the second and third wk., and the remaining triplets in the same manner.

§ 27

Tab. IX, Fig. 2. In (*b*) it may be taken as a rule that three notes of this kind must always be expressed in a flattering manner, that is, the first cr., the dot decr., the following two notes slurred quickly and wk. In (*c*) the first and third notes cr., the second and fourth wk., and those in (*d*) in the same manner. In (*f*) the dotted notes cr., the four quick notes wk. In (*g*) C cr., the four quick notes wk., E str., and the following notes the same. In (*l*) the first note str., the triplets wk. and e₁ual. In (*ll*) the triplets str., the semiquavers wk. In (*m*) the first note str., the following five wk. In (*o*) the first note str., D-E-D decr., C wk., and the remaining notes the same. In (*p*) the first note str., the quick notes wk. In (*q*) C cr., E wk. and very short, the appoggiatura cr., D wk., F str., E wk. The general rule for notes of the kind found in (*r*) is the first two notes wk. and precipitately, the dotted note cr. It is also a general rule that in (*s*) the first notes must be very short and rather str., and the dotted notes decr. and sustained, in both a fast and a slow tempo. The notes in (*v*) are more appropriate in a quick tempo than in a slow one; the first of every four notes must then be stressed. The same is true of those in (*y*).

§ 28

Tab. IX, Fig. 3. In (*b*) D cr., the dot together with the G and E decr., D cr., and the shake on C decr., C cr., B decr. In (*d*) D cr., E-F♯-G wk.,

---

[1] The musical illustrations for §§ 26 to 39 below appear in Chapter XIII, §§ 12–37. The examples illustrating §§ 41 to 43 below are found following § 24 of this chapter. The dynamic indications for the latter examples have been worked out with modern signs in Hans-Peter Schmitz, *Prinzipien der Aufführungspraxis alter Musik* (Berlin: H. Knauer, n.d.), pp. 1–3 following p. 32, and, less carefully, in the Appendix to Arnold Dolmetsch, *The Interpretation of the Music of the XVII & XVIII Centuries* (1946 edition; London: Novello), pp. 37–42. The embellished Adagio is also reproduced in Ferand, *Improvisation* pp. 132–4 but without the dynamic markings.

[2] *Nachschlag (coup de après)*. The termination is discussed in Chapter IX § 7.

A str., C wk. In (*f*) D str., C-B wk., and the same in the following notes. In (*g*) the shake str., the dot and the following two notes decr. Tab. X, Fig. 3. In (*l*) D str., B and the D after the rest wk., and the same in the following notes. In (*n*) D str., B wk., C-D cr., and the following notes in the same manner. In (*o*) the first note str., the second wk., and the following notes the same. In (*p*) D str., G-F♯-G wk., D cr., and the rest in the same manner. In (*q*) the first note of each triplet str., the second and third wk. In (*t*) D str., the four quick notes wk., and the following notes in the same way.

§ 29

Tab. X, Fig. 4. In (*e*) E str., F wk. and cr., G and A in the same way, C wk. In (*f*) E wk. and cr. to the dot, F and G wk. and cr., A and C wk. These two examples are in a kind of *tempo rubato*,[1] which may give occasion for further reflection. In the first example the fourth against the bass is anticipated, replacing the third, and in the second the ninth is held in place of the third, and resolved to it, see Tab. VIII, Fig. 4.[2] In (*m*) the first note str., the following four decr., and the rest in the same manner. In (*n*) the first note cr. to the dot, the following three wk., and the rest in the same manner.

§ 30

Tab. X, Fig. 5. In the two examples in (*a*) and (*b*) the situation is the same as in (*e*) and (*f*) in Fig. 4; (*e*) and (*f*) ascend, (*a*) and (*b*) descend. In (*a*) the second [above the bass] is anticipated, replacing the third, and is resolved to the third in the bass; in (*b*) the fourth is suspended, replacing the third, and then resolved to the third, see Tab. VIII, Fig. 5. Their execution is also the same as that of (*e*) and (*f*). In (*e*) the first note str., the following three wk., and the rest in the same manner. In (*l*) the first and fourth notes str., the second and third wk. If the same notes are played quickly, the third must be stressed more strongly than the others, since it is the lowest note. In (*n*) the first note str., the second and third wk., the fourth str. In a quick tempo the first note must be held a little and the fourth executed very quickly. In (*p*) the first note str., the second wk., the little note wk., and the remaining notes like the first two. In (*q*) the first triplet str., the second wk., and the rest in the same manner.

§ 31

Tab. XI, Fig. 6. In (*a*) E cr., F♯ wk. and briefly slurred,[3] the F♯ shake str., G wk. In (*b*) E str., C wk., the F♯ shake str., G wk. In (*d*) and (*e*) the four

---

[1] This passage is one of Quantz's rare references to *tempo rubato*. In the first example the four notes of the melody are written out in a syncopated form, so that the second, third, and fourth notes are anticipated. In the second example the process is reversed so that the appearance of the second, third, and fourth notes is delayed. For an excellent discussion of *tempo rubato*, which shows that this same understanding of the practice persisted in Mozart's day, see Eva and Paul Badura-Skoda, *Interpreting Mozart on the Keyboard*, trans. by Leo Black (London: Barrie and Rockliff, 1962), pp. 43–46.   [2] See Chapter XIII, § 4.   [3] To the preceding E.

semiquavers sustained equally,[1] the F♯ shake wk., G strgr. In (*h*) the shake str., D-C-B wk., A-F♯ str. The appoggiatura is completed with a *pincé* into the G. In (*i*) the dotted notes cr., the short notes wk. In (*ll*) E str., the high E-D wk. and slurred, F♯ str., G wk. In (*q*) E str., C-A wk., G-F♯ str., A-D wk., F♯-G strgr.

§ 32

Tab. XI, Fig. 7. In (*a*) E cr., G-E wk. In (*b*) E str., G-F-G wk., E strgr. In (*c*) E str., G-C wk., E str. In (*d*) E wk., F♯ str. and cr., G-E very wk. In (*n*) the shake str., D-C wk., G str., E wk. In (*p*) the first three notes str., the rest wk. (*q*) is treated in the same way. In (*t*) E cr., the rest wk.

§ 33

Tab. XII, Fig. 8. In (*c*) G-F-G-A str., B-A-B-C wk., D str. and short, D str., E-F cr. In (*d*) the demisemiquavers str., the quaver wk., and the rest likewise. In (*l*) G stressed, G-F-E wk., and the rest likewise. In (*m*) G-G cr., F wk. In (*o*) G str., from D to G wk., F str. In (*r*) G-A-B str., C-D-E-F decr., G-A-B-C cr., D-B-G-F wk. and sustained. In (*s*) D str., G wk. and short, F cr., E decr. In (*t*) D-E-D cr., E str., F wk. After the graces in (*v*), (*w*), (*x*), (*y*), (*z*), and (*aa*) the appoggiatura [before E] may now and then be raised a semitone with a sharp, as illustrated in (*v*). In (*gg*) G cr., the F shake wk., E-F decr.

§ 34

Tab. XII, Fig. 9. In (*a*), (*b*), (*c*) and (*d*) the descending leaps of thirds may be filled out with little notes, but the principal notes cr. In (*e*) C cr., E decr., E cr., G decr., the E shake cr. and decr. In (*g*) and (*m*) the principal notes str. and the passing wk.

§ 35

Tab. XIII, Fig. 10. In (*b*) and (*d*) the leaps of thirds may be filled out with little notes. In (*e*) the first five notes str. and the last three wk. In (*f*) C-A wk., G-F str., A-F cr. In (*g*) C str., D-E-F-G-A-B♭ decr., C str., A-G-F wk. In (*h*) the shake on C with the termination str., F wk., A str., F wk. In (*i*) the first and third notes cr., the second and fourth wk., and the rest likewise.

§ 36

Tab. XIII, Fig. 11. In (*a*) each note cr. In (*c*) C cr., D-E-F-G decr., G str., D-F wk. In (*h*) C-D-E-F sustained, G-G-G short and equal, D wk., G-F wk. In (*k*) C-B-C str., G-G cr., G-A-G-F wk., and also short and equally articulated.

[1] *Egal an einander gezogen* (*liées également ensemble*). *Gezogen* also may mean 'drawn out' or simply 'slurred'. Only the last three semiquavers, however, are marked with slurs in these examples.

§ 37

Tab. XIII, Fig. 12. In (*a*) G cr., A very wk. In (*b*) G str., E-C wk. In (*c*) G str., F-E-D-C wk. In (*f*) G str., F-E wk., F-E str., D-E wk., D strong.

§ 38

Tab. XIII, Fig. 13. In (*a*) A str., F-D wk. and sustained. In (*b*) A wk., D cr., C wk. In (*f*) and (*g*) four notes strong and four wk., whether the first or last makes no difference. In (*l*) the first five notes wk., C str.

§ 39

Tab. XIV, Fig. 14. In (*d*) B♭ cr., A-B♭-C-B♭ decr., G-E str. In (*g*) the first five notes str., the last three wk. In (*l*) E str., B♭-G wk., E str. In (*ll*) E cr., F-E str., B♭ wk., D wk. In (*n*) E-F wk., F♯-G str., B♭-G-E-D wk. In (*o*) E-G-B♭-A sustained and str., B♭-D wk. In (*s*) E-G str., B♭-A-G wk., F-E-D cr.

§ 40

The remaining examples, and whatever else I have passed over here, either have already been explained in the chapter on extempore variations or are found in the following example of the Adagio in Tables XVII, XVIII, and XIX.[1] Thus in the second staff in Table XVII, in which the variations are found, you should check the letters above the notes and the numerals beneath them, which indicate from which Figure the variations are taken.

§ 41

Table XVII. The first note G cr. At (*c*) (26) the two little notes wk., C strgr. and cr. At (*ll*) (9) E with the shake str. and decr., D-C wk. At (*d*) (28) D str., C wk., B str., A and G with the shake wk. At (*i*) (8) G wk., B-D strgr. At (*f*) (26) the two little notes wk., F-F cr. At (*aa*) (8) A-G wk., F-E-D strgr. At (*e*) (26) the two little notes wk. At (*b*) (28) E str., D wk., C str. and decr., E. cr. At (*a*) (3) D cr., F-E wk., D cr., C with the shake and termination wk., the appoggiatura C str., B wk. At (*f*) (7) E str., C wk., G str., E wk. At (*k*) (3) D str., G cr., D-C wk., A cr., C wk., the little note C cr., B with the shake decr. At (*v*) (8) D cr., C-B-C-D wk. At (*c*) (6) E cr., F♯-G wk. At (*g*) (6) F♯ str., D-E wk., F♯ str., G-A wk. At (*b*) (23) G with the shake str., F♯-E wk., D str. At (*t*)[2] (8) D str., E-D-E wk., F str. At (*v*) (6) F str., E wk., C-A-E decr., E str., F♯ wk., D-A-F♯ decr., F♯ str., G wk. At (*d*) (20) G-B-A cr., G-A-B decr., C cr. At (*ll*) (25) the four little notes wk. At (*m*) (25) A and B str. and with a hard attack, the four little notes wk.,

---

[1] These tables follow § 24 of this chapter. For modern interpretations of the dynamic markings, see the final footnote to § 25.

[2] (*f*) in the original text is incorrect.

C str. and with a hard attack, B wk., A with the shake cr., G wk. At (*a*)[1] (20) G cr., the four little notes decr. At (*g*) (20) A-Bb-Bᵇ-C-C# cr. At (*b*) (2) D wk. and cr., E-F wk. At (*k*) (2) E str., G-F wk., E str., F-G wk., F with the shake str., E wk., F cr., G str. At (*b*) (23) the shake str. and decr., G-F wk. At (*l*) (14) E str., Bb-G-E wk., D cr., the C# shake decr. At (*x*) (8) E cr., D-C#-B-C#-A decr., F-A cr. At (*c*) (13) A str., G-F-E wk., D str., C wk., the appoggiatura C cr., B with the shake decr. At (*p*) (18) D short and str., D-E-F wk., the E shake str., D-E wk. At (*c*) (5) F str., D cr., F wk., E str., C cr., E wk. At (*e*) (22) the E shake str., G-E wk., D str. At (*z*) (8) D cr., C-D-B decr., the appoggiaturas wk., C-A cr.

§ 42

Table XVIII. At (*e*) (14) F-D-F-E wk., D-C-B-A str., A with the shake str., G# wk. At (*a*) (8) E-G#-B cr., C-D wk., the C shake str., B wk., A str. and decr. At (*k*) (8) E str., G#-B-G# wk. [At (*dd*) (8)] D-G#-B-A-G# str., F-E-D wk., the C shake str., B wk., A str. At (*ff*) (8) A cr., G-F-E wk., the appoggiatura E cr., F wk., E-D-E-C str. At (*p*) (14) the six notes wk. and flattering, the G# shake str. At (*i*) (19) F-F-E-E-D very wk. At (*u*) (3) the two triplets together with the B shake str., A decr. At (*e*) (11) the four triplets together with the F shake and the following two notes very wk., and without much chest action. At (*q*) (8) the eight semiquavers together with the E shake up to the C str., but each note still cr., G cr., the four little notes wk. At (*c*) (5) A str., B-C wk., G str., B-C wk. At (*d*) (5) F cr., A-G-F wk., E-C cr. At (*c*) (25) D cr., the four little notes decr., E-F str., the little notes wk., G str. At (*m*) (13) A str. F-F-E wk. At (*n*) (13) D-F#-A str., C wk. At (*d*) (21) [perform the notes] as has been explained in detail in Chapter XIII, § 36, in Fig. 21 (*d*); to avoid unnecessary repetition, the explanation may be reread there. At (*c*) (20) G cr., the remaining notes decr. At (*l*) (9) C str., D-E wk., E-F-G str., E-F-G wk., E-D-C str. At (*o*) (24) str. to the G with the shake.[2] At (*f*) (27) G cr., the remaining notes decr. The triplets at (*s*) (1) and (*cc*) (8) wk., D str., F wk., the E shake and C str., A cr.

§ 43

Table XIX. At (*c*) (15) A-B-C-D str., G wk. and cr., C-B-C-E-G-F wk. and cr., B-D-F str., E wk. and cr., G-F-E wk. At (*kk*) (8) D and the following quick notes str., F and the following quick notes wk., A str., C wk. At (*h*) (4) the B shake together with A and G str. At (*m*) (25) from C together with the following notes and the shake to C str., the following C wk., B cr., C-D wk. At (*o*) (14) G-B-D-C str., D-F wk., the E shake and F-G str., C and the C at (*m*) (23) together with both triplets wk. At (*ll*) (8) the eight notes up to the E shake str. At (*b*) (20) G-A-G-F-G cr., B-C wk. and cr. up to C-D-C at (*d*) (16), B-C-A decr., D cr. At (*c*) (16) B-C-

---

[1] (*g*) in the original text is incorrect.
[2] No shake appears in Quantz's original example.

D str. At (*e*) (26) D-F-E wk. and cr. At (*a*) (16) G-F-E wk., F-F cr., A-G-F str. At (*hh*) (8) G str., D cr., F wk., the E shake together with the D and E str. At (*m*) (5) the eight notes wk. At (*n*) (22) F-E wk., C-G-E-D str., G and the following semiquavers together with the appoggiaturas at (*a*) (18) wk. and flattering. At (*o*) (5) the four triplets str. and sustained. Continue thus to the cadence, and end the last note with a diminuendo.

CHAPTER XV

Of Cadenzas

§ 1

By the word cadenza[1] I understand here neither the closes and stops in a melody, nor the shakes which some Frenchmen call *cadence*. I treat here of that extempore embellishment created, according to the fancy and pleasure of the performer, by a concertante[2] part at the close of a piece on the penultimate note of the bass, that is, the fifth of the key of the piece.

§ 2

It was perhaps less than half a century ago that these cadenzas became fashionable among the Italians, and were subsequently imitated by the Germans and others who devoted themselves to singing and playing in the Italian style.[3] The French, however, have always abstained from using them. Presumably cadenzas were still not the mode when *Lully* left Italy; otherwise he might also have introduced this ornament among the French. It is more probable that cadenzas first came into use after the time *Corelli* published his twelve solos for the violin,[4] engraved in copper.* Perhaps the surest account which can be given of the origin of cadenzas is that several years before the end of the previous century, and in the first ten years of the present one, the close of a concertante part was made with a little passage over a moving bass, to which a good shake was attached; between 1710 and 1716, or thereabouts, the cadenzas customary at pre-

[1] The German word *Cadenz* (French, *cadence*) and the English term 'cadence' in the eighteenth century were used to designate cadences in the modern sense, cadenzas, and shakes. Thus Quantz feels it necessary to indicate that the subject of this chapter is the cadenza. To avoid confusion, the translator feels that it is better to use the modern term. Tosi, *Observations*, pp. 126–39, has a similar chapter entitled 'Of Cadences'. In § 32 of this chapter the meanings 'cadence' and 'cadenza' are not as carefully distinguished. The 'half cadence' is a half cadence in the modern sense, with an embellishment.

[2] As in previous cases 'concertante part' indicates a solo part. See the Preface to the Translation.

[3] On the early history of cadenzas, see Heinrich Knödt, 'Zur Entwicklungsgeschichte der Kadenzen im Instrumental-Konzert', *Sammelbände der Internationalen Musikgesellschaft*, xv (1914), pp. 375–419, and Arnold Schering, *Geschichte des Instrumental-Konzerts* (Leipzig: Breitkopf & Härtel, 1905), pp. 111–13. The discussion of Vivaldi's cadenzas in W. Kolneder, *Aufführungspraxis bei Vivaldi* (Leipzig: Breitkopf & Härtel, 1955), pp. 67–82, also contains much information pertinent to this chapter, and valuable examples of Vivaldi's cadenzas. ←

[4] Corelli's Op. 5 was first published in Rome in 1700. The ornamented versions mentioned in Quantz's footnote were published some time before 1710 by Estienne Roger in Amsterdam. For a discussion of the embellishments in this edition, see M. Pincherle, *Corelli, His Life, His Work* (New York: W. W. Norton, 1956), pp. 109–20. ←

sent, in which the bass must pause, became the mode. Fermatas, in which one pauses[1] *ad libitum* in the middle of a piece, may well have a somewhat earlier origin.

*Soon after the first edition, these sonatas appeared again, engraved in copper, under the name of the author, and variations were included in the twelve adagios of the first six sonatas. But there was not a single cadenza *ad libitum* among them. A short time later the celebrated violinist *Nicola Mattei*,[2] formerly in the service of the Austrian court, composed still other graces for the same twelve adagios. The latter has indeed done somewhat more than *Corelli* himself, since he has concluded them with a kind of short embellishment. But there are still no cadenzas ad libitum like those made at the present time; they move in strict time, with no retardation of the bass. I have had copies of both for more than thirty years.

§ 3

Whether cadenzas were at first formed according to specific rules, or whether they were simply invented by a few skilful people extemporaneously and without rules, I do not know. I believe the latter, since more than twenty years ago the composers in Italy were already fighting against the abuses committed so abundantly in this respect by mediocre singers in operas. To remove the opportunity for unskilled singers to make cadenzas, the composers concluded most of their arias with bass-like passages[3] in unison.

§ 4

The abuse of cadenzas is apparent not only if they are of little value in themselves, as is usually the case, but also if in instrumental music they are introduced in pieces in which they are not at all suitable; for example, in gay and quick pieces in two-four, three-four, three-eight, twelve-eight, and six-eight time. They are permissible only in pathetic and slow pieces, or in serious quick ones.

§ 5

The object of the cadenza is simply to surprise the listener unexpectedly once more at the end of the piece, and to leave behind a special impression in his heart. To conform to this object, a single cadenza would be sufficient in a piece. If, then, a singer makes two cadenzas in the first part of an aria, and yet another in the second part, it must certainly be considered an

---

[1] In the *Easy and Fundamental Instructions*, p. 22, this phrase is translated 'General Pauses ad libitum'.

[2] Nicola Matteis (the more common spelling encountered today) was the son of the famous Italian violinist of the same name, who earned a considerable reputation as a performer and composer in England. His versions of the Corelli sonatas have not yet been located. On his activities at Vienna, see P. Nettl, 'An English Musician at the Court of Charles VI in Vienna', *The Musical Quarterly*, xxviii (1942), pp. 318–28.

[3] *Baßmäßige Gänge (passages de Basse)*, i.e. phrases written in the style of bass parts rather than in the style of solo upper parts.

abuse;¹ for in this fashion, because of the da capo, five cadenzas appear in one aria. Such an excess is not only likely to weary the listeners, especially if all the cadenzas are alike, as is very often the case, but also may cause a singer not too rich in invention to exhaust himself all the more quickly. If the singer makes a cadenza only at the principal close, he retains his advantage, and the listener retains his appetite.

§ 6

It is indeed undeniable that cadenzas serve as an adornment if they fit the requirements of the piece, and are introduced at the right place. It will also be conceded, however, that since they seldom are of the right sort they have grown into a necessary evil, especially in singing. If none are made it is considered a great defect, even though many performers would conclude their pieces with more credit without them. Meanwhile, all those who occupy themselves with singing or with playing solos want to, or must, make cadenzas. And since their nature and the proper way to perform them are not well known, the fashion generally becomes a burden.²

§ 7

As I have already said, rules have never been prescribed for cadenzas. And it would be difficult to circumscribe with rules ideas which are extemporaneous, which are not supposed to constitute a formal melody, for which no bass is permissible, in which the compass of keys that may be touched upon is very narrow, and which in general are only supposed to sound like impromptu inventions. Yet [knowledge of] the art of composition does provide some useful benefits if, unlike many, you do not wish simply to memorize cadenzas by rote, as the birds learn their songs, without knowing of what they consist, and where they are appropriate, sometimes allowing a gay cadenza to be heard in a melancholy piece, or a melancholy one in a joyful piece.

§ 8

Cadenzas must stem from the principal sentiment of the piece, and include a short repetition or imitation of the most pleasing phrases con-

---

¹ Tosi, *Observations*, pp. 128–9, writes: 'Every Air has (at least) three *Cadences*, that are all three final. Generally speaking, the Study of the Singers of the present Times consists in terminating the *Cadence* of the first Part with an overflowing of Passages and *Divisions* at *Pleasure*, and the *Orchestre* waits; in that of the second the Dose is increased, and the *Orchestre* grows tired; but on the last *Cadence*, the Throat is set a going like a Weathercock in a Whirlwind, and the *Orchestre* yawns.'

² In the French text the final portion of this sentence has been expanded. It reads: 'the fashion becomes very burdensome to the majority of singers, and sometimes makes them appear ridiculous in the eyes of true connoisseurs.' For further remarks on the subject, see Tosi, *Observations*, pp. 131–2.

tained in it. At times, if your thoughts are distracted, it is not immediately possible to invent something new. The best expedient is then to choose one of the most pleasing of the preceding phrases and fashion the cadenza from it. In this manner you not only can make up for any lack of inventiveness, but can always confirm the prevailing passion of the piece as well. This is an advantage that is not too well known which I would like to recommend to everyone.[1]

§ 9

Cadenzas are of either one or two parts. Those of one part are chiefly extempore, as stated above. They must be short and fresh, and surprise the listeners, like a *bon mot*. Thus they must sound as if they have been improvised spontaneously at the moment of playing. Hence you must not be too extravagant, but must proceed economically,[2] especially if you often have the same listeners before you.

§ 10

Since the compass[3] [of cadenzas] is very narrow, and is easily exhausted, it is difficult to keep them from sounding the same. Thus you must not introduce too many ideas.

§ 11

Neither the figures nor the simple intervals with which a cadenza is begun and ended may be repeated more than twice in transpositions or they will become disagreeable. I shall give two cadenzas in a similar style as an illustration of this point (see Tab. XX, Figs. 1 and 2). In the first, to be sure, there are two kinds of figures. But since each figure is heard four times, the ear is wearied. In the second, on the other hand, the figures are repeated only once, and are then interrupted with fresh figures. In consequence it is preferable to the first. For the more the ear can be deceived with fresh inventions, the greater is the pleasure it feels. The figures must therefore always alternate with one another in different ways. In the first cadenza another error is found : from beginning to end it employs the same metre and the same division of the notes. And this also is contrary to the nature of the cadenza.

[1] As A. Schering points out in his edition of the *Essay*, the practice of using thematic materials from the composition in the cadenza was not universal in Quantz's day. Many cadenzas consisted entirely of embellished scale figures and arpeggios.

[2] The French text has been followed here. German text: 'must proceed like a good innkeeper'.

[3] Here the term 'compass' seems to refer to the harmonic range of the cadenza. See § 7 above. The implication seems to be that the use of too many ideas within the restricted harmonies of the cadenza will soon become tedious.

TABLE XX

FIG. 1

FIG. 2

FIG. 3

If you wish to reduce the second cadenza to simple intervals, take the first note of each figure (as in Fig. 3); the latter will then be suitable for an Adagio, the former for an Allegro.

FIG. 3

§ 12

Since figures or phrases must not be repeated too often in transpositions, they certainly must not be repeated on the same pitch. In general, care must be taken that the notes with which phrases begin are not heard too frequently, particularly at the end [of the cadenza], where there is usually a slight pause on the sixth or fourth above the bass, since these notes leave a stronger impression upon the ear than the others. This would be just as disagreeable to the ear as to constantly begin or end several successive sentences in a discourse with the same word.

§ 13

Although cadenzas are extempore, the intervals in them must still be correctly resolved, particularly if you modulate to different keys by way of dissonances, which may be done through the leap of a diminished fifth or of an augmented fourth (see Tab. XX, Fig. 4).

FIG. 4

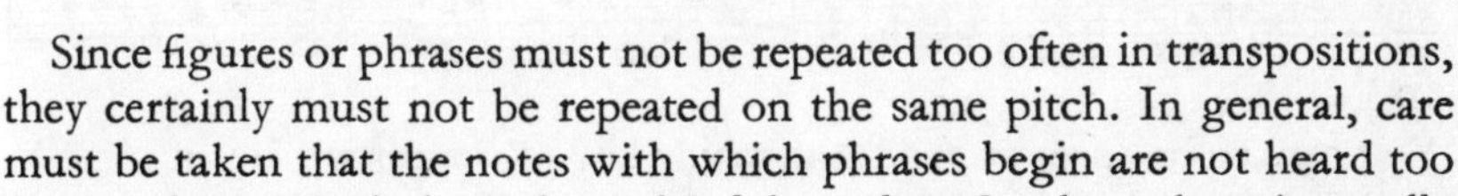

§ 14

You must not roam into keys that are too remote, or touch upon keys which have no relationship with the principal one. A short cadenza must not modulate out of its key at all. A somewhat longer one modulates most naturally to the subdominant, and a still longer one to the subdominant and the dominant. In major keys the modulation to the subdominant is made through the diminished seventh (see the D sharp[1] under the letter (*a*) in Fig. 5); the modulation to the dominant is made through the augmented fourth (see the B natural under letter (*b*)); and the return to the principal key is made through the perfect fourth (see the B flat below letter (*c*)).

Fig. 5

In minor keys the modulation to the subdominant is made through the major third (see the B natural under the letter (*a*) in Fig. 6); the modulation to the dominant and the return to the principal key, however, occur just as in major keys (see the C sharp and C beneath letters (*b*) and (*c*)).

Fig. 6

You can, to be sure, go from the major key to the minor, but it must be done briefly and with great circumspection, so that you may return to the principal key in good style. In minor keys you can ascend or descend by step in semitones, but no more than three or four must follow one another or, like all other uniform phrases, they become disagreeable.

§ 15

Just as a gay cadenza is formed from extended leaps and gay phrases interspersed with triplets and shakes, &c. (see Tab. XX, Fig. 7), a melancholy one, on the other hand, consists almost entirely of small intervals mingled with dissonances (see Fig. 8). The first of these is suitable for a happy piece, the second for a very melancholy one. In this regard you must take particular care not to lapse into absurd mixtures and confusions of the gay and the melancholy.

---

[1] In the example D sharp is marked E flat.

FIG. 7

All[egro]

FIG. 8

Ad[agio]

§ 16

Regular metre is seldom observed, and indeed should not be observed, in cadenzas. They should consist of detached ideas rather than a sustained melody, as long as they conform to the preceding expression of the passions.

§ 17

Vocal cadenzas or cadenzas for a wind instrument must be so constituted that they can be performed in one breath.[1] A string player can make them as long as he likes, if he is rich enough in inventiveness. Reasonable brevity, however, is more advantageous than vexing length.

§ 18

I do not pretend that the examples found here are complete and finished cadenzas; they are simply models from which you can, to a certain extent, learn to grasp the modulations, the returns to the principal key, the mixture of figures, and the characteristics of cadenzas in general. Many may wish, perhaps, that I had appended a number of finished cadenzas. But since it is impossible to write cadenzas as they must be played, any examples of finished cadenzas would still be insufficient to provide a genuine understanding of them. Thus, to learn how to make good cadenzas, you must try to hear many able people. And if you have some prior knowledge of the characteristics of cadenzas, such as that which I am trying to impart here, you will be better qualified to test what you hear from others, so as to be able to turn what is good to your own profit, and to shun what is bad. Weaknesses are frequently encountered even in the cadenzas of very able musicians, as a result of an unpleasant state of mind, or too much vivacity, or from indifference and negligence, barrenness of

---

[1] Observance of this rule would be of inestimable benefit to many modern performances of eighteenth-century flute concertos. Although there were undoubtedly exceptions to it, the same rule is repeated by Tromlitz in 1791. See his *Unterricht*, p. 298. Tromlitz's discussion of cadenzas in this work closely parallels that of Quantz, and provides many useful examples of late eighteenth-century flute cadenzas.

invention, disregard of the listeners, excessive artificiality, or other more intangible reasons. Accordingly, you must not allow yourself to be blinded by the preconception that a good musician cannot produce a bad or mediocre cadenza from time to time as well as good ones. Because of the necessity of speedy invention, cadenzas require more fluency of imagination than erudition. Their greatest beauty lies in that, as something unexpected, they should astonish the listener in a fresh and striking manner and, at the same time, impel to the highest pitch the agitation of the passions that is sought after. You must not believe, however, that it is possible to accomplish this simply with a multitude of quick passages. The passions can be excited much more effectively with a few simple intervals, skilfully mingled with dissonances, than with a host of motley figures.

§ 19

Cadenzas in two parts are not as arbitrary as those in one part. The rules of composition have even greater authority in them; hence those who wish to occupy themselves with cadenzas of this sort must understand at least the preparation and resolution of dissonances, and the laws of imitation, if they are to produce anything sensible. Most of these cadenzas are studied in advance and memorized by singers, since it is a great rarity to encounter two singers together who both understand something of harmony or composition. Most pretend, as a result of a prejudice propagated, mothered, and nourished by laziness, that such an exertion is harmful to the voice. Among instrumentalists there are still a few who possess the requisite knowledge.

§ 20

Cadenzas in two parts may be a little longer than those in a single part, since the harmony they contain is less likely to weary the ear, and also because taking breath is permitted.

§ 21

Those who know little of harmony usually content themselves with passages in thirds and sixths. These do not suffice to arouse the listener's admiration.

§ 22

Although it is quite easy to invent and to write down cadenzas in two parts, it is very difficult to invent them without preparation, since neither person can anticipate the thoughts of the other. Yet if you are slightly acquainted with the advantages that imitations and the use of dissonances offer, the difficulty is easy to overcome. The impromptu invention of cadenzas is my principal concern here. I shall therefore add several model examples; and these may be viewed as rough sketches in which the various kinds of imitations are found traced out together with the preparations and resolutions of the dissonances that must be used in them. The embellishments, however, which are the product of inventiveness, and cannot be circumscribed in a few examples, I leave to the invention and taste of each individual.

§ 23

Besides thirds and sixths proceeding together in regular motion, cadenzas in two parts generally consist of imitations, brought forward by one part and imitated by the other. Suspensions play an important part in these imitations. Either the *second* is suspended from the third and resolved to the third or sixth, or this is inverted, so that the *seventh* is suspended from the sixth and resolved to the sixth or third. Or you may go from the third into the *augmented fourth,* and inverted, from the sixth into the *diminished fifth.* Or you may delay the resolution of the diminished fifth in the upper part into the third, from which a *perfect fourth* results, which is then resolved into the third. If, then, two persons are thoroughly acquainted with these possibilities, they can move from one dissonance to another without prior consultation, and without overstepping the rules of composition.

§ 24

In a passage in sixths where you do not wish to touch any dissonances, one of the two parts must anticipate a note, whether ascending or descending, so that the other may adjust accordingly; see Tab. XX, Fig. 9, where the lower part has the movement, and indicates that in the first measure the upper part should ascend, and later that it should descend again.

Fig. 9

In Fig. 10 the upper part establishes the movement, and the lower one follows.

Fig. 10

If the upper part is substituted for the lower, and the lower for the upper in these two passages, you will discover the way to do passages in thirds.

§ 25

Passages in sixths mingled with sevenths are of two sorts, that is, ascending and descending. In the ascending passages, the upper part goes to the octave, and the lower part from the sixth to the seventh (see Tab. XX, Fig. 11).

FIG. 11

In descending passages in sevenths the lower part makes the suspensions, and the upper part resolves them. The lower can also make the suspensions and resolve them, as is to be seen in the second measure of the example in Fig. 12.

FIG. 12

If the first part is made the second, and the second the first in the two preceding examples, passages in thirds result, in which the second is suspended from the third and resolved to the third or sixth.

§ 26

The first part, which is generally the leader, not only must give the second the opportunity to answer, and wait for it to do so, but also must frequently know how to select during the answer an interval that permits a new suspension, so that all the suspensions are not of the same sort. In the example in Fig. 13 the first suspension consists of a minor second [E-F], and the following one of a diminished seventh [G sharp-F]; and while the second part imitates the figure of the first, the first prepares the following seventh [C-B] with the B, and then resolves it to the sixth. The second part then makes a new suspension of a seventh [B-A] with its B, and moves, through the C sharp against the G, or through the diminished fifth, to the suspension of the fourth [D-G] above its D, &c., thus deceiving the ear in diverse ways.

FIG. 13

§ 27

Cadenzas may also be arranged in the style of a canon, as illustrated in Tab. XX, Fig. 14. Here the imitation is at the fourth below.

FIG. 14

In Tab. XXI, Fig. 1, the imitation proceeds through fifths and sixths; in Fig. 2 through seconds, formed by crossing parts, resolved into thirds.

TABLE XXI

FIG. 1

FIG. 2

In Fig. 3 the imitation proceeds alternately through augmented fourths and the diminished fifths, as well as through fifths and sixths.

FIG. 3

In Fig. 4 the second is suspended from the third, and the seventh from the sixth. The former resolves to the sixth, and the latter to the third. This passage cannot be used more than twice in transpositions, however, because of the leaps of fourths.

FIG. 4

§ 28

In the examples quoted here most of the passages are so constituted that one part can imitate the other without previous agreement. It only remains to be noted that it is the primary duty of the first part, which usually makes the statement, to so order the passage that it is sufficiently distinct, and has the proper range, for the second to imitate it. If, however, the first of the two musicians understands nothing of the necessary rules, the knowledge of the second will be of no value. He must simply try to go along with the first in plain thirds and sixths as much as possible and avoid dissonances, since it produces a very unpleasant effect if dissonances are heard without resolution.

§ 29

With regard to the preparation for the close of a cadenza, it is to be noted that the fourth above the final note,[1] or the seventh above the bass note of the cadenza (which is the same note),[2] indicates the cadenza's end. It usually appears in the upper part, if, that is, the cadenza closes with a

---

[1] i.e. the tonic of the principal key of the composition.   [2] Translator's parentheses.

third to a unison. The second part must therefore regulate itself accordingly, and try to introduce the diminished fifth beneath the fourth, in
order to prepare for the close by a resolution into the third, as may be
observed in the examples described above. In Fig. 11,[1] Tab. XX, in the
penultimate bar, the suspended note C in the first part (see (*a*)), and the
F sharp in the second part (see (*b*)), announce the end. In Fig. 12 it is made
with the F and the seventh G (see (*c*) and (*d*)); in Figs. 13 and 14 with the
D and G sharp (see (*e*), (*f*), (*g*), and (*h*)); in Fig. 1, Tab. XXI, with E flat
and A (see (*i*) and (*k*)); in Fig. 2, G and C sharp (see (*l*) and (*m*)); in Fig. 3,
F and B (see (*n*) and (*o*)); and in Fig. 4, C and F sharp, and B flat and E (see
(*p*), (*q*), (*r*), and (*s*)); and these notes are always followed by shakes. If,
however, the cadenza closes with a sixth moving to the octave, the fourth
of the principal key comes in the second part, and the augmented fourth
comes in the first part, reckoned upwards from the lower part as an inverted diminished fifth.

§ 30

In statements and their imitations, just as in preparations and resolutions of suspensions, you can lengthen or shorten the figures or embellishments as you please. Look at Tab. XXI, Figs. 5 and 6, the first of which is
long, and the second short. Both examples are taken from the one in Fig. 2.
That in Fig. 5 is lengthened by the use of figures, and that in Fig. 6 is
shortened by their omission. The other examples may be treated in the
same fashion, so that, through the alteration and mixture of the figures,
the same passages will always be fresh and different.

FIG. 5

---

[1] See § 25 above for this Figure. The other examples cited below follow this one in the order
in which they are mentioned.

FIG. 6

§ 31

It is not always necessary to bind yourself to a regular metre in two-part cadenzas, as in the above examples, unless the figure stated requires an answer; then one part must imitate the other in the same tempo, and with the same number of notes. Otherwise, however, the less order you observe the better; in this fashion you avoid the appearance of premeditation. Yet this statement must not be interpreted as meaning that cadenzas should generally consist of an unintelligible maze of fancies, and should have nothing at all melodic in them. Such cadenzas would arouse little pleasure in your listeners. My meaning, as already touched upon with regard to cadenzas for one part, is only that cadenzas should not be formally unified melodies, like ariosos,[1] but should consist of detached, though still pleasing, phrases, and that these phrases may be akin both to duple and to triple time. You simply must not remain in one or the other too long, and must always be intent upon an agreeable alternation.

§ 32

The *half cadence*,[2] in which the upper part is suspended as a seventh against the bass and resolved through the sixth to the octave,* still remains to be considered. This half cadence usually appears in the middle or at the end of a slow piece in a minor key (see Tab. XXI, Fig. 7). It was used *ad nauseam* in former times, particularly in the church style, and has therefore almost gone out of fashion. Yet it can still be used with good effect, if it is introduced sparingly and in the right places.

FIG. 7

*This octave is on the fifth of the key of the piece, and always requires a chord with a major third.

[1] Quantz uses the term 'arioso' to indicate a slow composition in a sustained and singing melodic style. It does not refer to a style midway between recitative and aria.

[2] Since the term *halbe Cadenz* refers primarily to a particular type of cadence rather than a particular type of cadenza, *Cadenz* is here translated 'cadence'. For C. P. E. Bach's remarks on the half cadence, see *Essay*, p. 383.

§ 33

If such a half cadence is for only one part, the embellishments that may
be introduced have a very small compass. The principal notes must be
taken from the chord of the seventh, reckoned from the bass, and consist
of a third and fifth below and a fourth and a sixth above the suspended
seventh in the upper part. These notes may be taken both from above and
below (see Tab. XXI, Fig. 8). It is simply a matter of whether you wish ◄
the embellishment to be long or short. If it is to be short, you may touch
only the upper fourth (see the note G beneath the letter (*c*) of the Figure),
and from there move to the close. If it is to be somewhat longer, you can
touch the fourth and sixth in succession (see under the letters (*a*) and (*b*)).
But if it is to be lengthened still more, you can descend to the seventh
below, as is to be seen in Fig. 8, which indicates the principal notes. The
principal notes can also be varied and augmented by different figures
based on these notes.

Fig. 8

§ 34

In two parts, this half cadence is frequently used in trios. Its ornaments
consist of the very same intervals used in one for a single part. It is simply
to be noted that the part forming the suspension of the seventh against
the bass must make the statement. The other part must remain on the third
[of the chord] until the first has completed its figure and strikes the shake
on the sixth. The second part can then imitate at the lower fifth the figure
sounded by the first, as shown in the example in Fig. 9, Tab. XXI. ◄

Fig. 9

If, however, the seventh lies in the second part, then the second must
make the statement, and the first imitate it at the fourth above. If in
Fig. 9 the second part is transposed up an octave, and turned into the
first, you will have an example.

§ 35

A little still remains to be noted with regard to the *fermata* or pause *ad
libitum*,[1] which sometimes occurs in vocal pieces in the solo part at the

---

[1] The fermata is also discussed by C. P. E. Bach, *Essay*, pp. 143–6, 384–6. In Quantz's index
ad libitum and *pausa generalis* are both equated with *fermata*.

beginning of an aria, or very rarely in a concertante instrumental part, perhaps in the Adagio of a concerto. It usually consists of two notes forming a descending leap of a fifth, over the first of which stands a semi-circle with a dot (see Tab. XXI, Fig. 10); and it is set so that the singer, pronouncing a word of two syllables provided with a comfortable long vowel sound, such as *vado, parto*, &c., will have the opportunity to intro-duce an embellishment.

FIG. 10

Va - do

This embellishment must consist only of such principal notes as are per-mitted in the chord of the bass part, and cannot modulate to other keys. The example in Tab. XXI, Fig. 11, may serve as a model. A singer can imagine it in the range[1] suited to his own voice. The first note, beneath the semicircle with the dot, can be held as a *messa di voce*,[2] allowing the tone to swell and diminish, as long as your breath permits; but you must retain enough air to complete the following embellishment in the same breath.

FIG. 11

Va   -   -   -   -   -   -   -   do

If you wish to detach the figures that form this ornament, it can be divided into several parts, and regularly shortened by a figure, as the letters above indicate. For example, either the figures beneath the letters (*b*) and (*c*), or those beneath (*a*), (*b*), (*c*), and (*d*), or those beneath (*a*), (*b*), (*c*), (*d*), and (*e*), or those beneath (*a*), (*b*), (*c*), (*d*), (*e*), and (*f*) can be omitted without des-troying the substance of the embellishment. Although the intervals ascend through the chord here, they may also descend through the same chord, if the figures are arranged so that the opening note is touched again at the conclusion of the ornament, and the last figure is approached with a shake from above, and not from below, since this shake on the third must always commence from above. No termination must be made after this shake; and even if one is made by the greatest singers, it is, and remains, an error. This close should be sung or played as it is expressed in the notes here. In § 36 in the chapter on extempore variations this matter is treated more fully.

[1] Literally, 'clef'. In Quantz's day the various clefs were still closely correlated with the ranges of the various types of voices.

[2] *Haltung. Messa di voce* appears in parentheses in the German text.

§ 36

The closing shake of cadenzas in pieces in the minor mode is occasionally struck on the sixth instead of the fifth, though usually only in vocal pieces. It is treated in the manner shown in the caesura on the third in Chapter XIII, § 36, Tab. XV, Fig. 21 (*d*). Although this manner of terminating the cadenza does not have a bad effect if introduced at the right time, and with good grace, it is not advisable to use it too prodigally, as is the custom of some singers, who almost always make it in the manner described above on the final shake in the second part of an aria cadencing in a minor key. This shake sounds rather plain at the end of a piece, and although as described in § 36 of Chapter XIII it is still usual in the middle of a piece, it has almost gone out of fashion at the end, thus betraying its antiquity. The principal reason why it must be used only in very rare cases, however, is that the sixth and fourth would be required for it in the accompaniment. Since a chord with a major third and perfect fifth that has no relationship with the shake on the sixth ordinarily must be struck before the close of a piece, such a shake would leave a discord at the end of the piece, and thus would bring more distaste than pleasure to the ear.[1]

[1] For some further examples of eighteenth-century flute cadenzas, see Hans-Peter Schmitz, *Querflöte und Querflötenspiel in Deutschland während des Barockzeitalters* (Kassel: Bärenreiter, 1952), pp. 62–65). Haas, *Aufführungspraxis der Musik* (Potsdam: Athenaion, 1931), pp. 185–7, contains an interesting example of an aria with cadenzas as sung by Farinelli, which may serve as a useful basis for comparison of vocal and instrumental cadenzas in Quantz's day. For additional material on the subject, see Donington, *Interpretation*, pp. 185–96, and Lasocki and Mather, *The Classical Woodwind Cadenza*, pp. 56–60. Joan E. Smiles, in her 'Directions for Ornamentation in Italian Method Books', *Journal of the American Musicological Society*, xxxi (1978), p. 503, reproduces several examples of cadenzas by Antonio Lorenzoni (see pp. 347–8 for information on his *Saggio* of 1779) not included by Lasocki and Mather. My colleague, John Solum, has kindly passed on the following information about two manuscripts containing eighteenth-century cadenzas. The manuscript of the Gluck Concerto for Flute in G major in the Badische Landesbibliothek in Karlsruhe shows clearly that the cadenzas in the Scherchen edition of the work (Zürich: Hug & Co., n.d.) are in fact eighteenth-century creations, and not, as the title page of the edition would seem to indicate, by Scherchen himself. Scherchen's additions to them are confined to performance indications. Since the cadenzas are models of their kind, it is useful to know that they belong to the period in which the concerto was written. The new edition of the concerto edited by Rien de Reede and published by Amadeus Verlag (1980) is based on the manuscript, includes the cadenzas, and indicates editorial additions clearly. Further written-out examples from the period may be found in the manuscript of the Grétry Concerto for Flute in C major in the Library of Congress, Washington D.C. These cadenzas (one for each movement) are not the same as those added by Dieter Sonntag in his edition of the work (Wilhelmshaven: O. H. Noetzel, 1961), but they are included in an older edition, edited by S. Beck and published by the New York Public Library in 1937.

CHAPTER XVI

What a Flautist Must Observe if he Plays in Public Concerts

§ 1

If a receptive student has followed this method in all its parts, under the guidance of a good master, and has fully understood what it contains and correctly put it into practice, he will be in a position to allow himself to be heard with honour in public concerts.[1] With a few necessary rules, hints, and bits of good advice, I shall now strive to prepare him for these occasions, when he will seek to demonstrate the knowledge that he has acquired.[2]

§ 2

Above all he must be mindful of the accurate tuning of his instrument. If a harpsichord is present in the accompaniment, as is ordinarily the case, he must tune the flute to it. The majority take D″ as their rule and fundamental note; my advice, however, is to choose F″, if the natural intonation of the flute is as true as it should be.

§ 3

If he must play in a cold place, he can tune the flute consonantly with the harpsichord. In very warm weather, however, he must tune a little lower, since the nature of wind instruments is just the opposite of stringed instruments in this respect. With warmth, and hence with blowing, the former become higher; the latter, on the other hand, become lower. Coldness produces the opposite effects.

§ 4

For a piece in E flat or A flat the player can tune his flute a little lower than for all other keys, since the keys with flats are a comma higher than those with sharps.[3]

[1] *Öffentliche Musiken* (*Musiques publiques*). 'Public concerts' do not necessarily connote large public assemblies. They seem to indicate public performances before groups of any size, large or small, as opposed to 'independent practice' by oneself, discussed in Chapter X.

[2] Tosi, *Observations*, pp. 140–73, presents a chapter entitled 'Observations for a Singer', which parallels the present chapter of Quantz in some respects. It begins: 'Behold the Singer now appearing in Publick, from the Effects of his Application to the Study of the foregoing Lessons. But to what Purpose does he appear? Whoever, in the great Theatre of the World, does not distinguish himself, makes but a very insignificant figure.'

[3] On Quantz's distinction between sharps and flats, see Chapter III, §§ 3–5.

§ 5

In a spacious place, whether an opera house, a hall, or a place where two, three, or more rooms open into one another, he must never tune the flute at a distance from the other players, but always close by. For the sound of the notes becomes lower at a distance, and the further the distance, the lower it becomes. Although he may believe he has tuned quite truly at a distance, he will find that he is too low when he approaches the other players.

§ 6

In cold weather he must seek to keep the flute always at the same temperature; otherwise he will tune too low at one time, too high at another.

§ 7

Should, perchance, the violins be tuned higher than the harpsichord, which may easily happen if their fifths are tuned a little high instead of a little low (as care must be taken to do with the keyboard),[1] so that a considerable difference is apparent between the four strings tuned in fifths, then the flautist must necessarily adjust to the violins, since they are heard more than the harpsichord. To be sure, this produces a poor effect if one is accompanied alternately, now by the keyboard, now by the violins; and it is to be hoped that each person will tune his instrument truly by itself, as well as consonantly with the harpsichord, so as not to diminish the pleasure of the listeners. But it is understood, without my reminder, that this error is frequently committed only by those who practise their art as a trade, and then reluctantly and of necessity, and not by reasonable and experienced musical artists, who love music as they ought.

§ 8

If there is a large accompanying body, the flautist may tune the flute a little lower for the Allegro, rotate it a little further outward, and then blow more strongly, so that he is not covered up by the accompaniment, should it be intrusive at times. In the Adagio, on the other hand, he must tune so that he can play comfortably without forcing the flute by excessive blowing. For this it is necessary that he push the plug the width of a good knife's back deeper into the flute (see Chapter IV, § 26). In the following Allegro, however, he must not forget to draw the plug back to its former position.

§ 9

He must listen constantly to the accompanying instruments, to discover whether he is always in tune with them, so that he plays neither too

[1] Translator's parentheses.

high nor too low. For without this trueness of intonation the finest and most distinct execution remains imperfect.[1]

§ 10

He must hold the flute so that the wind may escape unhindered. He must be careful not to blow at some time into the clothes of those who stand very close upon his right side, since this makes the tone weak and muffled.

§ 11

If the novice flute player has accustomed himself in his prior individual practice to beating time with his foot, in public concerts he must refrain from this as much as possible. But if he is still unable to keep in time without its aid, let him use it secretly, so as neither to publish his weakness, nor vex his accompanists. If at times it seems to be absolutely necessary to beat time when someone rushes or drags, and thus hinders the soloist from playing the passage-work fully, distinctly, and in its proper speed, he should try to cloak this error by blowing a little more strongly, and by stressing the notes that fall on the downbeats rather than by beating his foot, a habit which few can tolerate.

§ 12

If sometimes a concerto accompanied by many persons is begun more quickly or slowly than it should be, and disorder and confusion are to be feared from an abrupt change of tempo if it is required forthwith, the soloist will do well to allow the ritornello to end as it was begun, if the difference is not too great. In the following solo passage, he can, by a clear and well-accented beginning, indicate the correct tempo.

§ 13

If the flautist who wishes to be heard publicly is timorous, and as yet unaccustomed to playing in the presence of many people, he must try while playing to direct his attention only to the notes before him, never turning his eyes to those present, since this distracts his thoughts, and destroys his composure. He should not undertake pieces which are so difficult that he has had no success with them in his individual practice, but should rather keep to those which he can play fluently. Fear causes an ebullition of the blood, which disturbs the regular action of the lungs,[2] and which likewise warms the tongue and fingers. From this a most obstructive trembling of the limbs arises in playing, and as a result the flute player will be unable to produce extended passage-work in one breath, or other specially

[1] The subject of intonation is taken up, with special reference to the accompanying instruments, still more thoroughly in Chapter XVII, Section VII, §§ 1–9.

[2] Rendered literally, this phrase reads: 'brings the lungs into unequal motion.'

difficult feats, as well as he does in a tranquil state of mind. In such circumstances, and especially in warm weather, it also may happen that he perspires about the mouth, and the flute in consequence does not remain lying securely at the proper place, but slips downwards, so that the mouthhole is too much covered, and the tone, if not lacking altogether, is at least too weak. Quickly to remedy this last evil, let the flautist wipe his mouth and the flute clean, then touch his hair or wig and rub the fine powder clinging to his finger upon his mouth. In this way the pores are stopped, and he can continue playing without great hindrance.

§ 14

For these reasons, anyone who must play before a large assembly is advised not to undertake a difficult piece before he feels himself perfectly at ease. The listeners cannot know his state of mind; hence they judge him, especially if it is the first time that he plays before them, only by what they hear, and not by what he is capable of doing alone. It is in general always more advantageous to play an easy piece truly, and without mistakes, than to play the most difficult piece unsatisfactorily.

§ 15

Should our flautist miss several passages of his piece in the public performance, he should play them through both slowly and quickly by himself at home until he can produce them with the same facility as the others, so that in the future the accompanists will not find it necessary to adjust to his mistakes,[1] since this neither brings pleasure to the listeners nor does honour to the flautist.

§ 16

If, by much practice, a person has achieved great facility, he must not abuse it. To play very quickly, and at the same time distinctly, is indeed a special merit; as experience teaches, however, it may also cause great errors. These are particularly apparent among young people, who possess neither ripe judgement nor a true feeling for how each piece ought to be played in the tempo and style appropriate to it. Such young people usually play everything that they encounter, whether it is Presto, Allegro, or Allegretto, at the same speed. In doing this they even believe that they are excelling others. Because of this excessive speed, however, they not only mar and destroy the most beautiful part of the composition—I mean the intermixed cantabile ideas—but also, by precipitating the tempo, accustom themselves to executing the notes incorrectly and indistinctly. Those who do not soon correct this error, which is caused by youthful fire, will persist in it, if not for ever, at least until far into their mature years.

---

[1] 'To his mistakes' appears only in the French text.

§ 17

In the choice of the pieces in which he wishes to be heard in public, the flautist, like every other soloist, must adjust not only to himself, to his powers and capacity, but also to the place where he plays, to his accompaniment, to the circumstances in which he plays, and to the listeners before whom he wishes to be heard.

§ 18

In a large place, where there is much resonance, and where the accompanying body is very numerous, great speed produces more confusion than pleasure. Thus on such occasions he must choose concertos that are written in a majestic style, and in which many passages in unison[1] are interspersed, concertos in which the harmonic parts change only at whole or half bars. The echo that constantly arises in large places does not fade quickly, and only confuses the notes if they succeed one another too quickly, making both harmony and melody unintelligible.

§ 19

In a small room, on the other hand, where few instruments are at hand for the accompaniment, the player may use concertos that have gay and *galant* melodies, and in which the harmony changes more quickly than at half and whole bars. These may be played more quickly than the former type.

§ 20

Anyone who wishes to be heard publicly must consider his listeners well, especially those whom it is most important that he please. He must consider whether or not they are connoisseurs. Before connoisseurs he can play something a little more elaborate, in which he has the opportunity to show his skill in both the Allegro and the Adagio. But before pure amateurs, who understand nothing of music, he will do better to produce those pieces in which the melody is brilliant and pleasing. To avoid boring such amateurs, he may also take the Adagio a little more quickly than usual.

§ 21

Pieces set in very difficult keys must be played only before listeners who understand the instrument, and are able to grasp the difficulty of these keys on it; they must not be played before everyone. You cannot produce brilliant and pleasing things with good intonation in every key, as most amateurs demand.

[1] On the term 'unison', see the Preface to the Translation.

§ 22

To ingratiate yourself with your listeners, it is most advantageous to know their humours. A choleric person may be satisfied with majestic and serious pieces; one inclined to melancholy with thoughtful,[1] chromatic pieces, and those set in minor keys; and a gay, wide-awake person with gay and jocular pieces. A musician must pay as much attention to this matter as he can; if he does not, he will never fully achieve his goal with listeners such as these.

§ 23

This prudent precept is generally observed least by those whom we must recognize in fact as learned and able musicians. Instead of first ingratiating themselves with their listeners with pleasing and understandable pieces, out of wilfulness they frighten them away at the outset with learnedness that is suitable only for connoisseurs; as a result, they often earn no more than the reputation for being a learned pedant. If they would accommodate themselves in a more reasonable manner, they would be more justly treated than is ordinarily the case.

§ 24

With regard to the embellishments in the Adagio, the flautist must, in addition to what has been said previously, consider whether the pieces are set in two or more parts. In a trio few embellishments may be introduced, and the second part must not be deprived of the opportunity to add his share. The graces must be of such a kind that they are both appropriate to the situation, and can be imitated by the performer of the second part. They must be introduced only in passages that consist of imitations, whether at the upper fifth, the lower fourth, or the unison. If both parts have the same melody in sixths or thirds, nothing may be added, unless it has been agreed beforehand to make the same variations.[2] With respect to the Piano and Forte one part must always adjust to the other, so that the swelling and diminishing of the tone occur at the same time. If, however, one of the two has a middle part from time to time, in which the notes are written chiefly to fill out the harmony, it must be played more softly than the one which has the principal melody at the time, so that the passages that have no melody do not stand out inopportunely. If both parts are imitative, or have a similar melody in thirds or sixths, both can play with the same strength.

---

[1] *Tiefsinnig (recherché)*.

[2] G. P. Telemann published a set of *III Trietti metodichi* in Hamburg in 1731 to illustrate the procedure for embellishing the two upper parts of a trio. A sample from this work is contained in Schmitz, *Die Kunst der Verzierung*, pp. 108–9. A reprint of the complete set has been prepared by Max Schneider (Leipzig: Breitkopf & Härtel, 1948).

§ 25

If one player makes a grace in a trio, the other, if he has the opportunity, as he should have, to repeat it, must execute it in the same way. Since it is easier to introduce something than it is to imitate it, if he can add something clever in addition, let him do so at the end of the grace, so that we may see that he can imitate it simply as well as vary it.

§ 26

A public performer who is a beginner should not undertake to play a trio with someone to whom he is not equal, unless he is assured that the latter will defer to and accommodate him; otherwise he will always be the loser. The trio is in fact the touchstone by which we can best judge the strength and insight of two persons. If it is to have a good effect, it requires a performance by two persons who have the same kind of execution; and if this is the case, it is in my opinion one of the most beautiful and perfect sorts of music. A quartet is similar to it, and still richer in harmony if it is written, as it should be, in four obbligato parts, that is, so that no part can be left out without harm to the whole. In it there is still less freedom to add extempore graces than in a trio. The best effect may be anticipated if the melody is played truly, and in a sustained manner.

§ 27

In a concerto you have more freedom in regard to the graces than in a trio, especially in the Adagio, but you must still pay constant attention to whether the accompanying parts have melodic progressions, or plain harmony. In the first case, the melody must be played simply. In the second, you may make whatever embellishments you wish, provided that you do not proceed in opposition to the rules of harmony, taste, and reason. You are better protected against error if in the Adagio you write the bass beneath the upper part in the scroll of the solo part; from it you can divine the other parts more easily.

§ 28

Were the flautist to join in the performance of a well-written ritornello in an Arioso that is played muted or Piano, and whose melody reappears at the beginning of the solo part on the flute, he would produce the same effect as that of a singer singing along in the ritornello of an aria, or of one player doubling the other's part instead of resting in a trio. If you leave the ritornello to the violins alone, the following solo of the flute will make a much better impression than would otherwise be the case.[1]

[1] It is not clear whether Quantz intends this rule to apply only to movements of this type. In a number of Quantz's concertos the flute part is written out as a doubling of the first violin part in the opening ritornello of both fast and slow movements. The fact that occasionally the violins' double stops are included in the solo flautist's music suggests that such passages were probably intended as cues.

§ 29

A solo[1] actually gives you the greatest freedom to allow your own fancies to be heard, if they are good, since you are concerned with only one opposing part. Here you may introduce as many embellishments as the melody and harmony permit.

§ 30

If a flautist has to play in concert with a vocal part,[2] he must seek to match it as much as possible in tone quality and manner of execution. He must vary nothing except where imitations give the opportunity to do so. The graces must be of a kind that the voice can imitate; hence extensive leaps must be avoided. But if the voice has a plain melody, and the flute has its own distinct progressions above it, the flautist can add as much as he deems suitable. If the voice rests, he can play with still more freedom. If the voice is weak, and the performance is in a chamber, the flautist must play more softly. At the theatre, on the other hand, he can play a little more loudly, since there soft playing on the flute has little effect. In any case, however, he must not overwhelm the singer with too many variations, lest the latter, having to sing from memory, be thrown into confusion.

§ 31

It is much more advantageous for a musician always to keep some of his skill in reserve, so that he can give his listeners more than one surprise, than to display all his skill at once, so that we have nothing more to hear from him.

§ 32

If someone requests him to play, let him do so at once, without grimaces or feigned modesty. And when he has finished his piece, he should not insist upon playing more than is demanded of him, lest we must beg him as many times to cease as we had to beg him to begin, a common reproach made against virtuosos.

§ 33

Although the approbation of your listeners may serve as an encouragement, you must not allow yourself to be led astray by the excessive praise that has become an unfortunate custom in music, perhaps because some fantastic dunces among the Italian singers, with all their crass ignorance, demand it almost as an obligation due to their very names. Such praise should be taken as flattery rather than truth, especially if received from good friends. The real truth can be discovered sooner from reasonable

---

[1] i.e. a solo sonata with thorough-bass accompaniment.
[2] i.e. if the flautist must play an obbligato flute part in a vocal work.

enemies than from flattering friends. If, however, you find a prudent, faithful friend, free of flattery, who praises that which should be praised, and censures that which should be censured, you must justly consider him a person to be greatly treasured, and must trust his verdicts, either taking heart from them, or concentrating on improvement. On the other hand, should you occasionally find some persons who only censure, and never praise, who, perhaps from hidden motives, seek to condemn everything produced by someone whom they consider less important than themselves, you must not allow yourself to be completely cast down. You should try to become gradually more certain of your ability, should determine carefully to what extent these persons are justified, and ask the opinion of other less biased persons. If you find something that could be better, strive diligently to improve it; and for the rest, bear excessive censure with a generous composure.

CHAPTER XVII

Of the Duties of Those Who Accompany or Execute the Accompanying or Ripieno Parts Associated with a Concertante Part

§ 1

Anyone who compares earlier music with that of the present day, and considers the differences manifest from decade to decade in only the past half-century, will find that, in regard to the invention of their ideas, composers have for some years striven to inquire into and perfect everything that contributes to the lively expression of the passions. These inquiries into composition would be of little use, however, if others were not also made into the art of performance (*exécution*).[1]

§ 2

Every musical idea may be executed in different ways, poorly, indifferently, or well. A good, distinct execution, appropriate in every respect, may sustain a mediocre composition; an indistinct and bad one, on the other hand, may spoil the best composition.

§ 3

Since experience shows that, as a result of the efforts of composers to invent new ideas, we expect far more of ripieno players now than formerly, and that today a ripieno part is perhaps more difficult to play than a solo in earlier times, it necessarily follows that the performers of the ripieno parts also must know much more today than was required earlier if the composers are to achieve their goal.

§ 4

Yet if we consider the condition of the majority of musical establishments[2] at courts as well as in republics and cities, we immediately note considerable defects with regard to accompaniment, stemming largely from the great disparity in the manner of playing found among the musicians of the same chapel or orchestra. No one can imagine the extent of these

---

[1] The French term *exécution* appears in parentheses in the German text. The German word is *Ausführung*.

[2] On the use of this term, see the Preface to the Translation.

defects unless he has personally experienced it, and has heard many different orchestras. We can only conclude that many beautiful compositions are mutilated, and therefore that it is necessary to remedy these mistakes made in performance.

§ 5

The basis for improvement can be established only through oral or written instruction. As oral instruction is rare, since most musical establishments lack good leaders with the necessary insight, and, to my knowledge, no written instruction has yet been published, I have resolved to make an initial essay, based on the little insight I have gained through long experience and practice, to serve those who have a firm desire to fulfil their duties in the accompanying body, and to explain, as fully as possible, the essentials that must be observed.

§ 6

So that each person may quickly find, without much searching, that which particularly concerns him, I shall divide this chapter into various sections; I shall first describe the qualities of a leader of an orchestra,[1] then note the particular duties incumbent upon the performer of each of the accompanying parts,[2] and finally append some necessary observations that concern all accompanists equally.[3] Instructions for bowing and all that pertains to it I present only in connexion with the duties of the violinist;[4] but since much appears there which may be of profit to the violists and bass players, and which I did not wish to repeat, lest the sections devoted to these instruments become unnecessarily long, all the remaining string players might well read through this section.[5] That which refers only to the bow-stroke of each of the middle and bass instruments I have indicated in the sections devoted to them.

SECTION I

Of the Qualities of a Leader of an Orchestra

§ 1

It is impossible for even a skilful leader of an orchestra to insure the good execution of a musical composition[6] unless each person associated with him is willing to contribute properly his own share. I have noticed, however, in large orchestras at various places, that if the very same people are

---

[1] Section I of this chapter.　　　[2] Sections II to VI.　　　[3] Section VII.
[4] Section II.　　　　　　　　　　　　　　　　　　　　　　　[5] Section II.
[6] The French text, which is clearer and more specific than the German in this case, has been followed in this portion of the sentence. In the German text the word *Ausnahme* again seems to be a misprint of *Aufnahme*.

led first by one person, then by another, the effect under the direction of the one has always been better than the effect under the other. I conclude that these varying results must be ascribed not to the ripienists, but to the leaders, and in consequence that much depends upon the leader.

§ 2

This being the case, it would be desirable, in order to gradually further the cause of music in general, to have at each place where an orchestra has been established at least one able and experienced musician who has not only insight into clear execution, but also some understanding of both composition and harmony, so that he can hit correctly upon the style in which each composition must be executed, and thus can avoid the numerous mistakes that might disfigure and spoil it. A man should be found who is gifted with both the capacity and the sincerity to impart to the others the skills that they need. Better solo performers as well as ripienists would then appear within a short time. For it cannot be said that it is absolutely necessary to have a good composer at every place, or in every musical establishment, to insure the growth or improvement of an orchestra. The number of good musical pieces is large enough, if one knows how to select them intelligently and well. A good leader, graced with the qualities mentioned above, is much more important. Unfortunately, however, it often happens that only those who move up in an orchestra through the right of seniority are chosen as leaders; or sometimes a person is pushed in who has had the good fortune to insinuate himself into favour with a solo or concerto, perhaps learned by heart, without further investigation into the matter of whether he possesses the proper knowledge to lead others. Sometimes the choice is even made quite accidentally. Hence it is not very surprising if, as frequently happens, the position falls to one who understands little or nothing of music. If some such error in selection has occurred, a decline rather than improvement in the orchestra may be surely predicted. And if such poor consideration is given to the choice of a leader, upon whom so much depends, it may be imagined how the choice of the other members of the orchestra is likely to be made. It would be well, therefore, to find for your leader a man who has played for several years in large and celebrated orchestras, and in them has acquired experience of good execution and the other necessary skills. It is certain that many of the ripienists in such large orchestras often have more insight into performance than many of the leaders of other orchestras; and it is truly a pity that such persons are not appreciated. If they were, they might do much more good than by remaining anonymous as ripienists.

§ 3

Whether a leader plays this instrument or that may be of no importance. Since, however, the violin is absolutely indispensable in the accompanying body, and is also more penetrating than any of the other instruments most used for accompanying, it is better if he does play the violin. Yet there is no urgent necessity that he demonstrate his ability to perform unusually difficult feats[1] upon his instrument; this may be left to those who seek to distinguish themselves only through the delicacy of their playing, of whom there are sufficient numbers. If, however, a leader does possess this talent, he deserves so much the greater honour.[2]

§ 4

The greatest skill required of the leader is that he have a perfect understanding of how to play all types of compositions in accordance with their style, sentiment, and purpose, and in the correct tempos. He must therefore have even more experience with regard to that which distinguishes one piece from another than a composer. The latter often troubles himself only with what he has written himself. Many do not know how to execute their own things in the correct tempos, whether from excessive indifference, too much ardour, or too little experience. A clever leader, however, can easily correct these errors, especially if he has been trained under a good leader in a well-disciplined orchestra in which he has played many different kinds of music. If he has not had this opportunity, he must at least have been at a *variety* of places where he could hear, and profit from hearing, good ensembles. If he is in earnest about presiding over his office well, he may also profit greatly from conversation with experienced persons; he will learn more of what he needs to know in this way than through striving to perform very difficult technical feats.

§ 5

The leader of an orchestra must also know how to keep perfect time. He must be able to pay the most exact attention to the value of the notes, and particularly to the short semiquaver and demisemiquaver rests, so that he neither rushes nor drags. For if he makes a mistake in this regard, he misleads all the others, and produces confusion in the ensemble. After short rests it would be less harmful to begin later and then rush the following short notes a little than to anticipate them. Before he begins a piece, he must carefully determine at which tempo it ought to be played. If it is a quick and unfamiliar piece, he will do better to begin too slowly than too quickly, since passing from a slow tempo to a fast one is easier and less apparent than passing from a fast tempo to a slow one. In this regard he must take great care to notice whether the ripienists are more

[1] *Schwierigkeiten (difficultés).* Eighteenth-century English writers refer to 'difficulties' in the same sense.

[2] In the French text the following sentences are added at this point: 'The Italians call the leader of an orchestra *il primo violino*, and the French *le premier violon*. We will employ the latter denomination.' In the German text, however, the less specific term 'leader' is retained.

inclined to rush or to hesitate and drag. Young persons fall easily into the former error, old people into the latter. Hence the leader must try to enkindle the latter, and moderate the former. If, however, he knows how to set the correct tempo immediately, the result is so much the better, and this precaution is then unnecessary. So that the other players will begin with him, especially in quick notes, he must accustom them to memorize the first measure of the piece, to hold the bow close to the strings, and to pay attention to his bow-stroke. Otherwise he will have to wait upon the first note[1] until the others come in, and so will lengthen the note, producing a poor effect in quick notes. He himself must not begin until he sees that all of the other musicians are in readiness, especially if there is only one person to a part; otherwise, the beginning, which should surprise the listeners and compel their attention, will be faultily done. In this respect the omission[2] of the bass parts will do the greatest damage.

§ 6

The leader must frequently direct his eyes and ears both to the performer of the principal part and to the accompanists, in case it is necessary to accommodate the one and keep the others in order. The leader must judge from the execution of the soloist whether the latter would prefer what he is playing either faster or slower, so that the others may be guided smoothly to the correct tempo. The leader must allow the soloist the freedom to set his tempo as he considers best.

§ 7

A good leader must try, in addition, to develop and maintain a good and uniform execution in the orchestra. Just as he himself must have good execution, he must also seek to make that of his colleagues alike, and always uniform with his own. To this end he must know how to introduce reasonable and proper discipline. If his services have earned him respect, and his friendly demeanour and affable conduct have brought him affection, this will not be difficult.

§ 8

The leader must take special pains to see that the instruments are correctly and uniformly tuned. The more prevalent the lack of correct common tuning, the greater is the damage done. Whether the pitch of the orchestra is high or low,[3] the effect of a composition will always be considerably impaired if the instruments are not in tune with one another. Hence if the leader wishes to maintain correct intonation in the perfor-

---

[1] i.e. hold the first note.
[2] In this case 'omission' seems to mean 'tardy entry'.
[3] On the different pitch standards used in Quantz's day, see Section VII of this chapter, § 7.

mance of a musical composition,[1] he must first tune his own instrument truly with the keyboard, and then have each individual instrumentalist tune to him.[2] That the instruments may not be put out of tune again if the performance does not begin immediately, he must not allow anyone to play preludes or other fancies[3] as he pleases; they are very unpleasant to listen to, and often cause the players to alter the tuning of their instruments, and finally deviate from the common tuning.

§ 9

Should there be some among the ripienists whose execution differs from that of the others, the leader must undertake to rehearse them separately, lest one, for example, add a shake where others play without it, or slur notes that are attacked by others, or make a mordent, omitted by the others, after an appoggiatura; for the greatest beauty of performance stems from the uniformity with which all the members of the orchestra play.

§ 10

The leader must see to it that all of his associates always play with him with uniform loudness or softness, as each idea requires, and especially that all express the alternations of Piano and Forte and their different degrees simultaneously at the notes where they are indicated. He himself must be regulated by whether the concertante part is loud or soft. And since he should serve as a model and leader for the others, it will be to his credit if he always shows the same attentiveness to each composition, and directs each, no matter whose it is, without partiality and with the same seriousness and diligence as if it were his own. Whether the composer is present or absent, whether he is fair or unfair, he will, in private at least, have to thank the leader for his honesty and for the good performance of his work, even if for some deceitful reason he does not wish to make a public acknowledgement; for both virtues and vices reward those who possess them.

§ 11

To give his instrumentalists a better foundation in good execution, and at the same time to make them good accompanists, the leader will do well to frequently rehearse, in addition to music of many other kinds, overtures, characteristic pieces,[4] and dances that must be played in an accented and

---

[1] 'Ensemble' may be meant at this point. See the discussion of 'musical establishment' in the Preface to the Translation.

[2] In the German text 'him' is ambiguous, and may refer to the keyboard. The French text seems to confirm that the leader is meant.

[3] *Zu präludiren und zu phantasiren* (*préluder ou de jouer quelque chose à sa fantaisie*). Although it was a common practice in Quantz's day to improvise preludes or fantasias (see Hotteterre, *L'Art de preluder sur la flûte traversiere*), here Quantz seems to indicate the 'warm-up' exercises still commonly heard before concerts today.

[4] See Section VII, § 56.

expressive[1] manner, with either a short and light bow-stroke or with a sharp and heavy one. In this way he will accustom his accompanists to play each piece in accordance with its character, with majesty, fire, and animation, and in a sharp, distinct, and uniform manner. Experience proves that those who have been trained in good town bands, and have long played for dances, make better ripienists than those who have practised only the *galant* manner of playing and only one type of music. Just as, for example, a delicate brush stroke does not have as good an effect in a theatrical set, which must be viewed by candle-light and from a distance, as in an intimate painting,[2] so an all-too-*galant* manner of playing, and a long, dragging, or sawing bow-stroke,[3] are less effective in the accompanying body of a large orchestra than they are in a solo or a small chamber ensemble.

§ 12

The brilliance of an orchestra will also be greatly enhanced if it contains good solo players on various instruments. Hence the leader must seek to encourage good solo players. To this end he must give those equipped to play alone frequent opportunities to distinguish themselves, not only privately, but also in public concerts. At the same time, however, he must endeavour to keep them from being led into a false conceit (a weakness of many young people)[4] which will persuade them that they are already the great musicians that they will become only with time. Those who might conceive such an unreasonable pride in themselves should not be favoured by the leader at the expense of others who would appreciate the opportunity to appear in public and would make every effort to profit from it.

§ 13

Finally, the leader must know how to distribute, place, and arrange the instrumentalists in an ensemble. Much depends upon the good distribution and placement of the instruments, and upon their combination in the proper ratio. In the orchestra pit of an opera house, the first harpsichord may be placed in the middle, with the broad end facing the parterre and the tip to the stage, so that the singers are visible to the player. The violoncello may be placed on his right, and the double bass on his left. The leader may sit next to the first harpsichord, on the right and slightly forward and elevated. The violinists and violists may form a narrow oval ring, beginning with the leader and continuing so that the violists have their backs to the stage and extend to the tip of the harpsichord, in such fashion that all may see and hear the leader. If, however, the pit is spacious enough to seat four people abreast, the second violins may sit, in two pairs, one behind the other, in the middle between the first violins and

[1] *Hebend (expressive).*   [2] *Cabinetstück (morceau de cabinet).*
[3] French text: 'a long, dragging stroke, that lacks a certain force'.
[4] Translator's parentheses.

the violists sitting with their backs to the stage; for the closer together the instruments are, the better the effect they produce. On the same side, at the end where the violinists stop, there still may be enough room for another violoncello and a double bass. Let the second harpsichord be placed on the left side of the first, parallel to the stage and with the tip turned toward the first, but so that room may still be found behind it for the bassoons, unless you wish to put them on the right side of the second harpsichord, behind the flutes. Another pair of violoncellos may be placed next to the second harpsichord. On this, the left, side of the pit, the oboes and hunting horns may sit in a row with their backs to the listeners, like the violins on the right side; the flutes, however, are posted in a diagonal line next to the first harpsichord, so that they turn their eyes toward the harpsichord, and the lower ends of their flutes toward the parterre. In some places, however, where there is an empty space between the pit and the listeners, the flutes are placed with their backs to the parterre, and the oboes are stationed in a diagonal line between them and the second harpsichord. The oboes produce an excellent effect, especially in the tutti, serving as a filler, and their sound justly deserves a free outlet, an outlet which the flutes also enjoy if no one stands close behind them and if the players turn a little to the side, and which they enjoy even more fully, since they are then closer to the listeners. The theorbo may find a comfortable place behind the second harpsichordist and the violoncellists attached to him.[1]

§ 14

In a composition for a large ensemble,[2] performed either in a hall or in some other large place where there is no stage, the tip of the harpsichord

[1] The following plan is based on that presented by A. Schering in his edition of the *Essay*, but has been revised in the light of the text and the seating plan of the Dresden orchestra, reproduced by Rousseau in his *Dictionnaire de musique* (1768). See C. Mennicke, *Hasse und die Brüder Graun als Symphoniker* (Leipzig: Breitkopf & Härtel, 1906), pp. 269–70.

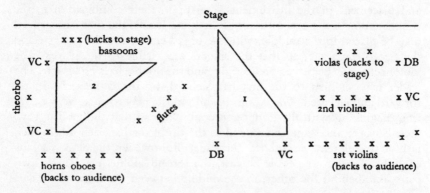

The number of players is not prescribed at this point in the text. I have therefore taken the figures for the largest ensemble mentioned in § 16. Alternatives mentioned in the text should
→ be noted.   [2] *Bey einer zahlreichen Musik (dans une Musique nombreuse).*

may be directed towards the listeners. So that none of the musicians turns his back to the listeners, the first violinists may stand in a row next to the harpsichord, with the leader on the right of the keyboard player, who has the two bass instruments playing on either side of him. The second violins may come behind the first, and behind them the violas. Next to the violas, on the right, place the oboes in the same row, and behind this row the hunting horns and the other basses. The flutes, if they have solo parts to play, are best placed at the tip of the harpsichord, in front of the first violins, or on the left side of the harpsichord.[1] Because of the weakness of their tone, they would not be heard if they were to stand further back. Singers also may take the same place; if they were to stand behind the keyboard player and read from the score, they would not only hamper the violoncellists and double-bass players, but would also obstruct their own breathing and stifle their own voices if poor sight forced them to bend over [to see the music clearly].[2]

§ 15

In a small chamber ensemble the harpsichord may be placed by the wall on the left of its player, but far enough removed from it so that all the accompanying instruments except the basses have room between him and the wall. If only four violins are present, they and the violists may all stand in one row behind the harpsichord.[3] If, however, there are six or eight violinists, it would be better to place the second violins behind the first, and the violas behind the second violins, so that the middle parts do not stand out above the principal part, for this produces a poor effect. The soloists, in these circumstances, can take their places in front of the harpsichord, in such a way that they have the accompanists in view to the side.[4]

[1] The following plan is again based on that of Schering, and has again been modified in the light of the text, especially the figures given for a large ensemble.

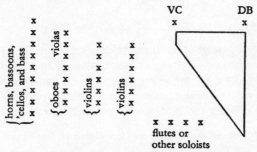

[2] In other words, if the singer were short-sighted, he would have to bend over the back of one of the players to see the notes properly, and this would hamper his breathing.

[3] *So können dieselben in einer Reihe, an dem Clavicymbal hin, und die Bratsche hinter demselben stehen* (*ils peuvent tous, aussi bien que la Violette se mettre d'une même rangée tout au long du Clavecin*).

[4] An eighteenth-century engraving that depicts Frederick the Great performing with his chamber musicians shows the players arranged in a fashion similar to that described here. See G. Kinsky, *A History of Music in Pictures* (New York: E. P. Dutton, 1929), p. 267.

§ 16

He who wishes to perform a composition well must see to it that he supplies each instrument in the proper proportion, and does not use too many of one kind, too few of another. I shall propose a ratio which, to my thinking, will satisfy all requirements in this regard. I assume that the *harpsichord* will be included in all ensembles, whether large or small.

With *four violins* use *one viola, one violoncello,* and *one double bass* of medium size.[1]

With *six violins,* the same complement and *one bassoon.*

Eight violins require *two violas, two violoncellos,* an *additional double bass,* larger, however, than the first, *two oboes, two flutes,* and *two bassoons.*

With *ten violins,* the same complement, but with an *additional violoncello.*

With *twelve violins* use *three violas, four violoncellos, two double basses, three bassoons, four oboes, four flutes,* and in a pit *another keyboard* and *one theorbo.*

Hunting horns may be necessary in both small and large ensembles, depending upon the nature of the piece and the inclination of the composer.[2]

§ 17

With this distribution in mind it will not be difficult to order even the largest ensembles in the correct ratios, if the increases from four to eight, from eight to twelve, &c., are properly noted. Since the success of a composition depends as much upon an arrangement of the instruments in the proper proportions as upon good execution, foresight in this matter is particularly important. Many compositions would be more effective if the distribution of the parts were arranged properly. For how can a composition sound well if the principal parts are drowned out and suppressed by the bass or even the middle parts? The former should stand out above all the others, and the middle parts should be heard least of all.

§ 18

If the leader is graced with all the talents mentioned heretofore, and if he has the requisite skill not only, where necessary, to develop all the good qualities required of an orchestra, but also to maintain them, he will bring honour to the orchestra and earn a special renown for himself as well. Since, as already stated above, an orchestra produces a better effect

---

[1] On the different sizes of double basses used in Quantz's day, see Section V, §§ 2–3, of this chapter.

[2] On the size of orchestras in the eighteenth century, and the distribution of instruments, see A. Carse, *The Orchestra in the XVIIIth Century* (Cambridge: W. Heffer and Sons, 1940), pp. 16–47. See also Mennicke, *Hasse,* pp. 269–70; the memorandum of J. S. Bach for 'a well-appointed church music' in Hans T. David and Arthur Mendel, *The Bach Reader* (New York: W. W. Norton, 1945), pp. 120–4; and the lists of players used in various performances of the *Messiah* in O. E. Deutsch, *Handel, a Documentary Biography* (New York: W. W. Norton, 1954. London A. & C. Black, 1955), pp. 751, 800.

under the direction of one person than under that of another, it follows that all musicians are not equally suited to lead. And since various persons who are excellent when well led do not have the slightest ability themselves for leading, it is not difficult to infer how much depends upon a man who possesses all the qualities required for the position of a good musical leader, and what great privileges he deserves in the ensemble.

SECTION II

Of the Ripieno Violinists in Particular[1]

§ 1

All bowed instruments in general, and the violins in particular, must be equipped with strings of a thickness commensurate with the size of the instrument, so that the strings are neither too taut nor too slack. If they are too thick, the tone becomes dull, while if they are too thin, the tone becomes immature and weak. Whether the pitch used in the orchestra is high or low also must be taken into consideration.[2]

§ 2

Since my observations about the correct tuning of the violin will apply to all the other bowed instruments, this matter will be dealt with in the last section.[3]

§ 3

In the performance of music on the violin and the instruments similar to it the bow-stroke is of chief importance. Through it the sound is drawn from the instrument well or poorly, the notes receive their life, the Piano and Forte are expressed, the passions are aroused, and the melan-

[1] A number of treatises on violin playing will help the student to see Quantz's instructions in historical perspective. L. Mozart, *A Treatise on the Fundamental Principles of Violin Playing* (1756) is the most important German treatise on the subject dating from the eighteenth century, and is close to Quantz in explaining a number of points. J. F. Reichardt, *Ueber die Pflichten des Ripien-Violinisten* (Berlin and Leipzig: G. J. Decker, 1776), suggests some changes in approach that occurred later in the century. G. Muffat, in his *Premieres observations sur la maniere de jouër les airs de balets à la françoise selon la methode de feu M. de Lully*, reprinted in *Denkmäler der Tonkunst in Österreich*, II Jahrgang (1895), Zweiter Teil, and in the Preface to his *Auserlesene Instrumental-Music* (1701), *DTÖ*, XI Jahrgang (1914), Zweiter Teil, provides much valuable information on string playing, particularly in the French style, during the period when Quantz was an apprentice. Eighteenth-century French violin tutors are reviewed in La Laurencie, *L'École française de violon de Lully à Viotti* (3 vols.; Paris: Librairie Delagrave, 1924). Other valuable works are G. Tartini, *Treatise on Ornaments in Music*, ed. by E. Jacobi, trans. by C. Girdlestone (Celle and New York: Hermann Moeck Verlag, 1961), and F. Geminiani, *The Art of Playing the Violin*, facsimile edition edited by D. Boyden (London: Oxford University Press, 1952). D. Boyden, 'The Violin and its Technique in the Eighteenth Century', *The Musical Quarterly*, xxxvi (1950), pp. 9–38, also contains much valuable information.

[2] On the various pitch standards of Quantz's day, see Section VII, §§ 6–7, of this chapter.

[3] See Section VII, §§ 1–9, of this chapter.

choly is distinguished from the gay, the serious from the jocular, the sublime from the flattering, the modest from the bold. In a word, like the
chest, tongue, and lips on the flute, the bow-stroke provides the means for
achieving musical articulation,[1] and for varying a single idea in diverse
ways. That the fingers must also contribute their share, and that you must
have a good instrument and true strings, is self-evident. But since, even
with all of these things, the execution may still be very defective, no matter
how accurately and truly you stop the strings, how well the instrument
sounds, or how good the strings are, it naturally follows that, with regard
to execution, the bow-stroke is of central importance.

§ 4

I will illustrate what I have said with an example. Play the passage in
Tab. XXII, Fig. 1, in a moderate tempo entirely with long strokes of the
full bow.

TABLE XXII

FIG. 1

Afterwards diminish the length of the strokes, and play the same notes
several times with successively shorter strokes. Then one time give a stress
to each stroke with the bow, another time play the example *staccato* (*abgestossen*), that is, with all the strokes detached.[2] Although each note will
have received its separate stroke, the expression will be different each
time. The expression will be equally varied if you try the example with
different kinds of slurs, and play the semiquavers with one stroke, then as
if dots beneath a slur appear above the notes, then two notes with one
stroke, then one staccato and three slurred, or the first three slurred and
the fourth staccato, the first and fourth staccato and the second and third
slurred, or the first detached and the remaining notes slurred with single
strokes for each pair.[3]

§ 5

This example is sufficient proof of the harm that incorrect use of the
bow can do, and of the varied effects that its correct handling can produce.
It follows that in a ripieno part neither the violinist nor any other performer upon a bowed instrument has the freedom to slur or detach the

---

[1] French text: 'true expression'.

[2] *Abgestossen (staccato), und mit dem Bogen abgesetzet (staccato c. a. d. que tous les coups soient de-
tachés). Abgesetzet (detaché)* is not the equivalent of the modern *détaché*. Quantz seems to use the
term to indicate actual removal of the bow from the string. 'Staccato', however, does not always
indicate a completely detached bowing. In this regard, see § 27 of this section.

[3] L. Mozart, *A Treatise*, pp. 114–31, presents a lengthy section, with many examples, that
enlarges on the point made in this paragraph.

notes as he pleases; he is obliged to play them with the bowing the composer has indicated at those places which deviate from the customary manner.

> Note here in passing that if many figures of the same sort follow one another, and the bowing of only the first is indicated, the others must be played in the same manner as long as no other species of notes appears. The same is true of notes with strokes above them. If, for example, only two, three, or four are marked with strokes, the following notes of the same species and value are also played staccato. If they are not, the desired effect will not be produced, and perfect uniformity of expression will never be achieved.

§ 6

It also follows that the effectiveness of the accompaniment depends more upon the violinists than upon the players of other instruments, since the former control the melody. If they play lethargically or carelessly, the others can do little to further the expression of the accompaniment. Since, then, the bow-stroke is so important to expression, everything that has to do with it will be treated together in this section, and in the other sections I will refer to what I have said in this one.

§ 7

To treat of all the precepts relating to the bow-stroke would be out of place here, since I assume a reader who can play the violin, and therefore understands bowing. Hence I will examine only certain doubtful situations, and those where some particular should be noted that the composer cannot always indicate. From these, decisions may be made about the majority of similar cases. Then I will show what kind of stroke should prevail in each category of pieces.[1] Finally I will add whatever else must be observed with regard to this subject.

§ 8

The principal characteristic of good bowing is that the notes belonging to an up- or down-stroke are played in this manner as often as possible.

If several notes are repeated and are intermingled with syncopated notes, each must have its separate stroke, that is to say, the bow-stroke[2] must be detached after the syncopated note (see Tab. XXII, Fig. 2).

FIG. 2

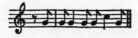

---

[1] Quantz refers to the various types of fast and slow pieces. See § 26 of this section.

[2] As the French text demonstrates, the noun *Bogen* is frequently used as a contraction for *Bogenstrich*. Where some confusion might result from this usage, the French text has been followed.

Were the quavers here played without repeating[1] or without detaching the bow, they would sound very lethargic, and a completely different effect would result. Rapid quavers or semiquavers of this type also must not be stressed with pressure of the bow; they must be given the necessary liveliness through the use of repeated strokes.

The quavers in Tab. XXII, Fig. 3, must all be stressed with a short bow-stroke; and if appoggiaturas follow such notes, the note before the appoggiatura must have a detached bow-stroke, so that the two notes on the same pitch may be heard clearly and distinctly.

FIG. 3

If in a quick tempo a crotchet on the downbeat is followed by several quavers or semiquavers which are repeated or which form a leap, the effect is good if the crotchet is stressed with a detached down-stroke, so that the following quavers may also be played with a down-stroke (see Tab. XXII, Fig. 4, the notes C-C and D-G).

FIG. 4

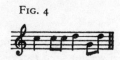

If two notes appear on the same pitch, and there is no slur above them (see Tab. XXII, Fig. 5), the bow-stroke must separate them rather than tie them together.

FIG. 5

In notes of the kind seen in Tab. XXII, Fig. 6, the last note in the bar must be detached a little, in order to separate it from the note on the downbeat.

FIG. 6

The second note in the bar, which is slurred to the first, may be expressed a bit more softly than the others.

---

[1] By 'repeating' the bow or bow-stroke, Quantz seems to mean taking a new stroke in the same direction, whether up or down. In some cases, however, he may mean simply taking a new stroke.

In gay and quick pieces the last quaver of each half bar must be stressed with the bow (see Tab. XXII, Fig. 7, the first G, the second E, and the F).

FIG. 7

If a short note is tied to a long one (see Tab. XXII, Fig. 8), the long note, and not the short one, must be stressed with a pressure of the bow.

FIG. 8

If two semiquavers follow a quaver, the quaver must be stressed and detached with the bow, as if there were a stroke above it (see Tab. XXII, Fig. 9).

FIG. 9

In Fig. 10 the second and third notes are taken with an up-stroke in the Allegro, but the stroke is stopped or detached a little at the dot;[1] the following two G's, however, must each receive down-strokes.

FIG. 10

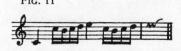

In Fig. 11 the down-stroke is repeated for the second C, and also for the C in the fourth crotchet of the bar, after the E.

FIG. 11

The same thing is done if semiquavers follow a minim. But if the first and third crotchets of the bar consist of four semiquavers, then the bow must be detached and repeated after the second and third crotchets.[2]

In crotchets or quavers mingled with rests of the same value, where the

---

[1] The French text is followed here. The German reads: *mit einem Einhalten oder Absatze gemacht.*

[2] As it stands in both the French and German texts, the last phrase makes little sense. Quantz may mean 'the bow must be detached after the second crotchet and a new down-stroke is taken on the third', or may have mistakenly said 'second and third' when he intended 'second and fourth'.

rests come first and fall on the beat (see Tab. XXII, Fig. 12) each note must be played with an up-stroke.

FIG. 12

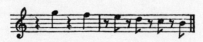

In a quick tempo notes of the kind seen in Tab. XXII, Fig. 13,[1] are played with a down-stroke for the first and an up-stroke for the following three. In a slow tempo, on the other hand, the effect is much more charming if all four notes are executed in one stroke, but with a slight detaching of the bow-stroke after the first note. The following four notes are taken in the same manner with an up-stroke. In the first case, in a quick tempo, a stroke is placed above the first note and a slur above the following three; but in the second, in a slow tempo, an additional slur is placed above all four notes, as this example shows.

FIG. 13

§ 9

The notes in Tab. XXII, Fig. 14, are played with alternating strokes, and not with repeated down-strokes; but the G in the first bar must receive just as much emphasis in the up-stroke as the C in the down-stroke, and also the G in the second bar.

FIG. 14

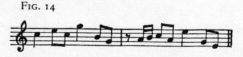

In Tab. XXII, Fig. 15, the notes are also played in the same fashion with alternating strokes, but with the difference that the fourth note is emphasized like the first.

FIG. 15

The notes in Tab. XXII, Fig. 16, may be executed equally well in two ways, if the violinist is as practised in the up-stroke as in the down-stroke. The effect will be equally good whether you provide each note with an

[1] As Quantz indicates in the following sentences, this figure illustrates two distinct ways of playing the same notes. In the first case the upper of the two slurs would not be used.

individual stroke or take the first A and C in an up-stroke with both notes well stressed and short; the latter type of execution, however, is also very useful in many other situations encountered in modern music.

FIG. 16

Proof of this is immediately apparent in the following example, Tab. XXII, Fig. 17. Here, because of what follows, the E and G in the first bar and the G and B in the second bar must be played with an up-stroke if the effect is to be good.

FIG. 17

The situation is the same in the notes in Tab. XXII, Fig. 18, when the tempo is very quick, especially if the notes are widely separated, as in the last two bars. This manner of playing is also much less tiring than playing each note with a separate stroke.

FIG. 18

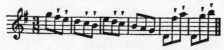

Notes of the kind seen in Tab. XXII, Fig. 19, may be performed in two ways. If the tempo is very quick, and no semiquaver passages are intermingled, they may be performed stroke for stroke, without repeated bows. If this intermingling is present, the bow must be detached and repeated[1] after the third note in the first half of the bar.

FIG. 19

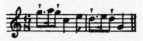

And since in this bar the accompaniment is usually constituted as in a Siciliano, that is, haltingly or *alla zoppa*, with each crotchet followed by a quaver[2] that must be played rather briskly[3] in a quick tempo, you must be careful to give these notes their proper weight, and must guard against breaking off some of the crotchet and adding it to the quaver; this would make the crotchets and quavers almost equal, and would transform the

---

[1] That is, a new down-stroke must be taken.

[2] As is actually the case in the accompanying parts of many sicilianos, Quantz imagines the movement as a regular alternation of crotchets and quavers: .

[3] *Hebend (vivement)*.

six-eight metre into two-four. You must also guard against making the crotchet too long and the quaver too short, or they will appear to be dotted notes in duple metre. To avoid both of these errors, however, you need only imagine during the crotchet two quavers of the same quickness as the one that follows, and all will be well.

§ 10

The equal strength and dexterity of the up-stroke and the down-stroke required above[1] is most necessary in the current musical style. For anyone who intends to perform the refined ideas that appear in this style will give them an offensive harshness[2] rather than a pleasing and light execution if he does not have this skill.

§ 11

To make your bow-strokes uniform, and to make yourself equally familiar with the up and down movement, practise a Gigue or Canarie in six-eight time which proceeds in quavers, and in which the first of each three of these quavers is dotted.[3] Give each note its separate stroke, so that, without repeating strokes, the first and third notes of each figure first receive down-strokes, then up-strokes; and always play the note after the dot very short and sharply. Or practise a piece in the above metre in which the first half of the bar consists of four notes, with two semiquavers replacing the middle quaver, while the second half consists of three, so that an odd number of notes occurs in each bar.[4]

Later try the same piece without dots, still without repeating strokes, [and imagine] triplets,[5] or rapid quavers in six-eight time.

In addition, take an example in duple time, in which either four semi-quavers follow each crotchet or two semiquavers each quaver,[6] and in which the notes move now by leap, now by step. Continue practising in this fashion until you perceive that the figures which begin with the up-stroke sound just the same as those beginning with the down-stroke. You will benefit greatly from practice of this sort, and will make your arm

---

[1] See the text accompanying Fig. 16 in the preceding paragraph.

[2] The French translator uses the word 'stiffness' (*roideur*), and this may indicate Quantz's meaning more clearly, although the German word is *Härte*.

[3] The following rhythmic pattern is meant; [musical notation in 6/8]

[4] The rhythmic pattern which Quantz describes would be written as follows: [musical notation in 6/8]

[5] The reference to triplets merely confuses the issue, since Quantz has been speaking in terms of six-eight time all along.

[6] These two figures would be written as follows: [musical notation in 4/4] or [musical notation]

competent to execute any difficult passage that may appear. Although certain notes must necessarily be taken with a down-stroke, an experienced violinist with the bow completely under control can also express them well with an up-stroke. This freedom of the bow must not be abused, however, since on certain occasions, that is, if one note requires considerably more sharpness than the others, the down-stroke remains superior to the up-stroke.

§ 12

In slurring notes in the Adagio, you must be careful not to make them seem detached,[1] unless there are dots beneath the slur that is above the notes (see Tab. XXII, Fig. 20). Likewise *pincemens* must not be introduced, especially if they are not indicated, lest the sentiment that the slurred notes are to express be in any way impeded. But if strokes are used instead of dots, as in the last two notes of this example,[2] the notes must be attacked sharply, in a single stroke of the bow. For just as a distinction is to be made between strokes and dots without slurs above them, that is, the notes with strokes must be played with completely[3] detached strokes, and those with dots simply with short strokes and in a sustained manner, so a similar distinction is required when there are slurs above the notes. Strokes, however, appear more often in the Allegro than in the Adagio.

Fig. 20

If semiquavers of the kind seen in Tab. XXII, Fig. 21, are to be elegantly performed in a slow tempo, the first of each two must always be heavier than the following one, both in duration and volume; and here the B in the third beat must be played *almost*[4] as though it were dotted.

Fig. 21

---

[1] *Im Adagio müssen die schleifenden Noten nicht mit dem Bogen gerücket, oder tockiret werden* ... (*En coulant les notes dans l'Adagio, il faut le faire de façon que les notes ne semblent point être detachées* ...).

[2] See the last two notes of Fig. 20. The term 'strokes' here refers to the vertical dashes above the notes.

[3] 'Completely' appears in the French text.

[4] 'Almost' is emphasized in the German text through the use of bolder type. J. F. Reichardt comments on this aspect of Quantz's teaching in the following manner: 'It would also be very faulty if one *always* observed the stressing of notes—about which Mr. *Quantz* speaks so much—with a particular pressure on the bow. This stress is nothing but a slight weight that everyone who plays with a good feeling for the beat naturally gives to the longer notes without thinking about it. ...' See his *Ueber die Pflichten des Ripien-Violinisten*, pp. 28–29.

§ 13

If in the Adagio slurs stand above dotted notes (see Tab. XXII, Fig. 22), the note after the dot must not be attacked; it must be slurred with the first with a diminuendo.

FIG. 22

If the second note is dotted, the first, whether a semiquaver or demisemiquaver, must be played very short in the Allegro and with a forceful bow-stroke; the dotted note, however, must be played more moderately, and must be sustained up to the following note. In the Adagio the first note must be as short as in the Allegro, but it must not be played as strongly (see Tab. XXII, Fig. 23).

FIG. 23

If these notes are to produce the desired effect, the bow-stroke must be repeated for each pair, so that there are two rather than four notes in each stroke.

The case is the same with notes of the kind found in Tab. XXII, Fig. 24. In them, however, you must employ a quiet and short bow-stroke, rather than a long, intense,[1] and dragging one. Otherwise the expression will sound too bold and offensive.

FIG. 24

In slow pieces dotted quavers and semiquavers must be played with a heavy stroke and in a sustained or *nourrissant* manner. The strokes must not be detached as is done when there are rests after the notes rather than dots. The dots must be held for their full value, so that you do not appear to be bored, and so that the Adagio is not transformed into an Andante. Strokes above the notes indicate that they must be stressed. The semiquavers following the dots must always be played very short and sharply in slow and quick tempos; and since dotted notes generally express something of the majestic and sublime, each note, if no slur stands above it, requires a separate bow-stroke; for it is not possible to express the short note after the dot as sharply with the same stroke, by detaching the bow,[2] as can be done with a new up-stroke.

---

[1] *Hastigen (rude).*   [2] *Durch einen Ruck des Bogens (par le même coup d'archet, en le détachant).*

§ 14

If in a slow tempo semitones are intermingled in the air (see Tab. XXII, Fig. 25), the notes raised by sharp or natural signs must be heard a little more strongly than the others; on stringed instruments this may be accomplished by a stronger pressure of the bow on the strings, in singing and on wind instruments by reinforcing the wind.

FIG. 25

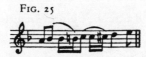

If two notes appear with a slur above them, the second raised or lowered by a semitone (see Tab. XXII, Fig. 26), the effect produced is better if the second note is taken with the next adjacent finger,[1] and the bow-stroke for it is simultaneously strengthened, than if it is executed by shifting the same[2] finger up or down. For in a slow tempo you must make the ear believe that you are playing only a single note.[3]

FIG. 26

In a quick tempo notice in general that if several crotchets or minims are raised with a sharp or lowered with a flat, and especially if several ascend or descend by step (see Tab. XXII, Fig. 27), they must be played in a sustained manner, and with greater strength and emphasis than the other notes.

FIG. 27

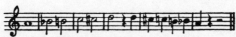

§ 15

Long notes mingled with quick and lively ones must also be played with the same strength and support of the tone. See, for example, Tab. XXII, Fig. 28.

FIG. 28

[1] *Mit dem folgenden Finger (avec le doigt suivant).*
[2] 'Same' appears in the French text.
[3] This is a literal rendering of both the German and French texts. Quantz may be trying to say that the movement from one note to the next must be so smooth that it is imperceptible.

§ 16

If demisemiquavers follow a long note and a short rest (see Tab. XXII, Fig. 29), they must be played very rapidly, both in the Adagio and in the Allegro. Hence, before playing the quick notes, you must wait to the very end of the time reserved for them, so that you do not lose the beat.

FIG. 29

If in slow alla breve or common time a semiquaver rest appears on the downbeat, and dotted notes follow (see Tab. XXII, Figs. 30 and 31), the rest must be regarded as if it were dotted, or as if it were followed by another rest of half the value, and the following note as if it were of half the value.[1]

FIG. 30   FIG. 31

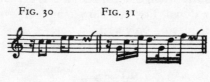

§ 17

If a slow and melancholy piece begins with a note on the upbeat, whether a quaver in common time or a crotchet in alla breve (see Tab. XXII, Figs. 32 and 33), this note must not be produced too vehemently or forcefully; the movement of the bow must be quiet and slow, strengthening the volume of tone, if the sentiment of melancholy is to be expressed properly.

FIG. 32   FIG. 33

If the other instrumentalists are to be able immediately to grasp the correct tempo, however, you must not dwell on notes like this longer than their duration requires. In the further course of the piece, similar slow notes may be treated in the same manner.

§ 18

Broken chords, where three or four strings are struck at once,[2] are of two kinds (see Tab. XXII, Figs. 34 and 35).

[1] This precept is an extension of Quantz's rules for the interpretation of dotted quavers, semiquavers, and demisemiquavers. See Chapter V, § 21.
[2] The third sentence of this paragraph makes it clear that 'at once' is an inaccurate figure of speech. The strings are actually struck as quickly as possible in succession.

FIG. 34   FIG. 35

In one a rest follows and the bow must be detached; in the other no rest follows and the bow remains resting upon the uppermost string. In both kinds the lower strings must not be held either in slow or quick tempos; they must be struck quickly one after the other, or the effect will be that of a chord arpeggiated in triplets.[1] And since these chords are used to surprise the ear with their unexpected vehemence, those followed by rests must be played very short and with the strongest part of the bow, that is, with the lower portion; and if many chords follow one another, each must be taken with a down-stroke.

§ 19

The different kinds of appoggiaturas and their duration have already been dealt with in Chapter VIII. Since, however, not all violinists understand tonguing well enough to regulate their bowing accordingly,[2] some explanations must be added here, and a general rule established, namely: each little prefixed note, be it long or short, since it is struck in place of the *following* principal note, requires a separate stroke of the bow, and must never be slurred to the *preceding* note. Proof of this may be found in the art of singing.[3] You will find that if a singer has to pronounce a word with an appoggiatura like this, he does not pronounce the syllables with the principal note to which they belong, and beneath which they are placed, but with the prefixed notes or appoggiaturas.[4]

§ 20

In the Adagio long appoggiaturas that derive their value from the notes following them must be so bowed as to increase in volume, without accentuation, and must be slurred gently to the following notes, so that the appoggiaturas sound a little stronger than the notes that follow them. In the Allegro, on the other hand, they may be slightly accented. Short appoggiaturas, among which those between descending leaps of thirds are reckoned, must be touched very briefly and softly, as though, so to speak, only in passing. For example, those in Tab. XXII, Figs. 36 and 37, must not be held, especially in a slow tempo; otherwise they will sound as if

---

[1] In other words, the notes of the chord must be struck more quickly than in the normal arpeggiated form.

[2] Quantz's first explanation of appoggiaturas in Chapter VIII is couched in terms used for articulation with the tongue rather than with the bow.

[3] German text: 'vocal music.'

[4] *Unter den vorhaltenden kleinen Noten (sous les notes postiches ou ports de voix).*

they are expressed with regular notes, as is to be seen in Figs. 38 and 39.[1] This, however, would be contrary not only to the intention of the composer, but to the French style of playing, to which these appoggiaturas owe their origin. The little notes belong in the time of the notes preceding them, and hence must not, as in the second example, fall in the time of those that follow them.

FIG. 36   FIG. 37   FIG. 38   FIG. 39

§ 21

If in a slow tempo two little quavers appear, the first of which is dotted (see Tab. XXII, Fig. 40), they receive the time of the following principal note, and the principal note receives the time of the dot.[2] They must be played with much feeling, and must be expressed as indicated by the notes in Fig. 41.

FIG. 40   FIG. 41

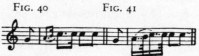

You must take the first double-dotted note with a down-stroke, allowing the tone to increase, slur the two following notes to it with a diminuendo, and stress the last short note with an up-stroke.

§ 22

If, however, embellishments like these are expressed with regular notes (see Tab. XXII, Fig. 42), in a ritornello they must be played with their proper value, especially if the part is doubled or another part plays the same figure in thirds or sixths. The first two notes above which the slur appears must be taken with a down-stroke, the last two with an up-stroke.

---

[1] The first of these two types of short appoggiaturas is discussed in Chapter VIII, § 6. The second, however, is completely new, and should be carefully noted, since it indicates an important omission in Chapter VIII. Quantz's statement that Fig. 37 must *not* be played as illustrated in Fig. 39 has been overlooked by the great majority of modern scholars who have drawn upon Quantz's exposition of ornamentation. The correct interpretation of this figure is indicated in the final sentence of the paragraph. In this case Quantz's short appoggiatura is the equivalent of C. P. E. Bach's invariable appoggiatura. C. P. E. Bach, however, and many other musicians of the day, state that appoggiaturas of this type should be performed very quickly on the beat. For further information on this point, see R. Kirkpatrick, *Domenico Scarlatti* (Princeton: Princeton University Press, 1953), pp. 369–71.

[2] This embellishment is generally known as a *Schleifer* or 'slide'. Another form of slide is discussed below in § 23. For further information on this grace, see Donington, *Interpretation*, pp. 217–28, and Neumann, *Ornamentation*, pp. 203–38.

FIG. 42

§ 23

The two little semiquavers in Tab. XXII, Fig. 43, more usual in the French than in the Italian style, must not be played as slowly as those described above; they are expressed precipitately, as is to be seen in Fig. 44.

FIG. 43   FIG. 44

§ 24

Shakes have already been dealt with in general in Chapter IX, and I refer my readers to that chapter. Here I would like to note in addition that if shakes are indicated above several quick notes, the appoggiatura and termination[1] are not always possible, because of the lack of time; often only half-shakes[2] are performed. If the appoggiatura and termination are indicated only for the first note (see Tab. XXII, Fig. 45), it is understood that the following shakes must be performed in the same way.

FIG. 45

If a shake is indicated above a triplet (see Tab. XXII, Fig. 46), the last two notes form the termination.

FIG. 46

If several notes are tied together on the same pitch and a shake is indicated above the first, the shake must be sustained to the end, without repeating[3] the bow-stroke (see Tab. XXII, Fig. 47).

FIG. 47

---

[1] *Nachschlag (coup d'après)*.
[2] The half-shake is discussed and illustrated in Chapter VIII, § 14.
[3] See p. 218, n. 1 of this chapter.

If an appoggiatura precedes two quick notes followed by a dotted note (see Tab. XXII, Fig. 48), this figure must be played very quickly and precipitately to the last note in a single bow-stroke. If a rest appears in place of the dot, the bow is detached.

Fig. 48

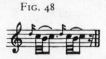

If appoggiaturas appear before dotted notes (see Tab. XXII, Fig. 49), neither shakes nor mordents may be introduced. If, however, shakes appear above either ascending or descending notes of this kind, or if rests take the place of the dots, it is understood that you make the shake without the termination, and detach the bow at the dots.

Fig. 49

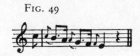

If all the instruments proceed in unison with the bass, that is, if all play just the same notes that the bass plays, even if one or several octaves higher, a slower shake executed by all at the same speed has a better effect than a very quick one. The very quick movement, when made simultaneously by all the instruments, leads to confusion rather than clarity, especially in a place that reverberates. Hence the fingers must be raised equally and at a moderate speed, yet somewhat higher than is normally the case.

§ 25

Thus far we have considered the bow-stroke in itself, and how individual notes must be apportioned in it and expressed with it. Now it is necessary to discuss the type of bow-stroke required by each piece, each tempo, and each of the passions that is to be expressed. These matters indicate to the violinists, and to all those who occupy themselves with bowed instruments, whether the stroke should be long or short, heavy or light, sharp or quiet.

§ 26

In general it is to be noted that in the accompaniment, particularly in lively pieces, a short and articulated bow-stroke, wielded in the French manner, produces a much better effect than a long and dragging Italian stroke.

The *Allegro, Allegro assai, Allegro di molto, Presto,* and *Vivace*[1] require a

---

[1] For Quantz's discussion of the relative speeds of the various tempos mentioned in this paragraph, see Section VII of this chapter, §§ 49–51.

lively, very light, nicely detached,[1] and very short bow-stroke, especially in the accompaniment, where you must play more sportively than seriously in pieces of this kind; and yet a certain moderation of tone must also be observed.

If the Allegro is interspersed with passages in unison,[2] it must be played with a sharp bow-stroke and an appropriate strength of tone.

An *Allegretto* or an Allegro modified by the presence of such words as non presto, non tanto, non troppo, moderato, &c., must be performed a little more seriously, with a rather heavy yet lively and suitably vigorous bow-stroke. In the Allegretto the semiquavers in particular, like the quavers in the Allegro, require a very short bow-stroke, made with the wrist rather than the whole arm, and articulated rather than slurred,[3] so that both the up-stroke and the down-stroke are concluded with uniform pressure.[4] The quick passage-work, however, requires a light bow-stroke.

An *Arioso, Cantabile, Soave, Dolce,* or *poco Andante* is executed quietly, and with a light bow-stroke. Even if interspersed with quick notes of various kinds, the Arioso still requires a light and quiet stroke.

A *Maestoso, Pomposo, Affettuoso,* or *Adagio spiritoso* must be played seriously, and with a rather heavy and sharp stroke.

A slow and melancholy piece, indicated by the words *Adagio assai, Pesante, Lento, Largo assai,* or *Mesto,* requires the greatest moderation of tone, and the longest, most tranquil, and heaviest[5] bow-stroke.

The *Sostenuto,* which is the opposite of the staccato that appears below, and which consists of a sustained, serious, and harmonious air in which many dotted notes slurred in pairs are encountered, is usually designated by the word *Grave.* Hence it must be played in a very sustained and serious manner with a long and heavy bow-stroke.

In all slow pieces the ritornello in particular must be played seriously, especially if dotted notes are present, so that the concertante part may distinguish itself from the tutti[6] when it has to repeat the same melody. If, however, flattering ideas are intermingled among other kinds, the flattering ones must be executed in an agreeable manner. In all pieces, but especially in slow ones, the performers must always assume the sentiment of the composer, and seek to express it. In this regard swelling and diminishing the force of the tone may be a great help in addition to the other requirements described above, provided that it is accomplished smoothly

---

[1] *Tockirter (bien détaché).*

[2] In many of the ritornellos in Quantz's concertos, a number of phrases are written in unison. Such unison phrases are also a common feature in the concertos of Vivaldi and many of the composers who followed in Vivaldi's footsteps.

[3] *Mehr tockiret als gezogen (plus frappé que tiré).*

[4] *So daß so wohl der Auf- als Niederstrich durch einen Druck einerlei Endigung bekomme (de sorte que tant le coup en haut que celui en bas soit fini par un pressement, d'une maniere égale).*

[5] Although 'heavy' seems contradictory at this point, the German text reads *schweresten* and the French *plus pésant.* Perhaps 'most sustained' is implied.

[6] French text: 'may distinguish itself from the melody of all the instruments when they play together, which the Italians call the tutti'.

and not with a vehement and disagreeable pressure of the bow. But should the piece have the misfortune to be fashioned with little or no sentiment on the part of its composer, no particular expression can be expected, in spite of all the pains taken by the performers.

An account of the kind of stroke to be employed in French dance music is found in § 58 of Section VII of this chapter.

§ 27

→ If the word *staccato* appears in a piece, all the notes must be played with a short and detached bow. Since, however, an entire piece is at present rarely composed in a single species of notes, and we take care to include a good mixture of different types, little strokes are written above those notes which require the staccato.

In notes of this kind you must be regulated by whether the tempo of the piece is very slow or very quick, and must not shorten[1] the notes in the Adagio as much as those in the Allegro; otherwise those in the Adagio will sound all too dry and meagre. The general rule that may be established in this regard is as follows : if little strokes stand above several notes, they must sound half as long as their true value. But if a little stroke stands above only one note, after which several of lesser value follow, it indicates not only that the note must be played half as long, but also that it must at the same time be accented with a pressure of the bow.

Hence crotchets become quavers, and quavers semiquavers, &c.

Previously it was stated that in playing the notes above which little strokes appear, the bow must be detached a little from the strings. This means only those notes in which the time permits. Thus the quavers in the Allegro, and the semiquavers in the Allegretto are excepted if many follow one another; they must be played with a very short bow-stroke, but the bow must never be detached or removed from the strings. If it were always raised as high as is required when we say that it is detached, there would not be enough time to return it to the string at the proper time, and notes of this kind would sound as if they were chopped or whipped.

In an Adagio the notes that provide motion beneath the concertante part may be considered as half staccato, even if no little strokes stand above them, and hence a little pause may be observed after each note.

If dots stand above the notes they must be articulated or attacked with a short bow, but must not be detached. If a slur is added above the dots, all the notes within it must be taken in one bow-stroke and stressed with a pressure of the bow.

§ 28

Those who wish to manipulate the bow correctly, and use it to good effect, must know not only the correct distribution of the bow-strokes and

---

[1] *Abstossen* (*pousser*). Literally, these words mean 'strike briefly'. In § 4 Quantz uses the terms to indicate staccato performance.

the proper time for a strong or weak pressure of the bow upon the strings, but also the place where the bow should touch the strings, and the weight which each part of the stroke must have. Much depends upon whether the bow is drawn close to or far from the bridge, and also upon whether you touch the strings with the lowest part of the bow, with the middle, or with the tip. The lowest part, or that closest to the right hand, is the most forceful; the middle is of moderate force; and the tip is the weakest. If, then, it is drawn too close to the bridge, the tone not only becomes piercing and sharp, but also thin, piping, and scraping, especially on spun strings. Next to the bridge the tension of the strings is too great, and the bow does not have the force to produce a motion proportionate with the remaining long portion of the string; thus the strings do not receive the necessary vibration.

When these faults produce so poor an effect on the violin, it is easy to imagine how much worse the effect must be on the viola, violoncello, and double bass, especially since the strings on these instruments are so much thicker and longer than on the violin. To find the correct distance, I hold that if a good violinist wields his bow the breadth of one finger below the bridge in order to produce a full, robust tone, a violist must take the distance of the breadth of *two* fingers, the violoncellist of *three* to *four*, and the double bass player of *six*. Note, however, that upon the thin strings of each instrument the bow may be wielded somewhat closer to the bridge, upon the thick strings a little farther from it.

If you wish to increase the strength of your tone, you may, during the stroke, press the bow more firmly against the strings and guide it a little closer to the bridge; this makes the tone stronger and more piercing. When playing Piano, however, the bow may be guided even a little farther from the bridge on each instrument than stated above, in order to set the strings in motion more easily with a moderate bow.

§ 29

In some pieces it is customary to place mutes or *sordini* on the violin, viola, and violoncello to express more vividly sentiments of love, tenderness, flattery, and melancholy, and also—if the composer knows how to adapt his piece accordingly—more violent emotions such as recklessness, madness, and despair. Certain keys such as E minor, C minor, F minor, E flat major, B minor, A major, and E major can contribute much [in conveying the latter emotions]. Mutes are made of various materials, such as wood, lead, brass, tin, and steel. Those of wood and brass are worthless, since they produce a growling tone.[1] Those of steel are the best, provided their weight is proportioned to the instruments. The size of the mutes for the viola and violoncello must be in the correct ratio with the size of these instruments, and hence must always be larger for the latter instrument

---

[1] *Schnarrender Ton* (*ton ronflant*).

than for the former. Let me say in passing that wind players would do better to insert a piece of damp sponge, rather than paper or other materials, into the opening of their instruments when they wish to mute them.

§ 30

It should be noted that when you play slow pieces with mutes, the greatest force of the bow should not be used, and you must avoid the open strings as much as possible. In slurred notes the bow may be pressed rather firmly against the strings. But if the melody requires frequent repetition of strokes, a short, light stroke, animated by a kind of inner stress,[1] produces a better effect than a long, drawn out, or dragging one. Above all, however, you must regulate yourself in accordance with the ideas that you have to express.

§ 31

Sometimes the fingers replace the bow with the so-called *pizzicato*, plucking or pinching the strings. By most players this is done with the thumb. That a good violinist should know how to [pluck the strings with the thumb] in an agreeable manner, and with such moderation that you do not notice the rebound of the strings upon the fingerboard, I will not deny. But since all do not possess the same skill in this regard the pizzicato often sounds very harsh, and the desired effect is not always obtained; hence I feel I must communicate my own views about this point. It is well known that upon the lute the upper part is played with the four fingers and the bass with the thumb; now, since the pizzicato on the violin is an imitation of the lute or mandolin, it should, as much as possible, be made to resemble these instruments. Thus I feel that it is better if it is produced not with the thumb, but with the tip of the forefinger. Do not grasp the string from below, but from the side, so that its fluctuation is in that direction, and not backward upon the fingerboard. This renders the tone much fuller and more natural than if the string is plucked with the thumb. The thumb, because of its breadth, occupies a larger portion of the strings and, because of its strength, strains them, especially the thin ones, as experience will show if you test the two methods. The pizzicato also must be played towards the end of the fingerboard, neither too close to the bridge nor too close to the fingers of the left hand. To strike each string more easily you may place the thumb sideways against the fingerboard. Nevertheless, in those chords where three strings must be sounded in quick succession, with the lowest first, the pizzicato must be practised with the thumb.[2] In a small chamber ensemble the strings must not be plucked too strongly or the effect will be disagreeable.

[1] *Durch einen Druck belebter, leichter Strich (le coup d'archet . . . animé par un certain poids interieur).*

[2] L. Mozart, *A Treatise*, p. 52, also mentions the two methods of playing pizzicato, and agrees with Quantz in preferring the index finger. Likewise, he cites the performance of chords as the one exception to the rule.

§ 32

As to the use of the fingers of the left hand, it is to be noted that the strength of the pressure applied by them must always be in the correct proportion to the strength of the bow-stroke. This proportion must be carefully observed.[1] If in a hold[2] (*tenuta*) you make the tone grow in volume, you must also increase the pressure on your finger. To keep the pitch from becoming higher, you must at the same time draw the finger back imperceptibly, or avert this danger with a good vibrato that is not too quick.[3] Those who raise their fingers too high usually produce a penetrating shake, but they expose themselves at the same time to the danger of incorrect intonation, ordinarily playing sharp, especially in minor keys. Usually these persons also execute running passages unevenly and indistinctly, since their fingers, due to inequality in length, relieve one another unevenly. Moreover, since the little finger is generally weaker than the other three, you must try to find a way to moderate the strength of the three longer fingers, and come to the aid of the little finger by striking it more promptly,[4] so that it attains the correct proportion with the others. In general all young violinists should exercise the little finger diligently; they will benefit greatly [from such practice] on many occasions.

§ 33

The manner of playing called *mezzo manico*, in which the hand is placed a semitone, whole tone, or several tones further up the fingerboard,[5] is particularly useful on certain occasions in avoiding the open strings, which sound differently than when stopped with the fingers, and also in many other situations, especially in cadencing. For example, in the notes indicated in Tab. XXII, Figs. 50 and 51, the shakes are generally better made with the third rather than the little finger.

FIG. 50   FIG. 51

---

[1] This sentence appears only in the French text.

[2] *Haltung (Tenue).* 'Tenuta' appears in parentheses in the German text.

[3] *Bebung (balancement).* Quantz refers to the embellishment that L. Mozart, *A Treatise*, pp. 203–6, calls a tremolo. For a fuller understanding of the term, see the passage cited in L. Mozart, and the discussion of vibrato in Donington, *Interpretation*, pp. 231–5. The French text of this sentence seems to contain one of the few genuine errors in the French translation. The French text indicates a 'good and quick' vibrato. *Nicht geschwinde*, however, appears in the German text.

[4] *Dem kleinen Finger durch eine Art von schnellem Schlage zu Hülfe zu kommen (secourir la foiblesse du petit; c'est-ce qu'on fait en le faisant battre plus promptement).*

[5] Quantz's *mezzo manico*, or 'half position', is actually the second position of today. For a fuller discussion of the half position, see L. Mozart, *A Treatise*, pp. 140–7.

If you try the three examples in Tab. XXII, Fig. 52 (*a*), (*b*), and (*c*) with the hand in the usual position,[1] and then move the hand a note higher, so that you use the second finger instead of the third in (*a*) and the first instead of the second in (*b*) and (*c*), you will soon notice a great difference with regard to uniformity of sound.

FIG. 52

§ 34

If a concertante part is accompanied only by violins, each violinist must pay close attention to whether he has a plain middle part to play, one in which certain little phrases alternate with the concertante part, or a high bass part.[2] In a middle part he must greatly moderate the volume of his tone. If he has something which alternates with the solo, he may play more strongly, and in the high bass he may play still more strongly, especially if he is at some distance from the soloist, or from the listeners. If both violins have only middle parts, they must play with equal strength. If in the ritornello the second violin complements the first with a melody similar to it, whether at the third, sixth, or fourth, the second may play with the same strength as the first. But if, as in the case indicated above,[3] the second violin is only a middle part, it must likewise moderate its tone somewhat, since the principal parts must always be heard above the middle parts.

§ 35

If the violinists have a weak concertante part to accompany, they must do so with great moderation. They must consider well the character of the accompaniment, that is, whether its movement is made up of quick or slow notes, and whether these notes advance by step or leap; whether they are placed in the same register or higher or lower than the solo part; whether the accompaniment is in two, three, or four parts; whether the concertante part has a flattering air to play or passage-work; whether the passage-work consists of extended leaps or of roulades; and whether the notes[4] are in a high or low register. All these matters require great circumspection. For example, a flute is not as penetrating in the low register as in the high, especially in minor keys; also, as a matter of course, it is not

---

[1] The 'usual position' would be the first position of today. The changes in fingering in the *mezzo manico* are indicated in L. Mozart, p. 141.

[2] On the meaning of this term, see p. 237, n. 1 below.

[3] Presumably Quantz refers to the second sentence of this paragraph. There he seems to have the first violins in mind.

[4] The notes of the solo part seem to be meant here.

always played with the same strength, but now weakly, now moderately, now strongly, as the case requires. The same is also true of weak voices, and of other instruments of medium force. Hence the violinists must be constantly attentive that the concertante part is always heard above the others and never obscured.

SECTION III

Of the Violist in Particular

§ 1

The viola is commonly regarded as of little importance in the musical establishment. The reason may well be that it is often played by persons who are either still beginners in the ensemble or have no particular gifts with which to distinguish themselves on the violin, or that the instrument yields all too few advantages to its players, so that able people are not easily persuaded to take it up. I maintain, however, that if the entire accompaniment is to be without defect, the violist must be just as able as the second violinist.

§ 2

He must not only have an execution equal to that of the violinists, but must likewise understand something of harmony, so that if at times he must take the place of the bass player and play the high bass,[1] as is usual in concertos, he may know how to play with discretion, and the soloist need not be more concerned about the accompanying part than about his own.

§ 3

The violist must be able to judge which notes in his part must be played in a singing manner or dryly, loudly or softly, with a long or short bow; likewise whether there are two or more violins against him, and many or few basses; and if he must play the bass part, whether the concertante part is being played loudly or softly, and whether the setting of the piece is melancholy, joyful, majestic, flattering, modest, or bold, since he must adjust his performance of the high bass to each sentiment, and accommodate it to the upper part.

§ 4

He must discern whether he has arias, concertos, or other forms of music to accompany. He has the easiest time in arias, since in them he usually only has to play a plain middle part, or perhaps double the bass.

---

[1] *Das Bassetchen (la petite Basse)*. In Quantz's concertos, and in those of his contemporaries, the basso continuo frequently drops out during some of the solo sections. In these places the accompaniment is often limited to one or two violins and a viola, and the viola thus serves as the temporary bass.

In concertos, however, there is often more to do, since an imitation or a melody similar to that of the upper part is sometimes given to the viola instead of to the second violin; and occasionally the viola must even play a singing ritornello in unison with the violins, [a doubling] that produces an excellent effect, especially in an Adagio. If in such circumstances the violist does not have a distinct and agreeable execution, he will spoil the most beautiful composition, especially if there is only one person to each part in the composition.

§ 5

It would not be too much to say that a good violist should be able to play even a concertante part just as well as a violinist, as, for example, in a concertante trio or quartet.[1] Perhaps the reasons why this beautiful form of music has declined in popularity is simply that so few violists devote as much industry to their work as they should. Many believe that if they only know a little about metre and the division of notes, nothing more can be demanded of them. This prejudice, however, is more than a little detrimental to them. If they employed the necessary industry, they could easily improve their lot in a large establishment, and gradually advance their position, instead of remaining chained to the viola to the end of their lives, as is usually the case. There are many instances of people who, after playing the viola in their youth, achieved great eminence in the musical world. And later, when already qualified for something better, they were not ashamed to resume the instrument in case of need. The accompanist actually experiences more pleasure from the music than the player of a concertante part; and anyone who is a true musician takes an interest in the entire ensemble, without troubling himself about whether he plays the first or the last part.

§ 6

A good violist must shun all extempore additions or embellishments[2] in his part.

§ 7

He must play the quavers in an Allegro with a very short bow-stroke, the crotchets, on the other hand, with a somewhat longer one.

§ 8

If he has the same kind of notes as the violinists, whether slurred or articulated, he must adjust to their manner of playing, whether it is cantabile or lively. This is particularly necessary if he has to play a ritornello in unison with the violins; for there he must play in just as cantabile and

---

[1] Quantz provides more detailed information about the type of trio or quartet that he has in mind in Chapter XVIII, §§ 44–45.

[2] Quantz refers here to the embellishments discussed in Chapter XIII.

agreeable a manner as the violinists themselves, so that one does not notice that different instruments are playing. If, however, his notes are similar to those of the bass, he must execute them just as seriously as the bass.

§ 9

In a melancholy piece he must moderate his bow-stroke greatly; he must not move the bow vehemently or with excessive quickness, make any harsh or disagreeable pressure with his arm, apply too much pressure to the strings, or play too close to the bridge; he must guide the bow the breadth of two fingers from the bridge, especially on the thick strings (see Section II, § 28). In slow pieces of this kind he must not play the quavers in common time, or the crotchets in alla breve, too briefly or dryly; they must all be expressed in a sustained, pleasing, agreeable, and tranquil manner.[1]

§ 10

In a cantabile Adagio that consists of quavers and semiquavers[2] and is interspersed with jocular ideas, the violist must perform all the short notes with a light and short bow-stroke, taken not with the whole arm, but with the hand alone, employing only the wrist, and also using less strength than usual.

§ 11

Since one viola, if a good and strong instrument, is sufficient against four or even six violins,[3] the violist must moderate the strength of his tone if only two or three violins play with him, so that he does not cover the others, especially if only one violoncello is present and no double bass. The middle parts, which, considered in themselves, provide the listener with the least pleasure, must never be heard as strongly as the principal parts. Hence the violist must decide whether the notes he is to play are melodic or simply harmonic. The former he must play with the same strength as the violins, the latter a little more softly.

§ 12

If at times the violist has the bass part, he may execute it a little more strongly than his usual middle parts. He must, however, always listen to the concertante part, so that he does not obscure it. If the latter is played more loudly and more softly by turns, the violist must adjust his own loudness and softness accordingly, and always observe the swelling and softening of the tone simultaneously.

[1] For further information on bowing, see Section II, § 26.
[2] i.e. when the basic rhythmic movement of the work is in these note-values.
[3] See Section I, § 16.

§ 13

If imitations of certain phrases of the principal part or the bass occur, they must be played with the same strength used in the part that is imitated. But a so-called *thema* or principal subject[1] of a fugue, and often-repeated ideas in a concerto, must be set off and stressed with emphasis and with conspicuous strength of tone. This also applies to long notes, whether crotchets, minims, or semibreves, that follow quick notes and form a respite in the liveliness [of the motion], especially those preceded by a sharp or a natural sign.[2]

§ 14

If the violist is required to play in a trio or quartet, he must carefully observe what kinds of instruments he has against him, so that he can adjust the strength and weakness of his tone accordingly. Against a violin he can play with almost the same strength, against a violoncello or a bassoon with equal strength, against an oboe a little more softly, since its tone is thin compared to that of the viola. Against a flute, however, he must play very softly, especially if it plays in the low register.

§ 15

In playing the viola, it is generally very important that the loudness or softness of the tone be well proportioned to that of the other instruments. It would be difficult to describe all the situations where this is necessary. Hence the judgement of the violist must be equal to that of a bass player.

§ 16

If, in the absence of the violoncello, the violist accompanies a trio or a solo,[3] when he plays in unison with the bass, he must, as much as possible, play an octave lower than he usually does, and must be careful not to go above the upper part, lest the fifths formed against the bass be transformed into fourths. Thus he would do well in a solo to keep an eye on the upper part, so that he can adjust to it if it plays in the low register. For example, suppose the upper part were to have A', and the bass its highest D [D']: if the violist were to take the latter on the thinnest of his strings,[4] the fifth which the parts form against each other would become a fourth, and thus would not produce the same effect.

---

[1] *Hauptsatz (Sujet).*

[2] For a fuller discussion of this point, and some illustrations, see Section II, §§ 14–15.

[3] Quantz indicates a situation in which the viola replaces the 'cello in playing the basso continuo of a solo sonata or a trio sonata.

[4] In other words, if the violist played the D an octave higher, actually sounding D''.

§ 17

The remarks about the other aspects of bowing, about attacks and slurs, the expression of the notes, the staccato, loud and soft playing, tuning, &c., to be found in the preceding and in the last sections of this chapter may be turned to as much account by the violist as by the ripieno violinist, not only because he needs to know all of these things, but also because he does not, I presume, wish to remain always a violist.

SECTION IV

Of the Violoncellist in Particular

§ 1

Those who not only accompany on the violoncello, but also play solos on it, would do well to have two special instruments, one for solos, the other for ripieno parts in large ensembles. The latter must be larger, and must be equipped with thicker strings than the former. If a small instrument with thin strings were employed for both types of parts, the accompaniment in a large ensemble would have no effect whatsoever. The bow intended for ripieno playing must also be stronger, and must be strung with black hairs, with which the strings may be struck more sharply than with white ones.

§ 2

The bow-stroke must not be guided too close to the bridge; it must fall at least the breadth of three or four fingers downward[1] from it (see Section II, § 28). Some move the bow as is customary on the viola da gamba,[2] that is, instead of a down-stroke from left to right for the principal notes, they make an up-stroke from right to left, beginning with the tip of the bow.[3] Others, however, proceed like violinists, and begin their strokes with the lowest part of the bow. This latter method is customary among the Italians, and produces a better effect, particularly in accompanying, but also in solo playing; for the principal notes require both more strength and emphasis than the passing ones,[4] and neither can be given them as well with the tip of the bow as with its lowest part. In

[1] 'Upward' from the point of view of the player.

[2] French text: *Basse de Viole* (*Viola da Gamba*).

[3] On the direction of the bow-stroke in viola da gamba playing, see C. Simpson, *The Division-Viol* (2nd ed.; London: W. Godbid, 1665), p. 6. Those interested in the technique of the gamba and its history should examine Jean Rousseau's *Traité de la viole* (1687) and Hubert Le Blanc's *Defense de la basse de viole* (1740). An informative picture of the relative positions of the viola da gamba and the violoncello in the chamber music of Quantz's day is found in R. H. Rowen, *Early Chamber Music* (New York: Columbia University Press, 1949), pp. 73–80. See also Donington, *Interpretation*, pp. 362–3.

[4] For fuller information on this point, see Chapter XI, § 12.

general the violoncellist must strive to draw a full, round, and virile tone
from his instrument; in this regard the manner in which he guides the
bow is of great importance, and whether it is too close to, or too far from,
the bridge. If, for example, in a large ensemble he carries delicacy too far,
and plays so softly that he seems to be touching the strings with a feather-
duster rather than a bow,[1] he will earn little praise. Certain little contor-
tions of the body, which are unavoidable when playing this instrument,
will, let us hope, be pardoned him.

<h2 style="text-align:center">§ 3</h2>

The violoncellist must take care not to garnish the bass with graces, as
some great violoncellists were formerly in the habit of doing; he must not
try to show his skill at an inappropriate time. If, without understanding
composition, the violoncellist introduces extempore graces into the bass,
in a ripieno part he will do even more harm than a violinist, especially if he
has a bass part before him above which the principal part is constantly embellishing the plain air with other additions. It is impossible for one
player always to divine the thoughts of the other, even if both have equal
insight. Besides, it is absurd to make an upper part of the bass, which
should support the embellishments of the other parts and make them
harmonious; by robbing the bass of its serious movement, the necessary
embellishments of the upper part are obstructed or obscured. It is undeniable that some melodic and concertante bass parts in solos[2] allow something in the way of additions, if the performer of the bass has sufficient
insight, and knows where it may be done; it is likewise true that the piece
becomes more perfect if on such occasions a few embellishments are
added in a skilful manner. But if the violoncellist cannot rely sufficiently
upon his knowledge, he is advised to play the bass as the composer has
written it, rather than run the risk of ignorantly adding many absurd and
discordant notes. Only in a solo is a skilful addition of embellishments
permissible. Even there, whenever it is essential that the principal part add
something to the plain notes, the notes of the bass must be executed entirely without extempore ornaments. If, however, the bass imitates some
phrases of the principal part, the violoncellist may repeat the same graces
used in the principal part. And if the principal part has rests or held notes,
he may likewise vary the bass in an agreeable manner, provided that his
principal notes are not obscured, and that the variations are so made that
they express no other passion than that which the piece demands. Thus the
violoncellist must seek constantly to imitate the execution of the player
of the principal part, with respect both to loudness and softness of tone
and to the expression of the notes. In a large ensemble, however, the
violoncellist must abstain entirely from extempore additions, not only

[1] French text: 'if . . . he wishes to play so delicately that he can hardly be heard. . . .'
[2] i.e. solo sonatas with thorough-bass accompaniment.

because the fundamental part must be played seriously and distinctly, but also because considerable confusion and obscurity would be caused if all the other bass players were to take similar liberties.

§ 4

In a melancholy Adagio, the slow notes, that is, the quavers in common time and the crotchets in alla breve, must be played with a quiet bow-stroke. The bow must not be drawn hastily or hurriedly to its tip, since this would impede the expression of the sentiment of melancholy, and would offend the ear. In the Allegro the crotchets must be played in a sustained or *nourrissant* manner, and the quavers very short. The same is true in an Allegretto written in alla breve time. But should the Allegretto be written in common time, the quavers are sustained, and the semi-quavers played short. The short notes must be played not with the whole arm, but with only the hand, by moving the wrist. Fuller instructions about this point are found in Sections II and VI.[1]

§ 5

All notes must be played in the register in which they are written; some must not be taken an octave higher at one time, an octave lower at another, especially those with which the other parts move in unison. Progressions of this kind constitute a formal bass melody that cannot and must not be varied in any way. Were such notes played on the violoncello an octave lower than they are written, the distance from the violins would be too great, and the notes would at the same time lose the sharpness and anima-tion that the composer[2] had in mind. Other bass notes which do not move in unison with the other parts may be played an octave lower now and then if no double bass is present; but they must be harmonic rather than melodic passages, that is, passages that do not form a truly independent melody, but serve only as the foundation for the upper melodies. Leaps of a third, fourth, fifth, sixth, seventh, and octave upwards or downwards must not be inverted, since these leaps often serve to form a distinct melody, and are rarely written without a special purpose on the part of the composer (see Tab. XXII, Fig. 53).

Fig. 53

The same is true if a passage of a whole or a half bar is often repeated in such a way that the same notes are set each time an octave lower or higher (see Tab. XXII, Fig. 54).

[1] See Section II, §§ 26–30. No such instructions have been located in Section VI. Section VII, §§ 10–18, may have been the reference intended.

[2] 'The composer' is found in the French text.

FIG. 54

A bass like this must be played as it is written. If the leaps are inverted, the effect will be entirely different.

§ 6

Since the violoncello has the sharpest tone of all the basses, and can state its part the most distinctly, its player is in an advantageous position to help the other parts in the expression of light and shadow, and can give vigour to the whole piece. In preserving the correct tempo in a piece, and the proper degree[1] of liveliness, in expressing the Piano and Forte at the appropriate time, in distinguishing and making recognizable the different passions that should be aroused, and hence in facilitating the performance of the concertante part, the violoncellist is very important. He must therefore neither rush nor drag, and must direct his thoughts with constant attentiveness both to the rests and to the notes, so that it is unnecessary to remind him to begin again after a rest, or to play loudly or softly. It is very disagreeable in an ensemble if all parts do not begin together in earnest at a new entrance after a rest, or if the Piano or the Forte is not observed where it is written, especially if the bass is remiss, since the precision of the execution depends largely upon it on these occasions.[2]

§ 7

If the violoncellist understands composition, or at least something of harmony, he will find it easy to help the soloist to bring out and make apparent the different passions expressed in a piece by its composer. This ability is required of the accompanying parts as well as the concertante parts, and it is one of the highest attributes of a superior accompanying body. For if only one person executes his part well, and the others acquit themselves of theirs indifferently and carelessly, one contradicts, so to speak, what the others affirm; and the listeners, if not completely vexed, are deprived of half their pleasure. The violoncellist can contribute much to the perfection of a good ensemble if he does not lack feeling, and if he directs the proper attention to the whole, and not just to his own part. He must also determine which notes must be stressed and brought out more than the others. These are, first, notes that have dissonances such as the second, diminished fifth, augmented sixth, or seventh above them, or

---

[1] 'The proper degree' appears in the French text.

[2] *Besonders wenn es an dem Basse fehlet, welcher der Sache den größten Ausschlag geben muß (surtout si la Basse manque, de laquel dépend le plus en cette occasion la justesse de l'exécution).*

those that are raised irregularly by a sharp or natural sign, or lowered by a natural or a flat. The same rule applies when the upper part makes a cadence, and the bass, which ordinarily must leap up a fourth or down a fifth in order to move to an octave with the upper part, by a deception or so-called *inganno* moves up or down only a step, as, for example, when the upper part cadences to C, and the bass, instead of the octave below C, has the lower third, A or A flat, or the diminished fifth, F sharp, as the key requires (see Tab. XXII, Fig. 55).

FIG. 55

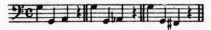

Here it is very effective if the notes mentioned, A, A flat, and F sharp, are stressed by the violoncello, and expressed a little more forcefully than the preceding notes. If, however, a piece, especially an Adagio, moves to its final cadence, the violoncellist may treat the preceding two, three, or four notes in the same fashion, in order to direct the attention of the listeners to the cadence (see Tab. XXII, Fig. 56).

FIG. 56

§ 8

In ligatures or tied notes[1] the 'cellist may allow the second note, above which the interval of the second or fourth is usually found, to swell by strengthening the tone, but he must not detach[2] the bow.

§ 9

If in a Presto that must be played in a very lively fashion several quavers or other short notes appear upon the same pitch, the first in each measure may be stressed by pressure on the bow.[3]

§ 10

Dotted notes must always be bowed more earnestly and heavily than the violinist would play them, but the semiquavers that follow must be executed very briefly and sharply, whether in a quick or a slow tempo.[4]

§ 11

If the violoncello has frets, as is customary upon the viola da gamba, the violoncellist must, in playing notes marked with flats, depress the

---

[1] Here, as in other cases, Quantz associates tied notes with suspensions. The French translator uses the more accurate term *syncope*.

[2] *Rücken (détacher)*.   [3] French text: 'by a certain weight given to the bow'.

[4] For further details on the interpretation of dotted notes, see Chapter V, §§ 20–24.

strings a little above the frets, and apply a little more pressure with his fingers, in order to stop them with the additional height (that is, of about a comma)[1] that their ratios require as opposed to those of notes marked with sharps.[2]

§ 12

Solo playing upon this instrument is not easy. Those who wish to distinguish themselves in this manner must be provided by nature with fingers that are long and have strong tendons, permitting an extended stretch. But if these prerequisites are found, together with a good method, much that is beautiful may be produced upon the instrument. I have myself heard several great masters who have accomplished near miracles upon it.[3] Anyone who practises the violoncello as an amateur is justly free to do whatever gives him the greatest pleasure, but somebody who intends to make it his profession will do well to apply himself above all else to becoming a good accompanist, for in this way he will make himself more useful and of greater service in ensembles. If, on the contrary, he rushes immediately into solo playing, before knowing how to perform a ripieno bass well, and in consequence perhaps strings his instrument so feebly[4] that he cannot be heard in the accompaniment, he will be of little use in the ensemble. He might well be put to shame by some amateur who excels both in playing solos and in accompanying. Good accompaniment is the chief quality demanded from this instrument. And even if accompanying and solo playing do not represent the same degree of excellence, a good accompanist is of greater service in an orchestra than a mediocre soloist. But the art of accompanying well cannot be learned either by oneself or by playing only in large ensembles. Anyone who wishes to give himself a secure foundation must accompany many able individuals; and if he does not allow himself to be vexed by accepting their advice occasionally, the benefits will be all the greater. There are no born masters, and one person must always learn from another.

SECTION V

Of the Double Bass Player in Particular

§ 1

The lot of the double bass*[5] is similar to that of the viola. As with the latter, many persons do not appreciate how valuable and necessary it is

---

[1] Translator's parentheses.

[2] On the distinction between sharps and flats, see Chapter III, § 8.

[3] In his autobiography, Quantz mentions having heard 'Giovannini, a strong violoncellist in Rome in 1724, and 'the incomparable violoncellist Franciscello' in Naples in 1725. See Nettl, *Forgotten Musicians*, pp. 302–3.

[4] Quantz apparently means with such thin strings. See § 1 of this section.

[5] This explanatory footnote appears only in the French text. Quantz uses the terms *grosse Violon* or *Contraviolon* for the double bass. In the French text it is called *la Grande Basse de Violon*.

in a large ensemble when it is well played. It may be that most of those who are assigned to the instrument do not have the talent to distinguish themselves upon other instruments that require both facility and taste. Yet it remains incontestable that, even if the double bass player has no need of great delicacy of taste, he must understand harmony, and must be no poor musician. In a large ensemble, and especially in an orchestra, where one person cannot always see the others or hear them well, the double bass player, together with the violoncellist, forms the point of equilibrium, so to speak, in maintaining the correct tempo.

* We speak here of that instrument with four strings tuned, from bottom to top, E, A, D, G, which the Germans call the contraviolon.

§ 2

In playing this instrument a special distinctness (which, unfortunately, few possess)[1] is required. Much depends upon a good instrument, but much also depends upon its player. If the instrument is too large, or is provided with strings that are too thick, its tone is indistinct and unintelligible to the ear. The same defect appears if the player does not know how to handle the bow as the instrument requires.

§ 3

The instrument in itself produces a better effect if it is of moderate size, and if it is provided with four strings rather than five. The fifth string, if it is to be in the correct proportion with the others, has to be thinner than the fourth, and in consequence produces a much thinner tone than the others. The disparity would be disadvantageous not only on this instrument, but also on the violoncello and the violin, if they were provided with five strings. Thus the so-called German violon[2] with five or six strings has been justly abandoned. If two double basses are needed in an ensemble, the second may be a little larger than the first; and if the first loses some of its distinctness, the second compensates for this with its gravity.

§ 4

The absence of frets upon the fingerboard is a great hindrance to distinctness. Some consider them unnecessary, or even injurious. This false opinion is sufficiently refuted, however, by the many able persons who, using frets, produce everything that can be done on the instrument truly and distinctly. The inescapable necessity of frets upon the instrument, if it is to sound distinct, is very easily demonstrated. It is well known that a short and thin string, if stretched tightly, makes much quicker

[1] Translator's parentheses.
[2] *Deutsche Violon* (*Basse de Violon Allemande*). For a description of a six-stringed instrument of this type, see J. F. B. C. Majer, *Museum musicum*, p. 80.

vibrations or oscillations than a long and thick string. If, then, you press a long and thick string, which cannot be stretched as tightly as a short one, against the fingerboard, the string rebounds against the wood, since its movement takes up a broader field. This not only impedes the vibrations, but also makes the string buzz afterward,[1] and produces an extraneous sound,[2] so that the tone becomes muffled and indistinct. It is true that on the double bass the bridge and the nut make the strings lie higher than on the violoncello, to keep them from rebounding against the fingerboard; but when the strings are depressed with the fingers this is still unsatisfactory. The obstruction is removed, however, if there are frets on the fingerboard. The strings are then held higher by the frets, and thus can vibrate freely; in consequence they can yield the most natural tone of which the instrument is capable. Other advantages provided by frets are that the notes may be stopped more truly with them than without them, and that the tone of the stopped notes more closely resembles that of the open strings. If it is objected that frets might cause difficulty in playing the flat semitones, since they could not be clearly differentiated [from the sharp ones], one may reply that this is not as harmful on the double bass as on the violoncello, since the difference between notes marked with sharps and flats is not as noticeable in the very low notes of the double bass as in the higher notes of other instruments.

§ 5

On this instrument the bow-stroke must fall about the breadth of six fingers from the bridge, must be very short, and must, if time permits, be detached from the string,[3] so that the long and thick strings can make the necessary vibrations. It must also be made nearly always from the lowest part to the middle of the bow, and jerked,[4] rather than sawed back and forth, except in very melancholy pieces, where the bow-stroke must still be short, but must not be taken with such haste. Except in passages marked Piano, the tip of the bow is generally of little effect. If a note is to be particularly stressed, the bow must be guided from left to right, since the bow then has more power to produce the stress. The short bow-stroke mentioned above applies only to notes that require majesty and liveliness. It does not apply to the long notes, such as semibreves and minims, that are frequently intermingled in quick pieces, either as a principal subject or as notes requiring special emphasis. Nor does it apply to slurred notes, which should express a flattering or melancholy sentiment; these the bass player must express in just as sustained and quiet a fashion as the violoncellist.

---

[1] *Nachsinget (siffle après).*   [2] *Nebenton (un autre son).*
[3] French text: 'must be detached as much as the duration of the notes permits'.
[4] *Mit einem Rucke (avec une tire).* This may possibly mean a down-stroke, but the context suggests that the normal meaning given here was intended.

§ 6

The bass player must strive to achieve a good and comfortable *application* or system of shifting fingers,[1] so that he can play whatever is written in the high register as well as the violoncellist, and does not garble the melodic bass parts, especially those in unison, which must be played on each instrument, including the double bass, in exactly the register in which they are written. In this regard look at the example for § 5 in the section on the violoncellist (Tab. XXII, Figs. 53 and 54).[2] Should bass parts like these be written higher than the bass player can reach on his instrument, he must perform the whole passage an octave lower, rather than divide it in a clumsy fashion; such passages, however, hardly ever go above G′, which some good players can produce and use accurately and distinctly.

§ 7

If in a bass part passage-work appears which, because of its great rapidity, the double bass player is unable to execute distinctly, he may play only the first, third, or last note of each figure, whether they are semi-quavers or demisemiquavers. In each case he must determine which notes are the principal notes in the bass melody. Illustrations are given in the following examples (see Tab. XXIII, Figs. 1, 2, and 3).

TABLE XXIII

FIG. 1

FIG. 2

FIG. 3

---

[1] *Uebersetzung der Finger (transposition de doigts).*
[2] These examples are reproduced in the paragraph cited in Section IV.

Except in passage-work of this sort, however, which some find too difficult to play rapidly, the bass player must omit nothing. If he were to play only the first of four quavers that appear upon the same note, passing over three, as some do at times, especially if they have to accompany a piece that they did not compose themselves, I do not know how he could avoid an accusation of laziness or malice.

§ 8

In general, the execution of the double bass player must be more serious than that of the other basses. Although the little refined embellishments are not required of him, he must strive constantly to give emphasis and weight to what the others play. He must express the Piano and Forte at the proper time, observe the tempo exactly, neither rush nor drag, execute his notes firmly, surely, and distinctly, and must be on guard against a scraping bow, which is a particularly ugly defect upon this instrument; and if he hears that the style of the performance is now serious, now jocular, now flattering, melancholy, joyful, bold, or so forth, he must always strive to contribute his own share, and not, from indifference, hinder the effects that the entire group seeks to bring forth. He must observe rests exactly at all times, but especially in concertos, so that when the ritornello commences, he can begin the Forte emphatically and at the proper time, without allowing several notes to go by first, as some do. The double bass player may also profit from many of the matters dealt with elsewhere in this chapter in connexion with other instruments, and from many of the rules of accompanying that, for reasons of space, cannot be repeated here.[1]

SECTION VI

Of the Keyboard Player[2] in Particular

§ 1

All those who understand thorough-bass are not necessarily good accompanists. Thorough-bass may be learned through rules, but accompanying must be learned through experience, and ultimately through individual sensitivity.

---

[1] Sections II, III, IV, and VII may be singled out as particularly important in this connexion.

[2] *Clavieristen (celui qui joue du Clavecin)*. *Clavier*, which means simply 'keyboard', may indicate any type of keyboard instrument, although Quantz seems generally to restrict it to keyboard instruments other than the organ. In identifying individual types of keyboard instruments, Quantz uses *Clavicymbal* and *Flügel* for the harpsichord, the latter indicating the wing-shaped type; *Clavichord* for clavichord; and *Pianoforte* for pianoforte. In the French text, *clavecin* is used as the equivalent of *Clavier*, and also for both forms of the harpsichord. A useful and stimulating introduction to keyboard technique in Quantz's day and earlier, and to the principal historical sources of information, is found in E. Harich-Schneider, *The Harpsichord* (Kassel:

§ 2

It is not my intention to deal with the former, since there is no lack of instructions for it.[1] But since the art of accompanying well is part of the design of this work, I wish, with the permission of my lords the keyboard players, to make a few remarks on that subject here, leaving the rest to the further consideration of each able and experienced keyboard player.

§ 3

As stated above, it is possible that a player who has an exhaustive knowledge of thorough-bass may nevertheless be only a poor accompanist. Thorough-bass requires that the parts which the player adds extemporaneously above the bass, in conformity with the figures, must be performed according to the rules, and as if they were written out on paper. The art of accompanying requires both this and much else besides.

§ 4

The general rule of thorough-bass is that you always play in four parts; yet if you wish to accompany well, a better effect is often produced if you do not bind yourself very strictly to this rule, and if you leave out some parts, or even double the bass an octave higher with the right hand. For just as a composer is neither able nor compelled to set a three-, four-, or five-part instrumental accompaniment to all melodies, lest they become unintelligible or obscure, so not every melody allows an accompaniment of full chords upon the keyboard; hence an accompanist must govern himself more by the individual case[2] than by the general rules of thorough-bass.

§ 5

A piece with full harmony, accompanied by a large body of instruments, also requires a full and strong keyboard accompaniment. A concerto executed by a few instruments already requires some moderation in this respect, particularly in the concertante passages.[3] You must then pay attention to whether these passages are accompanied by the bass alone or by additional instruments; whether the concertante part plays softly or

Bärenreiter, 1954). Donington, *Interpretation*, pp. 306–72, and 571–82, also contains much pertinent information. The most important source from Quantz's own time is undoubtedly C. P. E. Bach, *Essay*. But special attention should also be directed to F. W. Marpurg's *Die Kunst das Clavier zu spielen* (1750–1) and his *Anleitung zum Clavierspielen* (1755). In 1763 Marpurg reprinted this section of the *Essay* in the third part of his *Clavierstücke mit einem practischen Unterricht* (Berlin: Haude und Spener).

[1] F. T. Arnold, *The Art of Accompaniment from a Thorough-Bass as Practised in the XVIIth and XVIIIth Centuries* (London: Oxford University Press, 1931), presents a lengthy survey of the principal works on thorough-bass. See also Donington, *Interpretation*, pp. 288–305.

[2] French text: 'by what the composer wishes to express'.

[3] i.e. solo sections in the concerto.

loudly, and in the low or high register; whether it has a sustained and singing melody, leaps, or passage-work to execute; whether the passage-work is played quietly or with fire; whether the passage-work remains consonant or becomes dissonant in order to modulate to a new key; whether the bass moves slowly or quickly beneath the passage-work; whether the quick notes of the bass are written in steps or in leaps, or whether four or eight notes appear upon the same pitch; whether rests or long and short notes are intermingled; whether the piece is an Allegretto, Allegro, or Presto, the first of which must be played seriously in pieces for instruments, the second in a lively manner, and the third fleetingly and playfully; or whether it is an Adagio assai, Grave, Mesto, Cantabile, Arioso, Andante, Larghetto, Siciliano, Spiritoso, or so forth, each of which requires a special execution both in the principal part and in the accompaniment. If each person observes these matters properly, the piece will produce the desired effect upon the listeners.

§ 6

In a trio the keyboard player must adjust himself to the instruments that he has to accompany, noting whether they are loud or soft, whether or not there is a violoncello with the keyboard, whether the composition is in a *galant* or elaborate[1] style, whether the harpsichord is loud or soft, open or closed, and whether the listeners are close by or at a distance. The harpsichord is obtrusive and quite loud close by,[2] but at a distance it is not as loud as other instruments. If the keyboard player has a violoncellist with him,[3] and accompanies soft instruments, he may use some moderation with the right hand, especially in a *galant* composition, and still more if one part rests, and the other plays alone; with strong instruments, however, and if the piece is harmonically full and elaborate, and also if both parts play at the same time, he may play with much fuller chords.

§ 7

The greatest discretion and restraint are required in a solo; and if the soloist is to play his part tranquilly, without anxiety, and to his satisfaction, much depends upon his accompanist, since the latter can inspire his confidence or destroy it. If the accompanist is not secure in the tempo, if he allows himself to be beguiled into dragging in the tempo rubato, or when the player of the principal part retards several notes in order to give some grace to the execution, or if he allows himself to rush the tempo when the note following a rest is anticipated, then he not only startles

---

[1] *Gearbeitet (travaillée).*

[2] *Denn der Clavicymbal rauschet und klinget zwar stark in der Nähe . . . (Car le Clavecin sonne fort & fait beaucoup de bruit étant proche . . .).*

[3] i.e. if a violoncellist doubles the bass line.

the soloist, but arouses his mistrust and makes him afraid to undertake anything else with boldness or freedom.[1] In like manner the accompanist is to be censured if he uses the right hand too actively or if he plays melodically with it, or arpeggiates, or introduces other things in opposition to the principal part at the wrong time, or if he does not express the Piano and Forte at the same time as the soloist, but instead plays everything without sentiment, and with the same volume.

§ 8

What has been said here about the accompaniment of instrumental pieces may for the most part be applied also to the accompaniment of vocal pieces.

§ 9

It is true that on the harpsichord, especially if it has only one keyboard, volume of tone cannot be augmented or diminished as well as upon the instrument called the *pianoforte*,[2] in which the strings are not plucked with quills, but struck with hammers. Nevertheless, on the harpsichord the manner of playing is most important. Thus passages marked Piano on this instrument may be improved by moderating the touch, and by decreasing the number of parts, and those marked Forte by strengthening the touch, and by increasing the number of parts in both hands.

§ 10

The accompanist will often encounter notes that require more emphasis than the others, and thus he must know how to strike them with greater liveliness and force, and how to distinguish them clearly from the other notes that do not require emphasis. The former include the long notes intermingled among quicker ones, also the notes with which a prin-

---

[1] In this rather complicated sentence, the clearer French text has been followed in the main. The two versions follow : *Wenn der Accompagnist im Zeitmaaße nicht recht sicher ist, und sich entweder bey dem Tempo rubato, und durch das Verziehen der Manieren, welches eine Schönheit im Spielen ist, zum Zögern, oder, wenn anstatt einer Pause die folgende Note vorausgenommen wird, zum Eilen verleiten läßt; kann er den Solospieler nicht nur aus seinem Concepte bringen; sondern er versetzet ihn auch in ein Mistrauen gegen ihn, den Accompagnisten; und macht ihn furchtsam, weiter etwas mit Verwegenheit und Freyheit zu unternehmen. (Si l'Accompagnateur n'est pas ferme dans la mesure, & qu'il se laisse porter ou à trainer, dans le Tempo rubato, & quand le joueur de la partie principale retarde quelques notes, pour donner par là de l'agrément à l'exécution, ou à presser la mésure, quand à la place d'une pause la note suivante est anticipée; alors il peut non seulement rendre interdit dans cette occasion celui qui joue le Solo, mais il lui inspire aussi de la défiance pour tout le reste de la piéce, de sorte que le meilleur Musicien n'ose plus faire des agrémens hardis, de crainte qu'également ils ne réussissent point.)* For a fuller discussion of tempo rubato, see C. P. E. Bach, *Essay*, p. 161. See also Chapter XIV, § 29 above.

[2] Quantz's employer, Frederick II, was a great admirer of the early pianoforte builder Gottfried Silbermann (1683–1753), and is said to have collected fifteen of his pianofortes. J. S. Bach, on his visit to Frederick in 1747, performed on one of these instruments. For reports of Bach's reaction to this early type of pianoforte, see H. T. David and A. Mendel, *The Bach Reader*, pp. 259, 305.

cipal subject enters, and above all the dissonances. A long note, which may be struck with its lower octave, interrupts the liveliness of the melody. The *thema*[1] always requires an increase in the strength of the tone to make its entry clearer; and the dissonances serve as the means to vary the expression of the different passions.

§ 11

Indeed other long notes often appear in the accompaniment that require no special expression, but only accompany the melody, or set it in repose. These are not the object of the present discussion. Here we are concerned only with those notes that interrupt quick and impetuous motion with consonances as well as dissonances, but which immediately afterwards are in turn relieved by other quicker notes. Also to be reckoned with here are the notes through which the bass avoids a cadence with the principal part in order to create a so-called deception (*inganno*); the notes that prepare for the principal cadence; those that are raised a minor semitone by a sharp or natural sign and generally have a diminished fifth and a sixth above them; and finally those lowered by a flat, as has already been pointed out in the previous section dealing with the violoncellist.[2] Other cases may be discovered that are similar to those cited here, but each piece must be considered in its context, and with the proper attention; and the purpose of the music—to constantly arouse and still the passions— must never be forgotten.

§ 12

To excite the different passions the dissonances must be struck more strongly than the consonances. Consonances make the spirit peaceful and tranquil; dissonances, on the other hand, disturb it. Just as an uninterrupted pleasure, of whatever kind it might be, would weaken and exhaust our capacities for remaining sensitive to it until the pleasure finally ceased, so a long series of pure consonances would eventually cause the ear distaste and displeasure, if they were not mingled now and then with disagreeable sounds such as those produced by dissonances. The more, then, that a dissonance is distinguished and set off from the other notes in playing, the more it affects the ear. But the more displeasing the disturbance of our pleasure, the more agreeable the ensuing pleasure seems to us. Thus the harsher the dissonance, the more pleasing is its resolution. Without this mixture of agreeable and disagreeable sounds, music would no longer be able now to arouse the different passions instantly, now to still them again.

[1] i.e. the 'principal subject' mentioned earlier in the paragraph.
[2] See Section IV, § 7.

§ 13

Since, however, the displeasure cannot be always of the same vehemence, some of the dissonances have more effect, and so must be struck with greater force than the others. The ninth, the ninth and fourth, the ninth and seventh, the fifth and fourth are not as perceptible to the ear as the fifth with the major sixth, the diminished fifth with the minor sixth, the diminished fifth with the major sixth, the minor seventh with the major or minor third, the major seventh, the diminished seventh, the seventh with the second and fourth, the augmented sixth, the major second with the fourth, the minor second with the fourth, the major and augmented second with the augmented fourth, and the minor third with the augmented fourth. The former thus require less emphasis by far in the accompaniment than the latter. Even among the latter, however, distinctions must be made. The minor second with the fourth, the major and augmented second with the augmented fourth, the minor third with the augmented fourth, the diminished fifth with the major sixth, the augmented sixth, the diminished seventh, and the seventh with the second and fourth require still more emphasis than the others, and the accompanist must therefore execute them still more forcefully, using a stronger touch.[1]

§ 14

To make the matter still clearer, I shall append an example of the aforementioned dissonances, and of the differences in their expression with respect to the moderation and the strengthening of the tone (see Tab. XXIV, Fig. 1);[2] from it you will be able to perceive clearly that to express the sentiments properly the Piano and Forte are among the most essential elements of performance. Play this example several times as it is marked with the Piano, Pianissimo, Mezzo Forte, Forte, and Fortissimo;* then repeat it with the same strength of tone throughout, and pay close attention both to the diversity of the figures, and to their individual feeling.[3] I am convinced that if you once begin to accustom yourself without prejudice to this manner of accompanying; if you learn to recognize the different effects of the dissonances; if you pay close attention to the repetition of the ideas, to the held notes that relieve the flow of quick notes, to the deceptive passages that appear so often at the cadences, and to the notes raised by sharps or naturals or lowered by flats that lead to a foreign tonality: I am convinced, I say, that you will then easily be able to divine when to use the Piano, Mezzo Forte, Forte, and Fortissimo without their being written out. In consequence of what I have said above, and for the sake of

---

[1] C. P. E. Bach seems to have had considerable reservations about this theory of Quantz. See Bach's *Essay*, p. 163, n. 32.

[2] This example appears at the end of the present paragraph.

[3] i.e. the diversity of the chords *indicated by* the figures, and to their individual effects.

greater clarity, I divide the dissonances into three classes, according to their effects and the manner in which they should be struck. The *first* I mark *Mezzo Forte*, the *second Forte*, and the *third Fortissimo*. In the first class, *Mezzo Forte*, may be reckoned:

> The second with the fourth,
> The fifth with the major sixth,
> The major sixth with the minor third,
> The minor seventh with the minor third,
> The major seventh.

To the second class, *Forte*, belong:

> The second with the augmented fourth,
> The diminished fifth with the minor sixth.

In the third class, *Fortissimo*, count:

> The augmented second with the augmented fourth,
> The minor third with the augmented fourth,
> The diminished fifth with the major sixth,
> The augmented sixth,
> The diminished seventh,
> The major seventh with the second and fourth.

I have chosen an Adagio for this example because this tempo is the most convenient one for the more exact and distinct expression of the different kinds of dissonances. I assume that the consonant chords of the Adagio in a solo must be accompanied not with the greatest possible force, but generally Mezzo Piano, so that you retain the ability to play more softly or loudly wherever it is necessary. But when Piano or Pianissimo is indicated, the dissonances that appear must be expressed with a proportional force, in such a way that in the Pianissimo the dissonances of the third class receive only the force of the first, and in the Piano the force of the second, the others being moderated in the same ratio; otherwise the contrast, if it is too vehement, will awaken greater displeasure than satisfaction in the ear. With this manner of accompanying you attempt to give an imitation of the human voice, and of such instruments as are capable of swelling and diminishing the tone. Yet much must also depend upon good judgement and refined sensitivity of spirit. Whoever lacks these two qualities will make but little progress in this respect, unless he supplies himself with them by serious effort, and by much experience; for knowledge can be gained by industry, and by industry you can come to the aid → of nature.

* Where you find Mezzo Forte it applies to the note not above the M but above the F, since space does not permit it to be written otherwise; see the note to § 19 of the following section.

FIG. I
TABLE XXIV

§ 15

It remains to be noted that if several dissonances of different kinds follow one another, and these dissonances are resolved into dissonances, you must also allow the expression gradually to swell and diminish by strengthening the tone and increasing the number of parts. That the fifth and fourth, the ninth and seventh, the ninth and fourth, and the seventh if it alternates with the sixth and fourth or if it stands above a passing note, require no special expression you will be able to recognize sufficiently not only from the present example, but also, and indeed more fully, through individual experience and sensitivity. For, as already stated above, the dissonances are not all of equal importance, but must be regarded like salt and spice at meals, since the tongue always feels more effect from one kind than from the others.

§ 16

If the dissonances are to have their proper effect, however, that is, if the consonances that follow are to sound more agreeable and pleasing, they not only must be struck (as has been previously explained)[1] with varying degrees of emphasis, each according to its kind, but they must also be struck more forcefully than the consonances. And just as each consonant chord may be taken in three ways,[2] namely so that the octave, the third, or the fifth or sixth lies in the upper part, and produces a different effect in each case, the same is true of dissonant chords. If, for example, you try the minor third, augmented fourth, and sixth struck together with the fundamental note, and the first time take the third, the second time the fourth, and the third time the sixth in the upper part, or if you invert the seventh formed by two of the upper parts into a second, you will find that the dissonant notes sound much harsher if they lie close to one another

---

[1] Translator's parentheses.

[2] Quantz actually enumerates four ways. Here he seems to confuse the various possible notes in the upper part and the three possible positions of a triad.

than if they lie at some distance from one another. Distribution of the notes as the nature of the case[1] requires depends upon the good judgement of the accompanist.

§ 17

On a harpsichord with one keyboard, passages marked Piano may be produced by a moderate touch and by diminishing the number of parts, those marked Mezzo Forte by doubling the bass in octaves, those marked Forte in the same manner and also by taking some *consonances* belonging to the chord into the left hand, and those marked Fortissimo by quick arpeggiations of the chords from below upwards,[2] by the same doubling of the octaves and the consonances in the left hand, and by a more vehement and forceful touch. On a harpsichord with two keyboards, you have the additional advantage of being able to use the upper keyboard for the Pianissimo. But on a *pianoforte* everything required may be accomplished with the greatest convenience, for this instrument, of all those that are designated by the word keyboard, has the greatest number of qualities necessary for good accompaniment, and depends for its effect only upon the player and his judgement.[3] The same is true of a good clavichord with regard to playing, but not with regard to effect, since it lacks the Fortissimo.

§ 18

On each instrument the tone may be produced in different ways, and the same is true of the harpsichord, although it might appear that on this instrument everything depends not upon the player, but only upon the instrument itself. Experience shows, however, that if two musicians play the same instrument, one produces a better tone than the other. The reason for this must be the touch[4] peculiar to each person. In this regard it is necessary that each finger strikes the key with equal force and emphasis, and with the proper weight; that the strings are given sufficient time to make their vibrations unhindered; and that the fingers are not depressed too sluggishly, but are rather given, through a snap,[5] a certain force that will make the vibrations of the strings longer in duration, and sustain the tone longer. In this fashion you will obviate as much as possible the natural weakness of the instrument, which is that the tones cannot be joined to one another as upon other instruments. Whether you strike one finger more forcefully than another is also very important. This may happen if you have accustomed yourself to curve some fingers inwards while extending others straight forward, a habit that not only causes inequality in the force of your playing, but is also obstructive to the round, distinct and agreeable execution of quick passage-work. As a result many persons

---

[1] 'And the ideas' is inserted at this point in the French text.
[2] See, however, § 7 of this section.   [3] See § 9 and the accompanying footnote.
[4] *Anschlag (maniere de toucher).*   [5] *Schneller (tire).*

sound as if they were literally stumbling over the notes if they have to produce a run of several step-wise notes. If you accustom yourself at the very beginning to curving all the fingers inwards, each one as far as the others, you are less likely to make this mistake. In the performance of these running passages, however, you must not raise the fingers immediately after striking the key, but rather draw the tips of the fingers back towards yourself to the foremost part of the key, until they glide away from it. Running passages are produced most distinctly in this manner. I appeal here to the example of one of the greatest of all players on the keyboard,[1] who practised and taught in this way.

§ 19

If the principal part in an Adagio occasionally makes an appoggiatura before a third or sixth, so that the note before the third becomes a fourth, and the one before the sixth becomes a seventh (see Tab. XXIII, Fig. 4), a poor effect is produced if you strike the third together with the appoggiatura that makes the fourth, and the sixth together with that which forms the seventh.

Fig. 4

The accompanist would do better to strike only the other members of the chord, and to sound the third or sixth when the appoggiatura is resolved; otherwise dissonances arise that are neither prepared nor resolved, and in consequence strike the ear very disagreeably. In appoggiaturas taken from below, if a ninth is suspended before a third that lies in the upper register, the third produced by the harpsichord does not sound so badly, provided that the third proper to the chord of the principal note is not taken above but below the principal part, since it then becomes the seventh instead of the second against the appoggiatura.

§ 20

Any keyboard performer who understands the ratios of the notes will also know that subsemitones such as D sharp and E flat differ by a comma, and therefore cause, because of its lack of divided keys, some inequality in intonation upon this instrument as compared with other instruments on which these notes are produced in their true ratios, especially if the key-

---

[1] In his index Quantz identifies this player as J. S. Bach. While still in Dresden Quantz may well have heard Bach play, and was probably present when Bach performed for Frederick in 1747. The description that Quantz gives here of Bach's touch is expanded in J. N. Forkel's biography of Bach. See H. T. David and A. Mendel, *The Bach Reader*, pp. 307–8. For the views of some other eighteenth-century musicians, see Harich-Schneider, *The Harpsichord*, pp. 11–18.

board plays them in unison with one of the instruments just mentioned. Since, then, these notes cannot always be avoided, especially in those keys in which many flats or many sharps appear, the accompanist would do well to seek as much as possible either to hide them in a middle or lower part, or, if one of them forms a minor third,[1] to leave it out entirely. For these minor thirds in particular sound very bad and imperfect if they are struck in unison with the principal part in the upper octave.[2] The minor thirds I refer to are principally the C, D, and E of the two-line octave, if a flat stands before them, or, to put it more briefly, C flat, D flat, and E flat. But I also refer to G′ and A′, and D″ and E″, if they are preceded by a sharp; for if they form major thirds, the interval is too large, and they are thus too high. It is true that you cannot perceive this difference as distinctly if you play alone on the harpsichord, or if you accompany a large ensemble, but if these notes are found in unison with another instrument, the difference is all too clearly heard, since the other instruments give them in their true ratios, while upon the keyboard they are tempered; for this reason it is better to omit them entirely than to offend the ear. But let anyone whom the omission does not please at least take the minor and major thirds indicated above in the low register, where the ear will better endure them, as I have indicated for the other subsemitones. Apart from this, the unison does not produce as good an effect with an instrument as with a voice. In addition the poor intonation is not as apparent to the ear in the low register as in the high. To be convinced of this, tune an octave either flat or sharp on one keyboard of the harpsichord, then on the other keyboard tune one string of the high note quite accurately with the low one. Then try the mistuned unison and see if it does not displease the ear more than the mistuned octave.

§ 21

It has long been the rule in playing thorough-bass that you should not remove your hands too far from one another, and in consequence that you should not play with the right hand too high. This rule is reasonable and good, and should be consistently observed. For it produces a much better effect if the accompanying keyboard parts are taken below the principal part, than if they are taken with the upper part, or above it. When the old composers wished to have the accompaniment an octave higher, they placed the figures 10, 11, and 12 above the bass instead of 3, 4, 5, &c. And since the distinction to be made between these figures is not the same as that between 2 and 9,[3] they served a legitimate purpose. For the reasons stated above, you must not accompany a violoncellist, if

---

[1] Quantz seems to mean a minor third in relation to the bass.

[2] In other words, the minor third of the keyboard above the bass does not agree with the minor third of the principal part.

[3] These two figures require different resolutions. Three and ten, four and eleven, &c., do not.

he plays a solo, as you would a violinist. With the former the right hand must play everything in the low register; and if, through the ignorance of the composer, the bass at times is written too high, and rises above the principal part, it too may be played an octave lower, so that the fifths are not transformed into fourths.[1] In accompanying the violin, which has a greater compass of notes, the accompanist must pay attention to whether the violinist has much to play in the very low or in the very high register, so that he neither rises above the low notes, nor becomes too distant from the very high ones.

§ 22

If in slow pieces the bass has to repeat several notes upon the same pitch that are figured $\frac{5}{3}, \frac{6}{4}, \frac{7}{5}, \frac{6}{4}, \frac{5}{3}$, &c., since the principal part probably has the upper figures in its melody, it sounds very good if the accompanist plays the upper figures in the low register, thus transforming the thirds which the two parts form against one another into sixths. These sixths will not only sound more harmonious, but will also give the piece the effect of a trio rather than of a solo. The effect is still better if the accompanist plays only the lowest figures, and leaves out entirely those of the principal part. If he proceeds in this fashion on all such occasions, and makes the second part the upper one, and the upper one the lower, the principal part will never be obscured, and the soloist will receive the freedom that he requires. If the accompanist does not do this, it may seem that he wishes to play the piece in unison with the soloist.

§ 23

In the Adagio the accompanist must neither arpeggiate nor play melodically with the right hand, unless the soloist has sustained notes or rests. He must not allow the accompanying parts to become more prominent than the bass. In an Adagio in common time, he may strike each quaver with the right hand. But in an Arioso where the bass has a quicker movement, whether in quavers, semiquavers, or triplets of either species of notes, it is not necessary to strike chords with the right hand for each note; it sounds better to allow one note to go by in equal notes,[2] and two in triplets, provided that the passing notes have no figures of their own above them.

§ 24

If in the Adagio a singer or solo player allows the tone of a long note to swell and diminish, and the movement of the bass beneath it is in different values, it is good for the accompanist likewise to strike each note more strongly and again more softly, in accordance with the example of the principal part.

---

[1] For a fuller discussion of this point, see Section III, § 16.

[2] In other words, it sounds better to play chords with only the first of each pair of quavers or semiquavers, or with the first note of each triplet.

§ 25

If the principal part in an Adagio expresses something forceful with quick dotted notes, and the bass must imitate it with notes of the same kind, the accompanist must strike them, whether consonances or dissonances, majestically and with very full chords. But if the principal part has a melancholy or flattering melody, the accompanist must moderate his touch, decrease the number of parts, and accommodate himself on all occasions to the principal part, taking all the passions to heart as much as if he were himself playing the solo part. If the composer unfortunately expresses little sentiment or none at all, the accompanist can nevertheless, by using a stronger touch, bring out some notes from time to time as he sees fit, and moderate the following notes. This practice may be best applied to similar or repeated ideas, whether they occur in the same key or in transpositions, or, as already mentioned, when dissonances appear.

§ 26

Imitations[1] that consist of running or melodic passages have a better effect if they are doubled with the right hand at the upper octave than if they are accompanied with full chords. Unisons may be treated in the same way.

§ 27

If the bass quits its customary register, and has something to play in the register of the tenor, as often happens in vocal music, the right hand must accompany with only a few parts and very close to the left hand, so that what follows in the bass register may be expressed with so much the greater emphasis.

§ 28

If suspensions figured for the most part with the second, fourth, and sixth occur in the bass in a very slow piece, and if the accompanist is not joined by another bass instrument, he may, in spite of the rule of thorough-bass, strike the tied notes with the dissonances belonging to them, since the tone of the harpsichord soon diminishes, and without the fundamental note the dissonances are transformed into consonances by the ear, destroying the desired effect. Similarly, if several notes filling whole bars are tied upon a single pitch, each may be struck separately.

§ 29

If the soloist has not taken the tempo that he ought to have taken at the beginning, the accompanist must not obstruct him in altering it in any way that he wishes.

[1] i.e. musical ideas that are treated imitatively.

§ 30

In order not to disrupt the tempo, especially in very slow movements, the keyboard player must take care that he does not raise both hands too high or unequally, and that he does not strike the accompanying notes, such as crotchets or quavers, too briefly, and withdraw his hands from the keyboard too quickly. For if he holds his hands above the keyboard longer than upon it, he loses the advantage of being able to measure each note correctly. But if he makes an equal movement with his hands, so that he holds them above the keyboard just as long as he allows them to remain upon it, the division of the crotchets into quavers, and of the quavers into semiquavers, is made correctly and without much reflection; the notes also receive a more sustained sound, and the instrument becomes more agreeable. If, on the other hand, this practice is not observed, the strings are too soon stopped by the rapid backward fall of the quills for the necessary vibration to occur, and the natural tone of the instrument cannot come out as it should. Likewise there would be no distinction between the staccato notes and other kinds. In a sostenuto, however, the fingers must remain upon the keys right up to the following note.

§ 31

If in an Adagio both parts rest at a caesura, and the upper part must begin again with a note on the upbeat, the following note standing a fourth, fifth, sixth, or seventh higher on the downbeat, at which point the soloist is free to introduce an extempore embellishment, the accompanist, whose first note usually begins only with the downbeat in such cases, must wait until the upper part touches the note on the downbeat, and must not rush the tempo, since it is not strictly observed in such cases. But if the principal part has suspensions or other sustained notes, and the bass has moving passages beneath them, the accompanist must observe the tempo strictly, no deviation being permitted, since the soloist is then obliged to adjust his embellishments to the bass.

§ 32

The statements made thus far apply principally to the Adagio. Although all these matters cannot be observed in fast pieces with the strictness required in the Adagio, most of those that pertain to discretion and expression may also be applied in the Allegro. The primary matters in the Allegro are as follows. The accompanist must keep the tempo with the greatest strictness, neither allowing himself to drag or to rush. He must possess sufficient facility in his left hand to play everything distinctly and accurately. In general, instrumental music is more advantageous in developing this skill than vocal music, since less facility and fire can be required in the latter than in the former. If many quavers appear on one note, he must strike them all, and must not, for the sake of an ill-timed convenience, strike one and then allow three or even seven to go by, as some do occasionally, especially in vocal pieces. He must proceed quietly and modestly with the right hand. He must not play with chords that are too full, and must not play in unison with the principal part. He must not raise his hands too high after short rests, since in this way he may easily disrupt the tempo; hence he may strike the chord for the following note in place of the preceding short rest.* He must not make such quick movements with his right hand that he may be beguiled into dragging, thus impeding the liveliness of the soloist. He must not burden passing notes with too many parts. He must express the Piano and Forte at the proper time. He must play the bass notes in their register, and the intervals as they are marked, adding nothing to them. Finally, with respect to loudness and softness of tone, he must adjust himself to the volume of the principal part. If the latter is a flute, and it plays in the low register, he must moderate the accompaniment, especially in minor keys.

> * This applies only to accompanying notes. But if the principal subject of a fugue or some other imitation begins on the upbeat, it would be obscured if you struck the following chord during the preceding rest. In such circumstances the effect is better if you double the principal subject at the upper octave with the right hand than if you accompany it with full chords.

§ 33

In a recitative sung from memory it is much easier for the singer if the accompanist anticipates the singer's first notes at each caesura, and, so to speak, puts them into his mouth for him by striking the chord with a quick arpeggiation, in such fashion that, where possible, the singer's first note lies in the upper part; immediately afterwards he should strike separately several of the following intervals that appear in the vocal part (see Tab. XXIII, Fig. 5).

FIG. 5

This is most helpful both to the memory and to the intonation of the singer. Other matters that should be noted in the recitative, and those that must be observed in accompaniment in general, will be explained more fully in the following section.

SECTION VII

Of the Duties That All Accompanying Instrumentalists in General Must Observe

§ 1

If an orchestra is to produce a genuinely good effect, all of its members must be provided with good and true instruments, and all must know how to tune them correctly and uniformly.

§ 2

It may seem superfluous to offer instructions about the tuning of stringed instruments; nothing would appear easier than to tune an instrument with four strings in fifths, since the fifth is an interval that the ear naturally learns to distinguish more readily than others. Nevertheless, experience teaches that although some experienced violin players or other instrumentalists fulfil their duties in this regard, the majority do not, either because of ignorance or negligence; if each instrument in a large accompanying body were tested separately, it not only would be found that almost every instrument is untrue in itself, but also that frequently not even two or three would be in tune with one another. Considerable damage is done as a result to the good effect of the ensemble.

§ 3

Let anyone who demands proof of this imagine an able keyboard player performing on an out-of-tune instrument, and note whether an ear sensitive to the beauties of music[1] is not more offended by the impurity of the intonation than pleased by the good style of the player's performance. If such is the case on a single instrument, where the notes may be doubled with only two unisons[2] or, at most, two octaves, how poor the effect must be in a large ensemble, where the unison is doubled so many more times, if the instruments are not in tune with one another! It is true that each of the string players follows the judgement of his ear when he plays, and can shift his fingers up or down accordingly; but untrue tuning can still be detected on each instrument from time to time through the open strings, especially the low ones, which cannot always be avoided. In addition, it may be conjectured that somebody who so thoughtlessly accustoms himself to tuning his instrument truly only on rare occasions actually lacks the capacity to play it in tune, since one infelicity produces the other. And even if a violinist were skilful enough to play everything by changing positions, without recourse to the open strings, he could not avoid playing

---

[1] The French text has been followed here. The German text reads: 'a sensitive musical ear'.
[2] Quantz apparently has a harpsichord with two keyboards in mind.

leaps of fifths with the same finger. And these leaps of fifths will likewise remain untrue in quick pieces if the individual strings are not accurately tuned.

§ 4

To tune the violin quite accurately, I think you will not do badly to follow the rule that must be observed in tuning the keyboard, namely, that the fifths must be tuned a little on the flat side rather than quite truly or a little sharp, as is usually the case, so that the open strings will all agree with the keyboard. For if all the fifths are tuned sharp and truly, it naturally follows that only one of the four strings will be in tune with the keyboard. If the A is tuned truly with the keyboard, the E a little flat in relation to the A, the D a little sharp to the A, and the G likewise to the D, the two instruments will agree with each other. This suggestion is not presented as an absolute rule, however, but only as a matter for further reflection.

§ 5

In warm weather the wind instruments can be tuned a little lower than the violins, since their pitch rises with blowing, while that of stringed instruments is lowered by warmth.

§ 6

The pitch regularly used for tuning in an orchestra has always varied considerably according to the time and place.[1] The disagreeable choir pitch[2] prevailed in Germany for several centuries, as the old organs prove. Other instruments, such as violins, double basses, trombones, recorders, shawms, bombards, trumpets, clarinets, &c., were also made to conform to it. But after the French had transformed the German cross-pipe into the transverse flute, the shawm into the oboe, and the bombard into the bassoon,[3] using their lower and more agreeable pitch, the high choir pitch began in Germany to be supplanted by the chamber pitch,[4] as is demonstrated by some of the most famous new organs. At the present time the Venetian pitch is the highest; it is almost the same as our old choir pitch. The Roman pitch of about twenty years ago was low, and was equal to that of Paris. At present, however, the Parisian pitch is beginning almost to equal that of Venice.

§ 7

The diversity of pitches used for tuning is most detrimental to music in general. In vocal music it produces the inconvenience that singers performing in a place where low tuning is used are hardly able to make use of arias that were written for them in a place where a high pitch was em-

---

[1] For a detailed discussion of the various pitches used in Quantz's day, see A. Mendel, 'On the Pitches in Use in Bach's Time', *The Musical Quarterly*, xli (1955), pp. 332–54, 466–80. ←
[2] *Chorton (ton de Chœur)*.   [3] See Chapter I, § 5.   [4] *Kammerton (ton de la chambre)*.

ployed, or vice versa. For this reason it is much to be hoped that a single pitch for tuning may be introduced at all places. It is undeniable that the high pitch is much more penetrating than the low one; on the other hand, it is much less pleasing, moving, and majestic. I do not wish to argue for the very low French chamber pitch, although it is the most advantageous for the transverse flute, the oboe, the bassoon, and some other instruments; but neither can I approve of the very high Venetian pitch, since in it the wind instruments sound much too disagreeable. Therefore I consider the best pitch to be the so-called German *A* chamber pitch, which is a minor third lower than the old choir pitch. It is neither too low nor too high, but the mean between the French and the Venetian; and in it both the stringed and the wind instruments can produce their proper effect. Although the shape of the instrument would remain, the very high pitch would finally make a cross-pipe again of the transverse flute, a shawm of the oboe, a violino piccolo of the violin, and a bombard of the bassoon. The wind instruments, which are such a special ornament of an orchestra, would suffer the greatest harm in consequence. Indeed they owe their existence to the low pitch. The oboes and bassoons in particular, which were made for the low pitch, would become completely false if forced up by shortening the reeds and mouth pieces.[1]* The octaves would be expanded, that is, the lower note of an octave would become lower, while the upper note would become higher; just as in the opposite case, when the reed is pulled out too far and the mouthpiece is lengthened,[2] the octaves contract, and the lower note becomes higher, the upper note lower. The flute has the same peculiarity when its plug is pushed in too deeply or drawn out too far. For in the first case the octaves expand in the manner mentioned above, while in the second they contract. To be sure, smaller and narrower instruments could be made that would improve the high notes; but the majority of the instrument-makers work according to accustomed models that are adjusted to the low pitch, and very few would be in a position to reduce the measurements in a sufficiently correct ratio that would make the instrument high yet also retain its trueness. And even if some were finally to succeed, the question would still remain: would the above-mentioned instruments, if adjusted to the high pitch, produce the same effect as with the old measurements peculiar to them? Partiality for an instrument is indeed in itself good, but only as long as it does not bring detriment to the other instruments. In some parts of Italy they prefer the heightening of the pitch referred to above. For there the wind instruments are less used than in other countries, and in consequence the inhabitants do not have such good taste with regard to these instruments as they have for other things in music. In Rome at one time the wind

---

[1] *Röhre und Esse (anches & des portes voix). Es* seems to refer specifically to the crook of the bassoon. The footnote is found only in the French text.

[2] Another slip appears in the French translation at this point. The French text reads 'and the mouthpiece is shortened'.

instruments were banned from the church. Whether the unpleasant high pitch or the manner of playing the instruments was the reason for this I must leave undecided. For although the Roman pitch was low, and advantageous for the oboe, the oboists then played on instruments that were a whole tone higher, so that they were obliged to transpose. And these high instruments produced an effect like that of German shawms against the others that were tuned low.

* The *porte voix* is what the Germans call the *S* [Es].

§ 8

Much depends upon a good musical ear in the accurate stopping of the notes on bowed instruments, particularly the violin. But this is not simply a matter of natural ability, and must be acquired by knowledge of the proportions of the notes. Many persons, through their natural ear, perceive whether others play falsely; but if they themselves commit the same error, they are either unaware of it, or do not know what to do about it. The best means to escape from this ignorance is the monochord or measurer of sounds.[1] On it you can learn to recognize the ratios of the notes most distinctly. Every singer and instrumentalist should be required to acquaint himself with it. With it he would acquire knowledge of the subsemitone much sooner and learn earlier that the notes marked with a flat must be a comma higher than those that have a sharp before them; for without this insight, he must rely entirely upon the ear, which is deceptive. Knowledge of the monochord is especially required of violinists and other players of bowed instruments, upon which there are no limits to the number of positions of the fingers, as there are upon wind instruments. Many would also play more truly in the high register if they knew that the notes on a string, from its lower to its upper part, are not all at the same distance from one another, but lie at reduced intervals, namely closer and closer to one another. For proof of this, divide a string into two equal parts on the violin or on the monochord. The first half produces the octave. If the second half is again divided into two parts, the first half of the latter produces the octave above that; and the same is true of the rest of the string up to the bridge. If in the second octave the fingers are depressed at the same distances from one another as in the first, thirds rather than seconds will be produced. It follows that the reduction must be begun in the proper proportion after the first note and continue to the end of the string, and therefore that the instrument must be played with considerable discrimination.

§ 9

If true subsemitones appear, that is, if a note lowered by a flat is transformed into the note immediately below it, raised by a sharp, or if a note

[1] *Klangmesser.*

raised by the sharp is transformed into one immediately above it that is lowered by a flat (see Tab. XXIII, Figs. 6 and 7), it must be noted, as mentioned in the preceding paragraph, that the sharpened note must be a comma lower than the one with the flat.

FIG. 6   FIG. 7

For example, G sharp must be a comma lower than A flat. If these two notes are tied to one another (see Tab. XXIII, Fig. 6), the finger must be drawn back a little for the sharp following the flat, if the major third is not to be too high against the fundamental part. But if a flat follows the sharp (see Fig. 7), for the note with the flat the finger must be advanced as much as it was drawn back in the preceding example, as must be done here from G sharp to A flat in the upper part, from E sharp to F in the second part, and from C sharp to D flat in the fundamental part. The same rule must be observed on all instruments, with the exception of the keyboard, upon which the transformation of the subsemitone cannot be produced, and which must therefore be well tempered[1] to sound endurable with both. Upon wind instruments this variation is accomplished through the embouchure. On the flute the pitch is raised by turning it outwards, and lowered by turning it inward. On the oboe and the bassoon the pitch is raised by pushing the reed further into the mouth, and by pressing the lips more firmly together, and is lowered by withdrawing the reed, and relaxing the lips.

§ 10

If an orchestra is to be good, it must strive for an execution that is both good and appropriate to the style and character of each piece. Whether the piece is gay or melancholy, majestic or jocular, bold or flattering, or of any other sort, it must be executed in a manner suitable to the passion to be expressed. If there is a concertante part to accompany, each of the accompanists must regulate himself in all cases by the execution of the soloist, and always do his share. There must be no partiality, so that the work of one person is poorly performed, and that of another well; each person must seek to perform whatever is placed before him, no matter who has written it, with the same zeal he would show in his own work, at least if he wishes to maintain that reputation for honesty which is such a laudable characteristic in a musician.

---

[1] *Eine gute Temperatur haben muß (doit avoir une bonne Temperature).*

§ 11

The general requirements for the development of good execution may be seen more fully in Chapter XI. The type of bow-stroke that each piece requires, however, is explained in the second section of this chapter, since the most essential matters in the accompaniment depend on the bowed instruments.

§ 12

Not only each particular piece and each passion that the piece contains, but also the place and object of its performance, provide certain rules and limitations for its execution. For example, a composition for the church requires more majesty and seriousness than one for the theatre, which allows greater freedom. If in a work for the church the composer has inserted some bold and bizarre ideas that are inappropriate to the place, the accompanists, and the violinists in particular, must endeavour to mitigate, subdue, and soften them as much as possible by a modest execution.

§ 13

A good and appropriate execution must also be extended to comical music. An *intermezzo (Zwischenspiel)*,[1] which represents the opposite or a caricature of a serious vocal composition, is fashioned by its composer more out of low and common ideas than of serious ones, and has at bottom no other object than satire and laughter. If this goal is to be reached, it must be accompanied, especially in the comical airs, in a low and very common manner by the attendant instruments, and not as in a serious opera. The same is true of a ballet that has a common character, since, as has already been said, the accompanying body must be sympathetic not only to that which is serious, but also to that which is comical.

§ 14

The execution must not only be good and appropriate to each piece, but must also be uniform and harmonious among all the members of a good orchestra. It will be conceded that a discourse makes a greater impression when delivered by one person than by another. If a German tragedy were presented in which characters supposedly born in the same country were played by persons speaking a variety of different dialects, such as High German, Low German, Austrian, Swabian, Tyrolean, Swiss, &c., the differences in the pronunciation would make the most serious tragedy comical. The case is almost the same in a musical ensemble, if each member has his own particular manner of playing. For example, if one were to put

---

[1] In the German and French texts 'intermezzo' appears in parentheses. The French term is *interméde*. On the history of the intermezzo, see Donald J. Grout, *A Short History of Opera*, second edition (New York: Columbia University Press, 1965), pp. 247-54.

together an orchestra in which some played only in the Italian style, others only in the French, and still others played in both manners, the diversity of execution in the performance would produce the very effect described above in reference to the tragedy, even if each person were skilful enough in his own style. Indeed, greater harm would be done, since in the tragedy the persons speak one after the other, while in the ensemble all play together most of the time. It is often believed that if only the principal parts are assigned to skilful players, the rest may be dismissed as unimportant. But just as a little vinegar spoils the best wine, an ensemble is damaged if only some of the parts are well played, and one or more of the others are badly done.

§ 15

If a soloist has a ripieno part to play, he must for the time being renounce the particular skills that he possesses for playing concertos and solos, and also the freedom permitted him when he alone is the star; when he merely accompanies, he must, as it were, place himself in a state of bondage. Thus he must add nothing to a melody that might obscure it, especially if several people are playing the same part. Otherwise he will produce considerable disorder in the melody. For it is not always possible for one person to divine the thoughts of another. For example, if one player were to make even a single appoggiatura that is not written, and the other were to play the note plain, an offensive dissonance, without preparation and resolution, would appear, and would greatly affront the ear, particularly in a slow piece. If he were to play the written appoggiaturas without their proper duration, making the long short, or the short long, an equally poor effect would be produced in conjunction with those who play with him. Ritornellos in particular must be played entirely without extempore additions. These additions are permitted only to the performer of the concertante part. Some musicians have the bad habit of introducing at times all sorts of fopperies even in the ritornellos, and meanwhile forget to read the notes correctly. Many also make a close, especially in arias, with a full chord where none should be. This they seem to have learned from tavern fiddlers. It is still worse if immediately after the close of an aria a pair of open strings on the violin are struck. If, for example, the aria is in E flat major, and E and A are tested immediately afterward, you can imagine the beautiful effect that is produced.

§ 16

Since, then, the beauty of an orchestra depends largely on the ability of all its members to play in the same manner, and since a good execution suitable to each piece is absolutely required of its leader, it is the duty of each member of the orchestra to defer to the leader in these matters; he must not oppose the leader's instructions, and he must consider it no disgrace if he must submit to a reasonable and necessary discipline, without which no good ensemble can exist. You will rarely find an orchestra that has been established for many years which does not contain both good and bad players, as you may perceive most easily if various parts of the orchestra are chosen in turn for small concerts. Both young and old people are found among the ignorant.[1] But neither the age nor the youth of the members of an orchestra make it good; this quality is the result of good discipline and order. An old ripienist, if he still has enough energy, and has been trained under good direction, may render much better service than a young one who is perhaps capable of executing more difficult things, but who has less experience, and who is not docile enough to submit to the necessary discipline. On the other hand, old men who have had inferior training are, because of the prejudice or prerogative of their years, often as refractory as the young, who, because of their pretended skill, presume too much upon their facility. The old men often think it mortifying to submit to a leader not so rich in years as they, and the young imagine that they have all the skill required of a good leader, notwithstanding the multitude of duties incumbent upon him. But how can an orchestra subsist or prosper if only obstinacy, envy, hatred, and disobedience prevail among its members, instead of a sympathetic and docile spirit? Can uniform and harmonious execution be attained if each insists on following his own lead?

§ 17

There is still another rule for developing harmonious execution in an orchestra that may be recommended to each person who wishes to become a good musician, and in particular a good accompanist: in performing a musical composition, he must apply himself well to the art of simulation. This art of simulation is not only permissible, but most necessary, and it does no offence to morals. He who strives all his life to master his passions as fully as possible will not find it difficult to counterfeit in himself the passion required in the piece to be performed. Only then will he play well and as though from the soul. Whoever does not understand this commendable art of simulation is no musician in the true sense, and is no better than a common labourer, even if he is thoroughly acquainted with all the counterpoint in the world, and can perform every possible technical feat upon his instrument. There are many, unfortunately, who prefer more often to practise the art of simulation in everyday life than to employ it in the service of music, where it becomes as innocent as in other circumstances it is unlawful.

§ 18

An honest musician must not be stubborn or be too enamoured of his rank. For example, an able violinist ought by no means to be ashamed if, in case of need, he must play the second violin, or even the viola. For in many pieces these instruments in their own way require a performer who

---

[1] 'Among the ignorant' is found only in the French text.

is just as able as a first violinist. It is ability that gives a good musician his best and most solid rank, and this he can demonstrate upon one instrument as well as upon another.

§ 19

The exact expression of the Forte and Piano* is one of the most essential matters in performance. The alternation of the Piano and Forte is one of the most convenient means both to represent the passions distinctly, and to maintain light and shadow in the execution of music. Many pieces might have a better effect upon the listeners than they do, if the Piano and Forte were observed by every player in the proper proportion, and at the correct time. One might imagine that nothing could be easier than to play loudly or softly in accordance with the indications of two letters. Yet many pay so little attention to the latter that a further oral reminder is sometimes necessary. Since a good number of professional musicians have little feeling for, and pleasure in, music, however, and devote themselves to it only to earn their livelihood, they often play without pleasure and without the proper attentiveness. Good and reasonable discipline can do much to remedy this evil; and if it is lacking, the orchestra will always remain defective, regardless of the number of able people it contains.

* It is well known that the words *forte* and *piano* are employed for the notes that must be played loudly or softly, and that these words are written or abbreviated simply with their first letters, that is, *f* and *p*, and instead of *fortissimo* and *pianissimo* two letters, *ff* and *pp*; also, if the tone ought to be augmented or diminished still more, yet another *f* or *p* is added, making *fff* and *ppp*. In addition, other words are sometimes added before forte and piano as is deemed fitting, such as *mezzo* (half), *poco* (little), *meno* (less), *più* (more), or still others after them, such as *assai* (very).[1] These epithets, however, cannot be marked with a single letter, since *mezzo* and *meno*, *poco* and *piu*, have the same first letters, and therefore confusion would result. Nevertheless, if only one *m* is employed, *mezzo*, which is more commonly used than the other term, is understood by it. Since these double letters and epithets take up more space than that covered by a note, there is a question as to which letter is actually supposed to indicate the first of the notes to be played loudly or softly. For example, if you write *piano assai*, or *poco forte*, what letter marks the note where you ought to begin to play with the required loudness or softness? You may avoid any equivocality, if in writing them you follow the rule that the first letter of the words *forte* and *piano*, the *f* and *p*, is always placed below or above the first note that is to be played loudly or softly, and regulate yourself by the first *f* or *p* even when the *f* and *p* are doubled, or have an epithet before or after them.

§ 20

The Forte and Piano must never be unduly exaggerated. The instruments must not be handled with more force than their constitution permits, since the ear will be most disagreeably affected, especially in a small

[1] These various degrees of loudness and softness were known and used rather earlier than some musicians assume. All appear in Brossard's *Dictionaire de musique* (1703). See also the list of dynamic markings found in Vivaldi's works in Kolneder, *Aufführungspraxis bei Vivaldi*, p. 25, and in Donington, *Interpretation*, p. 484.

place. You must always be able, in case of necessity, to express an additional Fortissimo or Pianissimo. It may often happen that you must unexpectedly bring out or soften a note, even if nothing is indicated. And this opportunity will be lost if you always play with the greatest loudness or softness. There are also many more degrees of moderation between the Fortissimo and the Pianissimo than can be expressed by words; these degrees must be executed with great discretion, and can only be learned through feeling and judgement from the execution of a good soloist. The Fortissimo, or the greatest volume of tone, can be achieved most conveniently with the lowest part of the bow, playing rather close to the bridge, and the Pianissimo, or the utmost softness of tone, with the tip of the bow, rather far from the bridge.

§ 21

To express the Forte and the Piano well, you must also note whether you are accompanying in a large place that reverberates, or in a small place, especially a tapestried one, where the tone is muffled; whether the listeners are at a distance or nearby; whether you are accompanying a strong or a weak part; and finally, whether the number of accompanying instruments is large, moderate, or small. In a large place that reverberates, you must not play a Piano that immediately follows a loud and noisy *tutti* too softly, since it will be engulfed by the echo. But if the Piano lasts a while, you may gradually moderate your sound. In other situations you will do better to take the Piano just as it ought to be at the note where it is indicated. If, on the contrary, a Forte follows a Piano, you may play the first note a little more strongly than the following ones. The Piano must be softer in the accompaniment of a weak part than in that of a strong one, softer in the Allegro than in the Adagio, and softer in the high notes or on the thin strings than on the thick ones. If in a concerto, especially if it is one for the flute, a Forte occurs during a solo passage, it must be performed only as a Mezzo Forte, particularly if the flute plays in the low rather than the high register; for in general the flute, like all soft voices, must be accompanied with considerable moderation. Each accompanist need merely pay attention to whether he himself hears the concertante part. If he cannot, he can easily perceive that the accompaniment is too loud, and therefore requires moderation. Finally, the number of accompanying instruments must also be considered. Suppose twelve violins play the same kind of Piano; if six stop playing, this will become a Piano assai. If four more stop, it will become finally a Pianissimo. If, then the Piano is to have its proper proportion, it follows that if two violinists play Piano, six must play Piano assai, and twelve must play Pianissimo. A very large place where the sound dies out is an exception; for here you must regulate yourself by whether the principal parts are strong or weak, whether they are trumpets or flutes.

§ 22

Since all the instruments, and especially the violins, do not have the same volume of tone, and this circumstance may cause lack of uniformity with respect to the Piano and Forte, the stronger instruments must adjust to the weaker in the Forte, and the weaker to the stronger in the Piano, so that one part is not heard more loudly than the other, especially if they have to play imitations against one another, and there is only one player to each part.

§ 23

If a concertante part is accompanied by more than one other part, the fundamental part must be heard more strongly than the others. This rule must also be observed in a tutti, unless the middle parts imitate the principal part or the bass, or have a melody in thirds or sixths with them. For parts that serve only to strengthen the harmony must never be more prominent than the principal parts. An elaborate or fugal piece that is imitative in all the parts must be played with the same volume in all the parts.

§ 24

If a Forte is indicated beneath a long note, and immediately after it a Piano, and no change of bow-stroke is possible, you must produce this note with the greatest possible force, using pressure on the bow, and immediately diminish the tone without breaking the movement of the stroke,[1] and through a diminuendo transform it into a Pianissimo. Such notes appear now and then when one part begins with a strong note on the upbeat and the others imitate it[2] on the downbeat (see Tab. XXIII, Fig. 8).

Fig. 8

§ 25

If in an Adagio the soloist alternately swells and moderates his sound, and thus plays more expressively by introducing light and shadow, the most beautiful effect is achieved if the accompanists aid him in the same manner, swelling and moderating their tone jointly with him. As was demonstrated in the previous section,[3] this is particularly important in dissonances, and in notes that prepare for a foreign tonality, or cause a halt in quick motion. If in such cases you play everything with the same colour

---

[1] *Ohne Rückung des Bogens (sans empecher la marche de l'archet).*
[2] i.e. imitate the Forte of the first part.   [3] See Section VI, §§ 12–14.

or volume, the listeners will remain completely unmoved. If, on the contrary, you express the Forte and Piano by turns, in accordance with the nature of the ideas, and employ them properly in those notes that require them, you will achieve the goal you seek, namely, to maintain the constant attention of the listener, and guide him from one passion into another.

§ 26

In the repetition of the same or of similar ideas consisting of half or whole bars, whether at the same level or in transposition, the repetition of the idea may be played somewhat more softly than the first statement.

§ 27

The *unison*,[1] which consists of a plain bass melody, and produces a particularly good effect when a large accompanying body is used, must be played in an elevated and majestic manner, with fire, with a vigorous bow, and with a more forceful tone than another kind of melody. The open strings, particularly the fifths on the violin, must be avoided.

§ 28

The *principal subject* (*thema*), particularly in a fugue, must be vigorously stressed in each part whenever it appears unexpectedly, especially if it begins with long notes. Neither a flattering style of playing nor extempore additions are permissible in it. If in the continuation of the fugue no rests precede its entry, you may moderate the volume of the preceding notes somewhat. You must proceed in the same manner with notes that resemble the principal ideas, or are inserted as new ideas in the middle of the piece, whether in the tutti or during the solo of a concertante part.

§ 29

In ligatures or tied notes that consist of crotchets or minims, the volume of the tone may be allowed to swell, since the other parts have dissonances either above or below the latter half of such notes. Dissonances in general, in whatever part they are found, always require special emphasis (see §§ 12 to 16 of the previous section).

§ 30

From what has been said thus far, it may be inferred that to observe the Piano and Forte only at those places where they are indicated is far from sufficient, and that each accompanist must also know how to introduce them with discernment at many places where they are not marked. Thus,

---

[1] i.e. phrases performed in unisons or octaves.

to achieve success in this regard, good instruction and much experience are necessary.[1]

§ 31

For all who make music their profession, hence for all good accompanists, it is a bounden duty to understand tempo[2] with particular thoroughness and to observe it with the greatest strictness. Otherwise performance will always be faulty, especially in a large accompanying body. For all its importance, however, close study of tempo will reveal that many musicians are still not secure in their time, notwithstanding their flattering themselves to the contrary, and perhaps that they are not aware of their errors themselves, but simply adjust to others and play haphazardly. This defect is not found simply among young people. Frequently one finds a seemingly skilful and experienced musician who hesitates in the time or who hurries too much. Considerable disorder can be caused in an orchestra by this, particularly if such people must play the principal parts and lead the others.

§ 32

Some consider hesitation and falling behind (dragging), or haste (rushing)[3] as errors resulting from one's disposition. It is true that each person's so-called ruling temperament[4] is important, and that a gay or hot-blooded and rash person is inclined to rush, while a melancholy, disheartened, or indifferent person tends to drag. It is equally true, however, that if attention is given to it, you can modify and improve your temperament. Simply take care that the aforesaid errors are not the result of ignorance. You run the risk of making these errors if in the beginning you try to learn note values and time in general from individual practice instead of from correct principles; if you venture too soon on difficulties beyond your capacities; if you practise alone too much, without accompaniment; and also if you choose only pieces that can be learned by heart (a practice harmful for reading as well as for learning time).[5] To become quite secure in both of these matters, you must begin by playing more middle parts than principal ones; you should play accompaniments more often than solos (since it is more difficult but also more useful to do the former);[6] you should play more concertante and elaborate pieces than melodic ones;

[1] For a detailed discussion of dynamics, intended primarily for the solo player, see Chapter XIV, §§ 25–43.
[2] *Das Zeitmaaß* (*la mesure*). Quantz himself, in his index, and his French translator in much of the remainder of this chapter, uses *mouvement* as the equivalent of *Zeitmaaß*.
[3] The two parentheses in this sentence are original. The German sentence is useful in indicating the various synonyms for rushing and dragging: *Einige halten das Zögern oder Nachschleppen, (trainiren) oder das Eilen, (pressiren) für einen Naturfehler*. The two terms in parentheses are German borrowings from French, and in the French text they alone are used.
[4] For a discussion of the theory of temperaments which was accepted in Quantz's day, see P. H. Lang, *Music in Western Civilization* (New York: W. W. Norton, 1941), pp. 436–7. See also Chapter XV, § 22.
[5] Translator's parentheses.   [6] Translator's parentheses.

you should listen not only to yourself but also to the other parts, particularly the bass; you must not rush notes, but must give each its proper value; you should mark the principal notes that underlie the tempo, namely the crotchet in the Allegro and the quaver in the Adagio, with the tip of your foot, and continue to do so until there is no longer any need for this aid (in this regard, see Chapters V and X).[1]

§ 33

Arriving at the notes on the downbeat of the bar at the right time does not indicate that your observance of the tempo is entirely accurate. Every note belonging to the harmony must coincide with the bass. You must therefore subtract nothing from the proper time of the principal notes, whether they are crotchets, quavers, or semiquavers, by rushing in such fashion that passing notes are heard instead of the principal notes, and both melody and harmony are obscured or mutilated.

§ 34

Rests require an exactness of observation with respect to tempo equal to that given to the notes themselves. Since no sound is heard, and the time must therefore be gauged only in thought, they cause a great deal of trouble, particularly short ones such as those with the value of a quaver, semiquaver, or demisemiquaver. This difficulty can be very easily overcome, however, if you secretly mark the principal notes in a piece with your foot, if you observe whether the notes that follow rests in the motion of the other parts fall on the rise or the fall of the foot, and if you guard against rushing.

§ 35

If a piece is to be effective, it must not only be played in the tempo appropriate to it, but also in the same tempo from beginning to end, not faster at one place, slower at another. Daily experience shows that very often this is not the case. To end either slower or faster than you have begun is in both cases an error. The latter, however, is not as bad as the former. The former, particularly in an Adagio, often makes it almost impossible to tell whether the piece is written in a duple or a triple metre. The melody is gradually obliterated and in its place almost nothing but harmony is heard. If a piece is not played in the appropriate tempo, it not only causes the listeners very little pleasure, but is also most disadvantageous to the composition. Sometimes the soloist is at fault, if, for example, in a fast piece he rushes the easy passage-work and then cannot manage the difficult, or if in a melancholy piece he loses himself so much in the sentiment that he forgets the tempo. Frequently, however, the accompanists are at fault for tempo changes, for example, if they are lulled into

[1] See Chapter V, §§ 17–19, Chapter X, § 3.

dragging in a melancholy piece, or even in a cantabile Andante or Allegretto, and yield too much to the soloist, or if in a fast piece they become too fiery and rush. If a good leader has the necessary alertness, he will find it easy to avoid these errors, and keep both the soloist who is not quite sure in the time, and also the ripienists, in order.

§ 36

The accompanists, however, must not demand that the soloist should adjust to them in regard to the speed or slowness with which he takes the tempo of a piece, but must grant him complete freedom to select his tempo as he sees fit. At the time they are only accompanists. It would be a sign of unbridled vanity if at some time any of the least important of the accompanists assumed control of the tempo (especially if he himself had no more interest in playing),[1] and decided to spite the soloist by increasing the tempo. If it appears that the tempo should be either faster or slower, however, and that a change is necessary, the change must not be made impetuously and suddenly, but gradually, or confusion may easily result.

§ 37

Because the style of playing an Adagio requires that the soloist allow himself to be carried along by the accompanying parts rather than lead them, it frequently seems as if he desires to have the piece slower. The accompanists must not be misled by this, but must adhere strictly to the tempo, and not yield unless the soloist gives a sign to that effect. Otherwise they will eventually begin to drag.

§ 38

If in an Allegro a ritornello has been played with animation, this same animation must be constantly maintained in the accompaniment to the end of the piece. The accompanists need not even pay particular attention to the soloist[2] if he executes the same principal subject in a flattering and cantabile manner.

§ 39

If notes such as those in Tab. XXIII, Fig. 9, occur in unison in a slow tempo, it may develop that they are held too long, because of the shakes, and disrupt the tempo.

FIG. 9

---

[1] Translator's parentheses.
[2] i.e. the accompanists need not alter their tempo.

To avoid this mistake, you must, in thought, divide figures of this type into two equal parts and imagine a counter-movement [of the foot] beneath the dot.

§ 40

It has already been explained in § 12 of Chapter XI that the quickest notes in every piece of *moderate tempo* must be played a little dissimilarly, so that the accented or principal notes in a figure, namely, the first, third, fifth, and seventh, are held a little longer than the passing notes, that is, the second, fourth, sixth, and eighth. In the same context I have also presented several exceptions to this rule, and refer the reader to them here.

§ 41

If the last note in a ritornello is a minim, and a minim rest follows it, with the solo beginning in the following bar, the final note of the ritornello must not be broken off too quickly. If the ritornello begins on the downbeat and the following solo begins with a new idea on the upbeat with ← either a crotchet or quaver (the accompanists cannot always be sure which),[1] the soloist will do well to begin in strict time, and stress the downbeat, so that no confusion can arise.

§ 42

Because a fast piece must be begun at the same time and at the same speed by all, each person must memorize the first bar of his part so that he can look at the leader and begin accurately in tempo at the same time with him. This is particularly necessary in an orchestra, or when playing in a large place where there is a large accompanying body, and the players are at some distance from one another. Because sound is heard later at a distance than close by, and you therefore cannot judge by ear, as in a small place, you must use your eyes, and look frequently at the leader, not only at the beginning of the piece, but also frequently as it progresses, in the event of some slight confusion. Those who understand a little about the violin will be able to regulate themselves in the best and surest manner by the bowing of the leader. If not all the accompanists can see or hear the leader, however, each must regulate himself by that neighbour who is closest to the leader, in order to remain in the same tempo.

§ 43

As to how long you should wait after a fermata or general pause, which is indicated by a semicircle with a dot over a note or rest, there is, strictly speaking, no fixed rule. In a solo, which is played by only two or three people, this uncertainty causes little trouble; but the difficulty is so

---

[1] Translator's parentheses.

much the greater with a large accompanying body. After a brief silence all the parts must begin again simultaneously, just as at the beginning of a piece. If this is not done quite accurately by all, the surprise that one antici-pates after the little silence is not achieved. I will try to propose and estab-lish a rule, derived from various metres, that admits only a few exceptions. It is this: in all triple metres, as well as in alla breve and two-four time, wait a bar beyond the bar above which the rest sign appears. In common time you should be governed by whether the caesura falls on the upbeat or downbeat. In the first case, wait a half bar, and in the second a full bar longer. This, I believe, will be sufficient, and will conform with the in-tention of the composer. A general observance of this rule would make it unnecessary to give the accompanists a further reminder to begin again together. If a fermata occurs in a concertante part, and the player makes a grace which he concludes with a long shake, the accompanying parts must not leave their notes before the shake is completed, or they must at least repeat their notes again at the conclusion of the shake. Observance of this rule is especially important if the bass note has two chords above it and the resolution[1] is delayed by the shake. Afterwards the accompanists can rest for the length of time suggested above.

§ 44

If the tutti following the completion of a principal cadence[2] begins on the downbeat, discreet accompanists will do well, particularly in the accompaniment of a voice or a wind instrument, not to wait until the extreme end of the shake, but to interrupt it, entering rather too early than too late. Both singers and wind players may easily run short of breath towards the end, and if this were to happen, the verve of the performance would be disrupted. If, however, the tutti begins on the upbeat and during the shake, it is no longer a matter of discretion to interrupt the shake, but an obligation. In this regard you must be governed by the performer of the concertante part, and by the power of his lungs. Some singers and instrumentalists who have good lungs try to show a special bravura with long shakes after[3] the cadence [cadenza]; thus one must not obstruct them. The interruption of the shake in both cases must not take place before it is perceived that the shake is beginning to become faint. The leader will pay particular attention to this, and it is thus the accompanists' duty to look at him here also, and to follow his bow-stroke.

§ 45

Having dealt thus far with tempo in general and that which must be observed in connexion with it, I now consider it necessary to give an idea

---

[1] i.e. the second of the chords.

[2] 'Principal cadence' seems here to indicate both a sectional cadence and a cadenza. The same term, *Cadenz*, is used to refer to both. See Chapter XV, § 1.   [3] i.e. at the end of.

of how the approximate tempo required for individual pieces can be determined. To determine a tempo is certainly not one of the easiest matters in music, but it is therefore even more necessary to establish the most definite possible rules. Those who know how much depends on correct tempo in each piece, and what great errors can be made in this regard, will not doubt this necessity. If there were definite rules, and these were properly observed, many pieces frequently garbled through incorrect tempos would be more effective, and would bring more credit to their composers than they do in many cases. With such rules a composer in absence could also communicate his desired tempo more easily in writing to another person who is to perform his composition. In large ensembles it is my experience that at the beginning of a piece the tempo is not always grasped by each player as it should be, and that sometimes one or more bars pass before all agree with one another. If, then, each player knew how to imagine the tempo at least approximately, many disorders and unpleasant tempo changes could be easily avoided. And if you heard a piece played by someone, it would be possible to note its tempo more easily, and to imitate it in just the same tempo at another time. To be still more convinced of the necessity of such definite rules, make an experiment and play an Adagio, for example, one, two, three, or four times slower than it should be. Is it not found that the melodies gradually expire and nothing but harmony is heard? And if an Allegro that should be played with particular fire were performed so much more slowly than it should be, the listener would certainly soon feel like going to sleep.

§ 46

There have long been attempts to discover a usable means for definitely establishing tempo. *Loulié* communicated the plan for a machine which he called the *chronomêtre* in his *Elements ou principes de musique, mis dans un nouvel order &c. à Paris 1698.*[1] I have not been able to see this plan and therefore cannot say how I feel about it. The machine would certainly be difficult to carry about on one's person, however; and since, as far as I know, no one has ever made use of it, the almost universal oblivion into which it has fallen arouses a suspicion as to its adequacy and soundness.

§ 47

The means that I consider most useful as a guide for tempo is the more convenient because of the ease with which it is obtained, since everyone always has it upon himself. It is *the pulse beat at the hand of a healthy person.* ←
I will attempt to give instructions as to how each of the various distinguishable tempos can be determined without great difficulty by regulating yourself with it. Indeed, I cannot boast of being the first to come upon

[1] For a full report on Loulié and his chronometer, see Rosamund Harding, *Origins of Musical Time and Expression* (London: Oxford University Press, 1938), pp. 9–10, plates 1–8.

this device,[1] but it is certain that no one has yet taken the trouble to describe its application clearly and in detail, or to accommodate it to the
practice of contemporary music. I do the latter, therefore, with the greater
meticulousness, since, with reference to the main principle, I am not, as I
have since learned, the only person who has come upon notions such as
these.

§ 48

I do not pretend that a whole piece should be measured off in accordance
with the pulse beat; this would be absurd and impossible. My aim is simply
to show how in at least two, four, six, or eight pulse beats, any tempo you
wish can be established, and how you can achieve a knowledge of the various
categories of tempo by yourself that will lead you to further inquiry. After
some practice, an idea of [each] tempo will gradually so impress itself upon
your mind that it will no longer be found necessary always to consult the
pulse beat.

§ 49

Before I go further I must first examine these various categories of
tempo a little more closely. There are so many in music that it would be
impossible to fix them all. There are, however, certain main categories
from which the others can be derived. I will divide these tempos, as they
occur in concerto, trio, and solo, into four classes, and will use these
classes as the basis [for determining the others]. They are based on common or four-four time, and are as follows: (1) the *Allegro assai*, (2) the
Allegretto, (3) the *Adagio cantabile*, (4) the *Adagio assai*. In the first class I
include: the Allegro di molto, the Presto, &c. In the second: the Allegro
ma non tanto, non troppo, non presto, moderato, &c. In the third class I
count: the Cantabile, Arioso, Larghetto, Soave, Dolce, Poco Andante,
Affettuoso, Pomposo, Maestoso, Alla Siciliana, Adagio spiritoso, &c.
To the fourth belong: the Adagio pesante, Lento, Largo assai, Mesto,
Grave, &c. Each of these titles, to be sure, has an individual meaning of its
own,[2] but it refers more to the expression of the dominant passions in each
piece than to the tempo proper. If the aforementioned four principal categories are clearly grasped, the tempos of the others can be learned more
easily, since the differences are slight.

§ 50

The *Allegro assai* is thus the fastest of these four main categories of
tempo.* The *Allegretto* is twice as slow. The *Adagio cantabile* is twice as
slow as the Allegretto, and the *Adagio assai* twice as slow as the Adagio

---

[1] The pulse beat was used at least as early as 1592 to establish tempos. See Harding, *Origins*,
p. 1.
[2] On the connotations of some of these terms, see the definitions of Brossard, Grassineau,
and L. Mozart quoted in Donington, *Interpretation*, pp. 388–90. See also the list of tempo
markings found in Vivaldi's concertos given in Kolneder, *Aufführungspraxis bei Vivaldi*, p. 17.

cantabile. In the Allegro assai the passage-work consists of semiquavers or quaver triplets, and in the Allegretto, of demisemiquavers or semiquaver triplets. Since, however, the passage-work just cited must usually be played at the same speed whether it is in semiquavers or demisemiquavers, it follows that notes of the same value in the one are twice as fast in the other. In alla breve time, which the Italians call *tempo maggiore*, and which, whether the tempo is slow or fast, is always indicated with a large C with a line through it, the situation is the same, except that all the notes in it are taken twice as fast as in common time. Fast passage-work in the Allegro assai is therefore written in quavers in this metre, and played like the passage-work in semiquavers in the Allegro assai in common time, or *tempo minore*, and so also with other values. Just as the Allegro in duple time has two principal categories of tempo, namely a fast and a moderate one, the same is also true of triple metres, such as three-four, three-eight, six-eight, twelve-eight, &c. For example, if in three-four time only quavers occur, in three-eight only semiquavers, or in six-eight or twelve-eight only quavers, the piece is in the fastest tempo. If, however, there are semiquavers or quaver triplets in three-four time, demisemiquavers or semiquaver triplets in three-eight time, or semiquavers in six-eight and twelve-eight time, they are in the more moderate tempo, which must be played twice as slow as the former. If the degrees of slowness indicated at the beginning of this paragraph are observed, and attention is paid to whether common time or alla breve is indicated, no further difficulty will be encountered in connexion with the Adagio.

* What in former times was considered to be quite fast would have been played almost twice as slow as in the present day. An Allegro assai, Presto, Furioso, &c., was then written, and would have been played, only a little faster than an Allegretto is written and performed today. The large number of quick notes in the instrumental pieces of the earlier German composers thus looked much more difficult and hazardous than they sounded. Contemporary French musicians have retained this style of moderate speed in lively pieces to a large extent.

§ 51

To get to the main point, namely how each of the types of metre cited can be put into its proper tempo by using the pulse beat, it must be noted that it is most important to consider both the word indicating the tempo at the beginning of the piece and the fastest notes used in the passage-work. Since no more than eight very fast notes can be executed in the time of a pulse beat, either with double-tonguing or with bowing, it follows that there is

In common time:

In an Allegro assai, the time of a pulse beat for each minim;
In an Allegretto, a pulse beat for each crotchet;
In an Adagio cantabile, a pulse beat for each quaver;
And in an Adagio assai, two pulse beats for each quaver.

In alla breve time there is:

In an Allegro, a pulse beat for each semibreve;
In an Allegretto, a pulse beat for each minim;
In an Adagio cantabile, a pulse beat for each crotchet;
And in an Adagio assai, two pulse beats for each crotchet.[1]

There is, particularly in common time, a kind of moderate Allegro, which is approximately the mean between the Allegro assai and the Allegretto. It occurs frequently in vocal pieces, and is also used in compositions for instruments unsuited for great speed in passage-work. It is usually indicated with the words Poco Allegro, Vivace, or, most of all, simply with Allegro alone. Here there is a pulse beat for every three quavers, and the second pulse beat falls on the fourth quaver.[2]

In two-four time or quick six-eight time a pulse beat occurs on each bar in an Allegro.[3]

In an Allegro in twelve-eight time, two pulse beats fall in each bar, if no semiquavers occur.[4]

In three-four time, if the piece is Allegro and the passage-work in it consists of semiquavers or quaver triplets, a definite tempo cannot be established in a single bar. Taking two bars together, however, it is possible to do so. Then a pulse beat falls on the first and third crotchets of the first bar, and on the second crotchet of the following bar; thus there are three pulse beats for six crotchets.[5] The same is the case in nine-eight time.[6]

In both very fast three-four and three-eight time, where only six quick notes occur in the passage-work in each bar, a pulse beat occurs with each bar.[7] This does not apply to a piece which should be a Presto, however, or the beat will be too slow by the amount of two quick notes. To deduce how fast these three quavers or three crotchets must be in a Presto, take the tempo of the fast two-four time, where there are four quavers to a pulse beat, and play these three crotchets or quavers just as quickly as the quavers in the two-four time already mentioned.[8] The quick notes in both metres mentioned above will then be in the proper tempo.

In an Adagio cantabile in three-four time, where the movement of the bass is in quavers, there is a pulse beat on each quaver.[9] If, however, the movement is only in crotchets, and the melody is more of an arioso than

---

[1] In § 55 of this section Quantz establishes eighty pulse beats per minute as the norm. Hence metronome markings for these tempos can be established as follows. In common time Allegro assai ♩ = 80; Allegretto ♩ = 80; Adagio cantabile ♪ = 80; Adagio assai ♪ = 80. In alla breve time Allegro assai 𝅝 = 80; Allegretto ♩ = 80; Adagio cantabile ♩ = 80; Adagio assai ♪ = 80. Quantz's suggestions for tempos should not be taken as absolute rules for all music of his time. C. P. E. Bach, *Essay*, p. 414, states that at Berlin 'adagio is far slower and allegro far faster than is customary elsewhere'.

[2] Thus ♩. = 80 or ♩ = 120.   [3] ♩ or ♩. = 80.   [4] ♩. = 80.
[5] ♩ = 80 or ♩ = 160.   [6] ♩. = 80 or ♩. = 160.   [7] ♩. or ♩. = 80.
[8] ♩. or ♩. = about 107.   [9] ♪ = 80.

a melancholy cast, there is a pulse beat on each crotchet.[1] The key and the words marked at the beginning must also be taken into consideration, however; for if Adagio assai, Mesto, or Lento are indicated, there are two pulse beats for each crotchet.[2]

In an Arioso in three-eight time there is a pulse beat on each quaver.

An alla Siciliana in twelve-eight time would be too slow if you were to count a pulse beat for each quaver. But if two pulse beats are divided into three parts, there is a pulse beat on both the first and the third quaver.[3] Having divided these three notes, however, no further attention must be paid to the movement of the pulse beat, or the third quaver will become too long.

If in a fast piece the passage-work is entirely in triplets, and no semi-quavers or demisemiquavers are intermingled, the composition may be played a little more quickly than the beat of the pulse if you wish. This is particularly true in quick six-eight, nine-eight, and twelve-eight metres.

§ 52

What I have pointed out thus far, as already stated above, is most specifically and fully applicable in instrumental pieces such as concertos, trios, and solos.[4] As to arias in the Italian style, each would seem to require its own particular tempo. But all these diverse tempos usually stem from one of the four main categories cited here, and it is only necessary to pay attention to the meaning of the words and to the motion of the notes, particularly the fastest ones, and in fast arias to consider the quality and relative facility of the voices of the singers. A singer who articulates all fast passage-work from the chest can hardly produce it as quickly as one who produces it in the throat, although the former method, because of its distinctness, is always superior to the latter, particularly in large places. If one has a little experience with arias, and knows that the majority do not usually require as fast a tempo as instrumental pieces, the proper tempo for them can be established without other special difficulties.

§ 53

What is true of arias is also true of church music, except that both the execution of the performance, and the tempo, if it is to be suitable for the church, must be a little more moderate than in the operatic style.

---

[1] ♩ = 80.

[2] ♩ = 40.

[3] In other words the pulse beat falls on the first, third, and fifth of six quavers. ♪ = 160, or ♩. = about 53.

[4] Quantz's suggestions for tempos are best studied in the light of his own music, and then through comparison with other works of his time. For a survey of various eighteenth-century attempts to clarify tempo markings, see R. Kirkpatrick, 'Eighteenth-Century Metronomic Indications', *Papers of the American Musicological Society* (1938), pp. 30–50.

§ 54

If you seek to supplement the method just described with long and abundant experience, you not only can learn to give each note its proper time, but can in most cases discover for each piece the appropriate tempo demanded by the composer.

§ 55

I must, however, anticipate some objections that may be raised to this manner of determining tempos. One might object that the pulse beat is neither constant at each hour of the day, nor the same in every person, as would be required to accurately fix musical tempos with it. It will be said that the pulse beats more slowly in the morning before meal-time than in the afternoon after meal-time, and still faster at night than in the afternoon; likewise that it is slower in a person inclined to melancholy than in an impetuous and jovial person. There may be some truth in these objections. Nevertheless, some definite standard can be set up to meet these circumstances. If you take the pulse beat as it is found from the midday meal till evening, and as it is found in a jovial and high-spirited and yet rather fiery and volatile person, or, if you will permit the expression, in a person of choleric-sanguine temperament, as your basis, you will have hit upon the correct pulse beat. A low-spirited, or melancholy, or cold and sluggish person could set the tempo in each piece a little faster than his pulse indicates. In case this is not sufficient, I will be still more explicit. Fix approximately eighty pulse beats to a minute as the standard. Eighty pulse beats in the fastest tempo of common time constitute forty bars. A few pulse beats more or less make no difference in this regard. For example, five pulse beats more in a minute, or five less, in forty bars shorten or lengthen each bar by only a semiquaver. This amounts to so little that it is imperceptible. Those with more or less than eighty pulse beats in a minute will then know how to proceed with regard to decreasing or increasing the speed. Even if it were admitted, however, that my proposed device could not, in spite of everything, be presented as generally and universally applicable, regardless of the fact that I had proved it with the beat of my own pulse and with many other tests with various people in connexion with my own compositions and those of others; my device would still serve to keep everyone who, in following the method discussed above, had gained an understanding of the four main categories of tempo, from departing too far from the true tempo of each piece. We see daily how often tempo is abused, and how frequently the very same piece is played moderately at one time, quickly at another, and still more quickly at another. It is well known that in many places where people play carelessly, a Presto is often made an Allegretto and an Adagio an Andante, doing the greatest injustice to the composer, who cannot always be present.[1] It is common knowledge

[1] That is, the composer cannot always be present to fix the tempo correctly.

that a piece repeated once or more times consecutively, particularly a fast piecé (for example, an Allegro from a concerto or sinfonia),[1] is played a little faster the second time than the first, in order not to put the listeners to sleep. If this were not done the listeners would believe that the piece had not yet ended. If it is repeated in a slightly faster tempo, however, the piece takes on a more lively and, as it were, a new and unfamiliar guise that once more arouses the attention of the listeners. This practice is not disadvantageous to the piece; it is used by both good and average performers and produces an equally good effect in either case. It also would do no harm in any case if a melancholy person, in accord with his temperament,[2] were to play a piece moderately fast, but still well, and if a more volatile person played it with greater liveliness. Beyond this, if someone could discover a simpler, more accurate, and more convenient device for learning tempos and establishing them, he would do well not to delay in communicating it to the public.

§ 56

I shall now attempt to apply this method of determining tempos through the guidance of the pulse beat to *French dance music*, which I feel I must also discuss briefly. Music of this kind consists for the most part of special types.[3] Each type requires its own tempo, however, since music of this kind is very circumscribed, and is not as arbitrary as Italian music. If, then, both the dancers and the orchestra can always arrive at the same tempo, they will avoid much ill humour. It is well known that most dancers understand little or nothing of music, and frequently do not know the correct tempo themselves; for the most part they regulate themselves only by their mood at that moment, or by their ability. Experience also teaches that dancers rarely require as lively a tempo at rehearsals that take place in the morning before eating, when they are calm and dance collectedly, as they do at the performance, customarily in the evening, when, partly because of the good nourishment taken beforehand, partly because of the multitude of spectators, who stimulate their ambition, they become more ardent. Their knees may easily become unstable as a result, and if they are dancing a sarabande or loure where only a bent knee must sometimes support the whole body, the tempo frequently seems too slow to them. In addition, French dance music loses much if it is heard in the middle of a good Italian opera; it sounds flat, and is not as effective as in a comedy, where nothing is heard with which to compare it. Disputes frequently arise between the dancers and orchestra for this reason, since the former

[1] Translator's parentheses.
[2] Literally, this phrase reads 'in accordance with the mixture of his blood'. In earlier physiology temperament was supposed to result from the mixture of various bodily fluids, called humours.
[3] *Gewisse Charakteren* (*piéces de Caractéres*). The terminology here helps to explain what Quantz means in his earlier references to 'characteristic pieces' (or *pièces caractèrisées*). Apparently this designation is used for special types of pieces with readily identifiable characteristic features.

believe that the latter either did not play in the right tempo, or did not perform their music as well as they did the Italian. It is, indeed, undeniable that French dance music is not as easy to play as many imagine, and that its execution must be clearly distinguished from the Italian style if it is to be suitable for each type of piece. Dance music is usually played seriously, with a heavy yet short and sharp bow-stroke, more detached than slurred. That which is delicate and singing is rarely found in it. Dotted notes are played heavily, but the notes following them briefly and sharply. Fast pieces must be executed in a gay, hopping, and springing manner with a very short bow-stroke, always marked with an interior stress.[1] In this fashion the dancers are continually inspired and encouraged to leap, and at the same time what they wish to represent is made comprehensible and tangible to the spectators; for dancing without music is like food in a painting.

§ 57

Although accuracy of tempo is very important in music of all types, it must be observed most rigorously in music for the dance. The dancers must regulate themselves by it not only with their ears but also with their feet and body motions. It is easy, therefore, to imagine how unpleasant it must be for them if the orchestra plays now slower, now faster, in the same piece. They must strain every nerve, especially if they engage in high leaps. Fairness demands that the orchestra accommodate itself to them as much as possible, and this is easily done if now and then one attends to the fall of their feet.

§ 58

I would be too diffuse if I were to describe and note the tempos of all the types of pieces that may appear in dances. I will therefore cite only a few, and from them the others can be easily understood.

When in common time the Italians make a stroke through the large C, we all know that this indicates alla breve time. The French make use of this metre in various types of dances, such as bourrées, entrées, rigaudons, gavottes, rondeaux, &c. Instead of the crossed C, however, they write a large 2, which likewise indicates that the notes must be played at twice their regular speed. In this metre, as well as in three-four time, the quavers that follow the dotted crotchets in the loure, sarabande, courante, and chaconne must not be played with their literal value, but must be executed in a very short and sharp manner. The dotted note is played with emphasis, and the bow is detached during the dot. All dotted notes are treated in the same manner if time allows; and if three or more demisemiquavers follow a dot or a rest, they are not always played with their literal value, especially in slow pieces, but are executed at the extreme end of the time allotted to

---

[1] *Durch einen Druck markirten Bogenstriche (un coup d'archet . . . marqué par un poids interieur qu'on lui donne).*

them, and with the greatest possible speed, as is frequently the case in overtures, entrées, and furies. Each of these quick notes must receive its separate bow-stroke, and slurring is rarely used.

The *entrée*, the *loure*, and the *courante* are played majestically, and the bow is detached at each crotchet, whether it is dotted or not. There is a pulse beat on each crotchet.

A *sarabande* has the same movement, but is played with a somewhat more agreeable execution.

A *chaconne* is also played majestically. In it a pulse beat takes the time of two crotchets.

A *passecaille* is like the preceding type, but is played just a little faster.

A *musette* is executed in a very flattering manner. In three-four time there is a pulse beat on each crotchet, or in three-eight time on each quaver. Sometimes, however, in accordance with the whim of the dancer, it is performed so quickly that a pulse beat falls only on each bar.

A *furie* is played with great fire. There is a pulse beat on every two crotchets in duple time, and also in triple time when demisemiquavers are used.

A *bourrée* and a *rigaudon* are executed gaily, and with a short and light bow-stroke. A pulse beat falls on each bar.

A *gavotte* is almost like a rigaudon, but is a little more moderate in tempo.

A *rondeau* is played rather tranquilly, and a pulse beat occurs approximately every two crotchets, whether in alla breve or in three-four time.

The *gigue* and the *canarie* have the same tempo. If they are in six-eight time, there is a pulse beat on each bar. The gigue is played with a short and light bow-stroke, and the canarie, which is always in dotted notes, with a short and sharp one.

A *menuet* is played springily,[1] the crotchets being marked with a rather heavy, but still short, bow-stroke, with a pulse beat on two crotchets.

A *passepied* is played a little more lightly, and slightly faster than the preceding. In it two bars are frequently written in one, with two strokes placed over the middle note in the second bar (see Tab. XXIII, Fig. 10).

FIG. 10

Some separate these two bars from each other, and instead of the crotchet with the strokes, write two quavers with a tie above them, placing the bar-line between. In performance, these notes are played in the same manner, that is, the two crotchets short and with a detached bow, and in the same tempo as in three-four time.

A *tambourin* is played like a bourrée or rigaudon, only a little faster.

---

[1] *Hebend*. Literally, this means in a lifting or rising manner.

A *march* is played seriously. If it is in alla breve or bourrée time, there are two pulse beats on each bar, &c.[1]

§ 59

In an Italian *recitative* the singer does not always adhere to the tempo, and has the freedom to express what he is to execute quickly or slowly, as he considers best, and as the words require. If, then, the accompanying parts have held notes[2] to execute, they must accompany the singer rather by ear, using their discretion, than by the beat. If the accompaniment is in notes that must be performed in tempo, however, the singer is obliged to regulate himself by the accompanying parts. Sometimes the accompaniment is interrupted to give the singer freedom to recite at will, and the accompanying parts enter only from time to time, namely at the caesuras when the singer has completed a phrase. Here the accompanists must not wait till the singer has uttered the final syllable, but must enter at the penultimate or preceding note,[3] in order to maintain constant animation. If, however, the violins have a short rest instead of a note on the downbeat, and the bass precedes them by a note, the latter must enter with certainty and power, especially in cadences, where the bass is most important. In general the bass in all cadences of theatrical recitatives, whether accompanied with violins or plain, must begin its two notes, usually forming a descending leap of a fifth, during the last syllable; these notes must be performed in a lively manner, and must not be too slow. The keyboard player executes them with an accompaniment in full chords, the 'cellist and double bass player with a short accent with the lowest part of the bow; they repeat the stroke, and take both notes with down-strokes. If in a lively recitative the accompanying parts at the caesuras have quick notes which must be played precipitately following a rest on the downbeat (see Tab. XXIII, Fig. 11), the accompanists again must not wait until the singer has fully articulated the last syllable, but must begin during the penultimate note, so that the fire of the expression is constantly maintained. They will start together more precisely, particularly in a large orchestra, if they use the penultimate syllable of the singer as their guide.[4]

---

[1] With a pulse of eighty beats per minute, the following metronome markings for the dances mentioned can be deduced: entrée, loure, courante, $\quad$ = 80; sarabande, the same; chaconne, $\quad$ = 80; passecaille, a little faster than the preceding; musette, $\frac{3}{4}$, $\quad$ = 80, or $\frac{3}{8}$, $\quad$ = 80; furie, $\frac{2}{4}$, $\quad$ = 80, or $\frac{3}{4}$, $\quad$ = 160; bourrée and rigaudon, full bar = 80; gavotte, a little more moderately; rondeau, alla breve, $\quad$ = 80, or $\frac{3}{4}$, $\quad$ = 160; gigue, canarie, $\frac{6}{8}$, $\quad$ = 80; menuet, $\quad$ = 160; passepied, slightly faster than a menuet; tambourin, a little faster than a bourrée or rigaudon; march, alla breve, $\quad$ = 80. On the relationship between Quantz's suggested dance tempos and those of other eighteenth-century writers, see Kirkpatrick, 'Eighteenth-Century Metronomic Indications', pp. 45–46, and Donington, *Interpretation*, pp. 392–404.

[2] *Haltende Noten (Tenuës).*

[3] *Vorhaltende Note (la note . . . précédente)*. An appoggiatura may be meant.

[4] For further material on the accompaniment of recitatives, see C. P. E. Bach, *Essay*, pp. 420–5.

FIG. 11

§ 60

These are the matters that I have considered it essential to discuss in regard to the duties of the performers of the ripieno parts. From them you can see that it is not easy to accompany well, and that much is required of an orchestra if it is to be truly excellent. And since so much is required of it, composers have an obligation to order their compositions in such a way that a good orchestra can gain honour with them. Many compositions are either so dry, or so bizarre, difficult, and unnatural, that even the best orchestra, in spite of all effort, industry, and goodwill, cannot make them effective, even if it is made up of the most skilful people. It is much to the composer's advantage if he writes his compositions so that they can be performed even by people of moderate ability. A composer acts most sensibly in this regard if he regulates himself by the capacities of ordinary people. If his work is destined for skilful people he can indeed venture a little further afield; but if it is to be for average players, he must aim at facility.[1] He must be especially careful to write naturally, vocally, and neither too high nor too low for singers, and to leave them enough time for breathing and for the clear enunciation of the words. He must familiarize himself with the characteristics of each instrument, so that he does not write contrary to the nature of each. For wind instruments he must not choose too strange keys in which only a few people are well-versed, and which put obstacles in the path of trueness and distinctness of performance as well as good execution in general. He must also pay close attention to the difference between ripieno and solo parts. He must try to characterize each piece in such a way that everyone can easily divine its tempo. To ensure a uniform interpretation by all, he must mark the Piano and Forte, the shakes and appoggiaturas, the slurs, dots, strokes, and everything else that belongs above or below the notes, as accurately as possible; and he must not, as many do who have no knowledge of bowing or pay no attention to it, leave slurring and detaching to chance, as if everything were to be performed on the keyboard, where one has no bow with which to slur. He must therefore compel the copyists (who, to the detriment of the composer, frequently commit the greatest errors in this regard, either from ignorance or from carelessness)[2] to copy meticulously everything he has

---

[1] French text: 'avoid great difficulties'. [2] Translator's parentheses.

written. The copyist must not position the heads of the notes in a doubtful manner, but must place them right in the middle of the lines or spaces; he must draw the stems and the lines very clearly; and he must put down everything else that the composer has written just as it is found, and at the place it is found, in the score. He must especially heed the Forte and Piano and the slurs over the notes, and must not believe it unimportant to indicate whether a slur covers two, three, four, or more notes, or none at all, an oversight that can greatly alter or even destroy the intention of the composer. He must also read the words correctly in vocal music, and copy them out clearly and accurately. Thus the composer's handwriting also must be legible and clear, so that it will not need special explanation. If a composer fulfils all his duties in this manner, he has the right to demand from the performers the kind of execution that I have described at such length here; then the orchestra will do credit to him, just as he will do credit to the orchestra.

CHAPTER XVIII

How a Musician and a Musical Composition Are to Be Judged

§ 1

No art is so subject to indiscriminate judgement as music. It would seem that nothing could be easier to judge. Not only professional musicians, but even those who pose as amateurs, would like to be regarded as judges of what they hear.

§ 2

We are not always satisfied if someone who performs in public strives to bring forth what is within his powers, and we not infrequently make excessive demands. If in an assembly[1] all do not sing or play with equal perfection, we often accord all excellence to one person and scorn the others, without reflecting that one may have his merits in this genre, another in that, for example, one in the Adagio, another in the Allegro. We do not consider that the agreeableness of music lies not in uniformity or similarity, but in diversity. If it were possible for all musical artists to play with the same proficiency, and with the same taste, we would miss the greatest part of our pleasure in music, because of the lack of an agreeable variety.

§ 3

Rarely do we follow that surest of guides, our own feelings; instead we seek eagerly to learn which singer or player is the ablest, as though it were possible immediately to survey and weigh the skills of different persons, just as one judges other things whose price and quality are determined by a pair of scales. Then we listen only to the person who passes for the strongest. A piece, often a very bad one, quite carelessly performed by him, and often deliberately so,[2] is proclaimed a marvellous work, and another musician, in spite of all his efforts to perform a choice piece well, is vouchsafed scarcely a moment of attention.

§ 4

We seldom grant a musician the necessary time to demonstrate his ability or lack of it. Nor do we reflect that a musician is not always in a

[1] French text: 'concert'.
[2] Why 'deliberately' is not clear. The wording in the German and French texts, however, is unambiguous.

position to show what he understands, and that frequently the slightest circumstance may easily destroy all his composure; hence that fairness demands that we hear him more than once before we pass judgement on him. Many a musician is imprudent and, with perhaps a piece or two in which he can show his entire capacity, displays all his skill at once, so that we have heard all he can do. Another musician, on the other hand, who is not so rash, and whose skill is not limited, as with the former, to one or two pieces, is at a disadvantage. For the majority of listeners are too hasty in their judgements, and allow themselves far too often to be taken in by what they hear for the first time. If they had the patience and the opportunity to hear each player frequently, they would not always have need of much discernment; they would only have to pay attention, without prejudice, to their own feelings, and see which performer eventually gave them the greatest pleasure.

§ 5

We fare no better with regard to composition. We would not willingly be considered ignorant, and yet we do not always feel that we are capable of deciding matters rightly. Thus, in order that we may regulate our judgements accordingly, our first question is usually, 'By whom is the piece composed?' If, then, the piece is by someone to whom we have previously given our approval, we immediately, and without further reflection, declare it beautiful. If the opposite is the case, or if we perhaps object to something about the person of the composer, the piece too is considered worthless. If anyone wishes to be palpably convinced of this, he needs only to put forth two compositions of equal quality under different names, one in good, the other in bad repute. The ignorance of many judges will soon be apparent.

§ 6

Those listeners who are more modest, and who do not credit themselves with the discernment to judge a piece, often have recourse to a professional musician, and believe his words as though they were incontrovertible truth. It is true that some knowledge may be acquired by listening to much good music, and to the judgements that experienced, upright, and learned musical artists pass upon it, especially if one inquires into the reasons why a piece is considered good or bad. Indeed this would be one of the surest ways to avoid error. But are all those who make music their profession actually true musicians or connoisseurs? Have not many of them learned their art merely as a trade? Thus the listener may easily address his questions to the wrong person; for the decisions of the professional musician, like those of many amateurs, also may be based on ignorance, envy, prejudice, or the desire to flatter. Yet such pronouncements spread like wildfire, and so completely take in the ignorant who appeal to one of these would-be oracles that there finally arises a prejudice that is not easily effaced. Furthermore, it is hardly possible for each musician to judge all the different matters that one encounters in music. Singing requires its special insight. The diversity of instruments is so great that the powers and the lifetime of one man would hardly suffice to learn all their peculiarities. And this is to say nothing of the many things one must know and observe to judge a composition properly. Thus, before accepting the judgement of a professional musician, the amateur of music must be careful to investigate whether the professional is in fact capable of judging fairly. He is on surer ground with someone who has learned his art thoroughly than with someone who has followed only his natural talent, although the latter is certainly not to be wholly rejected. And since few persons are so free of bias that their judgements do not at times conflict with their knowledge, the amateur must also take this matter into account when considering the judgement of the professional. There are some whom almost nothing pleases except what they have composed themselves. Woe then to all other pieces that do not stem from their own celebrated pens! If shame forces them to praise something, it is certain to be done in such fashion that they betray what pains this praise costs them. Other musicians praise everything without distinction, so that they will fall out with no one, and will make themselves pleasing to all. Many a young musician finds nothing beautiful but that which is in the style of his master. Many a composer looks for glory only in strange progressions, obscure melodies, and the like. For him everything should be unusual and uncommon. And if he has found some approbation through his other real merits or has obtained partisans through other means, it would be foolish to expect him, or those who blindly venerate him, to call something beautiful that does not accord with this turn of mind. Old musicians complain of the melodic extravagances of the young, and the young mock the dryness of the old. In spite of this, however, now and then some musicians are still encountered who examine a piece without prejudice and in accordance with its true worth, who praise what is praiseworthy, and reject what ought to be rejected. Connoisseurs of music such as these are the most trustworthy. Hence the honest, learned, and able musician must be very careful that bias does not produce injustice, and that he is not influenced by professional jealousy; for although his judgement may be the most equitable one, it may also be the most dangerous, because of the reputation he enjoys.[1]

§ 7

Music, then, is an art that must be judged not by personal whims, but by certain rules, like the other fine arts, and by good taste acquired and refined through extensive experience and practice; for those who wish to

---

[1] French text: 'he must be all the more careful to pronounce equitable judgements because these judgements carry great weight with the public'.

judge others should understand as much as, if not more than those they judge. These qualities, however, are rarely encountered among those who occupy themselves with judging music, the majority being governed by ignorance, prejudices, and passions that are most obstructive to equitable judgement. Thus many people who say that they enjoy music would do better to keep their judgements to themselves and listen with greater attentiveness. If they listen more for the sake of judging the performer than of enjoying the music, they voluntarily deprive themselves of the greater part of the pleasure that they might experience. And if, even before the musician has concluded his piece, they are at pains to press their false opinions upon their neighbours, they not only destroy the musician's composure, but also make it difficult for him to conclude his piece with good heart, and show his ability as well as he might. For who can remain unperturbed and calm when he perceives disapproving countenances here and there among his listeners? Moreover, the incompetent judge always risks betraying his ignorance to others who are not of his opinion and perhaps understand more than he, and therefore may expect little gain from his judgements. Thus you can see how difficult it actually is to take upon yourself the office of music critic, and to acquit yourself of it with honour.

§ 8

If the judgement of a piece of music is to be reasonable and fair, attention must always be chiefly directed to three things, namely: to the piece itself, to its performer, and to the listeners. A beautiful composition may be spoiled by a poor performance, and a poor composition is a disadvantage to its performer; hence you must first inquire whether the good or bad effect is due to the performer or to the composition. With regard to the listeners, just as to the musicians, much depends upon differences in temperament. Some love what is majestic and lively, some what is melancholy and sombre, and some what is delicate and gay, according to their various inclinations. Some possess knowledge that others lack. We are not always in the same humour when we hear a piece for the first time. Frequently it may happen that today a piece pleases us which tomorrow, in another state of mind, we can scarcely endure; and, on the contrary, a piece may be distasteful to us today in which we discover many beauties tomorrow. Although a piece may be well composed and well performed, it still may not please everyone. A poor piece with a mediocre performance may displease many, yet even it may also find some admirers. The place where a composition is performed may put many obstacles in the path of equitable judgement. Listen, for example, to one and the same piece close at hand today, and at a distance tomorrow. Each time the effect will be quite different. We may hear a piece intended for a spacious place and a large orchestra at the proper place, and it will please us uncommonly. But if we hear the same piece in a chamber, performed with a small complement of instruments, and perhaps also by different persons, it will have lost more than half its beauty. A piece that enchanted us in the chamber may be scarcely recognizable if we hear it at the theatre. If a slow piece composed in the French style is embellished with many extempore graces, like an Italian Adagio, or if, on the contrary, an Italian Adagio is performed decorously and dryly in the French style, with beautiful and charming shakes, the former will be completely unrecognizable, while the latter will sound very flat and insipid, and neither will please the French or the Italians. Hence each piece must be played in the style appropriate to it; and if this is not done, judgement is fruitless. And even supposing that each piece in these two styles is played in accordance with the taste peculiar to it, the French style cannot be judged by an Italian, or the Italian by a Frenchman, since both are strongly prejudiced in favour of their country and their national music.

§ 9

I believe that everyone will now grant that much insight and almost the supreme degree of technical knowledge[1] are required for the just and equitable judgement of a piece of music; that far more is essential to this matter than merely knowing how to sing or play something oneself; hence, that whoever wishes to judge must carefully strive for knowledge of those rules which reason, good taste, and art prescribe. I hope none will dispute the fact, that, since few of those who so frequently set themselves up as judges of music are equipped with this knowledge, a great disadvantage must accrue to music, to musical artists, and to the amateurs of music, who are thus kept in a state of perpetual uncertainty.

§ 10

I shall attempt to indicate certain signs by which the principal qualities of a complete musician and a well-written composition may be recognized, so that both musical artists and amateurs may have at least some instruction by which to regulate their judgements, and so that they may know to which musicians and to which pieces they may reasonably give their approbation. Everybody who wishes to judge something ought always to do so without prejudice, passion, or precipitation, and with equity and circumspection. He should examine the pieces themselves, and not allow himself to be blinded by certain secondary matters that are not to the purpose; for example, whether someone is from this nation or that, whether or not he has been in foreign countries, whether he is said to be the pupil of a celebrated master, whether he is in the service of a great or minor lord, or in no service at all, whether or not he has a musical title,[2] whether he is a friend or enemy, young or old, and so forth. In general you will not overstep the bounds of equity if, in speaking of a composition or a

[1] *Musikalische Wissenschaft (science de la Musique).*
[2] French text: 'whether he has a post in some chapel or ensemble'.

musician, you say that *they do not please you*, rather than that *they are worthless*. Everyone has the right to express himself in the first manner, since no one can be forced to find pleasure in a thing. The second expression, however, belongs only to true connoisseurs, and they should make use of it only when they are in a position to substantiate their judgements.

§ 11

The chief requirements of a good *singer* are that he have a good, clear, and pure voice, of uniform quality from top to bottom,[1] a voice which has none of those major defects originating in the nose and throat,[2] and which is neither hoarse nor muffled. Only the voice itself and the use of words give singers preference over instrumentalists. In addition, the singer must know how to join the falsetto to the chest voice in such a way that one does not perceive where the latter ends and the former begins;[3] he must have a good ear and true intonation, so that he can produce all the notes in their correct proportions; he must know how to produce the portamento (*il portamento di voce*)[4] and the holds upon a long note (*le messe di voce*)[5] in an agreeable manner; hence he must have firmness and sureness of voice, so that he does not begin to tremble in a moderately long hold, or transform the agreeable sound of the human voice into the disagreeable shriek of a reed pipe[6] when he wishes to strengthen his tone, as not infrequently happens, particularly among certain singers who are disposed to hastiness. The singer must be able to execute a good shake that does not bleat[7] and is neither too slow nor too quick; and he must observe well the proper compass of the shake, and distinguish whether it should consist of whole tones or semitones. A good singer must also have good pronunciation. He must enunciate the words distinctly, and must not pronounce the vowels *a*, *e*, and *o* all in the same way in passage-work, so that they become incomprehensible. If he makes a grace on a vowel, this vowel and none other must be heard to the very end. In pronouncing the words he must also avoid changing one vowel into another, perhaps substituting *e* for *a* and *o* for *u*; for example, in Italian pronouncing *genitura* instead of *genitore*, and as a result evoking laughter among those who understand the language.[8] The voice must not become weaker when *i* and *u* appear; during these vowels no extended embellishments should be made in the low register, and certainly no little graces in the high register. A good singer must have facility in reading and producing his notes accurately, and must understand the rules of thorough-bass. He must not express the high notes with

[1] *Von der Tiefe bis in die Höhe durchgehends egale Stimme* (*égale par tous les tons, depuis en bas jusqu'en haut*).

[2] See Chapter IV, § 1.   [3] See Tosi, *Observations*, pp. 23–25.

[4] *Das Tragen der Stimme* (*porter la voix*).

[5] *Die Haltungen auf einer langen Note* (*une Tenuë un peu longue*). See Tosi, *Observations*, pp. 27–28.

[6] *Rohrpfeife* (*Flute d'oignon*).

[7] Quantz refers here to the French *chevroté*. See Chapter IX, § 3.

[8] *Genitura* means 'semen', and *genitore* means 'parent'.

a harsh attack or with a vehement exhalation of air from his chest; still less should he scream them out, coarsening the amenity of the voice. Where the words require certain passions he must know how to raise and moderate his voice at the right time and without any affectation. In a melancholy piece he must not introduce as many shakes and running embellishments[1] as in a happy and cantabile work, since they often obscure and spoil the beauty of the melody. He should sing the Adagio in a moving, expressive, flattering, charming, coherent, and sustained manner, introducing light and shadow both through the Piano and Forte and through the reasonable addition of graces suited to the words and the melody. He must perform the Allegro in a lively, brilliant, and easy manner. He must produce the passage-work roundly, neither attacking it too harshly nor slurring it in a lame and lazy manner. He must know how to moderate the tone quality of his voice from the low register into the high and, in so doing, how to distinguish between the theatre and the chamber, and between a strong and a weak accompaniment, so that his singing of the high notes does not degenerate into screaming. He must be sure in tempo, not rushing at one moment and dragging the next, particularly in the passage-work. He must take breath quickly and at the proper time. And if this becomes rather trying, he must try to conceal the fact as much as possible, yet not allow it to throw him off the time. Finally, he must seek to rely upon himself for whatever he adds in the way of embellishments, instead of listening to others like a parrot[2] who knows only the words his master has taught him, as most do. A soprano and a tenor may allow themselves more in the way of embellishments than an alto and a bass. A noble simplicity, a good portamento, and the use of the chest voice are more suitable for the alto and bass than use of the very high register and the abundant addition of graces. This is a precept which true singers have respected and practised at all times.[3]

§ 12

If, then, you find all the good qualities cited here united in one singer, you may confidently assert not only that he sings very well and justly deserves the title of virtuoso, but that indeed he is almost a natural prodigy. Every singer who wishes to gain a reputation for excellence can and should provide himself with these qualities; but a singer who can boast of all these qualities is as rare as a man graced with all the virtues. Hence you must be more indulgent in judging a singer than in judging an instrumentalist, and must be content if you find only some of the principal qualities enumerated above together with various defects, not denying him the accustomed title of virtuoso because of this.

[1] *Laufende Manieren (roulemens).*
[2] The remainder of this phrase appears only in the French text.
[3] For related material on the qualities expected of a singer, see Tosi, *Observations*, pp. 10–30, 140–73.

§ 13

To judge an *instrumentalist*, you must above all understand the qualities and the attendant difficulties of the instrument, lest you consider what is difficult easy, and what is easy difficult. Many things that are difficult and often impossible on some instruments go quite easily upon others. Thus one instrumentalist is not in a position to judge the merits of another soundly unless he plays the same instrument. Otherwise he will admire in the other only that which appears difficult on his own instrument, and will esteem nothing that he can do easily himself. But consider a moment the differences that exist between certain instruments which are in some respects similar. For example, look at the difference between a violin and a viola d'amore, between a viola, a violoncello, a viola da gamba, and a double bass, between an oboe and a bassoon, between a lute, a theorbo, and a mandolin, between a transverse flute and a flute à bec, between a trumpet and a hunting horn, between a clavichord, a harpsichord, a pianoforte, and an organ. You will find that in spite of resemblances between these instruments, each must be treated in a special manner peculiar to it. You can imagine, then, how much greater the difference in treatment must be in dealing with those instruments that do not resemble one another.

§ 14

To prove this I wish to cite only two instruments; by comparing them you will be able to perceive that each has both particular facilities and difficulties. As examples I will use the violin and the transverse flute. On the violin arpeggios and broken passages[1] are very easy, while on the flute they are not only very difficult, but to a great extent impracticable; on the former frequently only the bow must be employed, while on the latter equal facility is required of the fingers, tongue and lips. On the violin many figures can be easily played with the very same fingers in transpositions up or down from one key to another and from the very low to the very high register simply by moving the hand (see, for example, Tab. XXIII, Fig. 12); on the flute each transposition must be taken with different fingers. In many keys such figures are completely impracticable.

FIG. 12

If a violinist has only one good finger for shakes, he can avoid the others by moving his hand; a flautist must use all his fingers, and must be able to execute shakes evenly with all fingers. On the violin you can always produce the same tone quality, even if you have not played for some time,

---

[1] French text: 'passages in which the notes of a chord follow one another'.

but on the flute, because of the embouchure, tone quality suffers if you leave off for even a few days; in addition, contrary weather, coldness or heat, and even certain foods and drinks can easily put the lips out of condition, so that it is almost or totally impossible to play. The bow-stroke on the violin and the tongue-stroke on the flute serve the same purpose, but it is easier to master the former. The violinist finds little difficulty in the diversity of the chromatic keys,[1] whether sharps or flats are used, and even if there are many accidentals; the flautist finds many difficulties. If the violinist has a good musical ear, and understands the proportions of the notes, he can play his instrument truly without particular labour. But even if the flautist possesses an equally good ear, he faces many additional difficulties with regard to correct intonation. Passage-work in the very high register is frequently heard on the violin; it is very rarely heard on the flute, because of difficulties with fingering and embouchure. On the other hand, there are some passages almost impossible to produce on the violin that are easy on the flute, for example, broken chords in which leaps of diminished fifths and augmented fourths occur, leaps that exceed the tenth and are frequently and rapidly repeated, and so forth (see Tab. XXIII, Figs. 13 and 14).

FIG. 13   FIG. 14

If, then, a violinist were to judge a flautist, or if the flautist were to judge the violinist, and both understood only the characteristics of their own instruments, they would hardly be able to pass judgement justly upon each other's taste and insight into music or appreciate each other's merits upon their respective instruments, even if they had both achieved an unusual degree of musical skill.

§ 15

Thus those who have some insight into music should judge an instrumentalist only by those general matters that all instrumentalists have in common. The judges must pay attention to whether the instrumentalist plays his instrument in tune, and knows how to produce a good tone quality; whether he plays the instrument with the requisite tranquillity and charm, or noisily forces the tone; whether he has a good bow-stroke or tongue-stroke, agile fingers, and a good even shake; whether he is sure of his tempo, or plays passage-work that is difficult for him more slowly and that which is easy more quickly, thus not ending the piece as he began it, and forcing the accompanists to adjust to him; whether he knows how

[1] *Der Verschiedenheit der chromatischen Tonarten (les modes chromatiques)*. The term 'chromatic keys' here seems to mean only keys with a number of accidentals in the signature, a meaning mentioned and disapproved of by Brossard.

to play each piece in its proper tempo, or plays everything marked Allegro at the same speed; whether he plays only technically difficult things, or also plays cantabile pieces; whether he seeks only to excite admiration, or seeks also to please and to move; whether he plays expressively or indifferently; whether his execution is distinct; whether he knows how to rescue and improve a poor composition through his execution, or obscures a good piece and makes the melody incomprehensible by elaborating and disrupting the notes too much,[1] a defect that is most easily noticed if you hear the same piece performed by more than one person. You may also observe whether an instrumentalist plays the Allegro in a lively, facile, clear, and true manner, and the passage-work in it roundly and distinctly, or whether he simply rushes hastily over the notes, or even leaves some out; whether he plays the Adagio in a sustained and flowing manner,[2] or dryly and flatly; whether he knows how to embellish each Adagio with such graces as are appropriate to the sentiment and to the piece; whether at the same time he observes light and shadow, or indiscriminately overloads everything with graces, and plays everything with the same colour; whether he understands harmony and adjusts the graces to it, or simply plays by ear at his own discretion; whether he succeeds in all that he undertakes and is in accord with other players both in harmony and tempo, or plays haphazardly, beginning a grace well, but ending it poorly. You frequently encounter mastery of great technical difficulties, even among very young people, but the masterful performance of the Adagio is found only among practised and experienced musical artists; it requires a thorough knowledge of harmony and much discrimination. Then, finally, you may examine whether an instrumentalist plays in a mixed style or in a single national style; whether he knows how to play at sight, or only after having studied his pieces; whether he understands composition, or has recourse only to the pieces of others; whether he plays all kinds of pieces well, or only those that he has written himself or have been written for him; lastly, whether he knows how to retain the constant attention of the listeners, and how to make them wish to hear him more often. All these advantageous characteristics united merit praise; their opposites require indulgence. If you wish to know which instruments are easier to learn, one not completely undependable indication is that those on which many people excel are easier to learn than those on which many play without making much progress.

§ 16

To judge properly the *composition* and the *performance* of a musical composition as a whole is a much more difficult matter than those considered above. You not only must have perfect good taste and an understanding

---

[1] *Durch allzuvieles Künsteln und Verziehen der Noten (par trop de raffinement & en dérangeant les notes).*

[2] *Unterhalten und gezogen (d'une maniere soutenuë & coulante).*

of the rules of composition, but also must possess sufficient insight into the nature and characteristics of each piece, whether composed in the style of this nation or that, for this purpose or that, so that you do not confuse one matter with another. The purposes for which pieces are composed may be very diverse, and thus a piece that is good for one purpose may be bad for another.

§ 17

I would be too prolix if I were to examine the particular characteristics of every type of piece. Hence I will attempt to touch briefly upon only the most important.

§ 18

Music is either vocal or instrumental. Only a few pieces, however, are intended for voices alone; instrumental music usually has a part in and is combined with the majority of vocal pieces. Yet these two kinds of music differ greatly from one another not only broadly, in purpose and therefore in organization,[1] but also in their subdivisions, each of which has its particular laws, and requires its particular style of composition. Vocal music is intended for the church, the theatre, or the chamber. Instrumental music is likewise performed in all these places.

§ 19

Church music is of two kinds, namely *Roman Catholic*, and *Protestant*. In the *Roman church* the *Mass*, the *Vesper Psalms*, the *Te Deum laudamus, the Penitential Psalms*, the *Requiem* or *Mass for the Dead*, some *hymns*, the *motet*,* the *oratorio, concerto, sinfonia, pastorale*, and so forth, are found. Each of these pieces in turn has its own particular parts, and each piece must accord with its purpose and with its words, so that a Requiem or Miserere does not resemble a Te Deum or a composition for Easter, the Kyrie resemble the Gloria in the Mass, or a motet a gay opera aria. An *oratorio* or dramatically treated sacred history is ordinarily distinguished from a theatrical composition only by its content and, to a certain extent, by its recitative. In general the introduction of more liveliness is permitted in the church music of the Catholics than in that of the Protestants. The extravagances sometimes encountered in this regard, however, should probably be entirely ascribed to the composers.

* Motets of the old kind, which, set to verses from the Bible, are composed in *a cappella* style with many voice parts and no instruments, and in which a cantus firmus from a chant melody is sometimes interwoven, have now been almost completely abandoned in the Roman Catholic Church. The French call all their church pieces indiscriminately *des motets*. Neither of these types is meant here. In Italy this

[1] *Einrichtung*. French text: 'the arrangement of their parts' (*l'arrangement de leurs parties*).

name is applied at the present time to a sacred Latin solo cantata that consists of two arias and two recitatives and closes with an Alleluia, and is ordinarily sung by one of the best singers during the Mass after the Credo. This is the type I refer to here.[1]

§ 20

Of the pieces enumerated above, the following also occur in the *church music of the Protestants*: *part of the Mass, namely the Kyrie and the Gloria, the Magnificat, the Te Deum, some psalms, and the oratorio*, to which the *Passion*, utilizing prose Biblical texts with interspersed arias and some poetic recitatives, is related. The rest are compositions set to free texts, the majority in *cantata style* with Biblical verses intermixed, which are elaborated in the manner of psalms. The texts are adjusted either to the Gospel for the Sunday or feast day, or to certain particular ceremonies, such as funerals or weddings. The *Anthems* of the English are ordinarily worked out after the manner of psalms, since they consist mainly of Biblical words.

§ 21

In general a serious and devout style of composition and performance is required in church music of any type. The style must be very different from that of an opera. To attain the desired object, it is to be hoped that this point is always properly considered, especially by the composers. In judging a church composition, which ought to stir us to praise of the Almighty, excite devotion, or engender gravity, you must consider whether its designated purpose is observed from beginning to end, whether the character of each type is maintained, and whether anything contrary to this character is introduced. Here the composer has the opportunity to demonstrate his ability both in the so-called elaborate style and in the touching and affecting style of composition (the latter requiring the highest degree of musical skill).

§ 22

You should not believe that church music must consist exclusively of pedantries. Although the object of the passions is different, they must be excited here with as much or even more care than in the theatre. Devoutness simply imposes some limits. But if a composer is not able to move you in the church, where stricter limits are imposed,[2] he will be even less

---

[1] A well-known example of this type of motet is Mozart's *Exsultate, jubilate* (K. 165). For discussions of other types see Mattheson, *Der vollkommene Capellmeister* (Hamburg: C. Herold, 1739), pp. 222–4, and J. A. Scheibe, *Critischer Musikus, neue, vermehrte und verbesserte Auflage* (Leipzig: B. C. Breitkopf, 1745), pp. 177–85. The same works provide useful information on the various types of compositions mentioned in the preceding and following paragraphs.

[2] Quantz here seems to mean that the composer was more limited by conditions of place, occasion, tradition, and performing body when writing for the church than when writing for the theatre. More specifically, however, he may have had in mind compositions such as those he later wrote himself, which were to be sung by the entire congregation. See the preface to his *Neue Kirchen-Melodien* (Berlin: Winter, 1760).

capable of doing so in the theatre, where he has more freedom. One who knows how to move you in spite of constraints promises to do much more when he has greater freedom. Likewise the poor performance of church music at many places does not provide sufficient grounds for rejecting all church music as something disagreeable.

§ 23

Theatrical music consists of *operas, pastorales* (*Schäferspielen*), or *intermezzi* (*Zwischenspielen*). Operas are either genuine tragedies, or tragedies with happy endings, similar to tragicomedies. Although each class of theatrical piece requires an individual and particular style of composition, on the whole composers take more liberties in them, and give freer rein to their fancies; but they must still respect their obligations, and regulate themselves in accordance with the words and with the nature and content of the subject represented.

§ 24

To judge an opera soundly you must examine whether the sinfonia is in keeping with the content of the piece as a whole, the first act, or at least the first scene, and whether it is able to transport the listeners into the sentiment of the first action, whatever it may be, tender, melancholy, gay, heroic, furious, or the like.* You should observe whether the recitative is set in a natural, speaking, and expressive manner, and is neither too high nor too low for the singers; whether the arias are provided with singing and expressive ritornellos, so as to give a brief foretaste of what follows, or whether they are written in the common humdrum style of the workaday Italian composers, where the ritornello seems to be made by one person, the rest by someone else. In judging an opera you should also pay attention to whether the arias are singable, and give the singers the opportunity to demonstrate their abilities; whether the composer has expressed the passions as the subject requires, clearly distinguishing one from another, and has introduced them at the proper places; whether he has provided impartially for each singer, from first to last, in accordance with his role, voice, and ability; whether he has observed properly the quantity of the syllables as the prosody and the pronunciation require, or has proceeded haphazardly, as many do, sometimes transforming long syllables into short ones and short ones into long for no reason, and thus not only distorting the words, but also giving them a different meaning. This fault is often found among the very persons from whom you would least expect it. It arises from negligence, or because a melody more convenient and suitable to the words did not immediately occur to the composer in his hurried state, or because he has not understood the language.** In judging an opera you must further note whether the composer has carefully observed the caesuras of the discourse in the arias, and particularly in the recitatives; whether in transposing certain words he has carefully avoided obscuring their sense, or giving them an opposite meaning; whether the arias in which the texts require certain actions have been set expressively and in such a way that the singers have the time and opportunity to introduce their action with ease, or whether the singers are forced to babble on in many arias that contain a vehement sentiment through having to pronounce the words too quickly, as was formerly the custom among the Germans. You must note whether the singers are hindered in the lively execution of the words, and in the action, by excessively long notes set to each syllable; and whether in such *parlante* arias[1] the composer has taken care to avoid passage-work in the vocal parts, since it does not belong in them and checks the fire of the action. Finally, you should seek to discover whether the composer has placed each aria in its proper place, so as to insure the coherence of the work as a whole, and whether he has sought to intermingle different keys and metres which are appropriate to the words, so that several arias in the same key or metre do not immediately follow one another; whether he has sustained the principal character of the work from beginning to end, and has preserved a suitable length; and then, whether the majority of the listeners have been touched by the music, and have been transported into the passions represented in the spectacle, so that they quit the theatre with a desire to hear the opera frequently. If all the good qualities enumerated thus far are found in a single opera, it may be considered a true masterwork.[2]

* In this regard see also § 43 of this chapter.
** Astonishing examples of this fault and many others are found in a certain serenata called *la Vittoria d'Imeneo*,[3] newly performed in Italy in 1750, as in other works of the composer; it is from the pen of an Italian who seems either not to have mastered his mother tongue, or at least to have seldom paid any attention to the sense of the words and their expression.

§ 25

In judging individual arias many people are easily deceived. The majority always judge only in accordance with the impression that they make upon the ear, and consider those the best that please them more than

[1] *Sprechende Arien.* Omitted in the French text. On the *aria parlante* and other standard types of arias in Quantz's day, see D. J. Grout, *A Short History of Opera*, pp. 187–8.
[2] For valuable related discussions of opera, see Mattheson, *Der vollkommene Capellmeister*, pp. 218–20; Scheibe, *Critischer Musikus*, pp. 219–45, 265–80, 316–23; C. G. Krause, *Von der musikalischen Poesie* (Berlin: Voss, 1752); and F. Algarotti, *Saggio sopra l'opera in musica* (1755), a portion of which is translated in O. Strunk, *Source Readings in Music History*, pp. 657–72. Krause was a friend of Quantz, and Algarotti an intimate at Frederick's court.
[3] This serenata was the work of Baldassare Galuppi (1706–85), one of the most popular composers of comic operas of the time. A libretto preserved in the Library of Congress indicates that it was first performed on 7 June 1750 on the occasion of the marriage of Vittorio Amadeo, Duke of Savoy, and Maria Antonia Ferdinanda, *infanta* of Spain. The text was by Giuseppi Bartoli.

others. The arrangement of an opera, however, requires, for the sake of the interrelationship of the whole, that not all arias should be of the same constitution or force; they must be of different types or natures. The principal roles must be given some preference over the lesser ones in both their music and their poetry. Just as a painting where all the figures are equally beautiful does not charm or move the eye as much as one in which several less beautiful figures are present, so also a principal aria frequently shows its true lustre only when it is inserted between two lesser ones. The listeners' tastes in arias vary in accordance with the differences in their temperaments. This aria will please one person the most, that aria another person. Hence you must not be at all surprised if an aria that pleases one person is quite disagreeable to another, and if judgements of a piece, particularly of an opera, turn out to be quite varied and unpredictable.

§ 26

If you wish to judge a vocal piece composed for a certain purpose in either the church or the theatre but afterwards performed in the chamber, great circumspection is needed. The circumstances bound up with its intended place, the different manner of performance and execution for both singers and instrumentalists, and the difference between hearing a whole work and only a part of it, all contribute greatly to the good or bad effect produced by the work. An aria with action[1] that has made a particular impression in the theatre will please far less in the chamber; for in the chamber it lacks an essential element, namely, the action and its motivation, unless you are able to recreate a vivid image of these matters from memory. Another aria, the words of which express nothing in particular, but which contains a pleasing melody, advantageous to the singer and well performed by him, may eclipse the aforementioned aria and may be preferred by the listeners in the chamber. In this case you may say that the latter pleases more than the former, but not that it is better in consequence. In arias the words and their expression must be considered as well as the melody. In addition, an aria with vigorous action must be more spoken than sung, and therefore requires, besides an experienced composer, both a good singer and a good actor.

§ 27

When a *serenata* or a *cantata* is expressly written for the *chamber*, the style differs from that suitable for the church or for the theatre. The difference is that the chamber style requires more liveliness and freedom in its ideas than the church style; and since it has no action, it permits greater elaboration and artifice than the theatre style. The *madrigal*, which, like a psalm, is a carefully contrived piece with many voice parts, usually with-

---

[1] 'Action' in this case seems to mean movement on the stage.

out instruments, is also appropriate in the chamber.[1] The *duet* and the *terzett without instruments*, and the *solo cantata*, are equally suitable there.

§ 28

If you wish to judge an *instrumental composition* correctly, you must have an exact knowledge not only of the characteristic features of each type of piece that may appear, but also, as stated above, of the instruments themselves. A piece may in itself conform to good taste as well as to the rules of harmony, and thus be considered well written, yet still remain unsuited to the instrument. On the other hand, a piece may conform to the instrument yet have no intrinsic value. Vocal music has some advantages that instrumental music must forgo. In the former the words and the human voice are a great advantage to the composer, both with regard to invention and effect. Experience makes this obvious when, lacking a voice, an aria is heard played on an instrument. Yet instrumental music, without words and human voices, ought to express certain emotions, and should transport the listeners from one emotion to another just as well as vocal music does. And if this is to be accomplished properly, so as to compensate for the lack of words and the human voice, neither the composer nor the performer can be devoid of feeling.[2]

§ 29

The principal types of instrumental music in which voices are not employed are the *concerto*, the *overture*, the *sinfonia*, the *quartet*, the *trio*, and the *solo*. Of these, the concerto, the trio, and the solo are each of two sorts. We have *concerti grossi* and *concerti da camera*. Trios are, as we say, either elaborate[3] or *galant*. The same applies to solos.

§ 30

The concerto owes its origin to the Italians. *Torelli*[4] is supposed to have made the first. The *concerto grosso* consists of an intermixture of various concertante instruments in which two or more instruments, the number sometimes extending as high as eight and above, play together in turn. In the *chamber concerto*, on the other hand, only a single concertante instrument is present.

§ 31

The nature of the *concerto grosso* requires the following features in each movement. (1) At the beginning a majestic ritornello must appear which

[1] From Quantz's description of the madrigal, it is not clear whether he knew of some examples of this type written in his own day. He may be referring to late sixteenth-century examples, which are discussed by Mattheson, *Der vollkommene Capellmeister*, pp. 78–79.

[2] German text: 'can have wooden souls'.

[3] On the 'elaborate' (*gearbeitet*) style, see Chapter X, § 14.

[4] Giuseppe Torelli (1658–1709). On Torelli's place in the history of the concerto, see A. Hutchings, *The Baroque Concerto*, 2nd ed. (London: Faber and Faber, 1978), pp. 89–96.

is more harmonic than melodic, more serious than jocular, and which is interspersed with unison passages. (2) There must be a skilful mixture of imitations among the concertante parts, so that the ear is surprised now by this instrument, now by that. (3) These imitations must consist of short and pleasing ideas. (4) Brilliant ideas must always alternate with flattering ideas. (5) The inner tutti sections must be short. (6) The alternations of the concertante instruments must be distributed so that one instrument is not heard too much or another too little. (7) After a trio a brief solo by one or another of the instruments must be inserted from time to time. (8) Before the close the instruments must effect a short repetition of what they had at the beginning. (9) The last tutti must conclude with the most forceful and majestic ideas of the first ritornello. A concerto of this kind requires a large accompanying body, a large place to perform it, a serious performance, and a moderate tempo.[1]

§ 32

Concertos with one concertante instrument, or so-called *chamber concertos*, are also of two classes. Some demand a large accompanying body, like *concerti grossi*, others demand a small one. And if this distinction is not made, neither type produces the desired effect. The class to which a concerto belongs may be perceived from the first ritornello. One that is composed seriously, majestically, and more harmonically than melodically, in which many unison passages are interspersed, and in which the harmony does not change by quavers or crotchets but by half and whole bars, must have a large accompanying body. A ritornello that consists of fleeting, jocular, gay, or singing melodies, and has quick changes of harmony, produces a better effect with a small accompanying body.

§ 33

A *serious* concerto *for a single solo instrument* with a *large accompanying body* requires the following characteristics in its first movement. (1) A majestic ritornello must be carefully elaborated in all the parts. (2) The melodies must be pleasing and intelligible. (3) The imitations must be correct. (4) The best ideas of the ritornello must be dismembered, and intermingled during or between the solo passages. (5) The fundamental part must sound well, and must be appropriate to the bass. (6) There must be no more middle parts than the principal part allows; a better effect is frequently produced by doubling the principal parts than by forcing in unnecessary middle parts. (7) The progressions of the bass part and the middle parts must neither impede the liveliness of the principal part nor

---

[1] For a review of the history of the concerto grosso in Germany, with a brief discussion of Quantz's own contributions to the literature, see W. Krüger, *Das Concerto grosso in Deutschland* (Wolfenbüttel: G. Kallmeyer, 1932). See also Hutchings, *The Baroque Concerto*, pp. 114–32, 201–51.

drown or suppress it. (8) The ritornello must be of suitable length. It must have at least two principal sections. The second, since it is repeated at the end of the movement,[1] and concludes it, must be provided with the most beautiful and majestic ideas. (9) If the opening idea of the ritornello is not sufficiently singing or is not appropriate for the solo, a new idea quite unlike it must be introduced, and must be joined to the opening materials in such a way that it is not apparent whether it appears of necessity or with due deliberation. (10) At times the solo sections must be singing, and at times these flattering sections must be interspersed with brilliant melodic and harmonic passage-work appropriate to the instrument; these sections must also alternate with short, lively, and majestic tutti sections, in order to sustain the fire [of the piece] from beginning to end. (11) The concertante or solo sections must not be too short, and the tutti sections between them must not be too long. (12) The accompaniment during the solo sections must not have progressions that might obscure the concertante part; it must consist alternately of many parts at one time and few at another, so that the principal part now and then has a chance to distinguish itself with greater freedom. In general, light and shadow must be maintained at all times. If it is possible, a good effect is produced if the passage-work is invented in such a way that the accompanying parts are able to introduce a recognizable portion of the ritornello simultaneously. (13) Correct and natural progression must always be observed, and any too-distant key that might offend the ear must be avoided. (14) Metrics,[2] which must be carefully attended to in composition in general, must also be carefully observed here. The caesuras or divisions of the melody must not fall on the second or fourth crotchets in common time, or on the third or fifth beats in triple time. The metrical scheme must be continued as it is begun, whether by whole or half bars, or in triple time by two, four, or eight bars; otherwise the most artful composition will be faulty. In an Arioso in triple time that has frequent rests, successive caesuras are permitted after three bars and then after two bars. (15) Transpositions of passage-work must not be tediously continued in the same way; the passage-work must be broken off and shortened imperceptibly at the proper time. (16) The end of the piece must not be hurried or cut short; it must be clearly confirmed. The piece must not conclude with entirely new ideas; in the last solo section the most pleasing of the ideas previously heard must be repeated. (17) Finally, the Allegro must be concluded as briefly as possible in the last tutti with the second part of the first ritornello.

---

[1] To save time and space, some composers, including Quantz, at times divided the opening ritornello with dark vertical lines in the score, and simply indicated a recapitulation of the second of the two sections at the end of the movement.

[2] *Das Metrum.* According to Brossard and Walther, *Metrum* refers to 'beat' or 'measure'. Quantz, however, uses the term to indicate phrase structure in general, and the position of caesuras in particular. For further information on the subject of caesuras, see the extensive treatise on *Vocalsatz* in the first and second volumes of F. W. Marpurg's *Kritische Briefe über die Tonkunst* (3 vols.; Berlin: Birnstiel, 1760–4).

§ 34

Not all the various types of metres are equally appropriate for the first movement of a majestic concerto. If it is to be lively, common time may be used, with semiquavers as the quickest notes, and the caesuras falling on ← the second half of the bar. If the aforesaid first movement is to be majestic as well, a broader metrical scheme should be chosen, in which the caesura regularly occupies an entire bar and falls only on the downbeat. If, however, the first movement is to be both serious and majestic, a more moderate quick movement in common time may be chosen, where the quickest notes may be demisemiquavers, and the caesura falls on the second half of the bar. Dotted semiquavers will contribute greatly to the majesty of the ritornello. The movement may be indicated with the word Allegretto. Notes of this kind can also by written in a moderate alla breve time. The quavers must simply be changed into crotchets, the semiquavers into quavers, and the demisemiquavers into semiquavers. The caesuras may then fall regularly on the beginning of the bar. Ordinary alla breve time, in which the quickest notes are quavers, should be viewed like two-four time, and thus is better suited to the last movement than to the first, since the character of the last movement, unless it proceeds in a strict harmonic style in full chords,[1] tends to be agreeable rather than majestic. Generally, triple time is little used for the first movement, unless it is three-four time with semiquavers intermingled, in which the movement of the middle and bass parts is in quavers, and the harmony usually changes only by full bars.

§ 35

In general the *Adagio* must be distinguished from the first Allegro by its rhythmic structure,[2] metre, and tonality. If the Allegro is written in a major tonality, for example, in C major, the Adagio may be set, at one's discretion, in C minor, E minor, A minor, F major, G major, or G minor. If, however, the first Allegro is written in a minor key, for example, C minor, the Adagio may be set in E flat major, F minor, G minor, or A flat major. These sequences of keys are the most natural ones. The ear will never be offended by them, and the relationships are acceptable for all keys, whatever their names. Anybody who wishes to surprise his listeners in a rude and disagreeable manner is free to choose other keys; but since they may be pleasing only to him, he should at least proceed with great circumspection.

§ 36

The Adagio furnishes more opportunities than the Allegro to excite the passions and to still them again. In former times the Adagio was usually set in a very dry and plain fashion that was more harmonic than melodic.

---

[1] *Wenn man nicht immer gebunden und vollstimmig darinne arbeitet (à moins qu'on n'y veuille pas toujours procéder harmonieusement & en pleins accords).*

[2] *Reimgebäude (le Metrum).*

The composers relinquished to the performers that which they should have done themselves, that is, make the melody sing; and the performers could do so only by adding many graces. Hence it was easier at that time to compose an Adagio than to play one. Since, as may be easily imagined, Adagios of this sort did not always have the good fortune to fall into capable hands, and their performance rarely succeeded as the composer might have wished, such movements began in more recent times to be written in a more cantabile style, thus causing a good situation to emerge from a bad one. As a result the composer is honoured more, and the performer has to rack his brains less, while the Adagio itself cannot be so diversely and so frequently distorted and mutilated as was formerly the case.

§ 37

Since, however, the Adagio ordinarily finds fewer admirers than the Allegro among those who are not well versed in music, the composer must seek in every possible way to make it pleasing to inexperienced listeners such as these. To this end he should observe the following rules in particular. (1) In both the ritornellos and the solo sections he must strive for the greatest possible brevity. (2) The ritornello must be melodious, harmonious, and expressive. (3) The principal part must have a melody that permits some addition of graces, yet can also please without them. (4) The melody of the principal part must alternate[1] with the interspersed tutti sections. (5) This melody must be just as moving and expressive as one with accompanying words. (6) From time to time some portions of the ritornello must be introduced. (7) The composer must not move through too many tonalities, since this is most detrimental to brevity. (8) The accompaniment during the solo passages must be plain rather than figured, so that the principal part is not hindered in making some embellishments, and retains complete freedom to introduce many or only a few graces judiciously and in a reasonable manner. (9) Finally, so that the required tempo may be easily divined, the composer must seek to characterize the Adagio with an epithet that clearly expresses the sentiment contained in it.

§ 38

The *final Allegro* of a concerto must be quite different from the first in the style and nature of its ideas as well as in its metre. If the first movement is to be serious, the last must be jocular and gay. Metres such as two-four, three-four, three-eight, six-eight, nine-eight, and twelve-eight may be serviceable in it. All three movements of a concerto must never be set in the same metre. If the first two movements are in duple time, the last must be set in triple; but if the first is in duple and the second in triple, the last may be set in triple time or in two-four time. It must never be in common time, however, since this would be too serious, and would suit the last

---

[1] *Concertiren (alterner).*

movement as little as two-four or a quick triple metre would suit the first movement. Neither must all three movements begin with the same note; if the upper part in one movement begins with the fundamental note, in another it can begin with the third, and in the third movement with the fifth. Although the last movement must be written in the same tonality as the first, care must be taken to modulate to successive tonalities in a different order than in the first movement, so that excessive likeness is avoided.

§ 39

Speaking generally, the last movement must have the following characteristics. (1) The ritornello must be short, gay, and fiery, and at the same time rather playful. (2) The principal part must have a melody that is pleasing, fleeting, and light. (3) The passage-work must be easy, so that quickness is not impeded; but it must have no similarity to the passage-work in the first movement. For example, if in the first movement it consists of broken or arpeggiated figures, in the last movement it may move by step or may consist of turns.[1] Or if there are triplets in the first movement, the passage-work in the last movement may consist of even notes, and vice versa. (4) Metrical structure must be observed with the greatest strictness; for the shorter and quicker the metrical units are, the more apparent it is if they are improperly treated. Thus in two-four and quick three-four, three-eight, and six-eight time the caesuras must always fall on the beginning of the second bar, and the principal breaks must fall on the fourth and eighth bars. (5) The accompaniment must not be too full or overloaded with parts. It must consist of such notes as the accompanying parts can produce without excessive motion or difficulty, since the last movement is ordinarily played very quickly.[2]

§ 40

A timepiece may be consulted to ensure *suitable length* in a concerto. If the first movement takes five minutes, the Adagio five to six minutes, and the last movement three to four minutes, the entire concerto will have the requisite length. In general it is more advantageous if the listeners find a piece too short rather than too long.

§ 41

Anybody who knows how to write a concerto of this kind will find it easy to fashion a jocular and playful *little chamber concerto*. Thus it would be superfluous to deal with it separately here.

[1] *Rollend seyn (etre roulants)*. The noun *Rolle* was used by some eighteenth-century writers to indicate a turn.

[2] For a pertinent related discussion of concertos, see Scheibe, *Critischer Musikus*, pp. 630–41. For a list of modern editions of Quantz's own concertos, see *Quantz and His Versuch*, pp. 155–7, and the supplement to that list, pp. 392–4 below.

§ 42

An *overture*, which is played at the beginning of an opera, requires a grave and majestic opening, a brilliant and well-elaborated principal subject, and a good mixture of various instruments such as oboes, flutes, and hunting horns. It owes its origin to the French. *Lully* has provided good models for it; but some German composers, among others especially
→ Handel and Telemann, have far surpassed him. The lot of the French with their overtures is almost the same as that of the Italians with their concertos.[1] Since the overture produces such a good effect, however, it is a pity that it is longer in vogue in Germany.[2]

§ 43

The Italian *sinfonias*, which have the same purpose as overtures, require the same qualities of majesty in their ideas. Since, however, the majority are fashioned by composers who have exercised their talents more fully in vocal than in instrumental music, there are at present very few sinfonias that have all the required attributes, and can serve as good models. Sometimes opera composers seem to set about fashioning their sinfonias like portrait-painters who use their left-over colour to fill in the background or the garments. As mentioned above, it would seem that a sinfonia should have some connexion with the content of the opera, or at least with its first scene, and should not always conclude with a gay minuet, as it usually does. I am unwilling to prescribe a model, since all the situations that might occur at the beginning of an opera cannot be put into a single class; but I believe an easy remedy for this abuse can be found. A sinfonia before an opera need not always consist of three movements; it could be concluded after the first or second movement. For example, if the first scene were to contain heroic or other fiery passions, the sinfonia could conclude after the first movement. If melancholy or amorous sentiments appear in the scene, the composer could stop with the second movement. And if the first scene contains no marked sentiments, or if these appear only in the course of the opera or at its end, he could conclude with the third movement of the sinfonia. In this fashion the composer could adjust each movement to the situation, and the sinfonia would still retain its usefulness for other purposes.[3]

§ 44

A *quartet*, or a sonata with three concertante instruments and a bass, is the true touchstone of a genuine contrapuntist, and is often the downfall

[1] i.e. Germans wrote better works in both forms than the native composers.

[2] For a related discussion of the overture, see Scheibe, *Critischer Musikus*, pp. 667–74. There also, the works of Handel and Telemann are singled out for praise. The first movement of the sixth of Quantz's *Sei duetti*, Op. 2, is a French overture.

[3] For another discussion of the opera *sinfonia*, and several other kinds of symphonies, see Scheibe, *Critischer Musikus*, pp. 595–629. The suggestions contained in § 43 are Quantz's small contribution to the current of operatic reform that was increasing in strength at that time.

of those who are not solidly grounded in their technique. Its vogue has never been great, hence its nature may not be well known to many people. It is to be feared that compositions of this kind will eventually become a lost art. A good quartet requires: (1) a subject appropriate for treatment in four parts;[1] (2) good, harmonious melody; (3) short and correct imitations; (4) a discerningly devised mixture of the concertante instruments; (5) a fundamental part with a true bass quality; (6) ideas that can be exchanged with one another, so that the composer can build both above and below them, and middle parts that are at least passable and not unpleasing; (7) preference for one part should not be apparent; (8) each part, after it has rested, must re-enter not as a middle part, but as a principal part, with a pleasing melody; but this applies only to the three concertante parts, not to the bass; (9) if a fugue appears, it must be carried out in all of the four parts in a masterful yet tasteful fashion, in accordance with all the rules.

A certain group of *six quartets* for different instruments, the majority for flute, oboe, and violin, which Mr. Telemann wrote some time ago, but which have not been engraved, may provide excellent and beautiful models for compositions of this type.[2]

§ 45

A *trio* does not require quite so much laborious effort as a quartet, but if it is to be good, it does require almost the same degree of skill on the part of the composer. It has the advantage that the ideas introduced may be more *galant* and more agreeable than in a quartet, since it has one less concertante part. Thus, in a trio, (1) the composer must invent an air that admits the addition of another melodious part. (2) The opening subject at the beginning of each movement, particularly of the Adagio, must not be too long, since it can easily become tedious when repeated at the fifth, fourth, or unison by the second part. (3) One part must not present anything that cannot be repeated by the other. (4) The imitations must be short, and the passage-work must be brilliant. (5) Good order must be preserved in the repetition of the most pleasing ideas. (6) Both of the principal parts must be written in such a way that a natural and harmonious bass part can be placed beneath them. (7) Should a fugue be introduced, it must be carried out, as in a quartet, both correctly and tastefully in all the parts, in accordance with the rules of composition. The episodes, whether they consist of passage-work or other imitations, must be pleasing and brilliant. (8) Although passages in thirds and sixths in the principal parts are one of the ornaments of a trio, they must not be abused or dragged on *ad nauseam*;

---

[1] *Ein reiner vierstimmiger Satz (un sujet susceptible de quatre parties).*

[2] It is not possible to identify this particular set of quartets as yet. Telemann was the author of several other sets that were published. See Telemann's autobiographies in W. Kahl, *Selbstbiographien deutscher Musiker*, pp. 213-14, 225. Scheibe, *Critischer Musikus*, pp. 679-80, also discusses the quartet, and likewise recommends the works of Telemann, which seem to have enjoyed a considerable esteem for many years.

they must be regularly interrupted with passage-work or other imitations. (9) Finally, the trio must be so created that it is almost impossible to divine which of the two [upper] parts is the foremost.[1]

§ 46

Writing a *solo* is today no longer considered an art. Nearly every instrumentalist tries his hand at it. If he has no inventiveness of his own, he helps himself to borrowed ideas. If he lacks knowledge of the rules of composition, he has someone else to write the bass. As a result, instead good models, a considerable number of monstrosities appear.

§ 47

As a matter of fact, it is not such an easy matter to write a good solo. There are some composers who understand composition perfectly, and are successful in works for several parts, yet write poor solos. Others, on the contrary, are more successful in solos than in pieces for several parts. One who is successful with both is indeed fortunate. Although it is not necessary to know all the deepest secrets of composition to write a solo, it is hardly possible to produce anything reasonable in compositions of this type without some understanding of harmony.

§ 48

If a solo is to do honour to its composer and to its performer, (1) the *Adagio*[2] must be singing and expressive in its own right; (2) the performer must have an opportunity to demonstrate his judgement, inventiveness, and insight; (3) tenderness must be mixed with ingenuity from time to time;[3] (4) a natural bass part, upon which it is easy to build, must be provided; (5) one idea must not be repeated too often either at the same pitch or in transposition, since this would weary the player, and would become tedious to the listeners; (6) at times the natural melody must be

---

[1] For some samples of Quantz's own trios, see the list of modern editions in Bose, 'Quantz', *MGG*, 10, col. 1805. Scheibe, *Critischer Musikus*, pp. 676–9, again provides an interesting discussion of the form. The duet, which Quantz omits in his survey here, is considered in some detail in the preface of his *Sei duetti*, Op. 2.

[2] Quantz here describes a three-movement sonata in a slow–quick–quick scheme. Although his early works show a variety of different patterns, this one is found in the majority of his sonatas. Tartini's sonatas are today the most well-known examples of the type, but there is no reason to believe that Quantz borrowed the pattern from Tartini. It was used by many Italian and German composers of the day, and Quantz does not seem to have been particularly fond of Tartini. Scheibe, *Critischer Musikus*, pp. 681–3, also describes this type of sonata. For available examples of sonatas by Quantz, see Bose, 'Quantz', col. 1805. For a rich and comprehensive survey of the sonata during this period, see W. S. Newman, *The Sonata in the Baroque Era* (Chapel Hill: University of North Carolina Press, 1959), pp. 163–200, 255–300, 367–92, and the same author's *The Sonata in the Classic Era* (Chapel Hill: University of North Carolina Press, 1963), pp. 216–57, 315–453, 604–47.

[3] i.e. a cantabile style must be blended with a certain amount of contrapuntal ingenuity.

interrupted with some dissonances, in order to duly excite the passions of the listeners; (7) the Adagio must not be too long.

§ 49

The *first Allegro* requires: (1) a melody that is flowing, coherent, and rather serious; (2) a good association of ideas; (3) brilliant passage-work, well joined to the melody; (4) good order in the repetition of ideas; (5) some beautiful and well-chosen phrases at the end of the first part which are so adjusted that in transposed form they may again conclude the last part; (6) a first part which is a little shorter than the last; (7) the introduction of the most brilliant passage-work in the last part; (8) a bass that is set naturally and with progressions of a kind that sustain a constant vivacity.

§ 50

The *second Allegro* may be either very gay and quick, or moderate and arioso. Hence it must be adjusted to the first Allegro. If the first is serious, the second may be gay. If the first is lively and quick, the second may be moderate and arioso. As to variety of metre, what was said above in regard to concertos must also be observed here, so that one movement is not similar to another. If a solo is to please everyone, it must be arranged so that the inclinations of each listener find sustenance in it. It must be neither entirely cantabile nor entirely of a lively character. Just as each movement must be quite different from the others, so each must have in itself a good mixture of pleasing and brilliant ideas. The most beautiful idea can eventually become dull if repeated endlessly; and although constant animation or uninterrupted technical difficulties do much to excite admiration, they are not particularly moving. Such a mixture of different ideas is necessary not only in solos, but in every type of musical composition. If a composer knows how to manage this matter successfully, and by this means to inspire the passions of the listener, it may justly be said that he has achieved a high degree of good taste, and that he has, so to speak, found the musical philosopher's stone.

§ 51

These, then, are the chief qualities of the principal types of musical pieces; they must be present in each according to its kind if a connoisseur is to declare it good, and worthy of his approbation. There will always remain some listeners, however, who find it impossible to acquire sufficient insight into music to perceive by themselves the characteristics of excellence in a piece. Hence such listeners are forced to rely on certain circumstances, not exclusively bound up with the person of the performer, but with little direct relationship to the music itself, which may give some indication of the excellence of a composition. They will be on the safest side if, in great assemblies where a piece is sung or played, they pay attention to the mien and gestures of the listeners (these assemblies must be the kind where the main object is to listen to music, however, and in which the music is not regarded as a purely incidental matter, assemblies where connoisseurs as well as people who are not conversant with music are among the listeners). They should try to perceive whether the attention of only a few or that of the majority of those present is aroused; whether the listeners make their pleasure or displeasure known to one another; whether some draw near to the performers of the music, or stray away; whether the listeners are silent or talk loudly; whether they mark the time with their heads; whether they are curious as to the author of the composition; and whether, when the piece ends, those present indicate a desire to hear it again. Finally, such listeners must also inquire into their own feelings a little, and seek to determine whether the music they have heard has moved them, even if they are not able to tell the reason for it. If all the advantageous conditions are met in connexion with a musical work, the unversed listeners may safely conclude that the piece is well-composed and well-performed.

§ 52

The *diversity of style* manifest in different nations that fancy the fine arts, although less related to the essentials than to the incidentals of music, has the greatest influence upon musical judgement. Thus it is necessary to inquire into this diversity of style a little more fully, even though, where necessary, I have already had something to say about it at various places in previous chapters.

§ 53

Except among barbarians there is not a single nation that does not have something in its music that is more pleasing to it than to other nations; but that which is individual to each is usually neither great enough, nor of enough importance, to merit special attention. In recent times, however, there are two peoples in particular who have earned considerable esteem through their improvement of musical style; led by their natural proclivities, they have each taken different paths to achieve this goal. These two peoples are the *Italians* and the *French*.[1] Other nations have given the greatest approbation to the styles of these two peoples, and have sought to imitate and adopt some aspects of the styles of either the one or the other. In consequence, the two peoples mentioned have been seduced into setting themselves up as sovereign judges of good style in music; and since none of the other countries has been able to oppose them, they actually have

---

[1] The following discussion of French and Italian styles is one in a long line of such works which goes back to F. Raguenet's *Paralèle des italiens et des françois* (1702) and Le Cerf de la Viéville's *Comparaison de la musique italienne et de la musique française* (1705). The subject was a mainstay of writers on music for over fifty years.

been, to a certain extent, the legislators in this regard for some centuries. From them, good style has since been transferred to other peoples.

§ 54

Without going back to primary origins, it is certain that in antiquity, music, like the other fine arts, came to the Romans from the Greeks, and that after the decline of the splendour of ancient Rome it nearly sank into the dust of oblivion. The question of which nation was the first to begin to rescue music from this decline and to re-establish it in its renewed form is the subject of considerable dispute. With a full and thorough investigation, however, the verdict would probably favour the Italians. It is certain that it took a long time to bring music as near to perfection as it now stands. At different times one nation or another may have been in the forefront, only to follow again at another. Charlemagne, however, when in Rome, already recognized the superiority of Italian musicians, especially with regard to the art of singing, and even had many of them come to his court. He strove to order his music after that of the Italians.

§ 55

There are solid reasons for believing that, long after the time of Charlemagne, the music of the Italians and the French differed far less than at the present time. It is well known that the French regard *Lully*,[1] an Italian, almost as a musical dictator; that his style is at present still applauded throughout all France; and that they carefully endeavour to restore this style, and keep its fashion unchanged, if at times some of their compatriots attempt to depart from it. I will concede that since this celebrated man came to France when he was very young, he accommodated himself to a certain extent to earlier French music, and embraced its style. But no one can say that it was possible for him to disavow completely the style peculiar to his nation, of which he must have formed some notion while still in Italy, and he could still less disavow his own genius. The simple fact is that he mixed the style of one nation with that of the other. Since, as everyone knows, the Italian style in music has changed very considerably since the death of Lully, while that of the French has remained exactly the same, the difference between the two has gradually become more and more pronounced since that time. We will examine this difference a little more closely.

§ 56

The *Italians'* inclination to change in music has yielded many benefits to true good style. How many great and celebrated composers Italy

---

[1] Although Jean-Baptiste Lully (1632–1687) had been dead for over half a century, some of his operas were still performed in Paris, and the style of later French operas was based on the foundations established by him. In general, German writers of the time show themselves unusually familiar with current developments in France, but Quantz may have been unduly influenced by impressions gained during his visit to France in 1726–7.

showed us, up to the end of the first thirty years of this century! Since Pistocchi[1] opened his singing schools towards the end of the last century, and from them presented so many fine singers to the world, the art of singing has likewise risen to its highest pinnacle during the first thirty years of the present century; through various justly celebrated singers it has demonstrated and adopted in practice almost everything moving and worthy of admiration that can be produced from the human voice. As a result, good composers have seized countless occasions to gradually improve vocal composition. Corelli[2] and his successors have sought to emulate them in a laudable manner in instrumental music.*

> * When I mention the Italian style, I mean chiefly the Italian style that was gradually introduced by so many well-grounded men during the time referred to above, and which since then has been further refined by some celebrated foreigners who followed them.

§ 57

About twenty-five years ago, however, this inclination towards change of style in music became apparent in a completely different manner among the musicians of the Italian nation. At present the style of their singers differs greatly from that of their instrumentalists. There is no longer agreement between them. Although the Italian instrumentalists have the advantage over those of other peoples, in that they hear so many good things sung from childhood on, they nowadays accustom themselves to employing a style so different from that of the singers, that one would hardly take them to be of the same nationality. For the most part this difference lies in the execution, and in an excessive addition of extempore embellishments. The change was originated by several celebrated instrumentalists who distinguished themselves from time to time in composition, but more particularly by performing many difficult feats upon their in-

[1] Francesco Antonio Mamiliano Pistocchi (or Pistochi; 1659–1726). Galliard, in his translation of Tosi's *Observations on the Florid Song*, pp. 101–2, provides the following information about him: 'Pistochi was very famous above fifty Years ago, and refined the Manner of singing in *Italy*, which was then a little crude. His Merit in this is acknowledged by all his Countrymen, contradicted by none. Briefly, what is recounted of him, is, that when he first appeared to the World, and a Youth, he had a very fine treble Voice, admired and encouraged universally, but by a dissolute Life lost it, and his Fortune. Being reduced to the utmost Misery, he entered into the Service of a Composer, as a Copyist, where he made use of the Opportunity of learning the Rules of Composition, and became a good Proficient. After some Years, he recovered a little Glimpse of Voice, which by Time and Practice turned into a fine *Contr'Alto*. Having Experience on his Side, he took Care of it, and as Encouragement came again, he took the Opportunity of travelling all *Europe* over, where hearing the different Manners and Tastes, he appropriated them to himself, and formed that agreeable Mixture, which he produced in *Italy*, where he was imitated and admired. He at last past many Years, when in an affluent Fortune, at the Court of Anspach, where he had a Stipend, and lived an agreeable easy Life; and at last retired to a Convent in *Italy*. It has been remark'd that though several of his Disciples shewed the Improvement they had from him, yet others made an ill use of it, having not a little contributed to the Introduction of the *modern* Taste.'

[2] Arcangelo Corelli (1653–1713). For a brief discussion of Corelli's influence in Italy and in France, Germany, and England, see M. Pincherle, *Corelli, His Life, His Work*, pp. 140–75.

struments. They must have been of very different temperaments, however, since one was mistakenly led into one style, the other into another, both of which have been subsequently propagated by their adherents, so that a bizarre and unbridled style has arisen from a well-grounded one. The antagonism that always prevails between singers and instrumentalists in Italy, and between vocal and instrumental composers, may also have contributed somewhat to this contrast. The singers do not wish to grant that the instrumentalists can move the listeners as well as they do with singable ideas, and abrogate to themselves without any distinction a superiority over the instrumentalists. The latter do not wish to submit to the former, however, and thus try to prove that it is possible to be just as pleasing with a different style. As a result, they have almost succeeded in doing the reverse, to the detriment of true good style.

§ 58

Two celebrated *Lombardic* violinists[1] who began to be known about thirty or more years ago, one not long after the other, have independently contributed much to this state of affairs. The *first*[2] was lively and rich in invention, and supplied almost half the world with his concertos. Although *Torelli*, and after him *Corelli*, had made a start in this genre of music, this violinist, together with *Albinoni*,[3] gave it a better form, and produced good models in it. And in this way he also achieved general credit, just as Corelli had with his twelve solos.[4] But finally, as a result of excessive daily composing, and especially after he had begun to write theatrical vocal pieces, he sank into frivolity and eccentricity both in composition and performance; in consequence his last concertos did not gain as much approbation as his first. It is said that he is one of those who invented the so-called *Lombardic style*, which consists in shortening the note [or notes] on the beat in a group of two or three short notes, and dotting the following unstressed note (see Chapter V, § 23), a style which had its beginnings about the year 1722.[5] There are some indications, however, that this manner of writing is found in Scottish music; it was also introduced, although less abundantly, by several German composers more than twenty years before its vogue in Italy. Thus the Italian style could be considered simply an imitation of the one just mentioned. Whatever the case may be, because of his character this change in his manner of thinking in his last

[1] From the descriptions which follow these two violinists can be identified as Antonio Vivaldi (1687–1741) and Giuseppe Tartini (1692–1770). They are also identified by the translator of the Dutch edition of the *Versuch* published in 1754, J. W. Lustig. See *Grondig onderwys van den aardt en de regte behandeling der dwarsfluit* (Amsterdam: Olofsen), p. 219.

[2] Vivaldi. [3] Tomaso Albinoni (1671–1751).

[4] For some indication of the popularity of Corelli's Op. V, see Pincherle, *Corelli*, pp. 209–11.

[5] In giving an account of his arrival in Italy in 1724, Quantz notes that one of Vivaldi's operas had made the Lombardic style very popular in Rome shortly before, and that it took him some time to develop a liking for it. See Nettl, *Forgotten Musicians*, p. 299.

years almost completely deprived the above-mentioned celebrated violinist of good taste in both performance and composition.[1]

§ 59

The *second* of the two Lombardic violinists mentioned above[2] is one of the foremost, and one of the greatest, masters at performing difficult feats upon the violin. It is asserted that he withdrew completely from musical society for several years in order to produce an individual style of his own making. This style proved to be not only completely opposed to his own previous one in certain respects, but also impossible of imitation in singing; hence it remains peculiar to just those violinists who seem to have little feeling for the good and true singing style. Just as the first violinist sank into frivolity and eccentricity as a result of the multiplicity of his musical works, and as a result departed considerably from the style of others, the latter completely departed from everyone else in abandoning the singing style, or at least its good and pleasing qualities.[3] Hence the success of his compositions has not been equal to that of the works of the aforementioned composer. In them one finds nothing but dry, plain, and very common ideas, which, in any case, would be more suitable in comic rather than in serious music. His playing, to be sure, since it seems to be something new, excites much admiration among those who understand the instrument; the pleasure it excites, however, is proportionately less among the others. And since he has invented many different kinds of difficult bow-strokes which distinguish his execution from that of all others, various German violinists have, out of curiosity, come under his influence, to their own detriment. Many have adopted and retained his style, while others have abandoned it after a good singing style has given them a better idea of what is truly beautiful in music. Yet just as a copy rarely mirrors the original exactly, and we often mistakenly imagine that we hear a master in his pupils, estimating the former by the latter, to his detriment, so it may well be that some of the pupils of this celebrated violinist (and he has already trained a considerable number of them)[4] have

[1] Quantz's criticism of Vivaldi here should be read in the light of the enthusiastic account of his first acquaintanceship with Vivaldi's concertos in 1714 found in his autobiography. See the translator's Introduction, p. xiii.

→ [2] Tartini.

[3] Quantz seems to have heard Tartini only once, at Prague in 1723. In his autobiography he makes the following remarks about Tartini's playing at that time: 'Tartini was indeed one of the greatest violinists. He created a beautiful tone on his instrument, and had equal control of both hands and the bow. He mastered the greatest difficulties without great effort, playing with pure tone. Shakes, even double shakes, he could execute with all fingers equally well. He mixed double stops in fast as well as slow movements, and he liked to play in the very high register. Yet his execution was not moving, nor his style noble; in fact, it was quite contrary to good singing style. Locatelli and Piantanita resembled this famous violinist in many ways.' The translation in Nettl, *Forgotten Musicians*, pp. 297–8, has been modified in the light of the original in Kahl, *Selbstbiographien*, p. 128.

[4] Translator's parentheses.

contributed much to the unfavourable opinion we have of him. Perhaps they have not rightly understood his style, or, carried away by its unusual character, have made it still more bizarre, thus reproducing what they have learned from him in a much deteriorated form. Hence it is probable that he himself would not consider many things to be good that are found in various persons who pride themselves on playing in his style.

Every young musician should therefore be counselled not to go to Italy until he knows how to distinguish that which is good from that which is bad in music; for anyone who does not bring a little musical skill in with him is unlikely, particularly nowadays, to take anything out with him. In Italy, a beginning musician must always seek to profit more from the singers than from the instrumentalists. Anyone who is not misled by prejudice, however, will now find in Germany whatever he might have profited from formerly in Italy and France.

§ 60

I have not cited these two celebrated and, in more than one respect, worthy men to assess their merits, or to disparage the genuinely good things they have done. My only purpose has been to reveal to some extent the reason why present-day Italian instrumentalists, particularly violinists, have adopted a style so contrary to good singing style, although a style which is good and true ought to be universal. Some among them do not lack either knowledge of, or feeling for, that which pertains to good singing; yet they do not try to imitate it upon their instruments, finding that which they hold excellent among the singers too poor and too slight upon their own instruments. They praise the singer if he sings distinctly and expressively, but consider it good to play obscurely and without expression upon their instruments. They approve of the singer's modest and flattering execution, while their own is wild and eccentric. If the singer makes no more embellishments in the Adagio than the melody permits, they say that he sings masterfully; yet they themselves crowd the Adagio with so many graces and wild runs, that you would take it for a jocular Allegro, and can scarcely perceive the qualities of an Adagio in it any more.

§ 61

You also find that almost all of the modern Italian violinists play in the same style, and that as a result they do not show up to the best advantage in comparison with their predecessors. For them the bow-stroke, which, like the tongue-stroke on wind instruments, is the basis for lively musical articulation, often serves, like the wind-bag of a bagpipe, only to make the instrument sound like a hurdy-gurdy. They seek the greatest beauty at the very place where it is not to be found, to wit, the extremely high register, or at the end of the fingerboard; they climb about in the high register like somnambulists upon the rooftops, and meanwhile neglect the truly beautiful, depriving the instrument of the gravity and agreeableness which the thick strings are capable of giving it. The Adagio they play too boldly, the Allegro too lethargically. In the Allegro they consider the sawing out of a multitude of notes in a single bow-stroke to be some special achievement. They perform shakes either too quickly and in a tremulous manner, which they consider a defect in a singer, or use shakes in thirds. In a word, their execution and their method of playing is such that it sounds as if an able violinist were giving a comic imitation of an old-fashioned fiddler. In consequence listeners of good taste must often take great pains to conceal their laughter. And if fashionable Italian violinists of this sort are used as ripienists in an orchestra, they usually do more harm than good.

> Certain very renowned orchestras that have Italians among their members could be cited as examples. If in them you remark some unaccustomed disorder or lack of uniformity in the execution, it will usually stem from an Italian who plays without using either his eyes or his ears. If an orchestra suffers the misfortune of being led by an Italian like the one I have described here, you may anticipate with complete certainty that it will entirely lose its former lustre. Fortunate indeed is the orchestra that is not so burdened! It is astonishing, however, that Italian instrumentalists of the kind discussed here often receive approbation and protection from the very connoisseurs from whom one would least expect it, from musicians whose insight and refined taste are far too elevated to find pleasure in such a bizarre manner of playing. Frequently it may simply be the result of hypocrisy or some equally unintelligible reason.

§ 62

In the *composition of the modern Italian instrumentalists*, with few exceptions, more eccentricity and confused ideas are found than modesty, reason, and order. They seek to invent much that is new, but as a result lapse into many low and common passages which have little affinity with anything good that they may intermingle with them. They no longer produce such moving melodies as they did formerly. Their basses are neither majestic nor melodious, and have no particular connexion with the principal part. Neither the fruits of labour nor anything venturesome is apparent in their middle parts; you find simply dry harmony. And even in their solos they cannot endure a bass that occasionally has some melodic motion. They much prefer it if the bass moves along quite tediously, is but rarely heard, or always drums upon the same note. They pretend that in this fashion the soloist is least obscured. But perhaps they are ashamed to admit that they write the bass, or have it written, in this manner so that the virtuoso who is completely unacquainted with harmony and its rules does not so often run the risk of betraying his ignorance. They pay but little attention to the proportions of the work as a whole or to metrics. They take too much liberty in harmonic progression. They do not seek to express and intermingle the passions as is customary in vocal music. In a word, they have altered the style of their predecessors in instrumental music, but they have not improved it.

§ 63

In the *vocal composition of modern native Italians*, the voice part has the best role. They take the greatest pains with it; they make it comfortable for the singer, and not infrequently introduce charming fancies and expressions. But they also lapse frequently into that which is inferior and commonplace. The instrumental accompaniments are but little different from the instrumental composition described in the previous paragraph. The ritornello is usually very bad, and sometimes seems as if it does not belong to the aria at all. Correct metrics are also frequently absent. It is a pity that the majority of the modern Italian opera composers, some of whom undeniably have good natural talent, begin to write for the theatre at too early an age, and before they understand something of the rules of composition; that subsequently these composers no longer take the time to study the art of composition thoroughly, as their predecessors did; and that they are negligent in this regard, and ordinarily work too quickly. I am forced to acknowledge that they would be, perhaps, still worse if some great composers among their northern neighbours,[1] and especially a celebrated man[2] to whom they seem almost to have completely ceded the truly good and reasonable style in vocal music, had not provided them with good examples in his operas; these are frequently produced in Italy, and often give them the opportunity to deck themselves out in his feathers. It is certain that the company of good native-born Italian composers suffered a great loss about twenty years ago with the premature deaths in quick succession of three young composers who left traces of superior genius and promised much more. All three died before reaching full maturity. They were markedly different from one another in the way they thought. One was called *Capelli*.[3] He was disposed to the majestic, fiery, and unusual. Another was *Pergolesi*.[4] He had much talent for the flattering, tender, and agreeable, and demonstrated a considerable inclination towards elaborate composition. The third was called *Vinci*.[5] He was lively, rich in invention, agreeable, natural, and often very happy in expression; and as a result he quickly received general approbation throughout all Italy with a rather small number of operas. He seemed only to be somewhat lacking in the patience and the desire to correct his ideas with care.

§ 64

For the rest, if you separate the defects of the composers from their genuinely good qualities, you cannot deny that the Italians have skill in

[1] Lustig, in his Dutch translation of the *Versuch*, p. 223, indicates that Quantz refers to Handel and Hasse.

[2] There is little doubt that Quantz here means his friend Johann Adolph Hasse (1699–1783), who was very popular in Italy and Germany. For a brief discussion of Hasse's work, with further references, see D. J. Grout, *A Short History of Opera*, pp. 208–11.

[3] Giovanni Maria Capelli (d. 1726). During a visit to Parma in May 1726, Quantz heard Capelli's opera *I fratelli riconosciuti*.

[4] Giovanni Battista Pergolesi (1710–36).   [5] Leonardo Vinci (*c.* 1690–1730).

playing, insight into music, and richness in the invention of beautiful ideas, and that they have brought singing to a greater perfection than any other nation. It is a pity, however, that the majority of their instrumentalists have for some time departed so far from the style demanded by singing; in this way they have not only led astray many of the people who have tried to imitate them, but have also induced many singers to abandon good singing methods. Thus it is not unjustifiable to fear that the good style that the Italians have possessed heretofore in fuller measure than the majority of other peoples may gradually disappear, and may become entirely the property of others. Some reasonable Italian connoisseurs who are free of prejudice will admit this themselves. They will even allow that it has already happened in composition and in the manner of playing. Whatever the case may be, good singing style, which extends to a certain extent even to their gondoliers, remains peculiar to the Italians above all other peoples.

§ 65

Among the *French* the opposite of what I have said of the Italians is found.[1] For just as the Italians are almost too changeable in music, the French are too constant and slavish in it. They bind themselves all too closely to certain characteristics which are entirely appropriate for the dance and for drinking songs but not for more serious pieces, so that what is new among them often seems to be old. The *instrumentalists*, especially the *keyboard players*, do not ordinarily devote themselves to the performance of difficult feats, or to the use of many embellishments in the Adagio; yet they execute their pieces with much distinctness and accuracy, and thus at least do not spoil the good ideas of the composer. Because of their distinct execution, they make better ripienists in an orchestra than the Italians. It is therefore advisable for a beginning instrumentalist to commence with the French manner of playing. Through it he will learn not only to execute the notes and the little embellishments truly and distinctly as they are written, but also, with time, how to mingle French brilliance with Italian flattery, and acquire by this means an even more pleasing manner of playing.

§ 66

The *French manner of singing* is not designed, like the Italian, to train great virtuosos. It does not at all exhaust the capacities of the human voice. French arias have a spoken rather than a singing quality. They require facility of the tongue, for pronouncing the words, more than dexterity of the throat. That which should be added in the way of graces is prescribed by the composer; hence the performers do not have to understand harmony. They make hardly any use of passage-work, since they maintain

[1] For Quantz's account of his reactions to French music during his visit to Paris in 1726-7, see Nettl, *Forgotten Musicians*, pp. 309-11.

that their language does not allow it. As a result of the lack of good singers, their arias are mostly written so that anyone who wants to may sing them; this affords satisfaction to the amateurs of music who do not know much, but offers good singers no particular advantage. The only distinctive quality of their singers is their acting ability, in which they are superior to other peoples.

§ 67

The *French* proceed very scrupulously in *composition*. In their church compositions, to be sure, you find greater restraint than in those of the Italians, but also greater aridity. They prefer diatonic rather than chromatic progressions. In melody they are more straightforward than the Italians, for the sequence of the ideas can nearly always be divined, but they are less rich in invention. They are more concerned with the expression of the words than with a melody that charms or flatters. While the Italians seek for the most part to save the beauties of the composition for the principal part, so that the bass is sometimes neglected, the French, on the other hand, ordinarily place more emphasis on the bass than on the principal part. Their accompaniment tends to be plain rather than elevated. Their recitatives sing too much, and their arias too little, so that it is not always possible to divine in their operas whether a recitative or an arioso is being heard. If an *air tendre* follows a French recitative, you are completely lulled to sleep, and lose all attentiveness, although the ultimate design of opera should be to sustain the listener's interest constantly with an agreeable diversity, to transport him from one passion into another, and to drive the passions to a certain pitch of intensity and then allow them to subside. This cannot be effected entirely by the poet, without the aid of the composer. Yet what French operas lack in vivacity, because of the slight difference between arias and recitatives, is compensated for by their choruses and dances. In considering closely the arrangement of a French opera as a whole, one might be tempted to believe that the excessively uniform mixture of arias and recitatives was expressly contrived to set the choruses and ballets in greater relief. Although these elements, and the decorations of the theatre as well, are to be regarded only as subsidiary matters in an opera (the choruses in particular being of little moment in the Italian operas),[1] they are nevertheless almost the greatest ornament of the French operas. It is indisputable that the music of the French, when it is considered in all its perfection, is much better suited to the dance than any other, while that of the Italians, on the other hand, is more effective for singing and playing than for dancing. Yet it cannot be entirely denied that many pleasing and agreeable ideas are encountered in French instrumental music, especially in their characteristic pieces,[2] which, because of their coherent and harmonious melodies, may be intermingled very well with majestic and elevated ideas in the Italian style.

[1] Translator's parentheses.   [2] See Chapter XVII, Section VII, § 56.

§ 68

Not all Italian operas are pure masterpieces either, if they are considered as a whole. Although their foremost operatic poets have taken great pains, especially from the beginning of this century, to purge their operas of many extravagances, and to make them conform to the rational taste of the French tragic theatre as much as possible; and although Italy may point to a number of beautiful and perfect operatic poems, while the French, on the contrary, still cling to fables, and delight in a number of unnatural and quixotic displays, many poets, as well as composers and singers, still commit grave errors in Italy. The poets, for example, do not always join the arias to the main subject, so that many that do not have a proper connexion with what preceded them seem to be shoved in at random. At times some of the poets may have lacked judgement or feeling, but at other times they may have been forced to write to please the composer. Or the poetry may fail for other reasons: the words, through the fault of the poet, may be unsuitable for a musical setting; or perhaps the composer has already completed an aria in which the words are inappropriate for the situation, and the poet must therefore invent new ones, a practice that, in truth, does not always prove to be successful. Sometimes the poet has only to find words provided with vowels that are suitable for passage-work; but if the poet is not rich in variety of thought and expression, the piece may lack coherence, and the beauty of the idea may suffer. You will notice that the great opera poets, with the single exception of *Metastasio*,[1] ordinarily make arias far less convenient for musical settings than the mediocre ones. The latter must accommodate the composer if they wish to prosper, while the former, believing themselves too lofty, often refuse to condescend at all in matters just and necessary for the benefit of the music. It is, however, certainly possible for poetry and music to be united without detriment to either, as has just recently been demonstrated with particular thoroughness in a German work, *Von der musikalischen Poesie*.[2]

§ 69

The French charge, not without some foundation, that the Italians indiscriminately introduce too much passage-work in their arias. It is certainly true that if the sense of the words permits, and the singer possesses the capacity to produce passage-work in a lively, equal, round, and distinct manner, it is an exceptional ornament in singing. But it is not to be denied that the Italians sometimes go too far in this respect, and make no distinction between different words, and between different singers, ordinarily following the established custom without exercising any judgement. It

---

[1] Pietro Antonio Domenico Bonaventura Metastasio (1698–1782), the most highly esteemed opera poet of the eighteenth century.

[2] Christian Gottfried Krause's treatise *Von der musikalischen Poesie* (Berlin: Voss, 1752). Krause was a friend of Quantz, who probably knew the work before it was actually published.

seems that originally passage-work was introduced so frequently only to oblige some good singers, and to show the dexterity of their throats. Afterwards an abuse grew up, and it was imagined that an aria without passage-work is not beautiful, or that a singer does not sing well or is completely worthless if he does not know how to produce much difficult passage-work like an instrumentalist, without reflecting whether the text permits it or not. Nothing is more absurd than putting many passages in a so-called aria of action,[1] in which a high degree of sentiment should be present, whether plaintive or furious, and in which a declamatory rather than a singing style should prevail. Passage-work interrupts and destroys all expression of the sentiment, and is also impracticable for many singers. Singers who have the capacity to produce passage-work roundly and distinctly, with all the force, and *none of the defects*, of the voice, are rare. On the other hand, many singers may be good without possessing this skill or natural gift. Great application and special practice are necessary to achieve facility in passage-work. But those singers to whom, in spite of all their application, nature denies this facility, ought to devote their time to something that is better, that is also frequently neglected, namely, singing tastefully and expressively, instead of martyring themselves with passage-work in order to be fashionable. From the excessive desire to sing passage-work the further evil frequently arises that for the sake of some singers whom it would be imprudent to offend, the composer and the poet are denied the freedom to think rationally. Yet it seems that nowadays the prevailing lack of accomplished singers in most of Italy often places almost too narrow limits on passage-work.

§ 70

There may be many other reasons why not all operas are written reasonably and well in Italy. If the invention and execution of the poet is wholly worthless, with all the subjects completely unsuited for music, even the best composer may fail, because he is not fired by the poetry. But even if the poet devotes all his powers to producing something good, his composition may still not receive the expected applause, since the majority, sometimes mistakenly, attribute the success or lack of success of an opera not to the poet, but entirely to the composer, ignoring the fact that one must contribute as much as the other if the opera is to be perfect. A good subject for an opera, well treated by the poet, may enhance mediocre music, and a subject that is poorly treated may make music that is very well set to it vexatious and boring when heard frequently, especially if the singers and accompanists do not fulfil their duties properly.

§ 71

If an Italian opera, or one arranged in the Italian manner, is to please everyone, and is to be held a most agreeable spectacle, it must have the

---

[1] The French version reads 'an aria in which a violent passion is represented'.

following characteristics. The poet must choose a good subject, and treat it with all possible verisimilitude. He must clearly distinguish the characters of the persons represented from each other, and adjust them as much as possible to the capacities, ages, temperaments, and mien of the singers. He must make each speak in a manner suitable to the character he represents. The recitatives must not be too extended, and the words of the arias must be neither too long nor too bombastic. From time to time some similes should be introduced that may be conveniently expressed in music, and these should be chiefly and necessarily from the language of the passions. The passions must be varied in an adroit manner, both with respect to the augmentation and diminution of their force, and with respect to general diversity. Convenient forms of verse must be chosen for the arias. Reasonable care must be taken to employ words especially suitable for singing, and to avoid as much as possible those that are unsuitable. The composer must have a refined taste, and the capacity to express the passions in accordance with the words. He must, without partiality, give each singer the role which accords with his strong points. He must join everything together with the proper coherence, and at the same time observe a suitable brevity. The singers must perform their roles seriously and diligently, in accordance with the characters to be represented, and the intention of the composer. The accompanists must fulfil the prescriptions of the composer, and discharge their duties properly. Finally, the décor and the ballets must accord well with the content of the opera.

§ 72

Neither an Italian nor a Frenchman can pass proper judgements upon these matters, however, especially if he has never left his own country, and if he has always been accustomed to only one style of music. Each will consider the best that which accords with his native style, and will scorn everything else. Long custom, or deep-rooted prejudice, will constantly hinder each in comprehending the good qualities of the opposite faction, and the bad of his own. A third person, if he possesses insight and knowledge and is impartial, can decide the issue most justly.

§ 73

In Italy, to my knowledge, neither French operas nor French arias or other vocal pieces have ever been performed either in public or in private; much less have French singers been imported. In France, on the other hand, although no Italian operas are performed in public, Italian arias, concertos, trios, solos, &c., are privately performed, and Italian singers are brought in and supported, to which fact the *Concert Italien* at the Tuileries[1] and other more recent events bear witness. The king has several

---

[1] Quantz here seems to mean the series of concerts founded in 1724 by Mme de Prie. See M. Brenet, *Les Concerts en France sous l'ancien régime* (Paris: Fischbacher, 1900), pp. 162–5.

Italian singers in his chapel, and Louis XIV took the famous Pacchini into his service.[1] In Germany both French and Italian operas were performed more than seventy years ago, and other pieces fashioned in both styles were performed long before that in public and in private. Hence use was also made of Italian and French singers. But since the Italians continued to perfect their style, while that of the French remained stationary, neither French operas nor other compositions of this type, with the exception of ballets, have been heard in Germany for about twenty or thirty years. Both operas and instrumental pieces written in the Italian style still meet with approval, not only in all Germany, but also in Spain, Portugal, England, Poland, and Russia. The majority of the peoples of Europe, and particularly the Germans, love all the good things the French have produced, their language, writings, poetry, etiquette, customs, and fashions; but their music is no longer loved as of old, except by some young people who make their first foreign excursion to France, who there perhaps begin to play an instrument, and find French music more comfortable to perform than Italian.

§ 74

It is true that attempts have been made for twenty-odd years, especially in Paris, to mix the Italian style with the French.[2] But till now no particular indications of good results are to be found. In vocal music the excuse is always made that the language is not suitable for the Italian manner of singing. But it may be that able composers and good singers were lacking to carry out the task properly. Both German and English words, which are even less esteemed among the French, have been set successfully to music in the Italian style; why, then, is it not possible to do the same with the very popular French language? To disabuse the French of this prejudice, an aria should be fashioned to French words by a composer who knows how to write a beautiful aria in the Italian style, and who understands the French language as well as the Italian; and this should be sung by a good Italian singer who also has good French pronunciation. This would show whether the language or the ignorance of French composers is at fault, and whether Italian music really will not suit the French language.

§ 75

In instrumental music the French might make more progress if they had among them good models from other nations for both composition and performance; or if their composers, singers, and instrumentalists were more inclined to visit other countries, in order to develop a reasonable

[1] This sentence appears only in the French text.

[2] Here Quantz seems to have operatic style specifically in mind. In his autobiography he mentions that *Pyrame e Thisbé* of Francœur and Rebel, which he heard in Paris in 1726, showed signs of foreign influence, particularly the portions by Francœur. See Nettl, *Forgotten Musicians*, p. 310.

mixture in their style. Yet as long as they allow themselves to be governed by prejudices in favour of their own country, having in their country no truly genuine and good examples from the Italians[1] or other peoples who compose, sing, and play in a mixed style; and as long as they do not seek to acquire this mixed style in other countries, they will remain just as they have been for a long time past. Otherwise, if they wish to introduce something new, it is to be feared that, because of the lack of good models, they will eventually lapse from excessive modesty into an even more excessive boldness, and transform the neat and distinct execution that has always been peculiar to them into a bizarre and obscure manner of playing. Usually we do not devote sufficient time to the investigation of new and unknown things; we tend to go from one extreme to another, especially when the option depends upon young people, who can be dazzled by anything new.

§ 76

If, finally, one wished to characterize briefly the national music of the Italians and the French, considering each from its best side, and contrast the differences in their styles, this comparison would, in my opinion, turn out something like this:

In *composition* the *Italians* are unrestrained, sublime, lively, expressive, profound, and majestic in their manner of thinking; they are rather bizarre, free, daring, bold, extravagant, and sometimes negligent in metrics; they are also singing, flattering, tender, moving, and rich in invention. They write more for the connoisseur than for the amateur. In *composition* the *French* are indeed lively, expressive, natural, pleasing and comprehensible to the public, and more correct in metrics than the Italians; but they are neither profound nor venturesome. They are very limited and slavish, always imitating themselves, stingy in their manner of thinking, and dry in invention. They always warm up the ideas of their predecessors; and they write more for the amateur than for the connoisseur.

The *Italian manner of singing* is profound and artful; it at once moves and excites admiration; it stimulates the musical intellect; it is pleasing, charming, expressive, rich in taste and expression, and transports the listeners in an agreeable manner from one passion into another. The *French manner of singing* is more simple than artful, more spoken than sung, more forced than natural in the expression of the passions and in the use of the voice; in style and expression it is poor, and always uniform; it is more for amateurs than for connoisseurs; it is better suited to drinking songs than to serious arias, diverting the senses, but leaving the musical intellect completely idle.

[1] Quantz was either not fully aware of the extent of Italian influence on French instrumental music, or the extent of Italian influence was not as apparent to him as it is to the modern scholar who looks back at the period.

The *Italian manner of playing* is arbitrary, extravagant, artificial, obscure, frequently bold and bizarre, and difficult in execution; it permits many additions of graces, and requires a seemly knowledge of harmony; but among the ignorant it excites more admiration than pleasure. The *French manner of playing* is slavish, yet modest, distinct, neat and true in execution, easy to imitate, neither profound nor obscure, but comprehensible to everyone, and convenient for amateurs; it does not require much knowledge of harmony, since the embellishments are generally prescribed by the composer; but it gives the connoisseurs little to reflect upon.

In a word, Italian music is arbitrary, and French is circumscribed. If it is to have a good effect, the French depends more upon the composition than the performance, while the Italian depends upon the performance almost as much as upon the composition, and in some cases almost more.

The Italian manner of singing is to be preferred to that of their playing and the French manner of playing to that of their singing.

§ 77

The qualities of these two styles could, of course, be described still more fully, and investigated more thoroughly. But that would belong more properly to a separate treatise devoted entirely to this subject. I have only attempted to note briefly the most important facts and characteristics concerning them. Each person may conclude for himself from the above description which of the two styles justly deserves the preference. I am sure that the fairness of my readers will not allow them to accuse me of any partiality in this regard, since I have travelled through these two countries with the express intention of profiting from that which is good in the music of both, and what I say about both styles is based on the evidence of my own eyes and ears.

§ 78

If *German music* for more than a century past is examined closely, it will be found that the Germans had fairly long ago attained considerable proficiency in correct harmonic composition, and in playing many types of instruments. With the exception of a few old church airs, however, few indications of good style and few beautiful melodies will be found. Both their style and their melodies were rather flat, dry, meagre, and paltry for a longer time than those of their neighbours.

§ 79

Their *composition*, as already stated, was harmonious and rich in full chords, but was neither melodious nor charming.

They sought to compose in an artful rather than in a comprehensible and pleasing manner, more for the eye than for the ear.

In an elaborate composition the very early composers introduced too many cadences in succession with no necessity for them; they hardly ever modulated from one key into another without cadencing beforehand, a forthright habit, but one which seldom surprises the ear.

Their ideas lacked discrimination and coherence.

Exciting and quieting the passions were things unknown to them.

§ 80

In their *vocal music* they sought to express the individual words rather than their total sense and the sentiment they contained. There were many who believed that they had done all they needed to do if, for example, they had expressed the words heaven and hell through use of the extreme high and low registers; accordingly, much that was ludicrous used to creep in. In vocal pieces they particularly loved the extreme high register, and constantly obliged the singers to pronounce words in it. The falsetto voices of the adult males, for whom the low register is ordinarily troublesome, may have given some occasion for this. The singers were given many words to pronounce in succession during quick notes, which is contrary to the nature of good singing, prevents the singer from producing the tones with their proper beauty, and is too little different from common speech.* Their vocal airs, consisting mostly of two repeated sections, were very short, and also very simple and dry.

* Although a few Germans, by imitating the Italian style, have cast aside this defect, which is a virtue only in comic music, it is still not completely rooted out at the present time.

What the German manner of singing was like in times past may still be perceived today from the singers in choirs and schools in most of the towns. These singers are better versed in note-reading than many *galant* singers of other nations, but they hardly know how to manage the voice at all. Thus as a rule they sing with a uniform volume of tone, without light and shade. They are hardly cognizant of those defects of the voice that stem from the nose and throat. Joining the chest voice to the falsetto is as unknown to them as it is to the French. As to the shake, they content themselves with what nature provides. They have little feeling for Italian flattery, which is effected by slurred notes and by diminishing and strengthening the tone. Their disagreeable, forced, and exceedingly noisy chest attacks, in which they make vigorous use of the faculty of the Germans for pronouncing the *h*, singing ha-ha-ha-ha for each note, make all the passage-work sound hacked up, and are far removed from the Italian manner of executing passage-work with the chest voice. They do not tie the parts of the plain air to one another sufficiently, or join them together with retarding notes [appoggiaturas]; in consequence, their execution sounds very dry and plain. These German choir singers lack neither good voices nor the capacity to learn; they lack good instruction. The cantors, because of the school duties bound up with their position, are also supposed to be partly scholars. Hence, in choosing them, more attention is often paid to the latter prerequisite than to their knowledge of music. The cantors chosen in accordance with such views deal with music, about which they really know very little, as a purely secondary matter. They desire nothing more than an early release, in the form of a fat country parsonage, from their school and musical duties. Even if a cantor is found here and there who understands his duties, and wants to administer his musical office honestly, at many places the authorities of the school (not excepting some of its spiritual overseers, among whom many are hostile to music) seek to hinder the practice of music. And even in those schools which, as their laws attest, have been established principally with the aim that music should be taught and learned, and *musici eruditi* should be trained, the rector supported by the directors is often the most open enemy of music. Being a good Latin scholar does not necessarily go hand in hand with being a good musician. At many places—indeed, at the majority—the advantages associated with the duties of a cantor are so slight that a good musician must have scruples about accepting such service, except of necessity. Because of this lack of good instruction in Germany, particularly in vocal music, and also because of the insurmountable obstacles placed in its way at many places, good singers cannot be trained easily. In these circumstances, it is to be supposed that good singing style may never become as general among the Germans as among the Italians, who have had the best institutions in this respect for a long time past; that is, unless the great lords advance money to found singing schools in which the good and genuine Italian manner of singing is taught.

§ 81

In former times most of the *instrumental music of the Germans* looked very confusing and hazardous on paper, since they wrote many notes with three, four, and more crooks. But since they performed them at a very deliberate speed, their pieces still sounded flat and indolent rather than lively.

They thought more highly of difficult pieces than of easy ones, and sought to excite admiration rather than to please.

They were more intent upon recreating the songs of birds, for example those of the cuckoo, the nightingale, the hen, the quail, &c., than upon imitating the human voice. The trumpet and the hurdy-gurdy were also not forgotten.[1]

Frequently their most agreeable pastime was a so-called quodlibet in which, in vocal pieces, ridiculous words with no connexion occurred, or, in instrumental pieces, the tunes of common and vulgar drinking songs were mixed together.

The Germans played the violin harmonically rather than melodically. They wrote many pieces for which the violin had to be retuned, that is, the strings had to be tuned in seconds, thirds, or fourths, instead of fifths, in accordance with the indications of the composer.[2] This makes the chords easier, but causes not a little difficulty in the passage-work.

Their instrumental pieces consisted mainly of sonatas, partitas, intradas, marches, *Gassenhauern*,[3] and many other often absurd characteristic pieces, which are no longer remembered.

[1] As A. Schering points out, Quantz probably had J. J. Walther's *Scherzi da violino solo con il basso continuo* (1676) and *Hortulus chelicus* (1688) in mind. He mentions Walther among the composers whose works he studied during his apprenticeship. See Schering's edition of the *Versuch*, p. 256.

[2] Quantz here describes the practice known as *scordatura*. It was employed by Heinrich Biber (1644–1704), among others. Quantz also cites Biber among the composers whose works he studied as an apprentice.

[3] *Gassenhauern* at this time were apparently popular songs arranged for instruments. C. P. E. Bach, *Essay*, p. 31, is very critical of keyboard pieces given this name.

The Allegro usually consisted exclusively of passage-work from beginning to end, nearly every bar like the next. These passages were repeated from one key to another by transposition, and in the end must certainly have caused aversion. Pieces were often written that remained in the same tempo for only a few bars, while slower and quicker sections alternated in the same movement.

Their Adagio had more of natural harmony than good melody. They also made few graces in it, other than filling out the leaps from time to time with running notes. The closes of their slow pieces were very simple. Instead of taking the shake on B or D to conclude on C, for example, as at present, they struck it on the C, to which they gave the time of a dotted note, then sounded the B by itself as a short note; but, as a special kind of ornament, a note standing a tone higher than the concluding note was slurred to it. Their cadences were realized in performance approximately as illustrated in Tab. XXIII, Fig. 15.[1]

FIG. 15

They knew little or nothing of retarding notes [appoggiaturas], which serve to bind the melody together and to transform the consonances into dissonances in an agreeable manner; in consequence, their manner of playing was flat and dry rather than moving or charming.

Instruments of all kinds, the names of which are hardly even known at present, were in use among them. Thus it is to be supposed, on account of their diversity, that there was more occasion to admire their industry in playing than their skill.

§ 82

Bad as the style of German singers and instrumentalists appears to have been in former times (despite the thorough insight of the German composers into harmony),[2] it did gradually take on a new aspect. Even if it cannot be said that the Germans have produced an individual style entirely different from that of other nations, they are all the more capable in taking whatever they like from another style, and they know how to make use of the good things in all types of foreign music.

§ 83

Toward the middle of the last century there were already some celebrated persons who began to effect the improvement of musical style, partly by visiting and profiting from Italy and France themselves, partly by imitating the works and the taste of these meritorious foreign lands. The

[1] As yet no other references or examples have been located which throw any light on the curious practice described and illustrated here.   [2] Translator's parentheses.

organ and harpsichord players, especially *Froberger*[1] and after him *Pachelbel*[2] among the latter, and *Reinken*,[3] *Buxtehude*,[4] *Bruhns*,[5] and some others among the former, wrote almost the first very tasteful instrumental pieces of their time for their instruments. In particular *the art of playing the organ*, inherited in large part from the Netherlanders, had already been carried a long way at about this time by the able men enumerated above and by some others. Finally the admirable *Johann Sebastian Bach* in more recent times brought it to its greatest perfection.[6] We should hope that, with his death, it will not suffer decay or ruin because of the small number of those who apply themselves to it.

It cannot be denied that at present there are many good keyboard [harpsichord and clavichord] players among the Germans, but *good organists* are now much rarer than formerly. It is true that here and there a few worthy and able organists are still to be found. Yet it is also just as certain that we frequently hear the organ abused, even in many of the principal churches of large towns, by wretches authorized by formal nomination who hardly deserve to be bagpipers in village taverns. Such unworthy organists are so lacking in any understanding of composition that they cannot even devise a harmonious and correct bass for the melody of a chorale, much less hit upon two correct middle parts besides. They do not even know the simple melodies of the chorales. Often the bleating schoolboys in the streets are their preceptors and models, in imitation of whose defects they spoil the melodies anew each month. Between keyboard [as above] and organ they make no distinction. The treatment peculiar to the organ is as unknown to them as the manner of making a suitable prelude before a chorale, although there is no lack of engraved and manuscript models from which they could learn both if they so desired. They prefer ideas of their own cooked up on the spur of the moment to the best organ pieces, worked out with reason and reflection, by celebrated men. Instead of keeping the chorale in order, they mislead the congregation with clumsy coloraturas, worthy of a bagpiper, which they din forth during each caesura of a chorale. Of the manner in which the pedals should be used, many have not heard a thing. Among many, the left foot and the little finger of the left hand are so closely connected with one another that one is not trusted to strike a note without the fore-knowledge and agreement of the other. I will say nothing of the frequency with which a poorly performed church composition is made even worse by a miserable accompaniment. What a pity it would be if Germany were gradually to lose the advantage of possessing good organ players. To be sure, the much too small wages at most places provide a poor inducement for application to the science of organ playing. And certainly many able organists will be disgusted by the arrogance and obstinacy of some of their spiritual overlords.

§ 84

The most notable epoch in the improvement of German taste, particularly in the composition of vocal music, may be placed around the year

[1] Johann Jakob Froberger (1616–67).   [2] Johann Pachelbel (1653–1706).
[3] Jan Adams Reinken (1623–1722).   [4] Dietrich Buxtehude (*c.* 1637–1707).
[5] Nickolaus Bruhns (1665–97). For brief discussions of these composers, see Bukofzer, *Music in the Baroque Era*, pp. 108–11, 265–8. Editions of their music are listed in the same work, pp. 464–9.
[6] C. P. E. Bach attests to the fact that Quantz heard J. S. Bach while Quantz was still in Dresden. See G. Norman and M. L. Schrifte, *Letters of Composers* (New York: Knopf, 1946), pp. 41–42. Quantz was also probably on hand when J. S. Bach visited Potsdam in 1747. On Bach's manner of striking the keys, see Chapter XVII, Section VI, § 18.

1693. At that time, Mr. *Mattheson*, whose distinguished talents in the defence of music and in its history are well known, reports in his *Der musikalische Patriot*, pp. 181 and 343,[1] that the chapel-master *Cousser*[2] introduced the new or Italian manner of singing into operas at Hamburg. At about the same time the celebrated *Reinhard Keiser*[3] began to distinguish himself with his operatic compositions. The latter seems to have been born with an agreeable disposition for singing and a rich inventiveness, and thus enhanced the new manner of singing in a most advantageous way. Good taste in music in Germany undeniably has much for which to thank him. The operas which, after this time, flourished for a rather long period at Hamburg and Leipzig, and the celebrated composers who, jointly with *Keiser*, worked for them from time to time, prepared the way well for the present degree of good taste in music in Germany, in spite of often bad and not infrequently vulgar texts. It might be judged superfluous if I were to name here all the great men in the times just indicated, some now deceased, others still alive, who became celebrated among the Germans both for church, theatrical, and instrumental composition, and for playing upon instruments. I am sure that all of them are already so well known in and out of Germany that their names will occur at once and without much difficulty to my music-loving readers. It is certain that those who stand out in the music of our times deserve the greatest thanks.

§ 85

Even with all these efforts by worthy musicians, however, different obstacles were found in the path of good taste. Often little attempt was made to give the inventions of these celebrated men their merited approbation, and to cherish them as they deserved. At many places people did not concern themselves about good taste at all, but remained attached to older ways. And, furthermore, there were various adversaries who, possessed of an absurd love for the old, believed that they had sufficient grounds to reject everything as extravagances in the excellent productions of the said men simply because they departed from the old mode. It was not so long ago that they still defended the old style, their fervour as great as their grounds were weak. Many persons who might have had the desire to learn did not have the means either to travel to the places where music flourished, or to order musical pieces from them. It is undeniable that the introduction of the cantata style in the churches of the Protestants was particularly advantageous to good taste. But how much opposition had to be overcome before cantatas and oratorios could secure a sure foothold in the church? Only a few years ago there were cantors who, after more than fifty years in office, could not have been brought to perform a church

---

[1] Johann Mattheson, *Der musikalische Patriot* (Hamburg, 1728).
[2] Johann Sigismund Cousser (Kusser) (1660–1727).
[3] 1674–1739. For a discussion of the works of Cousser and Keiser, with references to articles and music, see Grout, *A Short History of Opera*, pp. 121, 151–6.

composition of *Telemann*. Thus it is not surprising if one encounters good music at one place in Germany, and altogether tasteless and unseasoned music at another. And a foreigner who, unfortunately, has heard music at one of the latter places, and forms a similar judgement of all German music, certainly cannot have the most flattering conceptions of it.

§ 86

The Italians used to call the German style in music *un gusto barbaro, a barbarous style*. This prejudice gradually diminished, however, after it came to pass that some German composers went to Italy, and there had the opportunity to perform both their operas and instrumental works with approbation; the operas there that have the greatest vogue at present, and indeed justifiably so, issue from the quill of a German.[1] Yet it must be said that the Germans have much for which to thank the Italians and, in part, the French, with respect to this advantageous change in their style. It is well known that Italian and French composers, singers, and instrumentalists have been in service at various German courts, such as those in Vienna, Dresden, Berlin, Hanover, Munich, Ansbach, &c., and have performed operas at them for a century past. It is also well known that some great lords have let many of their musicians journey to Italy and France, and, as stated above, that many of the reformers of German taste have visited one or both of these lands. They have appropriated the style of one as well as the other, and have struck a mixture that has enabled them to compose, and to perform with great applause, not only German, but also Italian, French, and English operas and other *Singspiele*,[2] each in its language and style. The same can be said of neither Italian nor French musicians. The reason is not because they lack the talent to do it, but because they take few pains to learn foreign languages, are too taken in by prejudice, and cannot be persuaded that anything good can be produced in vocal music without their style and language.

§ 87

If one has the necessary discernment to choose the best from the styles of different countries, a *mixed style* results that, without overstepping the bounds of modesty, could well be called *the German style*, not only because the Germans came upon it first, but because it has already been established at different places in Germany for many years, flourishes still, and displeases in neither Italy nor France, nor in other lands.

§ 88

If *the German nation* does not again depart from this taste; if it endeavours, as till now its most celebrated composers have done, to make continued

[1] Quantz again refers to Hasse.

[2] Quantz uses the term *Singspiele* to indicate any kind of vocal work for the stage, and not exclusively for German comic operas with spoken dialogue.

progress in it; if its *young composers* take more pains than they unfortunately now do to learn the rules of composition thoroughly, like their predecessors, and to acquire the mixed taste; if they do not content themselves with pure melody and the fashioning of theatrical arias, but also exercise themselves both in the church style and in instrumental music; if in respect to the ordering of their pieces and the reasonable union and mixture of their ideas, they follow the models of composers who have received universal approbation; if they imitate the manner of composing and the refinement of taste [of these composers] without decking themselves out in another's plumes, and perhaps copying out or warming up the principal subject or even the whole sequence of ideas of this composer or that; if, on the contrary, these young composers make use of their own imaginations to demonstrate and to cultivate their talents without prejudice to others, so that they do not remain for ever copyists, but become [genuine] composers; if *the German instrumentalists* do not allow themselves to be led astray by a bizarre and comical style (explained above in connexion with the Italians),[1] but take as models the good manner of singing and those who play in a reasonable style; if, furthermore, the *Italians* and the *French* imitate the Germans in their mixture of styles, as the Germans have imitated them in their styles; if, I say, all these things are unanimously observed, in time *a good style—that is universal* can be introduced in music. And this is not so improbable, since neither the Italians nor the French—the musical amateurs more than the professional musicians among them—are now completely satisfied with their pure national styles. They have, for some time, shown more pleasure in certain foreign compositions than in those of their own country.

§ 89

In a style that, like that of the Germans today, consists of a mixture of those of different peoples, each nation finds something with which it has an affinity, and which thus can never displease it. In reflecting upon all of the thoughts and experiences mentioned previously in reference to the differences between styles, a preference must be granted for the pure Italian style over the pure French. Since, however, the first is no longer as solidly grounded as it used to be, having become bold and bizarre, and since the second has remained too simple, everyone will agree that a style blended and mixed together from the good elements of both must certainly be more universal and more pleasing. For a style of music that is received and approved by many peoples, and not just by a single land, a single province, or a particular nation, a style of music that, for the above reasons, can only meet with approbation, must, if it is also founded on sound judgement and healthy feeling, be the very best.

[1] Translator's parentheses.

A CHAMBER CONCERT

From an engraving by G. F. Schmidt in the first German and French editions of the *Essay of a Method for Playing the Transverse Flute*

BIBLIOGRAPHY

THE following bibliography is divided into two parts. In the first all the known versions of Quantz's *Essay*, or of excerpts from it, are listed. The citations are grouped by the country of origin and by the order of appearance within each country. All other works mentioned in the introduction and in the notes to the translation are listed alphabetically in Part II. For reasons of space, all the works that are relevant to various portions of the treatise cannot be set down here. For further references to works on almost every phase of performance practice, the excellent bibliography in Robert Donington's *The Interpretation of Early Music* is strongly recommended. A number of the other works cited contain more specialized bibliographies. Eighteenth-century treatises that have already been translated are listed here only in their translated versions, since these are the most likely to be used, and information about the original texts is easily accessible.

PART I

The Essay: Editions, Excerpts, and Borrowings

Germany and Austria

1. Johann Joachim Quantzens, / Königl. Preußischen Kammermusikus, / Versuch einer Anweisung / die / Flöte traversiere / zu spielen; / mit verschiedenen, / zur Beförderung des guten Geschmackes / in der praktischen Musik / dienlichen Anmerkungen / begleitet, / und mit Exempeln erläutert. / Nebst xxiv. Kupfertafeln. / Berlin, / bey Johann Friedrich Voß. 1752. Reissued in an abridged version, edited by Arnold Schering (Leipzig: C. F. Kahnt, 1906 and 1926).

2. Essai d'une methode / pour apprendre à jouer / de la / flute traversiere, / avec ← plusieurs remarques / pour servir au bon gout / dans la musique / le tout eclairci par des exemples / et par / XXIV. tailles douces / par / Jean Joachim Quantz / musicien de la chambre de sa majesté le roi / de prusse. / à Berlin, / chez Chretien Frederic Voss 1752. As is sometimes overlooked, this French translation was issued in Germany rather than in France. That Quantz himself was responsible for having the work translated is indicated in an added paragraph in the French preface. Albert Quantz reports having seen an edition of the *XXIV tailles douces* dating from 1765, but no copy of the work bearing that date has yet been located.

3. Application pour la flûte traversière, avec deux clefs, dont la petite est marquée avec le ♭, et la courbée avec le ♯. No copy of this elusive work has been discovered. It may have been a reprint of Chapter III of the *Essay*, or of Quantz's fingering charts. Gerber, in his *Historisch-biographisches Lexikon*, ii, p. 215, indicates that it was published about 1760, but that he had not seen a copy of it. It is also listed in Forkel's *Allgemeine Litteratur der Musik*, p. 322.

4. 'Discours des Herrn Quanz über das Clavieraccompagnement', in F. W. Marpurg's *Clavierstücke mit einem practischen Unterricht für Anfänger und Geübter*, part 3 (Berlin: Haude und Spener, 1763). This article is an unmodified reprint of Chapter XVII, Section VI, of the *Essay*. It has been reprinted in *Monatshefte für Musikgeschichte*, xvi (1884), pp. 120 ff.

5. 'Anweisung, wie ein Musikus und eine Musik zu beurtheilen sey', in Schiebler and Eschenberg's *Unterhaltungen* (Hamburg: Michael Christian Bock), ix (1770), pp. 445–83, and x (1770), pp. 3–38. This article is a reprint, without any alterations, of the entire eighteenth chapter of the *Essay*. The first instalment contains paragraphs 1–51, the second, paragraphs 52–89.

6. Second unrevised German edition of the entire treatise, under the same title as in 1, but issued by Johann Friedrich Korn the elder in Breslau, 1780.

7. The second edition of Johann Samuel Petri's *Anleitung zur praktischen Musik* (Leipzig: J. G. I. Breitkopf, 1782) reproduces Chapter IX, paragraphs 7–13 (on shakes) exactly, and also Quantz's fingering charts. Petri's remaining material on the flute is more freely based on Quantz's first nine chapters.

8. Gründliche Anleitung / die Flöte zu spielen / nach / Quanzens Anweisung. / Herausgegeben / von Franz Anton Schlegel. / Graz / bei F. G. Weingand und Fr. Ferstl. / 1788. A considerably abridged and freely modified version of the first sixteen chapters of the *Essay*.

9. Third unaltered German edition of the full *Essay*, again issued by Johann Friedrich Korn the elder, Breslau, 1789. *Dritte Auflage* is merely substituted by *Zweyter Auflage* on the title page. This edition has been reprinted in facsimile in the series 'Documenta musicologica' (Kassel: Bärenreiter, 1952).

10. Kleines Handbuch / der / Musiklehre / und vorzüglich der / Querflöte. / Aus den besten Quellen geschöpft / von Andreas Dauscher. / Mit Tabellen. / Kempten, 1801. Im Verlag bey Thomas Brack. This little tutor makes use of brief extracts from Quantz's introduction, his discussions of embouchure, posture, fingering, and the three chapters on execution. It also draws on the works of Tromlitz and Sulzer.

Holland

→ 1. Grondig Onderwys / Van den Aardt en de regte Behandeling / der / Dwarsfluit; / Verzeld met eenen / Treffelyken Regelenschat / van de / Compositie / En van de / Uitvoering / der voornaamste Muzyk-stukken, op de / Gebruikelykste Instrumenten; / Door lange ondervinding en schrandere opmerking, / in de Groote Muzykaale Wereld, verzameld / door / Johann Joachim Quantz, / Kamer-Musicus van Zyne Koninglyke Majesteit / van Pruissen. / Uit he Hoogduitsche vertaald / door / Jacob Wilhelm Lustig, / Organist van Martini Kerk te Groningen. / Te Amsteldam / By A. Olofsen, Boek- en Muziekverkooper, / in de Grave Straat, by de Voorburgwal. 1754. A full translation of the *Essay*, except for the omission of the dedication and Chapter V. The translator has added a lengthy and interesting preface of his own.

2. Grondig Onderwys / Van den Aardt en regte Behandeling / der Dwarsfluyt, / door lange ondervindige en schrandere opmerkinge / in der groote

Muzykaale Waereld, verzaameld / door / Johann Joachim Quantz, / Kamer-Musicus van Zyn Koninglyke Majesteit van Pruissen. / Met eene voor-treffelyke Inleidinge, nopens de Hoedanigheid in / iemand die zich tot de Muziek denkt to begeven, vereischt werdt. / Uit het Hoogduits na het echte Origeel door den / Kenner der Muziek J. W. L. vertaalt. / Met 21 Cierlyke op Koopere gesnidene Plaaten. / T'Amsterdam, / By A. Olofsen, Boek- en Musiekverkoper, aan de Nieuwe Kerk, over de Vooburgwal. An unaltered reprint of the introduction and first eleven chapters of Lustig's full translation, with a new title-page. No date is given. Dayton C. Miller suggests about 1765.

England

1. Easy and / Fundamental / Instructions / Whereby either vocal or instru-mental Performers / unacquainted with Composition, may from the mere / knowledge of the most common intervals in Music, / learn how to introduce / Extempore Embellishments or Variations; / as also / Ornamental Cadences, / with Propriety, Taste, and regularity. / Translated from a famous Treatise on Music, written / by / John Joachim Quantz, / Composer to his Majesty the King of Prussia. / Price 7^s-6^d / London Printed by Welcker in Gerrard Street St. Ann's Soho / Where may be had, Practical Rules for learning Composition by John Joseph Feux 10-6. The Art / of learning the Harpsi-chord by Heck 10-6. A Treatise on Singing by Dr. Nares 3-6 &. &. &. A slightly abridged translation of Chapters XIII and XV of the *Essay*. Published *c.* 1775.

2. An unaltered reprint of the *Easy and Fundamental Instructions* was issued at some time between 1780 and 1798 in 'London, Printed by Longman and Broderip No. 26 Cheapside, Music Sellers to the Royal Family', with a raise in price to 10^s-6^d.

3. Tables VIII to XIX of the *Essay*, illustrating the practice of extempore varia-tion, are reprinted with an acknowledgement in John Gunn's *The Art of Playing the German-Flute on New Principles* (London: Birchall, 1793). Although Gunn shows a familiarity with Quantz's work in a number of points, his tutor is independent in thought and expression.

Italy

1. 'Trattato di un Metodo per imparare a suonare il Flauto traversiere con / molte osservazioni che servono per il buon gusto della Musica ed il tut-/to viene reso chiaro da esempli e da ventiquattro Stampe di Rame / Dato in Luce da Gio: Gioachino Quantz Musico della Camera di sua Maestà / il Re di Prussia.' A hitherto unnoticed eighteenth-century manuscript translation of the entire text of the *Essay*, preserved in the Civico Museo Bibliografico, Bologna. The translation is based on the French edition of 1752, and the unidentified translator probably made use of the printed musical examples from that edition, since they are omitted here.

2. Saggio / per ben sonare il flautotraverso / con alcune notizie generali ed utili per qualunque strumento, / ed altri concernenti la storia della musica : / opera del / Dr. Antonio Lorenzoni. / Vicenza. Per Francesco Modena. / 1779.

An unacknowledged plagiarism of the work of Quantz, as well as treatises of several other authors. The borrowings range from single sentences to several paragraphs at a time. The work was also issued in Bologna in the same year.

France

No portion of the treatise is known to have been reproduced on French soil. An interesting article included in vol. iii of the *Supplément* (1777) of Diderot's *Encyclopédie*, however, indicates that the work was known in France (see → the article of Eric Halfpenny listed in Part II of the Bibliography).

PART II

General Bibliography

AMELN, K., and SCHNOOR, H. (eds.). *Deutsche Musiker*. Göttingen: Vanderhoeck & Ruprecht, 1956.

ANONYMOUS. Review of R. A. Schlegel's *Gründliche Anleitung die Flöte zu spielen nach Quanzens Anweisung*. *Allgemeine deutsche Bibliothek*, cv (1792), pp. 118–19.

—— Review of the treatises of Quantz, C. P. E. Bach, and L. Mozart. *Bibliothek der schönen Wissenschaften und der freyen Künste*, x (1763), pp. 50–53.

ARNOLD, FRANK THOMAS. *The Art of Accompaniment from a Thorough-Bass as Practised in the XVIIth and XVIIIth Centuries*. London: Oxford University → Press, 1931. Reprinted, London: Holland Press, 1961.

BABITZ, SOL. 'A Problem of Rhythm in Baroque Music', *The Musical Quarterly*, xxxviii (1952), pp. 533–65.

BACH, CARL PHILIPP EMANUEL. *Essay on the True Art of Playing Keyboard Instruments*. Translated and edited by William J. Mitchell. New York: W. W. Norton, 1949. London: Cassell & Co., 1951.

BADURA-SKODA, EVA and PAUL. *Interpreting Mozart on the Keyboard*. Translated by Leo Black. London: Barrie and Rockliff, 1962.

BAINES, ANTHONY. *Woodwind Instruments and their History*. New York: W. W. Norton & Co., 1957. 3rd ed., London: Faber and Faber, 1967.

BENZ, RICHARD. *Die Zeit der deutschen Klassik*. Stuttgart: Reclam, 1953.

BOSE, FRITZ. 'Quantz', *Musik in Geschichte und Gegenwart*, 10, cols. 1797–1806.

BOYDEN, DAVID. 'The Violin and its Technique in the 18th Century', *The Musical Quarterly*, xxxvi (1950), pp. 9–38.

BREITKOPF, JOHANN GOTTLOB IMMANUEL. *Catalogo de soli, duetti, trii e concerti per* → *il flauto traverso*. Leipzig: Breitkopf, 1763–1784.

BRENET, MICHAEL. *Les Concerts en France sous l'ancien régime*. Paris: Fischbacher, 1900. Reprinted, New York: Da Capo, 1970.

BROSSARD, SÉBASTIEN DE. *Dictionaire de musique*. 6th ed. Amsterdam: Pierre → Mortier, 1709 (1st ed., 1703).

BÜCKEN, ERNST. *Die Musik des Rokokos und der Klassik*. Potsdam: Akademische Verlagsgesellschaft Athenaion, 1929. Reissued, New York: Musurgia Publishers, 1950. 2nd ed., Laaber: Laaber-Verlag, 1979.

BUKOFZER, MANFRED F. *Music in the Baroque Era.* New York: W. W. Norton, 1947. London: J. M. Dent & Sons, 1948.

BURNEY, CHARLES. *A General History of Music from the Earliest Ages to the Present.* 2nd ed. Edited by Frank Mercer. 2 vols. New York: Harcourt, Brace and Co., 1935. Reprinted, New York: Dover Publications, 1957.

—— *Dr. Burney's Musical Tours in Europe.* Edited by Percy A. Scholes. 2 vols. London: Oxford University Press, 1959.

CARSE, ADAM. *The Orchestra in the XVIIIth Century.* Cambridge: W. Heffer and Sons, 1940. Reprinted, New York: Da Capo, 1965.

CORRETTE, MICHEL. *Methode pour apprendre aisément à joüer de la flute traversiere.* Paris: Boivin, *c.* 1740.

DART, THURSTON. *The Interpretation of Music.* 'Hutchinson's University Library'. 4th ed., London: Hutchinson, 1967.

DAVID, HANS T., and MENDEL, ARTHUR. *The Bach Reader.* New York: W. W. Norton and Co., 1945. Revised ed., 1966. London: J. M. Dent & Sons, 1946.

DEUTSCH, OTTO ERICH. *Handel, a Documentary Biography.* London: A. & C. Black, 1955. Reprinted, New York: Da Capo, 1974.

DOLMETSCH, ARNOLD. *The Interpretation of the Music of the XVIIth and XVIIIth Centuries Revealed by Contemporary Evidence.* London: Novello and Co., 1915. Revised ed., 1946. Reprinted, Seattle: University of Washington Press, 1969.

DONINGTON, ROBERT. *The Interpretation of Early Music.* New version, London: Faber and Faber, 1974. New York: St. Martin's Press, 1974.

FERAND, ERNEST T. *Improvisation in Nine Centuries of Western Music.* 'Anthology of Music'. Cologne: Arno Volk Verlag, 1961.

FRIEDLÄNDER, MAX. *Das deutsche Lied im 18. Jahrhundert.* 2 vols. Stuttgart and Berlin: Cott'sche Buchhandlung, 1902. Reprinted, Hildesheim: G. Olms, 1970.

FRIEDRICH II. *Musikalische Werke.* Edited by P. Spitta. 3 vols in 4. Leipzig: Breitkopf and Härtel, 1889. Reprinted, New York: Da Capo, 1967.

—— *Œuvres.* 31 vols. Berlin: Imprimerie Royale, 1846–57.

FÜRSTENAU, MORITZ. *Zur Geschichte der Musik und des Theaters am Hofe zu Dresden.* 2 vols. Dresden: R. Kuntze, 1861–2. Reprinted, Hildesheim: G. Olms, 1971.

GEMINIANI, FRANCESCO. *The Art of Playing the Violin* (1751). Facsimile edition, edited by D. Boyden. London: Oxford University Press, 1952.

GERBER, ERNST LUDWIG. *Historisch-biographisches Lexicon der Tonkünstler.* 2 vols. Leipzig: Breitkopf, 1790–2.

GROUT, DONALD J. *A Short History of Opera.* 2nd edition. New York: Columbia University Press, 1965.

HAAS, ROBERT. *Aufführungspraxis der Musik.* Potsdam: Akademische Verlagsgesellschaft Athenaion, 1931. Reissued, New York: Musurgia Publishers, 1949. 2nd ed., Laaber: Laaber-Verlag, 1979.

HABÖCK, FRANZ. *Die Gesangskunst der Kastraten.* Vienna: Universal-Edition, 1923.

HALFPENNY, ERIC. 'A French Commentary on Quantz', *Music and Letters*, xxxvii (1956), pp. 61–66.

HARDING, ROSAMUND E. M. *Origins of Musical Time and Expression.* London: Oxford University Press, 1938.

HARICH-SCHNEIDER, ETA. *The Harpsichord.* Kassel: Bärenreiter, 1954.

HEINICHEN, JOHANN DAVID. *Der General-Bass in der Composition.* Dresden: pub. by the author, 1728. Reprinted, Hildesheim: G. Olms, 1968.

HELM, ERNEST EUGENE. *Music at the Court of Frederick the Great*. Norman: University of Oklahoma Press, 1960.

HOTTETERRE, JACQUES (*dit* le Romain). *L'Art de preluder sur la flûte traversiere*. Paris: pub. by the author, 1719.

—— *Principes de la flute traversiere, ou flute d'Allemagne*. Paris: Christophe Ballard, 1707. English translation as *The Rudiments or Principles of the German Flute*. London: Walsh, 1729. Facsimile and German translation of the Dutch edition
→ of 1710, edited by J. J. Hellwig. Kassel: Bärenreiter, 1941.

HUTCHINGS, ARTHUR. *The Baroque Concerto*. New York: W. W. Norton & Co., 1961. London: Faber and Faber, 1963. 2nd ed., London: Faber and Faber, 1978.

. KAHL, WILLI (ed.). *Selbstbiographien deutscher Musiker des XVIII. Jahrhunderts*. Cologne: Staufen-Verlag, 1948. Reprinted, Amsterdam: Knuf, 1972.

KIRKPATRICK, RALPH. *Domenico Scarlatti*. Princeton: Princeton University Press, 1953.

—— 'Eighteenth-Century Metronomic Indications', *Papers of the American Musicological Society* (1938), pp. 34–38.

KNÖDT, HEINRICH. 'Zur Entwicklungsgeschichte der Kadenzen im Instrumental-Konzert', *Sammelbände der Internationalen Musikgesellschaft*, xv (1914), pp. 375–419.

KÖHLER, KARL-HEINZ. 'Die Triosonate bei den Dresdener Zeitgenossen Johann Sebastian Bachs.' Unpublished dissertation, Friedrich-Schiller-Universität, Jena, 1956.

KOLNEDER, WALTER. *Aufführungspraxis bei Vivaldi*. Leipzig: Breitkopf & Härtel, 1955.

KRÜGER, WALTHER. *Das Concerto grosso in Deutschland*. Wolfenbüttel and Berlin: G. Kallmeyer, 1932.

LA LAURENCIE, LIONEL DE. *L'École française de violon de Lully à Viotti*. 3 vols. Paris: Librarie Delagrave, 1924. Reprinted, Geneva: Minkoff, 1971.

LA MARA (pseud. for Marie Lipsius). *Musikerbriefe aus fünf Jahrhunderten*. 2 vols. Leipzig: Breitkopf & Härtel, 1886.

LANG, PAUL HENRY. *Music in Western Civilization*. New York: W. W. Norton, 1941. London: J. M. Dent & Sons, 1942.

MAHAUT, ANTON. *Nieuwe manier om binnen korten tyd op de dwarsfluit to leeren speelen* (with parallel French text, *Nouvelle méthode pour apprendre en peu de tems*
→ *a jouer de la flute traversiere*). Amsterdam: J. J. Hummel, 1759.

MAJER, JOSEPH FRIEDRICH BERNHARD CASPAR. *Museum musicum theoretico practicum*. Schwäbisch Hall: G. M. Majer, 1732. Facsimile reprint, Kassel: Bärenreiter, 1954.

MARPURG, FRIEDRICH WILHELM. *Des critischen Musicus an der Spree erster Band*. Berlin: Haude & Spener, 1750. Reprinted, Hildesheim: G. Olms, 1970.

—— *Historisch-kritische Beyträge zur Aufnahme der Musik*. 5 vols. Berlin: Schütz (i) and G. A. Lange (ii–v), 1754–78. Reprinted, Hildesheim: G. Olms, 1970.
→ —— *Kritische Briefe über die Tonkunst*. 3 vols. Berlin: Birnstiel, 1760–4.

—— *Legende einiger Musikheiligen*. Breslau: Korn, 1786.

MATTHESON, JOHANN. *Der vollkommene Capellmeister*. Hamburg: Herold, 1739. Facsimile reprint, Kassel: Bärenreiter, 1954.

MENDEL, ARTHUR. 'On the Pitches in Use in Bach's Time', *The Musical Quarterly*, xli (1955), pp. 332–54.

MENNICKE, CARL. *Hasse und die Brüder Graun als Symphoniker*. Leipzig: Breitkopf & Härtel, 1906. Reprinted, Hildesheim: G. Olms, 1977.

MILLER, DAYTON C. *Catalogue of Books and Literary Materials Relating to the Flute and Other Musical Instruments*. Cleveland: privately printed, 1935.

MOZART, LEOPOLD. *A Treatise on the Fundamental Principles of Violin Playing*. Translated by Editha Knocker, with a preface by Alfred Einstein. London: Oxford University Press, 1948.

MUFFAT, GEORG. 'Premieres observations sur la maniere de jouër les airs de balets à la françoise selon la methode de feu M. de Lully.' Reprinted in *Denkmäler der Tonkunst in Österreich*, II. Jahrgang, Zweiter Theil.

MÜLLER, GEORG. 'Die Quantz'schen Königs-Flöten', *Zeitschrift für Instrumentenbau*, lii (1932), pp. 238–41.

NAGEL, WILLIBALD. 'Miscellanea', *Monatshefte für Musikgeschichte*, xxix (1897), pp. 69–78.

NETTL, PAUL. 'An English Musician at the Court of Charles VI in Vienna', *The Musical Quarterly*, xxviii (1942), pp. 318–28.

—— *Forgotten Musicians*. New York: Philosophical Library, 1951.

NEWMAN, WILLIAM S. *The Sonata in the Baroque Era*. Chapel Hill: The University of North Carolina Press, 1959. 3rd ed., New York: W. W. Norton, 1972.

—— *The Sonata in the Classic Era*. Chapel Hill: The University of North Carolina Press, 1963.

NICOLAI, CHRISTOPH FRIEDRICH (ed.). *Anekdoten von König Friedrich II. von Preußen, und von einigen Personen, die um ihn waren*. 6 vols. Berlin and Stettin: F. Nicolai, 1788–92.

NORMAN, GERTRUDE, and SCHRIFTE, MIRIAM LUBELL (eds.). *Letters of Composers, an Anthology*. New York: Alfred A. Knopf, 1946.

PINCHERLE, MARC. *Corelli, His Life, His Music*. Translated by H. E. M. Russell. New York: W. W. Norton, 1956.

—— *Vivaldi, Genius of the Baroque*. Translated by C. Hatch. New York: W. W. Norton, 1957.

PRAETORIUS, MICHAEL. *Syntagma musicum*. 3 vols. Wittenberg and Wolfenbüttel: J. Richter and E. Helwein, 1614–20. Facsimile reprint, Kassel: Bärenreiter, 1958–9.

PRINTZ, WOLFGANG KASPAR. *Musica modulatoria vocales*. Schweidnitz: C. Okels, 1678.

—— *Phrynis Mytilenæus, oder ander Theil des satyrischen Componisten*. Sagan: C. Okels, 1677.

PROD'HOMME, JACQUES-GABRIEL. *Écrits de musiciens*. Paris: Mercure de France, 1912.

QUANTZ, ALBERT. *Leben und Werke des Flötisten Johann Joachim Quantz*. Berlin: R. Oppenheim, 1877.

QUANTZ, JOHANN JOACHIM. 'Hrn. Johann Joachim Quanzens Antwort auf des Herrn von Moldenit gedrucktes so genanntes Schreiben an Hrn. Quanz nebst einigen Anmerkungen über dessen Versuch einer Anweisung die Flöte traversiere zu spielen', in F. W. Marpurg's *Historisch-kritische Beyträge zur Aufnahme der Musik*, iv (1759), pp. 153–91.

—— 'Herrn Johann Joachim Quantzens Lebenslauf, von ihm selbst entworfen', in F. W. Marpurg's *Historisch-kritische Beyträge zur Aufnahme der Musik*, i (1755), pp. 197–250. Facsimile in Kahl, *Selbstbiographien deutscher Musiker des XVIII. Jahrhunderts*, pp. 104–57. Reprinted, Amsterdam: Knuf, 1972.

RASKIN, ADOLF. 'Johann Joachim Quantz. Sein Leben und seine Kompositionen'. Unpublished dissertation, Universität Köln, 1923.

REICHARDT, JOHANN FRIEDRICH. *Schreiben über die Berlinische Musik*. Hamburg: Bohn, 1775.

—— *Ueber die Pflichten des Ripien-Violinisten*. Berlin and Leipzig: G. J. Decker, 1776.

REILLY, EDWARD RANDOLPH. 'Further Musical Examples for Quantz's *Versuch*', *Journal of the American Musicological Society*, xvii (1964), pp. 157–69.

ROWEN, RUTH HALLE. *Early Chamber Music*. New York: Columbia University Press, 1949. Reprinted, New York: Da Capo, 1974.

SACHS, CURT. *Handbuch der Musikinstrumentenkunde*. Leipzig: Breitkopf & Härtel, 1920. Reprinted, Wiesbaden: Breitkopf & Härtel, 1965.

SCHÄFKE, RUDOLF. 'Quantz als Ästhetiker', *Archiv für Musikwissenschaft*, vi (1924), pp. 213–42.

SCHEIBE, JOHANN ADOLF. *Critischer Musikus, neue, vermehrte und verbesserte*
➤ *Auflage*. Leipzig: B. C. Breitkopf, 1745.

SCHERING, ARNOLD. *Geschichte des Instrumental-Konzerts*. Leipzig: Breitkopf & Härtel, 1905. Reprinted, Wiesbaden: Breitkopf & Härtel, 1965.

—— 'Zur instrumentalen Verzierungskunst im 18. Jahrhundert', *Sammelbände der Internationalen Musikgesellschaft*, vii (1905–6), pp. 365–85.

SCHMITZ, HANS-PETER. *Die Kunst der Verzierung im 18. Jahrhundert*. Kassel: Bärenreiter, 1955.

—— *Prinzipien der Aufführungspraxis alter Musik*. Berlin-Dahlem: H. Knauer-Verlag, [1950].

—— *Querflöte und Querflötenspiel in Deutschland während des Barockzeitalters*. Kassel: Bärenreiter, 1952.

SCHUBART, CHRISTIAN FRIEDRICH DANIEL. *Ideen zu einer Ästhetik der Tonkunst*.
➤ Edited by P. A. Merbach. Leipzig: Wolkenwanderer Verlag, 1924.

SIMPSON, CHRISTOPHER. *The Division-Viol*. 2nd edition. London: W. Godbid, 1665. Facsimile reprint, London: J. Curwen, 1955.

SORGE, GEORG ANDREAS. *Compendium harmonicum*. Lobenstein: published by the author, 1760.

STRUNK, OLIVER (ed.). *Source Readings in Music History*. New York: W. W. Norton, 1950. London: Faber and Faber, 1952.

SULZER, JOHANN GEORG. *Allgemeine Theorie der schönen Künste in einzeln, nach alphabetischer Ordnung der Kunstwörter auf einander folgenden, Artikeln abgehandelt*.
➤ 2nd ed. 5 vols. Leipzig: Weidmann, 1792–9.

TARTINI, GIUSEPPE. *Treatise on Ornaments in Music*. Edited by Erwin R. Jacobi. English translation by Cuthbert Girdlestone. Celle and New York: Hermann Moeck Verlag, 1961.

THOURET, GEORG. *Friedrich der Große als Musikfreund und Musiker*. Leipzig: Breitkopf & Härtel, 1898.

—— *Katalog der Musiksammlung auf der Königlichen Hausbibliothek*. Leipzig: Breitkopf & Härtel, 1895.

TOSI, PIER FRANCESCO. *Observations on the Florid Song*. 2nd ed. Translated by J. E. Galliard. London: J. Wilcox, 1743. Facsimile reprint, London: W. Reeves,
➤ 1926 and 1967.

TROMLITZ, JOHANN GEORG. *Ausführlicher und gründlicher Unterricht die Flöte zu spielen.* Leipzig: Adam Friedrich Böhme, 1791. ←

VAUCANSON, JACQUES DE. *Le Mécanisme du fluteur automate.* Paris: Jacques Guerin, 1738. Translated as 'Beschreibung des mechanischen Flötenspielers', *Hamburgisches Magazin* (Hamburg: G. C. Grund), ii (1747), pp. 1–24. ←

WALTHER, JOHANN GOTTFRIED. *Musikalisches Lexikon.* Leipzig: Wolffgang Deer, 1732. Facsimile reprint, Kassel: Bärenreiter, 1953.

WILHELMINE, FRÉDÉRIQUE SOPHIE. *Mémoires.* 5th ed. 2 vols. Berlin: Hermann Barsdorf, 1910.

ZOELLER, CARLI. 'Thematic Catalogue of the Compositions of Johann Joachim Quantz', British Museum Add. 32148, *c.* 1886.

APPENDIX

Introduction

page/line

xiii/fn. 5

For a well-documented account of the period that Veracini spent in Dresden, see J. W. Hill, *The Life and Works of Francesco Maria Veracini* (Ann Arbor, Mich.: UMI Research Press, 1979), pp. 19–27.

xvii/*11*

A translation by F. S. Stillings, *The Practical Harmonist at the Harpsichord*, ed. D. L. Burrows, has been published by Yale University Press (New Haven, 1968).

xvii/*36*

Franciscello's real name has now been identified as Francesco Alborea.

xx/*21*

In spite of my attempts, here and elsewhere, to stress the critical importance of Quantz's experiences in Dresden on the formation of his style as a performer and composer, this aspect of his career is still often slighted or overlooked because of his connections with Frederick the Great. As noted in the following paragraphs, however, Quantz could not be induced to leave Dresden until he was forty-four years old, when his mature style was certainly well formed.

xxiii/fn. 3

A much richer collection of *Solfeggi*, including excerpts from compositions by Quantz, Telemann, and a number of other composers, has been recently discovered in the Giedde Music Collection in the Royal Library in Copenhagen. It has been published under its original title: *Solfeggi pour la flûte traversière avec l'enseignement, par Monsr. Quantz*, ed. W. Michel and H. Teske (Winterthur: Amadeus Verlag, 1978). Also located in the same collection is an important collection of Quantz's unaccompanied *Fantasias*, *Capricci*, and other works for flute, previously believed lost.

xxiv/*1*

A facsimile edition of these catalogues has been published under the title *The Breitkopf Thematic Catalogue*, ed. Barry S. Brook (New York: Dover, 1966).

xxiv/*18*

Two doctoral dissertations will eventually help to remedy the problems noted here: Charlotte Crockett's 'The Berlin Flute Sonatas of Johann Joachim Quantz' (University of Texas) 1982, and Sunhild Eigemann's 'Studien an des Instrumentalkonzerten Johann Joachim Quantz' (Universität Bonn) in progress. A–R Editions has also announced plans to publish six sets of seven sonatas for flute and continuo, edited by Gilbert L. Blount and Charlotte Crockett, in the series *Recent Researches in the Music of the Baroque Era*.

page/line

xxiv/22

See Appendix III of *Quantz and His Versuch*, pp. 155–63, for a list of virtually all of the significant modern editions through 1968, and the supplement to that list pp. 388–94 below. The article by Gwilym Beechy, 'J. J. Quantz (1697–1773) and His Flute Sonatas', *Musical Opinion*, 101 (April 1978), pp. 298–9, 306, includes a brief list of some solo sonatas, duets, and trio sonatas.

xxvi/23

For a fuller discussion of Quantz's compositions, see *Quantz and His Versuch*, pp. 1–39. For more current work, see also the two doctoral dissertations cited above in n. xxiv *18*.

xxvii/fn. 1

English translation in Reilly, 'Quantz's *Versuch einer Anweisung die Flöte traversiere zu spielen*: a Translation and Study', unpublished doctoral dissertation, University of Michigan, 1958, ii, pp. 823–51.

xxviii/5

Translations of these letters, and of an explanation by Quantz for his inclusion of the engraving of Pythagoras at the forge in the *Versuch* (facing p. 11 in this translation) are included in *Quantz and His Versuch*, pp. 82–6. The account of his life that Quantz prepared for Padre Martini, which was missing at the time when the other documents were studied, has since been located. See Anne Schnoebelen, *Padre Martini's Collection of Letters in the Civico Museo Bibliografico Musicale in Bologna* (New York: Pendragon Press, 1979), item 4234, p. 502. This account, dated Berlin, 14 April 1762, is largely a very condensed summary of the published autobiography. The latter portion of this statement, however, contains material not in the autobiography which throws some additional light on his work as a composer and a few other matters. The concluding three paragraphs are translated below:

> My compositions, for the most part, are designed for the transverse flute, and consist of some concerti grossi for several concertante instruments [i.e. solo instruments]; of about 300 concerti for one concertante flute; as many solo sonatas; some *sonate a quatro*; many *a tre*; and some arias. In the solo sonatas I have always endeavoured to unite the ingenious [*il laborioso*—i.e. contrapuntal ingenuity] with the tasteful [*gustoso*]. I have proposed the inviolable rule to make trio sonatas in such manner that both the [upper] instruments, in [a] good relationship with [the] bass, have equal activity and when possible also equally good melody. Otherwise I believe that it might be possible to mistake a trio in which the first part has the preference for a solo sonata to which an accompanying middle part has been added. This law is also observed in *sonate a quatro*. Concerti I attempt to make (in so far as my feeble powers permit) in such a manner that the ritornelli maintain a continuing relationship with the concertante part, and which thus does not obstruct a well-regulated whole. A concerto in which the ritornelli have so little relation to the concertante part that one may be tempted to believe that the concerto has been put together by chance, or that one composer has made the ritornelli, another the concertante part, and perhaps a third the bass, I am not able to consider good.
>
> All my compositions being intended for the use of His Majesty, my gracious

page/line

Monarch, my situation does not permit me to offer much elsewhere either in manuscript or in print. Thus only *Sei Sonate a flauto traverso solo e Basso,* in the year 1734, and *Sei Duetti a 2 Flauti trav:,* in the year 1759, have been printed. The book which bears the title: *Essai* [full French title] was published in the year 1752 in the German and French languages. To make the intonation of the transverse flute more perfect, I found it necessary to add another key to it. The one key serves for the tones with flats, the other for the tones with sharps. A certain invention attempted with little success by others in the footpiece [*il piede*] of the transverse flute, I have found practicable in the headpiece [*la testa*] of that instrument. By means of this invention it is possible, without changing the middle pieces, to tune the flute a half tone lower or higher in a moment. Merely read pars. 14 and 15 of Chapter I in the book cited above.

The flutes which the King uses, and my own, I have manufactured in my own fashion [*a modo mio*], and tune them myself. In addition to His Prussian Majesty, I have also had the honour to teach the Margrave of Bayreuth and some other Princes and Knights to play the transverse flute; and not having children, I have undertaken the care of the education of some young persons, two of whom are now in fact in the service of His Prussian Majesty.

The reference to the number of his concertos and sonatas may be significant in trying to establish a chronology for these works. The comments that follow on his compositional goals may be correlated with those in the final chapter of the *Versuch*. Quantz's statement about his compositions being destined for the King should be read in the light of the information presented on pp. xxiii and xxiv of this Introduction. With regard to contemporary published editions of his works, it seems clear that he wished to acknowledge only those that had appeared under his supervision. On the numerous other editions, some of which certainly present genuine works, see the list in *Quantz and His Versuch*, pp. 144–54, and the supplement below, p. 384–8. References to flute design confirm those in the *Versuch*, but the concluding mention of his care for young people adds a new and personal note to this review of his life.

Quantz is also mentioned in several letters of Martini and other correspondents. See the index in Schnoebelen's work and H. Brofsky, 'J. C. Bach, G. B. Sammartini, and Padre Martini: A *Concorso* in Milan in 1762', in *A Musical Offering: Essays in Honor of Martin Bernstein* (New York: Pendragon Press, 1977), p. 66.

xxviii/fn. 5
This portrait has since also been reproduced in the facsimile of the French edition of the *Essay,* cited below in n. xxxv *12,* and on the cover of the new edition of *Solfeggi* mentioned in n. xxiii fn. 3, and in *The New Grove Dictionary of Music and Musicians*, ed. S. Sadie (London: Macmillan, 1980), vol. 15, p. 495.

xxix/7
A facsimile of Corrette's work was published by F. Knuf in 1978, and a complete English translation by C. R. Farrar is included in her *Michel Corrette and Flute-playing in the Eighteenth Century*, 'Musical Theorists in Translation', vol. ix (Brooklyn: Institute of Mediaeval Music, 1970).

page/line

xxix/fn. 3

An important letter from Quantz to Telemann has been located in the library of Tartu State University in Estonia. It confirms the fact that the two musicians were in contact with one another and provides interesting indications of Telemann's reaction to the *Versuch*. The letter is translated in full and discussed in *Quantz and His Versuch*, pp. 61–2. The original German text is included in G. P. Telemann, *Briefwechsel: sämtliche erreichbare Briefe*, ed. H. Grosse and H. R. Jung (Leipzig: VEB Deutscher Verlag für Musik, 1972), pp. 364–6. This same volume includes a number of other references to Quantz, including several (see pp. 273 and 350) that bear on Quantz's relations with L. C. Mizler and his *Societät der musicalischen Wissenschaften*. The connections between Quantz and Telemann have been reviewed in my article 'Quantz and Telemann, *NACWPI Journal*, xxi, no. 2 (Winter 1972–3), pp. 44–8, and in the monograph by Ingeborg Allihn, *Georg Philipp Telemann und Johann Joachim Quantz*, Magdeburger Telemann-Studien, vol. iii (Magdeburg: Arbeitskreis 'Georg Philipp Telemann', 1971). To the information included in these works should be added the fact that excerpts from a considerable number of compositions by Telemann are included in the recently located *Solfeggi* cited earlier. In this collection Telemann is the most frequently cited composer other than Quantz himself.

xxxi/11

For a much more extended review of the editions of Quantz's work and critical reactions to it, see Chapter II, 'The Dissemination of the *Versuch*', in *Quantz and His Versuch*, pp. 40–92. A further detail may be found in V. Duckles, 'Johann Adam Hiller's "Critical Prospectus for a Music Library"', in *Studies in Eighteenth-Century Music: A Tribute to Karl Geiringer on His Seventieth Birthday*, ed. H. C. Robbins Landon and Roger E. Chapman (New York: Oxford University Press, 1970), pp. 183–4, which shows that the treatise was among those works recommended by Hiller in his *Wöchentliche Nachrichten* in 1768.

xxxii/27

A copy of what appears to be a supplementary companion to the *Sei sonate* of Moldenit, with the title *Idea dell' articolare rapresentata nelle sei sonate da traversiere solo di Moldenit* (Hamburg: the author, n.d.), has been traced in the Royal Library in Copenhagen and in several other locations. The music confirms Moldenit's use of extraordinary high and low tones, some of which were impossible to play on flutes of the period. At the end of the sonatas, which include slashes under virtually every note in what was apparently Moldenit's own system of articulation, a considerable number of examples from Chapter 6 of the *Versuch* are reproduced, probably as objects of Moldenit's attacks. A copy of the poetical satire *on* Moldenit (not *by* him as the title suggests, as does also the listing under his name in RISM), entitled *Dritter, neuester, und letzter Discours über Sechs Sonaten für die Querflöte und Bass, wodurch die Art angezeigt wird, wie die darinn befindliche ausserordentliche tiefe und hohe Töne zu spielen möglich sind, da Gioacchino Moldenit Nobile Danese da Glückstadt, Dilettante in Hamburg.* (n.p., n.d. [Hamburg, 1753?]), has been traced in the Bibliothèque du Conservatoire in Brussels. No copy, however, has yet been located of Moldenit's *Schreiben an Hrn. Quantz*, to which the latter finally responded. Letters in the Telemann *Briefwechsel*, cited earlier, pp. 279 and 285, confirm Quantz's statement that he and Moldenit had earlier been on friendly terms.

page/line

xxxii/*34*

Quantz's principal students were Riedt, Lindner, Kodowski and Neuff. For information about them and their pupils, see N. Delius, 'Quantz' Schüler. Ein Beitrag zur Genealogie einer Flötenschule', *Tibia*, vii (1982), pp. 176–84.

Preface to the Translation

xxxv/*12*

An excellent facsimile of the French translation, with an introduction by Antoine Geoffroy-Dechaume and *réflexions* by Pierre Séchet, was published in Paris in 1975 by Editions Aug. Zurfluh.

Chapter 1

29/fn. 2

The article by Jane Bowers, 'New Light on the Development of the Transverse Flute between about 1650 and about 1750', *Journal of the American Musical Instrument Society*, III (1977), pp. 5–56, constitutes a valuable more recent review of one history of the instrument just before and after the addition of a key.

31/fn. 1

Most of the eighteenth-century references to Quantz's instruments, including the article by F. D. Castilon traced by E. Halfpenny, are reviewed in some detail in *Quantz and His Versuch*, pp. 93–104. The article by J. Zimmermann, 'Die Flötenmacher Friedrichs des Grossen', *Zeitschrift für Instrumentenbau*, lx (1940), pp. 134ff., includes discussions of the work of some of Quantz's contemporaries and followers. Michael Zadro discusses 'Quantz and Flute Tone in Prussia' in an article in *Divisions: a Journal of the Art & Practice of Early Music*, vol. I, no. 4 (1980), pp. 32–6. Although Georg Müller studied some of Quantz's instruments, and reported on them in an article in 1932 (see Bibliography), no comprehensive review of the surviving flutes and their locations has been undertaken in the period since World War II.

Among the notes of Dayton C. Miller in his collection at the Library of Congress is a valuable account of the background of his own Quantz-style two-keyed flute (acquired in 1930–1), and information about eight other instruments of this type, nine flutes of other kinds that had reportedly belonged to Frederick the Great, and three replicas. Miller's own Quantz flute is now listed as No. 916 in L. E. Gilliam and W. Lichtenwanger, *The Dayton C. Miller Flute Collection: A Checklist of the Instruments* (Washington: Library of Congress, 1961). A photograph is also included. A replica of another instrument is listed as No. 429. In Michael Seyfrit, *Musical Instruments in the Dayton C. Miller Flute Collection at the Library of Congress,* vol. I (Washington: Library of Congress, 1982), the same Quantz flute is listed as No. 208, and the copy by E. J. Albert as No. 127. Seyfrit provides a bore graph and X-ray of the Quantz flute. Another Quantz type of flute which was on loan at the Library of Congress in the 1950s was subsequently put up for auction, and now forms a part of the collection of Robert Rosenbaum of Scarsdale, New York. A photograph of it is found in the report by Graham Wells, 'The London Salerooms in 1972', *Early Music*, 1 (1973), pp. 97–9. An excellent photograph of another two-keyed instrument, with two head pieces and five alternative middle pieces, in the Musikinstrumenten-Museum des Staatlichen Instituts für Musikforschung Preussischer Kulturbesitz, is included in the facsimile of the French translation of the *Versuch* cited earlier. Two other instruments (one a single-keyed flute) attributed to Quantz are reported in the Hohenzollern Museum and at Sans Souci. The instrument maker Friedrich von Huene has now created replicas of two-keyed instruments of the Quantz type, and they display strengths and weaknesses noted by eighteenth-century commentators. A review of the current body of knowledge about Quantz's flutes is presented in a forthcoming article by the present writer and von Huene in *Pythagoras at the Forge: An Annotated Catalogue of the Rosenbaum Collection of Western European Musical Instruments*, by Robert M. Rosenbaum et al. (Boston: Philidor Press).

The original of an autograph receipt by Quantz for payment (1100 Thalers) for four of his flutes, dated Potsdam, 23 November 1751, cited in *Quantz and His Versuch*, p. 102, and reproduced in several works, has been located in the Miller Collection in the Library of Congress. Another receipt, for 1000 Thalers, for three flutes and seven concertos, dated Potsdam, 25 October 1754, was put up for auction in a sale of musical manuscripts held on 20 and 21 November 1978 at Sotheby's in London. It is listed as Lot 461 in the catalogue of the sale, and is also reproduced in the catalogue. Yet another document, still untraced, offers the possibility of a few further details about Quantz's work as a manufacturer of flutes. A letter by Quantz to an unknown recipient, dated 11 February 1756, was offered for sale in an auction catalogue for the 21–3 May 1909 by the Berlin dealer Leo Liepmannsohn (item 775 on p. 89 of the catalogue). Addressed to a 'Hochedelgebohrenen Herrn' (Honourable [lit. 'high-noble-born'] Sir), that portion of the letter quoted in the catalogue offers 'a transverse flute of the kind described in my *Versuch die Flöte zu spielen* bored and truly tuned by me, and indeed made of box wood with six middle pieces, may be had for 7 Louis d'or. Of ebony I have let none go except to His Royal Majesty. The reason is . . .' (The quotation breaks off here!) Accompanying the letter was also a receipt of the instrument maker Joh. Reinecke, dated Berlin, 29 April 1756, for 20 Thalers for a 'Flate traverse' which was 'found good' by the Royal Chapel (who specifically in the Chapel is not made clear).

32/fn. 2
A translation of Mahaut's work by Pauline E. Durichen has been published in *Divisions*, vol. 1, no. 1 (Sept. 1978), pp. 19–34 and no. 2 (Dec. 1978), pp. 28–46.

34/§ 17 9
For a recent re-examination of the various types of Baroque flutes, and Quantz's position in relation to his predecessors, see C. Addington, 'In Search of the Baroque Flute. The Flute Family 1680–1750', *Early Music*, xii (1984), pp. 34–47.

34/fn. 3
For further information on subsequent efforts to add the low C and C sharp to the range of the instrument, see M. Byrne, 'Schuchart and the Extended Foot-Joint', *The Galpin Society Journal*, XVIII (1965), pp. 7–13.

CHAPTER III

42/§4 2
A fingering chart formerly belonging to Frederick the Great, and dated by him 17

page/line

January 1753, is reproduced in the facsimile of the French translation of the *Versuch* cited earlier. It is preserved in the Musikinstrumenten-Museum des Staatlichen Instituts für Musikforschung Preussischer Kulturbesitz. The chart is for a one-keyed instrument and differs in some instances from the chart given here. Dr. D. Krickeberg has undertaken a study of these differences in a typescript 'Vergleich zwischen der Grifftabelle in "Versuch einer Anweisung, die Flöte traversiere zu spielen" von Johann Joachim Quantz und eine entsprechenden Tabelle aus dem Besitz Friedrichs des Grossen'. An English translation of this study is included in the article by von Huene and myself in Robert M. Rosenbaum's *Pythagoras at the Forge* cited above. Philip Bate has prepared a fingering chart, combining the two presented by Quantz in the *Versuch* for the two-keyed flute, in his work *The Flute* (New York: W. W. Norton, 1969), p. 245. Pierre Séchet has also included his own useful tablature for a one-keyed flute, based on several eighteenth-century sources, in his *réflexions* in the facsimile of the French edition of the treatise. Finally, it should be noted that sometime *after* the first edition of the *Versuch* the fingering for G sharp' was altered by the addition of a 7 (which looks like a 1) to the chart, and the fingering for G double sharp''' by the addition of a 1. Since both the second and third editions were published after Quantz's death, we have no way of knowing who introduced the changes. It is perhaps also possible that the changes were inserted by the owner of the copy used for the facsimile.

46/12

Elsewhere I originally indicated that Quantz makes use of an untempered system of tuning. In fact he advocates a *mean-tone* system. Although it is not his principal subject, J. M. Chesnut, in his article 'Mozart's Teaching of Intonation', *Journal of the American Musicological Society*, xxx (1977), pp. 254–71, clearly identifies Quantz's position in relation to his predecessors, contemporaries and followers. In that article Chesnut also cites the most important relevant material connected with this subject.

CHAPTER IV

54/fn. 1

A facsimile of the French edition of Vaucanson's work has recently been issued by Frits Knuf (Buren, 1979), together with that of an English translation originally published in 1742. In his introduction to this volume, David Lasocki explores the question raised here by Quantz.

CHAPTER V

67/fn. 2

The article by Neumann has since been published in translation as 'The Dotted Note and the So-Called French Style', *Early Music*, v (1977), pp. 310–24. The subject of over-dotting in French overtures has continued to be discussed by Neumann, David Fuller, John O'Donnell, and Graham Pont in a series of articles, mainly in the pages of *Early Music* (see the supplementary bibliography for the present edition of *On Playing the Flute*). A study by Stephen Hefling, 'Dots-Documents: A Dispassionate Review', as yet still in typescript, offers a solid and helpful review of the evidence found in treatises of the period.

For important related material on this subject within the treatise itself, see Chapter XVII, ii, § 16, 17, 21; iv, § 10; vii, § 58. An easily accessible example of a French overture by Quantz, the first movement of his Op. 2, no. 6 duet for two flutes or other instruments, shows very well that over-dotting is quite effective in his own idiom; but this idiom is substantially different in some respects from what one finds in the French overtures of J. S. Bach. That Quantz himself did not take a doctrinaire approach to matters such as this is suggested by his description of the performance of works by Fux and Lully in his autobiography. See Nettl, *Forgotten Musicians*, pp. 294–5.

68/fn. 1

In a review of Georg Simon Löhlein's *Clavier-Schule* (Leipzig and Züllichau, 1765) in the *Allgemeine Deutsche Bibliothek*, vol. 10, no. 1 (1769), Johann Friedrich Agricola (the author has been positively identified by Erwin R. Jacobi in his article 'Neues zur Frage "Punktierte Rhythmen gegen Triolen" und zur Transkriptionstechnik bei J. S. Bach', *Bach-Jahrbuch* (1962), pp. 88–92) makes the following most interesting comments on Löhlein's teachings:

> On p. 70 it is taught: in dotted notes against triplets the note after the dot would be struck with the third note of the triplet. This is true only [when playing] at the most extreme speed. Otherwise the note following the dot must not be struck with, but after, the last note of the triplet. Otherwise a distinction between duple time, in which such notes appear, and 3/8 6/8 9/8 [and] 12/8 would disappear. Thus J. S. Bach taught all of his pupils; thus Quantz teaches in his *Versuch*. No one can legitimately challenge the artistry in performance and the sensitivity (*feine Empfindung*) of these men.

This passage is of substantial importance in providing evidence from a student of J. S. Bach that links his views with Quantz rather than his own son, Carl Philipp Emanuel. The question of to what extent C. P. E. Bach represents the views of his father has been often raised. Agricola's statement provides clear and rather startling evidence of an important difference between the two. His comments also provide a basis for linking interpretation in this matter to tempo. Since Agricola was a student of both J. S. Bach and Quantz, it would be difficult to question his reliability. Löhlein was sufficiently impressed that he altered later editions of his work to conform with Agricola.

CHAPTER VI

71/fn. 1

As has been suggested in a review of the present work by Hans-Peter Schmitz, Quantz's references to the pronunciation of 'u or i' in his note to Chapter IV, § 17, may be pertinent here.

72/fn. 3

An excellent review of the various kinds of articulations employed by woodwind players in the eighteenth century is found in Betty Bang Mather, *Interpretation of French Music from 1675 to 1775* (New York: McGinnis & Marx, 1973), pp. 32–50. The recently located and published *Solfeggi pour la flûte traversière avec l'enseignement par Monsr. Quantz*, ed. by W. Michel and H. Teske (Winterthur: Amadeus Verlag, 1978), present many invaluable further examples of articulations in a wide variety of specific musical situations.

74/§ 10 2

Drawing on the examples of extempore variations in Chapter XIII below, Mary Rasmussen has attempted to establish some general rules for articulating and slurring varying combinations of notes in her article 'Some Notes on the Articulations in the Melodic Variation Tables of Johann Joachim Quantz's *Versuch einer Anweisung die Flöte traversiere zu spielen* (Berlin 1752, Breslau 1789)', *Brass and Woodwind Quarterly*, vol. I, nos. 1 and 2 (Winter, 1966–7), pp. 3–26.

CHAPTER VII

90/3

The *Solfeggi . . . par Monsr. Quantz* previously cited again provide valuable further examples for the student in this regard. See 'Atem/Breathing' in the subject index of the volume, p. 95.

CHAPTER VIII

91/fn. 2

For a summary review of Quantz's treatment of the different areas of ornamentation, see *Quantz and His Versuch*, pp. 104–16.

92/fn. 2

'Preceding' is an equally logical translation for 'prefixed' here and in the following sentence. Raymond H. Haggh in his translation of D. G. Türk's *School of Clavier Playing* (Lincoln: University of Nebraska Press, 1982), pp. 463–4, translates this sentence as 'Appoggiaturas are a delaying of the preceding notes', and then adds that it should be translated 'appoggiaturas are a retardation *by means of* preceding notes although the German does not literally say that.'

93/fn. 4

See R. Donington, *Interpretation*, pp. 226–8, and especially Frederick Neumann, *Ornamentation in Baroque and Post-Baroque Music* (Princeton: Princeton University Press, 1978), pp. 183–99. The *Solfeggi . . . par Monsr. Quantz* offer examples of short appoggiaturas in a variety of different contexts.

97/§–13 2

B. B. Mather, *Interpretation of French Music*, p. 63, provides a helpful guide to the performance of the appoggiaturas in this example. Unlike many of her predecessors, she provides realizations of the short appoggiaturas, in figures such as those found in bars 3 and 5, in accord with Quantz's instructions in Chapter XVII, Section II, § 20.

98/fn. 1

For F. Neumann's interpretation of Figs. 29 and 30, and 32 and 33 in the following paragraph, see *Ornamentation,* pp. 458–9. The use of Fig. 30 at letter (e) in Figure 26 (see § 17), however, does not support the view that the appoggiaturas should be of the passing variety.

CHAPTER IX

102/fn. 4

The fact that Quantz in § 7 equates examples with and without written appoggiaturas, and that the same situation occurs in his illustrations of fingerings for shakes, does not provide firm support for F. Neumann's view that this example shows that Quantz had a 'main-note anchor' in mind for the alterations. See *Ornamentation*, p. 376.

104/fn. 1

For several instructive illustrations of the problems connected with the duration of appoggiaturas preceding shakes in Quantz's works, see F. Neumann, *Ornamentation*, pp. 376–9. In his note 32, p. 376, referring to this translation, Neumann has apparently failed to read the definition of the verb 'to tip' on p. xxxviii of the Preface to the Translation. The *Solfeggi . . . par Monsr. Quantz* also provide further clues about the interpretation of shakes.

105/fn. 1

A useful composite table of fingerings for shakes, based on several different sources, is provided by P. Séchet on pp. 20–1 of the introductory material in the facsimile of the French translation of the *Versuch* cited earlier.

CHAPTER X

114/4

Although it has not been possible to locate the specific trios mentioned here by Quantz, clues to which works he may have had in mind are found in the *Solfeggi . . . par Monsr. Quantz*, pp. 55–6, which include a reference to a 'Trio alla Francese. di Telemann' and excerpts from what appear to be several such trios. In accord with the advice given here Quantz includes numerous passages from his own duets and trios as well as those of Telemann, Graun and others in the *Solfeggi*. And in his *Sei duetti*, Op. 2, published in 1759 (see the Introduction, p. xxiv), Quantz further stresses the importance of good duets in training students.

CHAPTER XI

124/§ 15 2

For a thoughtful exploration of the idea of the expression of the passions and its implication in the performance of a trio sonata by Quantz, see D. Lasocki, 'Quantz and the Passions: Theory and Practice', *Early Music*, 6 (1978), pp. 556–67.

124/fn 1

Although one may not agree with all of his conclusions, the connections between Quantz's practice and French use of *notes inégales* is, I believe, conclusively demonstrated by F. Neumann, 'The French *Inégales*, Quantz, and Bach', *Journal of the American Musicological Society*, xviii (1965), pp. 313–58. The question of to what degree and when the practice of inequality may have been adopted in Germany, and in what works it would have been used, are in my opinion unresolved. Views contrary to those of

page/line

Neumann are found in the article of Babitz cited in my original footnote, in Donington, and in the responses to Neumann cited by Donington in his bibliography. Neumann's subsequent article 'External Evidence and Uneven Notes', *Musical Quarterly*, lii (1966), pp. 448–64, should also be consulted. In Quantz's case, it is important to remember that he was almost certainly articulating a practice he himself, and probably other members of the Dresden orchestra, cultivated no later than the early 1730s, and perhaps well before that time. In this regard the later date of the *Versuch* can be misleading. B. B. Mather, *Interpretation of French Music*, pp. 3–31, provides detailed guidance, with numerous examples, in the use of *inégales* in French works. And the *Solfeggi . . . par Monsr. Quantz* offer many valuable additional examples. (See *inégalité* in the subject index for page references in that volume.)

CHAPTER XII

131/fn. 1
For a number of examples, with instructions, of the performance of triplets, see *Solfeggi . . . par Monsr. Quantz*, pp. 39, 49, 50, 57, 69, 71, 78, 79, 91, 92. In the majority of examples, rhythmic equality is stressed.

132/fn. 1
Sol Babitz, in his 'Additions to Bulletin 1', *Early Music Laboratory Bulletin 10*, 1973, p. 13, draws attention to the unacknowledged emendation of this passage by A. Schering in his edition of the *Versuch*. Schering has the 'principal notes descend and the passing ascend', an interpretation which Babitz supports, but which the French text does not. Examples of the kind of passages to which I believe Quantz refers may be easily located in his *Solfeggi*.

133/fn. 4, 5, 6
For a study of the expression of the passions in a specific work of Quantz, and the implications for performance, see the article of D. Lasocki cited in n. 124 § 15 2.

CHAPTER XIII

140/fn. 2
These dynamic markings have been carefully worked out by B. B. Mather and D. Lasocki in their *Free Ornamentation in Woodwind Music 1700–1775* (New York: McGinnis & Marx, 1976), pp. 56–67, and also, with French equivalents, in the introductory section of the facsimile of the French translation of the *Versuch*. The dynamic indications also provide valuable clues about rhythm and the interpretation of the ornaments.

153/Fig. 17 b) h)
As Neumann, *Ornamentation*, p. 191, correctly indicates, Quantz's notation is wrong in these two examples, although his intention is clear. The rhythmic pattern in each case should be:

CHAPTER XIV

164/fn. 4

A partial translation of Heinichen's work by George J. Buelow has been published under the title *Thorough-Bass Accompaniment According to Johann David Heinichen* (Berkeley: University of California Press, 1966).

165/fn. 3

A vivid account of the skill with which Michel Blavet used the *mesa di voce*, known in France as the *son enflé et diminué*, by Hubert Le Blanc (1740), is quoted in Mather, *Interpretation*, pp. 66–7.

166/fn. 4

A further reference to the vibrato by Quantz is found in Chapter XVII, Section II, § 32.

173/fn. 1

As noted earlier, the dynamic markings provided here for the examples in the preceding chapter and for the Adagio in § 24 of this chapter are now *all* conveniently and more satisfactorily worked out with the music in Mather and Lasocki, *Free Ornamentation*, pp. 56–74, and also in the introduction to the facsimile of the French translation of the *Versuch*, pp. i–xv.

CHAPTER XV

179/fn. 3

By far the most substantial recent research into the history of the cadenza is that by David Lasocki in his M.A. thesis, 'The Eighteenth-Century Woodwind Cadenza' (University of Iowa, 1972). Material from this work forms the basis of D. Lasocki and B. B. Mather, *The Classical Woodwind Cadenza: a Workbook* (New York: McGinnis & Marx, 1978), which contains numerous examples from tutors and manuscript sources from the time of Quantz through the end of the century.

179/fn. 4

According to the research of F. Lesure (see Bibliography), the ornamented versions of the Op. 5 sonatas were published *in* 1710. An example of the additions attributed to Corelli, and one of embellishments by an anonymous performer in 1707 in an arrangement for recorder, are presented in Mather and Lasocki, *Free Ornamentation* pp. 21–5. Schmitz, *Die Kunst der Verzierung*, includes examples by Corelli and Geminiani, pp. 55–69. Further examples of free variations applied to Corelli's sonatas are found in D. Boyden, 'Corelli's Solo Violin Sonatas "Grac'd" by Dubourg', in *Festskrift Jens Peter Larsen* (Copenhagen: W. Hansen, 1972), pp. 113–25.

182/fn. 1

See also Lasocki and Mather, *The Classical Woodwind Cadenza*, which confirms that the use of thematic material remained the exception rather than the rule long after Quantz's time.

page/line

185/fn. 1

See Lasocki and Mather, *The Classical Woodwind Cadenza*, which includes examples by Tromlitz and numerous other composers of his time.

193/§ 33 6

The various alternatives indicated in the following sentences are conveniently written out as they could be used in a Handel sonata in Lasocki and Mather, *The Classical Woodwind Cadenza*, p. 2.

193/§ 34 7

Again, Lasocki and Mather, p. 3, have provided an appropriate context for this example, in this case a Telemann concerto for flute and violin.

CHAPTER XVII

Section I

212/fn. 1

For a variant of this plan, presented together with one for the Turin theatre orchestra as shown by Francesco Galeazzi, *Elementi teorico-practici di musica, con un saggio sopra l'arte di suonare il violino*, 2 vols. (Rome, 1791–6), see Neal Zaslaw, 'Toward the Revival of the Classical Orchestra', *Proceedings of the Royal Musical Association*, 103 (1976–7), p. 161. Zaslaw, whose work adds substantially to our knowledge of the orchestra in the eighteenth century, also provides further information about the placement of members of concert orchestras on pp. 164–6.

214/fn. 2

Again, see N. Zaslaw, 'Toward the Revival of the Classical Orchestra', pp. 170–85, for extensive figures on the sizes of orchestras in the latter decades of the eighteenth century, and for a comparative table that shows Quantz's recommendations for the proper balances between the strings and those suggested in later treatises. It may be noted that Frederick's musical establishment, as reported by Marpurg in 1754, included 11 violinists, 3 violists, 4 cellists, 1 gambist, 2 bass viol players, 3 oboists, 4 bassoon players, 3 flautists (in addition to Quantz, who did not play in the opera orchestra), and 2 horn players. It is clear, however, that the entire group did not always play at the same time, and that Frederick often used a small ensemble for his chamber concerts. An interesting receipt, signed by Quantz, now in the Miller Collection in the Library of Congress, lists payments to musicians in Potsdam on 24 July 1750 for work during the preceding month. The personnel listed suggest that at least on some occasions Frederick's concerts, with their performances of his own and Quantz's concertos and sonatas, were presented by a string quartet and harpsichord. An eighteenth-century engraving by P. Haas of Frederick playing with his orchestra (a much more prosaic view than that found in the famous nineteenth-century painting of A. Menzel) suggests an ensemble of about the size of either the first or second alternatives listed in § 16. See also the picture of a chamber concert included in the original edition of the *Versuch*, facing p. 342 of this edition.

Section II

215/fn. 1

Boyden's book *The History of Violin Playing from its Origins to 1761 and its Relationship to the Violin and Violin Music* (London: Oxford University Press, 1965), now offers the most comprehensive treatment of the subject in English.

221/Fig. 18

The lack of strokes about the second and third quavers in bar 4 of this example corresponds with the original text, but the continuation of the preceding pattern would certainly have been assumed.

226/Fig. 30

The example in Fig. 30 (and also Fig. 31) is as it is found in the original work. The cross bars for the semiquavers, however, are a little muddy and look a bit like extra dots. In both examples a $\frac{4}{4}$ metre is assumed.

226/fn. 2

For additional discussions of multiple stops, see Boyden, *The History of Violin Playing*, pp. 435–48, and Neumann, *Ornamentation*, pp. 500–3. Neumann's interpretation of this example is certainly possible—perhaps even probable—and would be one way to resolve Quantz's own contradictory statements. It should be noted, however, that in the third sentence of this paragraph Quantz says that the strings must be 'geschwind nach einander berühret', an expression that seems unlikely if he wanted two or three strings struck simultaneously. It should be further stressed that this section is intended for orchestral players, and the kind of multiple stops that Quantz mentions are in fact used with some frequency in the ritornellos of his concertos (see for example Concertos 97, 104, and 115 in Frederick's collection). The fact that ensemble performance was what Quantz had in mind might also tend to support Neumann's view.

228/fn. 1

Neumann, *Ornamentation*, in countless references in the sections of his work devoted to 'One-Note Graces', pp. 47–199, provides the most exhaustive documentation presented to date for the use of short pre-beat and on-the-beat appoggiaturas, especially the former. Examples in Quantz's *Solfeggi* suggest that he used both pre- and on-beat short appoggiaturas, depending on the specific musical context and the sentiment he wished to express. The majority of the published modern editions of Quantz's music, except for a few of the most recent, tend systematically to overlook his directions for the use of short appoggiaturas.

231/34

See the article by D. Lasocki cited above, n. 124, § 15 2.

232/§ 27 1

For a useful review of the various uses of the term *staccato* by Quantz and other eighteenth-century musicians, see Boyden, *History of Violin Playing*, pp. 408–26.

235/fn. 3

See also, Neumann, *Ornamentation*, pp. 511–22, and the previous reference to vibrato by Quantz in Chapter XIV, § 19, with the accompanying notes.

page/line

Section VI

251/fn. 1

Special attention should perhaps be drawn to *L'armonico pratico al cimbalo* (Venice, 1708) by Francesco Gasparini, who was one of Quantz's teachers during his stay in Italy in 1724–7, and *Der General-Bass in der Composition* (Dresden, 1728) by Johann David Heinichen, who was active at Dresden at the time when Quantz was there. The former has been translated by Frank S. Stillings as *The Practical Harmonist at the Keyboard* (New Haven: Yale University Press, 1968), and the latter in part by George J. Buelow as *Thorough-Bass Accompaniment According to Johann David Heinichen* (Berkeley: University of California Press, 1966).

256/*38*

After the original publication of this translation, I located a realization of the figured bass in this example in Johann (or John) Casper Heck's *The Art of Playing Thorough Bass* (London: John Welcker, *c*. 1767; later editions John Preston, 1793 and *c*. 1795). About Heck (*c*. 1740–91) we know very little except that he was a German émigré to England, and the author of this and several other instructional works. Although his realization does not reflect all of the specific recommendations made by Quantz (see especially §§ 15–17 of this Section), he does hold to the basic principle of reinforcing stronger dissonances by adding a fourth part to a three-part realization, and by further emphasizing certain dissonances by also doubling the bass. This realization is reproduced below, pp. 373–6.) Curiously, Heck omitted virtually all of Quantz's dynamic markings. The realization is discussed in more detail in my study 'A Realization by J. C. Heck', in *Notations and Editions*, ed. Edith Borroff (Dubuque, Iowa: Wm. C. Brown, 1974), pp. 154–62. (Reprint, New York: Da Capo, 1977.)

Section VII

267/fn. 1

Mendel substantially revised his earlier work in later studies. His final examination of the subject appeared in 'Pitch in Western Music since 1500—A Re-examination', *Acta Musicologica*, L (1978), pp. 1–93. Quantz's position in relation to his contemporaries is considered most fully in pp. 73–80. It should be noted, however, that the reference on p. 21 to a flute by F. Boie 'that has belonged to Quantz' should be corrected in the light of the report of L. G. Langwill, 'Notes and Queries', *The Galpin Society Journal*, XIV (March 1961), pp. 72–3. Langwill shows that the flute dates from after Quantz's death. The flute by I. Biglioni, now in the Museum of Fine Arts in Boston, which is also supposed to have belonged to Quantz, differs from other instruments that have the characteristic features of his own two-keyed instruments.

281/§ 41 *4*

Although Quantz's statement here seems odd, the German and French texts are unequivocal. I believe that he is describing a situation which is in fact encountered in certain of his concertos which diverge somewhat from what is 'normal' at this time. More often than not, the opening solo section of a concerto would begin with a solo restatement of the opening idea of the ritornello. Thus if the soloist began with a different rhythmic pattern, it required special attention.

283/§47 *3*

For a recent reconsideration of Quantz's use of the pulse beat as a guide to setting tempi, see R. Erig, 'Zum "Pulsschlag" bei Johann Joachim Quantz', *Tibia*, vii (1982), pp. 168–75.

287/fn. 4

H. C. Wolff, 'Das Metronom des Louis-Léon Pajot 1735', in *Festskrift Jens Peter Larsen* (Copenhagen: W. Hansen, 1972), pp. 205–17, provides further details about Pajot's work, and includes many of the musical examples cited by him.

292/fn. 1

See also the article by H. C. Wolff, cited above, and especially the conclusions of N. Zaslaw cited by Donington in his 'Postscript to New Version', *Interpretation*, p. 404. It cannot be stressed too emphatically that Quantz speaks of tempos for genuine dances of the types presented in court ballets staged in Dresden and Berlin, where French ballet masters were hired to offer dance productions, often between the acts of Italian operas. Unfortunately, little of this music seems to have survived, and still less has been studied and made available in modern editions. The dances for Graun's opera, *Montezuma*, although they include a number with the simple heading 'Ballo' or only an Italian tempo designation, are in fact largely French types, and may give some idea of the kind of music that Quantz had in mind. These dances are reproduced in the modern edition of the opera published as vol. 15 of the *Denkmäler deutscher Tonkunst* (Leipzig: Breitkopf & Härtel, 1904), pp. 222–31. Although distinct relationships exist between dances intended for ballets, those intended for balls, and independent music using dance rhythms but not intended for dancing, the differences between these categories are perhaps even more important. To use Quantz as a guide to the tempos for the dances in J. S. Bach's keyboard, violin, 'cello or orchestral suites can lead to disastrous musical results.

The example of an accompanied recitative included in the following paragraph is also very similar to what one finds in *Montezuma* (see, for example, p. 167 in the edition cited).

313/*3*

Raymond H. Haggh, in his translation of Türk's *School of Clavier Playing*, cited earlier, pp. 506–12, provides a valuable discussion of the terms *Einschnitt* and *Cäsur* as they were used in eighteenth-century German sources.

CHAPTER XVIII

316/*6*

Telemann apparently raised some questions about distinctions between various types of French overtures, to which Quantz responded in his letter to the composer quoted in *Quantz and His Versuch*, pp. 61–2.

317/fn. 2

In the letter by Quantz to Telemann just cited Quantz also explains his reasons for his choice of this group of quartets, indicating that 'these very quartets are the ones that first made me personally most clearly aware of the characteristics of good quartets and inspired me some years ago to venture into just this field'. At present, unfortunately, none of Quantz's quartets has been located.

370

Appendix

page/line

318/fn. 1 2

For more comprehensive lists of trio sonatas by Quantz, see *Quantz and His Versuch*, pp. 157–60, and the supplement below, pp. 390–3.

318/fn. 1 4

The preface to this collection is translated in full, together with a discussion of the pieces included in the volume, in my article 'Further Musical Examples for Quantz's *Versuch*', *Journal of the American Musicological Society*, xvii (1964), pp. 157–69. Quantz's *Solfeggi* include many passages from duets, with a considerable number from works by Telemann, W. F. Bach, and compositions by Quantz himself that have been lost.

318/fn. 2

A more extended list of solo sonatas is found in *Quantz and His Versuch*, pp. 160–2, and its supplement below, p. 387–94.

320/fn. 1

Another valuable document related to the differences between French and Italian styles, somewhat closer in time to Quantz's maturity, is Charles de Brosses' *Letter on Italian Music* of 1739–40, recently translated and published by Donald S. Schier (Northfield, Minnesota, 1978). The contrasts between the styles were also reflected in specific compositions. As early as 1659 Lully wrote a 'Dialogue de la musique italienne et de la musique française' for his *Ballet de la Raillerie*, reproduced on pp. 16–19 of the 'Appendice Musical' of H. Prunières, *L'Opéra italien en France avant Lulli* (Paris: Librairie ancienne Honoré Champion, 1913). And in his *Nürnberger Partita* of 1701 J. J. Fux contrasted Italian and French styles in the upper parts of a trio sonata. The work has been published, ed. A. Hoffmann, in the *Corona* series, No. 18 (Wolfenbüttel: Möseler Verlag, 1939).

324/fn. 2

In his *Solfeggi*, however, Quantz does include passages from a few duets by Tartini.

328/fn. 1

It is perhaps worth noting that Quantz, who seems to have strong leanings toward the Italian style, was seen by at least one of his contemporaries as a representative of the French. Marpurg, in his *Des critischen Musicus an der Spree erster Band* (Berlin: Haude & Spener, 1750), p. 218, asks rhetorically, 'Do not Quantz, Benda, and Graun play in a very French manner?'

338/fn. 2

Quantz's example here remains something of a puzzle. F. Neumann, *Ornamentation*, p. 112, reproduces an example from the *Trifolium musicale* (1691) of Johann Christoph Stierlein (d. 1693) which shows a somewhat similar situation, in which the final D is called an *accent*, but it seems unlikely that Stierlein's example is intended to stop with the D. French *accents* would normally move on to a following pitch.

339/20

'The bleating schoolboys in the streets' (German: *die blökende Currentjungen*; French: *les garçons qui vont brailler dans nos rues*). The French text was used as a basis for interpretation of the German here, but misses some of the connotations. 'Currentjungen' was apparently used with the meaning of 'Kurrende-schüler', 'poor schoolboys singing in the street for bread' (as did Martin Luther). (*Cassell's New German and English Dictionary*, 1939 ed.)

page/line

Bibliography

Part I

345/23

A facsimile edition of the French translation, with an introduction by Antoine Geoffroy-Dechaume, and *réflexions* by Pierre Séchet on various aspects of the treatise, was published in Paris (Editions Aug. Zurfluh) in 1975.

346/31

Facsimile edition, Utrecht: Oosthoek, 1972.

347/23

Mr. Alan Preston has kindly informed me that the *Easy and Fundamental Instructions* are first listed in a catalogue of 1775. As indicated in n. 256 *38* above, a further English borrowing from the *Versuch*, predating the *Instructions* and also published by Welcker, is found in Johann Casper Heck, *The Art of Playing Thorough Bass* (London, *c.* 1767). Heck's work includes a realization of the figured bass of the *Affettuoso di molto* found on pp. 257–8 of this translation. This is reproduced on pp. 373–6 below.

347/43

Facsimile edition, Bologna: Forni Editore, 1969.

348/9

In the above list, I should have noted that I was principally concerned with documenting eighteenth-century editions of the *Versuch*. I have not attempted to list the numerous translations of brief or more extended passages from the treatise in modern works, many of which are included in Part II of this Bibliography. The unpublished dissertation of A. H. Christman, 'J. J. Quantz on the Musical Practices of His Time', Union Theological Seminary (N.Y.), 1950, should be added, however, to works noted here, as a work wholly devoted to the subject.

Part II

348/21

(ARNOLD) Also reprinted New York: Dover, 1966.

348/36

(BREITKOPF) Facsimile reprint, as *The Breitkopf Thematic Catalogue*, ed. Barry S. Brook, New York: Dover, 1966.

348/40

(BROSSARD) Facsimile reprint of 1st edition (1703), Amsterdam: Antiqua, 1964; of 2nd edition (1705), Hilversum: Knuf, 1965.

349/11

(CORRETTE) Facsimile edition, with an introduction and notes by Mirjam Nastasi, Buren: Knuf, 1978. English translation by Carol Reglin Farrar in *Michel Corrette and Flute-Playing in the Eighteenth Century*, 'Musical Theorists in Translation', vol. IX. New York: Institute of Mediaeval Music, 1970.

349/35

(GERBER) Reprinted Graz: Akademische Druck- und Verlagsanstalt, 1966.

page/line

349/49

(HEINICHEN) Partial translation by George J. Buelow, as *Thorough-Bass Accompaniment According to Johann David Heinichen*. Berkeley: University of California Press, 1966.

350/8

(HOTTETERRE) Translation with an introduction by D. Lasocki, London: Barrie & Rockliff, 1968. Translation with an introduction by P. M. Douglas, New York: Dover, 1968.

350/35

(MAHAUT) Reprinted, Buren: Knuf, 1979. Translation by Pauline E. Durichen, in *Divisions: A Journal of the Art & Practice of Early Music*, vol. 1, no. 1 (Sept. 1978), pp. 19–34 and no. 2 (Dec. 1978), pp. 28–46.

350/43

(MARPURG) Reprinted, Hildesheim: G. Olms, 1973.

351/17

(NETTL) Reprinted, Westport, Connecticut: Greenwood Press, n.d.

351/26

(NORMAN and SCHRIFTE) Reprinted, Westport, Connecticut: Greenwood Press, 1979.

352/18

(SCHEIBE) Reprinted, Amsterdam: Antiqua, 1966 and Hildesheim: G. Olms, 1970.

352/30

(SCHUBART) Reprint of the Vienna edition of 1806, Hildesheim: G. Olms, 1969.

352/39

(SULZER) Reprinted, Hildesheim: G. Olms, 1967–70.

352/49

(TOSI) Further reprints, New York: Johnson, 1969 (with an introduction by P. H. Lang) and Kennebunkport, Maine: Longwood Press, 1977. German translation, with important additions and modifications by J. F. Agricola, as *Anleitung zur Singkunst*. Berlin: Winter, 1757. Reprinted, Celle: H. Moeck, 1966 and Leipzig: VEB Deutscher Verlag für Musik, 1966.

353/2

(TROMLITZ) Reprinted, with an introduction and notes by Frans Vester, Amsterdam: Knuf, 1973. An English translation of the work is found in L. B. Hartig, 'Johann George Tromlitz's *Unterricht die Flöte zu Spielen:* a Translation and Comparative Study', doctoral dissertation, Michigan State University, 1982.

353/5

(VAUCANSON) Reprinted, with an introduction and notes by David Lasocki, together with an English translation entitled *An Account of the Mechanism of an Automaton or Image Playing on the German Flute* (London: T. Parker, 1742). Buren: Frits Knuf, 1979. Another English edition was published in London (*The Universal Magazine*, 1752), and another German edition in Augsburg (J. A. E. Maschenbaur, 1748).

Affetuoso di molto

Johann Joachim Quantz
Realization by J.C. Heck
ed. by Edward R. Reilly

BIBLIOGRAPHY II

Additional Books and Articles

ADDINGTON, CHRISTOPHER. 'In Search of the Baroque Flute. The Flute Family 1680–1750', *Early Music,* xii (1984), pp. 34–47.

ALLIHN, INGEBORG. *Georg Philipp Telemann und Johann Joachim Quantz. Der Einfluss einiger Kammermusikwerke Georg Philipp Telemanns auf das Lehrwerk des Johann Joachim Quantz 'Versuch einer Anweisung die Flöte traversiere zu spielen'.* Magdeburger Telemann-Studien, III. Magdeburg: Arbeitskreis 'Georg Philipp Telemann', 1971.

ANONYMOUS. *Dritter neuester und letzter Discours über Sechs Sonaten für die Querflöte und Bass, wodurch die Art angezeigt wird, wie die darinn befindliche ausserordentliche tiefe und hohe Töne zu spielen möglich sind, da Gioacchino Moldenit Nobile Danese da Glückstadt, Dilettante in Hamburgo.* Hamburg (?): n.d. (1753?).

ARNOLD, DENIS. 'Instruments and Instrumental Teaching in the Early Italian Conservatoires', *The Galpin Society Journal,* XVIII (1965), pp. 72–81.

——'Orchestras in Eighteenth-Century Venice', *The Galpin Society Journal,* XIX (1966), pp. 3–19.

Babitz, Sol. *Vocal De-Wagnerization & Other Matters.* Early Music Laboratory Bulletin, 10 (1973).

BATE, PHILIP. *The Flute: A Study of Its History, Development and Construction.* New York: W. W. Norton, 1969.

BEECHEY, GWILYM. 'J. J. Quantz (1697–1773) and His Flute Sonatas', *Musical Opinion,* no. 1206, vol. 101 (April 1978), pp. 298–9, 306.

BOWERS, JANE. 'New Light on the Development of the Transverse Flute between about 1650 and about 1770', *Journal of the American Musical Instrument Society,* III (1977), pp. 5–56.

BOYDEN, DAVID D. 'Corelli's Solo Violin Sonatas "Grac'd" by Dubourg', in *Festskrift Jens Peter Larsen.* Copenhagen: W. Hansen, 1972, pp. 113–25.

——*The History of Violin Playing from its Origins to 1761 and its Relationship to the Violin and Violin Music.* London: Oxford University Press, 1965.

BROFSKY, HOWARD. 'J. C. Bach, G. B. Sammartini, and Padre Martini: A *Concorso* in Milan in 1762', in *A Musical Offering: Essays in Honor of Martin Bernstein.* New York: Pendragon Press, 1977, pp. 63–8.

BROSSES, CHARLES DE. *Letter on Italian Music.* Translated and annotated by Donald S. Schier. Northfield, Minn.: the author, 1978.

BROWN, HOWARD MAYER. *Embellishing Sixteenth-Century Music.* Early Music Series 1. London: Oxford University Press, 1976.

BUELOW, GEORGE J. 'A Lesson in Operatic Performance Practice by Madame Faustina Bordoni', in *A Musical Offering: Essays in Honor of Martin Bernstein.* New York: Pendragon Press, 1977, pp. 79–96.

BYRNE, MAURICE. 'Schuchart and the Extended Foot-Joint', *The Galpin Society Journal,* XVIII (1965), pp. 7–13.

CHESNUT, JOHN HIND. 'Mozart's Teaching of Intonation', *Journal of the American Musicological Society*, XXX (1977), pp. 254–71.

COLLINS, MICHAEL. 'A Reconsideration of French Over-Dotting', *Music & Letters*, L (1969), pp. 111–23.

——'In Defense of the French Trill', *Journal of the American Musicological Society*, XXVI (1973), pp. 405–39.

CROCKETT, CHARLOTTE. 'The Berlin Flute Sonatas of Johann Joachim Quantz'. Ph.D. dissertation in musicology, University of Texas, 1982.

DAHLHAUS, CARL. 'Quantz und der "vermaniererte Mannheimer goût"', *Melos, NZ (Neue Zeitschrift für Musik)*, 2. Jahrgang, Heft 3 (May–June, 1976), pp. 184–6.

DEAN, WINTON. 'Vocal Embellishment in a Handel Aria', in *Studies in Eighteenth-Century Music: A Tribute to Karl Geiringer on His Seventieth Birthday*, edited by H. C. Robbins Landon and Roger E. Chapman. New York: Oxford University Press, 1970, pp. 151–9.

DELIUS, NIKOLAUS. 'Quantz' Schüler. Ein Beitrag zur Genealogie einer Flötenschule', *Tibia*, vii (1982), pp. 176–84.

DONINGTON, ROBERT. *A Performer's Guide to Baroque Music*. London: Faber and Faber, 1973.

——'A Problem of Inequality', *Musical Quarterly*, LIII (1967), pp. 503–17.

DUCKLES, VINCENT. 'Johann Adam Hiller's "Critical Prospectus for a Music Library"', in *Studies in Eighteenth-Century Music: A Tribute to Karl Geiringer on His Seventieth Birthday*, edited by H. C. Robbins Landon and Roger E. Chapman. New York: Oxford University Press, 1970, pp. 177–85.

DÜRR, ALFRED. 'Performance Practice of Bach's Cantatas', *American Choral Review*, XVI, no. 2 (April 1974), pp. 7–33.

EIGEMANN, SUNHILD. 'Studien an den Instrumentalkonzerten von Johann Joachim Quantz'. Ph.D. dissertation in musicology, Universität Bonn. In progress.

EIRIG, RICHARD. 'Zum "Pulsschlag" bei Johann Joachim Quantz', *Tibia*, vii (1982), pp. 168–75.

FARRAR, CAROL REGLIN. *Michel Corrette and Flute-Playing in the Eighteenth Century*. Musical Theorists in Translation, IX. Brooklyn: Institute of Mediaeval Music, 1970.

FULLER, DAVID. 'Dotting, the "French Style" and Frederick Neumann's Counter-Reformation', *Early Music*, 5 (1977), pp. 517–42.

FUX, JOHANN JOSEPH. *Nürnberger Partita* (1701). Edited by A. Hoffmann, *Corona* series, no. 18. Wolfenbüttel: Möseler Verlag, 1939.

GASPARINI, FRANCESCO. *The Practical Harmonist at the Harpsichord*. Translated by Frank S. Stillings. Edited by David L. Burrows. Music Theory Translation Series, 1. New Haven: Yale University Press, 1968.

GILLIAM, LAURA E., and WILLIAM LICHTENWANGER. *The Dayton C. Miller Flute Collection: A Checklist of the Instruments*. Washington, D.C.: Library of Congress, 1961.

GRAUN, CARL HEINRICH. *Montezuma: Oper in drei Akten*. Edited by Albert Mayer-Reinach. *Denkmäler Deutscher Tonkunst*, Erste Folge, vol. 15. Leipzig: Breitkopf & Härtel, 1904.

HANDEL, GEORGE FRIDERIC. *Three Ornamented Arias*. Edited by Winton Dean. London: Oxford University Press, 1976.

HEFLING, STEPHEN. 'Dots-Documents: A Dispassionate Review'. Typescript. 1980.

HILL, JOHN WALTER. *The Life and Works of Francesco Maria Veracini*. Ann Arbor, Mich.: UMI Research Press, 1979.

JACOBI, ERWIN R. 'Neues zur Frage "Punktierte Rhythmen gegen Triolen" und zur Transkriptionstechnik bei J. S. Bach', *Bach-Jahrbuch*, vol. 49 (1962), pp. 88–92.

KRICKEBERG, DIETER. 'Vergleich zwischen der Grifftabelle in "Versuch einer Answeisung die Flöte traversiere zu spielen" von Johann Joachim Quantz und einer entsprechenden Tabelle aus dem Besitz Friedrich des Grossen'. Typescript, n.d. Forthcoming translation in the Rosenbaum volume listed below.

LARSEN, JENS PETER. 'Handelian Tempo Problems and *Messiah*', *American Choral Review*, XIV, no. 1 (January 1972), pp. 31–41.

——'*Messiah* Performance Traditions', *American Choral Review*, XIV, no. 1 (January 1972), pp. 23–30.

LASOCKI, DAVID. 'Quantz and the Passions: Theory & Practice', *Early Music*, 6 (1978), pp. 556–67.

LASOCKI, DAVID, and BETTY BANG MATHER. *The Classical Woodwind Cadenza: a Workbook*. New York: McGinnis & Marx, 1978. (Based on the M.A. thesis 'The Eighteenth-Century Woodwind Cadenza', University of Iowa, 1972, by David Lasocki.)

LESURE, FRANÇOIS. *Bibliographie des éditions musicales publiées par Estienne Roger et Michel-Charles Le Cène (Amsterdam, 1696–1743)*. Publications de la Société Française de Musicologie. Deuxième série, 12. Paris: Société Française de Musicologie, 1969.

MATHER, BETTY BANG. *Interpretation of French Music from 1675 to 1775 for Woodwind and Other Performers*. New York: McGinnis & Marx, 1973.

——'Making Up Your Own Baroque Ornamentation', *The American Recorder*, xxii (1981), pp. 55–9.

MATHER, BETTY BANG and DAVID LASOCKI. *Free Ornamentation in Woodwind Music 1700–1775*. New York: McGinnis & Marx, 1976.

MENDEL, ARTHUR. 'Pitch in Western Music since 1500—A Re-examination', *Acta Musicologica*, L (1978), pp. 1–93.

MICHEL, WINFRIED. '*Solfeggi pour la Flûte Traversière avec l'enseignement, Par Monsr. Quantz*. Einige Bemerkungen über ein ungewöhnliches, lange vermisstes Dokument zur Auffürhrungspraxis des 18. Jahrhunderts', *Tibia*, I (1977), pp. 201–6.

MILLER, DAYTON C. 'Flutes of Frederick the Great: Authentic, Original Specimens and Replicas'. Manuscript notes (20 pp.), 1930–1, together with a typescript 'history of the Flute of Frederick the Great' (in the Miller Collection), dated 10 January 1930, from Dr. Achim von Arnim and Marie Waleska von Arnim. Washington, D.C.: Dayton C. Miller Collection, Music Division, Library of Congress.

MOLDENIT, JOACHIM VON. *Idea dell' articolare rappresentata nelle sei sonate da traversiere solo di Moldenit*. Hamburg: the author, n.d. (1753?).

MUNROW, DAVID. *Instruments of the Middle Ages and Renaissance*. London: Oxford University Press, 1976. (Available separately or with the EMI/HMV Angel record set, SLS 988, of the same name.)

NEW GROVE DICTIONARY OF MUSIC AND MUSICIANS, THE, edited by Stanley Sadie. 20 vols. London: Macmillan, 1980.

NEUMANN, FREDERICK. Communication to the *Journal of the American Musicological Society*, XIX (1966), pp. 435–7.

——'Couperin and the Downbeat Doctrine for Appoggiaturas', *Acta Musicologica*, XLI

(1969), pp. 71–85. Responses, XLII (1970), pp. 252–5, and XLIII (1971), pp. 106–8.

——*Essays in Performance Practice*. Ann Arbor: UMI Research Press, 1982.

——'External Evidence and Uneven Notes', *Musical Quarterly*, LII (1966), pp. 448–64.

——'Facts and Fiction about Overdotting', *Musical Quarterly*, XLIII (1977), pp. 155–85.

——'The French *Inégales*, Quantz, and Bach', *Journal of the American Musicological Society*, XVIII (1965), pp. 313–58. Responses, XIX, pp. 112–14, 435–9, and XX, pp. 473–85.

——'Letter to the Editor', *Early Music*, 6 (1978), p. 131.

——'Misconceptions about the French Trill in the 17th and 18th Centuries', *Musical Quarterly*, L (1964), pp. 188–206.

——'A New Look at Bach's Ornamentation', *Music and Letters*, XLI (1965), pp. 4–15, 126–36.

——'Notes on "Melodic" and "Harmonic" Ornaments', *Music Review*, XXIX (1968), pp. 249–56.

——'La note pointée et la soi-disant "manière française"', *Revue de Musicologie*, LI (1965), pp. 66–92. Translated by R. Harris and E. Shay as 'The dotted Note and the so-called French Style', *Early Music*, 5 (1977), pp. 310–24.

——'Once more: the "French overture style"', *Early Music* 7 (1979), pp. 39–45.

——*Ornamentation in Baroque and Post-Baroque Music. With Special Emphasis on J. S. Bach.* Princeton: Princeton University Press, 1978.

——'The Question of Rhythm in the Two Versions of Bach's French Overture, BWV 831', in *Studies in Renaissance and Baroque Music in Honor of Arthur Mendel*. Kassel: Bärenreiter, 1974, pp. 183–94.

——'The Use of Baroque Treatises on Musical Performance', *Music & Letters*, XLVIII (1967), pp. 315–24.

O'DONNELL, JOHN. 'The French Style and the Overtures of Bach', *Early Music*, 7 (1979), pp. 190–6, 336–45.

PONT, GRAHAM. 'Rhythmic Alteration and the Majestic', *Studies in Music* (Australia), no. 12 (1978), pp. 68–100.

PRUNIÈRES, HENRY. *L'Opéra italien en France avant Lulli*. Paris: Librairie ancienne Honoré Champion, 1913.

QUANTZ, JOHANN JOACHIM. Autograph letter to an unidentified correspondent, dated 11 February 1756. Location unknown. Described in an auction catalogue, item 775 on p. 89, for 21–3 May 1909, by the Berlin dealer Leo Liepmannsohn.

——Autograph receipt for four flutes, dated Potsdam, 23 November 1751, Dayton C. Miller Collection, Music Division, Library of Congress, Washington, D.C.

——Autograph receipt for three flutes and seven concertos, dated Potsdam, 25 October 1754. Location unknown. Described and reproduced in the sale of 20–1 November 1978 at Sotheby's in London. Listed as Lot 461 in the catalogue of the sale.

——Autograph receipt for payments to musicians, dated Potsdam, 24 July 1750, Dayton C. Miller Collection, Music Division, Library of Congress, Washington, D.C.

——Autograph untitled account of his life for Padre Martini, dated Berlin, 14 April 1762. Derived in part from his published autobiography. Civico Museo Bibliografico Musicale, Bologna. Item 4234 in the catalogue of Anne Schnoebelen cited below.

——On the facsimile of the French translation of the *Versuch* and other additions to the bibliography of his published works, see above, p. 000. On the *Solfeggi* with Quantz's

RASMUSSEN, MARY. 'Some Notes on the Articulations in the Melodic Variation Tables of Johann Joachim Quantz's *Versuch einer Anweisung die Flöte traversiere zu spielen* (Berlin 1752, Breslau 1789)', *Brass and Woodwind Quarterly*, I, nos. 1 and 2 (Winter 1966–7), pp. 3–26.

instructions, see below, p. 000.

REILLY, EDWARD R. *Quantz and His Versuch: Three Studies*. New York: American Musicological Society (distributed by Galaxy Music Corporation), 1971.

——'Quantz and Telemann', *NACWPI Journal*, XXI, no. 2 (Winter 1972–3), pp. 44–8.

——'A Realization by J. C. Heck', in *Notations and Editions: A Book in Honor of Louise Cuyler*, edited by E. Borroff. Dubuque, Iowa: Wm. C. Brown, 1974, pp. 154–62. The entire volume reprinted New York: Da Capo, 1977.

ROSENBAUM, ROBERT M. et al. *Pythagoras at the Forge: An Annotated Catalogue of the Rosenbaum Collection of Western European Instruments*. Boston: Philidor Press. Forthcoming.

SCHNOEBELEN, ANNE. *Padre Martini's Collection of Letters in the Civico Museo Bibliografico Musicale in Bologna*. New York: Pendragon Press, 1979.

SCHULZE, HANS-JOACHIM (ed.). *Bach-Dokumente*, vol. III *Dokumente zum Nachwirken Johann Sebastian Bachs 1750–1800*. Kassel: Bärenreiter, 1972, p. 206.

SEYFRIT, MICHAEL (compiler). *Musical Instruments in the Dayton C. Miller Flute Collection at the Library of Congress. A Catalog*. Volume I: *Recorders, Fifes, and Simple System Transverse Flutes of One Key*. Washington, D.C.: Library of Congress, 1982.

SMILES, JOAN E. 'Directions for Ornamentation in Italian Method Books', *Journal of the American Musicological Society*, XXXI (1978), pp. 495–509.

TELEMANN, GEORG PHILIPP. *Briefwechsel: sämtliche erreichbare Briefe*, edited by H. Grosse and H. R. Jung. Leipzig: VEB Deutscher Verlag für Music, 1972.

TÜRK, DANIEL GOTTLOB. *School of Clavier Playing or Instructions in Playing the Clavier for Teachers & Students*. Translation, introduction & notes by Raymond H. Haggh. Lincoln: University of Nebraska Press, 1982.

VINQUIST, MARY and NEAL ZASLAW. *Performance Practice: A Bibliography*. New York: W. W. Norton, 1971. Supplements in *Current Musicology*, no. 12 (1971) and no. 15 (1973).

VON HUENE, FRIEDRICH. 'Six Quantz Flutes'. *Continuo, An Early Music Magazine*, 3, no, 5 (1980), pp. 4–9.

WARNER, THOMAS E. An Annotated Bibliography of Woodwind Instruction Books, 1600–1830. Detroit: Information Coordinators, 1967.

——'Tromlitz's Flute Treatise: A Neglected Source of Eighteenth-Century Performance Practice', in *A Musical Offering: Essays in Honor of Martin Bernstein*. New York: Pendragon Press, 1977, pp. 261–73.

WELLS, GRAHAM. 'The London Salerooms in 1972', *Early Music*, 1 (1973), pp. 97–9.

WESTRUP, JACK. *Musical Interpretation*. London: British Broadcasting Corporation, 1971.

WOLFF, HELLMUTH CHRISTIAN. 'Das Metronom des Louis-Léon Pajot 1735', in *Festskrift Jens Peter Larsen*. Copenhagen: W. Hansen, 1972, pp. 205–17.

——*Original Vocal Improvisations from the 16th–18th Centuries*. Translated by A. C.

Howie. Anthology of Music Series, Cologne: Arno Volk Verlag, 1972 (London: distributed by Oxford University Press).

ZADRO, MICHAEL. 'Quantz and Flute Tone in Prussia', *Divisions: A Journal of the Art and Practice of Early Music,* I, no. 4 (1980), pp. 32–6.

ZASLAW, NEAL. 'The Compleat Orchestral Musician', *Early Music,* 7 (1979), pp. 46–57.

——'Toward the Revival of the Classical Orchestra', *Proceedings of the Royal Musical Association,* 103 (1976–7), pp. 158–87.

ZIMMERMANN, J. 'Die Flötenmacher Friedrichs des Grossen', *Zeitschrift für Instrumentenbau,* LX (1940), pp. 134ff.

BIBLIOGRAPHY III

Supplementary Lists of Quantz's Compositions, in Manuscript, Eighteenth-Century, and Modern Editions

A. QUANTZ'S COMPOSITIONS IN MANUSCRIPT.

The principal additions to the body of manuscripts listed in *Quantz and His Versuch*, pp. 134–43, are those made known through the publication of Inge Bittmann's *Catalogue of Giedde's Music Collection in the Royal Library of Copenhagen* (Copenhagen: Edition Egtved, 1976). Incipits of all of the works cited here are included in the catalogue. The collection contains the frequently cited 'Solfeggi pour la flûte traversière avec l'enseignement' [mu 6210. 2528 (I, 16)]; 12 Capricci, 8 Fantasias, and 21 Suite and Sonata movements [mu 6310. 0860 (I, 17)]; a 'Flauto Traverso Solo Dell Sig' Bezozzi o Quantz' [mu 6210. 1837 (I, 14)]; and a set of eight solo sonatas for transverse flute and continuo [mu 6210, 2526 (I, 13)]. The first of this set is a sonata in A minor not traced in other sources. The remaining seven are equivalent to Nos. 317, 312, 306, 354, 313, 348, and 301 in Frederick's collection. A single concerto for transverse flute in B minor [mu 6340. 2467 (VIII, 35)], has not been located in other collections. 'VI Sonates A Une Flute Traversier E Basse-Continue . . .' [mu 6210. 2530 (I, 20)], are a manuscript copy of the well-known *Sonates Italiennes*, presented in the order found in an undated Amsterdam edition (see *Quantz and His Versuch*, p. 151). 'Six Sonates pour la Flûte Traversière avec la Basse . . .' [mu 6210. 2529 (I, 19)], are manuscript copies of a collection of sonatas published in Paris, *c.* 1731 (see *Quantz and His Versuch*, p. 149). Three works entitled 'Trio a 3 D#' [mu 6212. 0328 (III, 28)], [mu 6212. 0327 (III, 29)], and [mu 6212. 0326 (III, 30)], are all works for three unaccompanied transverse flutes. The first is the same work found in Kat. Wenst Litt. L., No. 53 in the Universitetsbiblioteket in Lund. The second is unknown in other collections, but is found in another manuscript, [mu 6302. 1704 (III, 25)], in the Giedde Collection, attributed to 'Sign. Rinaldo Cesare', who may be Reinhard Keiser! The third sonata is the familiar work, also found in the Lund Library, and published in the eighteenth century in a collection issued by Boivin (see *Quantz and His Versuch*, pp. 145–6). A trio sonata for two transverse flutes and basso continuo in G major [mu 6212. 0330 (III, 27)], is not known from other sources; likewise a duet in D major [mu 6211. 1238 (II, 24)].

The Ms Litt. X.Y. 15, 115 in the Brussels Conservatory Library (recently published in facsimile by Éditions Culture et Civilisation, Brussels), contains two sonatas for flute and continuo connected with Quantz. One, Sonata XLII in B minor, is specifically attributed to the composer. It has not yet been traced in other sources. The second, Sonata XI, is a work in D major attributed in this source to 'M' Aug. Stricker', who is almost certainly the Augustin Reinhard Stricker cited by Walther in his *Musikalisches Lexikon* of 1732 (p. 582). This is also the same sonata noted in *Quantz and His Versuch*, pp. 141–2, found in one manuscript with an attribution to Handel, and in two eighteenth-century printed editions under Quantz's name. We shall probably never be entirely sure of the actual composer. If, however, the revised view of the two Walsh collections that I suggest below is accepted, this particular sonata would no longer be counted among the sonatas that Quantz identifies as genuine.

A facsimile edition of the Trio Sonata in E minor (K. 26), Mus. 2470/Q28 in the Sächsische Landesbibliothek in Dresden, together with the parts of the same work in M. Th. 178 in the Deutsche Staatsbibliothek in Berlin, was published in 1982 by the Reprintabteilung of the Zentralantiquariat der DDR in Leipzig. The Dresden score includes indications of the performance of the work either as a trio sonata or as a sonata with obbligato harpsichord. The Berlin parts are for the later arrangement, and include a number of ornaments not found in the Dresden manuscript. The editor of the facsimile, Horst Augsbach, believes the Dresden manuscript to be an autograph.

Attention should be drawn to the fact that the *Solfeggi* noted above, which are now available in a modern edition (see below), contain extracts from many of Quantz's own compositions. These excerpts establish the existence of a number of works unknown from other sources, and provide at the same time a wealth of information about the interpretation of specific passages in known works. Certain compositions are identified as by Quantz; others are not. Future editors of Quantz's music should not fail to make a careful study of this volume.

B.　　Eighteenth-Century Editions of Quantz's Music
　　　(see *Quantz and His Versuch*, pp. 144–54)

I.　　*Concertos.*
　　　No new editions traced. The concerto listed in RISM as Q23 is the one cited in my list. It is in E minor, however, not G major, as indicated in RISM.

II.　　*Trio Sonatas.*
　　　No new editions located. For the collection of Le Cène that I cite, however, the work of F. Lesure (see Bibliography II above) indicates that a date of *c.* 1732 is more accurate than 1734.

　　　Although not technically an edition in the usual sense, it is perhaps worth noting that a thirteen-measure excerpt from what appears to be a trio sonata by Quantz is cited by F. W. Marpurg in vol. 2 of his *Abhandlung von der Fuge* (Berlin: Haude and Spener, 1753–4), Tab. IV, Ex. 3. In the discussion of the passage, Marpurg describes it as an example of canonic imitation at the upper second and lower fourth. The passage is taken from the second movement of the Trio Sonata in G major, K. 6 and K. 7, found in two manuscripts in the Sächsische Landesbibliothek, Mus. 2470/Q 6 and Q 7. The former may be an autograph, since it carries the inscription at the end 'fatto per lei / e non per noi'. If this is an autograph, however, then the manuscript in the facsimile of K. 26 noted above is not.

III.　　*Duets.*
　　　Six Duets for two German flutes or violins, collected by Mr. Tacet (London: Welcker, *c.* 1770). (RISM Q22)

　　　In the period since I referred to this collection in the postscript to *Quantz and His Versuch*, p. x, it has been possible to confirm that this collection is in fact an unacknowledged edition of Quantz's *Sei Duetti*, originally published in Berlin in

1759. Mr. Tacet, of course, was Joseph Tacet. He and Pietro Grassi Florio were perhaps the two most famous flautists in England in the second half of the eighteenth century. Although Tacet only claims to have 'collected' the works, no mention of Quantz's name is found in the edition.

IV. *Solo Sonatas.*

As with the collection of trio sonatas noted above, the set of *Sei Sonate a Flauto Traversiere Solo* . . . published by Le Cène (*Quantz and His Versuch*, p. 149) can now be dated on the basis of the work of F. Lesure as *c.* 1732. The two collections of Walsh, *ibid.,* pp. 148–9 have now been published in facsimile editions by Afour Editions in London. The conclusions that I reached with regard to which works in these collections were genuine must now be revised in the light of the contents of the two Witvogel volumes cited below (see 2 and 3).

1. Sonates Italiennes, / Composée / PAR MR QUOUANCE. / Flûte Traversiere Seule, / et, / Basse Continue, / Très propres à former le gout, et, la / main de ceux qui veulent parvenir aux / difficultés, qui sont à present en usage / Sur cet Instrument. / Le Prix est de 3^{ll} en blanc / Se Vend / A Paris / chez Le St Boivin Marchand Rue St Honore / a la Regle D'or. (RISM Q16) [Accents are present or absent in accordance with the original source in this and following notes.]

The previously missing printed edition of these sonatas has now reappeared in the Deutsche Staatsbibliothek in East Berlin. The privilège is dated 8 July, 1729, however, rather than 9 July. The first of the two volumes published by Witvogel, cited immediately below, forms yet another edition of the complete set of sonatas; and the failure of these two volumes to coincide with those of Walsh may invalidate my conclusions that sonatas IV and VI are spurious. For more details, see the discussion below.

2. VI Sonate / a Flauto Traversa Solo e Basso Continuo / Del Signor / Quants / Opera Prima / Imprime aux Depens / de Gerhard Fredrik Witvogel, / Chez le quel on Les Trouve / a Amsterdam. / No 8. [1731 or 32] (RISM Q24)

3. VI Sonate / a Flauto Traversa Solo e Basso Continuo / Del Signor / Quants / Opera Seconda / Imprimé aux depens / de Gerhard Fredrik Witvogel / Chez le quel on Les trouve / a Amsterdam. No 9. [1731 or 32] (RISM Q27)

The approximate dates provided can be established from the publisher's plate numbers. The title pages, with their common spelling of Quants, would lead one to expect that these two volumes were the two missing Dutch collections that Quantz mentions in the *Avertimento* to his Dresden *Sei Sonate* of 1734, and thus that their contents would be identical to the two volumes of sonatas published by Walsh (see *Quantz and His Versuch*, pp. 148–9). In fact, however, the two Witvogel volumes further complicate the difficult question of which volumes Quantz meant when he wrote of 'twelve sonatas for transverse flute and bass divided into two books published in London and Amsterdam under the name of the author but without his knowledge'. The question is of some importance because he identifies four of them (Bk. 1, no. 3; Bk. 2, nos. 4, 5, and 6) as spurious. The Witvogel *Opera Prima*, rather than coinciding with Walsh's first volume, corresponds exactly in its contents with the *Sonates Italiennes.* Just as surprisingly, Witvogel's *Opera Seconda* contains the same works as Walsh's first collection, not his *Opera Seconda*.

Thus we still have no equivalent editions of twelve sonatas published in both London and Amsterdam. And since no further evidence has been found to suggest that still more unknown editions of solo sonatas were published in both of these cities, it may be appropriate to question whether Quantz had himself actually *seen* both editions. In his autobiography, published in 1755, he disavows 'other sonatas' published under his name 'in Holland' before 1734. No mention is made of London. An additional piece of evidence has also been located which points to the likelihood that Quantz was referring to the Witvogel volumes, but not those of Walsh. In the *Solfeggi* discovered in the Danish Royal Library already frequently cited, the flute part of the entire second movement of the sixth of the *Sonates Italiennes*, and thus also of Witvogel's *Opera Prima*, is found (see p. 24 of the published edition). No composer's name is given, but the majority of the unidentified passages are by Quantz; and the last composer cited before this passage is Neuff, a pupil of Quantz far too young to have written a work published in 1729. This same sonata is found as no. IV in Walsh's *Opera Seconda*; and if Quantz had been referring to Walsh's volumes this sonata would have been counted among the spurious ones. The very presence of the music in the *Solfeggi* volume suggests, although it may not conclusively prove, that the work is genuine. By default, the Witvogel volumes seem to be the only alternative to those of Walsh. Thus, at this time, the available evidence indicates that the third sonata of the *Sonates Italiennes* and of Witvogel's *Opera Prima* may not be by Quantz; and that the fourth, fifth and sixth sonatas of Witvogel's *Opera Seconda* and Walsh's first collection may be spurious. Thus the manuscript sonata mentioned above in the Brussels Conservatory Library attributed to Augustin Reinhard Stricker would fall among the works that Quantz himself disclaims. Works which also appear in other collections must be related to those noted here.

A further, rather unlikely possibility, however, needs to be explored in more detail before it can be entirely ruled out. This is the question of whether the contents of the Walsh editions varied. The matter cannot be settled until all of the surviving prints have been examined. One modern edition of what purports to be Walsh's *Opera Seconda*, edited by Dieter Sonntag, and published by Willy Müller, Süddeutscher Musikverlag in 1965, in fact contains all but one (the fifth sonata) of the works from Walsh's *first book*. The basis for this confusing situation remains unclear.

4.   SIX / SONATES / Pour / La Flute Traversiere; / Avec la Basse Chiffrée. / Composees / Par / Mr Quanze. / OEUVRE SECOND. / Prix en blanc 3^{ll} 10^{ss} / SE VEND A PARIS. / Chez [the following two lines bracketed] / le S^a Boivin, rue St. Honore a la Regle d'Or. / le S^a Le Clerc, rue du Roule a la Croix d'Or. / Avec Privilege du Roy. [*c.* 1731] (RISM Q28)

The privilège is preserved, and is dated 17 April 1731, and was apparently issued to J. Chauvelin rather than Jacques Charlier, as indicated by Brenet (see *Quantz and His Versuch*, p. 154).

This unique collection provides several further examples of the oddities of eighteenth-century music publishing, and of the problems connected with the early printed editions of Quantz's music. The volume contains six sonatas in the following keys: 1) G major; 2) D major; 3) E minor; 4) D minor; 5) G major; 6) D major. The second, third and fifth sonatas have thus far been traced in neither printed nor manuscript forms in other collections. The first sonata, however, is the same as Walsh's Op. 2, No. 5. The fourth sonata is the same as Walsh's first collection, No. 3, but transposed from E minor in the Walsh volume to D minor here. And the sixth sonata is equivalent to Walsh's Op. 2, No. 3; but the second movement of the work in the present volume differs from that provided by Walsh, and is in fact the same as the *first movement* from the opening sonata (No. 1) of Walsh's first collection!

With the discovery of this edition and those mentioned below, it is now possible to establish a sequence of four sets of solo sonatas by Quantz published by various members of the Boivin and Le Clerc families. These collections range from the *Sonates Italiennes* cited above through the present *oeuvre second* and the *oeuvre IV* noted below, and the *Livre III* described in *Quantz and His Versuch*, p. 149. An earlier *Oeuvre Troisième*, cited *ibid*, p. 46, published by St Boivin *c*. 1728 contains trio sonatas, however, and complicates the apparently neat series just outlined. And in its spelling of Quantz's name (Quanze) and the style of engraving, the trio sonata collection is more obviously related to the sonata collection described here than to the *Livre III*. The evident uncertainties remain unresolved.

5. VI. Sonate / a flauto traversiere solo, / é Cembalo / Dedicate / Alla Maesta D'Augusto III. / Re di pollonia / Elettore di Sassonia. / Da / Gio. Gioacchino Quantz Sonatore du [sic] Camera / di S. M. / Cette Edition a Esté Gravée Par J. L. Renou, sur celle / de L'Auteur fait a Dresden. / Prix 4^ll / A PARIS, / Chez [the following three lines bracketed] M^r Le Clerc le Cadet rue St Honore vis-avis l'Oratoire à la Ville de Constantinople. / M^r Le Clerc M^d rue du Roule à la Croix d'Or. / Me Boivin M^de rue St Honoré à la Règle d'Or. / Avec Privilege du Roy [1739?] (RISM Q34)

6. VI Sonate a flauto traversiere solo / é Cembalo / Dedicate / Alla Maesta d'Augusto III / Re di Pollonia / Elletore di Sassonia / Da / Gio. Gioacchino Quantz, Sonatore di Camera / di S. M. / Oeuvre IV / Cette Edition a été gravée Par J. L. Renou sur celle / de l'Auteur fait a Dresden / Prix: 4^ll / A Paris / Chez [the following three lines bracketed] M^r Le Clerc rue St Honoré *Avis* le Portail de l'Oratoire / chez le M^d Bonnetier / M^r Le Clerc M^d rue du Roule à la Croix d'Or. / Me Boivin M^de rue St Honoré à la Règle d'Or / Avec Privilège du Roy. (RISM Q20)

Although it has not been possible to examine item 6 directly, the information kindly provided by its late owner, André Meyer, makes it virtually certain it is the same as item 5, except for a new title page that differs in several respects from that for 5. Most notably *Oeuvre IV* is added to this edition; but the manner of advertising the address of the two Le Clercs also differs. With item 5, a catalogue is found but no privilège; and apparently no privilège is preserved for 6 either. The catalogue advertises 'Quantz nouveau F-S. Livre 4.' (F-S indicates *flûte seule*, which in this instance means sonatas for a solo flute with figured bass.) The volume listed may well be this collection. The address for Le Clerc le Cadet in item 5 is that at which he was located in 1739. And a privilège is known to have been issued to Nicolas Chedeville for 'les quatre de Quantz' on 12 October 1739. 'Les quatre' may perhaps be a misreading for 'Livre quatre'. The manner in which the first Le Clerc's address is listed in item 6 is given an uncertain date between 1740 and 1743 by Cecil Hopkinson in his *A Dictionary of Parisian Music Publishers, 1700–1950* (p. 73).

Whatever the uncertainties of the date of publication, the contents of the collection are just as indicated in both titles: a nicely engraved French edition of Quantz's 1734 *Sei Sonate . . . Opera Prima*, published in Dresden. Quantz's failure to mention these and other French editions of his music in his autobiography should perhaps be noted, since it leaves unanswered questions about whether he was actually unaware of these editions, in spite of his acquaintanceship with Blavet and Buffardin (who returned to Paris when he retired), or whether he simply did not wish to acknowledge them after he had formally entered the service of Frederick in 1741.

Copies of the *Suites des pieces a deux flutes* and the *Concerto 2ᵉ* listed in *Quantz and His Versuch*, pp. 153–4 remain unlocated. A *Catalogue of the Music Library, Instruments and Other Property of Nicolas Selhof, Sold in the Hague, 1759*, facsimile edition, with an introduction by A. Hyatt King (Amsterdam: F. Knuf, 1973), p. 109, lists as item 409 'XII Sonata (sic) a Flauto Traverso Solo e Basso Continuo di *Quants, Braning, Scherer*, & libro primo', which also remain untraced. This catalogue, pp. 107 and 146, also contains references to six sets of solo sonatas and two collections of trio sonatas which can be identified with volumes listed in *Quantz and His Versuch* and here. Valuable as the material contained in the RISM account of Quantz's works is, the division into presumably genuine and 'questionable' collections is both inaccurate and misleading. Item 5 above, for example, is included in the questionable group, while item 6 appears among the genuine.

C.   MODERN EDITIONS OF QUANTZ'S MUSIC
        (see *Quantz and His Versuch*, pp. 155–63)

The situation that I noted some years ago with regard to the haphazard selection of Quantz's works for modern editions remains generally true, with some happy exceptions. The most sizeable available segment of Quantz's work in a given form is found in the trio sonatas, but even in this phase of his output few of the three-movement works in the Fast–Slow–Fast pattern have been examined. The current work of Charlotte Crockett on the solo sonatas in Berlin and that of Sunhild Eigemann on the concertos will, it is hoped, lead to both fuller and more selective publication of Quantz's better works. The publication of 42 sonatas for flute and continuo, edited by Gilbert Blount and Charlotte Crockett, plans for which have been announced by A-R Editions, should mark a decisive step forward in making available a representative sample of Quantz's work in this genre, at present the most poorly represented in modern editions. In the following lists I have attempted to include only the more important and accessible of the editions that have appeared since *Quantz and His Versuch* was completed. As in the previous lists, the concertos and solo sonatas are identified, when possible, by their numbers in the collections of Frederick the Great, the trio sonatas by their numbers in the catalogue of Karl-Heinz Köhler in his unpublished dissertation 'Die Triosonate bei den Dresdener Zeitgenossen Johann Sebastian Bachs' (Friedrich-Schiller-Universität, Jena, 1956).

I. *Concertos.*

1. Concerto No. 1 in G minor for 2 Flutes and Orchestra. Edited by H. Voxman and R. P. Block. London: Musica Rara, © 1974. Pub. no. M. R. 1645.

    Not in Frederick's collection. The number is supplied by the editors. A good, straightforward edition of what is probably an early work, based on a manuscript in the Sächsische Landesbibliothek. Three other concertos for two flutes have been announced for publication by the same company, but have not yet appeared.

2. Concerto in E minor [No. 83] for Flute and Piano [sic]. Edited by Jean-Pierre Rampal. New York: International Music Co., © 1976. Pub. no. 2875.

    No indication of source. Possibly from a manuscript in the Library of Congress, Washington, D.C.

3. Concerto in D major [No. 92] for Flute and Piano. Edited by Jean-Pierre Rampal. New York: International Music Co., © 1976. Pub. no. 2874.

    No indication of source. Again possibly from a manuscript in the Library of Congress, Washington, D.C.

4. Concerto in C minor [No. 108] for Flute and Piano. Edited by Jean-Pierre Rampal. International Music Co., © 1976. Pub. no. 2696.

    Previously issued in an edition by Dieter Sonntag, upon which the present edition seems to be based. See item 4 in my original list of concertos. Available in full score in that edition.

5. Concerto in D minor [No. 113] for Flute, Strings and Basso Continuo. Edited by David Lasocki. Continuo realization by Robert P. Block. London: Musica Rara, © 1972. Edition no. M. R. 1567b.

    Based on a manuscript in the Staatsbibliothek Preußischer Kulturbesitz, West Berlin. An excellent edition of one of the most interesting of the concertos now available. Also published in an edition for flute with keyboard reduction of the orchestral accompaniment.

6. Konzert G-moll [No. 132] für Flöte, Streicher und Basso continuo. Edited by Klaus Burmeister. Continuo-Aussetzung von Lorenz Stolzenbach. Leipzig: Edition Peters, © 1976. Edition Peters Nr. 9696.

Based on manuscripts in the Deutsche Staatsbibliothek, East Berlin. Also available in an edition for flute and keyboard.

7. Concerto in Sol Maggiore [No. 161] per Flauto, Archi e continuo. Arranged for flute and piano, revised with cadences [cadenzas] and edited according to the original manuscript by Oliver Nagy. Budapest: Edition Musica, 1969. Pub. no. Z. 5568.

8. Concerto in G major [No. 161] for Flute and Piano. Edited and provided with cadenzas by Jean-Pierre Rampal. New York: International Music Co., © 1972. Pub. no. 2687.

Further editions of the most familiar of all of Quantz's concertos. The Eulenburg miniature score of this work (No. 7 in my original list) still offers the most straightforward version of the work.

9. Konzert für Flöte und Streicher A-dur [No. 256]. Edited by J. P. Müller and Z. Jeney. Klavierauszug von. I. Mezö. Budapest: Edition Musica and Adliswil-Zürich: Edition Eulenburg, © 1973. Pub. no. Z. 6597. Eulenburg General Music Series GM 105.

Based on manuscripts in the Staatsbibliothek in Berlin. The only edition currently available of one of the later concertos.

II. *Trio Sonatas*

1. Sonate en Trio pour deux Flûtes et Clavecin [in ré majeur] [K. 12]. Edited by C. Crussard. *Flores musicae* no. 12. Lausanne: Edition Foetisch, 1961. Edition no. F. 8075 F.

No source indicated. Two previous editions of this work are listed in *Quantz and His Versuch*, p. 158. That edited by H. Ruf still seems preferable to me.

2. Trio-Sonate für zwei Flöten und Basso continuo [E moll] [K. 24]. Edited by G. Pistorius. Wiesbaden: Breitkopf & Härtel, © 1972. Edition Breitkopf Nr. 6665.

No manuscript source indicated. This work is one of two (see *Quantz and His Versuch*, p. 142) which appear in different manuscripts attributed to Quantz and to J. D. Heinichen. At present a positive attribution to one or the other of the two composers cannot be made.

3. Triosonate [in] G major for German Flute, Oboe d'amore or Violin and B. c [K. 37]. Edited by Hugo Ruf. Wilhelmshaven: Heinrichshofen (New York: C. F. Peters), © 1972. Pub. no. N 1290.

4. Trio Sonata in G major for flute and oboe d'amore [K. 37]. Edited by Uwe Friedrichsen and Stellan Jonsson. *Ludus instrumentalis* no. 94. Hamburg: Sikorski, © 1973. Edition no. 778.

The source of these two editions is the manuscript Mus. 2470/Q/39 in the Sächsische Landesbibliothek. Both editions offer straightforward realizations of the continuo part.

5. Trio-Sonate g-moll für Flöte, Violine und Basso continuo [K. 32]. Edited by G.

Pistorius. Wiesbaden: Breitkopf & Härtel, © 1973. Ed. Breitkopf Nr. 6666.

No manuscript source indicated.

6.   Trio Sonata in F minor for 2 flutes [K. 34]. Edited by G. Pistorius. *Ludus instrumentalis* no. 102. Hamburg: Sikorski, © 1974. Edition no. 794.

Based on the manuscript of the sonata in the Sächsische Landesbibliothek.

7.   Trio Sonata in B minor for flute and violin [K. 29]. Edited by G. Pistorius. *Ludus instrumentalis* no. 101. Hamburg: Sikorski, © 1974. Edition no. 793.

Based on the manuscript of the sonata in the Sächsische Landesbibliothek.

8.   Trio Sonata in C minor for flute, oboe & basso continuo [K. 36]. Edited by D. Lasocki. Realization of the basso continuo by R. P. Block. London: Musica Rara, © 1975. Edition no. N. M. 103.

A critical edition based on all the existing manuscript sources, and a much more satisfactory presentation of this fine work than the old Zimmermann edition listed as no. 10 in my original survey.

9.   Trio Sonata in G major for oboe, violoncello or bassoon and harpsichord [K. 45]. Edited by Walter Bergmann. London: Schott & Co., © 1975. Edition no. 11254.

10.   Trio Sonata in G K. 46 [actually K. 45] for oboe, bassoon or violoncello & basso continuo. Edited by David Lasocki. London: Nova Music, © 1979.

Nos. 9 and 10 offer two quite different realizations of this work for an unusual combination of instruments. The source of both editions is a manuscript in the Queen's Music Library, British Library, London (R. M. 21. b. 7, ff. 1ʳ–5ᵛ).

11.   Trio Sonata in C major for flute, violin, and basso continuo (cello) [K. 2]. Kalmus Chamber Music Series no. 4816. Melville, N.Y.: Belwin Mills, n.d.

In spite of the title, this edition is in fact a reprint of the Sonata for recorder, transverse flute and basso continuo published in the *Hortus Musicus* series (see no. 11 in the original list).

12.   Trio Sonata in D major for flute (or oboe) violin and basso continuo [K. 12]. Kalmus Chamber Music Series no. 4817. Melville, N.Y.: Belwin Mills, n.d.

A reprint of the edition originally published as No. 32 in the *Organum* series (see no. 3 in the original list).

13.   Sonata E-moll für Flöte und Obligates Cembalo. Faksimile nach dem Autograph der Sächsischen Landesbibliothek Dresden nebst den ausgezierten Stimmen nach einer Handschrift der Deutschen Staatsbibliothek Berlin und ein Kommentar von Horst Augsbach. Leipzig: Zentralantiquariat der Deutschen Demokratischen Republik, 1982.

Facsimile edition of K. 26, presenting Mus. 2470/Q28 in the Sächsiche Landesbibliothek, believed by the editor to be an autograph of the composer, and M. Th. 178 in the Deutsche Staatsbibliothek. The Dresden manuscript provides alternative indications for performance by flute and cembalo, or for flute, violin and continuo. The variants in the Berlin manuscript, for flute and obbligato keyboard, are of considerable interest. A modern edition of the flute and keyboard version, based on the Dresden manuscript, is listed in section IV below.

14.   Sonata in D major for three flutes [K. 46]. Edited by John Wummer. New York: International Music Co., © 1975. Edition no. 2769.

15.   Trio in D-dur für drei Flöten [K. 46]. Edited by Hermien Teske. Camera Flauto Amadeus Nr. 16. Winterthur: Amadeus Verlag, 1981. Edition no. BP 2016.

16.   Sonata F-dur für drei Alblockflöten (Querflöten, Violinen) [K. 46]. Op. III, nr. 6. Edited by Hugo Ruf. Wilhelmshaven: O. H. Noetzel Verlag (New York: C. F. Peters), © 1974. Pegasus Ausgabe N 3380.

In spite of the different keys, nos. 14, 15, and 16 present the same work. The sonata is transposed up a minor third in the third edition to accommodate the range of the alto recorder. A similar transposed version is also available from the publishers of the second edition. Wummer's text seems to be based on other modern editions (see nos. 5 and 6 of the original survey). The opus number given by Hugo Ruf is that of the eighteenth-century French volume of Boivin, published *c.* 1728, upon which this version is based. Teske's edition derives from a recently discovered manuscript in the Royal Library in Copenhagen. As noted in the original list of modern editions, this work is not in fact a traditional trio sonata, but a piece for three equal instruments in the French style. For a genuine critical edition of this work and another of the same type, see no. 18 below.

17.   Trio in D-dur für 3 Flöten. Edited by Nikolaus Delius. Zürich: Eulenburg (New York: C. F. Peters), 1977. Edition no. GM 745.

This composition is of the same type as that listed in nos. 14 and 15 above, but is in fact a different work. It is not included in Kohler's list. This first modern edition is based on a manuscript at the Universitetsbiblioteket in Lund.

18.   Sonata in D (K. 46) and Sonatina in D for 3 flutes (oboes or violins). Edited by David Lasocki. London: Nova Music, © 1982. Edition no. N. M. 177.

Critical editions of the two sonatas for three flutes listed above, based on a careful study of all known sources. By far the best edition available of both works.

19.   Trio Sonata in E (K. 28) for 2 flutes and basso continuo. Edited by David Lasocki. London: Nova Music, © 1980. Edition no. N. M. 133.

Based on the manuscript in the Sächsische Landesbibliothek.

20.   Trio Sonata in C (K. 33) for 2 flutes and basso continuo. Edited by David Lasocki. London: Nova Music, © 1980. Edition no. N. M. 138.

Based on the manuscript in the Sächsische Landesbibliothek.

III.   *Duets*

1.   Six Duets Opus 2 for Two Flutes. Edited by John Wummer. New York: International Music Co., © 1976. 2 vols. Pub. nos. 2293 and 2294.

A new edition apparently based on previously published modern editions (see *Quantz and His Versuch*, p. 160).

2. Three Duets for two flutes op. 2 Nos. 1–3. Kalmus Wind Series no. 4741. Melville, N.Y.: Belwin Mills, n.d.

    A reprint of the first volume of the 1932 Breitkopf & Härtel edition.

    In preparation for publication by Nova Music are editions of these duets in most of the alternative versions suggested by Quantz in the preface to his original edition of 1759: 2 flutes; 2 alto recorders; 2 oboes; and 2 bassoons (cellos or violas da gamba). All will be edited by David Lasocki. Another new edition in which Quantz's original preface is included, and in which his instructions are worked out in detail is in preparation by Ms Priscilla Collins. Meanwhile, the firm Musica Musica (Mark A. Meadow) in Basel, Switzerland, has issued another facsimile of the original edition.

3. Sechs Duette für Flöten. Op. 5. Edited by Frank Nagel. 2 vols. Wilhelmshaven: Heinrichshofen (New York: C. F. Peters), © 1972. Pegasus-Ausgabe N 1338.

    These works were published as Quantz's Op. 5 by J. Walsh in London in 1750. If they are in fact works by Quantz, they must be very early ones; they are stylistically far removed from the mature duets in the Op. 2 collection prepared by Quantz himself. Their authenticity has been questioned by Eitner on stylistic grounds.

IV. *Solo Sonatas and other accompanied works*

1. 3 Sonatas for Flute and Piano [sic]. Edited by John Wummer. New York: International Music Co., © 1976. Pub. no. 2882.

    This edition is based directly on the Breitkopf & Härtel edition of 1963 listed as no. 10 in my original survey. As noted there, the first two sonatas are from Quantz's Op. 1 of 1734 and the third was published separately in the *Musikalisches Allerley* of 1761.

2. Sonata E-Moll für Querflöte und obligates Cembalo (Pianoforte). Edited by Hugo Ruf. Mainz: B Schott's Söhne (New York: Associated Music Publishers), © 1968. Edition Schott 5724.

    Based on a manuscript in the Sächsische Landesbibliothek. It is one of several trio sonatas by Quantz [K. 26] which exist in alternative versions for flute and obbligato harpsichord. The trio sonata text is not included in this edition. For a facsimile of the Dresden manuscript, and another important manuscript of the work in Berlin, see no. 13 in the group of trio sonatas listed above.

3. 28 Variationen über die Arie 'Ich schlief, da träumte mir'. Edited by Frank Nagel. Thorough-bass and cadenzas realized by Winfried Radeke. Wiesbaden: Breitkopf & Härtel, © 1975. Edition Breitkopf Nr. 6723. Pl. no. Wb. 1383.

    Based on a manuscript in the Staatsbibliothek Preußischer Kulturbesitz.

IVa. *Pieces and Exercises for Unaccompanied Flute*

1. Solfeggi Pour La Flute Traversiere avec l'enseignement Par Mons' Quantz. First

edition based on the autograph by Winfried Michel and Hermien Teske. Winterthur: Amadeus Verlag/Bernard Päuler, © 1978. Edition no. 686.

This volume presents a complete edition of the important manuscript in the Giedde Music Collection in the Royal Library, Copenhagen. In general it is a clear and helpful edition, with useful subject and composer indexes, and a critical report, provided by the editors. A number of the works by Quantz included in the *Solfeggi* can now be identified more precisely (including several concertos from Frederick's collections), and the presence of these works may affect attempts to date the collection. The *Solfeggi* in this collection differ in a number of respects from those previously available in *Das Flötenbuch Friedrichs des Grossen*, including a large number of excerpts from specific compositions by Quantz, Telemann, W. F. Bach, C. H. Graun and other composers, with brief but pointed comments on the interpretation of specific passages. A unique document.

2. Capricen, Fantasien und Anfangsstücke für Flöte solo und mit B. C./Caprices, Fantasias and Beginner's pieces for Flute solo and with Basso continuo. First edition by Winfried Michel and Hermien Teske. Winterthur: Amadeus Verlag/ Bernhard Päuler, © 1980. Edition no. Bp 2050.

Here the other most significant discovery in recent years connected with Quantz the composer is presented in a clear straightforward edition. The source is again a manuscript in the Giedde Collection. The Caprices and Fantasias vary in quality and individuality, but many are attractive and distinctive additions to the unaccompanied repertoire. A considerable number of questions about the authorship of many of the shorter pieces remain unanswered at the present time. Eight pieces have been found by Elissa Poole in a collection published by a Mr. Braun in Paris in 1740 (facsimile edition, Firenze, Studio per edizioni scelte, 1982), where they appear without attribution. The appearance of these works in the collection, however, does not disprove (or confirm) Quantz's authorship, since Braun mentions that the volume includes compositions by himself and *'divers autres'*. John Solum has also noted that these same pieces coincide with those found before World War II in a manuscript, since destroyed, in the Darmstadt Library. The Braun in question may well be one of two brothers with that name whom Quantz mentions as working in Paris during his visit in 1726–7. A Jean Daniel Braun in fact obtained the privilège for a collection of trio sonatas by Quantz published *c.* 1728 (see my *Three Studies*, pp. 145–6). And at least one of the brothers also became a member of the Paris opera orchestra in 1728.

The missing opening theme of piece no. 58 in this edition of the Caprices is certainly, as the editors suggest, by Blavet. The variations on the theme, however, differ from those by that composer, although they are very much in his style. Why the two pages containing the theme and opening variations were missing at the time Michel and Teske prepared their edition remains a mystery. They were found in a copy of the manuscript that I examined before publication, and are still found in a facsimile edition of the complete manuscript which has been issued recently (1983?) by Musica Musica (Mark A. Meadow) in Basel.

INDEX OF THE MOST IMPORTANT MATTERS

The basis for the following index is a complete translation of the distinctive and idiomatic one provided by Quantz himself. To this foundation have been added references to material provided by the translator in his introduction and notes; new entries and additional references to remedy gaps in the original; and cross-references for more familiar terms to their equivalents in the translation. The German and French words for the most important technical terms are enclosed in brackets immediately after the English terms. The spelling and capitalization are the same as those found in the German and French indexes. French accents are frequently missing. Since running chapter headings similar to those found throughout the original work could not be provided in the translation, in this revised and expanded form of the index, the chapter and paragraph numbers used by Quantz have been replaced by page references for the sake of greater ease on the part of the reader.

M